GORE VIDAL'S *BURR*

"OUR GREATEST LIVING MAN
OF LETTERS."
George Frazier, *Boston Globe*

◆•◆ •◆ •◆ •◆ •◆ •◆ ◆

"HERE WE HAVE BURR'S STORY—
A TRAGEDY, A COMEDY, A VIBRANT,
LEG-KICKING LIFE . . . All of this and
much, much more is told in a highly
engaging book that teems with bons
mots, aphorisms and ironic comments
on the political precess . . . Enlightening,
fresh and fun."
Margaret Manning, *Boston Globe*

BURR

Gore Vidal

BALLANTINE BOOKS • NEW YORK

Library of Congress Catalog Card Number: 73-3985

ISBN 0-345-30619-8

This edition published by arrangement with
Random House, Inc.

Manufactured in the United States of America

First Ballantine Books Edition: September 1982

FOR MY NEPHEWS

Ivan, Hugh and Burr

BURR

1833

One

A Special Despatch to the New York *Evening Post:*

SHORTLY BEFORE MIDNIGHT, July 1, 1833, Colonel Aaron Burr, aged seventy-seven, married Eliza Jumel, born Bowen fifty-eight years ago (more likely sixty-five but remember: she is prone to litigation!). The ceremony took place at Madame Jumel's mansion on the Washington Heights and was performed by Doctor Bogart (will supply first name later). In attendance were Madame Jumel's niece (some say daughter) and her husband Nelson Chase, a lawyer from Colonel Burr's Reade Street firm. This was the Colonel's second marriage; a half-century ago he married Theodosia Prevost.

In 1804 Colonel Burr—then vice-president of the United States—shot and killed General Alexander Hamilton in a duel. Three years after this lamentable affair, Colonel Burr was arrested by order of President Thomas Jefferson and charged with treason for having wanted to break up the United States. A court presided over by Chief Justice John Marshall found Colonel Burr innocent of treason but guilty of the misdemeanour of proposing an invasion of Spanish territory in order to make himself emperor of Mexico.

The new Mrs. Aaron Burr is the widow of the wine merchant Stephen Jumel; reputedly, she is the richest woman in New York City, having begun her days humbly but no doubt cheerfully in a brothel at Providence, Rhode Island. . . .

I DON'T SEEM ABLE to catch the right tone but since William Leggett has invited me to write about Colonel Burr for the *Evening Post*, I shall put in everything, and look forward to his response. "I don't think," he'll gulp air in his consumptive way, "that the managing editor will allow any reference to what he calls 'a disorderly house.'"

Well, the euphemisms can come later. Lately, mysteriously, Leggett has shown a sudden interest in Colonel Burr, although his editor, Mr. Bryant, finds my employer "unsavoury. Like so many men of the last century, he did not respect the virtue of women."

Because I am younger than Mr. Bryant, I find Colonel Burr's "unsavouriness" a nice contrast to the canting tone of our own day. The eighteenth-century man was not like us—and Colonel Burr is an eighteenth-century man still alive and vigorous, with a new wife up here in Haarlem, and an old mistress in Jersey City. He is a man of perfect charm and fascination. A monster, in short. To be destroyed? I think that is what Leggett has in mind. But do I?

I sit now under the eaves of the Jumel mansion. Everyone is asleep—except the bridal couple? Sombre thought, all that aged flesh commingled. I put it out of my mind.

The astonishing day began when Colonel Burr came out of his office and asked me to accompany him to the City Hotel where he was to meet a friend. As usual, he was mysterious. He makes even a trip to the barber seem like a plot to overthrow the state. Walking down Broadway, he positively skipped at my side, no trace of the stroke that half paralyzed him three years ago.

At the corner of Liberty Street the Colonel paused to buy a taffy-apple. The apple-woman knew him. But then every old New Yorker knows him by sight. The ordinary people greet him warmly while the respectable folk tend to cut him dead, not that he gives them much opportunity for he usually walks with eyes downcast, or focussed on his companion. Yet sees everything.

"For himself the Colonel, and not a dear worm in it!" Obviously a joke between Burr and the old biddy. He addressed her graciously. Business men hurrying across from Wall Street quickly take him in with their eyes; and look away. He affects not to notice the sensation his physical presence still occasions.

"Charlie, are you free for an adventure tonight?" This was mumbled. He lacks a full complement of teeth and the taffy was not helpful to Dr. Dodge's elaborate dentures.

"Yes, Sir. What sort of adventure?"

The large black eyes gave me a mischievous look. "Half the fun of an adventure is the surprise."

In front of the City Hotel an omnibus was stopped: its horses neighing, pissing, groaning. Stout prosperous men converged on the hotel: sundown is their time of day to meet, gossip, drink—then go home on foot because it is faster than by carriage. Now-a-days lower Broadway is blocked with traffic at this hour and everyone walks; even the decrepit John Jacob Astor can be seen crawling along the street like some ancient snail, his viscous track the allure of money.

Instead of going inside the hotel, the Colonel (put off by a group of Tammany sachems standing in the doorway?) turned into the graveyard of Trinity Church. I followed, obediently. I am always obedient. What else can a none-too-efficient law clerk be? I cannot think why he keeps me on.

"I know—intimately—more people in this charming cemetery than I do in all of the Broad Way." Burr makes a joke of everything; his manner quite unlike that of other people. Was he always like this or did the years of exile in Europe make him different from the rest of us? or—new thought—have the manners of the New Yorkers changed? I suspect that is the case. But if we seem strange to him, he is much too polite to say so, as he lives on and on amongst us: full of the devil, my quarry.

In the half-light of the cemetery, Burr did resemble the devil—assuming that the devil is no more than five foot six (an inch shorter than I), slender, with tiny feet (hooves?), high forehead (in the fading light I imagine vestigial horns), bald in front with hair piled high on his head, powdered absently in the old style, and held in place with a shell comb. Behind him is a monument to the man he murdered.

"I shall want to be buried at Princeton College. Not that there's any immediate hurry." He glanced at Hamilton's tomb. No change in expression in face or voice as he asked, "Do you know the works of Sir Thomas Browne?"

"No, Sir. A friend of yours?"

Burr only grinned, a bit of apple peel red as old blood on Dr. Dodge's incisor. "No, Charlie. Nor was I present when Achilles hid himself among women." Whatever that meant. I record it all. At Leggett's suggestion I have decided to keep a full record of the Colonel's conversation.

"I have always preferred women to men. I think that sets me apart, don't you?"

Knowing exactly what he meant, I agreed. New York gentlemen spend far more time with one another in bars and taverns than in mixed company. Lately they have taken to forming clubs from which women are banned.

"I cannot—simply—be without the company of a woman."

"But you've had no wife . . ."

"Since before you were born. But then I have not lacked for . . . gentle companionship." He gives me a swift grin; suddenly in the pale light he looked to be a randy boy of fourteen. Then he abruptly became his usual self; full of dignity save for that curious unexpected wit. I always find his brilliance disturbing. We do not want the old to be sharper than we. It is bad enough that they were there first, and got the best things.

"We shall be met presently at the hotel by my old friend Dr. Bogart. He has rented a carriage. We shall then drive to the Haarlem Heights—or *Washington* Heights, as I believe they are currently known." A fugitive smile. "What better name for an American height than 'Washington'?"

I have taken some notes already on Burr's view of General Washington. Unfortunately, his comments are cryptic, and seldom more than a single sentence like "How fitting that the first American president should have been a land surveyor." He knows so much; tells so little. Well, I have made up my mind to know what he knows before the end.

Burr delights in tomb inscriptions. "Elizabeth! Of all people! Never knew she was dead." Burr slipped on his octagonal glasses. "Died eighteen ten. That explains it. I was still in Europe. A fugitive from injustice." Burr removed the glasses. "I think her birth date has been—as Jeremy Bentham would say—minimized. She was older than I and . . . *beautiful*! Beautiful, Charlie." Burr pushed the glasses onto his forehead. In the churchyard trees birds chattered while Broadway's traffic was at its rattling, creaking, neighing worst.

"I know you're writing about my adventurous life." I was startled. Showed it. My face reveals everything; always has. I have no guile. Must learn it. "I've observed you taking notes. Don't fret. I don't mind. If I were not so lazy I would do the job myself, having done part of it already."

"An actual memoir?"

"Bits and pieces. I still have a lingering desire to tell the true story of the Revolution before it is too late, which is probably now since the legend of those days seems to be cast in lead if the schoolbooks are any guide. It is quite uncanny how wrong they are about all of us. Why do you see so much of Mr. Leggett at the *Evening Post?*"

I literally stumbled at the rapidity of his charge; and it was a charge, of the sort he is celebrated for in court during cross-examination.

The old man helped steady me.

I gabbled. "I see him because—I have known him since I was at Columbia. He used to come there, you know, to talk about literature. About journalism. I'd thought, perhaps, as a career, I might write for the press, before I took up the law . . ."

Whatever Burr wanted to get from me he must have got for he changed the subject as he led me out of the graveyard and into Broadway where the white-flaring hissing streetlamps were now being lit, and passers-by cast flickering dark shadows. I shuddered suddenly; thought of ghosts. After all, was I not with one who has so far refused to go to ground?

"When you next see Mr. Leggett, tell him how much I admire his editorials on the subject of nullification. I, too, am a Jacksonian, and oppose nullification." A clue. Recently South Carolina claimed that it had the "right" not only to nullify federal laws but also to dissolve, if challenged, its connection with the union. If Colonel Burr had indeed wanted to separate the western states from the east (as everyone believes), he would favour South Carolina's Nullification Act. Yet he does not. Or says he does not. He is a labyrinth. Must not lose my way.

Burr led me into the crowded bar-room of the City Hotel where we drank a good deal of Madeira (rare for him: tobacco is his one indulgence) until the arrival of Dr. Bogart, a thin white old man with a parrot's face and a most birdly manner.

Burr was exuberant, festive. I still had no idea why. "Dominie, you're late! No excuses. We must set out immediately! The tide is at the full."

He put down his glass. I did the same, noticing how the gentlemen at the nearest table were straining to hear our every word. Not an easy thing to do considering the rumble of masculine voices in the smoky room, and the sound of the bar-tender cracking ice with a hammer.

"Heigh-ho!" Burr started briskly to the door, causing a covey of lawyers—some with awed bows of recognition—to scatter. "To the Heights, gentlemen." He clapped his hands. "To the Heights! Where else?"

Two

I AM NOT USED to night travel. To be cooped up in a carriage in the dark is to be totally subtracted from the usual world. Non-existent yet perversely made aware of not existing by the clatter of hooves, jingle of harness, coachman's curses and—on this night—by a hideous white half-moon that had drained the world of colour, caused trees and fields to hemorrhage their green, turn to black, white, silver all nature. For a time, I thought I was dead.

Certainly the two old men opposite me did not dispel the mood. Burr: "Wasn't that the Wentworth place, the farm-house there, with the three chimneys?" Dr. Bogart: "No, Colonel. It was the Dutchman's place. You know his name. With the bald wife who drowned at Fishkill in seventy-two or seventy-three."

Will I be like them at their age? Talking of grisly

death-beds and redundant gallantries? But then I am to have a short life, according to the Italian fortune-teller at Castle Garden. No garrulous old age for me. Good.

Meanwhile, in the carriage, I practised being nothing; and achieved for quite a long time the perfection of the nought, the zero. Yet I cheated: thought of future time—contemplated the hatching of that zero which contains me now and when it does break open, oh, the world will know that Charlie Schuyler has been added greatly to its sum! Why am I writing in mathematical terms? I have yet to learn the entire multiplication table and grow uneasy faced with a long division.

Describe! as Leggett keeps telling me. Describe! Very well.

Through open gates. Stone? Wood? Could not tell. Down a curving carriage way. Tall black trees. A view of the river in the distance. Light on water like tarnished silver (cannot do better—will try again later). Then the dark bulk of the mansion. Lights blazing at every window. A party? No. Burr would have wanted us to dress appropriately. But if not a party, why the lights? Even Madame Jumel, rich as she is, does not light every room to celebrate the approach of midnight.

The carriage stops at the front door. A black groom appears from the side of the house. We get down. Steps go up to a columned porch (there is a second-floor balcony). The house is vast, extending to left and right, suggesting all sorts of unexpected wings, dormers, cellars. It was built before the Revolution by a Tory named Morris. Later it was confiscated by the state. My parents used to come up here on Sundays when the mansion was a popular inn. Then Stephen Jumel bought it for his new wife and old mistress, Eliza Bowen (or something else) of Providence, Rhode Island.

Front door opens. Oblong of golden festive light. Large butler welcomes us. Colonel Burr hurries inside.

I help the shuffling Dr. Bogart; weak in the legs, he staggers like a drunkard. Now for history—and a change in tense.

We entered the front hall just in time to witness Colonel Burr's (or is it Madame Jumel's?) mating dance.

At the end of a long entrance hall, ablaze with chandeliers, stood Madame herself; wearing what looked to be a French ball-gown. Sumptuous, I think, is the word. An imposing woman, with huge eye-sockets containing small gray eyes; a small mouth, square jaw. She was hung with bright jewels. Yes, it must have been a ball-gown (it came from France she told us later) of a style either not yet known to provincial New York or known and discarded. Probably the former. I seldom see the gentry close-to.

"Colonel Burr! I did not expect you, Sir!" These were, I gather, the first words she had spoken to him. They were still echoing through the hall as I propelled Dr. Bogart toward a liveried footman who paid us no mind at all, his attention like ours on the lady of the house who stood as though poised for flight, one hand on the railing of the staircase, the other more or less over her heart.

"My dear Madame, what I warned you of yesterday has come to pass." Burr galloped the length of the hall toward the fair Eliza who, having to choose between a retreat to the large many-sided drawing-room behind her and the safety of the rooms above, skipped onto the first step of the staircase, still clinging to banister, to heart.

"What was that, Colonel? I remember no warning."

"Madame." Burr took the hand which had been raised to protect her heart. She surrendered it with a show of reluctance. "I have come, as I promised, with a clergyman. With Dr. Bogart."

"Great honour, Mrs. Jumel . . ." began Dr. Bogart.

Burr talked through him. "And a witness. From my office. Charles Schuyler . . ."

The illustrious New York name diverted Madame for a moment. "Schuyler?"

Before I could assure her that I was not one of *the* Schuylers, Burr had matters as well in hand as her hand itself, which he had now managed to bring to his lips, still talking in a low and perfectly pitched hypnotic voice. "Dr. Bogart, my oldest friend—a clergyman known to all of us at the time of the Revolution. A patriot, a true and holy man . . ." Dr. Bogart looked stunned at this encomium. "And an intimate friend of General Washington—who had no friends—has consented to marry us. To-night. Now."

"Colonel Burr!" Madame Jumel then gave as good a performance as was ever performed at the Park Theatre. She tried to pull her hand free, failed; tried to mount the stairs, was restrained. Called for help to butler, footman, was met with nervous giggles and averted eyes by those satellites. After some eight minutes by the clock in the hall (given her by Napoleon Bonaparte, she told us later), Eliza Bowen Jumel consented to become Mrs. Aaron Burr.

By now rather red in the face, Madame ordered whiskey for herself, Madeira for us. Then as if by a pre-arranged signal, we were joined by Nelson Chase and his wife Mary Eliza, the niece of Madame Jumel (though it is rumoured that she might well be the fruit of one of Madame's early alliances). Nelson Chase is a plump, foolish young man, fascinated by Colonel Burr. For over a year he has been associated with our firm, pretending to practise law. I had not met Mary Eliza before; she is pleasant, not pretty but winning. Needless to say, she does not shine but then no woman can in Madame's glorious presence.

The Colonel and Madame (I can't call her Mrs. Burr) were married in a small parlour to the left of the main hall. Nelson kept murmuring "fabulous, fabulous!" The right word, I suppose. The brief ceremony was followed by a splendid supper in the dining-room. Obviously Madame's cook had anticipated what her mistress had not—that she would succumb to the Colonel's heralded unheralded assault.

It was the first time I had seen Colonel Burr "in society." I had known him only in the office—and in court. Not that he argues many cases now-a-days: there are still judges who feel that they must vindicate the death of Alexander Hamilton by addressing his murdered rudely. The last time I attended the Colonel in court, the judge unearthed—if he did not newly mint—an obscure state statute.

The judge roared at Burr. "Don't you know that law, Mr. Burr! *Don't you know it?*"

When the judge at last stopped shouting, Burr said, in his mildest voice, "No, Your Honour, I do not know it. But I *hear* it."

Last night, however, was my first experience of the legendary Aaron Burr, the one-time leader of New York fashion, the intimate of German princes, the lion of the London drawing-rooms, the man Jeremy Brentham regarded as perfectly civilised. Listening to the Colonel's conversation, I could see how he had so easily enchanted three generations of Europeans as well as of Americans, how he had mesmerized both men and women like the devil—no, more like Faust to whom everything marvellous comes, then on the midnight goes. Oh, what I would give to read that sulphurous contract in order to see what clauses the devil added and Burr accepted, knowing that they would not hold up in court. And signed with an elegant flourish. I don't envy the devil when he takes to court Aaron Burr.

We drank toast after toast. My head still aches: I wanted to vomit before I went to sleep but did not, fearing to disturb the lovers. Madame got moderately drunk on whiskey. Nelson was very drunk, embarrassing his wife but no one else.

"I swore I would never re-marry." Madame gave her niece a tender smile. "Didn't I, *petite?*"

"Certainly, *Tante!*" Both aunt and niece have spent many years in Paris where the girl was sent to school.

"When my beloved Stephen . . ."

"A true gentleman, Madame." Colonel Burr reacted superbly to the mention of his predecessor, and the source of his current wealth. "I should think the most beloved man of his generation, in this city." He stopped the qualifying just short of adding "in the wine business." Madame cares not for trade.

Madame blew her nose like a trumpet. "I shall never forgive myself, letting *le pauvre* go out in that cart, old and feeble as he was. Then when he *tombé* . . . how you say? fell off the cart and they brought him back to me, I held myself—*moi-même*—responsible. Night after night I sat up with him, nursing him, praying . . ." Obviously Madame assumed that we had all heard the rumour that one dark night she had slipped off her husband's bandages and let him bleed to death. Lurid stories cluster to her name—as they do to the Colonel's.

". . . yet despite my vow I was overwhelmed by Colonel Burr." Madame's harsh, curiously accented voice dominated the room. "A man I have known since I was a young girl."

"A child, Madame." Burr looked at her, and I detected something new in his smiling eyes: a proprietary look as he finally realized that he is married to the richest woman in New York City.

The last few months now make sense to me. I used to wonder why the Colonel would so often drop whatever he was doing in order to make the long drive up to the Heights to discuss Madame's legal affairs (currently she has three suits in the courts). Explained, too, were the long conversations with the egregious Nelson Chase in the inner office, talks which would break off whenever I or Burr's partner Mr. Craft appeared. And, finally, the matter of money.

From the law the Colonel makes a good income (by my standards magnificent!). But somehow at the end

of the month there is never enough money to pay all
the bills. For one thing he has huge debts from the
past. For another, he is the most generous of men. On
a round baize-covered table in his office he makes
a sort of Norman keep of lawbooks in the centre of
which he piles the cash as it comes in; then whoever
asks for money gets it: veterans of the Revolution,
old widows, young protégés—anyone and everyone, in
fact, save his creditors. But though he is permanently
short of money, he still dreams of empire. Last month
he confided to me his latest scheme.

"For only fifty thousand dollars one can buy a
principality in the Texas Territory, to be settled within
a year's time by Germans, who require nothing more
than passage money." The Colonel's eyes grew wide at
the thought of all that acreage planted with all those
Germans. "Charlie, do you realize that in twenty years
such an investment would be worth millions?" I dared
not point out that in twenty years he would be ninety-
seven years old.

Last week I overheard him discuss the Texas scheme
quite seriously with a banker and I thought him mad,
knowing that he did not have fifty much less fifty
thousand dollars. Now of course he has all the money
he needs, and so Aaron Burr who might have been
third president of the United States or first emperor of
Mexico is about to be, in the last years of his life,
a grand duke—at the very least—of Texas.

"Shall we tell them where we first met, Colonel?"
Madame was fanning herself. The night was warm and
her fair skin had begun to mottle with heat and
whiskey.

In unison the ancient couple pronounced an incom-
prehensible French name. Later I got Burr to spell it.
"Chenelette Dusseaussoir." It was Madame who explained. "A confectioner's shop, just across the street
from the City Hotel. Everyone went there in the old
days. The rum-cake was the best I've ever tasted, outside Paris."

"What year was this?" Nelson Chase arranged his smooth porcine features into what he doubtless took to be an interested frown. "Seventeen ninety-nine," said Burr. "Seventeen ninety," said Madame. A significant difference of opinion which neither bothered to sort out since they were now careening down parallel lanes of memory.

"I was new to New York, from Providence. But of course I had relatives. And knew everyone *de la famille.* Oh, it was a wonderful time! For America, that is." This last had a flat ring to it. "My true home is France. Isn't it, Mary Eliza?"

"*Mais oui, Tante.*" Dutiful girl. She has a fine figure.

"The only reason we came back was because of the Emperor." Madame was in full sail, drinking whiskey as fast as the butler served it. Burr was bright-eyed, expectant, like a squirrel waiting to be fed a nut.

"When my darling Stephen and I arrived at Rochefort in France aboard our ship—the *Eliza,* named for me—the Emperor was in the harbour." Madame addressed herself to me since the others had heard the story many times before. "Waterloo had been fought —and lost by us."

Madame's accent was shifting from New England Yankee to émigré French. "Our emperor was aboard his ship *but* the harbour was blockaded by the *Anglais.* What to do? We devised and discarded a thousand schemes. Finally, it was decided between my husband and Maréchal Bertrand—a man of the old school, let me tell you, loyal, honourable—that the Emperor come aboard the *Eliza*—in disguise—and since we flew the American flag, we would slip past the British fleet and carry him to New Orleans where he would be safe until France, until the *world* recalled him to his rightful place! You know his eyes were like yours, Colonel Burr. Burning, powerful."

"So I have been told, Madame." Burr did not mind having the resemblance noted. After all, each was an adventurer who succeeded for a time; then failed. The difference between them was simply one of degree.

"But *les sales Anglais* seized him and took him away to St. Helena and killed him, the greatest man that ever lived, my idol." Madame's eyes filled with tears. The curls on either side of her face are too symmetrical. She must wear a wig.

"When the Emperor left, he gave my aunt his travelling carriage and his military trunk." Mary Eliza sounded like a guide at the city museum, explaining for the hundredth time the history of the mammoth's tooth. "It contained his clock among other things."

"That clock!" Madame indicated an ornate clock with a portrait of Napoleon beneath the face. Madame then gave us a quick inventory of other Napoleonic items, each given her personally by the Emperor.

I could not resist the tactless question. "Did you actually meet Napoleon?"

"Meet him!" A resonant deep cry. Burr gave me a swift look that silenced me for the rest of the evening. "He was all I lived for! The reason I was driven from France by King Louis Philippe . . ." On and on.

Later, the Colonel reprimanded me. We were at the second-floor landing. Madame had already gone to the bridal chamber. "Madame has a vivid imagination," began the Colonel.

"I'm sorry, Sir."

"No harm done. In point of fact, she did not meet the Emperor—any more than I did—but the rest of the story is true. It was Napoleon's last chance to escape on an American ship. The ship just happened to be the *Eliza*. But the gods were against him."

Burr indicated a small room at the end of a short corridor. "That was General Washington's office in seventeen seventy-six. He lived in this house for three months, during which he managed to lose New York City to the British. But despite his incompetence, the gods always supported him in the end. I suspect Cromwell was right: the man who does not know where he's going goes farthest. Talleyrand used to tell me that for the great man all is accident. Obviously, *he* was not a great man since he survived by careful planning, by never showing his true feelings. You must learn that art, Charlie."

"I'm sorry, Colonel. What I said . . ."

"Think nothing of it, my boy. God mend you. Now," he rubbed his hands together to indicate mock rapture, "I go to the Hymeneal couch."

We exchanged good nights and he rapped on the door opposite Washington's study. Madame's voice, slightly thick with whiskey, exclaimed, "*Entrez, mon mari,*" and Colonel Burr vanished inside.

Three

"CHARLIE, THIS IS NOT FOR THE *Evening Post!*" Leggett looked at me with—well, amused scorn, as the English novelists say.

"Too long?" I had given him a straightforward two-page description of the wedding, scribbled on the ride back to New York. The newly wed couple had departed at dawn in Madame's yellow coach with six horses to visit the Colonel's nephew, Governor Edwards, at Hartford, Connecticut. Yes, I am trying to be a journalist, mentioning all facts.

Leggett sighed. "We are interested in destroying Mr. Biddle's bank, in promoting free trade, in the gradual abolition of slavery, in workers' unions. We are not interested in a retired whore's wedding to a traitor."

Although I am used to Leggett's furious style, I was obliged to defend the Colonel, or at least my version of his nuptials. "Aaron Burr is not a traitor, as far as we know. Madame Jumel is not a whore but a respectable and rich widow no matter what she might have been years ago. And this is damned interesting. The two most notorious people in New York have got married."

Leggett gave a long wheeze, to signify disgust. At thirty-two (seven years older than I), he looks like my father. We met when I was still at Columbia and he was writing theatre reviews for the *Mirror*, and trying to become an actor like his friend Edwin Forrest. He failed on the stage. Yet of course he *is* an actor, with a stage more important than that of the Bowery Theatre. As a journalist he has taken all politics and literature for his field, and is famous.

The curtain-raiser to Leggett's continuing drama occurred when he was cashiered from the navy for fighting a duel. At the court-martial he insulted his commanding officer with a tirade of quotations from Shakespeare. Then he set out to take New York by storm. Although he failed as an actor, he succeeded as an author with a book called *The Rifle*; he then published his own magazine *Critic* which failed. Now he is an editor of the *Evening Post* and a power in the city. Feared by everyone for his pen, not to mention his duelling pistols or, more precisely, the Malacca cane with which he has whipped at least one rival editor. Yet he is plainly dying: a once solid frame shattered first by yellow fever in the navy, then consumption.

When I was seventeen I thought Leggett a god. Now he annoys more than he charms me. Annoys himself, too. But I continue to see him and he continues to encourage (as well as annoy) me. He knows I am not happy with the law, that I want to free myself somehow to write. Unfortunately, only political journalists are well-paid for writing, and I am not interested in politics (but then neither was Leggett until recently). So I dream of a career like Washington Irving's; and write short pieces that were sometimes published here and there but were almost never paid for until last month when Leggett proposed that I do an occasional piece for the *Evening Post*. Also: "You should use your relationship with Aaron Burr."

"In what way?"

But Leggett would say nothing beyond "Take notes. Keep a record. Assay his wickedness . . ."

The story of Colonel Burr's marriage was, I thought, exactly what Leggett had in mind. Apparently, I was wrong.

"All right, Charlie, I'll take it in to Mr. Bryant. He'll decide. I won't." Leggett went into the next office. I could hear the low murmur of talk. Then Leggett returned, shutting the door behind him. "Your prose will have Mr. Bryant's full attention."

"Thank you. Thank you." I tried to sound sardonic, like Colonel Burr.

Leggett put his feet on the table, dislodging papers and books. With a dirty handkerchief, he rubbed the ink from the middle finger of his right hand. "Charlie, are you still leading your dissolute life?"

"I am studying law, yes."

"Good answer. I trained you well." He grinned; then coughed for a long bad moment into the inky handkerchief and I looked away, not wanting to see what I suspected would be there, the bright arterial blood.

Coughing stopped, handsome haggard face gray and beaded with sweat, Leggett spoke in a low tired voice. "I meant, of course, Mrs. Townsend's establishment."

"Once a week. No more. I have put away boyish things."

"In order to spend, to *die* alone!" Eyes shone with amusement and fever. "Tell me of Mrs. Townsend's latest wards."

"There are three very young Irish girls, only just arrived, positively dewy . . ."

"No more! I am married, Charlie. That's enough."

"You asked."

"Like Odysseus then, I must stop my ears. Sing to me no more siren songs of my youth. Of those fair Hibernian charms I once . . ."

We were joined by Mr. Bryant. A remote man with carved lips and full face whiskers, he looks to be in his forties; he has the New English manner which

effectively disguises whatever pleasure he takes in his
reputation as America's First Poet (Leggett likes to
think of himself as the Second Poet, particularly when
Fitz-Greene Halleck is in the room). But Mr. Bryant
has yet to mention anything so trivial as verse in my
presence. Each time we meet, he is very much the
assistant editor of the *Evening Post*, decorously devoted
to radical politics. Incidentally, he is probably the only
man in New York who still writes with a quill pen.
Even Colonel Burr prefers modern steel to classic
feather.

"Most interesting, Mr. Schuyler." I was on my feet.
Since Mr. Bryant made no move for me to sit, a short
interview was indicated. "Naturally we will record the
. . . happy event. We are a *news*paper. But to serve
the news—and our public—one sentence will suffice."

"You see?" Leggett was pleased at my failure.

I was angry. "I have obviously been misled. I thought
that you were interested in Colonel Burr."

"Mr. Leggett is perhaps more interested than I."
The two editors exchanged an uneasy look.

I persevered. "At Leggett's suggestion, I described a
wedding which is, you must agree, of some interest."

Mr. Bryant was conciliatory. "I agree that Aaron
Burr is one of the most interesting people in the city,
in the United States . . ."

"And if only Charlie could get him to talk freely,
candidly about his life, about his connections, particularly today."

"I doubt if the Colonel would be candid." Mr.
Bryant's view of Burr is the traditional one.

Leggett, however, had something else in mind. "As
you know, Charlie, we support President Jackson. The
Vice-President, however, is a puzzling figure . . ."

"I do not find him puzzling." Mr. Bryant was sharp.

"Well, I do. I think him a trimmer. Without principle. And I'd like to know what everyone would like
to know: the relationship between Vice-President Van
Buren and Aaron Burr."

"Naturally, it is the *political* relation which interests Mr. Leggett and me." Mr. Bryant gave Leggett a warning look that was ignored on principle.

"No!" Leggett was on fire. "The *whole* relationship." He turned to me. "I had a good reason for asking you to take notes, to ask the Colonel questions. It is important for us to know how close the two men are."

"The Colonel admires Van Buren." I tried to recall what, if anything, Burr had said of the Vice-President. "But I would not say they are 'close.'"

Leggett was decisive. "Well they are, whether you know it or not. Twenty years ago when Burr came back from Europe, he went straight to Albany, straight to Van Buren, and stayed with him in his house. Stayed with a leader of the Albany regency. Yet Aaron Burr was still under indictment out west for treason. Still charged by the state of New Jersey for the killing of Hamilton . . ."

None of this is quite true but Leggett feels that to be excitingly right in general is better than to be dully accurate in particular. That is why he is such an effective journalist. "Now the question to be answered is: why did the careful, clever Martin Van Buren befriend such a dangerous, such a compromising man?"

"Naturally, there has always been a political affinity between the two." Mr. Bryant's elevated dullness makes a nice contrast to the vividness of his young colleague. "Colonel Burr was a founder of Tammany Hall. Martin Van Buren is now, in effect, a master of Tammany. They share the same . . . uh, ideals."

"Ideals!" Leggett threw wide his arms as though for a crucifixion. "Neither man has any ideals. Power is all that either ever wanted. Burr of course no longer matters. He's history. But Matty Van, now there's our target. The little wizard. Our own Merlin who's led General Jackson through one term as president and is now leading him through a second and as sure as there is corruption in Albany, will try to succeed him in thirty-six if we don't stop him."

"Why should we? Most of the positions he has taken . . ."

But Mr. Bryant is no match for Leggett when he is afire with what, I suppose, is moral passion.

"Positions be damned! Matty will do what he has to do to be nominated and win. He is the perfect politician. On the surface. But I tell you, beneath Matty's pinky-blond Dutch exterior, behind that seraphic smile, there lurks something very odd, very rotten, very Aaron Burrish."

I had no idea what Leggett was talking about. "Surely you don't think a man should be denied the presidency simply because he befriended Colonel Burr."

"I don't think that that is precisely what Mr. Leggett has in mind." Mr. Bryant looked more than ever like an Old Testament prophet. "Now, if you'll forgive me, Mr. Schuyler." He was gone.

"Charlie." Leggett assumed his special schoolmaster's voice. "I shall now corrupt your innocence. Martin Van Buren is the illegitimate son of Aaron Burr."

I was stunned. "I don't believe it. And anyway, *how* would anyone know?"

"It is known that Colonel Burr used to stay at the Van Buren tavern in Kinderhook up the Hudson. It is widely suspected that he got with child the tavern-keeper's wife Mary, crowning with splendid antlers her husband Abraham."

" 'Widely suspected.' " I was scornful.

"As well as suspicion, there was a good deal of evidence of the circumstantial variety. Colonel Burr constantly befriended the entire family, particularly young Matty, short, subtle, large-eyed, high-browed Matty—sound familiar?"

It is true that there is a physical resemblance between the two, except "Van Buren is fair, Burr dark . . ."

"He had a mother." Airily Leggett set to one side contrary evidence. "Now all of this may be simply gossip. Or may be not. Certainly it's true that at a very young age Matty left Kinderhook, came to New York and promptly went to work in the law office of one of Burr's associates . . ."

"But suppose Burr is his father. What's the point?"

Leggett condescended to explain. "Think of the possibility. For *you*. A pamphlet—no, a book proving that Martin Van Buren is the son of Aaron Burr, why, that would make your fortune."

"Proof in law," I began, but Leggett was not listening.

"Even more important than your fortune, Charlie, is the fate of this republic. Jackson has begun great reforms. We are beginning to tend toward democracy. Van Buren will reverse that trend. Therefore let us prevent him from becoming president."

"By proving him to be a bastard?"

"Americans are a moral people. But even more damaging than his bastardy is his *political* connection with Burr, particularly in recent years. If we can prove secret meetings, dark plots, unholy combinations— then, by Heaven, Van Buren will not be chosen to succeed General Jackson."

"Does that mean you want Henry Clay for president?"

"No. I want the other senator from Kentucky, Richard Johnson. Despite his *penchant* for black ladies, Johnson will continue Jackson's reforms. Van Buren won't." Leggett became conspiratorial. "You've probably observed that Mr. Bryant and I are in disagreement. He trusts Van Buren. I don't. I like Johnson. He doesn't."

I have never seen Leggett so worked up. Eyes glassy with excitement; cheeks a dull red. A moment of silence, broken finally by a clam-seller singing his wares below in Pine Street:

> "Here's your fine clams
> As white as snow
> On Rockaway these clams do grow!"

(I record all the songs I hear—for a possible article.)

I was tentative. "First, I don't think Colonel Burr is apt to tell me the truth . . ."

"You see him every day. He's fond of you."

"My father was a friend of his but that's hardly . . ."

"Burr's old. He lives in the past."

"In the *past*? At this very moment he's planning to settle Texas with Germans."

"Good God!" Leggett was impressed. "Anyway, you're the only one in a position to find out. And didn't you tell me he was writing the story of his life?"

"So he says. But I doubt it. Occasionally he speaks of dictating to me but . . ."

"So encourage him! Get him to talk about old times, about Kinderhook, about the days when he was in the Assembly and impregnating Mrs. Van Buren . . ."

"I'm afraid he's more interested in telling the 'true' story of the Revolution."

"Have you no guile?"

"You don't know Colonel Burr. And even if I did get the truth from him—which is doubtful—he can always prevent me from using it. He's the best lawyer in the state, and there is such a thing as libel."

Leggett was brisk. "We have three years before the next elections. He's bound to be dead by then, and under New York law you cannot libel the dead."

"What about Van Buren?"

"It is not libel to prove that a man is a bastard." Leggett was on his feet. "Charlie, we may have found a way to keep Matty Van out of the White House, and democratic principles in."

I rose, too. "The *Evening Post* will print the story?"

Leggett laughed and coughed simultaneously. "Certainly not! But don't worry. I'll have a publisher for you." He shambled along beside me to the door, loose as a wired skeleton. "I'm serious, Charlie." He took my hand in his hot dry one. "How often do you get a chance to alter the history of your country?"

Leggett had managed the wrong appeal. It was my

turn to be condescending. "I'll tell *that* to Colonel Burr. Just by living and breathing he has altered the lives of every American a number of times, and I can't see that it has done him much good."

"Let *me* reflect ironically, dear Charlie. *You* change history."

Do I BETRAY the Colonel? In a small way, yes. Do I hurt him? No. An anonymous pamphlet maintaining that he was the devil would distress him not at all. Much worse has been written about him by such supremely non-anonymous figures as Jefferson and Hamilton. Also, if he is consistent, he could hardly complain if the world were to know he is the father of Van Buren. The Colonel often says, "Whenever a woman does me the honour of saying that I am father to her child, I gracefully acknowledge the compliment and disguise any suspicion that I might have to the contrary."

On the other hand, the Colonel would be most distressed if Van Buren were to lose the election because of the Burr relationship. Well, I have no choice. Leggett has offered me a way out of drudgery; a means to support myself by writing. I shall take it. Also, there is—I confess—a certain joy in tricking the slyest trickster of our time. I'm fond of the Colonel; but fonder still of survival.

Four

THE VOYAGE INTO CONNECTICUT was cut short by business." Colonel Burr sat wreathed in smoke from a long seegar. The inner office. Describe: torn felt curtains cover dusty window-panes, diffusing the

green summer light; the effect is infernal, no, suba-
queous, a watery world into which the visitor swims,
barely able to discern the tall break-front containing
tattered law books; the baize-covered table, the portrait
of a plump dark girl—the Colonel's daughter Theodosia
(according to legend, forced to walk the plank by
pirates). Burr has yet to speak of Theodosia to me
but then he seldom mentions the past, unless provoked
by a mischievous desire to deflate the reputation of
some famed contemporary.

"I spent the night in the office. So much work
to do." He motioned for me to sit in the visitor's chair.

"Mrs. Burr . . .?"

"Madame is on the Heights, where else? But she
comes to town later today. Charlie, what have you
done with the Texas papers?"

I got them from the cabinet.

"Today we buy the land!" Happily, Burr spread out
the papers. "Already there are a thousand immigrants
at Bremen ready to set sail." He unfurled a map of the
Texas Territory and Louisiana. "I used to know every
inch of this part of the world." With an elegant strong
finger (the hands are not old), he traced the Mississippi
River's course to New Orleans.

"Wild, empty, beautiful country." Suddenly he
poked the map hard. "Here's where Mr. Jefferson had
me arrested." He grinned like a schoolboy. "With forty-
five men I was, he claimed, going to separate the
western part of the United States from Greater Virginia, as the union was sometimes referred to by those
of us who took no pleasure in Mr. Jefferson and his
junto."

"What *had* you meant to do with those forty-five
men?"

Burr's face shut. There is no other way to describe
his expression when he chooses not to communicate.
Yet the politeness never falters; he simply ignores the
impertinence.

"Here we put our Germans." He indicated a territory

to the west of the Sabine River. "Water is plentiful. The grazing is excellent. And the land leases are all in order." He spun fantasies. But are they?

"Best of all, Madame is eager for us to invest." Burr pushed his spectacles onto his brow. "An astonishing woman, Charlie. Truly astonishing."

"I'm sorry about—well, questioning her about Napoleon."

"I am afraid that as people grow old there is a tendency for them to believe that what the past *ought* to have been it was."

"You don't suffer from that, Colonel."

"But I am not old, Charlie." His dark eyes opened wide; a trick he has in common with Tyrone Power but unlike that romantic Irish actor, Burr is full of self-mockery. "You see, I have had a special dispensation. Too bad, in a way. Not only do I know what my past ought to have been, I know what it *was*." An involuntary—what? Grimace? Look of pain? Or do I invent? He was himself again. "And I am the only one who knows. Probably a very good thing, all in all."

"No, Sir. I don't think it is a good thing. You owe it to the world to tell your side of the story." What I had planned to say ever since I spoke to Leggett, I proceeded to say; and cursed myself for sounding rehearsed.

Burr smiled. "My side of the story is not, necessarily, the accurate one. But you flatter me. And I like that!" He kicked a leather-bound chest beneath the table. "I have a good deal of history there: letters, newspapers, copy-books, the beginning of a memoir. Oh, I am marvellous at beginnings, Charlie, truly marvellous!" He almost struck the bitter—and for him uncharacteristic—note. Then quickly, lightly, "But is it not better to have begun well than not to have begun at all? And what a beginning! Not only was I the son of a famous divine but I was also the grandson of an even more famous holy man, of Jonathan Edwards himself, a prophet who—what is the phrase?—walked

with God. No, the traditional verb does not describe
the progress of the great Puritan. Jonathan Edwards
ran with God, and out-raced us all. God, too, I should
think. Me certainly. I never knew the saint from Stock-
bridge but I was brought up in his very long shadow,
and chilling it was until I read Voltaire, until I realized
there was such a thing as glory in *this* world for the
man who was not afraid to seize what he wanted, to
create himself. Like Bonaparte. So I began in the
Revolution, and became a hero."

He stopped. Relit the stump of his seegar. "So a
number of us began. But then who *finished?* Not I,
as we know." He blew rings of smoke in my face. "At
the end the laurels went to a land surveyor from
Virginia who became the 'father' of his country. But
let us be fair. Since General Washington could sire
nothing in the flesh, it is fitting that he be given credit
for having conceived this union. A mule stallion, as
it were, whose unnatural progeny are these states. So
at the end, not to the swift but to the infertile went
the race." Burr found this image amusing. I was a bit
shocked. Like everyone else I think of Washington as
dull but perfect.

Burr handed me a number of pages of faded manuscript. "I recently came across this description of my
adventures in the Revolution. Perhaps they will amuse
you."

I took the manuscript, delighted that the Colonel
has chosen to confide in me, even though I find the
Revolution as remote as the Trojan War, and a good
deal more confusing since the surviving relics agree on
nothing.

Leggett recently proposed that all those who claim
to have fought in the Revolution should be taken to
the Vauxhall Gardens and shot—except that not even
the vast Vauxhall could hold the claimants. Every
American man of sixty was a drummer boy; of seventy
a colonel or general.

"Matt Davis means to write my biography, once I am

gone. Of course Matt himself is hardly young." The Colonel chuckled contentedly at the thought of his old friend's mortality.

Matthew L. Davis is a newspaper editor, a Tammany Sachem, and a life-long Burrite, as the press still call the original republican followers of the Colonel—a noun used by many who have not a clue as to its origin, who would be surprised to learn that the progenitor of the Burrites has an office in Reade Street and is not himself a Burrite for that faction is currently opposed to Van Buren while their eponymous hero supports him (because Van Buren is his son?).

"Matt will no doubt do me fine. But while I am still here I would not in the least object to your having a look at my papers. After all, you are incorrigibly literary. So—who knows? Perhaps we can work out something together."

In the outer office a door slammed. Nelson Chase had come to work. I rose, ready to begin the day's work. "Why is Mr. Davis so opposed to Van Buren?"

"I am not sure that he is."

"But just recently he wrote . . ."

"Politics, Charlie, politics. Those who *seem* to oppose are often secret supporters. Anyway, Van Buren will be president in thirty-six. And Tammany will support him, which is what I told the Vice-President last time I saw him."

"Colonel Burr!" The door opened, letting in fresh air that made me cough, so used was I to devil's smoke. Nelson Chase's dull face hung in the middle distance like a jack-a-lantern. "Madame—your wife—Mrs. Burr is downstairs in the carriage."

The Colonel was, briefly, flustered. He sprang to his feet. "Charlie, you go down and tell her that I shall meet her, as *planned*, at the Tontine, at five. Tell her that I am engaged at the moment. No. Tell her that I am out at the moment. In court."

"No court is sitting, Colonel," Nelson Chase began. But Colonel Burr was on his feet. As he put on his tall black hat, I noticed a thick protuberance in the front of his jacket just over the heart. Then he was gone out the back way and I was able to say, in all honesty, that "Colonel Burr has just left the office."

Madame peered at me through the window of her golden carriage. "*Where* did he go?" The question could be heard all the way to the water tower.

"I'm not sure, Madame. I think he said that he had an appointment . . ."

"Get in, Mr. Schuyler. Charlie. No, I shall call you Charlot. Get in. I want to talk to you."

"But, Madame . . ." On the phrase "get in" one of the grooms, a monstrous black buck in livery, leapt to the ground, opened the door to the carriage, shoved me inside like a sack of apples; sprang onto the box, and before I could protest, we were hurtling toward the Bowling Green.

Madame took my hand in hers, breathed breakfast Maderia in my face. "Charlot, he has robbed me!"

I looked at her blankly; not breathing until she removed her face from mine, and sank back onto the velvet cushions.

"I have married a thief!" Madame clutched her reticule to her bosom as though I had designs on one or the other, and in a torrent of Frenchified English told me how she had owned stock in a toll-bridge near Hartford. During the first raptures of their honeymoon in the house of Governor Edwards, the Colonel persuaded her to sell the stock. So trusting, so loving, so secure in her new place as the bride of a former vice-president, Madame allowed the Colonel to sell the shares and himself collect the cash—some six thousand dollars which he insisted on having sewn into the lining of his jacket; for safe-keeping, he said.

"'*Ma foi!*' I said to him. 'It will be better to sew the money into *my* petticoat. After all, those shares belonged to me, *non?*' We were in our bedroom in the house *du Gouverneur* and I wanted to make no scene. *Naturellement*. So what did he say to that? Why, damn him for a bastard in hell, he said, 'I am your master, Madame. Your husband, and under law what you have is mine!' *Under law!*" The small bloodshot eyes started in the huge sockets: one can imagine her fleshless skull too easily. "Well, I know the law forward and back and if he wants to play at litigation with me there are a hundred lawyers in this city I can put to work, and beat him in every court!" She ordered the coachman to stop the carriage, just opposite Castle Garden.

"Then last night, after supper, he said he was unwell. Wanted to go early to bed. Not until this morning did I realize that he had slipped away in the night, having hired a farmer's wagon. So I hurried to town— too late! He has now disposed of my money, and broken my heart!"

The footman opened the carriage door, and helped Madame alight. "We shall take the air." Firmly she took first my arm, then the air in noisy gusts.

I like the Battery best in high summer: trees too green, roses overblown, sail-boats tacking on the gray river while the pale muslin dresses of promenading girls furl and unfurl like flags in the flower and sea-scented wind.

We walked toward the round rosy brick cake of Castle Garden—the old fort where a few weeks ago I saw the President himself arrive by ship. Slender, fragile, with a mane of tangled white hair, General Jackson crossed the causeway to the shore; he moved slowly, grasping here an arm, there a shoulder, anything for support. He will not live out his term, they say.

Colonel Burr stood with me at the bottom of Broadway; the roaring, drunken crowd below us like a dozen Fourth of July celebrations rolled into one. "Not even Washington got such a reception."

"What would the President do if he knew you were here?" I asked.

"He'd probably make the sign against the evil eye." Burr laughed. "After all, I am his guilty past. He

wanted to help me conquer Mexico. Now look at him!"
Burr spoke fondly, without bitterness, like a man whose
child has grown and gone. Then, as the President
vanished into the crowd, we were both delighted when
the causeway suddenly collapsed, dunking a number of
dignitaries in the river.

Madame bade me buy us ice-cream, sold by an Irish
girl. Irish girl. Must not write that phrase. Or think
such things. But I did. Do. So much for high resolve.
I knew that I would see Mrs. Townsend to-night. How
weak I am!

"I owe the Colonel a good deal." Madame marched
between the elms. Strollers leapt aside as she passed:
a man—no, woman-of-war on the high green flowery
Battery Sea. "In the past, he was good to me for I was
not always—how you say in English, *bienvenue?*"
When tension lessens, Madame's English deserts her.
When it mounts, she is the voluble Eliza Bowen of
Providence, Rhode Island.

"Where did you first meet the Colonel?" It is almost
impossible to get from any of these survivors such a
small thing as a fact.

"So handsome!" She smacked her lips: ice-cream
delicately beaded the hardly perceptible moustache that
fringed an upper lip not naturally red. "I first *saw* him
when General Washington took the oath of office. In
Broad Street. On the balcony. I can still see General
Washington on that balcony. Such a noble, commanding figure, if somewhat too broad in the *derrière.*"
Madame chuckled at some plainly non-inagural memory. But how could she have been there? Washington
became president in 1789. If she is fifty-eight now,
she was thirteen then. Well, it is just possible.

"Colonel Burr was at the reception, and I danced
with him. Then—right after—ah, *l'ironie*, the irony! I
danced with Mr. Hamilton. Curious, come to think
of it. I admired them both, yet both were tiny and
I've always been partial to tall men."

Madame's gaze took in my own less than tall figure.

She gave me a coquettish smile. "But my passion, my *adoration* seems reserved for men of small stature but unique quality, *comme l'Empereur. Vive Napoléon!*" She shouted suddenly, causing a group of upstate Quakers—Poughkeepsie writ large on their dull faces— to scatter before her furious progress.

Madame licked her lips; ice-cream quite gone. "Occasionally we saw each other during those years. But not often. Colonel Burr was busy with politics and the law, and I had my own pursuits. Yet how sad we all were when he allowed that despicable Jefferson to take his rightful place as president. The Colonel had the votes but he would not break his word. He was too honest . . ." Sudden frown as Madame recalled the honest Burr's theft of her money.

"No! Not honest! Weak! Bonaparte would have held firm, become the president, and if that Jacobite Jefferson had stood in his way, he would have seized the Capitol by force of arms! Then I might have been— what? Marie Louise? Only constant, not like that Austrian bitch who deserted the most splendid man that ever lived! *Pauvre homme!* Why are men so frail? Women so strong?"

Madame shoved me onto a bench; then sat herself, like a carnival tent collapsing. Overhead, scarlet birds fought among branches. "Charlot, you must be my friend."

"But I am. Really . . ."

"The Colonel admires you, thinks you clever."

"Oh, no . . ."

"Much cleverer than you look. Your eyes are too far apart. Certainly much cleverer than Nelson Chase who married my *adorable* niece, pretending to have money. But that is the age-old story. And if he makes her happy, I shall pay. Why not? I like to bring a little *douceur* into the lives of others."

For a moment we watched a group of pigtailed English sailors slowly fan out over the green, their quarry three complaisant girls at the Battery's edge.

As the sun rose to noon, I could think only of Rosanna Townsend and her rooms of delight.

"Charlot, the Colonel means to ruin me." Madame stopped me before I could object. "No, no. It is not wickedness. He is not capable of any meanness. But he is mad with grandeur. He will try to get his hands onto my small fortune . . ." Small fortune! "And he will ruin me as he spends my money trying to fill up Texas with Germans. I, who hate Germans and regard Texas with a cold eye."

"The Colonel is often impulsive."

"You must talk to him. I know he listens to you. He told me that you are doing his *biographie*—good luck to you there, *mon petit!* I would not like the job of figuring out that one's life." She clutched my arm. "You must persuade him that the goose will lay golden eggs only if treated properly. As for the Texas investment, reason with him. Tell him that if he returns me the money, I shall demand no interest. In fact, I shall make him a present. What about new quarters for his firm? *Je redoute* Reade Street. I am foolishly generous when not exploited. You must take my side in this, Charlot."

I promised to help her. As I was swearing fealty, one of the beautiful scarlet birds splattered Madame's shoulder with pale guano. Unaware of the benediction, she allowed me to escort her back to the golden carriage.

En route Sam Swartwout greeted us. He is the collector of the port of New York, appointed by President Jackson to the surprise of many since he is a devoted Burrite.

Madame greeted Swartwout with delight. The collector, too, was all smiles and compliments; and earthy bluntness. "So you finally landed the old boy."

"What a way to talk, Sam! He landed me. And why not? Ain't I a rich widow?" For a moment I had a glimpse of the fun that Eliza Bowen must have been for a whole generation. Gone were the French pretensions, the mannered hardness: she giggled like a girl just out of convent, meeting her first beau. As best he could, Swartwout played the part of roaring boy, despite whisky voice, round glazed eyes, thin hair combed forward like an ancient Roman. "When will you have me to the mansion?"

"Name the day, dear Sam. What a good friend!" She used me for this declaration, like a sounding brass. "And loyal to the Colonel through thick and thin."

"Certainly through thin, Liza. But now that it's thick, I'm not sure which way to jump." They roared with laughter at things unknown to me—to anyone not of their bawdy amoral generation. Swartwout often comes to the office to chat with the Colonel behind closed doors. They have so many secrets, these ancient adventurers.

Swartwout turned to me. "My respects to the Colonel. Tell him I'll see him soon. Tell him I don't like Clay as much as he may have heard. He'll know what that means. So when are you going to qualify yourself for the law?"

I gave my usual answer. "Soon, I think."

"You have the best teacher in the world, Charlie. Fact, if the Colonel had only had the luck to have been his own teacher, he would've been emperor of Mexico by now and the world a whole lot better place —at least for you and me, Liza." With a flourish, the aged satyr kissed Madame's hand and made his way to the apple-seller on the quay.

"He is loyal, loyal, loyal!" Madame was in a better mood; her husband temporarily forgiven. "But then except for *l'Empereur* no man of our time has commanded and *kept* the loyalty of so many as Colonel Burr."

As we got into the carriage, I knew what it felt like to be the president: everyone gaped at us.

"I wonder," said Madame, happily aware of the effect her carriage was having on the people, "if I should paint the vice-president's seal on the doors. And *is* there a seal for the vice-president?"

I said I thought it unlikely a former vice-president would be allowed to employ the emblem of his lost rank. But Madame paid no attention to me; talked instead of the carriage the Emperor had given her at La Rochelle. Apparently the imperial coat-of-arms on the door made France's police her footmen, France's army her body-guard.

"He was gallant, no doubt of that." I thought she meant Bonaparte but it was Burr she had in mind.

"Certainly he worships you, Madame." I saw no harm in making peace. The bird's dropping had dried on her silken shoulder.

Madame—no, Eliza Bowen—chuckled. "He don't worship nobody, Charlie. He don't love nobody either. Never did. Except Theodosia . . ."

"His first wife?"

"No, not that old woman, hollowed out by the cancer. The *girl* Theodosia. She's the one he loved—his daughter, and no one else!"

Madame suddenly looked grim, awed, puzzled. "Strange business, Aaron Burr and his daughter, and *no* business of ours. After all, what's dead is finished. Poor Aaron, I think sometimes he drowned along with her, and all we've got of him now—all that's left—is his ghost that floated to shore."

Five

A T MIDNIGHT the Five Points is like mid-day. Every week I make up my mind not to go there, ever again, and of course I cannot stay away. This time, however, I have come for a purpose. Rosanna Townsend was born in the Hudson Valley, not far from Kinderhook. She could very well know all about Colonel Burr and Van Buren. But I am lying as I write these lines. All day I have been thinking of muslin dresses on the Battery. Could not care less about Van Buren.

Where the five streets come together the world's worst people can be found—drunks, whores, thieves, gamblers, murderers-for-hire. I cannot think any city on earth has such a squalid district. Of course, I have seen no other city, except Albany, and maybe the Sultan's Sublime Porte is wickeder than Cross Street at midnight but I doubt it.

I went from bar-room to bar-room, drinking very little but—well, observing, listening to political gossip, perversely putting off pleasure. At the corner of Anthony Street, I made a dinner of clams. As always I was dazzled by the noise, the smells, the lighted tavern windows—muslin dresses.

At midnight, I made my way to 41 Thomas Street (just writing the address in this copy-book makes me short of breath: I don't know how I was able to endure my largely celibate life before I made the acquaintance of that old brick house with its flaking green shutters and Dutch front).

I rapped on the door. A pause. A woman's shout from somewhere deep in the house. The door opened, a black face. "Oh, it's you." I slipped into the foyer. The Negro maid shut and bolted the door.

"Is Mrs. Townsend free?"

"Don't you want to go straight up and see what we got?" Of course I did, could hardly wait. But I was on a mission. This was not simply a voluptuous errand. I have—now—given up that sort of thing, and never again shall set foot in 41 Thomas Street. That is a solemn vow.

Convinced that I was perverse enough to want to pass some time with the mistress of the house, the Negress showed me into the downstairs parlour where Mrs. Townsend and her teapot were arranged on a comfortable *chaise-longue*. She drinks tea constantly: "Coffee rots you, tea dries you out," she likes to say.

As usual, she was reading a heavy book. "Something frivolous, I fear, Mr. Schuyler." She put down the book and raised her hand in greeting. "*Pilgrim's Progress.*" Usually she reads works of philosophy, collections of sermons. "It is not that I am religious, perish the thought. But there must be some meaning to all this. Some great design." And she made a spiral in the air with a long yellow hand. "I search for clues."

Mrs. Townsend motioned for me to sit beside her on a straight chair, the gas-light in my face. She is most aristocratic-looking with a long nose and a bright startled expression. Her hair has been dyed an unconvincing red—*pro forma* obeisance to a profession of which she is neither ashamed nor proud. "Mr. Bunyan is deeply depressing but I assume—by the end of his book—I shall *see* the City of God, or at least its water frontage. Light reading, I admit, but a relief after Thomas Aquinas."

She offered me tea. I shook my head. She poured herself a cup. "You must marry, Mr. Schuyler. You are much too young—or too old—for this kind of thing." She frowned as she indicated the upstairs part of her house.

"Twenty-five is the best age, I would've thought, to visit you."

Mrs. Townsend shook her head. "Twenty-five is the best age for marriage. My establishment exists as a refuge for the old married man or as a training ground for the young inexperienced boy. It is simply *not* a fitting place for a young man in his prime who should be starting his family, laying the keel, as it were, to the vessel of his mature life." Mrs. Townsend's discourse is often lofty, and though it does not reproduce too well on my page, it falls most resonantly upon the ear.

"I'm too poor to marry."

"Then marry an heiress."

We have had this conversation before. I changed the subject. Asked if there were any new-comers to Thomas Street. There was. "A treasure come to me from Connecticut, where pretty girls grow like onions. I can't think why. It must be the air. She is—she says —seventeen. I would suspect younger. She is—she says— a virgin as of this morning. I would suspect that in her modesty she exaggerates, but not by much."

As Mrs. Townsend spoke, I was more and more excited. I must be deeply depraved for I am drawn to the very young, girls just *en fleur,* as Colonel Burr would say: his taste, too—at least in old age; as a young man he was notoriously attracted to women older than he.

"Will you present me to this—Connecticut onion?"

Mrs. Townsend made a price. I made a counter-price. We haggled as we often do when there is some-thing special.

Price agreed and paid, I did not immediately rush upstairs, to her amazement. "But, go to it, Mr. Schuyler. Her name is Helen Jewett. The back bedroom on the left. Or do you want me to present you formally?"

To her further amazement I requested tea. As she poured it, I asked her if she knows Colonel Burr (she has no idea where I work or even what I do). A smile revealed perfect dentures, of genuine Indian (from India) ivory. "Colonel Burr! There was a man! I think the handsomest in the city when I was a girl. Those black eyes! And how he loved the ladies! Really loved them. Why, he would *talk* to them by the hour, busy as he was. Not like General Hamilton who was always much too busy to talk to anyone who didn't matter. Too busy for almost everything. Why, he would leap upon a girl and before she knew what was happening he was pulling up his breeches and out the door. A handsome man, too, General Hamilton, but *foxy.* You know what I mean? He had that curious orangey hair and freckled skin, which some people like and some don't. I don't." The elegant nostrils flared a moment. "And he had a sharp foxy smell to him I never could bear."

"Then you *knew* them both?"

Mrs. Townsend gave a low laugh. "Yes, even—or especially—in the Biblical sense I knew them both. Between the two they must've gone through every gay girl in the town, and I was one of the gayest then. Now let me ring . . ."

"Like Madame Jumel?"

"Eliza Bowen?" The elegant head shook with disdain. "Never could bear that tart! Always being kept by Frenchmen. I don't know if that was her taste or theirs. She lived with a sea captain for a long time in William Street and tried to pretend she didn't know ladies like me existed, but of course we knew all about her. Our sorority is not that large, you know, or at least it wasn't thirty years ago when all the world was young. But Liza's done well, they tell me. She wanted money and a place in society. She got the money. I don't think the other is possible. Not in New York, thank God. There are some things money cannot buy."

I steered her back to Colonel Burr. But she had not known him for many years. "I never leave Thomas Street and he never comes here. I *think* I saw him once at the theatre, after he came back from Europe, that must've been in twelve or thirteen. But maybe it was someone else. He was a hero of mine. Even though I am still a Federalist at heart."

"Didn't you come from Kinderhook originally?"

Mrs. Townsend looked more than usually startled. "Did I tell you that?" But she was not interested in my reply; she forgave herself the indiscretion. "No, Claverack. Not too far away."

"You must have known the Van Buren family."

Obviously she wanted to find some sequential link but refused to humble herself by asking a question. She is a woman of answers only. "I was once or twice in their tavern. But I don't remember the son. I suspect he was already in New York. Then when I was seventeen I came to the city, too, eager to take my place in Sodom and Gomorrah. Like Milton's Satan, I would rather reign in Thomas Street than serve in Claverack."

"Did you ever hear that Colonel Burr was the father of Martin Van Buren?"

"One *hears* everything. But I tend to believe nothing. I do know that Colonel Burr has at least one son born beneath the rose, as they say, a silversmith, who lives in the Bowery. Aaron Columbus Burr he is called. His mother was French and he was conceived while the Colonel was in Paris. A charming youth. He came here once as a customer—and remained to take a dent out of a silver tray that I had, uncharitably, flung at the head of a certain poxy girl. If I were younger and so inclined, I might have served Monsieur Columbus Burr myself for he is a beautiful young man, or was. I haven't seen him in years either."

MUFFLED CRIES from upstairs.

A door slams loudly.

A man coughs.

Mrs. Townsend picks up *Pilgrim's Progress.* "Go to Miss Jewett," she commands.

Miss Jewett stands in front of an open window; behind her I can see by moonlight the bedraggled back yard whose ricketty fence keeps in Mrs. Townsend's cow. I am in the room I like best. In fact, it was in this room that I first enjoyed Mrs. Townsend's hospitality.

Helen Jewett shakes hands. She does not seem nervous, only grave . . .

I AM IN THE OFFICE making notes; it is the next morning and I am obliged to record that I have never been so well pleased as with this girl. Gray eyes, perfect skin, clean body—none of that drenching in cheap perfume that makes love-making with so many girls seem like a wrestling match in a chemist's shop.

We talked for some time. "I should like to be a dressmaker." She did not have a country accent. "But, you see, there was no place in New Haven. Two French-women do everything, and very jealous they are of anybody else. So I came here and met a girl who knew Mrs. Townsend, and here I am." She smiled; she is very straightforward.

"In a few years I should have enough money saved to open a shop. You don't need much, you know. And Mrs. Townsend says I can dress her and all the girls here."

I did not make the obvious remark that the girls seldom wear more than a shift (they are not often let out of the house) while Rosanna Townsend's only costume is a rusty, green-black bombasine shroud.

"Did you enjoy that?" The girl seemed really curious to know.

"Yes, very much."

"I'm glad."

"Were you a virgin when you came here?"

She smiled again, shook her head. "No. But I never kept company with a stranger, like this."

"Do you like it?"

"Well, I don't exactly know." Then laughed. "You look sort of like one of those cherubs in the hymnal." This so aroused me that I was ready to begin all over again but the Negress's heavy tread outside the door signified that my time was up. I said I would see her soon again. Will I? Yes.

As I left the room, started toward the stairs, I heard the sound of gagging. A door was flung open and there was Leggett, both hands over his mouth; behind him, on the bed, a startled girl without clothes.

Outraged, the maid slammed shut the door.

Leggett gave one last thunderous cough, wiped his lips with the back of his hand, opened his eyes, saw me and said, "Well, that was wasted money. I nearly *died*—in the non-Elizabethan sense. It's the dust here. I tell Rosanna, 'I'd rather have the clap ten times than choke on the dust from your counterpanes'!"

Shakily, he took my arm and we went downstairs.

The doors to the parlour were shut. Mrs. Townsend was at home only to John Bunyan.

Leggett and I went out into the warm night—morning—and made our way to the Five Points, to the tavern at Cross Street.

As we entered two pigs were being chased across the sawdust floor by the bar-tender, to the delight of the clientele.

Leggett was recognised immediately. The workies adore him as much as the rich detest him. Great pats on the shoulder caused him to stagger this way and that as we made our way to a table at the back.

Then Leggett ordered beer for two, pulled proofs from his pocket, began to correct an editorial, all the while quizzing me about the new girl from Connecticut. I told him little, not wanting him to have her. He nodded, coughed, read and marked proof—to my irritation.

"Can you really read and talk at the same time?"

"Of course." But he put away the proofs when beer arrived.

"On the house, Mr. Leggett!" An Irish face smiled down upon us. The lower orders of New York may not actually read Leggett's fiery editorials—or anything else—but the word has spread among them that he is a scourge to their employers. And of course any man capable of thrashing (as he did recently) a libellous editor is a true hero.

"What news of Colonel Burr?"

I told Leggett of my conversation with Madame, adding, "I'm collecting material." Actually I have done no more than record my few findings in this book, with altogether too many digressions of a personal nature. Yet like a criminal's deposition, one thing does lead to another. At first the testimony is garrulous, self-serving, repetitive; then, gradually, themes emerge, lies become evident, truths isolated. I believe that if I put down *everything* I know of Colonel Burr, I ought, at the end, to be able to make that riddling Sphinx rise and show me whether it be man or woman, brute or human, or some hybrid undreamed-of lying athwart my days. Who is Aaron Burr, and—again—what is he to me?

"You know my interest, Charlie. The Van Buren connection."

"I can hardly ask the Colonel directly . . ."

"Obviously not. But there are people who might know."

"Matthew Davis?"

Leggett made a face. "He would know but I doubt if he'd *tell*. The quintessential Tammany man, secretly at work for Henry Clay. Well, all that I can say is: if it's between Clay and Van Buren . . ."

Elections fascinate Leggett. He cannot exist unless he is plunged deep in some cause or quarrel. It actually matters to him that there are black slaves in the south and exploited working-men in the city. I envy him. He is never bored; lives on his nerves, hurling inky thunderbolts at those in power; all fire and aggression.

I am the opposite; drawn to the past, to what is secret; and prone to those dreams of domination that make it possible for the dreamer to subvert with the greatest of ease class, nation, honour. Bonaparte fascinates me. So does Burr. To Leggett they are blackguards, which no doubt they are. Even so, I prefer either to any dozen Andrew Jacksons.

Perhaps it is simply a liking for easy games of chance that draws so many Americans to politics of the usual sort. Yet affecting to love democracy, every last one of them does his best to make sufficient money in order to exclude himself from the common round. I suppose that kind of blindness to motive is normal. At best, however, I prefer the man like Burr who, failing to gain power in the conventional way, breaks up the game—or tries to—seizes the crown—or tries to—and in the failing . . .

But what do I really know of Aaron Burr? Or of

myself? I am only scribbling idly, trying to put myself
in his skin as I sit now at my desk in Reade Street,
waiting for him and the others to come to work on
a hot August morning. No breeze.

I tried just now to open the chest beneath the round
table but it is locked.

What else did Leggett and I talk about?

"If Matthew Davis is unsatisfactory, I shall try Sam
Swartwout."

Leggett was not enthusiastic. "They have every reason to hide the connection and no incentive to reveal
it. Sam dislikes Van Buren but not enough to betray
Burr, much less the President. Of course he would
know a good deal about Burr's adventures out west."

It was time to go. As we left the bar, we saw two
men fighting at the wooden pump. One was short and
stocky: he was pummelling a tall gangling creature
with loose flapping arms.

" 'Put out the light,' " bellowed the youth and we
recognised the most splendid voice in our city: Edwin
Forrest was giving a much deserved beating to William
de la Touche Clancey, the Tory sodomite.

"*And then put out the light!*" Forrest's voice echoed
through the Five Points like a bronze trumpet on the
day of judgement. He is the world's greatest Othello;
and in most classic roles, better than any English
actor (despite Mrs. Trollope's ignorant abuse of him).
Assuming Forrest is not ruined by drink or got up for
murder, he will be the best actor in the world. He is
only twenty-seven.

Leggett threw himself upon the pair, shoved Forrest
against the tavern wall, gave the swooning Clancey
a kick that sent him half-way to Anthony Street. "For
God's sake, Ned," said Leggett, "this is no Desde-
mona!"

"Very like," muttered Forrest ominously, holding
himself erect with some difficulty, the handsome young
bull's face red from whiskey.

Safe at the opposite corner, Clancey was himself

again—coolly disdainful despite dirt-smeared face, torn shirt. "Get that butcher boy to bed, Leggett!" Clancey's voice is like that of a furious goose, all honks and hisses.

"Not *your* bed!" thundered Edwin Forrest, holding on to Leggett's arm. The Bowery b'hoys were delighted by these insults. Delighted, too, to observe a pair of their favourites in league against the natural enemy, for Clancey detests our democracy, finds even the Whigs radical, the Adams family vulgar, Daniel Webster a *sans-culotte*. He fills the pages of his magazine *America* with libellous comments on all things American. Despite a rich wife and five children, he is a compulsive sodomite, forever preying on country boys new to the city.

Leggett tidied up his friend; asked what the quarrel was about. But Forrest only smiled (I do think him better than anyone I have ever seen on the stage. I often practice in front of the mirror the last scene from his *Spartacus*), and putting an arm around Leggett's shoulder, allowed himself to be led away.

" 'You know,' " he whispered Iago's line, " 'what you know.' " I shuddered at that thrilling voice. Shudder now as I record the scene (like Leggett I once thought of becoming an actor). I suppose Leggett's unfulfilled ambition explains his friendship with Forrest—the actor lives out a life the writer will never know.

I turn now to the manuscript Colonel Burr gave me.

ACROSS THE TOP of the first page:

"*An account of Lieutenant-Colonel Aaron Burr's Military Service at the Time of the Glorious Revolution.*" The word "Glorious" has been inserted in the narrow space between "the" and "Revolution."

"*On the strength not only of this Record but also of the enclosed Accounts of those Witnesses who still survive, Lieutenant-Colonel Aaron Burr most respectfully proposes himself to the Congress, in accordance*

*with recent legislation (documents enclosed), as one
to whom Recompense is now due for Expenses in-
curred during the just war against British Tyranny. At
New York City, January 1, 1825."*

I search for enclosures. There are none.

Then, scribbled in the margin: "Charlie—a petition
to Congress can never be entirely candid. When I was
bedridden three years ago, I re-read this tale of heroism
and decided that the *actual* story of those days ought
to be told. The truth cannot hurt us, as they say.
Most incorrectly, of course: it is the truth that blasts
us like a thunderbolt from the God my grandfather
regularly communed with. Incidentally, it has always
been my view that if God exists He is probably not
half so unpleasant as He has been made out to be.
But then, as usual, mine is a minority opinion.

"Amuse yourself with this telling of old things. Certainly it amused me to set it all down, a task begun
when I was in the Senate and had, for a brief period,
the run of our military archives."

I copy out the whole text, incorporating foot-notes
and asides in the text proper.

Cambridge, Quebec

I was nineteen and a student at Tapping Reeve's law
school in Litchfield, Connecticut, on the day that
American colonists and British soldiers met for the first
time in battle at Lexington. One day later (April 20,
1775) "victory" bells were ringing in Litchfield. The
long-awaited battle for American independence had
begun, and I was ready for it.

Actually, I was ready only for adventure. Unlike
Hamilton, I had taken no part in the various debates
that precipitated the revolution, as people inaccurately
term the political separation of the American colonies

from the British crown. Brought up in a family of
sermonizers, I have never responded to *any* political
rhetoric, save, on rare occasions, my own.

Until the actual fighting began, my days were devoted entirely to law and to one Dolly Quincy of
Fairfield. Although Dolly was the fiancée of John
Hancock, the Massachusetts delegate to the Continental Congress, she was a good friend to me, and played
with tact the Older Woman who is obliged to hold—
nearly at arm's length—an impetuous boy-admirer.

Dolly and I were part of a small crowd that stood
outside the Litchfield tavern and listened to a cutler
who had just escaped from British-held Boston. He
claimed to have been at Lexington. I am sure he gave
us many bloody details but I no longer recall a word
he said. I do remember walking across the muddy common, a silent Dolly holding tight my arm. I remember
daffodils in bloom—a goose with goslings gliding across
the still cold water of a pond.

"John will be pleased." Dolly picked flowers. "He
has wanted a war from the beginning. I think he's
mad."

"Are you a Tory?" I teased her. But she was serious;
not at all responsive to the war fever. "I fear what is
going to happen to all of us." I still remember the
exact inflection of her voice, and the look in her handsome, if slightly crossed eyes. So the long war began;
with bells ringing, and bright daffodils.

In July, through the offices of a friend (Dolly), I
received a letter from John Hancock, now president
of the Continental Congress, recommending my cousin
Matthias Ogden and me to the attention of the recently appointed commanding general of the Continental Army, George Washington of Virginia.

I ought to mention that Dolly was appalled when
news came to us that Washington had been chosen.
"John was supposed to command the army. I don't
understand it."

But then, at the time, no one understood how Wash-

?

ington and his Virginia confederates had managed to wrest for themselves the leadership of what was essentially a New England army. Working together in perfect concert and displaying at all times the most exquisite loyalty to one another, the Virginians pushed to one side not only John Hancock but such talented commanders as Gates and Lee and Artemas Ward. As a matter of course, John Adams would betray his fellow New Englander John Hancock. Lacking personal loyalty to one another as well as any true policy, the New Englanders and the New Yorkers from the beginning gave over to the Virginia junto the American republic—and with relish the junto proceeded to rule us for the better part of a half-century.

In July, a week after General Washington took command, Matt Ogden and I arrived at Cambridge to find the town full of officers and would-be officers.

The letter from John Hancock was duly delivered to Adjutant-General Gates who was amiable but harassed. He promised me an appointment with General Washington but I never did speak to the General in the two months I spent at Cambridge. Matt Ogden, on the other hand, was promptly commissioned.

I was forced to spend nights in the taverns in order to meet officers; days in the camp to get to know a few of the 17,000 would-be soldiers who were encamped beside the Charles River. Particularly striking were the frontiersmen from the forests of what was then the west. They wore fringed hunting jackets and lived like wild beasts in the open. Since they did not bother to dig "necessaries," wherever they were the stench was overwhelming.

For those who preferred a roof over their head, the range of impromptu dwellings was wide. A few officers were able to afford proper tents, even marquees like the British. Others were forced to make themselves houses of sailcloth or of boards tacked together at random, or of turf. The total effect was chaos, like something thrown up in the wake of a disaster on the order of the Lisbon earthquake, and like the survivors of a calamity a good many took delight in reverting to barbarism—to drunkenness, thieving, fighting.

I moved from company to company, learning what I could. One thing was plain. Certain officers had the knack of gaining obedience with no effort while others —the majority—were forced to shout and threaten, often to no avail.

Toward the end of July, I was watching a ragged company of New Yorkers at drill when General Washington approached, astride a black horse. It was my first glimpse of him close-to. He wore the recently designed blue and buff uniform of the army; across his chest a pale blue ribband signified that he was commanding general (lesser generals wore purple ribbands, staff officers green ribbands, and so on).

As the General passed me, I saluted. I was still in civilian clothes but then so were most of the army.

As Washington returned my salute, I looked up into his face: the yellow pock-marked skin was lightly covered with powder; the gray eyes sunk in cavernous sockets were lustreless; the expression was grave but somewhat vacant. I thought him old as God. Yet he was only forty-three!

Slowly the General rode toward a makeshift cabin of sailcloth in front of which a pair of drunkards were trying to kill one another to the delight of a number of equally drunk onlookers.

I followed the General, curious to see what he would do. Most officers would have looked the other way. Sober, the American soldier is not easily managed; drunk, he can be murderous.

"Stop!" Raised in command, the deep voice was thunderous. There was a brief murmur of dazed, rummy interest from the spectators. Then they turned back to the fight. One howling man was now trying to choke the other who seemed to have bitten off most of his adversary's ear.

For a moment Washington resembled one of those

equestrian monuments that currently decorate so many of the republic's vistas. Horse and rider were motionless until it was plain that Washington was not going to be obeyed. Then majestically he dismounted, and as if at the head of a stately procession he walked toward the two men grunting and writhing in the dirt. For a large, rather ungainly man (he had the hips, buttocks and bosom of a woman), Washington could move with brutal swiftness. He fell upon the two men. One large hand encircled the strangler's throat. The other seized the matted hair of the cannibal. He dragged the men to their feet; held them aloft; shook them like rats. All the while a series of sky-rending oaths emerged from the broad yellow face now brick-red beneath its powder. If he was not heard all the way to Boston, he was certainly heard by most of the encampment.

Aides hurried to support their commander. A sergeant put the two terrified men under arrest. The revellers even tried to come to attention as Washington mounted his horse, affecting a serenity that was truly marvellous except for someone next to him, as I was, who could see the trembling of the hand with which he held the reins. He must, secretly, have been terrified. After all, he had had no experience of modern warfare, while his exploits as an Indian fighter were a good deal less than glorious despite the legends that he and the Virginians used so relentlessly to circulate. But no matter what his military short-comings, at least he *looked* like a general.

President Hancock described to me most amusingly Washington's first appearance at Philadelphia. As a hint to the recently convened Congress, the delegate from Virginia insisted on wearing the same red and blue uniform he had worn during his skirmishes with the Indians a dozen years before. But although he made an excellent martial impression, it was also noted by certain irreverent delegates that a tendency to corpulence had now made him rather too large for the old uniform he was wearing.

"One expected," said Hancock, "the sound of rip-
ping and tearing every time he rose from dinner at
Barnes' Tavern, and waddled forth to mount his long-
suffering horse."

Hancock went to his grave furious that it was Washington and not he who had been chosen to command
the Continental Army. Narrowly to miss such greatness is a bitter thing; and greatness seemed inevitable
that summer. At Lexington and Bunker Hill we had
held our own in the face of the best army in the world.
Also, the British were 3,000 miles from home and
forced to fight in a wild country-side where their
specialty, the fixed battle, was of no use to them
against the strategy they most feared, the constant
sniping of invisible riflemen.

Despite our green confidence at Cambridge, Washington himself must have wondered if it was possible
to make an army out of such unlikely human material.
Beside the river Charles were assembled thieves, ruffians, wild men from the forest, murderers, Negroes
run away from their southern owners, European adventurers . . . every sort of scoundrel save one, the
soldier. Hardly a man cared about the issue of England.
The majority had enlisted because they wanted money,
paid in advance. Even the non-mercenary patriots were
of little use to Washington, particularly those New
Englanders who saw themselves as generals to a man
and refused to serve in the ranks. Yet we thought it
would be a brief war.

As Washington rode off, a stocky youth turned to
me and made some observation about His Excellency's
language. We both laughed; and together walked toward the river.

"I'm Captain James Wilkinson from Maryland." He
introduced himself. I was filled with envy. Here I was
an experienced nineteen-year-old man of the world
while Captain Jamie Wilkinson was an eighteen-year-
old boy with a face that had yet to know the scrape
of a razor. Jamie had enlisted in the army at Georege-
town, after a short career studying medicine. "Now

I want to see fighting. But where? When?" He indicated Boston in the distance—and the British headquarters. He shook his head. "A sweet situation."

We got on well from the beginning and Jamie always said that from that day he had found in me the best friend he was ever to have. Would that I had been his enemy!

"Indian shoes for sale!" Sitting cross-legged in the dust, a pale fat frontiersman displayed several pairs of crudely made moccasins to a crowd of idlers. It was a bit like a fair, those early days of the encampment before Washington's discipline was felt.

A bare-foot farmer bought himself a pair, the salesman talking all the while. "There's a lot of wear in them shoes, I promise. Made 'em myself. Tanned 'em, too." All around us a good deal of mysterious giggling as the moccasins were passed from hand to hand and carefully examined. Mysterious until we realized that these Indian shoes were just that.

"I shot me two braves on the way here from Frankfort where I live. Well, after I shot 'em, I took a good look at these two sizable bucks just layin' there. A shame, I said to myself, to let all that fine meat go to waste. So I skinned 'em both from the waist down and cured their hides in the sun. I'm a tanner by trade. And then I made up these nice shoes that are every bit as good as cow. See?" He held up one of the moccasins. "Here's some bristles left, a proper memento, you might say. Oh, it's real Indian hide, I promise."

At the bridge over the Charles River, we found General Washington and his aides. The General was staring at the far bank of the river where a number of men were bathing, entirely naked. With happy cries, they showed themselves off to a number of interested Cambridge ladies.

"He'll never make an army of this riffraff." Wilkinson thought that the men in their anarchy would prove stronger than Washington. But Wilkinson was wrong. In a matter of minutes, the bathers were driven up-stream by sergeants with muskets. The next day one colonel and five captains were broken. The following day, at the centre of the camp, appeared "The Horse," a notorious contraption to which culprits were tied and flogged. Washington had taken command.

The next week both small pox and the bloody flux began to go through the camp. General Washington maintained that the flux came from drinking new cider. But the cider-drinking continued, and so for that matter did the flux, which is a terrible death, the bowels emptying out one's life in bloody spasms.

I took to my bed with a fever that lasted two weeks. Matt and Jamie looked after me as best they could: I have never been so wretched. I had, in effect, run away from home to join the army but so far had found no way of joining it.

"It's your size." Matt fed me cabbage soup. "You look ten years old!" This was an exaggeration but I did look younger than the other officers, including Jamie whose youthful belly gave him an undeserved dignity. Yet I was confident that I was well-suited to the military life. I was a fair shot, good with horses and, I was fairly certain, good with soldiers, too. After all, I had the natural authority of the born pedagogue. I also wanted glory—a desire that must surely add a cubit to even the smallest stature.

Unable to sleep (the heat within me and the heat without for once unbearable), I heard Matt talking to friends in the next room. "They'll need at least a thousand volunteers."

"Here's one!" Another young voice. "I don't intend to stop the rest of my life in Cambridge." We found it mysterious that Washington seemed interested only in drilling the men and digging "necessaries" while within sight of our encampment beside the Charles, the British army at Boston each day stood formation like so many dangerous scarlet toys in the green distance.

Washington did nothing because, unknown to us, his supply of powder was limited, his artillery non-existent, his troops unproven. Washington's view of war was simple and invariable: do nothing until you outnumber the enemy two to one. So he waited for Congress to send him more men and to give him more supplies. Considering that the British forces were far from home and considering that there were over two million Americans in the colonies, it ought not to have been difficult for us to overwhelm them in every way. But difficult it was, always, for Washington to maintain an army. The rich tended to be pro-British while the poor were not interested in whether or not American merchants paid taxes to a far-away island. The truth is that except for a handful of ambitious lawyers, there were very few "patriots" in 1775. By the time the long deadly war came to an end, there were hardly any to be found. The best died; the rest grew weary.

But now, at least, the dull days for a few of us were over. Candle in hand, Matt sat on the edge of my sweat-soaked bed and told me that "We're going to invade Canada."

I was surprised. "Why not invade Boston? It's much closer, and most of the British army is there."

"Washington thinks the British are going to come down from Canada and cut off New England from the rest of the colonies. So he wants us to anticipate them. Volunteers are wanted for a battalion and at least three companies of riflemen."

My fever broke that night, never to return. On September 6, I enlisted in the company of Lieutenant-Colonel Christopher Greene. On September 13, Colonel Greene's detachment left Cambridge for Newburyport. A new and eager soldier, I went on foot. Matt sensibly took a carriage.

On September 16, eleven hundred of us—mostly Virginians and Kentuckians with one company of New Yorkers (demanding, as usual, their pay in advance) were drawn up at attention to be reviewed by our commander, Colonel Benedict Arnold, the first hero of the Revolution.

I have a vivid recollection of Arnold that day, standing tall and bulky against a bright sky. Hair black as ink; face a curious deep olive colour, as though stained with walnut juice; eyes marvellously strange like those of an animal or some predatory bird, pale as ice, unblinking: the Indians called him Black Eagle. Restless, brave, entirely lacking in judgement except on the battle-field, he was a fascinating figure, given to quarrels.

Arnold spoke to us briefly. Then he presented the various officers. Among them was Dan Morgan of Virginia, a famed Indian-killer in fringed jacket; nearly forty years of age, Morgan was the oldest of the officers. Arnold himself was about thirty-four. Although he had authority, he did not inspire awe the way Washington did. Arnold was more like the best athlete among boys; the one who holds most easily the centre of the stage. In fact, none of our officers looked particularly military except for Lieutenant-Colonel Roger Enos, who was to lose us Canada.

Until May 1775, Benedict Arnold had been an apothecary in New Haven. After news came of the fighting at Lexington, he shut up shop, raised a company of soldiers and put himself at the disposal of the commonwealth of Massachusetts. From the beginning it was his strategy to take Fort Ticonderoga from the British in order to open the way into Canada. He did take Fort Ticonderoga but was forced to share the glory with Ethan Allen (a contentious figure whose eventual capture by the British was a relief to the American command). Allen and Arnold promptly fell out with one another. Worse, the Massachusetts Assembly declared that they had no interest in Canada; apparently the only reason for capturing Fort Ticonderoga was to acquire much-needed artillery. Declaring himself ill-used and betrayed, Arnold resigned his commission at Watertown in August. Washington promptly commissioned him a colonel and then, "His Excellency did me the honour of accepting my strategy for the conquest of Canada."

In the church at Newburyport, Arnold addressed his officers from the pulpit. "I do not think we have lost too much by waiting. I had wanted to go straight on to Canada after I took Ticonderoga." Matt Ogden and I exchanged glances. It was our first experience with a military hero. Apparently, quite alone, the military hero reduces cities and makes history. "But that proved not to be possible." Arnold had sufficient sense not to denounce to his officers the magnates of Massachusetts who had stopped him.

A staff captain produced a map of Canada and tacked it onto the pulpit. We leaned forward in our hard pews while Arnold explained to us the route. The next day, we would board eleven transports and proceed to Gardinierstown at the mouth of the Kennebec River. There we would find 224 bateaux.

"In these flat-bottomed boats we shall make our way up the Kennebec River." A thick finger traced the route on the map. "At the head-water we cross over land some twelve miles to the Dead River. Meanwhile another force under General Schuyler will be moving from Fort Ticonderoga to Fort St. John to Montreal. Once Montreal is ours, General Schuyler will join us at Quebec. My best intelligence assures me that in all of Canada there are only seven hundred British troops, and no fleet. I shall begin the siege of Quebec no later than October fifteenth."

I record this speech from memory in order to give an idea of the vaingloriousness of certain of our commanders in the early days of the fighting. Yet I must say Arnold was able to convince us that before the first snow fell we would be the liberators of Canada. How could we fail? The Canadians themselves were with us. The province had been ceded only twelve years earlier to England by France, to the great distress (so we were told) of the French colonials who were waiting impatiently for our arrival and "freedom." I'm afraid we all believed this nonsense.

As it turned out, the French colonials liked us rather

less than they liked the English, whom they actually preferred to their own corrupt French governors. More important, they were quite aware of the hatred Americans have for their church. On reflection, it is very odd that Washington could ever have hoped to appeal to the French Canadians when hardly a day passed that in our press or in the Congress there was not some attack on the Roman Catholic Church and its diabolic plots to overthrow our pure Protestantism in order to make bright a hundred village greens with the burning of martyrs. This insensitivity to other people's religion and customs has been a constant in the affairs of the republic and the author of much trouble, as Jefferson was to discover when he blithely and illegally annexed Louisiana with its Catholic population.

At Gardinierstown the famed bateaux were waiting. Made of green pine in great haste, they sank like stones when loaded with cargo. With considerable effort, we made a sufficient number river-worthy. Then on a bright September morning, we set out to conquer Canada.

Like Napoleon Bonaparte, Benedict Arnold was too great a man to notice weather. Neither understood that autumn is invariably followed by winter and that in such northern latitudes as Russia and Canada winter is invincible. But then none of us anticipated what was ahead—like the grasshopper in the parable we enjoyed the warm September days, and dreamed of glory amongst the northern lights.

It soon developed that Arnold's map was inaccurate. The Kennebec River was wilder and swifter then we had been led to believe. Some thirty times we were forced out of the river and into the forest, carrying those infernal bateaux on our backs. Spirits plummetted. Nights were cold. Wolves howled. We saw few people, except at Fort Western, a small depressing outpost (now known as Augusta in the state of Maine).

A huge bear was chained outside the stockade at Fort Western. There were sores on his legs where the chains chafed. That sight stays in my memory. Also, damp odour of pine needles and dark earth. The flash of mica in gray rock. The cursing of men trying to keep their horns of powder from getting wet as we forded streams, took shelter from the cold rain.

On land I usually travelled with young Jonathan Dayton (a future speaker of the house and New Jersey senator); we shared the same rations; slept at night beside the same fire. Matt was with the forward company.

When we went by water, Colonel Arnold would travel in state aboard his own dug-out, manned by two Indians. At first there were good-natured jokes about our commander's unerring ability to find a settler's cabin for the night, denying himself the pleasure of sleeping like us *al fresco*. But when disaster struck, the jokes turned to curses and only the power of his formidable personality kept the men from open mutiny.

On October 8, we reached the head-water of the Kennebec River. We were exhausted but knew that we must hurry on into settled territory for the fire-red, sun-yellow leaves were turning brown, were falling, and there was a smell of snow on the north wind. Grasshopper weather was over.

It took us eight days to move over-land to the well-named Dead River. Sullen, swift deep black water twisting through a pristine forest that must have looked the same at the world's beginning. So deep was the water that we could not pole the bateaux and so had to pull them along with ropes, men doing the usual work of horses. Already the New Yorkers were talking about the beginning of the new year in ten weeks' time, and the end of their enlistment.

On the night of October 24, the Dead River flooded. We lost half our provisions and bateaux and most of our confidence. I spent the night with Jonathan Dayton in a tree. At dawn we looked with wonder at a vast lake stretching in every direction through the dark

coniferous forest. As the waters began to recede into
the earth, we assembled in the mud and tried to make
sense of the disaster.

Just as Colonel Arnold joined us, snow began to
fall. He promptly held a council beneath the trees. "I
leave it to you," he said to the men, "whether we go
on or turn back."

There was much debate despite the swirling snow
which made it hard for us to see one another in that
awful whiteness. But Arnold cleverly led the discussion,
forcing those who wanted to turn back to admit that
it was most unlikely that any of us could survive the
journey with half our provisions gone, most of the
bateaux scattered throughout the forest and the snow
mounting even as we spoke. It was decided to press on.

On the 30th, Colonel Arnold went to buy food at
Sartigan, a near-by village according to the fatal map.

"We won't see him again." Dayton was confident
we had been abandoned. Rations were exhausted. The
men had already eaten their dogs; they were now
chewing on belts, moccasins, bits of soap. Fortunately
Matt appeared on the scene from the forward detachment, and brought with him the last of the provisions;
a half-pound of pork and five pints of flour to last each
of us until, presumably, Quebec fell or Colonel Arnold
brought us food.

To the delight of all, supplies arrived three days later
from mythical Sartigan. There was a good deal of re-
joicing. Even the snow stopped falling for the occasion.

Then the bad news. An Indian guide reported that
our rear detachment under Lieutenant-Colonel Enos
had departed for Massachusetts, leaving us with only
500 effective troops.

Between November 7 and 13, our "army" assembled
at Point Levis on the St. Lawrence River across from
Quebec. We were relieved to be in civilised country;
we were alarmed at our situation. Two ships of the
British navy patrolled the river while within the citadel
of Quebec there were more than 500 British troops,

guarded by a frigate and a sloop whose combined guns numbered forty-two. Arnold's "best" intelligence reports were about as good as his map.

On the night of November 13, the British set fire to our remaining bateaux. Astonishingly, the green wood burned.

We moved to Wolfe's Cove below the walls of Quebec. It was here that a trapper told us how General Schuyler's replacement General Montgomery had captured the British forts of Chambly and St. John. Montgomery was now advancing upon Montreal. Delighted, Arnold ordered Matt to go to the citadel and under a flag of truce demand the immediate surrender of Quebec.

"Tell the British commander that we shall be most generous if they obey us promptly. But unrelenting—repeat—*unrelenting* if they do not recognise our sovereignty in Canada." I could hardly believe my ears. Poor Matt did as he was ordered.

We watched Matt as he approached the gates to the citadel, a small figure, carrying a dirty white shirt on a stick. To Arnold's fury and (once we knew that Matt was safe) to my amusement, the British fired a volley of grape-shot at Matt who scurried down the heights and joined us at the cove.

"I shall teach those bastards from hell a lesson they'll never forget!" Arnold's dark face was black with wrath; the gray-yellow eyes shone like a cat's. On the spot he ordered Matt to start down-river to Montreal, to find Montgomery wherever he was and to "tell him he must join us. Now! For a joint siege. Montreal is not important. Quebec is." Matt departed within the hour.

On November 19, we moved twenty miles west of the city to Pointe aux Trembles and established a camp. The next day a British sloop arrived from Montreal; aboard was the Canadian governor Sir Guy Carleton. Montreal had fallen to Montgomery! Our spirits soared.

"We would have been better off serving with

Montgomery." Dayton was sour. Like most of the young officers he tended to blame Arnold for our situation. In retrospect, Arnold's plan to take Canada was good. It was the sort of bold stroke that Bonaparte excelled in. Arnold was hardly Bonaparte but he was an imaginative and daring general. Unfortunately, he did not possess the *sine qua non* of the truly great general, luck. He had also, as I have mentioned, not taken into account the peculiar savagery of the Canadian winter.

On the morning of November 30, having heard nothing from Montreal, Arnold presented me with a letter to General Montgomery and ordered me out onto the river. I was delighted.

With an Indian guide, I departed Pointe aux Trembles in a canoe. The British ship *Horney* fired a careless musket or two in our direction but otherwise we were unmolested as we paddled against the current past the high rocky cliff on which sits Quebec City. Even the cold was delightful on that white morning, no sound but that of water softly lapping against the birch-bark hull.

I should note here that I did not ever disguise myself as a French priest in order to pass through the countryside unremarked. For one thing, any Frenchman would have remarked on my crude disguise. I have no idea where this story came from but like so many other absurdities it has been duly published. Nor did I conduct a tragic love affair with an Indian princess supposedly encountered at Fort Western and loyally my concubine until she was struck down trying to save my life in the assault upon Quebec. It has been my fate to be the centre of a thousand inventions, mostly of a disagreeable nature. I never deny these stories. People believe what they want to believe. Yet I do think that my name has in some mysterious way been filched from me and used to describe a character in some interminable three-volume novel of fantastic adventure, the work of a deranged author whose imagination never sleeps—although this reader does when he reads for the thousandth time how the hellish Aaron Burr meant single-handedly to disband the United States when a voyage to the moon would have been simpler to achieve, and a good deal more interesting.

We had not been three hours from Pointe aux Trembles when we saw on the horizon the American flotilla coming from the west. By sunset I had delivered to Richard Montgomery himself the message from Benedict Arnold in which I was introduced (as always in those days) as the son of the late president of The College of New Jersey.

"I've already sent Colonel Arnold supplies. They should have arrived." Montgomery was a tall noble figure with a handsome somewhat stupid-looking face due to a low brow that sloped back from his nose like one of those English dogs who, bred for speed, lose in the process the usual canine complement of intelligence. Although I did not know Montgomery long enough to be able to form a proper estimate of his intelligence, there was no doubting his charm and courage, and we got on famously. In fact, he made me, on the spot, a captain attached to his staff. It was my first promotion.

After Montgomery's arrival with 300 men, we had, all told, perhaps 800 effectives with which to take the most elaborate fortress in North America.

During the month of December, I was able to convince General Montgomery that our best hope was to wait for a snow-storm (every third day, it seemed, snow fell) and then scale with ladders Cap Diamond, the highest portion of the citadel and so the least guarded. Simultaneously, three other detachments would attack the fort, distracting the guards. Once atop Cap Diamond, we would then be able to penetrate the citadel and open the gates.

For two weeks I was allowed to train fifty men (and myself) in the art of scaling a high wall. Unfortunately, General Montgomery's mind was changed by two friendly Canadians who assured him that if he seized the Lower Town with its warehouses on the river, the merchant families that own Quebec would force Sir Guy to capitulate rather than run the risk of losing their warehouses, supplies, ships. I never thought this a good plan; and it was not.

Montgomery fixed the last day of the year for the attack. He had no choice. On the next day several hundred New Yorkers planned to leave for home, their period of enlistment at an end.

Arnold was to attack from the east; Montgomery from the west. Their two divisions would then unite in the Lower Town, and move on to the citadel. At first, all things favoured us. A full moon. A drunken British garrison celebrating the New Year. But just as we began our advance, out of the north swept a snowstorm hiding the citadel, shrouding with white the Plains of Abraham. Since it was too late to turn back, we went on with the consoling thought that though we could no longer see the enemy he could not see us either.

I was at Montgomery's side as we slowly moved along the river's edge. We could not see more than a few feet ahead of us. Snow stung our eyes. We came to the first row of wooden pickets. We broke through. Then the second. We broke through; and saw in front of us the first blockhouse, occupied by sailors who fled at our approach, abandoning a twelve-pound gun.

We were now in the deep ravine leading to the Lower Town.

· Montgomery was delighted. "The snow is our ally," he whispered to me; and came to a full halt. He had walked into the first of a number of blocks of ice recently deposited by the river.

"Push them aside," Montgomery commanded; and himself worked alongside us, wrenching the ice from our way, clearing a path. Then 200 men formed a column behind Montgomery, myself and a French guide. "Push on, brave boys!" Montgomery shouted. "Quebec is ours!"

Tall and dark against the fatal whiteness, Montgomery turned to me, excitedly, and said, "We shall be inside the fort in two minutes."

I remember thinking that one ought not to tempt fate. As I started to answer, I was abruptly lifted off my feet and flung into a snow-drift. Just as I struck the hard snow, I heard the delayed thunder of the twelve-pounder: one of the sailors who had fled the block-house had returned to see what was happening; observing our shadows up ahead, he fired the cannon.

When I got back my breath, I stood up, wondering if I had been wounded, wondering whether or not I would be able to recognize blood in that mono-chromatic landscape. Finding myself apparently intact, I hurried forward to where General Montgomery lay in the snow, head shattered. I tried to pick him up but he was dead-weight, and dead. Close-by, two aides and an orderly sergeant were also dead. The French guide had vanished. I turned back to the column.

"Attack!" I shouted. "The city's ours!" But at that interesting moment a certain officer named Campbell insisted on holding one of those caucuses so dear to the American soldier—and why not? When consulted in a democratic way, the American soldier invariably chooses retreat.

Despite my pleas, curses, threats, I was left alone in the ravine, beside the 200-pound body of my com-mander whose blood looked to be black as it stained the snow. Furiously, irrationally, I decided to return Montgomery's remains to our side; no doubt hoping, in my madness, to thaw him out, revive him. But I had not dragged the corpse a dozen yards when I was fired on from the blockhouse.

I abandoned the body to the enemy (who not long ago returned it to New York for a pompous re-inter-ment to which I was not invited). Incidentally, Trum-bull's recent and deservedly popular painting memori-alizing the death of General Montgomery omits me entirely while adding to the poignant scene several officers who at the time were nowhere in the vicinity but who are now, so to speak, everywhere.

Had the men followed me and met with Arnold's troops (waiting for us in the Lower Town), Canada would today be a part of the United States (happy fate, oh Canada!). But due to the untimely death of Montgomery, the cowardice of Campbell, the defection of Enos, we failed. In 1812 we again tried to conquer Canada; and again failed. This time we were defeated not by the winter but by our own commander James Wilkinson. Poor Jamie was worth a dozen snow-storms to the Canadians.

Two hundred of our men died in that disastrous assault while 300 were captured. Most of the others sustained wounds, among them Colonel Arnold whose foot was badly hurt.

I was promoted to brigade-major and my exploits were reported all over the colonies. I was even mentioned in the Congress while Matt Ogden saw fit to praise me personally to General Washington who, impressed by my precocity, offered me a place on his staff.

I was a hero, and still not twenty-one. Crude wood-block engravings of young Aaron Burr carrying General Montgomery through a snow-storm once edified and inspired an entire generation of American school-children. Had I died at Quebec, would I still be remembered today? Probably not.

Six

WHEN I MENTION to Colonel Burr how much I enjoyed his account of the invasion of Canada, he looks at me as though not knowing to what I refer; pokes the coals in the grate (yes, in midsummer he often has a fire). "I am always cold," he likes to say. "It is the fault of General Washington." When Burr smiles he looks like the bust of Voltaire in Leggett's office. "He disliked me and saw to it that I was always assigned to swampy and malignant places."

Finally, "Oh, yes. My scribbling about those days. I still make notes from time to time. Pointless activity, I suppose. No one likes truth. For instance, were are now told that Benedict Arnold was a bad general because he was a bad man. But of course he was one of our best commanders. Superior certainly to Washington."

"That's not the impression one gets from your account."

Burr is surprised. "But Arnold was *splendid*! It was Montgomery who made the fatal error at Quebec. Arnold favoured my strategy, which I think was sound. Certainly Montgomery's plan to attack the Lower Town was not. Arnold's judgement in the field was excellent."

Nelson Chase interrupts us with a message from Madame. The Colonel takes it and frowns. He is much distracted these days. Things go badly at the mansion. He has promised to show me his notes on Washington, but every time I ask for them he says he cannot remember where he last put them.

Seven

I HAVE GROWN lazy in the heat. August is nearly over. Colonel Burr is absent for days at a time. Sometimes he is at the mansion. Other times in Jersey City. I think he may have gone at least once to his old school Princeton College (his father was its president when it was called The College of New Jersey).

Although he is more than usually secretive, I gather that the Texas land leases may be invalid, and if they are, he has lost his (Madame's) entire investment.

Nelson Chase tells me that "There are terrible rows up there on the Heights!" Chase has also taken to questioning me about the Colonel's private life, an unbecoming subject considering how recently the Colonel married Chase's aunt or whatever she is to him. I say nothing. After all, I *know* nothing except that I have posted a number of letters from Burr to a certain Jane McManus in Jersey City. But *honi soit qui mal y pense.*

Yesterday Burr spent all afternoon with a Mrs. Tompkins and a five-year-old girl who was plainly his daughter though not, I should think, by the elderly Mrs. Tompkins.

Burr is marvellously patient with all children. Talks to them as though they were adult. Teaches them. Plays with them by the hour. Particularly with little girls, for "Women have souls, Charlie! They really do."

This evening, at five o'clock, I finally receive the Colonel's notes on George Washington. "It is a continuation of what you have already read. With some new marginal notes. It is a nice portrait, I think, but I am sure you will find it unrecognisable."

Burr looks pale and fragile today. This morning in court the judge saw fit to harangue for an hour the murderer of Alexander Hamilton. When at last the judge gave out of breath, the Colonel said with great mildness, "I am sorry that Your Honour is not feeling well today."

George Washington

IN THE EARLY SPRING of 1776, I decided that Colonel Arnold was mad. For days on end, he would march our shattered contingent back and forth before the walls of Quebec. Periodically, he would amuse the British with a demand for surrender. Asked to deliver one of these documents, I refused point-blank.

When it came time for me to go, Arnold forbade it. I told him that he could keep me only by force. He did not try to do that.

The middle of June, I arrived at General Washington's headquarters in the Mortier mansion at Richmond Hill, some two miles north of New York City.

I had never seen a house so fine. It commanded a superb view of the Hudson River. Gardens, pavilions, ponds, a stream (the Minetta which I was later to dam and make a small lake of). A perfect paradise, I thought, as I rode up to the front porch where a dozen officers stood, waiting for admittance.

Above the main door, on the second balcony, the Lady Washington sat with her needlework. She had a benign if somewhat wintry smile and a quiet manner. The face was ordinary—what you could see of it because she was addicted to large hats, usually some years out of fashion. She had been the richest widow in Virginia when the poor but ambitious squire Washington married her.

As I entered the high-ceilinged main hall, I never dreamed—well, perhaps *imagined* for an instant—that I would one day own Richmond Hill.

I was shown by a staff captain into the side parlour where a half-dozen officers were waiting to see the General, who daily held court in an upstairs bedroom (which I was to make into a library, exorcizing, as best I could, that stern mediocre ghost).

Among the officers unknown to me in the parlour was Captain Alexander Hamilton of the New York artillery. We did not actually meet, however, until the end of June. "But I knew right away it was you," he told me later. "We all did. And I was filled with envy!" When Hamilton chose, his manner could be enormously charming. "There you were, the hero of Quebec, looking like a child while I was just another officer!" As a youth, Hamilton was physically most attractive with red-gold hair, bright if somewhat watery blue eyes and a small but strong body. It was our peculiar tragedy—or glory—to be of an age and quality at a time and place certain to make rivals of us. Yet from the beginning we had a personal liking for one another. We where like brothers (yes, Cain and Abel come to mind with the difference that each was part-Cain, part-Abel). At first meeting I knew Hamilton straight through. I suspect that he knew me as well, and could not endure the knowledge that of the two of us I alone had the means and talent to be what he most wanted to be, the president. He came to hate not only my capacity but my opportunity. Yet I wonder if he knew all along that I would fail, saw the flaw in me as I saw the one in him? Speculation is idle now. Like brothers, yes; but unlike, too. He was envious. I am not. Thwarted ambition never turned me sour as it did Hamilton, who at the end could not endure the American world I was helping to make and so, quite irrationally, made me out to be that hideous reality incarnate. Curious to think that we would almost certainly have been friends had we not been two young "heroes" at the beginning of a new nation, each aware that at the summit there is a place for only one. As it turned out, neither of us was to reach the highest place. I hurled Hamilton from the mountain-side, and myself fell.

General Washington stood beside his desk as I entered. In response to my salute, he gave me his gravest stare. He was a master of solemnity.

"Major Burr, you are welcome to stay here in the house until you find yourself a proper billet."

"Thank you, General, I am most sensible of the honour . . ." I was about to ask, as tactfully as possible, for a command in the field when Washington began to speak, formally, somewhat hesitantly. Conversation was not easy for him with anyone.

"We have heard excellent reports of you, Major Burr. From every source except Colonel Arnold."

"Colonel Arnold and I had but one disagreement. I thought it pointless to continue to send insulting messages to the British governor when we were in no position to do him the slightest damage."

"Why did we not take Quebec?"

"May I speak candidly?"

His answer came smoothly, from much practice. "I have always laid it down as a maxim to represent facts freely and impartially."

"We failed, General, because my plan was not followed." I saw no reason not to go down firing.

"*Your* plan, Sir?" The small dull eyes in their vast sockets stared at me with wonder.

I told him in detail my strategy for scaling Cap Diamond. He was not impressed. "Wiser heads no doubt prevailed."

"One of those wiser heads, Sir, was shot off. I was at General Montgomery's side when he was killed. The other wise head now commands a depleted and broken force."

"You are most certain, Major, of your military gift."

"No, Sir. But it is a fact that the other strategy failed. I had hoped only to imitate the same tactic King Frederick set in motion during the siege of Dresden." Young and opinionated, I hoped to impress my commander not only with my own military prowess but with my wide knowledge of modern warfare. Like so many young officers in those days, I had studied closely the campaigns of Frederick the Great.

General Washington, however, did not read books; he knew as little of Frederick as I did of tobacco farming, a business in which he had only recently failed. The wealth of his wife notwithstanding, Washington was in some financial difficulty when he took command of the army. He had not done well farming despite all sorts of theories about river mud being the best of manures (it is not), and the invention of a plough (shades of Jefferson!) which proved to be so heavy that two horses could not budge it even in moist earth.

Although Washington was always short of money, he lived grandly. Later in the war, we were all startled and amused when his mother put it about that son George had robbed her of everything and so, being destitute, she was forced to apply to the Virginia Assembly for a pension. I am reasonably certain that Washington was innocent in this matter. He was, apparently, a dutiful son and the mother a source of much distress to him. When word came of her son's "victory" at Trenton, the virago was quoted as saying, "Here is too much flattery." It is plain she always disliked her son and he must, finally, have hated her. How odd not to like one's own mother! I always thought I would have adored mine, who saw fit to die before we could properly meet.

General Washington rang a bell. A staff colonel entered.

"Please instruct Major Burr in his duties. He will stay here, until billetted in the town." The General turned to me. "I shall want a full report of what happened at Quebec."

Interview ended, the General crossed to a long table covered with papers and began, at random I rather think, to read. From the back his heroic figure was only somewhat disfigured by a huge rump. Neither of us knew that even as we spoke, Montreal had been recaptured by the British, and our Canadian adventure was a failure.

Longing for military glory, I found myself seated at a desk for ten hours a day copying out letters from Washington to the Congress. Although defective in grammar and spelling, owing to a poor education, the General was uncommonly shrewd in the way he flattered congressmen. But then he had not spent fifteen years as a burgess in the Virginia Assembly without learning something of politics. Ultimately, I think, he must be judged as an excellent politician who had no gift for warfare. History, as usual, has got it all backward.

After ten days in which my most useful work was the examination of several bales of under-sized blankets from France, I was happy to receive from John Hancock an appointment as aide to General Israel Putnam

. . . yes, I had gone over General Washington's head to the president of Congress. I had no choice if I was to serve usefully in the war. In fact, as I pointed out to Hancock, I would rather be out of the army than clerk to a Virginia land-surveyor.

There are of course many legends about my relations with Washington during those two weeks I spent at Richmond Hill. He is supposed to have been shocked by my licentiousness. I daresay he would have been had he known how I and a number of other young officers conducted ourselves on those rare occasions when we were free to visit New York City. But he knew nothing of such matters. It is true, however, that he was most puritanical.

Soon after I arrived a soldier named Hickey had been hanged for treason, to the delight of 20,000 New Yorkers. I was not present at the execution but I did read with amusement Washington's statement to the troops. According to our commander, the English-born Hickey had gone over to the British not for money but because *he was a life-long prey to lewd women!* It was a sermon worthy of my grandfather. Incidentally, the private soldiers disliked Washington as much as he disdained them. On the other hand, the young officers (with at least one exception) adored their commander, and it is the young officer not the private soldier who eventually decides what is history.

I have never known New York so gay—despite the British fleet which materialised in the harbour June 29. The Battery was regularly subjected to bombardments that did no damage. The girls, however, enjoyed squealing with excitement and rushing for protection to our strong arms.

On July 3, the British army under General Howe disembarked on Staten Island, a Tory stronghold. Although our position was perilous, everyone had confidence in Washington. A confidence that was to evaporate when presently he contrived to lose both Long Island and New York City.

As I have already noted, Washington had had very little experience of actual war before 1776. Years before he had been involved in a few disastrous skirmishes with the French and their Indian allies on the Ohio. His first fame was the result of a despatch he sent to the Virginia governor in which he referred to the sound of the bullets that whistled past his head as "charming." Strange word. Strange young man.

In my view had Gates or Lee been placed in command of the army the war would have ended at least three years sooner. Each was brilliant. Each understood the enemy (Lee, in fact, knew personally the British commanders). Each won true victories in the field against the British, something Washington was never able to do. But though Washington could not defeat the enemy in battle, he had a fine talent for defeating rival generals in the Congress. At the end he alone was at the pinnacle, as he intended from the beginning.

Washington did have a most unexpected *penchant* for espionage. Our intelligence was almost always better than that of the British. Unfortunately Washington's judgement sometimes disallowed facts. For instance, despite every possible warning, he never believed that the British would attack New York Island when and where they did. Yet he must be given credit for tenacity. Although the war dragged on year after year due to his eerie incompetence, I suspect that the kind of victory he did achieve could only have been the work of a man who combined resolute courage with a total absence of imagination.

I fear that I did not properly appreciate being an aide to Washington. I did not enjoy copying out letters asking Congress for money that was seldom forthcoming: the American soldier was as mercenary as any Hessian. No money, no battle. Nor did I much enjoy listening to the worshipful talk of the other aides who flattered Washington monstrously, to his obvious pleasure. I, on the other hand, was prone to question his judgement although I had been advised by everyone that independence of mind was not a quality he demanded of subordinates. We were happy to be rid of one another.

I was to have a better time of it with my good, old General Israel Putnam whose headquarters I joined in July 1776 at the corner of the Battery and the Broad Way. A former tavern-keeper, Putnam had the amiability of that class as well as a good if crude intelligence. His only fault was a tendency to repeat himself. Whenever the enemy drew close, he would invariably instruct the men not to shoot "till you see the whites of their eyes!" Having made the line famous at Bunker Hill, he tended to plagiarize himself, to the amusement of everyone except those officers who thought the firing ought to begin long *before* the whites became apparent to some of our myopic riflemen.

On July 9, I took the salute at General Putnam's side in the Bowling Green. Then at the request of the Continental Congress, our adjutant read aloud to the troops a document newly received from Philadelphia.

I confess to not having listened to a word of the Declaration of Independence. At the time I barely knew the name of the author of this sublime document. I do remember hearing someone comment that since Mr. Jefferson had seen fit to pledge so eloquently our lives to the cause of independence, he might at least join us in the army. But wise Tom preferred the safety of Virginia and the excitement of local politics to the discomforts and dangers of war.

Living at Putnam's house was a pretty girl of about thirteen whom I have been accused of having seduced. Margaret Moncrieffe was the daughter of a major with the British army; she was also a cousin of General Montgomery (how tangled our personal relationships were in those days!). Since her father had been a friend of Putnam, the General took her in. If nothing else, the girl had spirit. I was present when she baited General Washington himself at Putnam's table.

As dinner ended, a toast was propsed to liberty or victory or some such sentiment. All drank but Margaret.

"You do not drink your wine." Washington gave the child that cold dull serpent's glance he usually reserved for those private soldiers who were about to be flogged on The Horse ("Discipline is the soul of an army" was his favourite maxim). A disagreeable child, Margaret was not without courage. She raised her glass. "The toast is—the British Commander General Howe."

Washington's face went red in blotches. "You mock us, Miss Moncrieffe . . ." Washington began and then stopped, unable as usual to organize a sentence that contained a new thought.

The good Putnam came to everyone's aid. "What a child says, General, should amuse not offend us."

Washington regained his usual serenity of expression. With an elephantine attempt at gallantry, he said, "Well, Miss, I will overlook your indiscretion on condition that you drink my health or General Putnam's when you next dine with Sir William Howe, on the other side of the water."

I did not like the girl at all. Thought her precocious and sly. When I discovered that she spent hours on the roof with a telescope, looking across to the British encampment, I cautioned General Putnam but he took no notice. She then began a series of flower paintings to be sent as presents to her father. Watching the girl at work one day, I said, "Do you believe there is such a thing as a language of flowers?"

Margaret blushed prettily (she was full-bosomed at thirteen) and stammered. "Yes. I mean no. Not really." Suddenly I was aware of a true alarm that had nothing of the flirtatious in it. Obviously the language of flowers could communicate troop positions. The girl was a spy.

With some effort, I convinced General Putnam that she would be safer and happier farther removed from the potential line of battle (I suspect the good general of having *known* the child best of all).

Margaret was removed to Kingsbridge. Later she was returned to the British. Her subsequent life has been romantic and untidy. She lives now in London. For some years she was the paramour of the King's minister Charles James Fox. I am told she gives to me the honour of having been the first to take her virginity. But I do not think that would have been possible.

By the end of August 1776, General Howe had assembled on Staten Island some 34,000 men. It was his intention to seize New York City, take command of the Hudson and split the colonies in two. May I say, what he intended to do, he proceeded easily to do.

Immediately after the arrival of the British, I was sent by Putnam to every one of our outposts from the Brooklyn Heights to the Haarlem Heights. I had never seen men less prepared for a battle with anyone, much less with fresh modern European troops. Junior though I was to the great commanders, I took seriously my task which was to assess our situation as accurately as I could. My gloomy written report to General Putnam was sent on to the commanding general.

Two days later I encountered His Excellency on the Battery. A sulphurous New York August day. Tempers were short. Sweat mixed with the chalk the General used to powder his hair trickled down cheeks fiery from heat and bad temper. His mood was not improved by the sight of the British fleet making complicated manoeuvres just opposite us, cannon beautifully polished, white sails pretty beneath a leaden sky.

"What, Sir, do you think the result will be should the enemy begin an assault?" I was taken by surprise: Washington seldom asked such questions of senior officers; never of junior officers.

"Why, Sir, we shall be routed," I said with stupid honesty.

"Never!" The "never" was from a permanent member of the chorus of worshippers that was to follow Washington throughout the Revolution . . . nay, throughout his long life, even to the grave! No man was ever so much praised and fortified by those about him.

I continued. "It is my belief, Sir, that the wisest course would be the one you have so far pursued with such success since Cambridge." Yes, I was a courtier, too.

"What, Sir, do you think that to be?" Our suspicious war-lord suspected even then that I was not entirely in thrall to his legend which, quite mysteriously, continued to grow from month to month no matter whether he won or lost or, as was more usual, did nothing.

"To imitate Fabius Cunctator. To avoid meeting head-on a superior enemy. To draw him away from his supplies. To draw him deeper and deeper into the continent where the advantage is ours not his. Sir, I would abandon New York City today. Give General Howe the sea-coast. He will take it anyway. But by withdrawing now, we keep intact the army, such as it is . . ."

I had gone too far. One of the aides reprimanded me. "The best troops of the colonies are here, Major Burr. The best commanders . . ."

"You under-estimate us, Major." Washington was unexpectedly mild. With a lace handkerchief, he mopped his chalk-streaked face; the pits from the small pox were particularly deep about the mouth.

"You have asked for my report, Sir."

"Yes." Washington turned his back to the port and gazed at the sooty old fort that used to dominate what was still a small Dutch town with rose brick houses and slender church-spires. But then John Jacob Astor was still a butcher boy in Waldorf, Germany.

"We shall defend the city." Washington's mistakes were always proclaimed with the sort of finality that made one feel any criticism was to deface a tablet newly brought down from Sinai.

"Sir, I would burn the city to the ground tomorrow and withdraw into Jersey."

"Thank you, Major. My compliments to General Putnam. Good day, Sir."

In defence of Washington, I must note that at the time very few of us knew much about the powerful secret forces at work upon him. There is evidence that he would have liked to destroy the city but was stopped by the local merchants (to a man pro-British) and by the Congress at Philadelphia which, eventually, *ordered* him under no circumstances to fire the city. Yet it was his decision—and no one else's—to confront the enemy with all his forces at Brooklyn in Long Island. This was to be Washington's first set battle; it was very nearly the last. Even today's hagiographers admit his sole responsibility for the disaster.

Right off, Washington split into two parts an army which, entire, was not capable at that time of stopping a British brigade. Then he chose personally to respond to a dazzling series of British and Hessian feints: in a matter of hours, he was out-manned and out-generaled.

Thrown back to his main line of defence, the Brooklyn Heights, Washington was faced with the loss of his entire army if he remained on Long Island or humiliating defeat if he chose to give up the Heights and withdraw to New York Island. He chose humiliation.

On the unseasonably cold and foggy night of August 29, I stood in a water-melon patch near the slip of the Brooklyn ferry and watched the evacuation of the army. All night boats went back and forth between New York and Brooklyn. Low dark shapes appearing and disappearing into a strange soft fog. The only sounds the soft moans of the wounded, the whispered commands of officers, the jangle of General Washington's bridle as he presided over the *débâcle* he had devised for us.

On September 15, 1776, the British fleet appeared at Kip's Bay about four miles north of the Battery. As usual, we were surprised. A powerful bombardment began at 11:00 A.M. Then the British and Hessians disembarked. Our troops promptly fled, despite the presence of Washington himself who shrieked at his own men like a man demented, broke his stick over a brigadier's head, cut a sergeant with his sword—to no avail. Raging and weeping, he was dragged away to the sound of British bugles mocking him with the foxhunter's "View, halloo! Fox on the run!"

Washington retreated up the island to the Morris mansion on the Haarlem Heights (now the home of Colonel and Mrs. Aaron Burr *ci-devant Jumel*) which was to be his headquarters for the rest of September. This must have been the lowest point of his career; worse, in some ways, than the winter at Valley Forge.

I sit now in what was his office, as I amend these notes, and think of him more than a half-century ago, scribbling those long, ungrammatical, disingenuous letters to the Congress, trying to explain how he managed at such cost to lose Long Island and New York City.

During this period I saw General Washington only once at the Morris mansion. It was September 22, and I had accompanied General Putnam to a meeting of the senior officers. There was a good deal to talk about. The previous night almost a third of New York City had gone up in flames.

"Someone has done us a good turn." Washington stood at the foot of the stairs with his plump favourite young Colonel Knox. Before General Putnam could say anything, Washington turned to me and I received for the first and only time his bleak dark-toothed smile. "I would not, Sir, have put it past you to have done this thing."

"Only at your order, Your Excellency."

General Putnam and Colonel Knox had no idea what we were talking about.

CHARLIE, I SHALL BURROW into my trunks and find you more of these notes—assuming that you are not too much ennuied by such old matters.

The other night as I wooed Madame on those very same stairs, I thought of Washington. For an instant I could *see* him, just next to Madame, with his dark smile, and the inevitable sprinkle of hair-powder on the shoulders of his buff and blue uniform.

Oh, there are ghosts among us! But then what are memories but shadows of objects gone to dust? Or in this case a smile that is no doubt preserved not only in my vivid if failing memory but actually on display somewhere, in the grisly form of a set of false teeth stained black with Madeira.

Eight

THE STORM BURSTS! Neither the Colonel nor Nelson Chase has been in the office for more than a week. Mr. Craft and I do the work as best we can. Among my recent duties was the reception yesterday of the Colonel's partners in the Texas scheme. As I suspected there was a flaw in the land leases; and the Germans are not coming. The Colonel has lost his entire investment. The partners are irritable. I put them off. "The Colonel is out of town." What else can I say?

Late this afternoon the great yellow coach, ominous as the chariot of the sun, came to a halt beneath my window. The coachman shouted up at me. "Madame expects you at the City Hotel." The coach departed— without me. I am to walk.

At the foot of the horse-shoe staircase in the main hall stood Madame and Nelson Chase. Both looked as if they had been weeping. Superficially, rage and sorrow are much alike.

Madame seized my arm, as though without it she would sink to the floor. "*He* has sold my second carriage and the gray horses, too!"

"*He* has vanished." Nelson Chase sniffed uncontrollably. Neither tears nor rage, as it turned out, but the hay fever.

Madame steered us into the Ladies Dining Room where she ordered tea which she promptly enhanced with rum from a silver flask, adorned with Napoleonic bees.

"It is unbelievable! *Incroyable, Charlot!*" The rum began slightly to mellow her. "On Monday he tells me he must go to Albany. He will travel by the boat. I say 'no'—like a fool—'take the second carriage.' So he departs, waving his hat from the window! *Ma foi!* I could kill him! For a week I hear nothing until . . ."

Rum and tea inhaled the wrong way brought on a fit of coughing through which Nelson wheezed the remainder of the story. "Madame saw her own carriage this morning at the Bowling Green. She thought the Colonel must have just returned. She asked the coachman—a stranger—and he told her that his master, a Jennings of Newburgh, had bought the carriage a few days ago from Colonel Burr for five hundred dollars."

"It was worth a thousand!" This came out clear.

"Where is he?" Case looked at me as though I must know; must tell.

"He said he was going to Albany." This was true. "But I don't know." Also true.

"He is *not* in Jersey City." Chase looked at me significantly.

"Oh, we know about Jersey City!" Madame put a jewelled finger alongside her nose the way Italian singers do at the opera; and then she winked with a lewdness that would have shocked Mrs. Townsend as much as it did me. "*Il y a une fille à Jersey City.*"

"Her name is Jane McManus." Nelson Chase was swollen and grim. "At his age, imagine!"

"His age has nothing to do with it!" Madame's

wrath, never for long settled in any one direction, was hurled like Greek fire at Nelson Chase.

"I only meant . . ."

"The Colonel is a *man* above all else! A creature of fire! A perfect balance between Apollo and Mars. Fidelity is for these wretches!" Madame grandly indicated the room of New York ladies and their swains, many of whom kept looking our way with obvious fascination. "I would not want a husband who was so lacking in *puissance!* Let him keep his girls in Jersey City, he is hardly old . . ."

I could not believe my ears. The Colonel is seventy-seven. That he is still active is miraculous; that Madame should condone such activity is beyond anything that I know of the world.

"It is not the girls I mind, Charlot. It is his God-damned incompetence with money! To sell my new coach and horses for *half* of what they are worth! He will ruin me!"

"He has already lost the money you gave him from the sale of the Connecticut shares." For reasons of his own Nelson Chase is now undoing the marriage he helped bring about.

"His is incorrigible! He has spent a hundred fortunes in his time. Well, he won't spend mine! Tell him that. Tell him if he does not pay me the thousand dollars he owes me for the carriage and horses, I shall divorce him."

"We have sufficient evidence." Nelson Chase was happy.

I assured them that whenever I saw the Colonel again I would tell him what Madame had said. Then I escorted them to the stairs that lead down to the internal carriage way. Face rosy with rum, Madame was now in a good mood.

"Tell him, Charlot, I wait for him eagerly."

"With the one thousand dollars," said Nelson Chase.

"With all my heart!" Lurching slightly, Madame made her descent, Nelson Chase at her side.

I went back to the main hall, passing the dining-room which was almost filled. For a moment I put my head inside the spacious, comfortable room that always smells so wonderfully of vinegar and roast meat. Sometimes the Colonel eats here, alone, in a corner. But not today.

I felt a tug at my jacket. I looked down and saw the ancient Dr. Bogart. He had recognised me through his veils of cataract.

"My boy! Sit down! I always eat at this hour. Sunrise and sundown. So should you." I sat next to him as he ate—gummed—boiled potatoes.

"I've not seen our friend the Colonel since the great day." Dr. Bogart chuckled horribly. "Everything as happy as can be?"

"Oh, yes, Sir."

"A pretty couple. But then it's the least that girl could do for Aaron. I mean one good turn deserves another."

"What good turn did he do her?"

But Dr. Bogart was on a different tangent. "The *other* wedding was different, let me tell you."

I did not actually let him tell me but of course he did. "A very plain woman, the first Mrs. Burr. Poor Theodosia. Ten years older than Aaron she was, with this terrible scar on her forehead. And sickly from the cancer even then. And four children by her first husband. And not a penny to her name. But Aaron adored her. So did we all. My people lived near by in Paramus."

"Where did he meet her?" Since I was to be told, I preferred an orderly presentation.

"The war." Dr. Bogart looked vague; mashed a potato with his spoon; gradually retrieved the past. "Colonel Burr was in the neighbourhood, at Orange County on the Ramapo River. I remember all this because, you see, I was there, too." Old eyes looked at mine; eyes that had seen not only battle but the young Burr who was "the handsomest boy you ever laid eyes on. Slender and wiry. Hard as a hickory limb.

And, oh, the mind! The mind! In those days there was hardly a girl who was not a little in love with Aaron Burr."

It was lucky for them, I thought, that he returned their interest so fully.

"Theodosia Prevost she was. She lived at the Hermitage. Across the way from Bogart Farm. Her husband was a British colonel, serving in the West Indies. By rights she should've been moved out as a Tory but since she was born American, since she was a friend to George Washington and to Jemmy Madison, she was allowed to stay on, and all our officers used to visit her. Even Washington came to call one day. Then the young Colonel Burr—the youngest in our army he was—started his night raids against the British. Everyone still talks of him down home. That is, those of us left who can still remember the night raids and our young days . . ." Dr. Bogart lost his train of thought. Stared vacantly at his plate.

"Colonel Burr," I prompted him. "Theodosia Prevost."

Dr. Bogart was recalled from whatever limbo it is that draws the ageing mind. "Her husband died, the war ended, and she married the Colonel at Paramus. What days those were!" And at some length Dr. Bogart spoke of a period in which skies were bluer, water purer, potatoes better-grained than now. I know the speech. It is the tirade of the old.

I asked about Burr's exploits in the Revolution.

"He knew what he wanted from the day he joined General Washington at Cambridge. Illegally, I might say, because he was not of age. His guardian was furious—you know, Aaron was orphaned from the age of two. So the guardian, an Edwards, sent him a messenger with a letter ordering him to come straight home on the ground that he was not only a minor but, according to the family's doctor, of too weak a physical disposition to survive any war."

Dr. Bogart's thin blue lips made a thin blue smile:

he too has outlived many a doctor. "Well, Aaron told
the messenger that if he tried to take him from the
camp, he would have him hanged. And so the man
gave him a second letter from the guardian—who
knew his ward, you might say—and that letter was
milder, and there was a bit of money in it, too. So
Aaron went to war, and was one of our first heroes.
After Quebec everyone knew his name."

Dr. Bogart was about to tell me more when William
de la Touche Clancey sat down next to me with an
insolent crash (do I resemble a country youth because
I am small?), and I made a quick farewell to Dr.
Bogart.

Clancey gave me a hard look. I think he recognised
me from the Five Points.

This afternoon I had the inner office to myself. Like
a thief I tried for the second time to open the trunk
beneath the baize-covered table. I succeeded. The
Colonel had only half-turned the key and the tongue
of the lock was not secure in its place.

The contents were pretty much what I expected.
Packets of letters. Newspaper cuttings. Toys for the
grandson who died shortly after the Colonel's return
from Europe in 1812. I note that he refers to the boy
and himself, interchangeably, as "Gamp."

I looked in vain for any reference to Van Buren.
But then it would take a month to study all the letters
and papers not to mention the thousand-page journal
the Colonel wrote while he was in Europe, to be presented to his daughter Theodosia on his return. Presentation was never made, of course. After the death
of her child, Theodosia set sail for New York. The ship
was lost at sea and so the journal rests in the trunk,
presumably unread by anyone. For the Colonel's sake,
I wonder if it ought to be read.

With startling candour the Colonel reports his
poverty in London and Paris; his attempts to get an
interview with Napoleon, to borrow money, to obtain
a passport from an American consul who detests him

and will not grant him what is any citizen's due. I was most struck by the way in which the Colonel describes each of his sexual encounters, using French words which I don't always understand as well as a private language shared by him and his daughter.

Sample pages for May 2, 1811, at Paris.

I forgot to tell you last evening again the vigils until the watchman called two o'clock. The tea at dinner was too strong and I too weak not to drink. Took my leisure in bed, and did not go out until three, after eating potatoes. Boiled.

Went to the Tuileries to look at beautiful women, and saw only one in a carriage. *Une duchesse au moins.* The above part most comforting, and full like Mrs. X at Hartford, remember?

Then to the Palais Royal to observe the *filles* (the word used here for public women).

Beautiful day. The arcades of the Palais Royal a-twitter with *filles.* A wide range like the Battery on a similar day in spring. But unlike the Battery a small price will gain you the world, and no talk of marriage.

Much attracted by a dark creature, the image of Beau Ned Livingston's Creole wife, with a mole at the corner of her full mouth. "*Bonjour, Mademoiselle.*" I was most courtly. Gave a deep bow. She gave me a majestic stare. I practised French. She practised mathematics. In a matter of minutes we were *en route* to her *atelier,* a single room on the fourth floor of a ricketty building back of the Palais Royal and from the sounds and sights (and smells!) much frequented by the *filles* and their *amis.*

Fairly clean (this is France). Linen passable. Spirit *brio.* We did first the *Camel.* Then an attempt at *la Tonnerre* which failed due to pique and false entry. Most pleasing, all in all. She is from Dijon in Bur-

gundy. Her brother is a clerk in the foreign ministry
(she says). I take Vanderlyn's advice based on the
latest medical· theory (*departement de Venise*) and
after the *splendeurs de l'amour* appropriate the *vase de
nuit* and take a hearty piss.

WHAT SORT OF MAN *is* the Colonel? What sort of
daughter was Theodosia? When I read his letters to
her, and hers to him, it is like an exchange between
Lord Chesterfield and his son (had the son been the
father's equal, for Theodosia's style is learned and
brilliant), but then when I read this journal and realize
the way they spoke privately to one another I am
mystified.

I wonder what will happen to the journal. I suppose
Mr. Davis will. destroy it. He ought to, if he wants to
make a case *for* the Colonel.

Nine

COLONEL BURR WAS in the office when I arrived this
morning. His spirits soar. "I gather you have seen
Madame. And know all!" He rubbed his hands together mischievously. "We are estranged. But only
temporarily. For the next few days I shall be stopping
with a young protégé in the Bowery. A rising silversmith, if silversmiths can be said, properly, to rise."

"That would be Mr. Aaron Columbus Burr." I was
pleased at my own boldness. But then the Colonel's
manner is contagious.

I was rewarded with the first surprised look I have
ever managed to extort from that old knowing face.
Pale eyebrows arched until they touched the rims of

the spectacles which, as usual, rested just below the becombed topknot. "Charlie, you interest me. You do." He paused, wondering no doubt just how to express his interest. "You have not been following me about, have you? Like Nelson Chase?"

"No, Sir. It was a guess. Someone mentioned that you had a son who was a silversmith."

"I suppose it can hardly be a secret. His mother saw to that by giving him my name, with the thoughtful addition of 'Columbus' in the hope that the child might one day imitate the original and discover not only his father but our new world—which he did when he was eighteen. Now he wants to bring his mother to New York." The Colonel sighed. "When I first met her she was the assistant to a watch-maker in the Rue Royale. She was superb with machinery. She could fix anything from a clock to a compass. I have not the slightest desire ever to see her again. I try to dissuade Columbus from importing '*Maman.*'"

Burr sliced the end from a seegar. "I told him that his house is much too small as it is for himself and his wife—a charming creature from Staatsburgh—and their two bright children not to mention myself from time to time, their old Gamp." As he lit the seegar, he looked positively tender: children, I think, mean more to him even than the company of women.

"You will meet Columbus, by and by. He is a handsome lad, who speaks English with a very bad accent. I have never had much time to give him, poor boy." Smoke wreathed the Colonel's head like a halo slightly askew. He changed the subject. "Our friend Nelson Chase arranged a bit of sport for me in Jersey City. That's why I am now removed to the Bowery."

"He is working for Madame." I declared my allegiance, such as it is.

The Colonel nodded. "As you know, I often visit a dear girl named Jane McManus. I find her company soothing—as I found her grandmother's some fifty years ago. She was also from Jersey City—obviously a

place for me of enduring magic. Anyway we were
surprised, Miss Jane and I, by her maid, a goggle-eyed
creature in the pay of Nelson Chase. I got the whole
story from the girl, with the help of a cane. Madame
paid the girl to discover Miss Jane and me in a compromised state so that she might be able to testify as a
witness should Madame choose one day to dissolve the
sacred bonds that exist between her and me. Well,
catch us the girl did. Miss Jane is still weeping at the
shame of it all. And Madame now possesses her
shoddy evidence."

"I think, Sir, Madame's objections are not to your
... your ..."

"Friendships?" There was an ironic glint in those
youthful eyes. For once everyone is right: Aaron Burr
has made an agreement with the devil. Every dark
legend is true.

"It's the money that upsets her. The money you've
lost on the Texas land grants."

The Colonel frowned. Whatever his arrangement
with the devil, competence in money matters was not
a part of the contract. Matthew Davis once told me
that, right after the Revolution, the Colonel acquired
the largest fortune of any lawyer in the history of
New York City, and lost every penny on speculation
and extravagant living.

"I admit I ought not to have sold *our* carriage without first telling her. That showed want of feeling. But
the offer was such a good one. The money so necessary.
And Jake the coachman—a capital fellow, by the way
—said the grays were not much good. Anyway, it's
done."

A sudden gust of wind caused the scarlet-leafed vine
outside the window to rap three times upon the dusty
glass like knuckles on a coffin lid. Why does that
image occur to me? Burr is eternal. Yet, inadvertently,
eternal or not, he shuddered at the sound. "We must
be on our guard, Charlie."

"Yes, Sir. Do they know where you are living?"

"Not yet. Let us keep them guessing a while longer. I am involved in a new scheme which . . ." The Colonel stopped. He is always discreet about divulging prematurely what he is up to. This may explain his disasters. No one is ever in a position to warn him.

"You must see the new play at the Park Theatre. I went last night with Columbus. A melodrama but not entirely stupid. We sat in a box which cost us seventy-five cents apiece. Such extravagance!"

Then the Colonel indicated several old books on the table. "I bought these for you, Charlie. Second hand, I fear. Gibbon's *Decline and Fall of the Roman Empire*. Take them. Read them. Become civilised."

Mr. Craft hurried in with work for the senior partner. The moment of intimacy was at an end.

Ten

A T EXACTLY six o'clock, I knocked on the front door of 3 Bridge Street. I was even more nervous than I thought I would be when Leggett told me that he had made the appointment.

A large woman opened the door. Without asking my name, she simply said, "*He's* in the front parlour." And vanished, into the back of the house where I could hear women laughing. There was also a pounding noise from upstairs, as though children were holding a foot-race. For a bachelor the great man was hardly lonely in his New York residence.

Standing at the fireplace, beneath a drawing of a Moorish-looking palace (the Alhambra?), was Washington Irving. In the books I read at school he is portrayed as a dreamy-looking, slender youth. No longer. He is now very stout and elderly, with a crooked but pleasing smile. The eyes are guarded, watchful; and he does take you in, every inch, the way painters do at the preliminary sketch. He affects to be shy. At first the voice was so low that I got only an occasional word. "So happy . . . Mr. Leggett . . . to Washington City soon . . . not used to . . . please . . . sit down . . . too warm?"

Mr. Irving sat us down face to face in the two wing chairs before the fire, our knees almost touching. A sharp wind made draughts in the room. He gave me another long look. "Schuyler. Which Schuyler?"

"No Schuyler." Invited to give my familiar demur, I lost some of my nervousness. I explained to him that my father had kept a tavern in Greenwich Village and was in no way connected with the glorious Schuylers.

"I am partial to the Dutch." Irving overcame his disappointment, finding what solace he would in the unmistakable physical fact of my Dutchness. With yellow hair and blue eyes, I look like every caricature ever drawn of a Dutch lout. I take after my late mother, a Schermerhorn; no, not the rich Schermerhorns, the others.

Irving tried speaking to me in Dutch and was disappointed when I did not understand. "The old talk is being forgotten. We're all of us the same now. Early this month I was at Kinderhook with . . ." The pause was marvellous. The whole world knows that he was visiting Vice-President Van Buren. ". . . with an old friend, of the Dutch stock. And we looked in vain for so many landmarks we used to know when we were young. The Dutch are like everyone else now. The colour goes." Irving's habitual tone seems to be melancholy, and his sentences tend to terminate in the dying fall.

"Is the Van Buren tavern still at Kinderhook?" I moved too swiftly.

"Yes, yes. Do you know it?" Polite interest, nothing more.

"I have heard so much about it from Colonel Burr. I am in his law office."

"Aaron Burr." Irving said the name softly and with some feeling. But precisely what emotion I could not determine. Certainly there is no hostility. Perhaps wonder. Regret. "Yes, Mr. Leggett said you were interested in Colonel Burr's career. My brother once edited a newspaper for Colonel Burr, a long time ago." The eyes shut. "*Morning Chronicle* it was called. Most political, my brother Peter was—and is. A dedicated Burrite. Colonel Burr was the vice-president when I first published my"—the eyes open wide—"*little* things in his paper. Over thirty years ago."

I told him that when I was in school I read his Jonathan Oldstyle letters. Apparently even then people were looking back to the "good days" of old New York. As much as I admire Irving's work, I do not share his delight in Dutch quaintness. I like nothing about being Dutch, including all the jokes about us.

"It is curious that one of the last of the *little* pieces I wrote for the paper was an attack upon the practice of duelling. That was just two years before . . ." Irving gestured. Eyes evaded mine; settled on the Moorish castle above the fireplace.

From upstairs came a terrible shriek. Irving gave a start; looked alarmed; sighed. "Children," he said, and for a moment lost his usual sweetness of manner. He is plainly not used to family life. But then he has been living a bachelor's life for the last twenty years in Spain and England. As a result, he is now more like an Englishman—of the polite kind—than an American. He could step on the stage of the Park Theatre tonight and play with the greatest of ease man-servant to a duke.

"You must have seen Colonel Burr at Richmond Hill?"

Irving smiled. "Oh, yes. But I was not one of The Little Band. That was what the Colonel's admirers called themselves. A most devoted group, and with good reason. Colonel Burr was New York's Maecenas. He loved artists. Liked to help them. No good artist who asked him for money was ever disappointed. Both he and Theodosia ..."

"Mrs. Burr?"

"No, she was dead by then. I mean Theodosia his daughter. The most extraordinary woman I ever met." Irving seemed genuinely moved; the round eyes glazed over. "She was small, dark and splendid, with the Grecian profile. She spoke a half-dozen languages. Knew every science. Read Voltaire. Corresponded with Jeremy Bentham. Yet was womanly and loving ..."

From all accounts Theodosia was indeed a paragon but for mysterious reasons of his own I have the impression that Irving exaggerates his passion for the long-dead beauty, expressing his adoration in complex complete sentences as a single tear rolls slowly down his cheek into the fortress of that tall starched stock there to splash in darkness from chin to chin like. . . . I am beginning to parody his style.

"Was Mr. Van Buren often at Richmond Hill?"

A silk handkerchief was used to remove the saline track the tear had made on the smooth plump cheek (I cannot forget that this is the man who wrote the favourite stories of my childhood). "I think not." Irving was cautious. "Their friendship has been made too much of."

"But didn't Colonel Burr stay with Mr. Van Buren at Albany when he came back from Europe ..."

"Mr. Van Buren was once a friend. Therefore he will always be—amiable. But there is no *political* connection." This was said sharply. Irving is often mentioned as a possible secretary of state in a Van Buren cabinet. After all, he is an experienced diplomat who was for some time chargé d'affaires at the American legation in London. In fact, he was there last year when Van Buren arrived as minister, appointed by President Jackson and then, humiliatingly, rejected by the Senate as a result of Vice-President Calhoun's malice. The subtle Irving, however, was most kind to the discredited ambassador and managed for him to be received by the King and made much of by London society.

Irving is also supposed to have told Van Buren that his rejection by the Senate would be the making of him. "For," Irving is reported to have said, "there is such a thing in politics as killing a man too dead. You will now be Jackson's next vice-president, and that will be the end of Calhoun."

The unworldly Irving proved to be as good a political prophet as he was a friend. No wonder the two men take trips together up the Hudson and moon about Dutch ruins. Rip Van Winkle has indeed waked up and returned to us, with a future president in tow.

"I am not so certain that I can be of any use to you, Mr. Schuyler." I was aware now of the diplomat on guard. "I do agree that a study of Colonel Burr's career would be fascinating to read. But don't you think it is—perhaps—too soon? So many people still alive . . ."

"Like Mr. Van Buren?"

"It is also *said* that President Jackson was even more deeply involved with Colonel Burr." There was a definite sharp edge to the melodious voice. "So was Senator Clay who—"

We were interrupted by a powerfully built blond youth. "Mr. Irving! Oh, I am sorry. You are not alone." The boy hesitated in the doorway. I got to my feet.

"This is John Schell, Mr. Schuyler." The boy's handclasp was bone-crushing. "I met John on the ship coming from London. He is staying here while he gets the feel of our new country."

"Excuse me, Sirs." The German accent was heavy. The boy bowed stiffly and left us.

Irving continued: "I was about to say that when I saw Senator Clay at the Park Theatre last night—"

"Last night? But Colonel Burr was there, too."

"I know." Irving smiled. "Did he tell you what happened?"

I shook my head.

"Henry Clay came in at about nine o'clock. Almost everyone stood. And cheered. A most tumultuous welcome." A delicate crooked smile. "I *somehow* kept my seat during this Whiggish display. Then, at the interval, as I was crossing the foyer, what do I see but Colonel Burr suddenly—by accident, I should think—face to face with Mr. Clay. The one lean and mad-eyed with that awful mouth like a carp, the other like some dark imp from the lower regions. The imp put out his hand and Mr. Clay *reeled*—there is no other word for the backward falling movement he made. Then well-wishers bore him away. I don't suppose a dozen people standing there recognised Colonel Burr and of those who did hardly one was aware how, years ago, Clay, a very ambitious young lawyer in Kentucky, successfully defended Aaron Burr against a charge of treason—and very nearly nipped his own political career in the bud. Oh, your Aaron Burr is the sprightly skeleton in many a celebrated closet!"

"Including the President's?"

"I think—don't you?—that their involvement was explained at the time in a most satisfactory way by General Jackson." The response was stiff, to say the least. But then Irving's friend cannot be our next president unless the current president chooses to promote him; therefore Andrew Jackson must be above suspicion. They all must. Yet there are those who believe that the whole lot were once involved in treason, Burr, Jackson, Clay. How many secrets there are! and Washington Irving is willing to betray none.

A clatter from the kitchen beneath reminded us that the family supper was almost ready. I rose. "You never see Colonel Burr?"

Heavily, Irving got to his feet. Our knees for an instant struck.

"I *saw* him last night. But we do not speak. What

would be the point? Of course he was once most admirable. But I do think—all in all—that he does himself—all of us—a disservice by . . ." The tentative crooked smile again, the voice suddenly, deliberately soft. ". . . well, by *living* so very, very long—so *unnaturally* long—a continuous reminder of things best forgotten."

"I think it splendid that he is still among us. Able to tell us the way things really were."

" 'Really were'? Perhaps. Yet isn't it better that we make our own *useful* version of our history and put away—in the attic, as it were—the sadder, less edifying details?"

Irving walked me to the front door, now blockaded by a child's hobby-horse. Together we lifted it out of the way.

"My compliments to Mr. Leggett. If you see him, say that I shall meet him Wednesday for our weekly *tête-à-tête* at the Washington Hotel. You must join us." The hand resting on my shoulder gave a sudden pinch, like a corpse's fingers going into *rigor*.

"I am sorry to be so little help to you." The hand and arm dropped to his side. "I do have the notes I made during the treason trial at Richmond. If you like, I shall have a copy made for you."

Eleven

THIS MORNING Mr. Craft and I worked on briefs. Colonel Burr meditated in his office. Creditors came and went—obviously distressed that the Colonel is again without money: everyone in the city still thinks that he is the master of the Jumel fortune. As usual, in his case, the truth is quite opposite.

At noon Matthew L. Davis arrived. He is a gray lean bespectacled man with a secret smile; very much the political mover and shaker; also, very much the newspaper editor—he has almost never been without a partisan newspaper to edit. Mr. Davis went into the smoke-filled lair and shut the door behind him. An hour later, Colonel Burr called for me.

The two ancient conspirators sat facing each other over the open trunk.

"Charlie, do give Mr. Davis my notes on the Revolution."

"Have you copied them out?" Mr. Davis has the confiding Tammany voice.

"Yes, Sir." I turned to Colonel Burr. "I hope you don't mind my copying them?"

"No. Not at all. Look to it, Matt! You have a competitor! And what a task! For both of you. The rehabilitation of a man who has been slandered by both Jefferson and Hamilton. A considerable honour, come to think of it. They never agreed on anything save that I was the true enemy of their schemes." He laughed merrily. I cannot think why. "If it's true that slander has slain more than the sword, then for all practical purpose I am long—and doubly—dead. But it may yet be possible for you two fine fellows to put it about that no matter how dark my villainies I was at least a good soldier." The Colonel was unusually elegiac.

"Hamilton was a poor soldier . . ."

But the Colonel cut Mr. Davis short. "No, Matt. General Hamilton was always a man of courage—at least when there was an audience."

The conversation then turned to the affairs of Tammany, which interest me not at all.

Mr. Davis was pleased about the immigrants who almost daily arrive in large numbers from Europe. He expects to enroll them in Tammany, and win elections.

Burr was not enthusiastic. "They will win elections all right, but not for you."

Mr. Davis did not understand.

The Colonel explained. "I don't want to sound like Hamilton who used to get white in the face at the thought of the wicked church of Rome, or like Jefferson who was mortally afraid of Jesuits, but I promise you, Matt, when these Catholics outnumber the old stock two to one . . ."

"How can they outnumber us when we'll be making good Americans of them?"

Burr's laugh was like an organ's bass note. "Whatever a good American is he cannot be a Roman Catholic at the same time. It is a contradiction. And when there are two of them for our every one, they will divide up the property. You'll see. And why shouldn't they? That is true democracy and they—not we—will be Demos." Burr turned to me. "You will live long enough, Charlie, to see an *elected* judiciary."

Mr. Craft's clerk entered with a letter. "Anonymous, Colonel. The author prays that you burn in Hell, Sir. Mr. Craft thought you would be amused."

"Most tickled." Burr threw the document into the smouldering grate. Then Mr. Davis left and Colonel Burr sent me on an errand to the Register's Office. Later I was to meet him at the City Hotel.

As I was crossing Wall Street, I saw my father coming out of the Post Office. He was well dressed and not drunk, though not sober either. "Charlie." He gave me a vague look. "It is you, Charlie?"

"Yes, it is." We had not met since he killed my mother three years ago.

"You are still in Colonel Burr's office."

"You are still at the tavern."

Two statements, requiring no answer.

"I've been sending letters, you know." My father indicated the Post Office as though it would corroborate his story.

"I must go meet Colonel Burr."

"He must be right old, the Colonel."

"He is."

"I always voted for the Colonel, you know." Neither could look the other in the eye. Since we had nothing further to say to one another, we parted.

The Colonel greeted me gaily at the corner of Wall Street and Broadway. I told him of my encounter. He knows I am estranged from my father; does not know why. "Charming gentleman, your father. Kept the finest tavern in Greenwich Village. Such a pleasant place." Colonel Burr took my arm. Together we crossed Broadway, avoiding a crowd outside the City Hotel.

"Mr. Clay must be stopping here," said the Colonel.

"No. He's at the American Hotel."

Colonel Burr gave me a side-long look. "You have heard of last night's encounter?"

"Someone mentioned it, yes."

"There are only two men on this earth who fear me. One is president and the other would like to be."

"And both were with you at the time of the . . ." I have yet to find the proper euphemism for whatever it was that Burr was planning out west. Jefferson called it treason. Chief Justice Marshall and a jury suspected a misdemeanour.

"A most curious man, Henry Clay . . ." The Colonel suddenly stopped; stumbled; brown face gone tallowy. "There's something wrong with my leg." He looked bewildered. "There's no feeling in it." He staggered. "I can't walk." He started to fall. I caught him. Propped him against the wall of the hotel.

"I'll get a carriage."

Burr nodded, eyes shut—leaning, no, collapsing against the wall.

In Reade Street, Mr. Craft helped me carry him upstairs to a small room with a cot where the Colonel sometimes rests. A doctor was sent for. Once on the cot, Aaron Burr took a deep breath and fainted dead away.

Twelve

I HAVE JUST COME BACK from two days at the mansion. All is forgiven.

Madame is in her element. "My brave warrior! Light of America! You have come into a safe harbour at last!"

Madame stands at the head of the Napoleonic sofa on which Colonel Burr is stretched out beside a roaring fire. He wears a quilted robe. The face is as smooth and keen as a boy's. To the doctor's bewilderment (but not mine), he is making a fine recovery from the stroke. The left leg is still partly paralyzed but he can now hobble about unaided—on the rare occasions when Madame lets him. She spends all day and night with him, assisted by the niece. The traitor Nelson Chase is not in evidence.

I spent two nights in the mansion. Having lived in boarding-houses since I was sixteen and went to Columbia, I found it a remarkable experience to be waited upon by eight servants, with a fire in my bedroom all day and night. I now see why everyone in New York is so eager to be rich.

Madame regales us with anecdotes of her career. At one point, she sends for the cook. "Norah, tell them about your dinner with royalty."

Norah knows exactly what to tell, and does so. "You see, I was in the kitchen one noon while Madame was away from the house, and I was fixing for us in the house some boiled pork and cabbage . . ."

"The best in the world!" Madame drinks to pork and cabbage while Mary Eliza does needlepoint beside me on a sofa and the Colonel reclines languorously, and smiles benignly; the satyr lips unwithered by time.

". . . when in comes this nice foreign gentleman, small and dark he was with an accent like one of the waiters at the French taverns in the Bowery. So he says

'Is Madame here' and I says 'No' and he says can he look about the house and I says he can and he looks about for a while and then he comes down to my kitchen and says kind of sad-like 'I have to go all the way back to Jersey now' and I says 'Well, have a little something to eat' and he says 'Pork and cabbage is my favourite' so I sit him down at the table . . ."

"And there I found them! Dining *à deux*. Norah *et son majesté le Roi de l'Espagne*."

I look blank. Madame promptly translates for me. Apparently it was Joseph Bonaparte, Napoleon's brother who was king of Spain and now lives in New Jersey.

Madame Jumel waves Norah back to the depths.

"*Le Roi* has all the Bonaparte *force*." More anecdotes. My head begins to ache.

"I was in Paris," said the Colonel, "for two years and never—but once—did a Frenchman ask me into his house."

"How odd! In Paris I paid calls daily and received callers." A point for Madame.

"How could they have deprived themselves, my dear Eliza?" Burr shut his eyes. "But then I was remarkably poor. I used to eat two pounds of grapes a day because they were cheap."

"Exile! What this country has done to you!" Madame is off again, and so am I. On the table beside my bed, I find a packet with a note in Colonel Burr's handwriting.

"For C.S. Although our merry caper in the Broad Way has had—to date (just before dinner)—a happy ending—or continuing—why am I using so many dashes? Like a schoolgirl. The dash is the sign of a poor style. Jefferson used to hurl them like javelins across the page. Yes. I ramble. Yet I *think* my mind is unaffected by the seizure, and the leg improves with every hour. Nevertheless, it is *possible* that I might, rather suddenly, die. So I give you now the rest of my notes on the Revolution. They are not complete.

"When I was in the Senate, I was briefly given free

access to all official documents pertaining to the Revolution. With a clerk to copy documents, I used to work from 5:00 A.M. until 10:00 A.M. at the State Department. I was able to crack many a mystery. But then on the spurious ground that a U.S. senator ought not to have access to the 'correspondence of existing ministers,' the whole archive was denied me. Later what I had managed to collect in the way of documentation was lost with my daughter at sea.

"Sometimes I have written only a paragraph, intending more. Other times, I reconstruct from memory. I doubt if I shall ever add to what I have done. Perhaps you can make something of these fragments. Matt Davis knows that you have them and should I be translated to a higher sphere you are to make them available to him. That is a sacred trust, Charlie, much the worst kind!"

A look at the "fragments." Some long. Some short. A kaleidoscope of those days. I start to copy them out.

General Knox

OF ALL THE MEN attached to Washington, Henry Knox was the most truly adhesive. Fat, slow-moving, crafty, an excellent man for the organizing of a headquarters, he lacked, however, the military gift and though he was our chief of artillery from 1776 to the war's finish he was never entirely certain which end of the cannon you lit. Yet he was a marvel at finding artillery whether cast by us at Litchfield from church-bells or from the remains of the Bowling Green statue of George III or simply stolen in the night from the British.

Knox had been a bookseller in Boston. He was one of the few men familiar with books (or at least their bindings) that Washington was at ease with. He served loyally in the first Cabinet.

I saw Knox in action—if that is the phrase—Septem-

ber 15, 1776, the day the Continental Army enjoyed its
resounding defeat at Kip's Bay and fled (or as Washington put it "withdrew") to the village of Haarlem.

With two junior officers I was caught in the melee.
Thinking to find Washington at Richmond Hill, I
rode in that direction. Communication had entirely
broken down, and if there were new orders none knew
them. It was, as usual, every man for himself.

Half-way across the island we came to a makeshift
fort of hastily prepared· earthworks behind which
cowered an entire brigade. I assumed that they had
not known or understood the original order to retreat
to Haarlem.

"Who commands?" I shouted to the first sentinel.

"Colonel Knox!" was the answer. Then himself
looked above the dirt like a fat mole just flushed from
ground. I introduced myself. Asked why the brigade
had not moved out.

"Not possible, Major. The British have split the
island. But we shall do our duty. We shall hold this
fort to the end." The young voice trembled. The staff
officers eyed us nervously. No one wants to hold a fort
to the end; particularly a non-fort.

"Sir," I was respectful but urgent, "you cannot
defend these earthworks against one howitzer."

"We are dug in, Major." For an instant it occurred
to me that Knox might not want to move his brigade
quickly because he was, simply, too fat.

I turned to a captain. "Have you water? Provisions?"

"No, Sir. We are only just dug in."

"Then, Colonel, I propose you obey His Excellency's
orders and withdraw to Haarlem."

"We cannot!" The usually brazen loud voice was a
squeak. "The British are already between us and
Haarlem."

"Sir, they are not." Knox's officers had now joined
us in that pleasant autumnal glade where yellow leaves
diffused bright sunlight. A cool breeze rattled branches
overhead; and carried to my nostrils that unmistakable

odour men exude when frightened: no one wants to be killed. And death was now at hand.

"My intelligence tells me that since three o'clock this afternoon the British are drawn in a line straight across New York Island, a half-mile to the northeast of us. Listen. You can hear them firing." Knox did his best to look martial in the presence of his own unimpressed staff. We listened. Heard scattered musketry to the south. Nothing more.

"Sir," I said, "I cannot tell whose muskets those are but I propose you move out of here as quickly as possible."

"Sir, I command here." The round face swelled like a bullfrog's at mating time.

I turned to the officers. "Gentlemen, if you stay here you will be slaughtered by the enemy. You are outnumbered and out-gunned. Worse, those who are not killed will be taken prisoner and hung as high as Master Hickey." I was inventing freely but in a good cause. The officers began to talk all at once. Knox was drowned out. A vote was taken. The brigade chose to move on to Haarlem.

"We cannot move!" Knox was furious. "We don't know the island. We're from Massachusetts."

"I know every path and trail from the Bowery to the Heights." Which was true: as a boy I had often hunted in the island. "I'll lead the way."

Knox protesting, the brigade assembled and we marched straight into a nest of British infantry who, seeing us like so many wild beasts bursting upon them from the yellow wood, ran as fast as they could, without firing a shot.

For two miles I rode at the head of the brigade. Knox did not speak to me once as I led the men through thick woods and across those deep swamps and sudden streams that are a characteristic of what is now called, so affectedly, Manhattan Island.

At only one point were we fired on. Knox was terrified. But before he could give the wrong order, I cantered in the direction of the firing, two officers beside me. On a rocky ledge we found a small company of British infantrymen. With wild Indian yells, we rode straight at them, as if we were the advance guard of a vast horde. They fled into the forest. We chased them for half a mile, killing several.

The sun was almost gone when we returned to the trail to find that the brigade had vanished. I was terrified that Knox had surrendered to the first passing British officer, but luckily he was only lost. We found the brigade marching serenely to the west.

Knox was bewildered when I pointed out to him that a trail that led toward the setting sun could not help but bring him eventually to the city of New York, and the British gallows.

The day was dying when we saw before us the single church spire of Haarlem Village, surrounded by the lights of the American camp. The men cheered. Colonel Knox said not a word to anyone as he led his brigade into the camp.

Although my exploit was presently known to Washington, no official mention of it was ever made.

Three months later (December 1776) Colonel Knox became chief of artillery and a brigadier-general.

Night-riders

IN JULY 1777, I was at Peekskill with General Putnam when my commission as lieutenant-colonel arrived from General Washington. I thought it overdue. I said as much in a letter to His Excellency, remarking that officers junior to me at Quebec and Long Island now took precedence. Those things mattered greatly to me then because they mattered to everyone else. We were hungry for honour in those days.

Washington's response was elevated and aside from the point. But then I was already known to be friendly with those commanders he disliked, particularly the

brilliant if unstable General Charles Lee, late of the
Polish army. It was a law of General Washington that
the mediocrities who worshipped him like Knox should
rise inexorably during the war, while the Lees, as
inexorably, sank.

I was to be second-in-command of a regiment stationed on the Ramapo River in Orange County, New
Jersey. The regiment was the creation of a wealthy and
genial New York merchant named Malcolm. This
gentleman desired nothing more than to be revered as
the father of his regiment, preferably at a comfortable
distance from any administrative or military duties.
We got on famously. He moved twenty miles away
from our encampment, rented a large house and there
lived happily (and paternally) ever after with his
family while I took command of the regiment.

I found the men lax because their officers were New
York gentlemen, more interested in parties than drilling. I was strict but seldom resorted to The Horse.
This meant constant vigilance. I was always on the
move. Slept in my clothes; when I slept at all. Got the
reputation for having a pair of eyes in the back of my
head. All this at age twenty-one. It was glorious!

During this time George Washington was conduct-
ing the war in his own mysterious way. After losing the
battle for Long Island, he was surprised at Kip's Bay
and so lost New York City to the British. He then
sustained a defeat at White Plains after which most
of the Continental Army went home. With what men
remained, Washington scurried across the North River.
Yet if in August of '76 Washington had abandoned
to the British everything east of the Hudson River, he
would have been able to keep intact his army, dig in
before Philadelphia, and hold that city. Instead he
devoted nearly a year to losing New York Island and
City, demonstrating to everyone that he had neither
the resources nor the craft to defeat the British. The
Revolution was nearly over and done with by the
winter of 1777.

A number of young officers prayed for Washington
to be relieved of command. Some of us wanted Lee.
Others Gates. No one but the sycophants on His
Excellency's staff wanted another winter of Washington and failure. Had the British realized the extent of
our confusion and weakness, they might then and there
have forced a peace upon us for with each passing day
Washington's conduct of the war was creating Tories
by the thousands, including a number of powerful if
secret ones in the Congress itself.

My task in September 1777 was to make the enemy
regret that they were not Americans. I think we succeeded. Certainly they were never able to adapt to our
Indian-style fighting which relied on darkness, stealth,
surprise. We knew the wild forests around Paramus.
They did not. We never met them in battle. Rather,
we were always near by, ready to shoot them down one
by one, preferably in the dark.

Our night-rides became famous through all that
part of New Jersey, and at least one young commander
thought this a delightful way of living. But then I had
met at the Hermitage, a fine house just beyond Paramus, the lady who would one day become my wife.

It was a peculiar joy to creep like an Indian through
dark pine woods, past enemy pickets, in order to join
a brilliant party at the Hermitage and then, at an alert
from a posted servant, to leap out a back window and
vanish like a shadow when the moon is gone.

Winter 1777–1778. Valley Forge

THOSE "BLOODY FOOTPRINTS IN THE SNOW" at Valley
Forge! I have never enjoyed anything so much as the
memoirs of James Wilkinson, author of this pretty
image. But then Jamie could not tell the truth even if
it were convenient to do so. There were ragged men
and broken shoes at Valley Forge but I recollect no
blood upon the snow. I do recollect the series of

disasters which brought us to that windy Pennsylvania hill-side, and the bleakest hours of the war.

In September 1777 the British out-manoeuvred Washington once again and occupied Philadelphia (the Congress now became a burden to the city of Baltimore). Contrary to accepted legend, the Philadelphians did not at all mind the presence of the British army in their city; in fact, many of them hoped that Washington would soon be caught and hanged, putting an end to those disruptions and discomforts which had been set in motion by the ambitions of a number of greedy and vain lawyers shrewdly able to use as cover for their private designs Jefferson's high-minded platitudes and cloudy political theorizings.

Shortly before Christmas 1777, I reported to General Washington at Valley Forge, some forty miles from Bethlehem in Pennsylvania. The commander's quarters were, as always, comfortable (in February the Lady Washington would arrive to preside over the court).

I waited alone in a cold ante-room. Aides came and went, including General Knox who bestowed on me his fish eye as he went inside. I recognised Colonel Hamilton who was pleased to see me, as well as an old friend and contemporary, Colonel Troup, who told me, "You're to be a diversion. Go on in. His Excellency is in a rage."

I entered what must have been the dining-room of the original house. Washington stood in front of a fire, facing two gentlemen in civilian clothes.

He responded to my salute without ceasing to attend the burghers. "You gentlemen will recognise, no doubt, Colonel Burr who was at Quebec with General Montgomery." My name was indeed known to these two members of the Pennsylvania Assembly who were also suppliers to the army—which is to say thieves. One was large; the other small. Their names are respectable now in the history of Pennsylvania and so I will not embarrass their descendants, who doubtless

venerate as noble patriots the heavy-set villain and his
slight accomplice.

The large one said, as though in explanation, "You
will admit, Excellency, that this site is ideally suited
for your purpose." He waved his arms to north and
south. "Plentiful water, a mill, timber from which you
can build cabins. I have a consignment of nails, just
arrived, at your disposal . . ."

"I trust the Pennsylvania Assembly has already paid
for the nails." One could hardly blame Washington
for his bad temper; he had wanted to go into winter
quarters at Wilmington in Delaware, but Pennsylvania's delegates to the Congress threatened to withdraw all financial support for Congress as well as for
the army if he did not remain in Pennsylvania. So
in order to make money for a pack of merchants, our
half-starved army was now perched on the side of a
wind-swept hill and those few who were not sick were
now expected to build a camp, and survive somehow
without provisions until the spring.

The small one got the subject away from nails. "We
have all manner of supplies at hand. Or nearly at hand.
Certainly you will lack for nothing a grateful colony
. . . uh, 'state' can offer."

There was a sudden loud noise of cawing. The small
man stopped talking. Even Washington allowed his
dull face to relax into bewilderment. The cawing grew
louder. A thousand crows, two thousand crows were
sounding in the winter stillness. "Caw, caw, caw!"

Colonel Troup entered. "It's the men, Your Excellency."

"Caw, Caw, Caw!"

"They want food, Your Excellency."

Washington turned to the Pennsylvanians. "There
are only twenty-five barrels of flour in the camp.
Presently the men will mutiny. If you do not supply
us by tomorrow, there will be no one to protect you
from the British hangman. Nor will there be anyone,
gentlemen, to protect you from me."

Colonel Troup showed the shaken Pennsylvanians out.

Washington proceeded to deal with me. "I have heard of your night-raids in Jersey. They have been appreciated."

"Thank you, Your Excellency." I wondered if I should drop to one knee. With each year's new defeats, the ceremony of Washington's court became more royal. "I had hoped I might be of the same service now."

"In Pennsylvania?" Washington waved a large ink-stained hand toward the window.

"No, Sir. Staten Island. I know every inch of it, and I know we can do serious damage to the British there. Particularly with night-raids."

"How many men would you need?"

"Two hundred, Sir. From my own regiment."

"You mean from Colonel Malcolm's regiment." This was flat. We were fated to dislike one another. On my side I found irritating the slowness of his mind; not to mention his awesome gift for failure in the field. In three years he had lost *every* engagement with the enemy except for a small victory at Trenton and that had been an accident: the Hessians had not posted guards the night of his attack. At this point in the war the only American victories were those of Gates at Saratoga and Lee at Charleston. Quite naturally, many officers wanted Washington replaced. They had my sympathy.

Caw! Caw! Caw!

As Washington invented reasons for keeping me at winter quarters with nothing to do, the crowing continued and I saw that he was much shaken by it. Finally he dismissed me with "You will employ Colonel Malcolm's men in the building of wooden cabins." Thus was I domesticated.

Outside headquarters, I found Colonel Hamilton. He was staring down the side of the hill to the first of the tattered tents where a number of patriots were crowing and flapping their arms. A comical sight when described on the page but downright sinister to observe in what was supposed to be an army. Interspersed with the cawing was the cry "No meat, no meat!"

"We must do something, Burr." This was one of the few occasions that I ever knew Hamilton not to begin a conversation with a charming salutation.

"Yes." I was agreeable. "We must find food for the men. It should not be hard . . ."

"You don't know these Pennsylvanians." He shook his handsome head; a thin little fellow with patched breeches like the rest of us.

"I would go to the nearest town and take what I needed."

Hamilton gave me a contemptuous look. "If we did, every last one of those 'business men' would take the oath to the King."

I was not impressed. "Then we can hang them." I enjoyed shocking Hamilton, or rather allowing him to play at shock. Actually, he was far more devoted to demonstrations of *force majeure* than I. Mischievously, I asked him if he enjoyed the position I had found unendurable on Washington's staff.

Hamilton was oblique. "I find my place discouraging. Between the fools in the Congress and the treachery of certain of our general officers . . ." He launched into a scathing attack on Gates. "A vile intriguer, constantly writing to Congress behind His Excellency's back, conspiring with officers right here in camp."

For the first time I learned of the so-called Conway Cabal which was, at that very moment, aiming to replace Washington with Gates. Although Hamilton was no admirer of Washington, he had elected to rise through him and so was not a part of the cabal whose leader was a newly-arrived French officer named Conway. An intelligent but impetuous man, Conway had somehow persuaded Congress to make him inspector-general of the army. This was a blow at Washington.

Fortunately for His Excellency, it was also a blow at every senior officer in the army and their bitterness at Conway's undeserved promotion enabled Washington to play on the common jealousy, thus isolating Conway.

But the Frenchman was resourceful. A series of letters between him and Gates convinced the latter (as if he needed convincing) that he alone could defeat the British. What an extraordinary winter it was! Within the log cabins of our starving, half-clothed army there flourished intrigues of a complexity unknown at the court of the Sultan, as hundreds of letters in cipher passed back and forth between the various conspirators. Close to the centre of all this activity was—who else?—James Wilkinson.

I saw Jamie Christmas day as he passed in splendour before my hut. In October he had been sent by Gates to Congress with the news of our army's first and only true victory of the war, the surrender of the British general Burgoyne and his army in the north. With the good news was a request from Gates that the bearer be promoted to brigadier-general. By this peculiar criterion, if the news had been bad, Jamie would have been broken to major. Without demur or reflection, the jubilant Congress complied. The promotion of Conway had been bad enough but Wilkinson's absurd elevation caused some twenty colonels to write in protest to Congress. I was not one of them: Jamie was still my friend. I was still his "idol."

We embraced in the snow. The beardless youth was now a man who looked older than his twenty years—a fortunate thing considering Gates's folly in placing him so high. Arm in arm, we strolled to his billet. He told me of the retreat from Canada (he had joined Arnold a week after I had left). I told him of the retreat from Long Island.

We made our way carefully among tree stumps, boulders, iced-over puddles. Everywhere the noise of axes; cursing of men. Some 1,100 cabins were going up amid a thousand small fires. So many bursts of hot orange against cold gray, resinous smoke that made eyes sting and water.

Most veterans tend to recall their youth as one of perpetual high-blooming summer. Perhaps it was for them, but for me it was always winter. Even now I suffer at bone-remembered cold, want more fire, more heat; recall with a shudder that steep bitter Pennsylvania hill-side where half-starved men huddled close to their fires, some wearing only blankets because Congress's money for us had been stolen by so-called suppliers. We felt abandoned. We were abandoned. Elsewhere, let it be noted, the nation's founders spent a comfortable winter, particularly Jefferson at Monticello where, in perfect comfort and serenity, he was able amongst his books to gather his ever-so-fine wool.

Jamie had found for himself a small out-building, well chinked with clay. A fire was going on the hearth. Two junior officers (in age at least five years our senior) saluted and departed.

We sat before the fire, each scratching furiously as one always did when those of lesser or greater rank were absent. With the possible exception of General Washington and his Lady, we were all of us lousy at Valley Forge.

"Burr, you are the greatest fool ever!" This was said lovingly. "*You* could have been the brigadier by now if you had stayed with Washington." Jamie offered me fire cake (a mess of flour and water baked on a hot stone).

I ate hungrily. "I have not a clerk's mentality."

"So make yourself other duties. You don't see Troup or Hamilton copying letters."

"I prefer having my own regiment."

"I prefer a headquarters." I could not get over the way Jamie had matured; in appearance, that is. In character he was the same odd mixture of impetuous youth and shrewd intriguer, to use General Washington's favourite word at Valley Forge. I have often reflected how curious it was that James Wilkinson, a born politician, should rise to the very peak of the American army and I, a born soldier, to the peak of American politics. Each lived the life the other should have led.

Soldier Burr was then swiftly brought by Politician Wilkinson into the heart of a complex intrigue. "Gates must take over the army. There's no one else."

I was stunned. I had assumed that Wilkinson was with Washington and against the cabal.

"A majority in Congress will support us." Jamie filled his chest with air. "But for the moment no one dares bring down the Demigod."

"They never will." I was sufficiently versed in Revolutionary matters to know that as bad a general as Washington was, without him there would be an even larger statue of George III in the Bowling Green.

At this point in our affairs Congress was faced with a true dilemma. It was now plain to everyone that Washington was not—and would never be—sufficiently competent to defeat the British. Either Gates or Lee was preferable. But neither Gates nor Lee nor anyone else had the authority to keep together what army we had while holding in check the pack of thieves and rhetoricians that called itself the Congress.

I HAVE LOOKED through the rest of Colonel Burr's notes but I find nothing more to do with Wilkinson or the Conway Cabal.

The next note describes Washington's assignment of Burr to a mutinous regiment at Valley Forge.

The Affair at the Gulf

"GENERAL MCDOUGALL ASSURES ME that you are an excellent disciplinarian, Colonel Burr. So I give you command of this most troublesome regiment." Washington was seated after dinner before the fire. Opposite him sat the Lady Washington, her small pleasant sly face looking out at us from under a large bonnet of the sort that was in fashion with the girls of Litchfield when I was studying law. She had a disquieting tendency to nod or shake her head for no particular reason, as though affirming or denying some inner voice.

Several members of the General's military family were also seated about the room, going through despatches, pretending to work. Only Hamilton simply read a book; his passion for reading was as great as my own. Like me he usually read history or philosophy. In private, however (if I may be allowed to traduce his memory and expose him to all the world), Hamilton was a devoted reader of women's novels, as I discovered one day at the New York Society Library when I came upon a note in his hand asking the librarian to reserve for him *Edward Mortimer* (by a Lady) and *The Amours of Count Palviano and Eleanora.* I was shocked. It was not until middle age that I allowed my own education occasionally to lapse and took to reading novels and foolish plays—in French as well as English.

I tried to be as much at my ease as was possible with the Demigod. "The regiment is stationed at the Gulf." This was the pass through which the British would come, if they ever did. "They lack discipline. They do not keep proper sentinels. Worse, they are prone to false and mischievous alarms."

Mrs. Washington nodded her head fiercely as though the more false alarms the better.

"I shall do my best, Your Excellency." This was the most one ever needed to say to General Washington.

In ten days I took a disorderly and incompetent militia (formerly commanded by a brigadier) and through vigorous drilling day and night deliberately inspired a number of them to attempt mutiny.

On the morning of the tenth day I learned that certain of the men had sworn an oath to kill me at the

next assembly. During the day I took precautions.
Then at midnight I ordered everyone out.

A cold night. A bright moon. The rattle of drums.
When the troops were at attention, I began my inspection, looking each soldier in the face. Half-way down
the line a man leapt forward, pointed his arm at me
and shouted, "Now is your time!"

Several muskets were raised and trained upon me.
"Fire!" he shouted. A flat sound of clicking: the bullets
had been removed.

I drew my sword and swung it as hard as I could
at the arm still out-stretched before me. There was a
thick snapping sound as metal cut through bone. He
screamed. White clouds of frozen breath hid his face.
Nearly severed, the arm fell to his side like a broken
doll's.

"Take your place in line, Sir." He obeyed, and I
dismissed the company. The man's arm was amputated
and he was sent home. There were no more false
alarms.

I am told that General Washington thought seriously
of court-martialling me for the dismembering of a
soldier. He was dissuaded.

It should be noted that my plan to harass Staten
Island was finally accepted by Washington, who entrusted the task to our drunken general, the Scots peer
Lord Stirling. Not knowing the terrain, he failed.

Monmouth Court House

ALTHOUGH I TEND to think of the Revolution as a time
of bitter cold, my own disaster took place on one of
the hottest days in the history of a long life, June 28,
1778. What the cold could not accomplish the brutal
heat very nearly did. My health was lost to me for five
years and any effectiveness I may have had as an
officer in the field ended at the battle of Monmouth
Court House.

There was a considerable celebration in early May at Valley Forge. Not only had the army survived the winter (and Washington outwitted the cabals against him) but word came to us that the French government had officially recognised the United States of America; best of all, not only were the French sending out a fleet to help us but their navy had already begun a blockade of the English Channel. We were certain now that we would win.

On a fine May morning Washington reviewed the troops, read the news from France, fired thirteen rounds of precious powder, arranged a good deal of food under a bower, gave a gill of rum to every man, and generally created the impression that all things were at last possible for us, not least victory.

General Lee was on hand, recently exchanged for a British general. Some time before Lee had been mysteriously captured while visiting a lady in a tavern: mysteriously because some suspected Washington of having arranged the capture to remove a rival. Lee was brilliant, vain, fascinating, and we soon became good friends. It is significant that the only general officer I was ever close to was the only one to be court-martialled and broken. I plainly lacked Wilkinson's doggedness in pursuing those commanders who might help me up in the world. Yet for all of Jamie's adroitness, he finally managed to get himself involved in so many plots and counter-plots at Valley Forge that General Gates eventually threatened him with a duel while Washington, whose nose for intriguers was keen, appointed him clothier-general to the army and sent him away. In this occupation Jamie was able to steal money in small quantities which was to be expected; unfortunately, he neglected to clothe the army and was let go.

I use the word "dogged" to describe Wilkinson's pursuit of honour—no, *place*—through the cultivation of important men. But Wilkinson was positively desultory in this occupation compared to Hamilton who wanted honour for itself alone, as did the best of us.

I have often thought what a difficult time Hamilton must have had, forced to serve a man whose mind he despised. Certainly they were an incongruous pair. The solemn slow general waddling with dignity through the camp, while like a ginger terrier at his heel frisked the young impertinent aide. Washington plainly adored Hamilton, and must never have realized to what extent the beloved youth disliked him. But then Washington was not in the habit of friendship with men or women (I have known well many of those who were close to him and I have heard of no women in his life except the wife of a neighbour in Virginia who was, according to Jemmy Madison, more spiritual sister than in-amorata). What affections he might have had were tightly reined in. The decorous relationship with his wife Martha was simply an alliance between properties, and typical of Washington's ambition, of his cold serpent's nature.

Also, from the age of forty-three Washington was forced not only to play but to *be* the god of America. This meant that he could have no friends among his contemporaries, for any one of them might have proved to be a rival. As a result, his affections tended to centre on young men who were no threat to his eminence. Watching him, however, with a contemporary and equal like Charles Lee was a marvellously droll spectacle. The usually majestic Washington would become the clumsy courtier: diffident, halting, given to sudden blushes, and then, at the right moment, a knife would flash in the dark and another rival would be stunned to discover that the dull, obsequious Virginia gentleman had effectively done for him.

If Washington's passion for Hamilton was plainly unrequited, it was more than compensated for by the adoration proffered him by that vivacious young Frenchman the Marquis de Lafayette, who joined our Revolution at Valley Forge. Lafayette was one of a number of glory-minded Europeans who came to help us battle tyranny. Of these foreigners, only Von Steuben had military talent. A marvellous liar who had put it about that he was lieutenant-general to Frederick the Great when the highest rank he ever held was captain, Von Steuben proved to be equally marvellous at training men.

As for Lafayette, he was all youthful enthusiasm and charm and silliness. Incidentally, he had the most unusual head I have ever seen; it came to a point at the top like a pineapple. He worshipped Washington, who was so overwhelmed by the young man's ardour that he allowed him nearly to lose us the battle of Monmouth Court House.

Thinking back, we must have been a strange-looking assembly. Although Washington was in full immaculate uniform, the rest of us were in rags except Lafayette and some of the foreigners. I should note that Benedict Arnold had arrived on the scene; he was constantly hobbling along at Washington's side, talking into his ear. Arnold had recently been passed over for promotion, which did his native bad temper no good. Gates was there, too, much chastened since the collapse of the conspiracy. And of course the burly Lord Stirling who was always attended by his aide James Monroe, whose principal task during the Revolution was to keep His Lordship's cup filled until it was time to put him to bed. What a small group it was that fought the Revolution, founded the republic, and governed the better part of a continent for a quarter-century! And so many of the future governors were present at Valley Forge, drinking rum and water in a bower of green branches, and toasting the king of France.

When the celebration was done, I joined General Lee and several of his admirers in a farm-house. Dishevelled, ill-shaven, eyes a-glitter, Lee sat with feet on the fire fender, a Pomeranian dog (rather resembling him) at his feet, and regaled us with tales of his captivity at Philadelphia. "Most civil the British were to me. Particularly the senior officers. Good fellows mostly. And how they hate this war! Blame it all on their politicians. Every night we'd drink together and toast the end of the war and the hanging of the politicians; of *all* the politicians in the world except His Excellency." Lee winked. He had a special way of saying "His Excellency" that conveyed in each respectful syllable absolute contempt.

"General Clinton wants to give up Philadelphia. Move back to New York. He's trying to persuade the ministry in London either to abandon the colonies altogether, which is not likely, or settle for holding New York indefinitely. He's sick of the war. They all are. If he does move out of Philadelphia, I told His Excellency that we should do nothing to stop him. Quite the contrary. Build the British a bridge of gold, I said. Throw flowers in their path because we've won. It's all over. The French have decided the war in our favour and the day their fleet appears off Long Island the British will go home. Unhappily, His Excellency hungers for a victory in the field. I think he has grown tired of exaggerating what happened during that skirmish at Trenton. Although he now believes that he ranks with Marlborough and Frederick, he also knows that when people speak of American *victories* they speak of mine and Gates's and never, never of his. So I predict that as the British withdraw he will attempt a set battle with the British. I also predict that no matter how great our initial advantage, he will fail as he always does." If nothing else, Lee was a good prophet.

In June the British under General Clinton evacuated Philadelphia and began the long trek to New York City.

I attended the staff meeting where Washington presented his plan for attacking the enemy while they were in train. As usual, he elicited agreement from nearly everyone. Only Lee made his case for allowing the British to withdraw. As much as I respected Lee,

I think Washington's strategy, in theory, was sound. But in execution it was, as always with our famous commander, a disaster—or in this case a near-disaster.

Washington made his error at the very beginning. Overwhelmed by the exuberant Lafayette's passion for renown (not to mention for his commander's august legend), Washington first proposed that the French youth lead the assault with *General Lee's* troops. Lee was rightfully angry. So Washington patched together, as only he could, a fatally divided command. If Lafayette attacked the enemy first, Lee would stand aside while he earned glory. Should Lafayette *not* have seized a hero's laurels by the time Lee appeared on the scene, then Lee would take command. It was the sort of stupid compromise that works marvellously well in a congress but not at all on the field of battle. Final idiocy, Washington at the last moment re-arranged a number of companies in such a way that many of the division commanders had no idea whom they were commanding.

So much for the grand design.

Although not a general, I was given command of a brigade that included my own regiment and parts of two other Pennsylvania regiments. I had an excellent second-in-command, Lieutenant-Colonel Bunner, and, all in all, I was content. Yet by the morning of July 27, as I mounted my horse in a rain which was, without too much exaggeration, scalding, I began to sense disaster. Soldiers often do. Some electrical quality in the air communicates hours in advance victory, defeat, pain, death.

I was part of Lord Stirling's division that commanded the American left, to the west of Monmouth Court House where the British army was entrenched. On orders from Stirling we spent the entire day and night of the 27th in the open, under a tropical sun that did us more damage than British guns. We were all light in the head. Many fainted; and some suffered paroxysms from the stroke. We were also prey to clouds of Jersey mosquitoes, the world's largest and most resourceful.

Before the sun was up on the 28th I was leading my brigade along a sandy lane to the west and south of Monmouth Court House. There was a constant ringing in my head. Yet I was lucid, and can recall to this day the look of the spindly heat-withered pines that edged the road—trail, rather; can recall how the sergeant just behind me kept whistling over and over again the same two bars of "The World Turn'd Upside Down," a song popular with the British army.

By noon we were on the high ground just west of a certain ravine on whose opposite side the advance troops of our wing of the army were supposed to make their first attack. I ordered a halt, to await orders.

Beneath us was a mosquito-whining swamp crossed by a narrow footbridge. On the far side, a forest and, somewhere, the enemy. I ordered the men into battle position. This was not easy, for every few minutes someone fainted. Colonel Bunner's thermometer registered ninety-four degrees.

I exhorted the men not to drink too much water but since I could not be everywhere, dozens of bellies were soon swollen and cramped from guzzling. I, too, was inconvenienced by a diarrhoea that was to remain with me for the next five years, despite an invalid's diet.

Shortly after noon we heard the first loud hollow blast of cannon. In all there were five reports from the direction of the court-house. Then silence. Another hour passed. Alarmed, I despatched a lieutenant to Lord Stirling with a request for orders.

At about three in the afternoon when the sun burned like a flaming cannon-ball above the pine-wood, battle was joined. Off to our right, but out of sight, we could hear the clatter of musketry fire; the whiz and thud of artillery. The Lafayette-Lee division after a long mysterious delay had begun to fight.

Suddenly I saw a flash of scarlet in the woods opposite. Simultaneously, scouts reported that a British detachment was now advancing through the woods, hoping to outflank General Lee's advance position.

I gave the order for attack. Indian file, the men started to cross the bridge while I maintained a covering fire. In a matter of minutes the entire brigade would have been safely across the bridge and under cover. But fate intervened.

One of Washington's aides materialised. "Stop those men, Colonel!" Wild eyes met mine.

I thought him mad. "I can't stop them. They're moving to take cover before the British get our range."

"Stop them! Recall them! It is General Washington's order."

I swung my horse in such a way that it looked as if he had shied from the sound of bullets. Pretending to have heard nothing, I rode to the bridge. Something like a third of the brigade was now on the other side. Behind a row of pines the British were getting our range.

The aide followed me. "Colonel, I order you in the name of the commanding general to withdraw those men." Sick from heat, the aide was interpreting, literally, an order based on Washington's ignorance of the terrain, not to mention terror at the thought of yet another defeat: unknown to us at the edge of the swamp, General Lee had abruptly withdrawn from the advance position and many of his troops had interpreted the command to withdraw to mean retreat; and for the American soldier retreat is best done through flight.

Washington himself stopped the rout and ordered General Lee back to his post with a series of violent oaths. Then, after some hesitation, Washington decided to remain where he was and to stop the rest of us from advancing. Thus we lost, fatally, the initiative, thanks to Lee's abrupt withdrawal and to Washington's refusal to do more than make a perfunctory feint at the British position. What might have been a clear-cut victory for us was no more than a skirmish, ultimately beneficial to the outnumbered British who ought, in the normal course, to have been destroyed.

"These men will be murdered!" I shouted at the aide but he was adamant: right or wrong, Washington must be obeyed.

I stopped the crossing of the bridge. Safe in the woods, the enemy was now able to pick off one by one our men.

As I rode up and down our side of the swamp, shouting at the men to take cover, to return the enemy's fire, I suddenly found myself flung like a stone through the air. The whole world had indeed gone upside down, I remember thinking as pine-trees up-ended around me.

I fell with a crash onto a sandy bank, winded but not hurt; my horse killed.

As I got to my feet, I saw Colonel Bunner being shot dead at the bridge. One third of the brigade was now dead; as many wounded.

The night was as hot as day. A copper moon illu-minated the pine-wood where exhausted men slept; where the wounded moaned, gasped for breath, trying to live, to die.

I nursed the wounded until shortly before dawn when I collapsed in a field and did not awaken until the sun was well up. As a result I was dried out like an Egyptian mummy which I somewhat resembled. I had also been bled while I slept by a thousand mos-quitoes. I could hardly walk.

In this highly debilitated state I learned to my disgust if not surprise that (unknown as usual to Wash-ington, who had spent the night sleeping at the side of Lafayette on a mantel beneath the stars) the British army had departed, and were now safely on their way to Staten Island. The plan to intercept them had entirely failed; and we had sustained heavy casualties for nothing. Such was the "victory" for George Wash-ington at Monmouth Court House.

When awakened by the news that the British army had escaped, Washington's response was characteristic. He arrested General Lee for disobedience, and ordered a court-martial. I openly supported Lee, as did many others. Washington took note of us all, and few of Lee's admirers were to earn promotion.

I even corresponded at some length with Lee while he was under arrest. At one point he wrote me that regardless of whatever sentence was imposed (a year's suspension from duty, as it turned out), he intended to quit the army and "retire to Virginia, and learn to hoe tobacco, which I find is the best school to form a consummate general."

I should note here two curious pieces of information that I was given in London by a permanent clerk at the war ministry. I do not vouch for their authenticity. The first was that when Charles Lee was captured by the British, they threatened to hang him for a deserter from the British army. To save his neck he persuaded them to let him go on condition that he persuade Washington not to interfere with their withdrawal to New York. When he failed to persuade Washington, he ordered the disastrous retreat at Monmouth Court House, saving the British army. The other information I find easier to believe: that during the Adams administration Alexander Hamilton was British Agent Seven, and paid for by London. Jefferson suspected this, but then Jefferson suspected all his enemies of treason and I never took his charges seriously.

With the breaking of Lee, Washington reigned supreme as military genius in the eyes of the states. Although Washington was never to defeat an English army, he had now won a far more important war—the one with his rivals.

"What was Washington's most notable trait?" I once asked Hamilton when we were working together on a law case. The quick smile flashed in that bright face, the malicious blue eyes shone. "Oh, Burr, self-love! Self-love! What else makes a god?"

West Point

I SPENT TWO DAYS' sick-leave near Paramus, at the
Hermitage, with my future wife Theodosia Prevost.
Then, ill as I was, I accepted Washington's appointment as a sort of spy to try and discover whatever possible about the enemy's shipping.

With a small group of men we ranged up and down
the North River from Weehawk to Bergen, collecting
gossip, some of it useful.

I was then given the task of escorting by barge a
number of wealthy Tories from Fishkill to British-held
New York City. This might have been enjoyable duty
had I not been suffering from debilitating headaches
as well as diarrhoea.

In October I asked to be given sick-leave *without*
pay. I wanted to be under no obligation to Washington who granted the leave but insisted that I take full
pay. Since this was unacceptable, I felt obliged to
rejoin my regiment at West Point where I was
promptly mistaken by a local farmer for Colonel
Burr's *son*.

THIS SECTION breaks off.

The Westchester Line

JANUARY 13, 1779, I ARRIVED at White Plains to take
command of the Westchester Line that stretched some
fourteen miles between the Hudson River and Long
Island Sound. Below the line was New York City, the
British army, and their friends the American Tories.

It was my task to regulate the passage of traffic
between Tory New York and Whig Westchester. As
it turned out, my actual work was to stop the plundering of the civilians who lived in the area. Stealing was
the chief occupation not only of the troops under my

command but of their officers as well. In fact, plunder
was the principal occupation of what seemed to be
half the population of Westchester. Those who stole
from the Tories and the British were called Skinners.
Those who stole from us were called Cowboys. By
the spring of 1779, Skinners and Cowboys had been
largely done away with; my health, too.

On March 10, I sent my resignation to General
Washington who accepted it with the polite sentiment that he "not only regretted the loss of a good
officer, but the cause which made his resignation necessary."

Through Enemy Lines

AT THE END of May 1779, I was at West Point visiting
General McDougall. Despite poor health, he was a
fine officer and eloquent despite a stammer.

We sat out-of-doors beneath tall elms, overlooking
the Hudson River. Aides came and went from the
large frame-house he used as headquarters. There was
a certain amount of stir that day, for 6,000 British
troops had just left New York City and were now
landing on both sides of the river below Peekskill.
McDougall had been trying for some days to get word
to Washington in New Jersey. But none of his messengers had got through.

McDougall was indignant at the course the war had
taken, or not taken. "That Congress!" He spoke with
a trace of Scots accent. "I swear they are the worst men
in the country!" All soldiers agreed. It was well-known
that those few delegates who bothered to attend the
Continental Congress preferred currency speculation
to supporting the army. But then Congress thought
that the war was as good as over. Washington himself
had led them to believe that with the arrival of the
French fleet our victory was assured.

In due course, the French fleet did arrive and Wash-

ington was able to make his long-anticipated strike at
New York. Between the French fleet and the American army the British were as good as dead or so everyone thought, not taking into account Washington's
gift for defeat which once again carried the day.

To begin with, no one saw fit to acquaint the
French admiral d'Estaing with the mysteries of New
York's port. As a result, when the hour of battle arrived, the French fleet could not pass the bar at the
harbour entrance while Washington's favourite general,
John Sullivan, in attempting to carry out his master's
strategy, ignominiously lost the field to the British
garrison. In disgust, the French fleet sailed south.

"I tell you, Burr, if it wasn't for the French fleet in
the English Channel, the British would drive us clear
to the Ohio." McDougall stammered over the second
"b" as though the word so begun was too vile to
complete.

We would have been even more disturbed if we had
known that the war was going to continue in desultory
fashion for three more years with Washington avoiding, as much as possible, all military action. Partly
because inaction was now congenial to his nature;
partly because the army of some 14,000 he had commanded at the famous "victory" of Monmouth Court
House had now dwindled to almost nothing through
lack of funds, and through a mystical faith on the part
of Congress in the victory that was somehow bound to
be ours simply because of the French alliance.

At the end of the war when Washington arrived in
Virginia to join the siege of Yorktown, he commanded
only 2,500 men while French troops at Yorktown
numbered 3,000 in addition to their fleet of more than
thirty ships of the line. So in a sense Congress was
right. The French did defeat the British for us. Certainly without them we would still be British colonies;
a distressing fact we have long since forgotten just as
we are currently trying to forget how easy it was for a
small British army detachment to drive President

Madison from the White House and set the torch to Washington City. Fortunately our people have always preferred legend to reality—as I know best of all, having become one of the dark legends of the republic, and hardly real.

McDougall listened to the whisper of an aide. Swore another oath. "You go to Washington, Burr. You know the country." The mule story. Washington and St. Clair. New Haven. Yale.

COLONEL BURR'S NARRATIVE stops at this point. Then another fragment, on different paper, of recent date.

Benedict Arnold. Noted June 4, 1833

IN THE AUTUMN of 1780 I was at the Hermitage with Mrs. Prevost, who had kindly undertaken the considerable task of keeping me alive. At her insistence I drank a gallon of spring water a day and felt rather the worse for it.

The treachery of Benedict Arnold was exciting the country that season. For some time Arnold had been disaffected. He had been unjustly passed over for promotion. Then because of his damaged foot, he was not suited—it was thought—to take an active command. So Washington made him military governor of Philadelphia after the British left.

In this post, Arnold strutted about like a Roman proconsul; all he lacked was lictors at his portly side. His quarrelsome and autocratic nature was further exacerbated by too much drink. Yet he did contrive to marry the prettiest girl in town, Peggy Shippen, whose family had been kind to me in my orphaned youth. Like most of the American gentry, the Shippens were pro-British Tories. In fact, during the British occupation of Philadelphia, Peggy had nearly married an attractive British officer named Major André.

Careless, venal, offensive in his manner, Arnold got himself into all sorts of trouble not only with the Pennsylvania Assembly but with the Congress itself, a group of thieves quite capable of recognising Arnold as one of their own, and in need of watching. Various charges were brought against him. Although he was eventually exonerated, the trials he had undergone made him more bitter than ever—if that was possible. To placate Arnold, Washington offered him an attractive field command. Arnold rejected it; his health was not good. He would accept, however, the command at West Point on the Hudson, a most insignificant post for an important general. Taken aback, Washington pointed out to Arnold that West Point's garrison was made up of invalids while the post's only function was surveillance of the river and as a centre for information. That of course was why Arnold wanted it.

Unknown to us all, Arnold was now a British agent with instructions to turn over West Point to the enemy. He would have succeeded if the British spy Major André had not been captured with incriminating documents. Simultaneously, Washington, Lafayette and Hamilton arrived at West Point on a tour of inspection. In a panic, Arnold abandoned the beautiful Peggy and took refuge aboard the British ship *Vulture* in the river.

Peggy then went mad; raved at Washington, accused him of murdering her child whose father, she declared, was Hamilton, much to that young satyr's embarrassment. I can imagine His Excellency's thoughtful dull gaze as he slowly, slowly considered the pros and cons of the matter. Finally, Washington sent Peggy home to Philadelphia under military escort. This much of the story was known to us in Paramus that autumn evening when a carriage and horsemen clattered up the drive.

Servants answered the door. Theodosia was alarmed. So was I. For all we knew the British were on the move.

From the hallway, a resounding shriek. Then a veiled figure appeared in the doorway. "The iron! The *hot* iron!" The voice rang out. The figure staggered. Theodosia rushed forward to support her old friend Peggy Shippen Arnold.

Servants and children gathered wide-eyed as Peggy reeled toward the sofa by the fire. "My baby! They have killed my baby!"

But a nurse with a child looked in for a moment and said, "I have baby. She wants a bed." Theodosia sent a servant to prepare beds for mother and child. Then Major Franks from Washington's staff entered and saluted me. "I am Mrs. Arnold's escort to Philadelphia. She particularly wanted to spend the night here."

"You are all welcome." The bewildered Theodosia ordered a room for the Major who immediately went upstairs, whispering to me as he did, "She's in one of her fits now. They come and go."

Peggy, meanwhile, had taken up her position before the fireplace. She looked uncommonly pretty, despite wild hair and a sparkling demented gaze. She had known Theodosia all her life, regarded her as an older sister.

"There he is, the murderer!" Peggy pointed a long finger at me. It was most effective. I later used with much success the same gesture and tone of voice in the course of a murder trial.

Peggy grasped her brow. "The iron! Hot! Hot! Hot as the flames of Hell!"

This would not do, even from a madwoman. Theodosia made a shushing sound and sent everyone from the room except me.

Peggy sobbed for a long time in her veil. Then she dried her eyes briskly and said, "By God, Theodosia, if I have to go on like this one more day I *will* go out of my mind. Hello, Aaron. We've not seen each other since . . ."

"You were a child. How," I could not help asking the actress, "is the hot iron now?"

"Considerably cooler, thank you!" Peggy burst into laughter, was again the most charming girl of her day.

Theodosia was more puzzled than I. "Are you really all right, Peggy?"

"Of course she is. Peggy has been play-acting." I had suspected her from the moment of her entrance.

"Better play-acting than a jail." Peggy gave me a hard look. "Is Aaron all right?"

"In what way?" Theodosia was an innocent in these matters.

I was not. "She means will I tell General Washington that she fooled him. No, I won't. That is, if she doesn't try to fool us."

"I would never do that! Well, I would if I had to. You're not Tory, are you?"

I said I was not. I had been devoted to the Revolution from the first day, and so was a proper Whig.

Peggy made a face. "Well, I have hated your 'Revolution' from the first day."

"So apparently did General Arnold." This was bold of me but Peggy was boldness itself.

"I have no way of knowing." Peggy was matter-of-fact. "That was before I met him. I do know how badly he was treated by the Congress, by Mr. Washington who . . ." She suddenly broke out laughing, and I feared that she was about to favour us with another mad scene but she was sane, and much amused. "You should have seen His Excellency! When I realized my husband was in danger, I took to my bed. I had to convince everyone that I knew nothing of what was going on. So I claimed that Colonel Varick was trying to kill my baby and that a hot iron was burning my head and . . ."

"Where did you get that marvellous hot iron from?" Theodosia had an inquiring nature.

"I read it somewhere, a story about a poor woman in Bedlam. 'The iron, the *hot* iron'!" Peggy boomed until we begged her to stop. "I pretended I didn't recognise Mr. Washington who looked frightened to death and sent for Mr. Hamilton, that lovely young goose . . ."

"Peggy!" Theodosia obviously did not like to think of us precocious colonels as geese, lovely or otherwise.

"Oh, a perfect goose, believe me. With him I changed my manner. Became conspiratorial. *Tête-à-tête*. I was wearing a handsome lace bedgown, the latest thing from London, sent me last summer by Major André." Peggy frowned. "They won't shoot him, will they?"

We did not know it but Major André had already been hanged as a spy. "I rather think we will." I was hard, too hard, for I have since been told not only that Peggy and the Major were lovers before she married Arnold but that their affair continued even after, and that Peggy helped André to corrupt her new husband. Between the wife playing on Arnold's sense of injury and Major André offering him money (and the King's commission), it is no wonder that that unstable man went over to the enemy and, good commander that he was, did our cause much injury in the field before the French won the war for us. As I have said before, Arnold was a superb commander.

"Of course, Major André might be exchanged for General Arnold." I could not resist playing on her terror. She was also devoted to her lunatic husband.

"The British would never give him up. Not even for—for him."

Theodosia and I often discussed this scene during the years of our marriage, meditating upon Peggy's exquisite dilemma. The old lover's life and the new husband's life for an instant were in the balance.

Peggy was a remarkable girl, with a quick intelligence. Tribute to her quickness was the fact that she was able in one day to dupe Washington, Hamilton and Lafayette. But then she was a professional spy. When I was in London, I learned that in 1782 she received some 400 pounds from the British government for services rendered. Of those services, the greatest was

her marriage to Benedict Arnold, and her conversion
of a truculent malcontent into prodigious traitor.

Peggy was in her glory that night at Paramus. She
must have thought herself a perfect success. Yet she
had destroyed her husband, for the British were plainly
losing the war. But then she had the sort of febrile
personality that is happy only in a desperate, preferably losing situation in which a vivid role can be
enacted like Joan at the stake. Politically she was uncommonly zealous. Her father had been a Tory judge
in Philadelphia and she had learned from him and
his circle of friends to detest anyone who questioned
England's majesty and the rights of property.

Feet on the fire fender, like a handsome boy, Peggy
told us of her interview with Colonel Hamilton at
West Point.

"I said I knew nothing of my husband's activity.
And then I wept, very softly, holding his arm very close
to me. He is most susceptible, isn't he?"

I looked at her politely. Actually, Hamilton's "sus-
ceptibility" was unknown to me at that time. Later
of course he became notorious for his—I almost wrote
"lecheries" but who am I to use such a word for life's
best pleasure? I will say that Hamilton was a fool where
women were concerned, and often embarrassed his
partisans, not to mention his noble, long-suffering
Schuyler wife.

"Anyway I persuaded him that I wanted only to
come home to Philadelphia, to my family. I threw
myself upon his mercy. He was so moved at this that
he put his free hand on my arm ever so gently . . ."

"Peggy, you should be soundly spanked." Theodosia
was more direct than I; also of the two of us, she was
the more knowing in the ways of people.

"You are unkind." But Peggy enjoyed arousing her
old friend; wanted to disturb my impassivity. "I said
that I feared the crowd. Feared for my life." She
frowned. "I *am* afraid, as matter of fact. What will
the Whigs do to me in Pennsylvania?"

"Invite you to all their parties, I should think, and

ask you to play Ophelia." Theodosia was not as amused by Peggy as I was.

"Colonel Hamilton said that he would intercede with General Washington, which he did. I then had almost the same interview with the Marquis de Lafayette *in French!*"

A servant entered to call away the mistress of the house. When Theodosia was gone, Peggy stretched like a cat in front of the fire. Then she looked me straight in the eye, the way she used to when we were children and wanted her way. "Well?" from Peggy.

"Well?" I did not respond.

She crossed to me. Took my hands in hers and looked me in the eye. "I've talked too much. I don't usually go on like this."

"It was most interesting."

"You don't approve of what we did?"

"I do not."

"I hate the enemies of England!" There was real passion in her voice. "I hate what your Virginia dolt is doing to our world."

I assured her that it would still be *our* world when the war ended; but without the inconvenience of paying taxes to England. She would not believe me.

"It will not be ours but theirs, those wild men from the woods, from the water frontage, from the worst stews of the towns. They'll take *everything!*" Peggy sounded like one of today's New York ladies deploring Andrew Jackson. Only she had done more than deplore; she had sacrificed everything.

"Well, no matter who owns the country, Peggy, you'll have no part in it. The English will go home and you will go with them and never come back."

"I believe we'll win. But if we don't, I will be happy to go." She was so close to me that I could smell the sharp odour of her breath, a feminine odour I had even then learned to recognise as corresponding with a phase of the moon. She tried to draw me toward her but I got my hands free.

"I am to marry Theodosia."

Peggy gave me a furious look, threw herself into a chair beside the fire. "She is old enough to be your mother."

"Hardly." But Theodosia was ten years older than I. Her late husband had been a colonel in the British army. She had no fortune. I was aware that in the world's eye this was the poorest sort of match for a rising young man to make. Yet to me Theodosia was everything I ever wanted in a woman except that she was not my daughter, too; fortunately, she provided me with a second Theodosia before her death and my happiness—for a short time—was complete. Yet I confess that evening at Paramus I did not much enjoy Peggy's taunt.

"Now you'll betray me." Peggy's face was foolish with fear.

"It's not possible. You have anticipated me."

Put briefly, Benedict Arnold was a fool and Peggy was a greater one. Fearing that I might reveal the extent of her complicity, Peggy promptly put it about that I had made advances to her at Paramus. This was in character. Actually, I kept her secret until now. I like to think that my discretion was equally in character.

1834

&

One

SHORTLY BEFORE NOON, the main door to the office was flung open. Icy air filled the room. Mr. Craft's latest brief floated toward the grate. One of the young clerks rushed to slam the door only to find that it framed a bright-faced Aaron Burr and two heavy-set men who looked rather the worse for what must have been a long walk in the cold. Their hands and cheeks were flame colour.

The Colonel simply looked fresh. "Heigh-ho!" he exclaimed. "I am—as you see—back!"

He is as hearty as ever; does not even walk with a stick.

Burr led the men into the inner office, calling out, as he did, for various papers that he wanted.

Mr. Craft was quietly pleased. "*They* cannot kill the Colonel." The dour face was filled with dark significance.

"You mean Madame and Nelson Chase?"

Mr. Craft shook his head. The dark significance, apparently, is his way of expressing undue pleasure, some-

thing I have not often noted in the five years we have
worked together. He seldom discusses anything with
me except our work and the day's temperature.
Weather means a lot to him.

"Life!" Mr. Craft exclaimed. Apparently life could
not kill Aaron Burr. I left the sense of that unexplored.
"You would do well to study his . . ." Mr. Craft
lowered his voice to make sure that the two clerks
did not hear him. ". . . style. In his day he was the first
gentleman of New York. And one of the first gentlemen in the land."

"He was vice-president, of course . . ."

"*Gentleman*, Mr. Schuyler, not office-holding knave!
His father, his grandfather, his great-grandfather, back
to the beginning, were great divines and presidents
of universities. That is why he was so envied by Hamilton, by that . . ." The voice lowered to a whisper in
my ear. ". . . that West Indian *bastard!* How they all
envied him! From the gutter *they* came, while Aaron
Burr was our first gentleman." After all our years of
work together, Mr. Craft has at last revealed himself
to be, most unexpectedly, a classic New York snob.
I have always thought that the most appealing thing
about Alexander Hamilton was his illegitimacy. But
then I am not impressed by "divines."

There was the sound of voices raised in disagreement
from the next room. Then Colonel Burr called my
name. I went inside.

"I would," said one of the men sharply, "like very
much to be paid the money."

"And I would," said Colonel Burr in his courtliest
fashion (three, four, five generations of "divines"?),
"like very much to pay you the money. But I cannot—
for the present. Mr. Schuyler, you will now have my
full attention. Gentlemen, good day."

As the Colonel shut the door after his creditors, he
was in a merry mood. "We must complete your education to-night with something truly profound." He
bit the end from a seegar. "You have been reading
Gibbon?"

"I am in the third volume." I lied.

"I shall query you about him to-night. At the Park Theatre. I have bought tickets to see the unique Miss Fanny Kemble and her father in what I fear is a foolish play called *The Hunchback*."

I expressed delight that was not feigned. Actually I had seen Miss Kemble in the part last September when she made her first appearance here, and took the town by storm. She is a marvellous fiery creature on stage, though not beautiful. She is supposed to look like her aunt Mrs. Siddons.

Colonel Burr lit his seegar and did what can only be described as a dance step. "Free!" he intoned. "Free!"

Then he confided to me that he had left the Heights, "for the last time. A heart of gold, Madame has. No doubt of it! What fills her purse, you might say, also beats in her fine bosom. The tick-tick of gold, Charlie, what a sound! The world dances to its measure." Another half dance step and he was at his chair beside the baize table. The fire glowed in the hearth. I thought, suddenly, here is a happy man. Why?

"For reasons of temperament, we have decided to go our separate ways for a time. Our marriage is in abeyance. I need the stimulus of the town. Madame is happy only at the mansion, receiving Bonapartes. It is possible she will try to divorce me, but I hope not. I have promised to reimburse her—God willing—for the sale of her four broken-down bays. Make a note to send her a barrel of salted salmon. It is her favourite. My first wife's favourite, too." The Colonel shut his eyes. With pain? Recollection? Neither. "Have you prepared the bill of particulars I wanted for the De-Peyster case?"

"I have begun it, only . . ."

Through the smoke he gave me his most Burrite aphorism. "Excellent, Charlie. Never do today what you can do tomorrow because who knows what may turn up?"

Miss Kemble was superb as Julia. Her father was

also effective as the Hunchback. The theatre's new decorations are most sumptuous—everything gold and crimson on cream, with a portrait of Shakespeare over the proscenium arch and representations of comedy and tragedy on either side of the stage where mirrors used to be.

Only the audience was a disappointment. The boxes were half-filled with enthusiastic gentry, including the Colonel and me. The pit, on the other hand, was crowded with loud, drunken men recruited from the Five Points to boo not the performers—or there would have been a riot—but the theatre's manager, Mr. Edmund Simpson, who is thought to prefer British to American players, which is nonsense because his principal attraction is our own Edwin Forrest. It is nothing more than a foolish competition between the Park Theatre and the Bowery Theatre, whose manager Tom Hamblin hired these ruffians to shout and bray, particularly during the orchestral interludes. This rattles all the musicians except the Cockney known as Mr. Drum. Between bars Mr. Drum sleeps, as oblivious to the noise in the pit as he is to the conductor. But somehow he never misses a cue. He is the loudest drummer in New York.

The Bowery Theatre has also enlisted the *Evening Post* in its support, and Leggett himself has taken to attacking the Park Theatre. Understandably, Mr. Simpson has banned him from the theatre. Meanwhile, in a cheap gesture for sympathy, the Bowery Theatre changed its name to the American Theatre on the sensible ground that no one can attack anything wrapped in the stars and stripes.

During the *entr'acte*, I stand with Colonel Burr at the door that looks out onto Broadway and St. Paul's. The church is lighted within. A service? Between the golden glow from the church's windows and the white glare from the theatre's lobby, large snow-flakes like feathers slowly turn and fall. The Colonel, as usual, pretends to keep his eyes on me, as though rivetted by what I am saying. Actually, it is to avoid the possibility of being publicly cut by someone.

"She is a fine animal, Charlie, no doubt of that!" Miss Kemble had stimulated him but then is there any man who can resist that mighty yet womanly voice? I have written a study of her acting which *The Mirror* is considering for publication.

"I thought, Colonel, you believed that women had souls, were not animals." I was amused.

"But the soul has its fleshly envelope. Besides, I have yet to think through whether or not animals might also possess souls, too. So many people who do have souls are bestial."

As we talked, I glanced at the people in the audience. Many of the older ones were aware of the Colonel's presence and stared at him with fascination, even horror. The young know him not, or anything else. Patrons of the Park Theatre boxes tend to be rich. They hate the President, adore Clay and Webster. I am writing now about politics not because I care how the Park Theatre audience votes but because I was jostled twice by a man with a heavy beard and thick spectacles. The first time I simply moved away. The second time, when he stepped on my foot, I turned, ready to do battle—and then recognized through a full dark false beard William Leggett.

"Don't I look like the prophet Isaiah?"

"I don't know what the prophet Isaiah looked like." My toe hurt. Then I introduced him to Colonel Burr who was as gracious as Lord Chesterfield with a groom.

"I am not supposed to be here," Leggett whispered. "Simpson has threatened to fight a duel with me. For me, the cane. For him, the adverb." Leggett suddenly stopped: in the house of the hanged man, do not mention rope.

But the Colonel was serene. "A most sensible choice of weapons. Personally I have always regarded duelling as a terrible business."

"Of course. Barbaric. But then . . ." Leggett actually stammered. The false whiskers slipped a bit; the moustache covering under as well as upper lip.

"But in my barbarous day, we had no choice. It was a code we felt obliged to live by."

Leggett straightened his beard. "But you were fortunate, Colonel. You were a fine shot and so had every advantage in those barbarous days."

Leggett had gone too far but the Colonel handled him with his usual niceness of manner. "I seldom try to correct legend. For one thing, it is not possible. But I shall tell you a secret unknown until now."

Leggett's eyes gleamed. He leaned down, ear close to the Colonel's mouth.

Burr was suitably mysterious. "Despite all my years as a soldier, Mr. Leggett, I can seldom at twenty paces hit with accuracy a barn-door."

"You are too modest, Sir."

Burr laughed. "Not at all. But perhaps I have been too lucky. Some years ago in Utica, a group of men asked me to give then an exhibition. I said I was indisposed. But they said they *must* see Aaron Burr display his marksmanship. So I indicated a notch on a tree some distance away. Would they like me to hit it? Indeed they would." Burr's eyes glittered. "Well, with a single casually aimed shot, I pierced the centre of the notch."

"You see . . ." began Leggett.

"You see," finished Burr, "it was my luck. Nothing more. The men were delighted. They prepared another target but I begged off. As a result, to this day there are people in Utica who will swear on oath that I am the best marksman that ever lived."

"But of course there were other equally famous occasions when you hit your target." I was ready to throttle Leggett right there in the lobby.

Although the Colonel's face remained fixed in a gentle smile, the voice dropped to a deeper but still amiable register. "Mr. Leggett, the principal difference between my friend Hamilton and me was that at the crucial moment his hand shook and mine never does."

The bell rang behind the green baize curtain. We went back to our seats. The rowdies were roaring in the pit. Mr. Drum was asleep on his stool. The orchestra fell silent as the oil lamp dimmed and the curtain rose. But I could not think of the play, only of Colonel Burr's remarkable candour. It is the first time I have heard him mention the duel.

After the play, the Colonel wondered whether or not to pay his respects to father Kemble whom he knew in order to meet daughter Kemble whom he did not. Finally he decided against going back-stage. "It's too late, and I must go to Jersey City."

Outside the theatre, I helped him on with his coat. The slow snow had been replaced by a cold steady wind from the North River that made the near-by museum's shutters snap back and forth. Carriages crowded Broadway, waiting for the theatre-goers.

The Colonel and I crossed over to St. Paul's (the lights were gone). At the corner of Fulton Street we saw the now beardless Leggett; he was supposed to have been picked up by a friend. "I can't think what went wrong."

"Perhaps," said the Colonel smoothly, "he did not recognise you clean-shaven."

Leggett laughed, coughed. "Without the beard I might have been assaulted by a murderous adverb."

" 'Ultimately'?" inquired the Colonel. "It is the fatal adverb in wait for us all."

"Did *you* like the Kembles?" I changed the subject. Leggett said yes, he admired the Kembles very much, and so I said that I thought it shameful the *Evening Post* continues to attack them simply because of the management.

As we argued, the Colonel started briskly down Fulton Street toward the docks. We hurried after.

When told that the Colonel was going to Jersey City, Leggett was surprised. "But it's too late. The ferries don't run. And there's a storm coming up."

We were now on West Street just back of the funereal bulk of the Washington Market. "Ephraim!" Burr shouted.

"Here, Colonel!"

We made our way toward the dark slip where the son of one of the Colonel's Revolutionary friends waited in his small boat.

"Nice night, Ephraim."

"Real nice, Colonel." A tall figure stood up in the shadowy boat and pulled tight the mooring line until the boat was against the dock, rising and falling at a great rate in the boiling river.

"My God, it's cold!" Leggett was shivering uncontrollably.

The Colonel took Ephraim's arm and like a cat sprang into the boat.

As Ephraim cast off, the Colonel waved to us. "Don't you boys see that *this* is what makes it all fun?"

"I'm freezing." Leggett wrapped his cloak about his ears.

Colonel Burr had heard him through the wind. "Put your beard back on, Mr. Leggett. It will keep you warm."

Then boat and Colonel vanished into sleety darkness and Leggett and I walked—no, ran—all the way to Thomas Street and Mrs. Townsend who took us into her front parlour, made us drink Columbia County apple-jack until the cold was out of our bones.

Leggett spoke with reluctant admiration of Colonel Burr.

Mrs. Townsend gave us a somewhat mystical smile. "I have been reading his grandfather all evening. But then I often read Jonathan Edwards, *for the terror!*"

Mrs. Townsend believes in a dramatic creed. Before we could stop her she had picked up a volume from the pile of books on the floor beside her sofa. Pages were marked with slips of paper. She opened at seeming random and read. " 'As innocent as children seem to be to us, yet if they are out of Christ they are not so in God's sight, but are young vipers.' Young vipers," she repeated with satisfaction. She is celebrated for her loathing of children. Once in the street when a small child grabbed at her skirt, she wrenched it free, shouting, "Unclean!" Some thought she referred to her skirt or, more likely, soul. But those who admire her know that she meant the child.

" 'Will those children . . . that lived and died insensible of their misery, until they feel it in Hell, ever thank parents for not letting them know what they were in danger of?' "

"Dreadful stuff," said Leggett. "The sort of thing that would make a traitor to God and man of any child brought up on it."

"The Colonel is hardly a traitor to either God or man." I came to Burr's defence.

But Mrs. Townsend was not finished with Jonathan Edwards. She had opened a larger volume, blew dust from a page, reducing Leggett to a fit of coughing as, inexorably, she read, " 'Let it be considered that if our lives be not a journey towards Heaven, they will be a journey to Hell.' " She gave Leggett a long look. "It's not the dust," she whispered stagily, "but *the dust to dust.*" That stopped his coughing. " 'The two great receptacles of all that depart out of this world; the one is Heaven, whither a few, a small number in comparison, travel.' Ah, Mr. Leggett, contemplate those *few!*"

"I would rather contemplate Black Bess."

"It is her time of the month. We have something even better, twenty years old, from Ohio." The voice was matter-of-fact. She returned to her page. " 'And the other is Hell, whither the bulk . . . the bulk . . . the bulk of mankind do throng. And one or the other of these must be our journey's end; the issue of our course in this world.' "

Her voice fell silent; the book shut softly; dust motes spiralled in the lamplight. "I have been told, Mr. Leggett, Mr. Schuyler, too" (I was also Hellward bound), "that on his death-bed John Randolph of Roanoke suddenly sat up, a top hat on his head, and said, over and over again, 'Remorse, remorse!' "

"Randolph was mad and a eunuch. I am neither, dear Mrs. Townsend." Leggett was irritable. I was restive. Mrs. Townsend gave us her yellow-fanged, dry-lipped smile and rang for the maid. "We have new delights, gentlemen."

Then she remembered. "But for you, Mr. Schuyler, there is an 'old' new delight. So enjoy yourselves—in this world." Mrs. Townsend opened a copy of Jonathan Edwards' *The Freedom of the Will* (apparently, he does not believe in it) as the maid arrived to show us to Hell's ante-room.

Helen was loving but hates the winter. Talks of spring. Of leaving Mrs. Townsend. I promise—before—to help her find work; and mean what I say because—after—I tell her that I will ask friends who know about dress-makers. She told me that she has yet to see the Vauxhall Gardens. I promise to take her there the first good day in spring.

Why is it no girl I meet in the usual way appeals to me the way she does? even though I know she appeals in exactly the same way (no, that is not possible, *not* the same) to anyone who pays the price.

Since there is no Heaven, how can there be Hell?

Leggett and I left Thomas Street together. He was pleased; not ill as before. He walked me part way to my lodgings. The apple-jack and the girls had warmed us up; and the north wind had dropped. "I had not expected the Colonel to be so youthful."

"He is extraordinary!"

"You are fond of him." This was almost a reproach.

"Well, yes. I suppose I am. He takes an interest. How many people do in someone younger—in *anyone* for that matter?"

"What have you discovered?"

I confessed to very little. I did not tell him about the notes on the Revolution.

"What about Mr. Irving?"

"Not informative, I'm afraid. He's very cautious, particularly on the subject of Van Buren."

"Sly old tabby-cat! I do hate those comfortable stories of his."

I was shocked. "He is the best we have . . ."

"That's not saying much. You know, we've just made an arrangement with Cooper to write for the *Evening Post*, under a pseudonym." Last month James Fenimore Cooper returned to New York after many years abroad. His arrival was hardly noticed; unlike that of Irving, who took the town by storm. But then Irving is tactful while Cooper enjoys pointing out to his countrymen their shortcomings. He is too prickly for our flag-waving patriots.

"You know," said Leggett, "after studying as carefully as I could Colonel Burr's head, I am more than ever convinced that he is the father of Van Buren."

Leggett is fascinated by the new science of phrenology. Apparently all the secrets of character are revealed by the bumps on the head. He has even suggested that I write something about phrenology for the *Evening Post*.

For the moment, however, he had given me the last word. "I prefer looking carefully *inside* the Colonel's head. That's the only way of finding out who he is, and what he is to Van Buren."

"There is a contagion to the Colonel's style." That was the best he could do. "I hope *your* hands don't shake."

As Leggett galloped down the street, the false beard slipped from his pocket and fell onto the icy cobbles where it lay like a dead kitten.

Two

IT IS APRIL. I have not had time—no, I have had the time but not the will—to continue this record.

The Colonel lives either at Jersey City or in the office. There has been, as far as I can tell, no communication from Madame. Nelson Chase has gone to another law firm. I don't know which. Some say he is working for Alexander Hamilton, Junior. That would be, as the Colonel would say, most neat.

The Colonel is in fine spirits. He has taken on several new cases. He has also become somewhat absent of mind. Recently a client paid him fifty dollars. When she left, he put the money in a dictionary. As he was about to leave the office, he started to go through his pockets. "Charlie, I have no money. Not a cent. And the bank is closed. Do you have ten dollars?"

"No, Sir. But *you* have fifty dollars in the dictionary."

Startled, he opened the book and took out the money he had only just hidden there. "You are my benefactor. It is a gift from Heaven." But light as the manner was, I saw his distress: Burr without the splendid mind is nothing at all.

But the Colonel's memory of the past is as sharp as ever. Shortly after New Year (1834 according to the gypsy woman will be the best year of my life; but then she said that about 1833), the Colonel asked me my opinion of his notes on the Revolution.

"What is 'the mule story'?"

Burr looked blank. " 'Mule story'? Oh," he laughed. "I tell it only to children. You are much too big a boy. It's a very long story about the mule I rode from West Point to Newburgh. I wanted to go south. The mule wanted to go north. We ended up in a westerly direction, through a coal-mine. If you were younger, I would add many, many details, with appropriate sounds."

Then he spoke of the possibility of dictating to me his recollections. "While they are still lodged in what is left of my mind."

I encourage him; am eager. But he is reluctant to begin; delays.

LEGGETT INVITED ME for lunch at the Washington Hall Hotel. At our table were Washington Irving, the literary congressman Gulian C. Verplanck (currently the anti-Tammany candidate for mayor), and Fitz-Greene Halleck. Mr. Cooper and Mr. Bryant were supposed to join us but sent regrets. "Cooper detests Irving," Leggett whispered in my ear as we sat down. But Irving detests no one or, if he does, is a capital actor.

"I had looked forward to seeing my old friend Cooper." Irving seemed most sincere. "He is not only a great man, he is a good man." A waiter carrying beef brushed Irving's shoulder: drops of gravy fell onto his sleeve.

"It's not Holland House," said Halleck, meaning I suppose some noble English house.

"The food is excellent." Irving glumly mopped up the gravy.

Then Verplanck mentioned an attack on Irving in the *North American Review*. Irving affected not to have read it.

"They say that you denigrate America, praise only things British. Imagine! When you alone gave America a literature. Somewhat at the expense of us poor Dutch . . ." In his gruff way, Verplanck is not without malice.

"I shall have a glass of claret." Irving had finally caught a waiter's attention, and leaned nervously to one side as wine was slopped into a dusty glass.

Verplanck detailed, with obvious delight, the terrible charges the reviewer had made against Irving. But our lion of literature merely smiled and nodded and murmured for the historic record, "I never ceased to represent my country abroad. And now that I am home—

see the changes—all things *ongoing*—happy—represent
—fulfilment." First the verbs began to drop from his
sentences; then the nouns. Finally, silence, as he drank
his wine, cut turkey deftly, looked somewhat sleepy.

Leggett questioned Verplanck about the election
next week. Because Verplanck opposed Jackson who
wants to replace the Bank of the United States with
a number of local banks, he has been purged by Tammany but taken up by the Whigs (the new name for
those who are not Jacksonian Democrats). Verplanck
expects to be elected mayor though he is happy in
Congress.

Leggett treats Irving deferentially but with a certain
edge. "The *Evening Post* is printing Mr. Cooper soon.
When will you write for us?"

Irving blinked his eyes rapidly. Cleared his throat.
"Mr. Bryant's poetry seems to me to be unique.
Superior to Wordsworth's, don't you think? Without
Byron's vulgarity or Coleridge's opacity." I gather most
famous men are like this. They answer the same question so many times a day that sometimes, absently,
they answer the wrong question.

But Leggett pressed him. "We suspect you, Mr.
Irving, of democracy."

Irving responded with his crooked smile. At heart
he is very much a Tory. One can see that in his manner, in his love of the past, of the quaint and the
traditional; not to mention in the company he keeps:
he is friends with all the rich merchants of the city.
But the sweep of the times is toward democracy, if
Leggett is to be believed. Secretly I think Irving must
hate what is happening; yet, "I spent the winter at
Washington City. Haunted the Capitol. Heard every
debate, good and bad. What great orators we have!
Clay, Webster, Calhoun!"

"All Tories." Leggett was relentless.

"All brilliant men. But"—Irving looked to left and
right to make sure that the other diners could not
hear him, as if anyone could hear anything through the

crash of plates, the shouts of waiters, the muffled bellowing of cooks in the far-off kitchen—"but mistaken, I think." Cautiously, Irving came out against the Nullifiers. "The southerners are, you know, once you observe them in the Congress and talk to them in private, not entirely without—well, a degree of justice." Irving is incapable of offending any part of his audience. "Yet," he spoke before Leggett, "it is plain to me that if they have their way our general union will dissolve."

"A bad thing or not?" Although Halleck has the reputation for brilliance, today he was somewhat subdued; stared at me when he thought I was not looking. Obviously puzzled to see me there.

"I should think it a bad thing." Irving was dry. "But the south might be happier without us."

Leggett tried to question him about Van Buren but Irving affected to know nothing of the Vice-President's plans.

In a low voice Fitz-Greene Halleck asked me what I did. "I am in a law office."

"Everyone is. But are you . . . literary or political?"

"I hate politics!" Why not jump in with both feet?

Halleck smiled. "Good. So do I. But then I am an enemy of the people, and regard the ship of state like any other ship: for the captain to sail it safely he must never ever consult the crew. That is why I am for a king, any king, the more tyrannical the better. I also incline to the Roman Church because it saves you such a lot of bother. Your salvation is entirely taken care of by priests who are paid to do nothing else." And so on. I found Halleck refreshing, and though he seems to be making jokes I think he is probably quite serious.

As we rose from table, Halleck said something to Irving who turned and looked at me, and nodded. At the door to the dining-room, I stood back for the lions to pass. But Irving took my arm and led me out into the hall.

"You have made a most vivid impression on poor Halleck."

"Oh?" was the best I could do, wondering why Halleck was "poor."

"You look so like his friend Joseph Rodman Drake. He was Halleck's closest friend, lived with him, worked with him. Then the boy quite suddenly died. That was nearly fifteen years ago, and Halleck has not recovered to this day. Like Damon and Pythias. Jonathan and David . . ." We were outside in the street. Brusquely Halleck shook my hand; hurried away.

As Verplanck and Leggett argued politics, Irving turned to me. "I have not forgotten your interest in Colonel Burr. Would it amuse you to go and see Richmond Hill?"

I said that I would be most amused. Colonel Burr is at Albany and Mr. Craft can always do without me for an afternoon.

I got into Irving's open carriage. Leggett and the others waved good-bye and Leggett gave me a schoolboy's wink, as though I was truckling to a teacher. Feeling rather conspicuous, I sat back in the carriage. The great man at my side nodded to gentlemen, lifted his hat to ladies, as we jolted along Wall Street.

"I have not seen Richmond Hill in twenty years. But I believe . . . Driver, stop! Stop!" Irving's voice can be loud when he wants. The coachman pulled over to the side just as the carriage in front of ours disgorged the stout slow ermine-clad Mr. Astor, just returned from Europe to find his wife dead. He looks half-dead himself but, apparently, business goes on as usual. Irving leapt with singular grace from the carriage, leaving me to decide whether or not to follow or stay. I stayed.

The two stood in the doorway of the Merchants' Bank, heads together, a family of piglets racing around their legs. Mr. Astor is reputed to like literature, to help artists. According to Leggett, he also wants to be thought well of as he buys up our city; to that end he has hired Fitz-Greene Halleck to be his secretary-companion and live with him at the Hell Gate mansion. Halleck's job is to scc that Mr. Astor is treated with respect in the newspapers.

Interview done with, Irving returned to the carriage, moving slowly now, as befits a great and heavy man. "I need advice in financial matters." He sat back in the seat, and sighed. "I am prone to speculation. Usually with disastrous results. Poor—no, *rich* Mr. Astor tries to be helpful. You know, he took over Richmond Hill, after Colonel Burr lost it. In fact, breaking up that estate into lots was the beginning of the Astor fortune in New York. It seems so simple, doesn't it? To make a fortune."

Irving talked a good deal about houses and property and money. I listened attentively, hardly able to believe that I was the sole auditor of this famous man who was recognized and waved at by several strangers in City Hall Park where a number of people were enjoying the pale April sun.

But though I was somewhat disappointed by the material cast of Irving's mind, he compensated by telling me a dozen stories about landmarks present as well as gone. "This was where we used to hunt duck." He pointed to a row of tenements. "Just past those houses begin—or began—the Lispenard Meadows. And beyond them was Richmond Hill."

As we were crossing an open stretch between buildings, Irving was suddenly agitated. "That's it! There! Look. See that well?"

I saw nothing but an empty field. But Irving is able to people landscapes with his own imaginings. "*It is the Manhattan Well!* In the early spring of eighteen hundred, one Elma Sands was found at the bottom of that well, murdered." A slight colour rose in his cheeks. The small eyes gleamed. "A young Mr. Levi Weeks was accused of the murder. He claimed innocence of the murder but guilt of having enjoyed the favours of Elma Sands. Everyone was most excited in the city and the two most brilliant lawyers of the day defended Weeks—Aaron Burr and Alexander Hamilton. I was in the court-room during Colonel Burr's performance. By the time he had finished, the jury and the judge—and no doubt the devil himself—were convinced that Elma Sands was a woman of no virtue while Levi Weeks was a young Galahad."

"Do you think this was true?" I know the effect a good lawyer can make on a jury. The sun at noon can become the moon at midnight if Colonel Burr has decided that such a replacement is in the interest of his client.

"Who knows? But of course Weeks was let free. Then . . ." Irving turned toward me and I noticed tiny broken veins on his nose. He actually licked his lips with pleasure in recollection. ". . . as the judge, Burr and Hamilton were talking to one another outside the court-house, a relative of Elma Sands approached and said, 'You are eternally cursed, the three of you, for what you have done to the memory of Elma Sands.' Shortly afterward, the judge vanished from his hotel never to be seen again. Burr then killed Hamilton, and now lives on and on"—the voice was clear and soft, each syllable distinct—"under the dread mark of Cain." It was most moving to hear an unwritten tale by Washington Irving. I must ask the Colonel if there is any truth to the story.

The city has pretty much overwhelmed the Lispenard Meadows and most of the lands of Richmond Hill (now bordered by Varick and Charlton streets). But the mansion itself still stands, somewhat altered since I was a child in Greenwich and used to play in the grounds, or what was left of them.

Recently the hill beneath the mansion was removed; the house is now at street level and no longer commands a view of the Hudson. It is simply a large old frame building with wings. A sign above the front door proclaims "Richard Hill Theatre." A smaller sign announces "Virginius—or, The Liberator of Rome, with Mr. Ingersoll."

Irving looked about him, at the new houses to left and right. He shook his head, mournfully. "I first set foot in this house when Colonel Burr was the vice-president. My brother Peter brought me. A third of a century ago."

With half-shut eyes, Irving stared at the front of the building (no sign of life inside or out), as though he might through sheer force of imagination evoke the young Burr and his Little Band. So Irving must have looked when his genius summoned from the Alhambra the phantom Boabdil. I do like his kind of writing, no matter what Leggett says. There is not much magic in the world these days.

Irving moved to the front door, rapped on it. No answer. He opened the door and we went inside. A foyer had been achieved by blocking up a part of what had been the downstairs hall. On the walls play bills flourish on penny sheets.

Irving opened the next door and we stood alone at the centre of the gutted mansion. The main hall has been turned into a pit with stage at the far end; the curtain was up on some poorly painted scenery depicting a castle. Where the second-floor landing had been, boxes had been built in a semicircle.

"That was the Blue Room." Irving pointed to the theatre pit. "You know, Colonel Burr had the first Venetian blinds I ever saw." He walked carefully among the rows of benches to what had been the Blue Room. "Oh!" Triumph. He had found the outline of a sealed fireplace visible through whitewash. "That is where he was standing when my brother and I came in after dinner."

Irving became an awkward young man, moved uncertainly toward the whitewashed wall. I could almost see Aaron Burr, sleek and dark and elegant at the fireplace (seegar in hand? no, there would be ladies present). "Over there at a card table sat Vanderlyn, the young painter—most handsome, most talented. Burr met him when he was a starving boy at Kingston. Saw one of his pictures, told him all he needed to make his way in New York was a clean shirt. One day, in this very room," Irving was embroidering freely but I was mesmerized, to think of old Vanderlyn as ever young and starving, "a servant brought the Colonel a package. He opened it. Inside was a rough but clean shirt. The boy had arrived. Burr paid for his training, sent him to Paris, got him commissions. At Colonel Burr's insistence Vanderlyn painted a minature of my mother which I still have."

Irving paused, looked down at the dirty floor. "I remember a red Turkey carpet. But not much furniture. Colonel Burr had been forced to sell most of his possessions just before he went to Washington City. He was always in debt."

Irving made a sweeping gesture. "Just think of all the remarkable men who have been in this room." I looked dutifully at the stage, the boxes, the rows of benches. "During the Revolution, Washington. Then Adams lived here when he was vice-president. And the visitors! Talleyrand, Jérôme Bonaparte, King Louis Philippe." Irving said the famous names like a witch casting a spell until I half-expected to see General Washington himself come out on the stage and sing "Yankee Doodle."

"I pinched myself that first evening—to think that I was *here*." Irving moved to a sort of bay to the left of the fireplace. In it was a ladder and a bucket of whitewash turned to chalk. "*She* sat there. On a cabriole sofa, covered in velvet."

Irving approached the ladder on tiptoe. Smiled tenderly at the bucket of whitewash. "Theodosia," he whispered. "Are you still here?"

But Theodosia was long gone to her grave at the bottom of the sea and we were quite alone in the wreck of Richmond Hill, except for a drunken janitor who suddenly emerged from a back door. "What're you two doing?"

"Forgive us." Irving was benign. "The door was open. I used to come here when it was a private house."

"This is a theatre, man, can't you read? If you want to come in you can buy a ticket like the rest." Suspiciously the man bore down upon us. Although Irving did his best to charm the janitor neither Aaron Burr nor Washington Irving was a familiar name to one who knew a pair of thieves when he saw them; and saw them off the premises.

Irving was full of talk all the way back into the city. Apparently there was never a person as marvellous as Theodosia. A scholar, a wit, a beauty, able to preside over her father's table at the age of fourteen. I must say she sounds like the sort of girl I would run from. Yet everyone seems to have come under her spell.

When Theodosia was ten or eleven her mother died, and she became her father's only confidante. "He never loved anyone else, I am certain of that." Irving echoed Madame. All New York seems to be of the same mind —a Byronic theme if ever there was one.

"The Colonel was devastated when she married Mr. Alston who took her to live in South Carolina—so far away. I think the last time they ever saw one another was at Richmond, Virginia, during his trial for treason. I confess he was superb then! The hero of the whole affair. With Theodosia beside him like—like a consort! And how all we young people paid court to them."

There was more in this vein. Also a second promise to find for me his account of the trial.

Only by mentioning Leggett could I shift Irving's conversation from the luminous past to the dull but to me vital present.

"Such a sharp young man, Mr. Leggett. But learned. Very learned. Of course his politics are, well . . ." Irving gave his little hand gesture, like a lady's fan.

"I think Leggett will oppose Mr. Van Buren."

"Two years is a long time in politics." The dreamy magic voice was replaced by a practical if still ingratiating tone. One can see why Irving is admired not only by Van Buren but by General Jackson. "I am sure the *Evening Post* will eventually do its duty, aren't you?"

I was not certain; spoke of political differences. Irving affected to know nothing of such matters other than the observation that "the Democratic interest is not apt to produce anyone else in the next two years."

"Colonel Burr speaks most highly of Mr. Van Buren."

"Does he?" Irving looked at me with a sharpness that seemed to peel away clothes and flesh. Yet the half-smile never left his lips.

"Oh, yes," I said. "He regards him as—well, like a son." I had said it.

Irving continued to smile; he was now counting the ribs of my skeleton in the April-Fool's light. "I would not . . . believe that story." To my relief, Irving turned his gaze from me. "Mr. Van Buren's mother was a most godly woman, and many years older than Colonel Burr . . ."

"Who married a woman ten years older than he." When in doubt attack.

Irving showed displeasure. I was complimented. I had shaken that constant benevolent blandness. "I knew her, Mr. Schuyler, and know that she could not have—done what they say she did."

"Yet the Colonel took Mr. Van Buren into his office, helped him, promoted him . . ."

"Colonel Burr, as you know better than I, is a born pedagogue. He loves the young. He loves to teach them. After all he is the son and grandson of presidents of Princeton College." I feared for a moment that Irving would again sink like some huge river animal into the swamp of the past and I would be told more than I could bear to hear about Princeton College. Fortunately, sensing danger from me, he was to the point. "There is nothing more in character than for Colonel Burr to advance the career of a brilliant young man."

"When the Colonel came back from France, Mr. Van Buren let him stay at his house in Albany."

"Mr. Van Buren is a good and generous person, to a fault, some say . . ."

"And Colonel Burr helped him with legislation for the Assembly." For the moment I had forgotten just what it was that the Colonel had helped the young assemblyman to do but it was something significant.

Irving was now alarmed. "The Colonel is an old man, given to—I should think—exaggeration."

"No. He is always precise. He is still an excellent lawyer. He does not stray from *facts*." I could not resist this thrust at the master of fancy himself.

Irving parried the thrust. "When occasion warranted, Colonel Burr could be as free with the truth as any other politician or adventurer."

"But since he speaks with admiration of Mr. Van Buren . . ."

"My dear boy, there are those who wish to destroy Mr. Van Buren with *any* weapon. So why not love? The kiss in the garden of Gethsemane. For years the Vice-President's enemies have put it about that he is Colonel Burr's natural son, that he is Colonel Burr's *un*natural political creation. Both are lies."

I had stirred him at last. "If so, then, why did Mr. Van Buren meet the Colonel last summer . . ."

"Here we are. Reade Street."

The carriage stopped. Irving pointed to the water-tower at the far end of the street. "Colonel Burr's monument. You know, he founded the Manhattan Water Company in order to start, clandestinely, a bank."

"But we still have the water."

Irving laughed. "Yes, and the bankers have the Bank of Manhattan. I enjoyed our afternoon. It is such a pleasure to meet someone young who is interested in old matters."

I thanked him at length for his kindness. He patted my knee. "Your investigation will lead you down all sorts of paths. You must be careful. There are pitfalls for the unwary."

Irving's fingers again administered the same savage pinch as at our first meeting. The eyes that studied mine were clear, and hard. "I trust that no one will try to make anything of the *casual* friendship that once existed between the Colonel and the Vice-President. Because Mr. Van Buren is certain to be our next president, and he will remember his enemies every bit as vividly as he does his friends." The warning—threat—was even more shocking to me than the pinch.

As I got out of the carriage, Washington Irving was his usual shy, diffident self. "So happy—excursions elsewhere—oh, Knickerbocker, Knickerbocker!"

This evening when I undressed for bed, I saw on my thigh a dark bruise. I am convinced now that the story of Van Buren's illegitimacy is true, and that the election could well depend on the Aaron Burr connection.

Three

FOR THREE DAYS there has been rioting in the streets. Certainly we are living through some sort of revolution. There has never been an election as bitter as this one.

This morning (the third and last day of the election), Colonel Burr gave me some material to take to Matthew Davis. "It's of no importance." He tapped the folder in my hand. "Simply a ruse to find out what is happening."

Colonel Burr adjusted the muffler at his neck (the office was hot; the day warm). He is always excited at election time. "In my day it was so simple. Only a thousand men voted for governor."

"Not exactly democracy, was it?"

"No, it was not. In fact, New York state was the private property of three families." He quoted. " 'The Clintons have power, the Livingstons have numbers, the Schuylers have Hamilton.' Now of course every man over twenty-one can vote. It is quite astonishing." Burr looked dreamily into the ashy grate. "None of us —not even Jefferson—foresaw this democracy. I suspect it will prove a bad thing. But the other was certainly worse, though Heaven knows convenient if one . . ." There was a sound of shouting just north of us, from Duane Street.

"Go out! Reconnoitre! See the *sans-culottes!* Tell Matt Davis my heart is with him, as always. But nothing more. Jackson is the best of all our presidents . . . for what that is worth."

In Duane Street I saw my first battle, and wondered if Monmouth Court House had been similar.

All morning a procession of Whigs had carried through the town a miniature frigate labelled *The Constitution* which they finally set down outside the Masonic Hall. They then went inside the hall for a meeting. At about noon a mob of drunken Irish attacked the frigate but were driven off by the Whigs.

When I arrived at the hall, several hundred angry Whigs (a curious mixture of workies and wealthy merchants) were milling about, examining one another's blackened eyes and broken heads while their frigate was slowly being pulled across the street into the safe harbour of New York Hospital's front yard.

I found Mr. Davis in front of the hall. With him was a portly man with a furious face.

"Charlie Schuyler! My fellow historian." The glass in one of Mr. Davis's steel-rimmed spectacles was shattered, making him look odd but happy.

"Davis, I insist you call for the Mayor." The portly man was edgy. "We need protection."

"Nonsense. A few playful b'hoys, no more. Think nothing of it." Mr. Davis looked at me. "The vote's going our way, Charlie! We're winning the city, and— best of all—we're going to elect Verplanck."

A rock from nowhere landed at our feet. The portly man gasped.

Mr. Davis ignored it. "If we can elect Verplanck

mayor today, we shall elect Henry Clay president two years from now."

On this prophetic note, we were engulfed by the democracy.

Waving clubs, throwing paving stones, several thousand drunken savages from the Sixth Ward swept into Duane Street.

A rock struck me in the shoulder. I fell back against the wall. A lout pummelled the portly man until Mr. Davis raised his walking-stick and with a splendid thwack broke the man's nose. Then, gleefully, Davis aimed his stick at the crutch of a lad with a shillelagh. The boy doubled up, vomited beer, ceased to be with us in spirit. The elderly Mr. Davis was plainly in his element. I was not in mine.

Ducking from side to side, I managed to get clear of the worst of the fighting just as His Honour Mayor Gideon Lee appeared with a number of armed watchmen.

The Mayor stood very tall and stern at the head of his men. "Stop!" he shouted. There was a sudden quiet as the invaders from the Sixth Ward turned to see what new entertainment was at hand.

"This is your mayor. Disassemble. And go back to your houses. Peacefully. That is an order."

A well-aimed rock removed the Mayor's tall hat. Sticks at the ready, the city watchmen moved upon the mob, and the mob charged.

I ran as quickly as I could to the grounds of New York Hospital where I found Mr. Davis and the portly gentleman.

"They are desperate, our friends at Tammany." Mr. Davis was ravished by the disorder. "This"—he indicated the roaring battle all around us—"is the beginning of the end for Mr. Van Buren, and the making of Henry Clay. My boy, we have created a truly *new* party!"

I cannot fathom Mr. Davis. Originally a leader of Tammany, originally a backer of Jackson, originally an

ally of Van Buren, Mr. Davis split with all of them
on the issue of the Bank (he likes it; they don't; why
does he care?). Now Mr. Davis has helped put together
a new Whig party made up of the wealthiest people
in the city, and the poorest. Two groups with nothing
in common save support for Mr. Biddle's Bank of the
United States and a passion for Henry Clay. Yet why
should the poor care about the Bank? And why should
the rich care about Henry Clay? To me it is a perfect
mystery.

Respectfully, we stood aside as two watchmen carried
the unconscious mayor of New York into the hospital,
a dented top-hat resting on the proud curve of his
stomach.

"Let us go some place less turbulent." Pleased despite the beating the Whigs were taking, Mr. Davis led
us to the seedy Broadway House whose large bar-room
is the unofficial centre of the Whig party.

Mr. Davis established his headquarters in a far
corner of the noisy crowded smoky room. Nearly everyone was drunk; the price of a vote, in fact, is beery
oblivion *after* the vote is cast.

A dark man, not in the least drunk, reported to Mr.
Davis. "We took care of the lot of them in the Fourth
Ward."

"No one hurt?"

"No one dead." As the man moved to go, his coat
swung open and I saw both a knife and a knobbed
stick stuck in his belt.

The portly man was not pleased. "We must not
resort to their tactics."

"We must protect ourselves." Tea was brought Mr.
Davis and beer for me and for the portly man who
turned out to be the notorious Mordecai Noah. Ten
years ago he was the first—and only—Jew ever to be
appointed sheriff of New York. When there was criticism of a Jew being put in a position where he might
hang Christians, Noah is supposed to have said, "Pretty
Christians to require hanging at all!" Noah is a re-

markable creature who writes melodramas for the stage, edits newspapers, and serves—or used to serve—Tammany as one of its leaders. President Madison made him consul at Tunis (this was during the time of the trouble with the pirates); and President Jackson appointed him surveyor of the port of New York, a post he recently resigned when he broke with the President over the Bank. Until the last election he was co-editor of the *Courier and Equirer*, a newspaper favourable to Jackson until Mr. Biddle's Bank became an issue. Then Noah and his newspaper turned around completely and began to attack the Administration. During the election it was discovered that Noah and his fellow editor were secretly taking money from Mr. Biddle. This scandal was helpful to the Administration; harmful to Mr. Biddle, the corruptor of the press.

At the moment Noah edits the *Evening Star* which openly supports the Bank and the Whig interest. After a lifetime of loyalty to Tammany and the workies, Noah is now devoted to the rich Mr. Biddle and to his creature Henry Clay.

Leggett thinks Noah mad. "But colourful. A compulsive actor. And of course he's the king of the Jews, or thinks he is." Leggett described how Noah, wearing a crown and velvet robes, took "possession" of Grand Island in the Niagara River and there proclaimed the City of Ararat, to be a home of refuge for the Jews. Needless to say, the city fathers of Buffalo quickly put a stop to that.

This afternoon Noah was not very kingly—simply nervous and complaining. "How stupid it was of those employers to shut down their businesses and *order* their workers to vote Whig."

"Don't fret, Mordecai. The tide that will soon bring us in will carry out our Nestorian skipper." Mr. Davis turned to me as though to allay any possible shock on my part. "Whom we applaud. What good domocrat does not? But we recognise that the President has grown old serving the people and now—poor old man

—he listens to Van Buren and to the other enemies of the people. Oh, there will be changes soon!"

I cannot for the life of me understand why men like Davis and Noah care so much about the election or rejection of other people. I don't care who is alderman in the First Ward or president in the White House. But then that is not the point. For the true and effective partisan who supported Jackson in '28 or '32 there was bound to be money or office or both. Currently half of Tammany Hall are now directors of those new banks that came into existence after Jackson struck at Nicholas Biddle and the Bank of the United States. Incidentally, no one—not even Leggett—has yet made clear why the federally supervised Bank is so much worse than a thousand banks that are unsupervised. Yet for some mysterious reason the Bank is thought "aristocratic" while the banks are "democratic." The poor of course are as certain to be fleeced by the many as they were by the one.

"I am not confident. Not confident at all!" There was an explosion near by. The windows of the barroom rattled.

"Exactly what we want! Let Tammany take the credit for burning the city!" Mr. Davis was euphoric. I was alarmed. And so was everyone else. Fighting and plundering and arson have erupted all over the city.

"Now what has Colonel Burr sent me?" Mr. Davis opened the folder.

For the first time Noah was aware of my presence; asked me if I was indeed a messenger from Aaron Burr.

"Not only a messenger," Mr. Davis spoke for me, "but he is also composing a life of that much maligned man."

"I come to appreciate Burr more and more." Noah was suddenly alert. "What do you know of his business out west?"

Again Mr. Davis answered for both of us. "We know —I think—everything, and the Colonel was innocent of all charges."

"Of course. But what about the involvement of President Jackson?"

"It was no greater . . ." In the best court-room manner I decided to move to the sort of offence that stops entirely the prosecution's manoeuvre. ". . . than the involvement of Henry Clay."

Mr. Davis actually laughed, a whispering dry sound like law books being rubbed together. "He's got you there, Mordecai."

Noah was not distressed. "Clay only defended Burr in court. Nothing more. But Jackson was ready to go to Mexico with him. Everyone knows that."

"Everyone except his two biographers. No, Mordecai. That line of attack will do us no good. Andrew Jackson is too beloved to treat in such a manner. Besides, he'll be gone in two years' time; if not sooner."

"That would not stop me from telling the people what they ought to know about the sort of man who . . . Davis, do you see what I see?" So Edmund Kean looked when he saw Banquo's ghost at the Park Theatre. A tall smiling man had entered the bar-room. Although clean, he was dressed like a labourer.

Mr. Davis lost his usual composure. "Let us look the other way," he announced too late, for the man, blinking his eyes in order to adjust them to the dimness, came to our table. Glumly, Mr. Davis introduced me to Thomas Skidmore.

Five years ago Leggett lent me Skidmore's pamphlet "The Rights of Man to Property!" but I never read it. In those days Skidmore was considered to be the anti-Christ—no, worse, the anti-property! A self-taught machinist, Skidmore argued (brilliantly but wildly, according to Leggett) in favour of putting an end to imprisonment for debt, an end to private ownership of land, an end to all inherited wealth. He even favoured the taxing of churches—and just about every other measure the mind of a crank could conceive if he wants really to be hated in our city. Leggett finally attacked him as the apostle of a system of "public robbery."

Nevertheless, for a single season Skidmore had been the hero of the workies, and the terror of the property owners.

"We shall win the city." Mr. Davis was polite but cool.

Noah was neither. "We shall prove, Mr. Skidmore, that reform is possible *without* destroying society."

"But that makes no sense, Mr. Noah. No sense at all." The mild whiny voice contrasted with the blunt words. "Until we give to each man his due there is not a society here but a tyranny of the few."

"That is what the Tammany men say in the Sixth Ward."

"But, Mr. Noah, they don't mean what they say and we do."

"*We*, Mr. Skidmore?" Noah was most unpleasant.

But Skidmore was serene. "An idea so basic as true equality, Mr. Noah, cannot be the sole possession of a single mind, no matter how—radical." With a pleasant nod, Skidmore moved on to a table of low types, swilling beer. As he sat down, he suddenly said in a loud voice, "Mr. Davis, the Whig party will fail. Because the others have more than you."

"What did *that* mean?" Noah turned to Mr. Davis. "More what?"

Mr. Davis shrugged. "He is a bad man."

Having listened so much to Leggett, I made the obvious answer. "He means that if you are going to have a world with a few people rich and a good many poor then the party with more rich people than the other will win."

For the first time Noah did me the honour of listening. "He's right." He spoke to Mr. Davis as if I was not there.

"Charlie is a clever boy."

"Then why is he working for Colonel Burr?"

"Why indeed?" Mr. Davis gave me the Tammany look which means "nothing is what it seems."

"I admire him, as a lawyer." I was defensive, and ought not to be.

"Charlie is onto something golden." Mr. Davis sounded as if he had just bought a judge's decision. "He will write the true story of Colonel Burr while I shall write the official memoirs. That means Charlie will beat me all hollow." We are to be in competition, Matthew L. Davis and I? I am suspicious.

Noah showed interest. "You have arranged for publication?"

"Yes." Mr. Davis answered for me. "Charlie is dealing with William Leggett."

I was startled. How did Mr. Davis know? "But I am not writing for the *Evening Post* . . ."

"Leggett!" Noah proceeded at length to accuse Leggett of every crime. Then, "Thank God, Webb beat him to the ground! In the street! With a cane!" I said that it was Leggett who had beaten Webb. We were interrupted by a clatter of horses in the street, the jangle of armour, a shout: "It's the militia!"

"Let us hope they get to the ballot-boxes before our friends at Tammany do." For the first time Mr. Davis showed some anxiety. Certainly he showed none at all a few moments later when a rock broke through the window just above his head and fell to the table with a crash, rather delicately jostling my beer mug as it rolled to the floor.

Noah and I both leapt to our feet. Not Mr. Davis. Coolly he combed the glass shards from his thin gray hair.

A red face poked through the hole in the widow and bellowed, "There they are, the . . ."

We never heard just what we were, for Mr. Davis in a swift gesture raised his cane and cracked smartly the red face. "Out, you whoreson!" rang the voice of Tammany's one-time Grand Sachem. The red face was seen no more.

The bar-room broke into cheers. Mr. Davis accepted the homage of his people with a gracious, thin-lipped smile. "Quite like the old days!" he said to me. "When Burr and Hamilton were dividing the people. I confess to nostalgia."

"You're mad! They'll burn the city now! They're capable of anything if they think they're losing the election." Noah was trembling.

"Most unlikely." Mr. Davis assembled the fragments of window glass into a neat pile. Then he put Burr's message into his coat pocket; turned to me. "The Colonel thinks I should give you any notes I might have."

"I don't want you to give me anything if you really believe that I intend to . . ."

"Charlie, Charlie! Whatever you want to read you can. I shall send you what I have." Mr. Davis was now on his feet. "Try to publish as soon as you can."

I thanked Mr. Davis. He is remarkably kind. But then he cannot publish his own book for several years at least and perhaps he thinks my effort will whet the public's appetite for the entire story. My effort? What am I writing about?

I now act even to myself as if I were writing the full story of the Colonel's life when, actually, I am only on the track of one small portion of it which Leggett assures me will change history. Though I sometimes wonder how different history will be if the president is Clay rather than Van Buren. Also, do I want to be the key that opens such a door? Odd situation to be in for someone who dislikes politics and politicians. It is my secret dream to live in Spain or Italy and write stories like Washington Irving. I am counting on this work to bring me the money to travel. I only hope that the Colonel is dead when I publish. No. I cannot hope or want that. But I must publish within the next year and a half. *Before* the presidential election. It is a hard business I have got myself into.

Four

VERPLANCK WAS DEFEATED for mayor by 179 votes out of some 35,000 cast. Tammany Hall is victorious but shaken, for the Whigs have taken the city's common council. Mr. Davis must be happy. Colonel Burr is happy—no, amused. "It's the new people, Charlie. They're going to take it all one of these days."

"Mr. Davis thinks Clay will be the next president."

"Poor Matt! He lacks judgement in the big things but is a master of the small. Van Buren will be nominated and he will defeat Clay or any other National Republican—no, no, *Whig*, I must get used to calling them that. How topsy-turvy it is! Those of us who were for the Revolution were Whigs. Those for Britain were Tories. Then there was the fight over the federal Constitution. In our state Governor Clinton wanted a weak federal government. So some of the Whigs became anti-Federalist, and some like Hamilton became Federalist. Then the Tory-Federalists became Republican. Now Tory-Federalist-Republicans call themselves Whig though they are anti-Whig while the anti-Federalist Republicans are now Jacksonian Democrats. Oh, names are magic here!"

"What were you, after the Revolution?"

"Neutral. I inclined to the anti-Federalists, but I took no part in the long debate. I do recall my first reading of the Constitution. 'It will not last fifty years,' I said. Obviously I was wrong—about the fifty years. But I am right in principle. The Constitution is much too brittle a document for a country like ours. By the way, I saw a dead man on West Street when I got off the boat this morning. He was killed last night at the polling-place, and no one has thought to take away the corpse. 'Thy hand great Anarch lets the curtain fall and universal darkness buries all.' " I know the quotation by heart because Burr so often quotes it.

"Do *you* favour Van Buren?" I asked. A single drop of sweat trickled down the centre of my spine. It is a warm day.

"Yes, I do."

"Because of your old connection?"

The eyes were shut now; small feet on the edge of the grate. "I am old and therefore moderate. The only old man I know who loves danger and surprise is Andrew Jackson. But then I think there must be a medical explanation. Too much blood in the brain. At least I prefer the decorous way Matty Van does things. He is without ferocity, while Clay is unstable and corrupt."

"Does Mr. Davis know you prefer Van Buren?"

"Oh, yes. He pays no attention to me. He knows that Aaron Burr—what's left of him—is not a Burrite."

Five

T HE CITY IS A WRECK from the rioting. In some streets every window is broken. But who cares? The day is beautiful, the militia have been withdrawn, the Irish are sick with sore heads, and I go with Helen Jewett to the Vauxhall Gardens.

We took a coach up the Bowery to the point where it meets Broadway. Helen was like a child. Since she joined Mrs. Townsend's establishment she has never been beyond a block or two of Thomas Street. She wore a high-necked dress, and looked as much a lady as ever drank tea in the Ladies Dining Room of the City Hotel.

"Oh, it took me hours and hours to convince her that I did have an aunt who lived here and that one of the—one of our guests knew her and told me that she often wondered where I was and so I said, 'Mrs.

Townsend, I must tell my aunt I'm alive and well because suppose she asks the police about me?' " Helen has a smile like an isosceles triangle long side down. "So she let me off for the day, very put out she was, too, and told me that God punished liars. Do you think this is true?"

I said I doubted it. But assured her that if there is a Hell, it would one day include a marvellously learned lady, able to drive Satan mad with scripture and theology.

The evening was warm and the gardens crowded with couples. No one seemed aware that we are living through what Leggett terms a revolution.

After a promenade beneath coloured lanterns, dutifully breathing in and out of the country air, scented with hyacinth, we found ourselves in a bower close enough to the band to hear the music but not so close as to be forced to shout at one another. A Negro waiter brought us vanilla ice-cream and cake. I have never been so nervous, and I cannot think why.

Helen was not at all what I expected—or *she* expected? At first she had been like a dog unchained from a gate. She could not get enough of the sights and the sounds the rest of us take for granted. The Gingerbread Man on Broadway particularly intrigued her as he ran by, coat-tails streaming in the wind, pockets bulging with gingerbread, his only food. No one knows who he is or where he lives because he never speaks, just runs, eats gingerbread, sips water at the public pumps.

By the time we were seated in the bower, listening to the band play marches, Helen had grown very quiet, even sullen. "What's the good of coming out like this when I must go back to-night?"

I suppose from the beginning I knew what I was doing. It was not possible to show freedom to that unchained dog and expect it to want to be leashed again to the gate. Was I deliberately cruel in showing her this much of the world beyond her room in Thomas Street? Or simply stupid? Both, I suppose.

"I thought you—well, didn't dislike it, where you are."

"I hate it." She crumbled cake disagreeably. I hoped I would not have to touch her hand and feel the stickiness of sugar. Once I got honey on my neck as a child. My mother said that I screamed for an hour.

"There is never hot water." Helen frowned. "The Negro woman doesn't like me. The others get hot water twice a day. Most days I get this barely warm water, only *once*. And in the winter it's ice cold. I tell Mrs. Townsend this is no way to live. She speaks to me of *moral* courage and promises to tell the Negro woman but it's the same thing the next day, and the woman—she just smiles at me when I say where is my hot water? Just smiles and looks happy and shoves the tin at me, slopping water on the floor." Helen swept the fragments of the cake onto the ground. "You see? I have nothing to talk to you about."

I told her I liked her whether or not she talked. I was sincere. She was indifferent. The evening was going all wrong. "What do you talk to the others about?"

Helen shrugged. "Everything. Nothing. We talk about the customers. They say shocking things—the girls."

"Such as?"

"Shocking, I said." She would not indulge me. What, I wonder, do they say of me? "Then we talk about clothes, and I like that best. I sew for them. I like sewing. Do people come here *every* night?" She looked about her, eyes dazzled by the pink and yellow of lanterns. The music was slow now; a single fiddle played a mournful solo off-key. Yet the whole effect was ravishing: hyacinths, coloured lights, the half-shadowed sullen pretty face of a prisoner made free for a single evening by me. It was like a fairy-tale, particularly the ending when she must return at midnight to Thomas Street and its guardian witch Rosanna Townsend, nevermore free again. Though why should I not set her free permanently? I could, with some effort, rent a room for her. And she could earn money by sewing. I proposed the matter to her.

Helen smiled at last, looked happy. "Oh, good!"

I was alarmed. It is one thing to talk like this during a fiddler's off-key aria, and another to wake up in the morning and find another person lying beside you forever, and no more choice.

Either Helen sensed my fear or she is truly unusual. "But that would be wrong. I could never live with a man I wasn't married to." This was breath-taking but she meant it. "I'm not like that."

"What about—what you do at Mrs. Townsend's?"

"That's different." Helen was firm. "You wouldn't want to marry me, would you?" She laughed before I could think of anything to say. "No, you wouldn't. Besides, I'd be a bad wife. I'm not good with children. They frighten me. That's why living at Mrs. Townsend's is really not bad, most of the time. If there were a different maid . . ." The face became heavy with resentment, an ugly expression which made her all the more appealing to me. "But you will remember to find me work where I can be paid as much as I get now and start a business of my own, though where I shall get a hundred dollars I don't know. I try to save but it all goes. I don't know where. My mother said I would die in the poorhouse which is where she is, poor thing."

"What about your father?"

The first warm laugh, not heard by me since one of Mrs. Townsend's customers vaulted the back fence and landed in the neighbour's piggery. "What about my father? You tell me. I never knew him. Neither did my mother, I should think. She drank a lot when she was young, and worked as a dress-maker. Only cutting—which is all she did—not really sewing. Her eyes were too weak. She lacked the touch. You can tell me about your people, if you like."

At last a personal exchange; the first in our seventeen encounters. I keep count, being on a strict budget.

"My father kept a bar in Greenwich Village. My mother worked there, too. I suppose he's as much a drunkard as your mother."

"They were rich." A long sigh.

"No. But the bar did well."

"Brothers, sisters?"

"All dead. Five, I think, there were. I was the only one to grow up."

"That must've been hard on your mother."

"It was. She hated my father. That was harder still." I told Helen everything—or almost everything. She listened like a child being read a story. Ever since I was born there had been quarrels between my father and mother. He drunk, abusive; she tearful, frightened. One November night he locked her out of the house. Too proud to go to a neighbour's, she slept in the shed at the back, got a chill, a fever, a pleurisy, a coffin and a grave. Since I was living in the city, going to classes at Columbia College, I did not know for a week that she was dead. "When I came home, we fought in the yard, my father and I. I bloodied him. And to this day I've not set foot in Greenwich." Telling this story, I felt strong, masterful, a king out of legend; and what I told her was true though I did not mention that my father nearly put out one of my eyes with a stool.

"You've never seen him since?" There was—I shivered with pleasure—awe in her voice.

"Recently. In the street. We were polite." Murderer, murderer, murderer, a drum beats in my head when I think of him, write of him, look at the miniature of my mother, painted on ivory by Vanderlyn—she was a pretty woman, never happy.

Together Helen and I strolled through the gardens and Helen took careful note of every dress. "See those muttonchop sleeves? They took days and days to sew! And the *material!* French watered silk. And look at that *fichu!* Belgian lace." She gave me a carefully detailed report on the cut and cost of every lady's clothes.

As we rounded a small pavilion, we nearly stepped

into a pair of figures—who leapt apart. One was William de la Touche Clancey. The other was a well-made boy of perhaps sixteen, carefully got up to resemble a swell; only the red blunt hands betrayed the fact that he was a workie.

"So!" Clancey gave his accusing goose-like hiss.

The boy looked embarrassed, as well he should. There are some things that the poor ought not to do even for money.

"So how is your friend the radical Mr. Leggett?" Yes, Clancey remembered me from the Five Points.

"Very well. And how is *your* friend Mr. Edwin Forrest?" I was bland.

"I've seen you before, Miss." The boy looked at Helen who stared at him with a blankness that would have done credit to an Assembly matron. "I work for Joseph Hoxie, Miss. You must know him. He's a friend of Mrs. Townsend."

Helen did not blink. "I think," she said to me, "it's time to meet our friends."

But Clancey was eager to balance an account. "Townsend? Townsend? Surely you don't mean the Townsends who live in Gramercy Park?"

"No, Mr. Clancey. The lady we know lives in Thomas Street." The boy was obviously set on preparing a defence for himself if Helen was ever tempted to put it about that he, too, was a prostitute.

"I fear that I know not a soul in that colourful part of town, except for my old friend the estimable Mr. Hoxie for whom young Richard works."

"Part-time?" I could not resist the final thrust. In the lamplight the boy's face went dark with rage.

"I did not hear your name . . ." began Clancey to Helen but by then we were gone.

To my surprise, Helen began to laugh. "I can't wait to tell the others. Do let's get a carriage. Quickly! I always suspected something was wrong with Mr. Hoxie. Now I know. Those handsome apprentices! And it's true, what the boy said, I *have* seen him before. Sometimes he stops and stares up at the house for the longest time. I guess he hasn't the money or the courage to come inside or—or he doesn't *want* to, that's it! To come in and visit us. Oh, what a day! You are sweet, Charlie!" She kissed my cheek like a sister.

I was shocked by her response. Although I have spent many pleasant hours in establishments like Mrs. Townsend's, I must, at heart, be very innocent or perhaps simple is the word. There is so much going on that I know nothing of. This was not the magic *sad* ending I had in mind for our evening.

Six

I HAVE READ several hundred pages of M. L. Davis's memoirs of Aaron Burr and have learned almost nothing that I did not know. He might have outlined the material as follows:

After the British left New York City, the Tory lawyers were disbarred, leaving an opening for Whig lawyers, particularly heroes of the Revolution. But the rule in New York state is that one must have read law three years before being admitted to the bar. Burr was in a hurry. He went to Albany, presented himself to the three justices of the state supreme court, got them to bend the rule for him (particularly helpful was Justice Robert Yates) and on January 19, 1782, he was admitted to the bar. Among his first clients were his old commander, Colonel Malcolm, the dePeysters of Albany, and Robert Livingston.

April 12, 1782, he became a counsellor-at-law.

July 6, 1782, he married Theodosia Prevost at Paramus, New Jersey. He was twenty-six. She was thirty-six.

June 21, 1783, their daughter Theodosia was born at Albany. In November the Burrs moved to New York City, arriving just as the British army departed.

The Burrs lived first at the Verplanck house two doors from City Hall. Then they moved to the corner of Maiden Lane and Nassau Street (their back yard was famous for its grape-vines and arbours, their household for a drunken maid named Hannah). In 1791 they moved to 4 Broadway. As a summer house, the Colonel took a lease on the mansion at Richmond Hill.

From the beginning Colonel Burr was a successful lawyer. With his first partner, William T. Broome, he began to make and spend the first of several fortunes. As a lawyer he was—is—meticulous. Yet he has a certain contempt for the whole business. "The law," he likes to say, "is simply whatever is boldly asserted and plausibly maintained."

Burr's rivalry with Hamilton began in those days. It was inevitable. Both were heroes, both were ambitious, both were lawyers. Of the two Hamilton was considered to be the more profound philosophically as well as the more long-winded, with a tendency to undo his own brief by taking it past the point of successful advocacy.

Burr was the more effective in a court-room because his mind was swifter than Hamilton's; also, of an entire generation of public men, Burr was free of cant: he never moralized unless to demonstrate a paradox. As a result the passionate believers thought him evil on the ground that the man who refuses to preach Goodness must be Bad. Yet juries are often gratful to the Colonel for *not* preaching at them. Neither Burr nor Hamilton was a natural orator like Clay or Webster. They could not move multitudes; on the other hand, they were effective with juries and with their peers.

Despite their rivalry, Burr and Hamilton sometimes worked together. On one case, the vain and edgy Hamilton insisted that Burr precede him and give the first argument. Without protest, Burr took the inferior position. Then, blandly, he used all the arguments that he knew Hamilton was going to make. Hamilton was furious—and uncharacteristically short and to the point when it came time for him to speak.

These are the facts for those years and Mr. Davis simply puts them all down, pasting an occasional platitude over the Colonel's wax-like effigy. I have just sent him back the manuscript with a grateful letter. Now I must begin the real work: finding out what is true, if possible, or if not true useful to my purpose.

One important detail from the Davis manuscript. He reproduces a letter Colonel Burr wrote from the Columbia county estate of the Van Ness family. The text of the letter (to a Colonel Claypoole) is of no particular interest. But the date and the place are vital.

The Van Ness house in which Burr was staying is only a few miles from Kinderhook where Martin Van Buren was born December 5, 1782.

The date of the letter is March 11, 1782. (Yes, I have ticked off the months on my fingers.)

Burr's last line is cryptic. "I disport myself as best I can in this wooded valley, and you know what I mean by that."

Seven

LEGGETT TOLD ME the lastest Van Buren story. One senator bet another senator that he could get Van Buren to commit himself publicly on a public issue. "Matt," said the senator, "there's been some talk that the sun rises in the east. What do you think?"

"I have heard the same rumour, Senator, but since I never get up until after dawn, I have no useful opinion in the matter."

Eight

COLONEL BURR and I watched with child-like pleasure the demolition of a whole block of houses on Broadway just across from the Park Theatre. We were not alone. What looked to be half the town had turned out to watch as a huge iron ball attached to a crane smashed in the wall of the first house. Mr. Astor intends to build on the site a hotel that will eclipse the City Hotel. No doubt he will succeed. He always does.

"Splendid!" The Colonel clapped his hands as the narrow Dutch building buckled in upon itself with a hollow cascading sound. But then as a thick cloud of gray dust slowly began to rise, the audience fled.

The Colonel and I crossed to the City Hall Park. Although we had an appointment at the Register's Office, the Colonel was in no mood for work. Instead we sat on a bench beside a purple lilac hedge.

Burr breathed contentedly; looked about the well-kept park. "This used to be called the Fields." He pointed to a high place on a line with the City Hall. "And over there were the gallows. But not just an ordinary commonplace gallows. Oh, no! New Yorkers have always liked their pleasures exotic. So our gallows was designed to resemble a Chinese pagoda. Very pretty it was, too. And what a lot of poor wretches they used to hang there. In the first year of the federal government, when New York was the capital, there were five hangings in a single afternoon, one right after the other. The town was thrilled. President Washington was no doubt impressed."

"Were there as many murderers then as now?"

"Murderers? Hardly! We hanged only burglars in those days. Murder was practically unknown."

"There is so much I'd like to know about that time."

"Yes, I know you would." With a stick, Burr drew suns and stars in the dust at his feet. Emblems of his Mexican empire?

"I've read some of Mr. Davis's book."

"Don't tell me."

"I won't."

"Must I do it myself?"

"I see no choice."

The Colonel gave a soft moan. "You know, Charlie, I made a great error—that is, of the *many* great errors I have made in my life, the worst was supposing that one could not be hurt by a lie. As a result, I never corrected a slander. I simply assumed that since there were so many honourable men in the world who knew my character, matters would be set straight in time. Well, I was wrong. Friends drop away, die. While the slanders never cease, never!" Burr spoke with a stoic wonder. No bitterness that I could detect.

"When my daughter was alive, I was intent upon clearing my name for her, for my grandson. Then . . ." He removed his hat, as if at grave-side—no, *water*-side. ". . . for a good many years I have been perfectly indifferent. But now your interest . . ." He looked at me (he must know!) and smiled. "Well, I do enjoy teaching though I would prefer a subject other than my career, despite its cautionary aspects. Very well. We shall talk and you may write down, if it amuses you, what I say in your short hand, which is so much more dextrous than my long."

Thus it was agreed.

I have now begun to drive the Colonel a bit hard but there is not much time to assemble all the details. Leggett wants the Van Buren connection made explicit, with as much documentation as possible for an anonymous pamphlet. Later, under my own name, I will write the whole life, anticipating Mr. Davis. A prospect that excites me though Leggett is full of foreboding. "You will be favourable to Burr, and so must fail because the American reader cannot bear a surprise. He *knows* that this is the greatest country on earth, Washington the greatest man that ever lived, Burr the wickedest, and evidence to the contrary is not admissible. That means no inconvenient facts, no new information. If you really want the reader's attention, you must flatter him. Make his prejudices your own. Tell him things he already knows. He will love your soundness."

"Then explain your success at the *Evening Post*. Every day you attack your advertisers' prejudices . . ."

"And every day we lose another advertiser because of what Bryant calls my fierceness. I am also in constant danger of a knife in the ribs. Be warned by my 'success.'" I shall be.

Nine

IT TOOK THE COLONEL and me several days to learn how to work together. He is not used to dictation; he also refuses to rely on memory. "After all, I am a lawyer. Therefore I need evidence—books, letters, newspapers: things I can refute!"

Our first attempts were simply fragments. The Colonel could not connect episodes. He tended to wander from the point. But now (the middle of May) we are working well and what began as a series of random anecdotes is becoming such a full narrative that as we sweep down the years I am at last able to detect, here and there, a glimpse of my quarry, and I am certain now that once I have thoroughly mapped the jungle it ought not to be too difficult to find whatever beast I want, no matter how hidden the lair!

Ten

THE COLONEL is unusually nervous today. "I feel like an actor who does not know his lines." He has been sitting with a packet of letters and some old newspaper cuttings on the table in front of him. Also, an open much-marked copy of *The Life of Alexander Hamilton*, recently published by Hamilton's son, John.

"For once, Charlie, I wish that I had sired a proper son. There is a good deal to be said for filial piety, no matter how infelicitous. Naturally, I assume that any son of mine would write better than this boy who sounds like a combination of his father at his most windy, and his grandfather Schuyler at his most confused. Well, I shall be my own son—with your help."

The Colonel puts his feet up on the grate; shuts his eyes as if he expects some inner curtain to rise upon past spectacles. "You asked me about Hamilton." I had asked him about Van Buren. "Let me recall a scene or two for you." He closes his throat. "It is November . . ."

The eyes open for a moment and he glances at a newspaper cutting. "November 25, 1783. I have just come to New York City from Albany, with my wife and daughter. The American states have made peace with England. The British are about to depart. General Washington is to make his triumphant entry into the city."

I record now the Colonel's recollections—not as he dictated them to me but as they currently exist after a number of revisions in his own hand.

Memoirs of Aaron Burr—One

AT ABOUT NOON, I arrived with my wife Theodosia at Cape's Tavern in the Broad Way. The streets were filled with veterans, many drunk, all happy. New York City was a small place in those days but the people, despite a certain Dutchness, were as lively then as now.

The assembly-room of the tavern was crowded with former officers wearing cockades of black and white, as well as sprigs of laurel to attest to our gallantry and patriotism. I knew most of the officers, though not their wives. I particularly recall General McDougall; between the stammer and the Scots burr he was quite incoherent with joy.

Theodosia hung back, intimidated by so many strangers. But then Elizabeth Hamilton took her firmly by the hand, in that effective Schuyler way, and presented her to various ladies. Elizabeth was uncommonly handsome as a girl, if too square-jawed. I have been told that Hamilton used to discuss his infidelities with her. If he did, they must have had a good deal to talk about.

My old friend Troup greeted me; he was now a lawyer like me (after two weeks in the city I had more business than I could handle).

"A great day!" we both agreed and of course it was, despite the fact that the war had been over for some time. Today's ceremony was a tribute to the dilatoriness of Sir Guy Carleton, the British commander in New York. He kept finding excuses not to go home: the weather was bad, the ships in disrepair, His Excellency indisposed. But now it was finally ended.

As we waited in the tavern, Sir Guy's troops were slowly embarking from the Battery. At last General Washington could make his "triumphal" entry into the city that he had lost to the British seven years earlier and never, by arms, regained.

Hamilton hurried into the long room, cheeks bright with excitement. He greeted Troup and me warmly. Though rival lawyers, each intent on being first in the town, we were all of us friends that day.

What a vivid, bright, pretty little man Hamilton was! And oh, what a gift he had for making a *moral* point while destroying the reputation of an adversary. The malice in him was as spontaneous as the brilliance. "*He's* in Chatham Street, at the Tea Water Pump!" We knew who *he* was. "Governor Clinton will escort *him* here."

We congratulated one another on our good luck in so soon having the glorious Washington amongst us. But human pageantry is peculiarly vulnerable to the ridiculous. The only time I saw the Emperor Napoleon he was proceeding up the marble stairs of a Paris theatre, moving with all that sombre elegance he had learned from the actor Talma. But then, at the very top of the stairs, as all of us bowed reverently, he shrilly broke wind.

Today's comedy had been prepared by two British soldiers who had slyly greased the flag pole on the Battery. When our flag and its attendant tried to mount the pole, flag and attendant dropped in a heap to the ground, deeply mortifying General Washington.

Colonel (now Brevet-General) Malcolm joined us. Like so many senior officers who have not seen combat, this good man wanted to discuss the war. But the young men—and Hamilton, Troup and I thought we had invented youth—spoke only of the present and the future.

I twitted Hamilton. "How are your rich and well-born friends?" Hamilton was representing half the wealthy Tories in New York.

"They suffer, too."

"I wish they would suffer me." Troup wanted clients.

"I shall send you an occasional rich widow." Hamilton's passion for the rich and the well-born was, doubtless, the result of having been born poor and illegitimate.

Although the Constitution and the federal government would not be invented for another five years, the division in our ruling class was already apparent. The Tories who had opposed the Revolution now had no choice but to accept a new American order. But though

the army of their king was no longer installed on the
Battery, the principles of British government were still
very much installed in their minds. They believed that
we must have a government in which the privileges of
the rulers are as well-defined as are the obligations of
the ruled. In other words, we must re-create the British
system. Hamilton was so devoted to all things English
that if I had been he, I would have set sail for England
that afternoon with Sir Guy, gone into British politics,
and become prime minister. But Hamilton chose to
stay and fight not only the pernicious idea of democracy but the craftiest of all its proponents, Thomas
Jefferson—soon to be American minister at Paris, a
post to which the Congress hustled him in the wake of
his disastrous governorship of Virginia.

The noise of cheering caused us to hurry to the
windows. Washington the demigod—no, the god!—was
dismounting. The crowd waved their hats. He raised
his hat once and put it under his arm. Then accompanied by Governor Clinton His Mightiness entered
the taven. Incidentally, when Washington became
president he wanted to be styled His Mightiness. The
Senate was agreeable. The House of Representatives
was not, and referred the other house to the Constitution which speaks of the chief executive as, simply,
the president. In fact, the Speaker—the droll Mr. Muhlenberg—went so far as to suggest that perhaps the
General would like to be known as "His High and
Mightiness." Muhlenberg's mild pleasantry was not
well received by the greatest man in the world who
would very much have enjoyed, I suspect, being king
had he not lacked a son, a prince of Virginia, to succeed him.

But that was in the future. At the moment it was
quite enough that the most famous man on earth was
in the assembly-room of Cape's Tavern.

We formed two lines. Washington walked slowly between the rows, turning from side to side, his cold
slow gaze mitigated by a hesitant almost boyish smile
when he chose to favour a particular aide.

He stopped when he came to Hamilton who was standing next to me. Suddenly the General looked positively merry, even animated; for an instant his face like a dull mirror reflected the bright intelligence of the other's image. "My boy." He was like a father.

"It is your day, General. Your country."

"*Our* day, Sir." Then the light went from his face as he turned to me and saw himself in a very different sort of mirror.

"Colonel Burr. You are recovered in your health, I trust?"

I said that I was and presented to him his old friend, my new wife. Theodosia curtsied, as to the King.

Washington smiled and lifted her up. "Colonel Burr like the rest of us is . . ." Words, as usual, failed him. I was embarrassed. Theodosia looked pale. Hamilton did the work Heaven had designed for him. "Bewitched by the mistress of the Hermitage."

"Just so." Washington moved on and Hamilton gave me an imperceptible wink—no, *flick* of his bright blue eyes. What did he really think of Washington? We come to that.

Eleven

COLONEL BURR IS NOW delighted with our sessions, particularly when he re-reads his dictation and makes changes. "It is like preparing a brief—for the defence, of course!"

He is still reading and annotating his copy of *The Life of Alexander Hamilton*. The ancient rivalry is much on his mind. "You know, my friend Hamilton thought me 'equivocal' on the subject of the Constitution. For once in describing me he used the exact word. I was—I *am* equivocal. I have told you I did not think the Constitution in its original form would last fifty years. Nor has it. The habit of amendment continues to alter its nature—though not enough.

He opened a volume of Hamilton's works; riffled the pages. "No one can say that the Constitution was framed by innocent men. They were—and I knew most of them—as able a group of lawyers as ever argued a client from his rightful place on the gallows. They were most cynical. Listen to Hamilton." Burr read: "'Men will pursue their interests. It is as easy to change human nature as to oppose the strong current of selfish passions. A wise legislator will gently divert the channel, and direct it, if possible, to the public good.' I like the 'if possible.' What does the wise legislator do if it is *not* possible? Feather his nest, I fear."

The Colonel laughed suddenly, and recalled "the time Hamilton made an election speech to a group of mechanics. Unfortunately Hamilton always addressed his inferiors as if they were his inferiors. This is never charming, and I fear the crowd made fun of him. Furious, exasperated, he shouted, 'You are your own worst enemy!' What would he think now when 'the beast,' as he used to call the generality, governs, or at least we flatter it into thinking that it governs."

He put down the book. Began the day's work.

Memoirs of Aaron Burr—Two

IN 1787, I TOOK NO PART in the arguments for and against the Constitution. Like everybody else, I read Publius in the newspapers. Like everyone else, I soon worked out which Publius was Hamilton, which Jay, which Madison. Like everyone else, I knew Hobbes and his extraordinary belief (shared by Hamilton) that *any* form of government no matter how tyrannous is better than anarchy. I had also read Montesquieu whose work so influenced the three Publiuses. Yet at heart I was more pleased than not by the loose confederation of states that existed between 1783 and 1787. All in all, New York was agreeably governed by the Clinton faction. If certain of the other states were less well-governed, that was their affair; to be set right by them and not by a group of clever lawyers in Philadelphia. Yes, I was equivocal. A degree of anarchy is no bad thing.

Contrary to tradition, the movement for a strong Constitution and federal government began not with Hamilton but with General Washington. It is usual to picture him as a worthy, slow-witted man, a latter-day Cincinnatus only happy on his farm—trying to move that leaden plow he invented. He was of course worthy (if inordinately vain) and slow-witted in matters of the mind. But no man was cleverer when it came to business and to the promotion of his commercial interests. For very practical reasons, he wanted a strong central government with himself at its head. He was from the beginning a perfect federalist, and used Hamilton far more than Hamilton ever used him in order to make safe his investments in land.

Jefferson told me that for all of Washington's innumerable complaints about the exigencies of public life, he was actually bored to death after the Revolution. "They are making a damned tavern-keeper of me!" he used to swear when yet another party of curious guests descended upon him at Mount Vernon. It should be noted that at the time of Washington's election he was, as usual, short of cash and his first act as president was to get from the Treasury an advance on his salary.

I recollect only one private interview with Washington after the Revolution. It was in October of 1791, shortly after I arrived in Philadelphia as senator from New York. At the time I was most ambitious to write the true history of the Revolution. Each morning I would get up at five o'clock and go to the State Department, accompanied by a clerk. Together we would study and copy out documents until ten o'clock when I would attend the Senate.

Puzzled by certain military details, I requested an audience with His Mightiness. It was granted me so promptly that I ought to have been suspicious. Not only had I replaced Hamilton's father-in-law in the Senate, but the French Revolution was under way and I confess to having believed for a time that a new era in the world's history had begun. Later of course I realized that the same bad old era had simply shown us a new face whose smile would presently reveal bloody fangs. But in 1791 I was, like Jefferson, a devotee of the *other* Revolution and so anathema to the Federalist faction.

The President received me in his stately office. He had entirely redone the Morris House to make it resemble a royal palace. A diffident young secretary bowed me into the presence.

Washington stood before the fire, as though expecting to be painted. The altogether too famous sallow face was considerably aged. He was also in pain from carbuncles. He greeted me solemnly. Since he remained standing, we faced one another before the fire like ill-matched andirons.

I asked him questions about the Revolution; he made evasive answers. Both questions and answers are now lost. I do recall his cold benediction: "It is a most useful task, Senator Burr, that you are engaged upon." Plainly he was not happy with my line of questioning which seemed to stress unduly his defeats.

The secretary brought him despatches from the west; he glanced at them, then dismissed the secretary and bade me sit. Slowly, carefully, painfully, Washington arranged himself in a throne-like chair, favouring one huge buttock: the dread carbuncle had erupted in that sensitive fleshy quarter. I commiserated with him over the recent news from the west where his favourite General St. Clair had lost nearly a thousand men to the Indians.

Washington was cold and grim. "I shall presently send the Congress a report on this tragic matter. I firmly believe that if we do not destroy these warlike savage tribes, we shall lose the whole of our new lands west of the Ohio." He spoke the way one imagined a statue would speak.

But then he sat too far back in his chair. Gasping with pain, he swore mightily. Aware that he was now no longer royal in my eyes but simply a Virginia planter whose bottom hurt, he said, "I deteriorate before your eyes, do I not?"

"You seem most vigorous, Sir."

"I come from a short-lived family. I do not complain. That is fate. But I did not think that the last stages would be so humiliating." For the first and only time in our dealings with one another he was almost human —an extraordinary condescension considering that I was not a junior officer enamoured of him but an anti-Federalist senator detested by the beloved Hamilton.

"Glory is a good medicine, Sir."

"It is palliative." I caught a glimpse of the wintry dark-toothed smile. "But of course I shall not accept a second term." As we now know, all presidents talk in this fashion. But at the time none of us understood the nature of the executive disease; after all, we were at the beginning of the adventure.

"Colonel Burr, I dislike the spirit of faction. I cannot fathom why gentlemen of similar interest quarrel so bitterly with one another when they ought to unite in the face of the mob and its excesses." I was touched by his candour and—for him—ease of manner with someone he had no reason to trust and less to like.

"There are honest differences, Sir, on how best to govern . . ."

"It has come to my attention, Colonel Burr, that you admire much of what is presently happening in France."

"I think, Sir, that the reasons for their revolution are understandable and the principles they assert are admirable."

"Yet were it not for King Louis, the British might still be on this shore."

"I agree that their treatment of him is deplorable . . ."

Washington spoke through me, but not to cut me off: he was going deaf and did not hear half what was said to him. "When word came to me of the treasonous acts of a certain Captain Daniel Shays—a dirty fellow once known to me—it was apparent that we must have a strong government to protect our property. Mr. Hamilton concurred with me and we summoned a constitutional convention at which I, at great personal sacrifice, let me say, presided. I regard, Sir, that convention as the most important event of my own career. Because had we not invented this federal government, *they* would have taken away *everything*."

The face was dark with sudden colour. The hands that were stretched to the fire trembled. "By now that Massachusetts rabble would have divided all property amongst the worthless classes. Not even your French have dared go so far. This is not natural, I said at the time. This must be stopped. We did not fight and win a war with a despot across the sea to be in turn tyrannized by a bloody mob whose contribution to our victory, if I may say so, was considerably less than that of those gentlemen who sacrificed all that they had in order that we be a separate nation. So what we won in that war we mean to keep, Colonel Burr. And I am sure that you agree with that sentiment."

Political theory was the last subject I ever expected to hear from General Washington. He did not read Hobbes or Montesquieu or Plato, or any book at all. But he could add and subtract sums in a ledger, survey a property, recognise with an eagle's eye the vermin that infest the crops—*his* crops—and like that eagle pounce and kill.

"I certainly did not support Captain Shays and I do not believe in a promiscuous division of property but . . ."

"I am relieved to hear you say that." I was being

sounded out. Heaven knows what Hamilton had been telling His Mightiness about me.

"But I favour a looser federal structure."

"Yes. You are like my old friend Governor Clinton. Such *amicable* divisions are natural and healthy in a society."

The secretary slipped into the room, and whispered something in the General's good ear.

"Send them in." Washington heaved himself with a groan from his chair. Several liveried Negroes entered the room carrying trays of sample tableware. Washington indicated that the various knives, forks, plates be displayed on a table. "You may give us your opinion, Colonel Burr. I am told that you have redone Richmond Hill in a most splendid way."

"Yes, Sir, I have. But I must warn you that splendour is expensive."

"We are in sad accord."

So for half an hour the President and I examined tableware, trying to find a truly republican balance between too plain democratic ware and too rich royal plate.

I have never known a man so concerned with the trifles and show of wealth and position as Washington. But then it was his genius always to look the part he was called upon to play, and it is not possible to create a grand illusion without the most painstaking attention to detail. Much of his presidential day was occupied with designing monograms and liveries and stately carriages, not to mention inventing, with Hamilton's aid, elaborate court protocols.

Incidentally, at about this time, the Pennsylvania legislature passed a law that anyone moving into the state with full-grown Negro slaves must free them after six months. Although it was a moot point whether or not the President qualified as a Pennsylvanian simply because the capital was located in that state, Washington thought it best to whisk back to Virginia his personal slaves in order that they not get ideas about

a freedom he had no intention of granting them. He
was the total Virginian.

We parted on the most friendly terms. The next
day when I went to the State Department to consult
the archives, an embarrassed clerk told me that Secretary of State Jefferson was obliged to close the archives
to me on the flimsy ground that since certain documents might involve current executive matters the
constitutional separation between legislature and executive would be breached. Although Hamilton liked
to take credit for my exclusion, Jefferson told me privately that it was actually President Washington who
did not want me examining too closely his military
record. Yet Washington had nothing to fear from me.
Although I would have depicted him as the incompetent general he was, I would also have demonstrated how he was the supreme creator of this union;
how his powerful will and serpentine cunning made
of a loose confederation of sovereign states a strong
federal government graven to this day in Washington's
sombre Roman imperial image.

Twelve

SOME DAYS later. Colonel Burr goes over what I have
written. He makes corrections.

"How hungry for all credit, all glory, poor Hamilton
was! Among his papers they found a note swearing
that he had written more than sixty of the *Federalist*
papers when, in fact, he had written at the most fifty.
He made claim to some of Jemmy Madison's best
efforts."

Burr blows three blue-white rings of smoke at me;
becomes suddenly mischievous: "Now let us examine

Mr. Jefferson. He is sometimes known as the Great
Leveller of society. Actually, the only levelling he ever
did was of me!"

Memoirs of Aaron Burr—Three

OF ALL THE new republic's political leaders, I was the
most reluctant. Washington, Adams, and Jefferson had
spent their lives serving in congresses and assemblies
or dealing with them as governors and generals. Hamilton realized from the beginning that only through
politics could he make the United States the sort of
aristocratic pond in which he would most like to swim
and glitter. On the other hand, I was interested chiefly
in my wife and daughter, and in the law as a means
of providing for them.

But six months after I settled in New York (April
1784), I was elected to the Assembly. "It will be helpful for your career as a lawyer," said Hamilton, who
dreamed of election but wisely never proposed himself to our small electorate (of the 13,000 men who
lived in New York City only 1,300 owned sufficient
property to qualify as voters). I thought of Hamilton
a few years ago when the franchise was extended to
every man twenty-one or over. Had Hamilton lived,
he would have been apoplectic at so much democracy,
and made Chancellor Kent sound like a *sans-culotte!*

After a single term in which I was not only bored but
resentful of being separated from my family, I did not
stand for re-election. In 1788 I was again put up for the
Assembly on an anti-Federalist ticket and, to my relief,
I was defeated. I was still largely indifferent to public
matters, and took no active part in the making of the
Constitution.

My political career began, properly, with the contest
for governor in the spring of 1789. Out of friendship,
I supported the Federalist candidate, my old friend
Judge Yates. I had warned Clinton that I owed a good

deal to the Judge and that, though I was ordinarily a Clinton supporter, this time I must vote against him. "I unnerstan', I unnerstan'." The Governor gave me his jovial smile which usually presaged political assassination. But I was not to be assassinated since I did not want any political office. For once I was above the battle, much the best place to be for one who craves the victor's laurel.

Clinton was narrowly re-elected. To bind me to him, he offered me the attorney-generalship of the state, a position I did not want. But pressure was brought to bear on me. As Troup said: "You will be the centre of our profession in the state. You will never regret it." Translated this meant that I was to be useful to my Federalist friends at the bar.

As it turned out, I was not particularly useful to anyone in a post that for the most part involved steering clear of the various land-selling schemes of the Clintonian faction. Without going into melancholy details, let me simply say that the state administration was as corrupt then as it is now. No doubt this has something to do with the mephitic air of Albany.

Meanwhile, my friend Hamilton was like a rocket in the ascent. We now had a republic, a congress, a first magistrate and a *de facto* prime minister—Hamilton himself. He had achieved mastery in New York by getting the state to ratify the Constitution, to the fury of Governor Clinton. Hamilton then selected the first two senators, his father-in-law General Schuyler and his old Massachusetts friend Rufus King. In the process, he enraged his natural allies the Livingstons, denying them what they considered to be *their* seat in the Senate. The wrath of the Livingstons proved to be the unmaking of Hamilton, and my opportunity.

During the early months of the Washington administration I travelled a good deal about New York state and occasionally I would stop at Clermont, the Livingston palace on the Hudson where that great disaffected family spent its days brooding and plotting the destruction of my friend Hamilton who had so neatly excluded them from the high offices of the republic.

It was in the drawing-room at Clermont that I was included in the most audacious of the Livingston plans. My relations with Chancellor Livingston were always good though hardly intimate. For one thing he was stone-deaf. For another he was very much *de haut en bas* but then he was, in every sense, *de haut,* and the rest of the world, relatively speaking, *en bas.*

At the Chancellor's request, a dozen of us met on one of those silvery October days when the leaves at Clermont are a most furious red-yellow and skittish deer cast violet shadows on the lawn, and watch us watching them.

The Chancellor came agreeably to the point. "General Schuyler's term as senator will end March fourth. I see no reason, Colonel Burr, why you should not replace him."

The true politician like the true general is never surprised. I knew that an alliance between the anti-Federalists (that is to say, the anti-Hamiltonians) and the Livingston faction was under way. Governor Clinton had taken to praising the Chancellor at dinner parties. "Wunnerful deep he is, knowin' so much law!"

Now I was to be the symbol of this new alliance. I was more curious than surprised. "I am not at all certain, Chancellor, that I want to be a senator." This was true. In those days the Senate's function was a mystery to everyone, including its presiding officer John Adams who simply could not fathom the duties of a vice-president. "But what am I to do *next?*" he would pitifully cry from the chair. To which the only answer was "preside"; and wait for the President's death or retirement. A seat in the House of Representatives, on the other hand, was most desirable, for that House controls the Treasury. Jemmy Madison much preferred it to the Senate.

The Chancellor was brisk, once he had understood my shouted demurs. "We have the votes in the state Senate. Governor Clinton assures me you will have the

votes in the Assembly, which is his peculiar territory.
I see no reason for you not to accept."

I saw at least one reason. What was their price? We
did the stately minuet of politicians manoeuvring. "I
am curious," I said, "as to *why* you chose me?"

"You are the best-fitted!" This came from a Livingston relation by marriage. I cannot remember which
one. But then who can ever get them all straight?
There are so many.

"You are also the most acceptable." The Chancellor
was benign. "Your support of our friend Judge Yates
was taken as a sign of independent mind. And though
you are no professional anti-Federalist, your relations
with our good governor are excellent. In fact, he told
me that yours was the best legal mind in the state."

"Tactless of him to say so in *your* presence, Chancellor."

"Tact is not that good man's strongest point. But
he has his virtues even if they are not those of a gentleman." How vigorously the Livingstons used to employ
that noun to cast in bold relief the few of us who
were born gentlemen and thus in permanent opposition to that shadowy multitude from among whose
seedy dangerous ranks Alexander Hamilton had vaulted
to our high bright roost.

"But marrying Elizabeth Schuyler was hardly enough,
do you think?" as the mistress of Clermont liked to
say. "No wife can *entirely* change what her husband
is." Make him legitimate, she meant; make him one
of us.

It is ironic that Hamilton who worshipped the aristocrats was never taken seriously by them except as a
tool. He might have been president had he turned to
the people he came from, to the mechanics who had
the vote, to the men in the taverns who could appreciate in him their own selves made large by intellect
and cunning. But Hamilton wanted no part of the
lower orders. He rejected his own origins and con-
sorted only with the well-born and the rich, serving
them truly and himself, at the end, not at all.

"It would seem to me, Chancellor, that your claim on the Senate seat is greatest of all."

"Of course it is." The Chancellor was bland. "But at the moment no Livingston can be elected. You can. It has been arranged. Will you accept?" Expectantly, he cupped a hand to his ear.

"Yes," I bellowed. "But without ties to either faction."

The Chancellor stared thoughtfully at the dusty family portraits. The Livingstons think, not incorrectly, of New York as being their personal property, a gift from King Charles forever threatened not only by the democracy but, most bitterly, by their rivals the Schuyler family. The Livingstons of those days would have preferred the tumbril and the guillotine to playing second fiddle to the Schuylers.

"Of course," said the Chancellor. And so because of the rivalry between two proud, foolish clans, I was chosen, in January of 1791, the third United States senator from New York.

The fact that I had not sought the office nor wanted the office gave me strength. Although I was anti-Federalist, I was on good terms with many Federalist leaders and so could act with perfect freedom. I was not thirty-five years old, and from an important region. I accepted my destiny. I would become the president, an office for which I believed that I was by temperament and training uniquely qualified. Why else had fate set me so high on the ladder? All I need do was ascend. I had no fear of Hamilton. His limitations were already apparent to me. The man I should have feared I thought my friend. By allowing Jefferson to deceive me, I lost all.

Memoirs of Aaron Burr—Four

THOMAS JEFFERSON has written that he did not meet me until I came to the Senate in Philadelphia (the capital kept moving farther and farther south thanks to the Virginia junto). Although often prone to truth, Jefferson was never a fanatic when his own legend was at stake. We had met earlier than that.

Since Congress did not meet until the autumn of 1791, I spent the summer at home with my wife and child, knowing that we would soon be separated for long periods. Houses were hard to come by in Philadelphia; and my wife was ill.

During the summer, Jefferson and Madison made their famous tour of New York and New England. They were interested, they said, in botany as well as the vicious habits of the Hessian fly.

Actually they were creating support for themselves against Hamilton who now controlled President, Congress and Cabinet. Quite alone in the Cabinet, Jefferson fought to uphold the republic that Hamilton wanted to turn—so Jefferson maintained—into a corrupt replica of the British system, with Commons, Lords and Crown.

About the middle of June, I was invited by Henrietta Colden to a small dinner for the Secretary of State. Since my wife was ill, I attended alone.

Henrietta was a great favourite in the society of that era. She had a lively, bright manner that acted like champagne on even the dullest guest. In fact, the widower Jefferson was suspected of being more than just a friend to the widow Colden who was, for a time, Hamilton's mistress. But then what lively lady in New York had not been, more or less seriously, addressed by Hamilton? I should think that his amative bump was uncommonly large.

There were a dozen men and women in Henrietta's flowery drawing-room. When I was announced, she seized my arm; led me to the tallest man in the room.

"Our new senator!" she cried, assuming that the tall man needed no introduction, that I needed no name to go with my new title.

A rather large limp hand touched mine. I am not usually conscious of height but with Jefferson I always felt in danger of a crick in the neck as he obliged me—obliged everyone except those few who were at his eye level—to look up into that freckled fox face with the bright hazel eyes, and delicate thin-lipped smile.

"Colonel Burr, what an honour!" The voice was low but beguiling. Even face to face (or face to chest) one had to strain to hear him, particularly when he slipped into one of his reveries and the words would flow beautifully, inexhaustibly, sometimes interminably, yet never entirely without interest for one always found good things even as *he* found them in that fine speculative torrent. He was the most charming man I have ever known, as well as the most deceitful. Were the philosopher's charm less, the politician's deceit might not have been so shocking.

We exchanged compliments.

"Mr. Madison is ill!" Henrietta announced gaily to the company.

"So you must make do with me." Jefferson gave her a fond look. "One Virginian is very like another, according to Mr. Hamilton."

Henrietta defended Hamilton. She knew nothing of politics but everything of politicians.

Jefferson discussed at length his recent trip to New England. "A botanical excursion," he said quite seriously. "Mr. Madison and I have been fascinated by what we have seen and learned, particularly about the mating habits of the Hessian fly."

Jefferson affected great interest in my views. Wanted to know my estimate of Governor Clinton whom he had briefly met at Albany. Betrayed a detailed knowledge of my election. Wanted to know my precise relations with the Livingston family. Since the Chancellor was at the other end of the table, my decorous praise of him was no doubt repeated.

In my view Jefferson wrote rather less well than he talked, but no less copiously. From the colour of Negroes (the result, he felt, of a peculiarly virulent form of leprosy) to the proper building of walls, Jefferson not only had an opinion on everything but was driven to express it. Indiscreet letters of his will one day delight and trouble unborn historians. Certainly his letters to me (most of them lost at sea) were marvels of wit and good sense.

Unfortunately Jefferson did not always know when to be silent. A few months before our meeting at Mrs. Colden's, Tom Paine's *The Rights of Man* was published, with words of praise from Jefferson on its cover. Since the author had been recently indicted for treason by the British government, it was thought tactless of the American Secretary of State not only to praise the traitor but, gratuitously, to remark upon the danger to the United States from "heresies" of the sort Paine was indicting.

The Hamiltonian *Gazette of the United States* promptly published an attack on Jefferson by one "Publicola," thought to be John Adams. Actually Publicola was the Vice-President's son, John Quincy Adams.

"I cannot for the life of me think why Mr. Adams should be so distressed." Jefferson was disingenuous.

"Possibly because he is a heretic." This from Philip Freneau who was then writing savage indictments of Hamilton and Adams for the *Daily Advertiser*.

I later discovered that Jefferson had expressly asked Henrietta to invite Freneau to dinner. Respecting ideas not men, Freneau was not the sort of prickly person Jefferson usually liked in attendance. But two months after our dinner party Freneau was drawing a good salary as clerk of foreign languages in Jefferson's State Department at Philadelphia, and editing for Jefferson a new anti-Administration newspaper called the *National Gazette*. Everyone was shocked. It is not usual to give government money to an editor whose policy is the destruction of that government. Quite sensibly, if maliciously, Hamilton proposed that both Jefferson and Freneau resign if they did not approve of the government which paid their salaries. From time to time,

Jefferson would deny that he had any connection with Freneau's newspaper, but then he had the fortunate gift of believing implicitly anything he himself said at the moment he said it.

For our benefit, Jefferson spun his version of the quarrel with Adams. "I confess that when I wrote of heresies in my letter—which I never gave the publisher permission to use . . ." True or false? With Jefferson one could never be certain. ". . . those heresies I referred to were the ones to which Mr. Adams inclines. He is a monarchist through and through, and has told me as much."

This was later denied to me by Adams himself. "I never in my life had a serious conversation with Mr. Jefferson on any subject," said Adams two years later. "But if I *were* a secret monarchist, Mr. Jefferson would be the last person I would confide in. He knows of course I am no such thing nor is that Creole bastard. But Mr. Jefferson does know that the surest way for him to rise is to excite the people against Hamilton and me by pretending that we want a king when all we want is a strong federal government." Of the sort Jefferson himself was to achieve some years later.

Chancellor Livingston wondered if perhaps the Secretary of State was exaggerating.

The bright hazel eyes grew round as a child's and the voice dropped so low that we were all leaning forward across our Madeira glasses to hear his sudden warning. "Gentlemen, there is—I assure you—a plot at the highest level of this country to change our institutions. To make them over in England's image. Once, in my presence, Hamilton described our Constitution as a 'shilly-shally affair.' Oh, his contempt for this republic is as brazen as that of any Catiline!"

Little did I know then that in time's womb the classic traitor's name would be used to describe me, with Jefferson himself as happy midwife at that so unnatural birth. But ignorant of the future, I listened raptly to the beautiful low voice describe Hamilton's habit of giving speculator friends secret Treasury information, all the while attempting to set up a monarchy with British gold. In retrospect, this sort of talk sounds perfect madness. At the time, it sounded perfectly plausible.

Freneau was obviously much taken with this discourse. So was I. There was something in Jefferson's manner that *held* me as no other man was ever able to do. Even after I came to know well his recklessness with the truth, I never failed to respond to that hushed voice, to those bright child's eyes, to his every fanatical notion, to his every rich slander. He was a kind of wizard, no doubt of it.

The Chancellor teased Jefferson about his famous remark during Shays's rebellion—that from time to time the tree of liberty's proper manure is blood. Jefferson responded with all seriousness. "I meant only that we should congratulate ourselves that in two hundred years we have had only one such internal uprising. It is a tribute to our sense of justice that redress comes before rebellion."

"Even so, you are now the hero of all the Shaysites." At heart the Chancellor was a Federalist, forced to pose as a Republican. Had he not been passed over for chief justice, he would have found the ideas—if not the company—of Jefferson most uncongenial.

"We met many of these poor men in New England." Jefferson looked mournful. "They were misled by Shays. They had too little faith in our ability to set things right . . ."

"Like forty-per-cent interest rates? like crushing taxes? like thousands of men in prison for debt?" Eyes fixed on Jefferson, Freneau resembled a doctor who is waiting to see if the patient will recover or succumb to a radical dosage of mercury.

"Of course many of their complaints are justified. I find it a frightful business imprisoning men for debt." As well he might! The one thing that Jefferson, Hamilton and I had in common was indebtedness. We all lived beyond our means and on the highest scale.

Hamilton died owing money. Jefferson died a pauper, with Monticello collapsing about his head. Fortunately, unlike the average farmer or mechanic, we could not be jailed for debt. We could indefinitely collect signers and co-signers to our notes until the sordid conditions of our borrowings entirely vanished under the scrolls and flourishes of those wealthy magnates who are always anxious to befriend a man of state.

Freneau added to the dosage. "In Massachusetts, ninty per cent of those in prisons are debtors. Well, Sir, if I had been a poor man in that state, I would have marched with Daniel Shays."

"Mr. Freneau!" The Chancellor was appalled. "Surely you do not favour what that man favoured? Surely you do not want *all* property evenly divided among the citizens?"

There was an expectant moment at the table. From the drawing-room we could hear the harsh rather unlovely laughter of the lovely Mrs. Colden.

Jefferson slumped down on his spine, shoulders hunched, head to one side, freckled hands covering the lower part of his face. He did not intervene.

Freneau chose lightness. "I would let your family keep Clermont, Chancellor. But Mr. Jefferson would have to give up Monticello for he believes in democracy and you do not."

Jefferson laughed a bit too merrily. The others pretended to enjoy a joke that amused no one present. Two years later such a joke would have been impossible; by then the excesses of the French Revolution had made of the dream of Daniel Shays a nightmare. In fact, with the murders in Paris, no serious person in the United States has ever again suggested a division of wealth.

When the party ended, Jefferson and I walked out into Hanover Square. A waning moon was visible in the west. In the pale glow, Jefferson seemed to hang over me like a tree or like the sharp rise of some cliff (yes, and wait for the avalanche to bury you alive). He suffered from chronic headache, and used to wonder why.

"Perhaps," I said in response to the familiar complaint, "it is your height. You are too close to heaven, to the thunder and lightning." Instead of smiling at this pleasantry, he frowned. "Do you think so? I must ask Dr. Rush."

Jefferson walked loosely, in a shambling way—he was, I should note, very much the French exquisite during this period. His clothes were sumptuous; there was always a good deal of red, of silver, of lace about his long person, and a huge golden topaz on his finger. Later when he became president and the leader of the democracy, he took to wearing old slippers and frayed jackets in the presidential palace. Like Napoleon, he was a fascinating actor but far more subtle than the Corsican and ultimately far more successful.

"You speak of Montesquieu," said Jefferson, taking my arm. "At worst he is a bit too English in his bias. Yet on most issues I find him congenial and wise. Certainly he is a true republican." We made our way around a family of sleeping pigs in the Broad Way. Darkness was almost total; the moon had gone; the streets were empty.

I mention Jefferson's comment on Montesquieu's *Esprit des Lois* because twenty years later he was to turn fiercely on its author who had maintained that a true republic of the democratic order can exist only on a small scale. Certainly this "ideal" form of government is not practical for an empire of the sort Jefferson gave us when he illegally bought Louisiana—thereby doubling the size of the United States and putting an end once and for all to any hope of our society evolving into a true republic of the sort dreamed of by the Baron de Montesquieu and proclaimed by Jefferson. To justify himself, Jefferson turned on his old idol and attacked him for (favourite and characteristic Jefferson word) "heresy." But of course it was Jefferson who was the heretic, and Montesquieu the true believer in democracy.

I got the subject onto political matters. It was already apparent that Adams would succeed Washington. But

then what? I feared Hamilton would succeed Adams.
The only alternative was Jefferson. I did not rule out
myself as leader of the anti-Federalist faction but I was
practical enough to realize that as a Virginian, Jefferson
would have first call on the presidency once Massachusetts had been served by Adams. But no matter
what the future held, I was necessary to Jefferson that
summer night as we slipped in the garbage, and tried
not to step on sleeping pigs whose shrieks could awaken
the dead.

"We are apparently doomed to political faction."
Jefferson sounded melancholy. "I put the blame on
Hamilton. He is corrupt through and through."

I did not disagree although my personal feeling for
Hamilton was most friendly. (I did not know to what
extent he was slandering me even then.) But Jefferson
had no illusions about our enemy. "He is driven to
make a monarchy out of this republic."

"With himself as Alexander the Great?"

Jefferson had no humour. "With Adams as king, I
should think, and himself as permanent prime minister,
another Walpole. I must warn you, Colonel Burr,
Hamilton is treachery incarnate!"

I changed the subject. "How did you find Governor
Clinton at Albany?" Jefferson tended to obsession on
the subject of monarchy, a vice he attributed to anyone who stood in his way. It was Jefferson's conceit
that he alone represented democracy and that all the
rest of us from Washington to Adams to Hamilton
wanted to wear crowns and tax his cup of tea. Fortunately George Clinton was always a safe subject. He
was not a monarchist—he was simply the absolute
ruler of New York, and an enemy to the Federalists.

Jefferson's soft voice purred when he discussed his
meeting with Clinton. "A vigorous man, don't you
think? With unusual theories about the Hessian fly.
Of course your governor is not exactly a man of learning but there is something likeable in his roughness.
You know, he is much pleased with your election."

"Yes, I know."

A night-coach nearly ran us down in front of Trinity Church.

"I must confess that the loss of Senator Schuyler pleased me quite as much as the knowledge that such a distinguished supporter of the democracy as you would be joining us in Philadelphia." When Jefferson wanted one's support, he was shameless in his flattery. "Hamilton may lose his majority in the Senate."

"He still has the President."

Jefferson sighed. "Our good President thinks that Hamilton is the cleverest man in the world."

"Let us hope, Mr. Jefferson, that the President is wrong."

Even in the darkness I was aware that those bright eyes were looking down upon me. He did not answer immediately.

"Perhaps," he said at last, "it might be useful to form a series of clubs or associations, for those who are devoted to the democracy."

"There is the Society of St. Tammany." Tammany had been founded four years earlier as a patriotic club where solid New York greengrocers and upholsterers pretended to be Indians.

"But the Tammany membership is mostly Federalist." Jefferson's pursuit of the dread Hessian fly had not entirely distracted him from the political realities of the small but crucial New York electorate.

"Not entirely. Anyway, I have friends in the Society. They can be guided."

"It might be useful if our friends were to set up Democratic societies, particularly now when the revolution in France is so popular."

I agreed. As we parted, in the dark, Jefferson took my hand in both of his. "We have, dear Colonel Burr, so much to do. So many battles to fight, so many heresies to refute. We must stand by one another."

"You may depend on me in all things," I said. I was sincere. Was he? It is hard to say. Jefferson was a ruthless man who wanted to create a new kind of world, dominated by independent farmers each living on his own rich land, supported by slaves. It is amazing how beguilingly he could present this contradictory vision. But then in all his words if not deeds Jefferson was so beautifully human, so eminently vague, so entirely dishonest but not in any meretricious way. Rather it was a passionate form of self-delusion that rendered Jefferson as president and as man (not to mention as writer of tangled sentences and lunatic metaphors) confusing even to his admirers. Proclaiming the unalienable rights of man for everyone (excepting slaves, Indians, women and those entirely without property), Jefferson tried to seize the Floridas by force, dreamed of a conquest of Cuba, and after his illegal purchase of Louisiana sent a military governor to rule New Orleans against the will of its inhabitants.

Finally, in his second term, when Jefferson saw that he could not create the Arcadian society he wanted, he settled with suspicious ease for the Hamiltonian order, and like a zealous Federalist proceeded to levy taxes, and to create a navy (admittedly on the cheap—his famed gunboats had to be scrapped), while setting for the west and the south an imperial course as coldly and resourcefully as any Bonaparte. Had Jefferson not been a hypocrite I might have admired him. After all, he was the most successful empire-builder of our century, succeeding where Bonaparte failed. But then Bonaparte was always candid when it came to motive and Jefferson was always dishonest. In the end, candour failed; dishonesty prevailed. I dare not preach a sermon on *that* text.

At the beginning of October 1791, I arrived in Philadelphia and took lodging at 130 South Second Street in the house of two elderly widows, one mother to the other, one deafer than the other. Very kindly the ladies suggested that I not strain my senatorial voice in trying to communicate with them. Since I was their only lodger, silence reigned in South Second Street and I slept marvellously well in a back bedroom.

On the 24th of October the Second Congress convened, and the next day President Washington haltingly read to us a message prepared for him by Hamilton. I remember thinking how uncommonly healthy the President looked, his normally sallow face quite ruddy. It was Senator James Monroe of Virginia who enlightened me.

"He's taken to painting himself like a tavern sign whenever he appears in public. At home, he looks to be a hundred." Monroe's contempt for the father of his country was apparent even then while Washington detested the senator from his home state: thought him a regular Jacobite.

I was selected by the Senate to respond to the presidential address. After composing some elevated nonsense (fear of the Indian tribes was that session's crisis), I went with the other members of Congress to the Morris mansion in High Street (called without irony "the palace").

Like schoolboys we filed into the great man's presence. Magnificently dressed, holding a cocked hat, sword at his side, heavily and plausibly painted, George Washington stood before the fireplace with Jefferson to his right and Hamilton to his left. Hamilton looked more than ever like a small ginger terrier at the side of those two giants—each was more than six feet tall; does such physical altitude insure greatness? Even Monroe was tall though constantly stooped.

Vice-President Adams mumbled a few remarks (he at least was comfortingly small and fat). Slowly and with care, the President inclined his head (when newly applied, the fine white powder he used to dress his hair sometimes gave the startling effect of a cloudy nimbus about that storied head).

I responded in the name of the Congress to his address, and he responded to me briefly. All the while Hamilton stared at me, smiling a most curious, perhaps involuntary smile. Then doors were flung open and there in the drawing-room stood the Lady Washington surrounded by various Philadelphia ladies. White servants in royal red livery dispensed sweet plum cake and wine to us loyal commons.

I found myself with the fiercely republican Senator Maclay (who had lost his seat in March but was still in Philadelphia), an angry figure whose loathing of monarchy made Jefferson seem a mere dilettante on that sore subject.

"Look at King George!" Scornfully Maclay indicated the President who was stationed now in the centre of the room receiving ladies who curtsied deeply to him. "If the people could see this . . ."

"They would be delighted." It is my view that the people themselves are not democratic; only slave-owning aristocrats like Jefferson can afford to believe in democracy.

"I am not delighted." Maclay watched with disgust as Washington inclined his head to each of a number of gentlemen who filed slowly past him. "Note how he never shakes a man's hand. He deems it vulgar."

Then I was taken up by the beautiful Mrs. Bingham (a cousin of Peggy Shippen Arnold). "We expect you later. After this!" Mrs. Bingham's gesture toward the plump Lady Washington indicated serene condescension. The Washington court was a source of much amusement to Philadelphia's high society, and particularly to its queen Mrs. Bingham whose mansion on Third Street was the most elaborate private house in the United States. "And you, too, Mr. Hamilton," for that handsome little figure had suddenly appeared at my elbow.

I put out my hand in greeting only to realize too late that the Secretary of the Treasury had taken to imitating his chief. He gave me a decorous bow, arms to his side. "It is a pleasure, Colonel Burr, to see you here."

We played at friendship. "I regret that my presence should be at the expense of General Schuyler."

"There will be other elections." Hamilton's curious

smile seemed permanently fixed to his lips. "I hope that you and I can avoid the spirit of faction which has begun."

"I belong to no faction." I was blunt, and spoke the truth. "I was chosen by both Federalists and Republicans."

"I know, and they could not have chosen more shrewdly."

Whatever that meant. But I was as intent as he on playing out the scene, and with the same urbanity. "Yet the divisions here do not seem to me to be too deep."

"You have just arrived." The smile went (as did Mrs. Bingham); the succeeding frown was real. "Jefferson is intent on destroying this administration from within." In a tirade it all came out. Hamilton's tragedy was also his gift: he was a man of high intellectual passion whose weapon was language. Unable to remain silent on any subject that excited him he, literally, dug his own grave with words.

"I know that you met with Jefferson and Madison in New York . . ."

"Only with Mr. Jefferson. I'm afraid that your informant . . ."

"Was a Hessian fly!" Hamilton's eyes flashed with sudden good humour. He was as mercurial as the weather of that tropical West Indian island from which he came. "I am sure Jefferson did his best to convince you that I want to put a crown on the General's head."

"No, on your own." If this was to be badinage, I would sustain my end. But it was not.

The frown returned. "I think, Burr, that Jefferson is mad. Certainly on that subject. First, he has been away too long in France, and has a womanish attachment to that nation. He has also decided that their present form of anarchy is highly desirable—at least to contemplate at a distance. I doubt if he will ever surrender that Virginia farm of his to the people. Oh, Burr, I tell you he is the perfect hypocrite!"

I was embarrassed by the suddenness of this outburst, particularly since Jefferson was dreamily watching us from the far end of the room; but Hamilton was not to be stopped. "You know what a bloody time of it we had in the last Congress, over my plan for the Bank." I said that indeed I did. The dispute over the United States Bank was, in effect, the dividing line between two factions which, presently, became—and continue to be—two political parties. The northern states interested in trade and manufactures favoured the Bank. The agricultural southern states detested it; farmers are always short of cash and to a man they fear banks, mortgages, foreclosures.

Hamilton's grievances against Jefferson were manifold and such was his passionate nature that he could not keep from confiding them to me, a potential enemy but then, for all he knew, a potential ally, since I was senator from a state devoted to trade and manufactures.

"Three years ago when Jefferson became secretary of state, we made an arrangement. I wanted the federal government to assume the debts of the states. But as Virginia had paid off most of her debt, the Virginians in Congress were opposed. I appealed to Jefferson. We were standing outside the President's house in New York. I practically got down on my knees to him, begged him to help me change the Virginia votes. Warned him that other states would secede if we did not help them pay their debts. He entirely agreed, he said, and—now this is crucial—he agreed that the assumption of debts was in the interest of *all* the states. He then suggested that I put my case to Madison at a dinner in his house. I repeated for Madison what I had said to Jefferson but Madison was cool to the plan, and so to my surprise was Jefferson, who kept changing the subject. Spoke of climate. Of flora. Of fauna. Of the natural beauties of Virginia. I did my best to appear spellbound when he favoured me with a long digression on the physical nature of the opossum. There is a pouch, it seems, in the stomach of the opossum. Jefferson was worried about that pouch. Finally, I realized what our deep philosopher was after. He wanted the new capital of the country to be placed in Virginia—specifically on the banks of the Potomac River near Georgetown. If I gave him the capital, he and Madison would support me on the assumption of debts. I agreed. I had no choice. And that is how my bill to assume the debts of the states promptly passed the Congress, with the aid of the Virginia delegation, and that is why nine years from now Virginia will have the capital of the country, assuming those desultory farmers remember to build a city between now and then."

At the time I rather doubted Hamilton's version. Later I discovered it was correct. But then he was always truthful in such matters. Unlike Jefferson, Hamilton never lied about issues, only men.

"It would seem to me," I was thinking rapidly, "that if Jefferson is so agreeable to arrangements, you must simply keep on making it worth his while . . ."

"Unfortunately he has discovered *the people*. That beast attracts him. He would like to level everyone, and not because he has any abiding love for the majesty of the multitude but because he is a demagogue and thinks that to cry 'monarchist' at the President or at me is the surest way of inciting the people against us. Well, if he succeeds, Heaven help him! No Washington, no United States. No United States, no Jefferson. He is without conscience."

I made my only objection. "I would not underestimate his zeal. He strikes me as a man addicted to the most rigid principles . . ."

"Principles! You should have seen the letter he recently wrote a friend in Paris." During this period the one certain way of gaining total publicity was not through the newspapers but through the postal service. In consequence, most of us wrote in cipher; even so, letters were constantly intercepted and the ciphers regularly broken. Hamilton and Jefferson spent a good deal of time reading one another's private correspondence.

"Jefferson wrote to advise a Mr. Short to invest his money *in the bank*! In the very bank Jefferson is publicly accusing of being a menace to the republic! Oh, he is as two-faced as Janus! Do you know why he is so eager for a war in Europe? Because it will increase the price of the wheat he is growing in prospect of just such a war. He has also instructed his farm agent to grow hemp, cotton and flax because when the fighting begins in Europe he will be able to make a huge profit here at home. So Jefferson actually promotes war as being—in his very phrase—'helpful to domestic manufacture'!"

I have no idea if any of this was true. The important thing is that Hamilton believed it to be true. What zealots those two were! Yet of the two I regard Hamilton as the more honourable. Certainly he had the more realistic view of the world. Trained as a boy by Jews in the Indies, he understood money and commerce in a way that no one else at that time did, excepting Gallatin. Personally Hamilton was probably honest, though surrounded by thieves. One such thief was his close friend and assistant secretary of the Treasury, William Duer. Hamilton allowed Duer to sell Treasury secrets to speculators until Duer went to jail. But then Hamilton was no judge of character. He lived in a rarefied world of theory; unlike Jefferson who *appeared* unworldly yet understood human character better than any other politician I have ever known. Had the two been combined into a single statesman, we might have been governed by Plato's philosopher-king, and I would have gone rather earlier to Mexico, my Syracuse!

I recall no more of our exchange. Hamilton was desperate for votes in the Senate now that he had lost Schuyler. He was counting on my neutrality—on my accessibility to reason in the coming sessions. As it turned out, much of the time we were allied.

As I was leaving "the palace," I found myself walking beside Adams—known behind his back as His Rotundity. Round, plump, tactless, with a nose like a parrot's beak and a cold piercing eye, Adams was an imposing if somewhat comical figure, famed for his *gaffes:* as president he once told a hostile Republican Congress how honoured he had been to be presented to the King of England. He never did understand men, but he was quite at home with their ideas.

As we waited for our carriage (this was a part of our pretentiousness in Philadelphia: although most distances were short we all owned or hired carriages to take us from Congress Hall to "palace" to boarding-house), Adams said, "Your family is highly regarded in New England, Senator." This sort of pronouncement was purest Adams. "Your grandfather Jonathan Edwards might be said to have shaped our very being."

"Then I understand New England better."

For all Adams' bluntness, he was not—like Jefferson—immune to irony. "Yes, I suspect you do. You are a contemporary of Mr. Hamilton. I saw you speaking to him just now."

"We are almost exactly contemporary. But no more."

"Faction! Faction! This place stinks of political faction!" Fisher Ames heard this as he passed us on his unexpectedly democratic way home by foot. "For some," Ames flung at Adams, "this stench is like attar of roses."

Adams was joined by his wife, a lady always amiable to me. She spoke of Hamilton with a degree of fondness. "I have the desire to be like a mother to him." Mrs. Adams was not particularly motherly in manner.

"Well, I have no desire to be his father, and could not!" Adams' mind was indeed shaped by my grandfather's puritanism. So much so that John Adams was not, finally, a creature of our century at all but a relic of old New England days, of a wrathful god delighting in the ubiquity of sin and its terrible punishment. Yet Adams' intelligence, though limited, was profound.

What he knew he knew well. Unfortunately what he did not know he did not suspect existed.

Hamilton's bastardy used to exercise Adams even before they quarrelled (led to the quarrel?). Mrs. Adams reproved her mate. But Adams was not done with the subject. "One day the world will understand that young man you want to be a mother to for what he is: a *natural* orphan."

"Charity, John."

"I merely observe. Hamilton needs, *lusts* for fathers and mothers and he picks them up wherever he goes. The President did not adopt him as a son, he adopted the President as a father. He has been attaching himself to older men since he was a boy, an orphan, an outcast from the respectable world and quite rightly, too, considering *how* he was born, and of what blood. Senator Burr, the world is stern but the world is just."

The vice-presidential carriage arrived, splattering us sternly but justly with mud.

As the groom descended, Adams turned to me. "I trust, Sir, that this Congress will be the better for your attendance."

"As it is better, Sir, for your presidence of our chamber."

A wide cold stare raked my face like grape-shot. "I fear this Congress may be like the first, full of faction. I also fear those members who are too attached to France's vicious revolution."

"I fear all attachments which are excessive."

Adams took this ambiguity in stride. "We are in danger of government by professional office-holders ..."

"Come, John." Mrs. Adams was impatient and uneasy.

Adams was not finished. "By men of party rather than by men of state."

"It is sometimes hard to tell the difference."

"I can tell." From inside the carriage Mrs. Adams yanked hard at her husband's arm which was just inside the door.

"Can you also tell change when it comes, Mr. Adams? And whether it be for good or ill?"

"When it is for ill . . ."

Mrs. Adams and the groom had now got the Vice-President by sheer force into the carriage.

Mine was the last word as the groom shut the door. "New occasions, Mr. Adams, require new men and new ideas."

The carriage started with a jolt. I heard Adams say to his wife in a tone of exasperation, "Look at him, sleek as a duck!" I felt a certain distress. What he said was true. I had gained weight with all the party-going. I vowed a new regimen the next day.

As I waited for my carriage, I noticed James Monroe behind me. He had heard the end of our conversation. He made a face. "They're powerful enemies, those old Tories."

"Shall we replace them presently?" Almost casually, I set about the first of my alliances.

"Can it be done, without bloodshed?"

"It can be done, and it will be done, if we are wise."

"Are you a prophet?"

"No, Sir. But I can see what is in front of me. This faction mistrusts the people. All we need do is let the people know in what contempt their masters hold them, then *they* will do the rest." I got into my rented carriage.

"Are you with Jefferson?" Monroe called after me.

"In *this* matter, what republican is not?" On that equivocal, as Hamilton would say, note, we parted—with Monroe shouting after me to beware the Philadelphia tradesmen as "sharpers." In those few minutes on the steps of Washington's "palace" I had made my first move toward the presidency.

Thirteen

THIS MORNING I found Colonel Burr in his office, much amused by an account of a recent Senate performance by Henry Clay. "Mr. Clay apparently made the rafters ring, denouncing Andrew Jackson. He then turned to the Vice-President who was in the chair. Pleaded with him to bring his friend the President to reason. Listen to this. 'Entreat him to pause,'" Burr caught marvellously Clay's plangent frontier voice, "'to pause and to reflect that there is a point beyond which human endurance cannot go, and let him not drive this brave, generous and patriotic people to madness and despair!'"

Burr even managed the half-sob Clay sometimes works with such effect into his codas. "Then Mr. Van Buren turned over the chair to a senator, made his way down the aisle to where Henry Clay still stood with arms out-stretched in a gesture of pleading and, as everyone stared, said in a soft little voice, 'Mr. Clay, might I have a pinch of your fine maccoboy snuff?'" Burr's laughter echoed in the stuffy office.

"He sounds like *you*, Colonel."

"I was never so superbly deflationary. But then we had no audience in the early days of the Senate. Our proceedings were secret until I insisted on making them public. The level of our debate changed over night. Nothing so improves a senator's speech as an audience."

Sam Swartwout threw open the door, unannounced as always. "Colonel—leader!"

"You exaggerate, my boy."

"I was passing in the street and thought I'd bring you the news straight from the port. Lafayette is dead!"

"One cannot say that he was taken before his time.

We must restrain our grief." The Colonel was suitably dry. "He must have been—what, eighty?"

"Seventy-seven. Younger than you, Colonel."

"Then I shudder at this cold premonitory wind from France. Poor boy! So much to look forward to. I trust he is now in Heaven with General Washington and, side by side, they rest on a cloudy mantle of stars for all eternity, dreaming up disastrous military engagements."

"News from Washington City." Swartwout looked conspiratorial. I withdrew.

Later when the Colonel began his dictation, France was on his mind.

Memoirs of Aaron Burr—Five

IT IS DIFFICULT for people in 1834 to understand to what extent the life and politics of the early republic were governed by the fact of Europe, particularly by France and England. Yet no one preferred it that way; not even the Tories who loved the King wanted us to be embroiled in the problems of Europe. Unfortunately, we had no choice.

At the beginning France was our chief ally. After all, had it not been for the French fleet, there would still be a British garrison on the Battery. But the Revolution in France distressed our Tories—or Federalists as they came to be known; a nice irony since they had not wanted any federal government, preferring the King. But after we forced independence on them, the Tories wanted a strong federal government in order the better to protect their property and to keep the people in their place.

Looking back, we Republicans were not much different. Neither Jefferson nor I fretted particularly over the Constitution's limited franchise. I recall that in the election of 1789 there were over 300,000 residents of New York state of whom only 12,000 were qualified to cast a vote for governor. Needless to say, no one was allowed to vote directly for president. That was considered much too dangerous a privilege even for our small propertied electorate. They could vote for state legislators who in turn would select a president.

Between the First and Second Congresses, what Adams called "the spirit of faction" emerged. Hamilton was no more monarchist than Jefferson but he did see the American future as being dominated by manufacture and commerce which, in turn, required banks, taxation, cities, an army and a navy. Jefferson saw the whole continent as a kind of Virginia, filled with honest yeomen enjoying the fruits of black labour. Jefferson wanted no cities, no banks, no manufactories, no taxes. Jefferson was wrong and Hamilton was right. Worse, Jefferson was impractical.

The divisions in Washington's cabinet were exacerbated by the French Revolution. When the Bastille fell in 1789 even the Federalists were for a moment thrilled. Although every American owed a considerable debt to Louis XVI, we were all of us certain that he would be a better and happier king if he presided over a republic. I fear we were a bit simple at the time, interpreting everything that happened in Paris as a sort of Gallic repetition of our own glorious experiment.

Sometime in April 1793 we learned of the execution of Louis XVI. Republicanism had truly triumphed. Pigtails were cut off and hair worn à la Brutus. Trousers replaced small-clothes. Everyone started calling everyone else "citizen" and "citizeness," and the bad manners so many foreign visitors remark upon when they come to our shores (the children who do not respond politely to adults, the surliness of tradesmen and servants) began that spring with the arrival of the French ambassador Citizen Genêt. Over night it was considered slavish for the lower orders to be polite to anyone. Yet before Genêt's arrival, Americans were considered the politest people in the world—resembling the British but with greater sweetness and less servility. After Genêt they became what they are today—truculent, sullen and envious.

At the time of the execution of the King and Queen, their portraits hung on the walls of our Senate chamber (and everyone, including Mrs. Bingham, remarked how much she resembled Marie Antoinette). After the beheadings, various Republicans—including Freneau—wanted the portraits taken down. Jefferson's view of the portraits is unknown but he did delight in the executions. "After all," he said to me, "was ever such a prize won with so little blood?"

I said that from all accounts the prize had cost a good deal of blood.

But Jefferson was hard. "Rather than their revolution fail, Colonel Burr, I would see half the earth desolated! After all, if in every country there was but one Adam and Eve left, one *free* Adam and one *free* Eve remaining, the world would be better than it is now." I could not believe my ears. Either Jefferson was a fool in his zealotry or an active principle of evil.

Since France was now at war with England, Austria, Russia, Sardinia and the Netherlands, President Washington wisely insisted on our maintaining a strict neutrality. This enraged Republicans and Federalists. The first wanted war with England; the second with France. As a result, there were now two plainly recognisable political parties: the Republican party which was pro-French, anti-British and in tone egalitarian; the Federalist party which was the reverse. The Republican national leadership consisted of Jefferson, Madison, Clinton and myself. The Federalists included Hamilton, Adams, Jay, Knox and, more or less covertly, Washington himself.

On Thursday, May 16, 1793, Citizen Edmond Genêt arrived in Philadelphia to present his credentials to the President. He had already presented his credentials to the American people. Arriving some weeks before in Charleston, South Carolina, he had made a triumphal progress toward our capital, addressing along the way—and in excellent English—cheering crowds. The Federalists were alarmed. Jefferson, however, was benign. Do we not all detest tyrants?

An enthusiastic Philadelphia crowd assembled at Gray's Ferry to welcome Genêt. Unfortunately, the ambassador had appeared at the wrong wharf where he delivered a powerful address to a dozen startled loungers whom he took to be the Republican party. But the next few days more than compensated for the comedy of this début.

A splendid dinner was given him at Oeller's Hotel. Because of the Neutrality Proclamation, those of us who held public office were requested to attend *ex officio*. Needless to say the entire Republican delegation to the Congress was on hand.

Monroe and I sat together at the end of a long table in the main assembly-room. I confess we spent a good deal of time looking about to see if Jefferson, the enthusiast of the rights of man, would be present or whether Jefferson, the signer of the Neutrality Proclamation, would be absent. Wisely, as it turned out, the apostle of democracy chose not to be present.

Wine was drunk in large quantities, and Citizen Genêt, a lively fat fellow of thirty with a face somewhat like that of the young Benedict Arnold, made the rounds of the company on the arm of Governor Miflin who solemnly presented Monroe and me to the representative of liberty, equality, fraternity.

"I visit your state soon, Senator Burr." The Citizen held both my hands in both of his. He had a most histrionic way of talking. "We shall do good work there for freedom."

"It is an open field, Citizen."

"I want very much to meet your Governor Clinton."

"I am sure that he will want to meet you." That proved to be something of an overstatement. Within a year the Girondins (Genêt's faction in Paris) had been slaughtered by the Jacobins and the new government recalled Genêt to Paris in order that his head be cut off. Reluctant to lose such a fine docoration, Genêt chose to marry Governor Clinton's daughter and to settle down on Long Island; and with her money he became the gentleman-farmer that he is today. "Burr, I despise the French!" The crude Clinton was distraught. "A nation of hair-dressers and dancing masters! And my girl, my own girl has to go and pick a crowing, penniless French cockerel as a husband!"

But Clinton's cockerel was very much cock of the walk that night at Oeller's Hotel. There were at least twenty toasts to him or to his country. In fact, I proposed one to "the republics of France and America—may they forever be united in the cause of liberty."

A cap of liberty was placed upon Genêt's head. Bellowing the "Marseillaise" at us, he then passed the hat around the table. For a moment each of us put it on while Philip Freneau led the singing of a hymn he had himself composed extolling the rights of man and uneasily set to the tune of "God Save the King."

The usually glum Monroe was delighted with the evening. As we left Oeller's together, he said, "I should like to be in the room tomorrow when Hamilton and the President get their report on what happened tonight." Monroe looked almost gleeful.

"I should like to be in the room when Jefferson presents Genêt to His Mightiness."

We were just opposite Ricketts' Circus when a half-dozen villainous-looking French sailors leapt at us from a darkened alley, knives drawn. "You English!" one of them shouted. While another placed a knife at my throat. "We kill all English."

"You kill an American senator," I spoke in French, "and you will be hanged."

"You speak French like an Englishman!" One of the sailors reached for my watch fob.

Just at that moment, luckily for us, a group from the Oeller's dinner approached, and the sailors ran off.

Monroe and I were both shaken, and angry. I wanted

to have the men arrested. We were fairly certain that they were from the *Embuscade* which was docked at the Market Street wharf.

"No." Monroe was more cautious than I. "We must say nothing. We must not play into Hamilton's hands." So we said nothing.

That summer was for Philadelphia a miniature Terror, and the cause of France's revolution suffered accordingly. French sailors in unholy combination with refugees from Santo Domingo (ousted by their Negro slaves) preyed on the people of Philadelphia in the name of liberty. At one point it looked as if the bandits, in league with a number of native malcontents, might overturn the government and chop off Washington's head. Though the danger of this was never as great as Hamilton and Adams pretended, Genêt did manage to shadow the President's popularity amongst the lower orders to such a degree that His Mightiness was often—unthinkable *lèse-majesté*—booed at the theatre and in the streets. Knowing the high almost sacred regard Washington had for himself, it must be said that he handled, with admirable restraint, not only Genêt but himself, allowing the cockerel to destroy itself.

Fourteen

I MET MR. DAVIS BY CHANCE in the lobby of the City Hotel where I had been waiting, vainly as it turned out, for a client of the firm to appear and pay his bill. Money is in short supply these days. I have received no salary for two months. As a result, Mrs. Townsend has not seen me in a month.

Mr. Davis asked me into the tap-room where we were

served a rum concoction by the bar-tender who works in a sort of cage. In the afternoon the bar of the City Hotel is like a club with certain tables always occupied by the same men. I must say I enjoy the smoky room's air of opulence and mystery as large prosperous men whisper together of money, the low murmur of their talk sharply punctuated at regular intervals by the sound of the bar-tender's hammer breaking ice.

Mr. Davis knew half the room, and was greeted warmly. The other half presumably know him, but pretend not to. Political divisions are particularly bitter since the riots in April.

"We're going to win, Charlie. No doubt of it." Mr. Davis peered at me through spectacles that magnify large honest eyes, but then *all* eyes magnified look honest. I would not trust Matt Davis to tell me the right time of day.

"You'll be contributing your bit, won't you?"

I was mystified, and showed it, as always. I could never be a conspirator; and begin to wonder if I can ever be a proper lawyer.

"We're looking forward to your little book." Mr. Davis winked at me.

Before I could ask him just what he meant, whether or not he knew of my arrangement with Leggett, he changed the subject. After much admiring talk of Henry Clay whom he affects to know well and thinks to be in the true line of Jefferson, I asked him suddenly, "When did Jefferson first fall out with Colonel Burr?"

"The election of 1792." I realized then that Colonel Burr's narrative—seemingly so ample—had discreetly omitted the events of 1792 when George Washington and John Adams were re-elected president and vice-president, and John Jay was defeated by George Clinton for governor of New York. "The state—the country —was bank-mad in those days, thanks to Hamilton. But by election time, there was a depression. Hamilton's friend Duer went bankrupt, and to jail. The

Federalists were in despair. Many wanted Burr to be their candidate. Hamilton put a stop to that. He persuaded John Jay, the chief justice, to make the race. He did and almost won."

"With the help of Tammany?"

"We had no help to give. We were still a fraternal order. I don't suppose twenty braves were committeemen in that election and they were pretty evenly divided between Clinton and Jay."

Nelson Chase entered the bar. Saw me. Paused. Then came over to our table. "I have a message for Colonel Burr. Could you tell me where he is stopping?"

I was not about to tell him that the Colonel is currently in the Bowery with Aaron Columbus Burr. "Jersey City," I said.

Nelson Chase thanked me, and departed. Mr. Davis nodded; enjoyed the lie. Then continued: "It was a tribute to Colonel Burr that after only one year in the Senate, he was regarded by many Republicans as a future president. It was Jefferson's plan to undermine Adams as vice-president. Washington would be re-elected unanimously but Adams must be defeated, or at least diminished. To Jefferson's amazement, votes began to accumulate for Colonel Burr and votes for Jefferson did not materialise. Finally, a meeting was held in which the Republican leadership, directed by Jefferson, persuaded Burr to give up his votes to Governor Clinton with the understanding that in 1796 Burr would be our vice-presidential candidate."

"When *did* Tammany become political?"

"During the French Revolution. Oh, we were blood-thirsty Jacobins in those days! Citizen Genêt was our god. By the way, I saw him right here in the bar last spring, looking fat and old and rich! But it was thanks to him that those braves who disliked the French revolution began to drift away. By the election of 1800 we numbered—all told—perhaps a hundred and fifty braves who wanted Jefferson for president and Clinton for vice-president."

"Not Colonel Burr?"

"Not Colonel Burr."

"Then why does everyone think the Colonel was the creator of Tammany?"

"Because Tammany is considered evil. Burr is considered evil. All evil is the same. You know the world."

I do not; but am beginning to.

Memoirs of Aaron Burr—Six

JOHN ADAMS WENT TO HIS GRAVE believing that the entire Administration was in danger of the guillotine during the summer of 1793. Certainly Philadelphia's July 4 celebration was of Citizen Genêt personally and of the rights of man generally, and everywhere the Federalists were in retreat.

At the beginning of September 1793, Jefferson sent me a note to Richmond Hill asking me if I would come see him at the capital. I consented despite an epidemic of yellow fever in Philadelphia. But then we used to pride ourselves on our *sang-froid*. Lesser mortals might fear contagion and death; we gods ignored such things. As a result, the god Hamilton was thought to be dying the day I rode through Philadelphia's streets, empty of all traffic save those heavy carts whose drivers would shout at regular intervals, "Bring out your dead!," their voices harsh with command and loathing—the fever makes an ugly corpse, fit only for the flames.

There is, I am certain, a correlation between temperature and yellow fever. The disease only arrives in summer, and only in those summers that have begun cold and wet then become unseasonably hot and dry. The epidemic always ends with the first cold weather. Whatever the cause of the contagion (Jefferson suspected a mass of bad coffee left to rot on a Philadelphia wharf), it is fed by rain then nursed by heat and passed on from one person to the next until the cold weather puts a stop to it. The wise man retreats to the cool country-side at the first sign of the contagion. Unwisely, I chose to expose myself at the height of the epidemic, riding through the city, a handkerchief soaked in camphor held to my nose (we used to think this the best prophylaxis). Fortunately I did not have to stay in the city. Jefferson had rented a summer place at Gray's Ferry on the Schuylkill River, just outside the worst of the fever districts.

At the top of Jefferson's house, there was a sort of widow's walk where I saw him standing with two men as I got down from my carriage. He waved to me and vanished within.

I was received in the cool parlour by one of Jefferson's daughters. "You are very brave to come here. I hope you will help me convince my father to leave before we're all of us sick."

"But your house is on high ground." It was thought that those who lived on hills would not get the fever—until of course they did. There seems to be no rule in these matters; and there is still no cure for the disease. A few always recover despite their doctors; most die.

Jefferson greeted me, face flushed with what I took to be the first symptom of the fever but what proved only to be the response of a fair-freckled skin to heat. With him were Dr. James Hutchinson (a man nearly as fat as General Knox) and Jonathan Sergeant, two leading Republicans.

"Another fearless man!" Jefferson was in good spirits.

"No, simply a fatalist."

"It comes to the same thing. Come look at what I've just installed." It was not possible to visit Jefferson without being shown some new invention. Even his rented houses were "improved" by that restless tinker's mind. I affected interest.

We were led into a small room between two parlours. "Stand back." We did so. "Now watch."

Jefferson took the end of a rope that dangled from the ceiling, and gave a tug. There was a loud crash as a heavy bed landed at the inventor's feet, nearly sparing us the Jefferson administration. "Good God!" The American Archimedes was crest-fallen. "I can't think what went wrong."

"The ropes were too fragile." Dr. Hutchinson was profound.

"A marvellous invention, in theory at least." I was polite. I had already seen a similar invention in Jefferson's town house. During the night the bed would rest on the floor; during the day it would be hauled up to the ceiling by ropes. I cannot think why.

For some time, Jefferson discoursed impressively on Newton's theory of gravity and the inverse square which entirely accounted for the delicious fact that a heavy bed unless secured by strong ropes will always fall to the floor.

Dinner was served at three o'clock on the lawn where we were tolerably shaded by tall plane-trees. Despite the heat we did more than justice to the wonders from the Jefferson kitchen and cellar, served us by a French major-domo named Petit. One always dined royally at the great democrat's table.

Among the other guests were Philip Freneau and John Brown, the senator from Kentucky. It was, in effect, a gathering of Republicans for a most interesting purpose.

As always with Jefferson, the conversation at first touched on a thousand matters other than the business at hand. Although Madeira was considered the best drink to ward off the fever, a cold white French wine emerged in quantities from the cellar, and we drank much too much of it; like characters in Boccaccio, we played at enjoying ourselves during a plague year (each wondering to himself who would be next to die).

Jefferson gave us news of Hamilton. "Apparently he became sick a few nights ago, after dinner with the President."

"One should bring a taster to King George's table."

Freneau's attacks on Washington were particularly
savage during this season—which proved to be the last
for the *National Gazette*. A month later the newspaper
failed.

"The wise man eats *before* going to the Washing-
tons'." Jefferson was as droll as he could be. "Whatever monarchical tendencies the President may have,
he sets a republican table. Anyway, Hamilton has summoned not one but two doctors to save his precious
life." Jefferson was disdainful. "He is in terror of death.
But then he has a fearful nature. He is timid on a
horse, timid on the sea—timid in battle, too, was he
not Colonel Burr?"

"Actually he was a good officer on those rare occasions when he was in the field . . ."

"But a better officer at headquarters, playing Jonathan to the General's David." Freneau was as relentless
as Jefferson, and far more bitter since he had that ill-
proportioned passion for the abstract that is peculiar
to so many literary men. There is some evidence that
Freneau really did believe in the rights of man.
Although Jefferson's dislike of monarchy was sincere,
he knew as well as anyone that there was never the
slightest danger of any American wearing a crown; thus
his constant harping on the subject was simply a way
to blacken the reputation of anyone unfortunate
enough to stand between him and that throne he
meant, from the beginning, to occupy. With Jefferson
everything was personal; with Freneau, theoretical.
Naturally, each appeared to be opposite to what he
was.

They spoke with such contempt of Hamilton's record as a soldier that I found myself coming to my
rival's aid. "To his credit Hamilton was always there
with the rest of us. He did fight in the battle for New
York Island. He did suffer with the rest of us at Valley
Forge. He was at Yorktown. He never shirked his duty
. . ." I am not often tactless but as I spoke I felt a
definite drop, as it were, in the temperature at table.
I glanced at Jefferson and saw that he was blushing,

always a sign in him of distress. Obviously he thought that I was alluding to the ignominious role he had played in the Revolution. It was the one subject (aside from Hamilton and later me) whose very mention made him irrational—with some reason. At the approach of the British army, Governor Jefferson fled to Monticello, leaving the state without an administration. At Monticello he dawdled, thought only of how to transport his books to safety. Not until the first British troops had started up the hill did he and his family again take to their heels. Later Patrick Henry's faction in the Virginia Assembly demanded an investigation, but fortunately for Jefferson the proud Virginia burgesses did not want to be reminded of the general collapse of their state and so their hapless governor was able to avoid impeachment and censure. He did not, however, avoid ridicule; and that is worse than any formal censure.

Dr. Hutchinson changed the subject for us; spoke of Citizen Genêt. Who did not that year?

Jefferson was sad; genuinely, I think. "A passionate good man." Jefferson was never so animated as when he was carving in marble, as it were, a contemporary's epitaph. "Certainly the cause of our own republic is forever in his debt."

"But if he makes one more attack on the President he will ruin us all." Senator Brown was drinking too much wine in the western way.

"I know. I know. I have tried to restrain him." Jefferson smiled. "But I simply could never make myself *heard*." We all laughed rather more loudly than this pleasantry required. But then one could wait a year for Jefferson to say anything ironic or, Heaven forbid, self-deprecating.

"Citizen Genêt's voice is very loud." Thoughtfully, Jefferson explained the irony to us; laughter diminished appreciably. "But then so is Mr. Hamilton's. You know he wants us to deport Genêt and shut down the Democratic Societies. He made three long speeches—

in succession—to the Cabinet. It was like being at a murder trial. The President was not pleased, particularly when General Knox, your friend . . ." He inclined his head to me; the ironic mood was really upon him. No doubt the plague had inspired him. ". . . showed the President your cartoon," this to Freneau, "depicting him as a tyrant whose head was about to be chopped off. I thought we would lose that great man then and there while you, Freneau, would go down in history as his assassin. The President was in a fury such as I have never seen. Veins knotted at his temples. He flung his hat to the floor. Swore he would rather be a farmer than emperor of the world. Swore he had no desire of being a monarch or anything else to do with the governing of this country. I thought he would die of rage."

"I have gone too far." Freneau was demure.

Jefferson smiled a small fox smile. "The President is particularly angry because you always send him three copies of every issue. 'Why three?' he cried. 'Does this dirty fellow expect me to be his distributor?' "

"He responds ill to healthy criticism." Freneau looked very pleased with himself.

"He will have to take worse criticism," observed Sergeant, "if he continues to be Hamilton's creature, and a Treasuro-bankite." This cumbersome phrase was of Jefferson's coinage. With a slight bow, he acknowledged authorship. He then gave us his unique thoughts on how best to destroy the Bank of the United States.

"When a branch of the Bank is projected, let us say, for Richmond in Virginia, the governor of that state should then invoke the clause of the Constitution which leaves to the states all powers not plainly given the federal government. Since the federal government is nowhere given the power to create such a bank, only the states themselves can create such a bank. Now, Colonel Burr, you are the ablest lawyer at this table. Give me your view of the following proposition. Is it not true that any person who recognises a foreign legislature in a case belonging to the state commits treason against the state?"

I could not believe him serious. "You are asserting that the federal government is *foreign?*"

"I am."

"You would then have a state court indict for treason any Virginian who consented to act as director, say, of the Bank of the United States?"

"If he did so on Virginia soil, yes, I would."

"And should the court find him guilty of treason . . ."

"Under our Constitution, the state court would be *obliged* to find him guilty."

"You would then have him executed as a traitor to the state of Virginia?"

"Yes, and that would put an end once and for all to Mr. Hamilton's bank, for no one would serve as director if he knew he would be hanged." Jefferson was no Jonathan Swift. He meant exactly what he said. Years later Madison told me that Jefferson had used the same argument with him. Needless to say, Madison was as appalled as I and dissuaded Jefferson from pursuing the matter. If he had, the Constitution would have been put aside long before the fifty years' life I gave it!

The Republican sycophants at table thought the plan superb. Freneau was for implementing it immediately. I made gentle objections until the conversation flowed into other more congenial channels.

As we sat over peach ice-cream, drinking more chilled wine than was entirely necessary, watching the long shadows stretch across the lawn, the first fireflies glow in the shrubbery, Jefferson told us the reason for the dinner.

"I wanted my good friends to know that I have given the President my resignation as secretary of state." A chorus of "oh no!" "To take effect the first of October. I told the President that it is no longer possible for me to continue usefully as a member of his government."

"Now it will be Hamilton alone as chief of state." Senator Brown broke the silence.

"If," said Dr. Hutchinson enthusiastically, "he does not presently die."

"We cannot count on that." Jonathan Sergeant was grim.

But Jefferson had not done with surprising us. "The President came here—to this house—last week. Declared himself most bitter at my decision. 'You and Hamilton persuaded me—against my deepest wish—to serve a second term as president. Now I am to be left entirely alone.' "

"Hamilton is resigning, too?" I could not believe it.

"At the end of this Congress, according to the President."

I said I did not believe it, and I was right. Hamilton stayed on two more years, until the beginning of 1795. But that warm evening beside the Schuylkill River, Jefferson was a happy man. Like Washington, he did nothing but complain of the horrors of political life and, like Washington, he had no desire to let go of power. But for the moment he knew that his usefulness was at an end. The Genêt business had exhausted him. Unknown to us at dinner, Jefferson had already requested the French to recall their ambassador in a document which, I am told, was a masterpiece of diplomacy. This meant that Jefferson would be able to leave office in a blaze of glory, keeping, on the one hand, the loyalty of those rabid Republicans who worshipped Genêt and the Revolution while, on the other hand, demonstrating to the Federalists that he placed the interest of the United States before that of France. Talleyrand used to say that if ever he was an emperor he would want Jefferson to be his foreign minister.

In the cool of the evening we rose from dinner and strolled beneath the trees. Jefferson's daughter urged us singly and jointly to insist upon the Secretary of State's immediate departure from Philadelphia but Jefferson would have none of it. "I do not like," he said severely, "to exhibit the appearance of panic."

"But the President goes next week."

"And we go, as planned, two weeks later. One ought to sustain at least the semblance of a government here —even though I am now reduced to only one clerk." Jefferson looked at Freneau and quickly amended himself. "One clerk and one superb translator."

At the river's edge, beneath the many-rooted willows, Dr. Hutchinson spoke sadly of Jefferson's retirement. "It will be three years before the next election, and long before that time Adams and Hamilton will possess the nation." The good doctor was vehement, eyes flashing, colour high.

Senator Brown and I also urged Jefferson to remain in office but he was adamant. He did have a scheme, or rather several schemes, for the extension of our democracy. Senator Brown alluded to the boldest. "Your Frenchman should be in Kentucky now."

"*My* Frenchman?" Jefferson looked pensive. "No, he is not my Frenchman. And if he fails he is no one's Frenchman."

"In that case," Senator Brown agreed, "he will be a dead Frenchman."

Jefferson turned to Dr. Hutchinson and me. "You may know of the botanist André Michaux."

Dr. Hutchinson did know; praised the young man's recent address to the Philosophical Society. It seems that Michaux had been particularly revelatory on deciduous trees.

"Citizen Genêt asked me if I would send Michaux to Kentucky, with a letter to the governor asking that Michaux be supported in a venture to take New Orleans from the Spanish."

"At last!" Dr. Hutchinson was afire. "You agreed, didn't you?"

Jefferson's features were indistinct in the failing golden light. "I gave Michaux the letter."

Senator Brown was explicit. "For three thousand

pounds, two of our generals, Clark and Logan, will raise an army of frontiersmen and occupy New Orleans. We shall then have what we *must* have, control of the Mississippi River."

I, too, was thrilled. I did wonder how Jefferson intended to cover his tracks. He told us, quite candidly, "This will be entirely—on the surface—a French affair. Citizen Genêt's government will provide the three thousand pounds . . ."

"But we are at peace with Spain," I said, thinking like a lawyer when I should have thought like a philosopher and so gained the world.

"And we shall continue to be at peace." Jefferson was mild. "I have stipulated that the men are not to be trained on American soil."

"What happens," I asked, "if they succeed? If they capture New Orleans?"

"That whole area will then join our union while enjoying a special relation with France."

"Are the Spanish so weak?" I was curious; my destiny not yet begun—no, at this very moment begun—in that enticing part of the world.

"It is our impression."

"What happens should you—should they fail?"

"I warned Michaux that in such a case we do not know their names. Fortunately he is a stoic young man." Jefferson's voice was beginning to blend with the soughing of a warm wind. I could no longer make out his face. In the house lanterns were being lit.

"There's no chance of failure, Mr. Jefferson. You will have the support of every man in Kentucky." Senator Brown had the expansive manner peculiar to the frontier where one is always offered the world while settling for a mug of home-made whiskey.

"I hope you are right. After all, this is my last . . . activity in the government."

"Until we make you president!"

Dr. Hutchinson put his arm through Jefferson's and we made our way across the lawn to the house while

Jefferson explained to us what it was that made the firefly glow.

I left Jefferson at the carriage path.

"I am grateful," he said, "that you braved the fever to visit me at the end of my political career."

"I suspect it is the beginning."

"No, no, no." The soft voice trailed off. "But I do think we must keep an eye on the monocrats, you in New York and I in Virginia. We shall correspond."

Dr. Hutchinson appeared, and asked if I would take him home in my carriage. I agreed. We then exchanged bows with our host (no one shook hands during the fever season).

As we drove off, Jefferson waved to us. Suddenly I saw him as a monster scarecrow silhouetted against the lights from the house. So death must look, I thought, and shuddered: a nightmare figure with attenuated limbs and a whispering voice. Then slowly, slowly, with distance, he shrunk from troll to doll to nothing, darkness.

Dr. Hutchinson was eloquent with praise. "There has never been such a mind! Not even Franklin, and I knew him well, too. If anyone can make us into a true republic, it is Jefferson."

"Or an empire. What he plans to do in Kentucky is very bold."

"Boldness is what the world respects. We need new territory."

"But do we need . . . can we afford a war with Spain?"

Dr. Hutchinson laughed. "Jefferson told me he has a perfect pretext if we ever need it. The Spanish control the Creek Indians. The Creek Indians have been harassing our settlers. If the Creeks are not restrained by their Spanish masters, Jefferson will threaten Spain with . . ." Dr. Hutchinson suddenly gagged. "Too much wine. Forgive me. Do stop the carriage."

He got out and vomited. I sat very still, holding a camphor-soaked handkerchief to my face; certain that

I was now at the end of my life and that the vision of Jefferson as death had been premonitory.

When Dr. Hutchinson got back inside we both knew that he had the yellow fever—which explained the red lips, the glassy eyes.

"He feeds us much too well for a summer day," said Dr. Hutchinson.

I agreed.

In silence we drove to the doctor's house. We bade one another good night. The next day Dr. Hutchinson was dead.

A few weeks later Jonathan Sergeant was also dead, to the delight of John Adams who always maintained, perhaps seriously, that only the yellow fever had saved the United States from revolution that summer.

The Michaux expedition failed but Jefferson was in no way compromised. He had seen to it that Citizen Genêt got the full blame from everyone.

Amusingly enough, a few days after our dinner party where Jefferson had refused to "exhibit the appearance of panic," he fled to Monticello after first borrowing, so Hamilton told me with delight, a hundred dollars for travelling expenses from the evil Bank of the United States.

Fifteen

COLONEL BURR AND I WENT this day for dinner at the City Hotel. Contrary to his usual custom, the Colonel took a place near the end of that table which is always occupied by the old bachelor Charles Baldwin. Fat, red of face, boisterous in manner, Baldwin was delighting a number of cronies with his various opinions, delivered in what he took to be the style of Samuel Johnson.

"Ah, Colonel Burr! Our Themistocles. How do you do, Sir?" He turned to the friends about him. "The death's-head at our feast."

Colonel Burr inclined his head gravely. I pretended to distract him with an aside; and he pretended to listen to my nonsense.

But Baldwin was not to be stopped. Tearing apart a large roast duck, stuffing chunks of it into his mouth, swilling claret, he gabbled (and gobbled): "Astonishing sight, to see such a man abroad, amongst honest men. With hands—what is the word?—all encarnadined!"

Baldwin suddenly grabbed at his throat; tried to breathe. Could not. He fell forward into the plate of torn duck.

Much confusion. A doctor arrived from the next room. Efforts were made to revive the fat man as he lay on the floor, his head resting on a low spittoon.

The Colonel rose, rather fastidiously. "I do believe, Charlie, that poor Mr. Baldwin is dead." And so he proved to be. "Of *gluttony*." The Colonel shook his head solemnly. "There is a lesson here for all of us," he said at large, and then he led me from the shocked table, as though to preserve my youth from further contagion.

In the street we made a dinner of oysters; and Burr chuckled in a *macabre* way at Charles Baldwin's unexpected departure. The old are merciless.

Later this afternoon, just before Colonel Burr and I began work, I asked about the Michaux expedition.

"Everything went wrong." The Colonel carefully shut the dusty window to keep from circulating a most refreshing breeze. "It is a bit chilly in here, isn't it?" He poked the fire. I sweated in miserable silence.

"You must understand that it was Jefferson's dream to annex Canada, Cuba, Mexico and Texas. He also favoured some sort of dominion over South America, as did Hamilton, as did I."

"It seems like a lot of territory for a republic to govern."

Burr grinned. "Republics can change form quite as rapidly as empires. Look at France under Bonaparte. The only true republican of us all was little Jemmy Madison." Burr opened a thick file of papers. "Whom we shall consider today. I have been making notes."

Memoirs of Aaron Burr—Seven

I FIRST MET JAMES MADISON when I was thirteen years old and in my first year at the College of New Jersey (as I continue to style what is now Princeton College). This was in 1769. Madison was five years older than I but somewhat less precocious (that is, neither his father nor grandfather had been president of the college, a fact that had made it possible for me to begin my career as a sophomore).

I graduated in 1772. Madison graduated in 1771 but remained on for another year, preparing himself for the ministry. He belonged to a wealthy Virginia family and, as far as I know, did nothing much beyond desultory study at home until 1775 when he became a member of the Committee of Public Safety for Orange County. A year later he was drafting the state constitution, to which he contributed a "radical" clause insuring religious freedom. It was briskly rejected by the Virginians.

From 1780 to 1783 Madison was a delegate to the Continental Congress where he became a master of parliamentary procedure and able at last to bring his considerable if somewhat eclectic learning to bear on the urgent matter of framing that triumph of the lawyer's peculiar art, the American Constitution. For good or ill, this document is largely Madison's creation.

Even more important than the putting together of the Constitution was the ability with which Madison defended it in the so-called *Federalist* papers and the cunning with which he got the reluctant Virginians

to accept the federal republic. In fact, so brilliant was
Madison's advocacy (and so bitter his enemies as a
result), that he lost a bid to be the first senator from
Virginia. But he did contrive to win election to the
House of Representatives in 1789, defeating James
Monroe.

Because Madison was so small and so insignificant-
looking, people tended to ignore him until he began
to speak (in a voice nearly as weak as Jefferson's);
then, very gradually, listening to him, one became most
vividly aware of what a great little man he was. Yet
I confess I never dreamed that he would be president.
Neither perhaps did he. His elevation was Jefferson's
work.

When I was thirteen and Madison was eighteen I
was as tall as he. Full grown, he was smaller than I.
We were not intimate at Princeton. For one thing, he
was a strange pale youth, all head and no body, addicted to theology—a subject with which I wanted
nothing ever to do. Then I was worldly while he most
definitely was not. As far as I know he had no inter-
course with a woman until, in his thirties, he became
enamoured of a sixteen-year-old girl at New York.
Eventually the girl threw him over for a young minister. From that time on Madison was everyone's
bachelor friend, and deeply sad.

After the plague summer of '93 the government
re-assembled at Philadelphia, and though some 4,000
people had recently died, everyone in society was remarkably gay. Between the theatre and Ricketts' Circus
and the receptions *chez* Madame Bingham, Philadelphia was a sort of provincial Babylon, reborn after
Jehovah's wrath and every bit as impenitent as the
original no doubt would have been.

On May 18, 1794, my wife Theodosia died, after a
long and vicious illness that destroyed mind as well
as body. For her sake, I was glad the suffering was at
an end; for my own and that of our daughter, I was
much shaken, and could not believe that I would not
know her ever again.

At the end of May, while I was still in New York seeing to my late wife's affairs, James Monroe was appointed minister to France, a post that both Madison and Monroe insisted should go to me. The President said no, at Hamiltonian length; he was willing, however, to appoint either Madison or Monroe. Madison refused. Monroe accepted. Later, at Monrovian length, the new ambassador explained to me that I had been rejected on *regional* grounds. Apparently the post had first been offered New York's Robert Livingston. When he refused it, the President did not want to offer it to another New Yorker, thus giving the impression that this particular embassy was somehow exclusive to New York. Monroe actually expected me to believe this nonsense.

I daresay I shall never know the actual story. After all, it was years before I discovered the role Monroe played in denying me certain southern votes in the vice-presidential election of 1792. I was, he felt, too young. This no doubt was true but in that case why had he agreed to support me?

It is hard now-a-days when senators are so splendid and ambassadors so obscure to realize what the possession of an embassy meant to us. For one thing it took one away from America, a considerable pleasure (publicly denied by all ambassadors from Franklin to Adams to Jefferson to Monroe to Jay) but no less true despite their solemn patriotic demurs. To represent the American republic at a foreign court was a marvellous thing to do. Also, practically speaking, the existence of the United States depended on playing off the European powers one against the other. To be one of thirty senators was simply to be a single "aye" or "nay" in a chorus. To represent the republic in France was to be the republic personified and decisions made by the ambassador could affect the whole world—witness, Livingston's manoeuvring that ended with Jefferson's purchase of Louisiana.

I was deeply disappointed, and said so to Madison as we walked away from Congress Hall in Chestnut

Street. Conversation was not exactly easy. Fearing a
recurrence of fever, we spoke through camphor-soaked
handkerchiefs.

Madison was distressed for my sake; but he was also
placating. "Monroe has many gifts . . ."

"Name one." I was in no mood for the usual
amenities.

"He studied law with Jefferson." Madison could
always make me laugh.

"All right. I grant you that all-important gift. But
he knows nothing of France . . ."

"If only he knew less! He loves their revolution even
more than Jefferson does. Even more than they do,
I should think. He will never be able to represent us
properly. The way you could."

I do not think Madison was flattering me. In any
case, two years later Monroe was recalled in near-dis-
grace. Furious with Washington, he then wrote as unpleasant an account of that paladin's administration
as has ever been published. Washington never forgave
him. In fact, I am told that the General used secretly
to read and re-read the offending pamphlet, shouting
curses and writing in the margins.

Suddenly Jemmy Madison asked me in his little
voice, "Burr, you are most attractive to the ladies. Pray,
tell me why?"

"Because I treat them as if they were men."

Jemmy gave me an amused frown. "How then, Burr,
does one treat men?"

Madison's wit was amiably dry, unlike the brilliant
humourless Jefferson whose creature, like it or not, he
was. I assumed he liked it. Yet Jefferson's second fiddle,
I always thought, made the better music.

I had been living for some time at a boarding-house
run by a Quaker lady named Mrs. John Payne. Stopping
with Mrs. Payne was her daughter, Mrs. Todd,
widowed six months before in the yellow fever epidemic. Mrs. Todd was a pretty if coarse-looking girl
with thick brows, an endearing husky laugh and rather

too much flesh on her bones for my taste, which often rules me but is no tyrant.

I suppose Mrs. Todd and her mother had designs on me. I was as new a widower as she was a widow. She had a small son; I a daughter. I was a senator and thought to be rich. The two Quaker ladies, in the nicest way, set out to snare me. But I was not for snaring. Yet I liked Mrs. Todd and wanted to be of use to her.

After the Senate sessions I would drink coffee with the two ladies in their parlour, and Mrs. Todd would ask me about the political happenings of the day and I would answer, as brightly as I could, realizing that her interest was not in the politics but in the personalities of the politicians. Yet she was not ignorant. She enjoyed the play of politics; she was also moderately well-connected; her mother was related to Patrick Henry while her fifteen-year-old sister had, scandalously, run off and married a nephew of President Washington. For all practical purposes, however, these relationships were much too tenuous and the ladies themselves much too poor to give them entrée at the Tuesday levees of King George and Queen Martha. Without an important marriage, Mrs. Todd was doomed to obscurity, and not-so-genteel poverty.

At Mrs. Bingham's house, I stopped, ready to go in.

"Oh, Burr!" Jemmy looked up at me with the saddest expression. "Another *voluptuous* evening!"

"Share it with me. Come in. Mrs. Bingham will be delighted."

Madison shook his head. "No one is ever delighted when I join the ladies."

"Is this self-pity?"

"Of the most profound order."

Then it was that inspiration seized me. "Come to Mrs. Payne's boarding-house tomorrow evening." I gave him the address. "There is someone I want you to meet."

"He wants to be a postmaster."

"*She* wants to meet James Madison."

Jemmy gave me a look of perfect disbelief. "My dear Burr, no woman has ever wanted to meet me, and at my advanced age it is not likely that any woman will."

I must say I privately agreed with him. He was forty-three (which I thought old); he was also dwarfish, and shy with women. But I have always enjoyed giving pleasure to others. I was certain that Mrs. Todd would overlook his appearance and manner, and if she were not wise enough to understand the depth of his intelligence, she was clever enough to know that the most powerful member of the House of Representatives (and lord of that fine estate Montpelier) was a bachelor, and lonely.

The evening is now history, and I have not much to add to what everyone knows. My servant Brooks prepared a dinner for four: Mrs. Todd, her duenna Mrs. Lee, Madison and myself. According to legend, Madison is supposed to have asked me to present him to the beautiful Mrs. Todd. This is not true. I simply told Madison that the lady would like to meet him and then I told the lady that he would like to meet her. These two amiable lies got them off to a splendid start and there is some evidence that neither knows to this day that the other did not request the meeting. It was all my work as Eros.

Mrs. Todd glittered at the elegant table Brooks had set up in the front parlour (Mother Payne was presented and then set about her business). At first Madison was shy but Mrs. Todd soon warmed him up, filled his glass again and again with my best claret. She was very much the Quaker girl *en fleur* that evening (this was long before she took to wearing expensive clothes from Paris, not to mention those exotic turbans which, as Dolley Madison, she has made her emblem).

But Dolley did delight Madison when he asked if he might take snuff and she graciously allowed him to. When he had finished whisking his small mouse nose with a huge lace handkerchief, she said, "And what about me, Mr. Madison?"

To Madison's astonishment, Dolley took a pinch of snuff, as unheard-of in those days for ladies as now; and with a snort said, "It is to ward off the fever."

Dolley has always struck a fine balance between the bold and the maternal, and no man can really resist her when she means to charm which is most of the time. Over the years she has proved to be as loyal a friend to me as possible. She was most devoted to my daughter.

The Madisons were as *good* a couple as ever occupied the president's mansion. Recently a friend saw them at Montpelier where they now live, age, die. The pale fragile little Madison was stretched out on a sort of day-bed.

"Don't speak," said our common friend, wanting to be helpful. "Not while you're lying down."

To which Madison replied in a perfectly normal voice, "My dear fellow, I always talk more easily when I lie."

Sixteen

FOR OVER A WEEK I have had no chance to continue with Colonel Burr's reminiscences.

On July 12, Madame filed suit for divorce, naming one Jane McManus as his principal mistress. Other adulteries were noted in the interest of verisimilitude. Madame also filed a separate petition requesting the court to keep her property out of the Colonel's hands. In fact, she has hurled a vast amount of law at the Colonel who is now furiously counter-suing, naming all sorts of lovers. This activity has rejuvenated him to such a degree that he does not require a fire in the office.

"She claims I spent thirteen thousand dollars of her money! If only I had!" The Colonel has every state divorce statute in front of him on the baize-covered table. "I have never taken a penny that was hers. Quite the contrary." He had obviously forgotten the sale of the carriage and horses, the money from the toll-bridge shares. But then I have noticed that whenever Burr contemplates money—spending it or borrowing it—he becomes irrational.

Madame's choice of lawyer has particularly incensed him. "What a sense of fitness that woman has displayed!" As all New York now knows, Madame has engaged for counsel the young Alexander Hamilton. "I am half-tempted to name the dead, too. God knows she knew the original Hamilton in the Biblical sense."

"When was that?" My fingers itched for pen and paper but he no longer has time for the past.

"Madame has led a life even more gallant than my own. Well, the world shall know it!"

After I had helped him draft several indictments of his wife's behaviour, he set out for Jersey City, leaving me with Mr. Craft who simply shakes his head and murmurs, "Those who would roll in the gutter . . ."

Seventeen

TOGETHER WITH LEGGETT I rolled in the gutter last night.

For two days the Abolitionist leaders have been attacked by mobs. Leggett wants to know who is inciting them. "I suspect the Whigs."

"You always suspect the Whigs," I said. Actually

the movement to abolish black slavery in the south is
deeply unpopular. It is not that New Yorkers so much
like the institution of slavery as they dislike the sort
of righteous people who want to abolish it.

We were in Centre Street, the heart of the Negro
neighbourhood and close to the Five Points. Just opposite us was the Episcopal African church whose
pastor the Reverend Peter Williams came out to greet
Leggett.

The pastor feared that his church would be the next
to suffer. He is a small black man with an insinuating
voice, and a gift for politics. Understandably he was
frightened. "They attack *us* when the ones they ought
to be attacking are white radicals."

"But surely *you* want slavery abolished in the south."
Leggett was the questioning journalist.

"I *want* it, Mr. Leggett, but I am not about to lend
myself to violence, and that is what it will come to."

As the streetlamps were lit in the spreading twilight,
shutters began to slam up and down the street. Slam
only to re-open a crack as the black population kept
an eye out to see if the enemy was near. The enemy
was. We could hear the sound of a drum's irregular
beat in the Five Points, of Irish voices raised in songs
of the most bloodthirsty sort.

Friday evening a meeting of Abolitionists in the
Chatham Street Chapel was attacked, and an attempt
was made to kill the brothers Arthur and Lewis Tappan
who are the leaders of the movement in New York.
Luckily the Tappans were able to escape without injury. Lewis Tappan's house, however, was burned down.

Last night it was rumoured that the mob was planning to make a clean sweep of every known Abolitionist
by setting fire to their houses and their churches (most
of these high-minded meddlers are clergymen; I have
not Leggett's enthusiasm for the movement). As it
proved, the mob was not so ambitious. But they did
attack the Episcopal African church.

The half-dozen policemen who had been called out

to guard the church quietly vanished as the now familiar mob (I am beginning to recognise some of those b'hoy faces) came roaring toward us from the Five Points.

As the mob stormed the church, its pastor vanished into an alley. Windows were smashed. The door stove in. The pews thrown out the window and set afire in the street. They do hate the blacks, the poor who are white.

Flames appeared in the empty windows of the church. The bonfire of pews in the street cast a terrible glare over everything and everyone, including Leggett and me who were promptly recognised as not of the mob and so hostile. In an instant we were overturned —there is no other word for it—by a dozen demented-looking youths.

Soaked with mud and bloody chicken feathers (as luck would have it we were rolled in the gutter just in front of a poultry shop), we ran as fast as we could: not even the belligerent Leggett was willing to face that mob.

Since my boarding-house was closest, we went there; and while the landlady got us hot water, she swore that she too had been assaulted the month before—the word "assault" in her loose-toothed mouth carried with it the awful spectre of Sabine lewdness—by rioting stone-cutters.

"If I was the Mayor, I'd shoot every last one of them Abolitionists who is burning down the city." Hating the Abolitionists, Mrs. Redman has, like so many simple people, confused them with their persecutors.

Leggett and I removed our be-feathered suits and handed them over to Mrs. Redman to clean; then, in our shirts, we washed up as best we could.

Leggett's hands were not steady as he scrubbed at his shirt front. But then neither were mine. Yet I could not help but notice how heavily he was breathing and how the skin of his stocky bare legs resembled —well, the tallowy skin of a freshly plucked chicken. Chickens are still on my mind.

I found some Dutch gin and we toasted the Abolitionists. The hot night was filled with shouts and
screams and the noise of glass breaking while through
the open window we could see, over the dark rooftops,
the pretty pink glow of a church burning in the next
ward.

"The whole city could come to a stop." By nature I
am more alarmed than Leggett by the thought of
anarchy.

"Unlikely." Shirt unbuttoned, Leggett leaned back
on the bed; his hairy muscular chest glittered with
sudden new sweat. The lungs within are torn past
mending. Conscious of the dying body on the bed, I
looked away, embarrassed by death. Luckily he had
no clue to what I was thinking. He takes for granted
the blood he spits, the sudden chills, the sick sweating.

I showed Leggett certain of these pages and explained to him that I was, like it or not, assembling
a memoir of Colonel Burr, in his own words. Leggett
was delighted by the letter that established Burr's
presence near Kinderhook at the time of Mrs. Van
Buren's impregnation with the future vice-president.

"But that's it, Charlie! He was there! You have the
proof. What more do you need?"

For once I was able to laugh at Leggett. "We lawyers
have different standards from you journalists. This is
no proof. It is merely circumstantial."

"But what circumstances!" Unconsciously Leggett
was massaging his chest with an odd circular movement, as though trying to help the lungs do their
work. "That letter as well as a few reminiscences from
Colonel Burr on the subject of his protégé . . ."

"He hardly ever mentions him . . ."

"Well, that's your fault. Be guileful. He wants vindi-
cation, doesn't he? He as much as admits it to you and
Davis. And he certainly wants to be thought a power
to the end. So get him to tell you how he was the one
who launched Matty Van in politics, how he was . . ."
A sudden quick spasm, a contraction of the entire body
stopped Leggett in mid-sentence. He gasped. Seemed

to hold his breath. "No cause for alarm," he mumbled at last. "But I will rest a bit." He fell back onto my bed, and there remained in a drugged sort of sleep the entire night.

I curled up in a chair and wondered if I would find my guest alive in the morning.

Leggett woke me up. He was fully dressed and looked in perfect health. "It's dawn. My wife'll be worried. Thanks for the bed. Start on the pamphlet now. Right away. We must have it ready before the convention, before October. If you don't feel up to writing it alone, we can do it together."

Leggett was gone. It is July. How can I be ready in three months with so much unknown?

Eighteen

THE COLONEL IS HAVING second thoughts about his counter-suit. "Perhaps it is not the gentlemanly thing to do."

I give no advice. Not that he wants it; he talks often to himself with me as mute audience.

"Yet it is a blow, that petition, as if I wanted to take her money. But then she thinks the rest of the world like herself. In her day she took money from everyone. From me. From Hamilton. And we never —I never—asked for it back."

"Did Hamilton?"

But the Colonel did not hear me. "When that first French lover of hers turned her out, I gave her the money to keep her from debtors' prison, and never asked for a penny back. But she is what she is. I am what I am."

The Colonel stopped abruptly; pushed aside the various depositions on the baize-covered table.

"Let us turn to less weighty matters. Let us consider the home life of Massa Tom, in the autumn of 1795."

Memoirs of Aaron Burr—Eight

DURING THE LAST SESSION of the Third Congress I led the battle in the Senate against ratification of Jay's treaty with England. The treaty was clumsily drawn and to our disadvantage. It actually contained a clause forbidding us to export cotton in *American* ships. In effect, the treaty made us a colony again. It also revealed for the first time the deep and irreconcilable division between the Republican and the Federalist parties—and they were now actual political parties, no longer simply factions. One was pro-French, the other pro-British. One wanted a loose confederation of states; the other a strong central administration; one was made up of independent farmers in alliance with city workers; the other was devoted to trade and manufacturing. One was Jefferson; the other Hamilton.

Since Hamilton's forces in Congress outnumbered ours, the treaty was duly ratified. I was now accepted as not only first among the Republicans in the upper house (the equivalent to Madison in the lower) but also the leader—with Governor Clinton—of the party in New York state. Meanwhile, I had made a series of personal alliances: with Gallatin in Pennsylvania; with various Edwards cousins in Connecticut; with Jonathan Dayton in New Jersey; with Madison and (I thought) Monroe in crucial Virginia. I had also fought hard for the entrance into the union of Tennessee. This won me the friendship of that state's first representative, who introduced himself to me outside Congress Hall.

"By the Eternal, Colonel Burr, I am your admirer for life!" Andrew Jackson was a handsome, fiery-tempered young man who tended to incoherence when passionate, which was much of the time. He used also to drool at the corners of his mouth, a disagreeable habit since overcome. Jefferson called him "the mad dog."

I gave Jackson a fine dinner party but I don't think he enjoyed the company as much as he did the wines. He disliked Congress and Congress reciprocated. Later Jackson resigned his seat, out of boredom I suspect. Although our friendship was to prove most useful to me in the election of 1800, six years later it was nearly fatal to him, poor man, when I was arrested for treason and he was named my accomplice.

In 1792 the Virginians had promised me that if I stepped aside as vice-presidential candidate for George Clinton they would support me in that position four years later. In politics, as in life, one ought to do what one has promised to do. This has been my Quixotic code. The Virginians, however, were not so— I search for a word. Punctilious? Therefore I thought it time to remind the chief Virginian of the junto's promise.

Yellow fever had broken out in New York City when I left Philadelphia by stage on September 18, 1795. I was accompanied by my valet Alexis. Why is it that a man's servants figure not at all in his story, as told by himself or others? and yet our lives are mostly spent in the company of such true intimates. I have never had a friend as true as the black Santo Domingan Alexis who once—but that is for a different memoir.

By the time I arrived at the "city" of Washington I was feeling curiously stupid. There was a ringing in my ears. I was feverish. Nevertheless, I was taken in by a Miss Duncanson who displayed the courage of which martyrs and saints are made. Anyone else would have turned me out of the house to die in the woods as so many did die during the summer of '93 when, fleeing the contagion in Philadelphia, they were kept at bay with rifles by the country-folk. Even President Washington when he left Philadelphia for Mount Vernon was not allowed to stop in several villages, and

His Mightiness was obliged to sleep not surrounded by adoring subjects but beneath indifferent trees.

When Alexis drew the curtains the next morning and saw my face, he realized that his term of employment was practically at an end. "*Diable!*"

"*Qu'a-t-il?*" I could hardly speak. He brought me a mirror. My face and neck were swollen and the whites of my eyes were as scarlet as those poor Dr. Hutchinson surveyed me with for the last time. Worst, I could hardly swallow, speak.

Miss Duncanson was tact itself. The fever was never mentioned and—not mentioned—amiably did not go to its next phase. I ate nothing; allowed no doctor to bleed me; sprang a new man from my bed a few days later and in perfect health explored the new capital of our country.

I confess that I have never seen such a disheartening wilderness. Parts of the Capitol and presidential mansion were going up, but nothing else. The builders lived in shacks which, at the time of my last visit to the city in 1806, were still intact, still occupied.

I speculated in land like everyone else, including General Washington who had just bought two lots near the Capitol. I put a down payment on a lot near the White House. We were a mad sight! Grown men on horseback riding through dark woods, consulting maps in order to be able to point knowledgeably to this or that section of marshy soil and say, "Now that is the corner of such-and-such a street. Most convenient to the Capitol. I shall build a house—no, an hotel—there." Yet those who persevered in that wilderness made vast fortunes. As usual I did not.

I then rode on to Monticello through a perfect wilderness crossed by some of the most treacherous streams and fords that I have ever encountered.

At about ten in the morning toward the end of September, I stood below the hill on which the mansion Monticello was a-building. All was confusion. A large forge manned (or rather boy-ed) by a dozen black children was turning out nails. The apostle of the agrarian life gaily admitted to now being a wholesale manufacturer.

"I have no choice," said Jefferson who greeted me at the smithy. "The crops pay for re-building the house. The nails pay for groceries. I calculate at my present rate of production I shall be out of debt in four years." I complimented him. I too have had my nail manufactories which were to get me out of debt. But somehow the nails never do the trick.

Jefferson mounted his horse and rode with me up the hill, chattering all the while. He was then about fifty, beginning to go gray, and very stiff with the rheumatism which he was gloomily certain was heralding his life's end.

I was complimented for my opposition to Jay's treaty. "Yours is the finest legal mind in the Senate."

I said that, considering my peers, this compliment was not of the highest order.

Suddenly Jefferson's horse shied. Savagely he jerked at the animal's mouth till blood came with the foam; all the while using his whip until the poor creature was heavily wealed. It was my first experience of the way he always treated horses.

At the top of the hill I was invited to admire what looked to be a Palladian ruin. The main part of the house was half-dismantled. Bricks flew in all directions as walls came down; then, slowly, went up again, according to Jefferson's latest design. "I think there is nothing so much in the world I like as tearing down and building up."

We rode through a meadow filled with brick kilns. Slaves were everywhere, hard at work. I was surprised to see how "bright" they were. I do not know if that word is still in use in the south, but in those days a slave with a large degree of white blood was known as "bright." It made me most uneasy to see so many men and women whose skins were a good deal fairer than my own belonging to Mr. Jefferson.

A number were remarkably handsome, particularly those belonging to the Hemings family whose most illustrious member was Jefferson's concubine Sally, by whom he had at least five children. Recently I learned that Sally is living with one of her sons in Maryland. Apparently the son is now considered white, obliging his mother to keep her identity a secret from their neighbours in Aberdeen.

"I inherited the bright slaves from my father-in-law John Wayles." Jefferson sighed. "It is no secret—there are no secrets in Virginia—that many of them are his children." Sally Hemings was a daughter of Wayles which made her the half-sister of Jefferson's late wife. Certainly the girl bore a remarkable resemblance to Martha Wayles, if the portrait in the dining-room at Monticello was to be trusted. Amusing to contemplate that in bedding his fine-looking slave, Jefferson was also sleeping with his sister-in-law! One would have enjoyed hearing him moralize on that subject.

Sally greeted us at the door. She was a good-looking fair-complected girl. In her role as unobtrusive house-keeper she was exactly what Jefferson wanted a wife to be—submissive, shy, and rather stupid.

"It is plain to me that women are intellectually inferior to men." This was over wine at dinner. "Excepting present company—and I do not subscribe to the Adam's rib theory but to plain evidence." He then made a number of foolish points that I refuted, referring to my own educational experiments with Theodosia who knew far more Greek and Latin—if such knowledge is to be a criterion—than this Virginia farmer and intellectual dabbler. But our discussion was amiable, what I could hear of it for the dining-room rang with the sound of falling bricks, the shouts of slaves, the rumble of carts coming and going.

My fellow guests at table were all neighbours of Jefferson; the sort of Virginia gentry that is rather more drunk than not at dinner's end. Jefferson's daughter Martha presided. Although her husband and a pair of

Jefferson's sisters were in the house, due to illness they did not join us. "I have been doctor and nurse all summer," Jefferson said. Unlike his guests, he drank very lightly of his good French wine, and ate mostly vegetables, a sensible regimen I often follow.

Inevitably, the subject turned to Hamilton. Jefferson was like a man possessed whenever he contemplated his rival. "This colossus of monarchy—and he is a colossus, there is no denying his brilliance. It is self-evident like his corruption and his relentlessness even in what he calls retirement."

I could and did testify to that relentlessness. Hamilton was currently managing a series of Federalist victories in New York state, and our party was in full retreat. As a result, I would lose my seat in the Senate to Hamilton's father-in-law while the governorship would pass from our Clinton to his John Jay.

Jefferson was particularly interested in the fact that Hamilton has at last "revealed his love of force. Who else but a monocrat would lead twelve thousand militia into western Pennsylvania? to capture a few farmers who put up no resistance, who simply do not want to pay his whiskey tax, and should not pay it either."

"The tax is a stupid one," I agreed. Needless to say, I did not remind my host that, as secretary of state, he had raised no objection to the Whisky Tax Act.

"We fought a revolution to put an end to such iniquities."

"So we did. But now we have a Constitution which says most clearly that Congress shall have power to levy and collect taxes, and so the taxes must be paid."

"*Congress*, yes! The Executive, no!" Jefferson was a marvellous nit-picker when he chose. In this instance, however, as in the earlier matter of the Bank, he was laying the ground for the principle of nullification that will, I am certain, eventually disintegrate the union of these states. To Jefferson the Constitution was simply a convenience when it allowed him to do what he wanted to do, and a monarchical document when it stayed his hand. He regarded domestic government as the business of the states and foreign affairs as the business of the Executive, and he was naïve enough in those days to think that the two businesses could be kept separate. Enlightenment came when, as president, he decided to fight pirates in the Mediterranean, to buy Louisiana, to steal the two Floridas and, if possible, to annex Cuba. By the time Jefferson's presidency ended, the Executive was more powerful than it had ever been under those two "monarchists," Washington and Adams.

Jefferson's daughter (who resembled him closely) tried to change the subject but Jefferson was now in full flow. I have not the art to give a proper rendering of his discourse, which came in floods. He seemed to think aloud and, as he did, one was obliged to think *with* him, in the process becoming so much a part of his mind that each time he hesitated for a phrase, one's own brain stopped all functioning and waited upon his to think for us all, to express for us all. What a devilish gift!

"We should have indicted Hamilton as soon as we knew about his friend Duer. I am convinced that Hamilton knew exactly what Duer was doing at the Treasury. They were in it together. Two conscienceless speculators like those informers, Mr. and Mrs. Reynolds!" The bright eyes flashed at me; then looked away as I turned toward him, mesmerized as is the rabbit by the snake. Incidentally, Jefferson had the shiftiest gaze of any man I have ever known. But then after a lifetime of cross-examination in court, I have come to the conclusion that the man who cannot meet your gaze is the one who is telling the truth while the witness who looks you straight in the eye is lying. Naturally, my rule is proved by this one exception!

Conscious of the ladies at the table, Jefferson said no more of the Reynolds *affaire*. Not until much later did I learn the whole strange story of how Hamilton had been black-mailed by this strange lewd couple.

Jefferson now started to muse on the character of Washington, to the delight of the squires (excepting one who, presently, vanished from view beneath the table, signalling the end of our feast).

We moved outside onto the lawn—or rather a section of turf between two roaring kilns. The Virginians were so used to the noise and confusion that they entirely ignored it, as did our host.

Jefferson could not understand Washington's response to the attacks that were now being made more and more frequently not only upon his administration but upon himself. "After all, it is the price of a free press, and small to pay considering the advantages."

"Perhaps," I said, "the President is distressed by the *source* of the attack?"

Jefferson looked at me with true innocence. "Source?"

"Freneau's newspaper was devoted to your interest."

"But surely we must try to strike a journalistic balance at Philadelphia. Besides, I have never complained about Fenno's newspaper and its attacks upon me." On almost every occasion that I spoke with Jefferson, he had bitter complaints to make about the calumnies, heresies, seditions, libels and licentiousness of the "free" press which, on at least one occasion, he tried to suppress.

"A great man ought to ignore such pin-pricks. Washington's place in history is secure—if he is not subverted entirely by Hamilton." Jefferson frowned and then, as bricks cascaded down the side of a near-by wall, he launched into a fine tirade. "I am besieged with visitors from abroad who come not to see me but to see the republic we are making, to see if this sort of life"—he waved his arm to include his mountain top, his kilns, his slaves, his vista of bronze-leaved trees in the valley below—" can be made to work. That a man on his own land—and I want every man to own at least fifty acres, even if the government must pay for it or otherwise acquire it from the Indians to the west—a man and his family on a farm can be entirely self-sufficient, growing their own food, making their own clothes—yes, nails, too! I tell you, Colonel Burr, there is nothing that a man cannot do in this marvellous climate, on this rich earth, and that includes," his voice became solemn, the usual slight breathiness was replaced by an unusual clearness of tone, "the making of a republic, a *true* republic of the kind that no nation —until us—has attempted since classical times. That is why the alliance with France means so much. For we are the only two republics on earth, and we have much to teach one another."

Indeed we had! As we were speaking, a French army officer named Bonaparte was being congratulated in the name of the republic for having opened fire on a Parisian crowd, killing 200 "malcontents"; the eagle had begun that spreading of wings which would presently leave us the sole republic on earth. Yet, finally, who was more truly imperial? Bonaparte with his military conquests now vanished? Or Jefferson with his strategic acquisitions that endure to this day?

The subject of France then suggested the troubles in Santo Domingo to our host's allusive mind. "There is a lesson for us in what is happening." He particularly addressed the Virginians. "Blacks have murdered whites. Slaves have murdered their masters. And I tell you that if we do not find some way of eliminating—gradually—the institution of slavery, our children's children will be slaughtered just the way the French have been slaughtered on Santo Domingo."

I recall this dialogue on a day when New York City is a battle-ground between Abolitionists and their enemies. Both factions are exploiting Jefferson's name. What one would give to have him with us now, trying to explain himself!

Forty years ago, Jefferson was not an Abolitionist, to say the least. He detested and feared what was happening in Santo Domingo. "We cannot condone anarchy —in no matter what cause." He prayed that France would soon restore good government to the blacks of Santo Domingo, even if this meant the restoration of slavery. He saw but one solution to the problem in the United States. "We must ship our black people to the Indies—as well as to Africa—and hope that restored to their original longitude they will enjoy the same freedoms we do, with whatever wisdom we might have imparted to them."

On that note the Virginians wandered inside, and Jefferson offered to show me a plow he had invented; spoke fondly of his grandson. "He is a regular Indian, goes bare-foot in the winter. We have to tie moccasins on his feet."

As we walked, Jefferson discoursed learnedly on Indians. "I think they must be of a similar stock as ourselves. Their intelligence *seems* equal to ours but unfortunately they are slaves to old, bad customs, and so will not work the soil, preferring the aimless life of the hunter. Yet if this American environment has made them what they are, will it have the same effect upon us?"

"Will we become hunters, do you mean? Abandon our cities . . ."

". . . our *farms*." The emphasis was plain. A small sandy-haired boy was throwing stones at the master's recently invented (and highly successful) plow.

Benignly Jefferson watched the boy, his mind on Indians. "Buffon of course was wrong. He thought Indians physically degenerate because they are smaller than Europeans. Which is nonsense. The Iroquois are considerably larger than most Europeans. The lack of facial hair Buffon took to be a sign of effeteness—not noticing how painfully they extract those hairs. He was also confident that their organs of generation are smaller than ours which has not been true in my experience. Has it been so in yours?"

"I fear that my studies along that line are incomplete." My small irony was lost. Buffon was refuted at length.

Then Jefferson referred again to the massacres in Santo Domingo. It was much on his mind. The nightmare of every slave-owner had finally become reality. Not only was it possible for slaves to seize a plantation, they could also seize an entire nation. "It is incredible! Yet how will they govern themselves? How will they survive? For one thing, Negroes are not like Indians, not like us. They have less intellectual capacity than we. Of course I should like to think that it is the fact of their unfortunate condition which has made them stupid. But then how explain the intelligence of the Roman slaves, the *white* Roman slaves? Their condition was the same as that of our Negroes but look at what they accomplished! Why, the slave Epictetus was the wisest man of his time. No. I fear that it is not the condition of slavery itself but some defect in nature that has denied to the Negro the highest intelligence." Jefferson waved at a well dressed black man riding toward us from the woods. "Though certainly in matters of the heart, nature has more than done the Negro justice."

The black man was the renowned Jupiter who was often entrusted with such headful tasks as collecting money from those who bought Jefferson's nails.

Jupiter saluted; reported on a transaction; departed. "White blood," said Jefferson, aware of what I was thinking, "alters them." Jupiter was black as onyx.

I indicated the small boy who was now perilously climbing a tree. "Your grandson is going to hurt himself."

Jefferson flushed deeply. "That is a child of the place. A Hemings, I think."

Since the child was obviously son or grandson to him, I had seriously blundered and, as in law, ignorance is not a defence. It was a curious sensation to look about Monticello and see everywhere so many replicas of Jefferson and his father-in-law. It was as if we had all of us been transformed into dogs, and as a single male dog can re-create in his own image an entire canine community, so Jefferson and his family had grafted their powerful strain upon these slave Africans, and like a king dog (or the Sultan at the Grande Porte) Jefferson could now look about him and see everywhere near-perfect consanguinity.

"We cannot let them go free in their present state." For the first time I detected a certain tentativeness in Jefferson. "How would they live? Who would look after them?" He sighed. "Yet it is wrong that half the population trample on the rights of the other half."

"Do you ever free your slaves?"

Jefferson nodded. "I am about to lose an excellent cook. I told him I would let him go as soon as he teaches my new cook everything he learned with me in France."

"He is superb."

"I know. Unfortunately, he's found an employer in Philadelphia who will pay me for his freedom." Later I discovered that Jefferson never simply freed anyone. On occasion, however, he would allow those slaves who had found employment to *buy* their freedom, usually with money advanced by a future employer. But then the hundred or so men, women and children Jefferson owned at Monticello were his capital. Without them, he would have been unable to till the soil or to manufacture nails and bricks, to build and re-build houses, to write the Declaration of Independence. From all accounts, he was a kind master. Yet today I find it hard to reconcile the Jefferson whom the Abolitionist demagogues enjoy quoting with the slave-owner I saw at home in Monticello.

It was of course Jefferson's gift at one time or another to put with eloquence the "right" answer to every moral question. In practice, however, he seldom deviated from an opportunistic course, calculated to bring him power. The Jefferson who denounced bills of attainder and outlawry when he prepared a draft

for the Virginia constitution in 1783, five years earlier
had declared it lawful for any person to pursue and
slay one Josiah Philips, on a mere supposition of guilt.
Later in life, Jefferson decided that, all in all, such
writs were valuable.

John Marshall once told me that much of the contempt he had for Jefferson derived from the illegal
execution of Philips. "Either one respects due process
of law," said Marshall, "and the right of every citizen
to a trial, or we live in a lawless jungle where any one
of us might be the victim of a mad executive or even
of a wrong majority. In a civilised society, you may not
kill a man because you think him, as Jefferson thought
so many people to be, a bad man."

Jefferson also believed that any soldier who used
"traitorous or disrespectful words" against the authority
of the United States or the legislature of any state was
guilty of a crime. The monarchical Adams concurred,
and this stern inhibition became a part of our military
code in 1776, and was only expunged in 1806.

Presently I shall deal with the Jefferson who brought
me to trial for treason, who fabricated evidence, who
threatened witnesses, all on the ground that we could
not have won the Revolution "if we had bound our
hands by the manacles of the law" and that there are
"extreme cases where the laws become inadequate
even to their own prosecution, and when the universal resource is a dictator, or martial law." Startling
to think that Hamilton thought of me as an "embryo-
Caesar" at a time when Jefferson was that Caesar, born
full-grown and regnant.

But all this was ahead of us. On that pleasant hill-top
we were allies. "Madison came to see me—with the
bride you found him."

"My best work in the Third Congress."

"Madison is a new man, and perfectly content—he
says—to go home for good."

"It will be bad for us if he does. With him gone
from the House, and you from the Cabinet . . ."

"There is only Aaron Burr to defend our interest at Philadelphia." We were now at the edge of the slave cabins. Large women in gaudy dresses washed clothes in tubs. Children played in the dust. Over all presided the kindly figure at my side, glancing at me from time to time; yet whenever I tried to fix his hazel gaze, he would look away like some shy creature of the woods.

It was time now for politics. "You know to what the Federalists owe their recent victory in New York . . ."

"Hamilton!" It was a cry.

"And the incompetence of Clinton," I continued. "Which is why I leave the Senate after next year."

"That is the end of us in Congress!" He played at despair.

I continued. "I plan to return to the state Assembly where I am certain that in two years' time I can obtain a Republican majority."

"You believe such a majority is possible?" Unconsciously, he was clasping and unclasping his two large freckled hands—Pontius Pilate comes to mind (in retrospect!).

"Yes. For one thing Clinton lost us New York rather more than Hamilton won it." I stopped; became direct. "What are your political intentions?"

"I am retired, my dear Burr. Look about you! I have more than enough work up here to last me the ten, the fifteen years of life left me." Actually it was to be nearly thirty years. "The last thing I desire is to hold office." I will not record the familiar speech. Washington, Jefferson and Madison gave it in one form or another at regular intervals throughout their political (and they had no other) lives.

The retirement speech done with, we both continued as if he had not made it.

I continued to the point. "Four years ago I stepped aside for Clinton, with Virginia's assurance that in '96 I would have their support for the vice-presidency."

"It seems to me," Jefferson picked up from the dust

a fallen horse-shoe and examined it with wonder, as
if it were the first of its kind, "that Adams will succeed,
easily, to Washington."

"It may not be such an easy succession." I was able
to tell him something he did not know. "Hamilton is
secretly supporting Pinckney of South Carolina. Hamilton believes that Pinckney is manageable. Adams is
not."

"Pinckney is not electable." The dreamy tone was
now very matter-of-fact.

"I agree. But Hamilton will split the Federalists.
That is our opportunity."

"*Our* opportunity?"

"I assume that you are still interested in the Republican movement."

"Yes, yes, but at a distance . . ."

"And I assume that you will be our presidential
candidate and that I will be—as we agreed—the vice-
presidential candidate."

Jefferson tried to straighten the horse-shoe. "In all
honesty, I would prefer Madison . . . for president,"
he added quickly.

"But Madison prefers you."

A swift bright glance to satisfy himself that Madison
and I had indeed been in communication. "So he does.
But I mean to be firm."

"Then I shall expect you to support Madison and
me."

The horse-shoe, unstraightened, fell to the ground.
"Whatever I can do, Colonel Burr, I will do." The
voice broke with feeling. We shook hands awkwardly.

I spent a pleasant evening with him and his neighbours. He played his fiddle—not as badly as I had
feared. At dawn I departed.

"Whatever I can do, Colonel Burr, I will do."

Yes. Whatever Jefferson could do for himself he did!
He was the Republican candidate for president and,
as agreed, I was the vice-presidential candidate. In the
electoral college Adams was elected president with

seventy-one votes. Jefferson was elected vice-president with sixty-eight votes (in those days the man with the second most votes was automatically vice-president). Pinckney was third with fifty-nine votes, and I was fourth with thirty votes. On the face of it this was to be expected. But when I examined the way each state cast its votes, I learned that I had been given by Tennessee three votes, by Kentucky four, by North Carolina six, by Pennsylvania thirteen, by Maryland three, and by Virginia, by my good friends and allies, only one vote.

"Whatever I can do, Colonel Burr, I will do." I never trusted Jefferson again. But since we needed one another, I pretended to forgive.

Later Madison tried to explain Jefferson to me. "Politically, he thinks you too independent. Personally, he fears a rival."

"He does not fear you."

"Because I am a part of him, and no rival."

"I am?"

"He *thinks* you are, and so he is afraid of you."

"What should I do?"

Madison simply grimaced. Obviously there was nothing to be done with such a man. I shall never know—who will ever know?—what Madison really thought of his remarkable friend.

Memoirs of Aaron Burr—Nine

IN THE SUMMER of 1797 I was involved with Monroe and Hamilton in a curious affair of honour or perhaps it might better be termed an affair of curious honour. Five years earlier when Hamilton was creating his bank and otherwise moulding the republic, Jefferson suspected him of mismanagement at the Treasury. Jefferson persuaded John Beckley, the clerk of the House of Representatives, to conduct a private investigation of his enemy.

I do not know all the ins and outs of the intrigue. I do know that at about this time an unsavoury speculator named James Reynolds was put into prison for having bought up at discount the arrears in pay of various Revolutionary soldiers. Apparently he knew *in advance* what value the Treasury planned to set on those arrears. As a result of this information, Reynolds was able to make a good deal of money before he went to prison.

At Beckley's suggestion, Congressman Muhlenberg and Senator James Monroe paid a visit on Reynolds who hinted that, once free, he could and would implicate Hamilton.

The inquisitors next paid a call on Mrs. Reynolds, a good-looking, low woman who wept a lot; then showed them various slips of paper addressed to her husband, purportedly written by Hamilton in a "disguised hand." So far there was no evidence of any kind. At this point I would have abandoned the chase and I think that Muhlenberg wanted to, but Monroe was dogged. Jefferson used actually to complain of Monroe's honesty. "Turn him inside out, and you'll find not a stain, not a stain!" He would shake his head with wonder.

Monroe, Muhlenberg and a third congressman presented themselves to the Secretary of the Treasury and asked that great minister to explain his connection with James Reynolds.

"If ever there was a guilty man it was that little Creole!" Even in retrospect, Monroe's cold gray eyes shone with delight at the thought of Hamilton's humiliation. "He was speechless. Just think! Hamilton speechless! Finally he said that he would receive us at his house that evening where, in private, he would tell us the truth." Monroe's sudden laugh, quite bereft of mirth, was always a chilling thing to hear.

That evening Hamilton described with remarkable candour how a year and a half before Mrs. Reynolds had come to his house and asked him for aid. Although she was a stranger to him, Hamilton was moved by her story of a cruel husband from whom she wished to flee. Hamilton was also moved by her physical person—all his life he was attracted to women of the lowest class, among them my own dear wife Eliza Bowen. For the record, I was always attracted, when young at least, to older women while Jefferson liked only the sort of pretty woman who was safely married, preferably to one of his friends.

To Monroe's astonishment—and disgust—Hamilton then told how he had gone with money to In-Skeep's boarding-house (a place so obviously devoted to sordid intrigue that one could only assume that it was this very sordidness which made him lustful), and there was received into the bed of Mrs. Reynolds.

"I tell you, Burr, I could not believe my ears! There we were in his wife's parlour. Children's toys on the floor . . ." Monroe shook his head. Hamilton then showed his inquisitors illiterate letters from Mrs. Reynolds. One letter said that her husband had discovered everything and meant to reveal what he knew to President Washington, to Congress, and to Mrs. Hamilton, in that order. The Secretary of the Treasury paid up. At first six hundred dollars. Then four hundred. He was properly bled at regular intervals for almost a year.

So embarrassed and confused were the congressional investigators that they insisted on bringing to a close the confession.

"I then made a report which we agreed not to release to anyone. And Hamilton swore the three of us to secrecy." But of course Monroe immediately told Jefferson what had happened. Jefferson's response was predictable. "Hamilton is corrupt," he told me later. "Why else would he be so willing to plead guilty to adultery? He thinks it the greater sin, and so will divert attention from the lesser—which would end his career."

As soon as Adams and the Federalists came to power, they dismissed Beckley as clerk of the House. Wanting

revenge, Beckley promptly gave to the gutter-journalist
Callender his notes on the Reynolds-Hamilton affair.

In June 1797, the full story of Hamilton's adultery
was published in an anonymous pamphlet, written by
Callender from Beckley's notes and paid for by Jefferson.

A few weeks later, Monroe appeared at my house in
New York where I was camping out. Theodosia was
away; Richmond Hill had been stripped of furniture
to pay creditors; I was a most lugubrious bachelor.

Monroe was deeply agitated. "It is to be a duel, a
duel!" He thrust his face downwards into mine, and
I remarked to myself as always upon the deep cleft
in his chin that made his face look so like an apple.

"Hamilton has called you out?"

Monroe sat with a heavy crash in a chair. Without
asking, Alexis brought him brandy. He drank it down.
"Hamilton came to see me yesterday. When I said
I was in no way connected with this damned pamphlet,
he called me a liar."

"Dear God!" Gentlemen do not speak to one another
in this fashion unless prepared to die; such was our
code of honour in those days. Despite a lifetime
amongst the rich and well-born, Hamilton remained to
the end a strange wild little boy thrust by his bastardy
outside society, forced to rely on his beauty and wit to
get himself what he wanted, usually from older duller
men. I think this constant serving of others savaged
his pride, made him eager to do others damage with
pen, tongue—though never sword.

"I want you to be my second in the duel." Monroe
poured himself more brandy; as Lord Stirling's aide
in the Revolution, he had learned, if nothing else, how
to drink. But unlike the noble lord, he had also learned
to keep his head since it is the aide who must put to
bed the general and see that he is on his horse the
next day.

"I have every confidence," said Monroe gravely, "in
your judgement, honour and friendship to me." I was

deeply moved; quite forgot his role in denying me the vice-presidency five years earlier.

"I accept, of course. But I think this matter can be resolved without relying on—what are the weapons?"

"Pistols." A slight sound, as if Monroe had difficulty swallowing.

"For one thing, I am certain that Hamilton is not as eager to fire those pistols as *we* are."

Monroe looked at me gratefully as I maintained the myth of *our* eagerness to risk death on the field of honour. "It strikes me," I continued, "that we must contrive a statement from you which he can accept . . ."

"I have said all that I can say. I even gave him a written statement, reminding him that at the time of his confession we had simply accepted his word—without proof—that he had been guilty of adultery but not of speculation."

"In other words, you have practically accused him of lying to you."

"Not lying. I simply reminded him that we never demanded *proof*. We just let the matter drop."

I saw the solution. I drafted a message from Monroe to Hamilton, re-asserting his innocence in the matter of the Callender-Beckley(-Jefferson?) pamphlet, and stating plainly that when a gentleman says that he is telling the truth, another gentleman has no choice but to believe him. This was wisely double-edged. "If I know Hamilton, he will be delighted to avoid meeting you."

"Do you think so?" Monroe was unconvinced; no doubt saw himself dead on the Jersey Heights. Who does not respond in this way to the prospect of a duel?

I arranged to meet Hamilton at Captain Aorson's tavern in Nassau Street. The good "captain" was with me in Quebec and so enamoured was he of our gallant youth that his tavern used always to be nearly empty, for strong men feared his reminiscences and fled rather than hear again how he stormed Quebec, marching between—so he tells it—Montgomery and me. Since

I was actually at Quebec, I was spared his memories and so could enjoy the pleasant room undisturbed.

I arrived first, set myself in a quiet corner of the tap-room; ordered tent, a Spanish claret I was partial to in those days (before I understood true claret).

Hamilton appeared a few minutes later, bright as always; a trifle plumper than when he had been in office.

"What a terrible business, my dear Burr! Terrible!" He sat beside me; drank tent, too, with—I noticed— a shaking hand. It was difficult to determine who was the more nervous, Monroe or Hamilton. "You know how much I disapprove of duelling!"

"No, I did not know. I recall that you challenged Charles Lee and lately Commodore Nicholson, and now you are challenging James Monroe."

"But what's to be done? You've seen the libels your Republican friends have written about me."

I told him then how Monroe had assured me on his word of honour that he had not broken his promise to Hamilton.

"Do you believe him?"

"Yes."

"Then who is responsible for what was published?"

"I have no idea."

"Massa Tom?" Hamilton's loathing of Jefferson was palpable in his voice.

"It is pointless to speculate. My only interest, frankly, is preventing a duel between you and Monroe."

"I called him a liar to his face." Hamilton was un-expectedly remorseful for one who regarded himself as always in the right and thus able to say whatever he pleased, no matter how libellous.

"That was foolish of you."

"You honestly do not think him a liar?" Hamilton had immediately seen his way out of the trap, and I helped him to safety. I showed him Monroe's state-ment. He glanced at it (Hamilton read more rapidly than any man I have ever known). He frowned. He smiled. The storm had passed. "I can accept this statement."

"I'll discuss the details with your second."

"This is very good of you, Burr."

"Yes, I know it is."

Hamilton gave me his beautiful boy's smile. "We must not let others come between us." He spoke with what was, for the moment at least, affection.

"How can they?" I asked innocently. "When we are both retired from political life."

"You are a most witty man, Burr. Come. Walk me to the City Tavern."

Together we made our way down Nassau and then across Pine to the Broad Way. It was a slow progress, because half the town wanted to pay homage to the leader of the Federalist party (even though his hold on that party was loosening due to the enmity of President Adams) while the other half found me interesting as a leader of the Republican forces in the state (I had been returned to the Assembly a few months earlier). Although we were political rivals, we were also practising lawyers who had to deal with one another in court and out. I think we actually were, to a point, friends in those days.

Hamilton tried to draw me out on Jefferson, but I took no bait from him. "Obviously I suspected Monroe of publishing the story. But if he is innocent—which we have agreed he is," he added quickly, "then Jefferson is responsible. And I know why, don't you?"

"I don't know that Jefferson has anything to do with it." I was wary.

Hamilton was reckless. "Because of Mrs. Walker."

"And who is Mrs. Walker?"

"Plainly she is the wife of Mr. Walker who was once a friend of Jefferson."

I recalled the gentleman. He had received an interim appointment as senator from Virginia.

"Mr. Walker was angry with Jefferson for not keeping him on in the Senate. As you know, politics for those Virginians is entirely a family affair."

Since Hamilton's father-in-law had only just replaced me as senator, I could not resist, "Unlike New York?"

Hamilton burst out laughing. "Well, let us say there are good and bad families. Anyway, Mr. Walker has disliked Jefferson ever since, and is now putting it about that Jefferson tried to seduce his wife."

"Unsuccessfully?"

"There are always two versions in such a matter. Of the two, the one version that never varies is that of the wife. In her husband's absence, Mrs. Walker virtuously resisted Massa Tom on a number of occasions."

"How long have you known this story?" We were standing in front of Trinity Church.

"Several years."

"Would you—would one of your newspaper writers use it against Jefferson?"

The storm returned to that bright face. We stepped off the busy Broad Way into the shady churchyard. Then, as now, those who wished to speak privately to one another strolled in pairs amongst the tombs.

"I am convinced that, to protect himself, Jefferson struck first at me—a sort of *tu quoque*."

In the green shade we stopped close to the church wall, and Hamilton said something most odd. "I wonder sometimes if this is the right country for me."

"You would prefer to live under the British crown?" I played with him.

"Of course not! But there *is* something wrong here. I sense it everywhere. Don't you?"

I shook my head and said what I believe to be true. "I sense nothing more than the ordinary busy-ness of men wanting to make a place for themselves. Some are simply busier than others, and so will take the higher ground. But it is no different here from what it is in London or what it was in Caesar's Rome."

Hamilton shook his head. "There is more to it than that, Burr. But then I have always thought we might be able to make something unique in this place."

"Our uniqueness is only geographical."

"No, it is moral. That is the secret to all greatness."

"Are great souls *ever* moral?"

"They are nothing else!" So spoke the seducer of Mrs. Reynolds. I should make it plain that I am not one to think such an intrigue of any *moral* importance —rather it was the way in which Hamilton revealed (revelled in?) a sordid seduction in order to cover up what Jefferson and Monroe went to their graves confident was dishonesty at the Treasury. Hamilton demonstrated a perverse—to say the least—morality. But of course his use of the word "moral" was practically theological in its implications; and mine is a secular brain.

Hamilton again thanked me most warmly for my good offices and we left the churchyard together, crossing the exact spot where seven years later I was to place him.

Hamilton's response to the Callender attack was to publish an extraordinary pamphlet in which he revealed to the world his adultery with Mrs. Reynolds while proclaiming his honesty as a public servant.

When Monroe showed me the pamphlet I was certain that someone else had written it but Monroe assured me that it was Hamilton's work. "He has put an end to himself politically," was my first response.

"I would not count on it." Monroe was cautious.

"But he can never be elected to offce."

"Why should he want to be elected? He already controls Adams' cabinet."

"But not Adams."

"He does not need him. He also has the support of that vain old man in Virginia." So Monroe referred to the founder of the Virginia dynasty that would, in time, give to him the crown.

Four or five years ago, crossing William Street, I saw an aged man getting into a carriage. I was struck by the powdered hair, the cocked hat, the black velvet smallclothes. He looked as out of his time as Rip Van Winkle. Then, with a shock, I realized that it was my

one-time friend James Monroe. Yet at first glance what
had struck me most forcefully was the uncanny resemblance he bore to his old enemy George Washington. I am sure that the resemblance was deliberate:
the last of the Virginia dynasty chose to imitate the
first whom he had detested and traduced—no doubt
this elegant performance was a form of expiration.

A few months later Monroe died in the house of
his son-in-law. Like the rest of us, insolvent!

Nineteen

COLONEL BURR HAS DETERMINED not to contest
Madame's suit. "It will be too costly in time, and
we must conserve what's left of my brain." He sat in
the centre of ledgers, newspaper cuttings, packets of
yellowed letters tied with faded silk ribbons (*"love
letters,"* Mr. Craft unexpectedly told me with a most
disagreeable smirk).

Day after day I take down the Colonel's narrative
which now flows so rapidly that I have developed a huge
corn on my right middle finger from the pen's chafing.

This afternoon, before we started work, Burr suddenly mentioned Hamilton. "Somewhere in the text
we must make the point that Hamilton and I continued friends for the next three years until I became
vice-president. We even worked together to create the
Manhattan Company . . ."

"Hamilton was involved with *you?*" This is not the
usual version.

"Oh, yes. The Manhattan Company was most respectable. In those days the city's principal water supply was in the Collect, a large pond that had become
foul. Most people felt that the yellow fever was, in

some way, caused by bad water. After the epidemic of
'98 it was agreed that the city must tap the Bronx
River. I favoured a private company. Others wanted
the city to pay for the new system but even Hamilton
admitted that this could not be done without unpopular taxes—and he was an expert on that subject!
So I persuaded a Federalist legislature to accept my
bill creating such a company, with a most distinguished
board of directors. In fact, at Hamilton's request, I
made his brother-in-law a director. And so we brought
fresh water to the city."

Burr suddenly laughed. "I understand that at Jefferson's request his tombstone tells us that he was the
founder of the University of Virginia. Well, let mine
declare that Aaron Burr with his rod struck the rock
Manhattan and the waters flowed. Drink, O Israel,
of Aaron's water! And drink they do to this day."

Then the Colonel poured himself strong tea, opened
a ledger in which he had made a series of notes, and
for the first time gave his version of what happened
when he and Jefferson were both elected president.

Memoirs of Aaron Burr—Ten

BY THE TIME of the presidential election of 1800 it
was plain to everyone except John Adams that he
would not be re-elected. His administration had been
a disaster, equalled in our history only by that of his
son John Quincy. It is odd that two such brilliant men
lacked so entirely the ability to conduct the public
business with any degree of intelligence or justice. Perhaps it was true that my grandfather had shaped their
characters. If he had, their careers become explicable,
for to the Puritan mind Hell is pre-ordained; therefore
it is impious to tamper with God's earthly arrangements; better to sing hosannas to His celestial arbitrari-
ness.

The Adams *débâcle*—and our opportunity—began

with the various Alien and Sedition Acts. They are
too well known to describe here other than to note
that fearing war with France, the Adams administration pushed through Congress four measures: one,
empowering the president to arrest foreigners in time
of war; two, to make it legal to deport them at will;
three, to lengthen the resident requirement for citizen-
ship from five to fourteen years (this was known
privately as the Gallatin Act—Albert Gallatin had
come to the United States from Geneva, been elected
to the Senate from Pennsylvania, and then unseated
by the Senate, despite my best efforts to save him).
Four, the Sedition Act: forbidden was the publication
"of any false, scandalous and malicious writing" aimed
at the government and its officers.

I was with Hamilton in July of '98 when the Sedition
Act was published. He affected despair. "I have spent
my life trying to prop up the frail and worthless fabric
of our Constitution and now that fool Adams wants
to establish a tyranny."

"Don't worry. He won't have the opportunity. He
has given us the presidency."

"I would not be so certain of that." The rosy face
was suddenly mischievous. "After all, deporting foreigners is a popular thing to do."

"What about arresting editors?"

"Personally I would draw and quarter them, and so
would you. But all may yet be well for us."

A week later I understood what he meant. At the
President's request, Washington took charge of the
army. Hamilton was made second-in-command, with
the rank of major-general. President Adams then proposed that I be promoted to brigadier-general, but
Washington turned me down on the ground that as
a friend of Jefferson I was the sort of crypto-democrat
who would try to overturn the government!

It was Hamilton's intention to promote a war with
France. Then the American army (together with the
British fleet) would attack not France directly but

the Spanish empire, annexing Latin America to the
United States, presumably with Britain's connivance—
a most unlikely prospect.

Fortunately for the Republican party, Adams had
no interest in war. Almost as fortunately, Washington died in December 1799. Then the French Direc-
tory made peaceful gestures and Major-General Hamilton's dream of military conquest à la Bonaparte collapsed, leaving him more than ever bent on punishing
the principal obstacle in his path, John Adams.

Shortly after the New Year, 1800, Jefferson called on
me at Francis' Hotel in Philadelphia where I had come
at his insistence. I had reserved the small side room
for what was bound to be a long meeting. We had a
good deal to say to one another, some of it unpleasant.

From the main parlour one could hear the loud
talk of those members of Congress whose best debates
were not in the Congress but in the unrecorded privacy
of the Francis establishment. They were, all in all,
jovial men to be avoided.

It was a cold day and the Vice-President was dressed
accordingly. The rusty head was framed by furs, the
freckles more pronounced than usual in the winter
pallor of his face.

My hand was warmly seized. Then Jefferson threw
off the fur-lined cape, addressed himself to the Franklin
stove, and thoughtfully explained to me its principle
(which I knew), meditated on Benjamin Franklin's
character (which I also knew), was willing to talk
with ease of everything except the reason why he had
wanted to see me—the alliance between Virginia and
New York that would make him president. Affecting
to be no politician, he was nothing else.

I asked him about Washington's funeral services.
Jefferson was unexpectedly cool. "I was not present.
Here or there. I understand he asked for no funeral
oration at the service."

"But then for ten years he had heard nothing but
eulogy."

"That was not the way he saw it." Then Jefferson repeated to me almost word for word his comments on Washington beside the Schuylkill River. I have noticed that even the greatest of men tend to redundancy. Doubtless, it comes of meeting too many people and having too little that is fresh to say to them.

That season Jefferson had been particularly busy. Outraged by the Alien and Sedition Acts, he had written a secret attack on them in which he boldly made the case for the right of any state to nullify any act of the federal government which it deems unconstitutional. He also made an excellent and highly dangerous case for secession. I was horrified. So was Madison who later told me, wearily, that when enraged Jefferson had no sense at all of what he was doing.

"Genius often expresses itself," said Madison sadly, "in a particularly fierce manner when confronted by sensations of the moment." Most unwisely, the Kentucky legislature accepted Jefferson's formulation (not knowing its author) while Virginia accepted Madison's much more reasonable document. Both resolutions were then presented to the rest of the states for ratification. They were rejected. The other states were unwilling to put an end so promptly to the federal union.

"I was in—I am in a most delicate position. I am a federal officer. Yet I oppose the tyranny of the federal system." Jefferson invariably managed to get himself into the position of double agent. As secretary of state he had agreed to the whiskey tax; then he sided with the farmers who revolted against it. As vice-president, he was now making the case for disunion.

I always found that with Jefferson one had to begin all over again with each meeting in order to establish —not intimacy, but a certain community of interest. I have several letters from him sent at not-too-distant intervals in which he seems to be introducing himself to me for the first time. There was not much *continuing* with him. I daresay this was his policy.

A black servant brought us hot rum, and we both

drank a good deal considering our usual abstemiousness. The arrival and departure of the Negro reminded Jefferson of a bill before Congress to grant limited recognition to Toussaint L'Ouverture, the black master of Santo Domingo.

"We cannot recognise him. Ever. If only for the sake of our French friends." Jefferson was emphatic. Our sister republic (whose motto was liberty, equality, fraternity) must be allowed to crush its black rebels. Meanwhile recognition was out of the question, and for an excellent reason: "Can you imagine what our southern ports would be like? swarming with former slaves *who have killed their masters?*"

We discussed the editor James Callender, who had been arrested under the Sedition Act. "He is sure to be let go." Jefferson was sanguine; loved his creature. Yet the following August, Jefferson told me, sadly, "Poor Callender is in the Richmond jail, waiting to be tried. He reports that he is surrounded by Gabriel Prosser's people, and they keep him awake at night with their singing." Gabriel Prosser had led an uprising of slaves, inspired, according to Jefferson, by the terrible events in Santo Domingo. No one knows how many thousands of Negroes were executed that year by the frightened Virginians.

Jefferson spoke admiringly of Callender's book *The Prospect Before Us,* a vilification of Adams in particular and of the Federalists in general. We speculated what would happen when Callender came to trial. Jefferson was certain that the charges would be dismissed. But he was mistaken. When the trial took place, Supreme Court Justice Chase sentenced Callender to jail for nine months. This trial was to have a considerable effect on our joint destinies.

But to return to our winter meeting in Philadelphia. I observed that the government's arrest of some twenty editors could only help us in the coming election.

"But are these arrests simply the beginning?" Jefferson's face assumed that haunted visionary's look that

I had already come to know—and dread—for it always presaged a denunciation of "heresy," of "monocrats," of "Catalines and Caesars."

"You mean *General* Hamilton?"

"I do. He commands the army. He and he alone. Adams is too weak to restrain him. Washington is dead. Hamilton can seize power whenever he chooses." I did not listen as the familiar tirade swirled about that small parlour in Francis' Hotel.

When Jefferson had finished, I spoke of practical matters. "At the election Hamilton will support Pinckney's brother instead of Adams."

"So I have been advised. Naturally, this will weaken Adams further, particularly in South Carolina." I much preferred Jefferson the work-a-day politician to the inflated *philosophe*. Then: "How do you see your own position in New York?"

Due to the patriotic fervour Hamilton and the Federalists had drummed up, the New York Assembly now had a Federalist majority, and I was out of office.

"I expect to be re-elected to the Assembly on the first of May."

"You are optimistic." Jefferson was not. "It is my impression that New York is securely Federalist, and I expect no votes from your electors."

"You will receive every one of New York's electoral votes."

In theory, Jefferson knew of wit, of irony, of humour, as he knew of the opossum's pouch but like that singularity he could not achieve any of those things himself while, worse, he was never certain when a true specimen was at hand. My manner was constantly puzzling to him.

"You believe that *you* can produce a Republican majority?"

"I do."

"May I ask how?"

"You may." I was now prepared to pay him back for his treacheries. "But I must warn you that although

I expect my state to be Republican, it is by no means certain that you will be the candidate."

Jefferson gave me a hard look. "They would be wiser," he said evenly, "to take Madison." The humility was characteristically mechanical.

"Many would rather take *no* Virginian!"

"I see." I suppose that he did.

"You are also thought to be an atheist."

"My life has been devoted to guaranteeing religious freedom for all people." I feared that he would tell me more; but he cut himself short. "I know that religious bigotry is more acceptable than tolerance at the north where the clergy still govern."

"Then be prepared for their attacks. You are also thought to be a Jacobin who wants to level society, to destroy the rich . . ."

"That rumour will not cost us a vote."

"I agree. You will also be attacked as a libertine."

"By Hamilton?" The scorn was perfect. "By the lover of Mrs. Reynolds?"

"No. By a Mr. John Walker of Virginia."

The pale face blushed suddenly. "I am used to such attacks." He neither answered nor denied the charge. Later he confessed that he had been guilty on one occasion, and only one, of having "offered love" to a beautiful lady—who happened to be the wife of an old friend. At this time I knew nothing of his affair in France with a Mrs. Cosway whose husband, a miniaturist, had been (no doubt in a very small way) complaisant. Eventually all things are known. And few matter.

Having put Jefferson on the defensive, I moved to secure what was mine by honourable agreement: the Republican candidacy for vice-president.

"We have discussed this matter once before, Mr. Jefferson, and I do not mean to weary you, but I shall expect *all* of Virginia's votes to be cast for me, just as you will receive all of New York's votes."

Jefferson stared at the side of the Franklin stove.

The iron glowed red in patches; as if a black man were blushing red. "I think that this business of party is demeaning to all of us."

"None of us likes it. But since you helped devise the rules of the game you must now play accordingly." As if I needed to give the subtlest of our politicians any advice at all. He had already out-played me but I did not know it.

"Am I to understand that you are making a *condition*, Colonel Burr?" I had the full gaze at last.

"I am living up to an earlier agreement, Mr. Jefferson. I expect you to do the same."

"I live up to all agreements to the best of my ability." The gaze stayed upon me. He had made some inner resolve to overcome his natural shiftiness, and stare me down. This was not possible.

"Then you will support me for vice-president."

"I have not that much influence, Colonel Burr."

"What influence you do possess, would you be so good as to bring to bear. Just as my friend Madison—whose word I entirely trust—also intends to do."

The mouth set in precisely the same way it had set when he had beaten so savagely the horse at Monticello. "Influence is not measurable, Sir. I cannot speak for the consciences of other men."

"Then, Mr. Jefferson, you must take your chance as I shall take mine." I played the last of my cards.

"You would oppose *me* for president." I still recall how the freckles were suddenly as dark as plague spots in that ashen face.

"I do not want to oppose you. After all, there is time for me. But if I am again betrayed . . ." The word was said. The response was electric.

"You will have your Virginia votes, Colonel Burr." The eyes left my face. The contest was over. The war had begun.

"And you will have the votes of New York state and the presidency." I humoured him. "I shall simply be your vice-president, waiting to be asked to dinner, to take pleasure in your company which is about all a vice-president can do, as you know better than I. Fortunately, I would rather listen to you talk than to all the music in the world."

Jefferson took me quite seriously; became warm and confiding; led me on. Led me on!

Twenty

I HAVE TAKEN to writing pieces for the *Evening Post* under the pseudonym Old Patroon, a very conservative, very angry, very censorious old New Yorker. Mr. Bryant is delighted, Leggett is amused. "I never thought that beneath your stolid Dutch exterior there was so much fire and fury."

"Nor did I." Apparently everything offends me, including the voices of women raised in song. I have always hated the custom of the ladies coming forward to sing at polite evening parties (of the sort I seldom attend). They shout the house down; they screech; they have no sense of music—worse, they have no shame. They compete with one another to see who can holler the loudest; and we are expected to sit quietly and look as we do in church, beautifully elevated and inspired. My attack on lady singers distressed Mr. Bryant, but yesterday he allowed it to appear and everyone is angry. "The best response," said Leggett.

"I hope so," said Mr. Bryant. "But let your next Old Patroon subject be more . . . anodyne."

The Colonel is amused by Old Patroon. "You have a nice way with our difficult language. Obviously you are to be a writing-lawyer like Verplanck."

I am pleased with the Colonel's praise; but would prefer to be no lawyer at all.

Writing-lawyers made him think of Hamilton. He showed me a cartoon of his rival, holding in his arms a blowzy woman identified as Mrs. Reynolds. "There is a mystery to Hamilton, as there is none to Jefferson who simply wanted to rise to the top. Odd how Jefferson is now thought of as a sort of genius, a Virginia Leonardo. It is true he did a great number of things, from playing the fiddle to building houses to inventing dumb-waiters, but the truth is that he never did any one thing particularly well—except of course the pursuit of power. Yet his exuberant mediocrity in the arts is everywhere admired today, and quite unrecognised is his genius for politics."

The Colonel laid out on the baize table the papers he would need for the day's work. "If I were young and," he grinned, "a *writing*-lawyer instead of a scheming-lawyer, I would do a life of Hamilton and I would go to the Indies and spend as much time as I could trying to find out about a Mr. Nicholas Cruger. He was a young bachelor with a business in that part of the world. When Alexander became an orphan at twelve or thirteen, Cruger took the boy in. They lived in the same house until Hamilton was seventeen or so and came to America to study. Two things amaze. One, at fourteen, Hamilton was running Cruger's business. The other, in later life, Hamilton came to detest his original benefactor. Why? A falling out? The way Hamilton always fell out with his surrogate fathers? Most mysterious. I have my theories but . . ." The Colonel stopped, and before I could get him to expand on those theories he had begun the day's dictation.

Memoirs of Aaron Burr—Eleven

I RETURNED TO NEW YORK STATE to find George Clinton in a bad mood. He disliked Jefferson, would take no part in the election. I was able to change his mind by telling him that I thought Governor John Jay could be defeated, and that I would be happy to take his place. The thought of me as governor aroused the old man wondrously well. He would have canvassed the Sixth Ward on his knees to get me safely out of the state as vice-president.

The Livingstons were useful allies; and as long as one listened attentively to their advice one was not actually bound to take it. Edward Livingston, in particular, was devoted to me, "and if the presidency should ever be between you and Jefferson, I am for you." Fortunately for him, I never held him to his promise.

I had my own Little Band: the Swartwout brothers, Matt Davis, the Van Ness brothers (newly arrived in the law office of Peter Van Ness was a young clerk from up-state named Matty Van Buren), the Prevost family, and so on. Through Davis, I also had some support within the Society of St. Tammany.

Suspecting that Hamilton would nominate a number of nonentities for the various legislative seats, I waited until after the Federalist caucus. When I saw Hamilton's lack-lustre nominations, I knew I would beat him all hollow for I intended to nominate the most famous men in the state as Republican legislators.

General Gates was now living in New York. He still possessed a famous name despite Washington's best efforts to consign him, like poor Lee, to darkness. Gates agreed to stand. So did Washington's postmaster general Samuel Osgood; also Brockholst Livingston—easily the most brilliant member of that family. Finally, I prevailed upon George Clinton to allow his name to go on the ballot. May I say that I could not get these distinguished men to run for such unimportant offices without convincing them first that we were indeed going to win.

"It is madness, Burr, just madness!" Clinton was outraged at having to appear to seek a seat in the legislature. "It looks all wrong for me who am the governor . . ."

"The former governor . . ."

"For me the governor that was to be going to that

Assembly of yours that I never liked, and all for some
Frenchified trimmer of an atheist from Virginia. No,
Sir. Now if it was *you* for president, why, it would be
well worth it, but not for Massa Tom."

It took me a long time but, finally, the governor-
that-was agreed to have his name on the ballot. "But
I won't work to be elected and if anybody asks me
what I think I'll tell 'em I don't want to be elected."
Old Clinton was emphatic. He always made me think
of a dancing bear on a chain: clumsy, clownish, good-
humoured, until he got his arms about you.

I myself stood for election in Orange County where
friends looked after my interests, allowing me time
to organize the city.

From April 29 to May 1, the polls were open. During
this time Hamilton and I shared a number of plat-
forms. Courteously we deferred to one another in public, as each went about the urgent business of defeating
the other. A few weeks earlier, as a demonstration of
our god-like serenity, we even joined forces to defend
a man accused of murder—and we got him off.

By the evening of May 2, it was evident that the
Republican party had swept the city, giving us a clear
majority in the legislature. All twelve of New York's
electoral votes would now be cast for Jefferson and
Burr.

Hamilton's response was characteristic. He wrote a
"secret" letter to Governor Jay, asking him to call an
immediate session of the current legislature (with its
Federalist majority) in order to change the laws of
election. No longer would presidential electors be
chosen by the legislature; rather they would be elected
directly by the people. It is a nice irony that the only
time Hamilton ever sought to broaden the franchise
was to steal an election. Aware of the fraudulence of
what he was proposing, he assured Jay that "scruples
of delicacy and propriety . . . ought to yield to the
extraordinary nature of the crisis." To Jay's credit he
ignored the suggestion.

It is curious how Hamilton (who was capable of

any illegality including a military coup) should have
attached so securely to me the unlikely epithet
"embryo-Caesar." Whatever my ambitions, none was
ever the cancellation of a legal election or the overthrow of the Constitution. I suspect that when Hamilton looked at me he saw, in some magical way, himself reflected. And so if one is an embryo-Caesar,
accuse the looking-glass of that high treason and divert
thereby the wrath of the plebes. Best of all, smash
the glass and free the self therein—to range at will.

At the last moment Hamilton gave us the presidential election just as his inept selection of candidates
had given us the state election. Unable, as usual, to
resist a public expression of his rage, he wrote a pamphlet (his tombstone should have been carved in the
shape of a pen) denouncing John Adams, the leader
of his party. Wiser—and more frightened—Federalist
heads persuaded Hamilton not to publish. But they
could not stop him from printing his pamphlet for
private circulation. Fortunately, Eliza Bowen secured
for me a copy which I then published in the Republican newspaper *Aurora*. President Adams was not
happy; and Hamilton forever after held me (and poor
Eliza) responsible for what *he* had written.

I then travelled through New England and New
Jersey to see what support might be forthcoming. Jefferson by now was entirely happy to leave the election
in my hands. "You have done," he wrote to me from
Philadelphia, "what I thought could not be done" (he
was referring to the Republican majority in the New
York legislature) "and so I leave to you the entire
undertaking, and will not be surprised to see you turn
Massachusetts itself to democracy, clergy and all!"

I did not turn Massachusetts Republican but I did
cultivate those Federalists who disliked and mistrusted
Hamilton. It was later charged that I did this in order
to gain their support for the presidency. The charge
is half true. I *always* wooed Federalists in the general
interest. For one thing I was trusted by many of their

leaders because I was not thought to be a zealot like Jefferson, intent on levelling the rich and exalting the poor.

Jefferson's later charge that I wanted to take the presidency away from him was not unlike Hamilton seeing in me a military adventúrer. Jefferson would never honour an agreement if it was inconvenient and naturally he assumed that I was like himself. But then Jefferson was not, even in Chesterfield's sense, a gentleman (of the Virginians only Madison qualified); unfortunately, I was one, or did my best to be. I worked only for what we had agreed upon at Philadelphia, the ticket of Jefferson and Burr.

The summer and autumn of 1800 were the busiest time of my life, and a torture to both Jefferson and me, as well as to poor John Adams. I had thought to secure New Jersey to us, but that state went Federalist as did Connecticut. By late autumn the struggle was now centered upon Pennsylvania, where all was confusion, upon Rhode Island which tended to be for us, and upon South Carolina which had the dubious fortune to be the home of the egregious Pinckney brothers, the second of whom was, thanks to Hamilton, an active national candidate.

Jefferson was in despair. I did my best to cheer him: "With Rhode Island, you will still have a majority," I wrote. But he was no more convinced of the certainty of his election than I was convinced that I could rely on the Virginians to honour their commitment to me. Fortunately, I had an ally in James Madison. He forced the southerners, as a point of honour, to support me.

At the beginning of December, Pennsylvania chose a legislature in which Republicans outnumbered Federalists by a single vote. South Carolina voted last. It was now plain that Jefferson would be president; but if South Carolina voted for their own Pinckney, he (or Adams) would be vice-president. Happily, I had sufficient friends and allies in that charming state. As a result, South Carolina's electoral votes were cast entirely for Jefferson and me. We had won the election —with the aid of Alexander Hamilton's busy pen.

I was at Richmond Hill when the word came of South Carolina's vote. The Little Band was ecstatic. But I was not. I knew something was wrong. I excused myself and went immediately to the upstairs study where I sat down with a copy of Blackstone's on my knees (my desk had been sold) and began to add up the electoral votes for all the United States. My apprehension was justified. Jefferson: 73. Burr: 73. Adams; 65. Pinckney; 64. Jay: 1.

Jefferson and I had tied, and the Federalist House of Representatives would now have to choose between us for president. A second scrutiny of the figures proved that the election had been decided by the electors of New York state. Without New York, Jefferson was seven votes short of his total in '96 while Adams, without New York, had gained nine votes. No matter what happened in the House of Representatives, I had carried New York and New York had decided the election.

I slept remarkably well that night, and woke the next morning to find that we had been splendidly snowed in. It was like Revolutionary days, and I was young again.

At about this time Jefferson wrote me one of his most disingenuous letters. He congratulated me on my victory. Noted that the vice-presidency was a higher post than any he could offer but regretted deeply "the loss we sustain of your aid in our new administration. It leaves a chasm in my arrangements which cannot be adequately filled up. I had endeavoured to compose an administration whose talents, integrity, names, and dispositions should at once inspire an unbounded confidence in the public mind. I lose you from the list, and am not sure of all the others."

This was a most gracious tribute from a man who has since claimed that he *always* mistrusted me, and doubted my integrity. The date of the letter was significant: it was just before South Carolina had voted. I am convinced that Jefferson had made an arrangement (or had heard that some arrangement was being made) that would have resulted in my losing the vice-presidency to Adams or Pinckney. The letter was to forestall my anger with the promise of a Cabinet post. Fortunately I was strong in South Carolina, and got the same vote he did.

The Federalists were in a turmoil. There were those who inclined to me on the ground that whatever my faults of character (and Hamilton saw fit to describe these, I later learned, in alarming detail to every congressional leader of weight), I was not a fanatic like Jefferson. At worst, I was suspected of being a Bonaparte. This was bad enough. But Jefferson was suspected of being a Robespierre, and that was worse.

I moved as swiftly as I could to see to it that no one put me forward as a possible alternative to Jefferson. It was of course feared that the Federalists in Congress might entirely go mad and, exploiting the ambiguity of the Constitution, elect a president *pro tem* who would then, if the ambiguity was acceptable, become president instead of Jefferson or me.

Having effectively destroyed Adams and split his party, Hamilton was now forced to choose between Jefferson and me, the two men he most despised and feared. Curiously enough he preferred Jefferson to me, the fanatic leveller to the Caesar-self in the looking-glass. In a perverse and bitter way, denying me the presidency was like denying himself, and he was a born destroyer of his own interest. Yet a sane man choosing between what he thought to be a fanatic and a political adventurer would obviously choose the adventurer who was known to practise the arts of accommodation. In any case, let it be said once and for all, I would have refused the presidency on the practical ground (putting aside honour like a Virginian) that it was plainly the sense of the people of the United States that Jefferson be the president and that to usurp his rightful place would have made it impossible for me to govern. Also, at the age of forty-five, I expected the highest office to come to me in due course as it had come to previous vice-presidents, not to mention as a reward for my having won for the Republican party its first national election. I did not know that once Virginia again had control of the Executive, she would not give it up for a quarter-century.

Finally, with the French republic in the hands of a military despot and our own Constitution looking more absurd than ever, any sudden illegal—or rather immoral—exertion on my part would have torn apart our new republic.

I despatched several letters to Washington. The letter to Samuel Smith of Maryland was published. In this letter I disclaimed firmly all competition with Jefferson. I thought that was that.

In January, I went to Albany to take my seat in the Assembly where my days were devoted to the contemplation of New York's ˙canals and inland waterways, and my evenings to the charms of boarding-house life. Hardly what an intriguer would have done.

Curiously enough my only serious tempter was Theodosia. The night before she was to be married to Joseph Alston of South Carolina, she came to my room for what I took to be a last meeting with her father as a virgin—this sentence is all wrong, Charlie, but I do like it!

I was closetted with John Swartwout who had also been elected to the Assembly. We were studying the latest newspapers from the south, as well as a long memorandum from a persistent admirer at Washington who wanted me to make myself available to the Federalists, and so become president on the first ballot. Swartwout and I were discussing this letter when Theodosia joined us. John turned to go.

"No, no! Please!" She put her hand on his shoulder: she was like a sister to the three Swartwouts. "I've been listening to the two of you in the next room."

"Then I have failed as a parent."

"Quite the contrary! You have made me wiser than you."

"She is to be married tomorrow," I said to Swartwout, "and so is crazed with vanity. The fit will pass."

"It will not!" I realized then that this was not her usual banter. She turned to Swartwout. "He must be the president. He has no other choice."

Swartwout was as taken aback as I by her vehemence. I remonstrated. "It is not possible."

"Of course it is possible, if you want it! Write Congressman Bayard tonight, tell him what he wants to hear. He'll get you Vermont on the first ballot. He can bring you Maryland."

"Why are you suddenly so interested in the grubbier aspects of political life?"

"Because I am interested in you and I know that this is the only opportunity you will ever have to be first, and if you don't take it you will regret it as long as you live."

I was overwhelmed by her so uncharacteristic passion. "Child, I have given my word to Jefferson."

"Break it! He will deeply respect you, as he is bound to respect any bold gesture. He betrayed you four years ago, and he will do it again, if he can. So *remove* him."

"The people want him . . ."

"The people will want you when they know you better. You admire Bonaparte. Well, think of him. He took his opportunity and now he is the first man in Europe just as you can be the first man in America, and may God strike us where we stand there is no point to being second."

"I think I made you read too much Plutarch."

Theodosia laughed. "I learned that the wise man does what events compel him to do . . ." She indicated the admirer's letter from Maryland.

"I cannot break my word."

"Then you will regret that you did not all your life."

Like the Sybil at Cumae my daughter stood before the prophetic fire and I, foolishly, thought her deranged by the excitement of her approaching wedding.

"You would now, I assume, enjoy your father's words on the subject of marriage, and the brute needs of the male."

Theodosia smiled; was no longer Sybil but her usual gay self. "The Senior Miss dePeyster has told me all that I need to know. During the worst of it I am to pray in a very loud voice. This is certain to shame the brute."

"Amen," I whispered. We laughed. She was married the next day. I made no move to gain the presidency. I behaved honourably and, as Theodosia foretold, I have regretted it all my life.

On February 11, 1801, the ballotting began. Each state delegation cast one vote. Had the president been chosen by a majority of the members of the House of Representatives, I would have been elected, despite all my protests, on the first ballot with fifty-five votes to Jefferson's fifty-one. As it was, of the sixteen states in the union, Jefferson won eight (New York, New Jersey, Virginia, Pennsylvania, North Carolina, Kentucky, Georgia and Tennessee). Six states voted for me (Massachusetts, Connecticut, South Carolina, Rhode Island, New Hampshire and Delaware). Vermont and Maryland were divided evenly between us. There were nineteen ballots on the first day, and no resolution. To a man the Federalists had disregarded Hamilton's advice, and were determined to support me as the lesser of the two democratic evils.

On the second day of the ballotting Jefferson made a note in his journal about the Federalist representative Bayard. As the lone representative of Delaware, Bayard was the key to the election. According to Jefferson, Bayard offered Smith of Maryland any appointment he wanted in a Burr administration. Fortunately, Smith was still alive when Jefferson's comment was published, and he denied it on the floor of the Senate while

Bayard used often to say, "The means existed to elect Burr, but he would not cooperate." And because I would not so much as lift a finger, the election went to Jefferson after a dead-lock of seven days.

Meanwhile, Jefferson presiding over the Senate in the next chamber of the unfinished—ever to be finished?— Capitol was not above meddling in the matter, despite all protestations that he had never sought the office, and so on.

Jefferson told me at our first private meeting after the inaugural that when the Federalists threatened to interpret the Constitution to mean that Congress had the power to disregard both of us and choose any one of its number as president, "I instructed Mr. Adams that if his party attempted to do any such thing, the middle states would go into insurrection, and with guns see that the people's will be done." I do not know John Adams' response. I can guess it. Like so many bookish men who have never been in battle, Jefferson enjoyed the threat of bloodshed.

Proudly Jefferson told me that he had been approached by Bayard who agreed to support him if he would promise not to dismiss certain Federalist office-holders. "I told Mr. Bayard that I could not in conscience make such a promise in order to gain an office I did not seek. General Smith made the same request, and received the same answer."

Some years later General Smith swore that Jefferson had agreed to the *principle* that officers of the government ought not to be let go on political grounds. With this assurance, Bayard had then allowed the presidency to go to Jefferson—who dismissed every Federalist office-holder he decently could, except those he had privately promised Bayard to retain. He was never *not* in character.

Twenty-one

I HAVE SHOWN these last few pages to Leggett who predictably seized upon the reference to Van Buren. "Pursue the matter!" We were in his office at the *Evening Post*.

"Certainly not. When I pursue, I learn nothing."

Mr. Bryant entered. I rose respectfully. "Ah, the biographer of Colonel Burr." Apparently that is now my principal identification.

"Charlie is unearthing all sorts of fascinating things."

Mr. Bryant looked pained. "I cannot help but think, Mr. Schuyler, that the Colonel's intrigues are best forgotten."

"I disagree, Mr. Bryant."

"Of course. Of course." The great man backed away. Like Washington Irving, he suspects that his hero Jackson is going to be revealed as a traitor to the union along with Henry Clay. If they were indeed conspirators with Colonel Burr nothing would give me more pleasure than to publish the fact.

Mr. Bryant gave Leggett a slip of paper. "Tomorrow the Vice-President will give an address on democracy."

"I shall be there, in workie disguise."

"There is also a reception for him this afternoon at the American Hotel." With a bow, Mr. Bryant vanished.

Leggett stood up. "It's time you met the man we are about to destroy."

THE ASSEMBLY-ROOM at the American Hotel was crowded with politicians. Every Democratic office-holder in the city was there as well as the leadership of Tammany. Sam Swartwout was moderately drunk and until the Vice-President arrived, the centre of attention.

Leggett and I stood on a small dais at the far end of the room and so had an excellent view when the doors were thrown open and a Tammany lout bellowed, "The Vice-President!"

Martin Van Buren appeared in the doorway. The slanting rays of the sun struck his golden hair so as to make him seem positively a figure of gold, of fire.

For a moment there was absolute silence in the room. Then the small, elegant, graceful figure proceeded slowly through the crowd that parted for him. He was superbly dressed (Helen has taught me to note such things); his suit a rich dark brown with a velvet collar; heavy lace fringed his cravat; yellow kid gloves held in the left hand; morocco leather shoes. As Van Buren turned this way and that, shaking hands, a half-smile on his lips, I had the dizzying sense of all power being concentrated in one small frame.

When the Vice-President saw Leggett, the smile widened. "Mr. Leggett." The small hand darted forward; touched Leggett's hand; was swiftly withdrawn (the professional politician's way of avoiding having his hand crushed). "How does Mr. Bryant?" Yes, Van Buren lisps; he also speaks with a slight Dutch accent.

"Very well. He applauds your every move, excepting your recent support of slavery in the south."

The challenge went entirely unremarked. Van Buren turned to me. Leggett pronounced my name. I felt giddy as the small hand briefly touched my own. We are exactly the same height. For an instant, we were so close to one another that I literally got his scent, a combination of Spanish leather and expensive snuff.

"Mr. Schuyler is a clerk in the law office of Aaron Burr." Leggett did his bad-actor imitation, the voice deepening melodramatically on "Aaron Burr." But the Vice-President's face and manner betrayed nothing at all. He simply looked at me politely. The large golden eyes are exactly like Aaron Burr's but drained of darkness. "How does Colonel Burr?"

"Oh, very well, Sir," I stammered like an idiot, "and

wishes to be remembered, Sir, and he says how much—"

Abruptly Van Buren said something to me in Dutch. A long sentence in which the lisp was not apparent. Then not waiting to see if I understood or not, the small golden historic figure moved away from us, leaving me bewildered and Leggett furious. "What's the good of being a Dutch oaf if you can't speak the goddamned language?"

Later I described the scene (with obvious omissions) to Colonel Burr, and wondered what it was the Vice-President had said.

"He probably wished you a good day, and good fortune. Matty Van has fine manners. He ought to. I took enough time with him. Though I fear not enough with you." And that was all.

In the flesh the resemblance between the two is striking, particularly in the way they move. Each has a kind of majesty—and no other word will do. I almost regret the role I am to play in ruining Van Buren.

"Now," said the Colonel, "let us consider Washington City in the spring of eighteen oh one."

Memoirs of Aaron Burr—Twelve

AT THE BEGINNING of March, Theodosia, her husband and I arrived at the new capital city (which lacked both city and capitol). On a slight rise in the wilderness was the Senate chamber. Some yards distant was a small ellipse-shaped building, recently thrown together to shelter the House of Representatives and known to its unhappy occupants as "The Oven." Between the two buildings was a covered passage-way. That was all there was to the Capitol. Today's noble brown dome was only a dream.

Close to the unfinished Capitol a few dozen houses formed the core to the city. At that time the most desirable place to live was on top of the F Street ridge or, if one did not mind the distance, at George-town.

A mile and a half from the Capitol, the Treasury building was nearly complete, as was its neighbour, the executive mansion. Connecting Capitol and president's house was a long cow-trail on either side of which Jefferson was to plant several rows of rather forlorn-looking trees, eagerly explaining to anyone who would listen how exactly like a Paris boulevard it looked. Actually Pennsylvania Avenue was good only for shooting the partridges that nested among the elder bushes or for perch-fishing in the little stream (called the Tiber!) that crossed the "avenue."

We stayed the first few nights at Conrad's boarding-house, near to the Capitol. Because of the crowding, I slept in a room with Theodosia and her husband. Across the landing, Jefferson lived in luxurious solitude. The other rooms were crammed with congressmen—of whom a number were forced to sleep on the floor.

That night we were extremely happy in the dining room of Conrad's. Jefferson was elsewhere (usually he sat at the end of the table farthest from the fire, slyly drawing attention to his democracy; gone forever was topaz ring, silver, lace). Theodosia reigned at the table, and I was never more proud of her.

In those days there were thirty-two senators and one hundred six representatives of which not quite half were Republican. That night nearly all the Republicans were at Conrad's. Toasts were delivered, bottles passed from hand to hand, and it seemed as if the good had for once in a wicked world prevailed.

Shortly after midnight, I excused myself, left Theo-dosia and her husband in command of the revels and went upstairs. The door to Jefferson's sitting-room was open. He was half-reclining on a sofa, reading aloud to his secretary. They gave me a startled look. The secretary made as if to shut the door.

Jefferson stopped him. "Come in, Colonel." Both rose as I stepped into the small parlour.

"You see me for the last time comfortable in Washington." The secretary presented a chair for me to sit in. Jefferson stretched out on the sofa. "I dread that house." He waved in the general direction of the executive mansion. "It is too large. It is uncomfortable. It will never be finished in our lifetime. And there are no stables."

I told him that I had yet to see the inside. "You must come and stay. Keep me company. Having no wife makes it worse." Jefferson turned to the secretary. "When does Mr. Adams depart?"

"The last report was that he would be gone at midnight."

Jefferson glanced at the clock on the mantel. "He is gone now." He turned to me. "Mr. Adams has decided not to attend our inaugural tomorrow."

"That seems most—unkind." Affecting grief over the death of a son several months before, Adams chose not to attend the usurpation of what he considered his rightful place.

"I intend to be conciliatory." Jefferson touched the sheaf of papers which proved to be his inaugural address.

"It is a marvellous work!" The secretary was devoted. He was also one of the ugliest men I have ever known.

"I certainly look forward to hearing it."

"Well, I certainly do not look forward to reciting it." Jefferson was genuinely distressed at the thought of speaking in public—he who in private never ceased to talk! He slapped hard a fly that had stopped on the back of his hand. "Particularly in front of my disapproving cousin." Some weeks before Adams had appointed the secretary of state John Marshall chief justice of the United States. Marshall deeply mistrusted Jefferson who responded with a continuing hatred of his cousin. Eventually the two were to collide at my trial for treason.

"I have asked the Chief Justice—most humbly—to

administer the oath of office and, to my surprise, he has agreed. For such good behaviour we are now in honour bound to build the Supreme Court a little house somewhere in the city." The secretary laughed immoderately at this pleasantry. Jefferson was in an excellent mood. But what new president is not? His mistakes unmade, the future bright.

As I said good night, Jefferson took my hand in his, looked me in the eye. "We are now at the beginning of the *actual* American Revolution."

The next morning Theodosia, her husband and I walked from Conrad's to the Capitol. In those days the population of Washington was perhaps 3,000 souls if one included the residents of Georgetown. All 3,000 were on hand that morning, trampling the bushes that edged the Capitol, shivering in a sharp north wind.

A ragged company of riflemen came to attention as I appeared at the Capitol entrance. Those people who recognised me applauded. At that time politicians were not known by face to the degree that they are today. We also did not often show ourselves to the people, except in small canvasses on home ground. Jefferson was known to be tall and red-haired; I to be small and dark. Beyond that, the people only had cartoons to go by, and the artists who drew us were under no obligation to be accurate.

I stepped into the Senate chamber and found that despite the raw newness of everything, the interior had been made most impressive with Doric columns and marble entablatures. On the walls of the semicircular chamber hung the controversial portraits of Louis XVI and Marie Antoinette. The fireplaces at either end provided a good deal of smoke and insufficient heat. Beneath the ceiling was a spacious gallery crowded with spectators. On the dais three chairs had been arranged. In the centre chair sat John Marshall; he was nearly as tall as Jefferson but with black hair on a head much too small for so large a body.

I stood with the sergeant-at-arms until the chamber was quiet; then I made my way down the aisle. As I stepped up on the dais, the Chief Justice rose to greet me.

There was a moment of confusion. Was I expected to make an address? No one seemed certain. We stood there rather foolishly. Finally the Chief Justice whispered, "I think it best to administer the oath *first* to the President."

I then saluted the Chief Justice with a few decorous words; bade everyone welcome; instructed them that the President-elect would arrive at noon, which they already knew; and took my seat in the centre chair as presiding officer of the Senate, the Chief Justice to my left.

A few minutes later a thin volley of rifle-fire signalled the approach of the President-elect.

The sergeant-at-arms threw open the doors and, to applause from the gallery, Jefferson stepped into the chamber. He wore plain dark clothes. He was exceedingly nervous; face flushed; eyes darting this way and that; tongue repeatedly moistening dry lips. As he proceeded down the aisle, clutching his manuscript, artillery began to sound and did not stop until he was beside us on the dais.

I indicated that he take the centre chair. I took the one to his right. Again we were at a loss what to do. Jefferson stood awkwardly, holding the sheaf of papers to his breast.

"You had better begin," I said, establishing a precedent. Without further ceremony Jefferson read to the Chief Justice and me his inaugural address. I say read to *us* because no one else in the chamber heard a word of what he was saying and even Marshall and I were forced at times to lean forward in our chairs to catch the wisdom as it fell from those eloquent lips.

Marshall looked startled and pleased when Jefferson declared, "Every difference of opinion is not a difference of principle. We have called by different names brethren of the same principle. We are all republicans, we are all federalists."

I was merely startled, and somewhat overwhelmed at the hypocrisy: Jefferson more than any other American had poisoned the political life of the nation by slandering as "monarchist" anyone who stood in his path. Nevertheless, the aim of the speech was, if not a *mea culpa*, at least a tacit admission of past excess, and this was a good thing: the public is always relieved to find that once the chief officers of the state are elected they do not sincerely want change.

On one occasion Marshall and I looked at each other and nearly broke out laughing. Jefferson had a strange propensity for confusing metaphors. At one point he graced us with the image of infuriated man's "agonizing spasms" which promptly became through the alchemy of his literary art, "billows" that reached our distant and peaceful shore.

Jefferson then sat down to the somewhat strained applause of a Congress which had not heard a word of what he had said.

The Chief Justice came forward and Jefferson stood up again, dropping a number of pages. I collected them for him. He was then administered the oath of office. Then I, too, swore to uphold the Constitution of the United States. Thus it was that on March 4, 1801, Thomas Jefferson became the third president and Aaron Burr the third vice-president of the twelve-year-old American republic.

We all went back to Conrad's boarding-house for dinner, and the new president modestly took his place at the far end of the table, despite the attempts of Mrs. Senator Brown to give him her seat near the fire. His only word to me that evening was, "The revolution has begun." I was relieved. Apparently there was still a difference between Republicans and Federalists.

Twenty-two

Mr. DAVIS SENT ME A NOTE this morning, requesting the honour of an interview at the City Hotel.

I arrived to find him seated alone in a corner of the bar, drinking beer from a pewter mug.

"How is the Colonel?"

"Flourishing." The Colonel has indeed been in good form lately. "At least when I saw him last. That was two days ago. He's at Jersey City."

"Today, yes." Mr. Davis was, as usual, conspiratorial. "Yesterday, however, he was in the city. In this very hotel. At half past five. Upstairs. In a private reception room."

Mr. Davis likes mystery. I do not. "No doubt." I was flat.

"I think you would be very interested if you knew who it was that he was visiting upstairs?"

"Would I?"

"He was with Mr. Van Buren for over forty minutes. Just the two of them."

"They are old friends." I was not going to allow Mr. Davis the pleasure of surprising me. Instead I changed the subject, surprising *him*. "I would like to know what happened between President Jefferson and Colonel Burr after the inaugural."

"What happened?" Mr. Davis pursed his lips; looked puzzled—to lie or not? "Well, Colonel Burr asked for only three appointments. He got two. I was the third. For my work in the campaign I was to be made naval officer for New York. But I did not get the post, nor did any other friend of Burr get an appointment. Jefferson dropped the Burrites in favor of an alliance with old Governor Clinton and his nephew young DeWitt Clinton."

I asked Mr. Davis why it was that Jefferson wanted

to destroy Colonel Burr. The question is a simple one, and I have asked it a number of times. Unfortunately I never get an entirely convincing answer.

Mr. Davis sighed. "It is so obvious. When Burr got as many votes as Jefferson, and then did nothing to promote himself, Jefferson was undone. Men like Jefferson can never forgive a rival who behaves honourably. Also, Jefferson had already decided—for the good of the nation, naturally—to promote another Virginian once his second term was over."

"Jefferson was without gratitude?"

"Entirely. That was the secret of his strength. Unlike Colonel Burr, he had no friends. Only servants like Madison, Gallatin, Monroe."

"But he rewarded them."

"Madison and Monroe *extended* the Jefferson administration another sixteen years. Friendship had nothing to do with it. Jefferson continued to be the master of the republic."

I think this highly exaggerated; must ask Colonel Burr's view. Certainly Jefferson died poor, and I should not think he was particularly influential at the end.

We were joined by a stolid young man with enormous chin whiskers and a bald head. "This is Reginald Gower." The name was said to me as if I ought to know it. I did not. Soon learned the plot. Gower is a printer. Owns a bookstore. Wants to publish my pamphlet establishing the paternity of Martin Van Buren "and—even more important, Mr. Schuyler—Colonel Burr's *political* influence on the Vice-President. Their meeting yesterday was most significant." Gower nodded to Mr. Davis who nodded back. They were like a pair of Chinese mandarin dolls.

"Does Colonel Burr know what you are doing?" I turned to Mr. Davis, the Colonel's oldest friend and political ally.

"Does Colonel Burr know what *you* are doing?" This was to the point.

"No." I cannot lie; nor tell the truth either, it seems.

"Leggett wants Van Buren removed because he is not radical enough. We want him removed because he is too radical. Leggett wants Johnson for president. We want Clay. You, Charlie, my boy, can satisfy us both. A rare thing indeed!" Mr. Davis' magnified eyes looked at me in a kindly, twinkly way.

I started to ask him how he knew of my arrangements with Leggett but decided that would gratify him too much. "Why don't you write the pamphlet yourself?"

"You have material that I don't." The answer was prompt—too prompt? "Also, I have not the time to spend with the Colonel, to—*extract* the information."

Mr. Gower turned to me. "I understand you've already begun. I want you to know, Mr. Schuyler, that I am willing to advance you five hundred dollars now and another five hundred if you can finish by September."

I was not prepared for such a huge temptation. I have never had more than a hundred dollars in hand at any moment of my life. I paused. Could think of nothing to say.

Gower was quick. "Naturally you will get a certain royalty . . ."

"Depending on the size of the printing." Mr. Davis tried to save Gower money but I, too, moved swiftly, and we came to terms.

In the tap-room of the City Hotel I found myself with a draught on the Bank of Manhattan (Colonel Burr's invention, what else?) to the amount of $500. I am rich.

I went straight to Thomas Street. Mrs. Townsend greeted me in her parlour which was now dominated by a large gilded statue of an unclothed fat man.

"It is the Buddha." Mrs. Townsend indicated a number of thick dusty volumes piled to left and right of the idol. "I am extending my religious range to the East."

"Is that wise?" The God of Jonathan Edwards is, notoriously, a jealous God.

"I have taken precautions," she said cryptically. "We've not seen you in some time. Helen pines for you."

"I've been interviewing Mr. Van Buren." This was stupid but I could not contain myself.

Mrs. Townsend nodded, apparently pleased that I had not been robbing a bank or leading a riot. "A gracious young man, as I recall, who has lived by the Golden Rule." She gave the Buddha a tiny smile. They appear to have an understanding.

"He was with Colonel Burr yesterday."

"So?" Mrs. Townsend lit a stick of sandalwood and set it upright in front of the statue. Sweet-smelling smoke swirled ceiling-ward. "Colonel Burr was a good friend to that young man."

"Is he the Colonel's son?"

Mrs. Townsend put a long finger to thin lips, and motioned to the Buddha whose smile was visible through the shifting smoke. Apparently one must be discreet, or the god would be angry.

"I have heard the story in Kinderhook, and thought nothing of it. After all, I knew old Mrs. Van Buren, and a very plain woman she was, much older than the Colonel . . ."

"Did you know the Colonel's first wife?"

"Oh, yes. I used often to see her out marketing. Always with two blackamoors in livery. A gracious lady."

"Was she also a plain woman, and much older than the Colonel?"

"Yes." Mrs. Townsend looked at me thoughtfully. "I see." If there is one thing Mrs. Townsend understands (other than the manifold faces of God) it is the private eccentricities of men.

"Is there anyone who might know the truth?"

"Is it important?"

"I think so. Not that such a thing could be published. But it goes a long way toward explaining why the two men are so close."

Mrs. Townsend nodded. "Aaron Columbus Burr

once told me that he took a trip up the Hudson River
with Mr. Van Buren and the Colonel. He remembered Mr. Van Buren as being quite the nicest man he
had ever met."

I asked her where the young silversmith might be
found. She told me. I almost did not go up to see
Helen, so eager was I to earn my freedom. But I could
not leave Mrs. Townsend—or myself—unsatisfied.

Helen was in a bad mood made worse by my proposal that she move out of Thomas Street. "Where
on earth am I supposed to go, to the Five Points?"

"I will find you a room."

"And what on earth am I supposed to do *in* the
room all day?" She was suddenly furious; very white
in the face; eyes fever-bright.

"Anything you like. Work. Earn money."

"Like *this*?" She indicated the wash-basin, the
pitcher of permanently cold water.

"If you want to." I was growing more excited as
she grew more obdurate. "But I thought you would
want to start work on your own, making clothes."

"What would you do?"

"I would see you."

"You see me now, and it's a lot cheaper this way
than paying for weekly room and board, as I know
pretty well."

We left it at that: she will think the matter over.
I am out of my mind, I know, but I have never before
been this free, this rich!

Twenty-three

AARON COLUMBUS BURR IS AS TALL as the Colonel
is short, and quite as dark; he is uncommonly
handsome. Although he bears no particular re-

semblance to the Colonel, he does share the same excellent manners, enhanced more than marred by a strong French accent.

As we talked in his small crowded shop, he hammered a thin sheet of silver over a wooden mould. In his hands the hammer moves with such speed that it blurs before the eye; like the wings of a humming-bird.

I had introduced myself as a friend of Mrs. Townsend. The thick dark brows shot up with amusement. White teeth flashed. "Then we have this much in common."

I had contemplated a dozen possible introductions for myself, realizing that I could not pass myself off as a journalist or politician without giving away the game. Nor could I say that I knew Colonel Burr without running the risk of being doubly revealed. But a fellow client of Mrs. Townsend meant that we belonged to the same club, as it were, shared a secret that was made all the more enjoyable by my inspiration: "I'm being married next month, Mr. Burr. To a girl from Connecticut." A half-truth always sounds truer than truth. I told him that I wanted to know the prices of silver, old and new: my future father-in-law was generous.

The French Burr was most obliging; spent half an hour showing me about his shop, and another half-hour enquiring after Mrs. Townsend, and did I know Cora? Had I been with Marguerite? Was the black from Santo Domingo recovered from the mysterious knife-wound?

I invited him to drink with me at a near-by bar. He shouted something to his wife in the upper part of the house. Then he locked up and we crossed the crowded Bowery to a small French café with a sign out in front which said "Marquis de Lafayette."

At round marble tables, Frenchmen played chess and dominoes; and spoke of home—usually some West Indian island. I find them exotic. Will I ever see France?

Columbus was embraced by the patron who showed us to a table in one corner where we ate bread and cheese and drank harsh red wine, all ordered by Columbus (as I took to calling him at his request) in rapid French. Delicately I mentioned the obvious fact of his Frenchness which appeared to deny the Englishness of his name.

"That is because of my father. You see, he is American. A lawyer. Very old. Very distinguished. My mother is French. They are married in Paris. She likes Paris. He likes New York. When I am very little I am in Paris. When bigger, I come to New York."

"Burr? I seem to know the name." I frowned.

But Columbus was not about to be helpful. "He is old, old man. My mother is very young when they marry." Columbus wanted to talk of girls, and so we did, and I kept pouring him more and more red wine which he kept on drinking. From girls and Mrs. Townsend we moved—naturally—on to religion (he is a devout Roman Catholic: I look suitably awed by this exoticism); then from religion the conversation shifted—almost naturally—to politics.

Yes, he has met Mr. Van Buren. "I meet him on the boat to Albany—oh, when I am first here—maybe ten years ago." Actually it was six years ago. I have worked out the date to be either May or June 1828. Columbus accompanied Colonel Burr and Senator Van Buren from New York to Albany where—something which I ought to have known but did not—Van Buren appeared as Colonel Burr's junior associate counsel before the Court for the Correction of Errors in the case of Varick v. Jackson (Mr. Craft has promised to find me the record of the case. He recalls that the fee was a good one and that Senator Van Buren argued the case which Colonel Burr had prepared for him).

"It is my first trip on the river-boat. Colonel Burr takes me along because he wants me to go to a school in Albany but I don't like school and come back here very quick. Mr. Van Buren tries to tell me how important an education is. 'Oh,' he says, 'what I would give if I had been to college!' And Colonel Burr laughs and agrees with him and says if Mr. Van Buren was an educated man, he would be something a lot more than just a senator from New York which is a ridiculous thing to be, he says. He laughs a lot, Colonel Burr."

I did my best to appear casual. Not to press. To keep Columbus to the subject. "I thought Mr. Van Buren was governor in 1828, not senator."

Columbus shook his head. He sliced thick bread and ate it with pickled onions. I could almost taste the sourness, and winced as he chewed happily, mouth open.

"Mr. Van Buren is governor soon after because on the boat that's what they talk about. 'I must carry the state for Jackson,' says Mr. Van Buren. 'Indeed you must,' says Colonel Burr. 'But with old Governor Clinton dead we have nobody who can win this year,' says Mr. Van Buren. 'There's you,' says the Colonel. 'But I am just elected again to the Senate,' says Mr. Van Buren. 'Yes,' says Colonel Burr, 'and now you be governor and you make General Jackson president and you will be secretary of state next year.' And they argue about what to do but by the time we get to Albany Mr. Van Buren says the Colonel is right and he will do just what he says and he does. Very *affreuse*, Albany is, and the Dutch girls are ugly. You're not Dutch, are you?"

"No. No. I'm Irish."

As best I could I tried to discover if Columbus knows anything of Van Buren's true paternity but he does not or else is more discreet than I give him credit for.

I did acquire one useful detail. Some months before the trip up-river, Van Buren had made a speech in the Senate favouring half-pay for all surviving officers of the Revolution: " 'The best speech I ever wrote for you, Matty,' says the Colonel. 'But not,' says Mr. Van Buren, 'the last.' "

Twenty-four

I HAVE GONE over this conversation with Leggett who is delighted. "You have enough to start." He handed me a number of pamphlets from a drawer in his desk. "A few libels for you to study."

As luck would have it the first was an attack on his own candidate Richard M. Johnson. Apparently the senator from Kentucky has just lost his mulatto concubine, one Julia Chinn, by whom he had two daughters. Although the girls were highly educated, he failed to introduce them to society. He has now bought another mulatto girl, and taken her to bed. I read aloud one of the gaudier passages.

Leggett waves anxiously in the direction of Mr. Bryant's office. "Don't! He's already suspicious enough."

I desist. "Is this the style I'm to imitate?"

"Yes. With a phrase or two from me, if you like."

I told him of the meeting with Gower, but did not mention the price I am to get. Leggett is thoughtful. "I'd be wary of anything Matt Davis is involved with."

"He wants the same result you do."

"Perhaps." Leggett shook his head with wonder. "I had no idea Van Buren and Burr were so close. Practising law together as recently as—when?"

"Six years ago. And a forty-minute meeting yesterday at the City Hotel."

"We'll have to guess at what went on there."

"Shall we say that they were planning to restore slavery to New York state?" I grow irritable with my task.

"You can *say* anything as long as it sounds reasonable, plausible. That is the beauty of anonymity."

"But one ought not to lie, particularly about a man one admires."

"Burr or Van Buren?"

"Guess?" I found myself disliking Leggett; myself more.

"You cannot hurt your friend the Colonel. He is used to slander. Besides, do your work well and he will never suspect you. Do your work well and we shall have Johnson in the White House."

"A thrilling prospect. And what will you get out of it? Will you be collector of the port, or ambassador to England?"

"Virtuous, Charlie! I shall be virtuous, and a new world will begin, without slavery, without . . ." He made a speech.

Twenty-five

THE COLONEL CONTINUES to be in good spirits. As we prepared for today's session, he remarked upon the death a few days ago of Genêt. "The last time I spoke to him, he told me that it was Jefferson who had convinced him that he should appeal directly to the people; that he should attack Hamilton and Washington openly, and by name. I wonder if Jefferson really gave him such malicious advice."

The Colonel whittled at a seegar. Before him on the baize-covered table were arranged the usual newspaper cuttings, campaign tracts, letters.

We are now ready to deal with the Colonel's vice-presidency. I am armed with pencil, pad; and an aching forefinger. I grip too hard the pencil. The true professional holds it lightly, saves himself.

"How is Mr. Van Buren?" I was bold. This business must end soon, one way or the other.

Burr blinked at me; bit his seegar; exhaled smoke.

"I told Matty it was too public a place but he had no time to go elsewhere. What a clever man he is! I am continually awed by the *neatness* with which he accomplishes things. If only he could spell, knew grammar, didn't have that uncouth Dutch accent. Your friend Leggett will support him, won't he?" The Colonel has got the general range. But I hope no more.

"Well, he thought Mr. Van Buren's position on slavery weak."

"Matty will be impeccable on that subject come election day." Burr put his feet up on the fire fender. "Matty flatters me shamelessly. He asks my legal advice. Imagine!"

And that is all I shall probably ever know about what transpired at the City Hotel. Will I have to invent something suitably sinister? I cannot say I much enjoy the *manner* of the political pamphlet. But at least I am now rich, and have Helen Jewett in a room back of the Washington Market.

She agreed last night to join me, "For a while anyway but we better not let Mrs. Townsend know. I've said I'm going to have a baby and leave it with my aunt who wants a baby—funny kind of aunt—but Mrs. Townsend seems to believe me and says she'll take me back when I'm 'restored,' that was her word."

Memoirs of Aaron Burr–Thirteen

SIX MONTHS AFTER our inauguration, Jefferson joined forces with the Clintons to eliminate me from politics not only in the nation but, rather more seriously, in New York state.

Young DeWitt Clinton was a formidable antagonist. Clever, drunken, ruthless, there was nothing he would not do to achieve his ends. First, he restored his uncle to the governorship. Then, coolly, through a series of amendments to the state constitution, he removed all power from the governor and bestowed it upon a council which was his creature. "The boy's strong-minded, Colonel. Strong-minded." George Clinton's mouth worked nervously; thick tufted brows arched over small eyes. "There's times he scares me half to death when he's on the war-path."

Clinton was indeed terrified of his nephew, and with good reason. In a matter of months, the young man had secured the state for himself by, among other things, the elimination of nearly every Federalist office-holder: in all, he made some 6,000 appointments, including that of himself to the United States Senate. I know of no conquest quite so total or so rapid as DeWitt Clinton's annexation of New York. I do not think that it would have happened had I not been removed from the scene by the vice-presidency. No matter. At the age of thirty-three, DeWitt Clinton was master of the Republican party in the state of New York.

I cannot say that I look back on this period as entirely happy. I was in debt. I was trying unsuccessfully to sell Richmond Hill. Theodosia was at the other end of the world in South Carolina. Washington City was a depressing village set in a wilderness, and not even the best efforts of the Madisons to create a salon quite made up for the sense of constriction in that makeshift capital—tribute to Jefferson's will.

One afternoon in March of 1802, I was at John Marsh's bookstore in M Street when I heard a familiar voice asking for a novel. I turned and saw Hamilton, swiftly thumbing through a stack of English periodicals; no doubt committing them to memory at a glance!

As I approached him, he looked up; gave a start; then bowed deeply. "The Vice-President himself—and in the flesh."

"I'm afraid there is too much of the latter . . ."

"And not enough of the former?" The response was sharp, as always. He, too, was heavier than in the past. We all were. It is my recollection of those days that we did almost nothing but eat and drink at Washington City.

Hamilton was in the city for "Litigation. What else? How lucky you are to be out of all that!"

"Considering my poverty, I wish I were *into* all of that."

Mr. Marsh brought Hamilton the novel he had asked for. The commanding general of the American army placed a copy of the *Anti Jacobin Review and Magazine* around the book, hoping I had not noticed the title.

"Do you enjoy yourself?" Hamilton was most amiable, and though we were contemporaries I found myself responding to him the way older men did when he meant to charm: I played Achilles to his buoyant Patroclus.

"Tolerably. I am stern with my flock. I have, this session, forbade the eating of cakes on the floor of the Senate chamber. We already have rats as well as mice at every session. Apples are next for proscription."

"You are so decorous, Vice-President!"

"Obviously I have found my proper place in life. Decorum is all that the position requires."

Hamilton invited me to join him at the Union Tavern farther along M Street (are these places still there? it has been thirty years since I have set foot in Washington City).

Shivering in a cold wind, we walked briskly along the muddy Georgetown street. And it was a proper street unlike the cow-paths and uncharted woods of near-by Washington City—a capital, as one tactful foreign minister used to say, "of magnificent distances."

As always, Hamilton tried to draw me out on the subject of Jefferson and, as always, I was not to be drawn out. I gave him only the idlest gossip. "The roof of the mansion leaks. The walls of the bedrooms are still unplastered. And Mr. Adams forgot to order a proper staircase between the floors, so the President must climb a sort of ladder when he goes to bed."

"You visit there often?"

"Twice a month we dine and settle all the matters of the universe."

Hamilton frowned; and wondered if I was lying. But I was not. Jefferson was eager that we maintain—socially—the appearance of amity.

The owner of the Union Tavern arranged two comfortable chairs for us on the stone hearth of the empty bar-room. Slaves worked the bellows; made the fire crackle; brought wine.

This was the first time I had been alone with Hamilton since the election. Before 1800, I had always thought of him as a *friendly* rival. Now I knew otherwise. Letters he had written about me had come my way. It seemed that every thought, whim, fancy that came into his irritable mind was sooner or later put in writing. I ought to have hated him, but did not. Some flaw in my nature has made me indifferent to slander—and thus much slandered? Certainly my indifference seems to excite such attentions.

As I held up my glass, I repeated, somewhat mischievously, the toast I had made at the recent Federalist celebration of Washington's birthday. "To the union of all honest men!"

Hamilton frowned; and did not drink. "Your attendance at *our* dinner was most . . . effective."

"I merely stated the theme of this administration."

"Others saw it as a deliberate bid for Federalist support."

"Support for what?" I was as bland as if I had never seen a copy of Hamilton's newspaper, the *Evening Post* (so superbly edited today!), nor read a single one of his current attacks on Jefferson, on me, on the entire Republican hierarchy.

"The President must have been startled by your appearance in the enemy camp."

"But I was simply there as a guest, as the eminently neutral presiding officer of the Senate."

"Neutral!" Hamilton had finished one glass of wine. He poured himself a second, and drank it down quickly. I noticed how unhealthy he looked. The usual rosy brightness looked curiously glazed while the small body was so unwholesomely bloated that the brass buttons of his waistcoat looked ready to burst free; in fact, one had broken its mooring and swung like a pendulum on the frayed thread. He, too, had been going through a bad time personally as well as politically.

I said what I had to say. "I was most sorry to hear of your son Philip's death."

Hamilton rubbed a hand across his features, as though to re-arrange them. But into what? For he looked no more sad, no more misty-eyed than before.

"Political faction . . ." He began; did not go on. Philip Hamilton had challenged a friend of mine at a theatre in New York. In the subsequent duel my friend shot and killed young Hamilton whose sister, Angelica, had gone mad. The girl had been a good friend of my Theodosia: at so many points did our lives touch one another in that small society.

"Do you not wish at times that you were free of political faction?" I could not resist the question.

"I am!" The answer was swift, and disingenuous. "I have got myself a farm some eight miles from the Bowling Green. For a disappointed politician, there is nothing like growing cabbages. Why, I would not give up my cabbages for an empire. I am like Domitian."

"Diocletian." I fear that Hamilton had only glanced at Gibbon while I had made the mistake of reading the master's every word.

"What a scholar you are!" Hamilton looked to see if the novel he had set down on the table was still discreetly wrapped in the *Anti Jacobin Review*. Aware that my eye had followed his, he provided a distraction. He pointed to a print of General Washington and his mother, a popular engraving of the day. "That look of pain on the General's face is most accurate."

"I think the artist meant it to be one of filial devotion."

"Then his error was on the side of accuracy. Poor General! How that woman made him suffer." Hamilton regaled me with several anecdotes about the stormy relations between George Washington and his mother who attempted, on several occasions, to extort money from her glorious son. Then, quite carried away by indiscretion, he told me the "true" story of Jefferson's resignation as secretary of state.

"You will recall that summer at Philadelphia, when the yellow fever struck and I nearly died?"

"I recall it most vividly." Saw again Dr. Hutchinson's bright red lips, bloodshot eyes, shambling gait, the noise of his retching beside my carriage.

"Shortly before I took ill, the President and I were discussing how best to eliminate Jefferson from the Cabinet . . ."

"Washington wanted him gone?" I had not known this.

"Most fervently. But most privately. It was our strategy that Washington must always appear above the battle, trying to mitigate the excesses of his two ministers. Actually Washington was a most bitter partisan. Particularly that summer. The Genêt business infuriated him . . ."

"And he thought that Jefferson was conspiring with Genêt?"

"How could he not? For months we had only one dream, the two of us, how best to restore Jefferson to the tranquil beauties of Monticello."

"I should not have thought that hard to do. Jefferson wanted to go."

"He had no intention of ever going home if I remained in Philadelphia. So it was then that the President and I devised our intrigue—oh, yes, Colonel, in a good cause even I will intrigue."

"Do you mean to astonish me, General?"

Hamilton was amused. "Note how I said 'good' cause."

"Duly noted."

"After a Cabinet meeting where I had managed to distress Jefferson by attacking his democratic societies, the President took Jefferson aside and said, most sadly, in that grave tone with which he used to memorialize fallen comrades of the Revolution, 'You know that we are to lose Mr. Hamilton at the end of the year. And you must help me to persuade him to remain. Otherwise I shall resign my office, and let Mr. Adams succeed to this dreadful place.' Jefferson was horrified at the thought of Adams succeeding but delighted that I was going. He then 'persuaded' the President to remain in office, and promised to appeal to me. But of course he did not. He simply told me that he, too, was leaving." Hamilton drank more wine. "The General was thrilled, if such a word can be used to describe so phlegmatic a man. 'Naturally,' he said to me, 'I must now do my very best to persuade Mr. Jefferson to stay.' To which I replied 'Naturally' and so the President drove out to Gray's Landing and gave a splendid performance of a man deserted by his two principal supports. This, in turn, delighted Jefferson for whom any sort of betrayal is always a kind of ecstasy." A swift look at me to judge response; none was visible. "So it was that Jefferson resigned as secretary of state and I remained in the Cabinet for one more year."

"During which time Mr. Jefferson and I were able to create a republican party and win the late election."

"During which time I was able to set this nation on sound financial principles. Now rapidly being undone." I was treated to a discourse on Jefferson's folly in abandoning the 'sinking fund.' When I pointed out that any leader who reduces taxes as Jefferson had done is apt *never* to be replaced in a republic, Hamilton's response was, "Demagoguery! And as for that ridiculous speech of his . . ."

I am afraid that I, too, had laughed at Jefferson's address to Congress (read by a clerk because Jefferson thought it "monarchical" to speak from the throne, as it were; actually, he simply dreaded speaking in public). Displaying a more than usual infelicity of style, Jeffer-

son had written of "a conscientious desire to direct the
energies of our nation to the multiplication of the
human race, and not to its destruction." This produced
(for the wicked Vice-President at least) a vision of
constant Dionysian revelry, interrupted only by much-
applauded pregnancies.

Then Hamilton complimented me for my part in
the debate on the Judiciary Bill. The Republicans had
wanted to repeal the National Judiciary Act, thus eliminating those Federalist judges John Adams had created
his last day in office. Although I disagreed with the
Federalists who took the absurd line that Congress
could not undo what it had done in the creating of
judges, I did find it immoral, to say the least, to eliminate a score of judges simply because a new and
hostile majority existed in Congress.

On a move to submit the bill to a vote, the Senate
tied: fifteen Republicans to fifteen Federalists. As vice-
president, I broke the tie in what appeared to be the
favour of the Republicans. I wanted the bill to come
to a vote because, with my friend Jonathan Dayton
(the Federalist senator from New Jersey), I thought
the whole matter should be referred to a select committee whose task it would be to review the *entire*
judiciary system. I was aiming at reconciliation. When
Dayton's proposal came to a vote, the Senate again
tied, and this time I broke the tie in a way that many
thought favoured the Federalists. I sent the bill to
committee for further review.

"I cannot imagine Jefferson forgiving you easily."
Hamilton's voice was somewhat blurred. He was never
a heavy drinker yet at times drink seemed to go more
rapidly to his head than to that of other men. Perhaps
he was constitutionally frailer than any of us knew.
I have often found that those who "recover" from the
yellow fever are seldom again whole.

I was relieved when I heard the familiar clatter of
Senator Gouverneur Morris's wooden leg behind us.
That exquisite gentleman was always most civil to me,
although he hated the French Revolution and its

American supporters. As our minister to France he had actually conspired to free Louis XVI. When this adventure failed, he consoled himself by buying up at bargain prices furniture from the royal palaces. Reverently, he would show his visitors the Queen's fauteuil, the King's chamber-pot.

"Dear God, the two of you in one room! I smell sulphur, brimstone. *Excellence!*" He gave me a mock court bow; gave his hand to Hamilton. "*Mon Général.*"

"We were reliving old times." Hamilton had quite recovered himself.

Morris looked at the two of us most shrewdly. "You could do a lot worse, General. And you probably will."

Hamilton was genuinely puzzled. I was not. I knew what Morris meant. "I don't think," I said, "that I am ever apt to be the *Federalist* candidate for president." I was mild, realizing that every word I said would soon be repeated from one end of the country to the other.

"Is *that* what you intended, Mr. Morris?" Hamilton stared at the senator as if he had at that moment recognised in him the first sign of plague.

Morris sank into a chair beside the fire and I thought for a moment how like to one of the burning logs was his wooden leg. "Yes, General, that is just what I meant. We have no one. No one at all. And I will say this." He looked at me. "If Colonel Burr had cast his *first* vote, breaking the tie vote in our favour, he would have been the unanimous choice for president of all the Federalists in Congress. As it is, thanks to the second vote, you have support, Sir. You have important support from our side."

Hamilton's face was—well, not a mask. One saw everything. The possibility that I might now become the leader of *his* party was a nightmare he could not wake up from fast enough. "Surely Colonel Burr has not changed so rapidly his Republican principles."

"No, he has not." I made light of the matter. "But it is my fault to see both sides to every matter." This was demure if not entirely true.

"Yes. He is a gentleman, you see." I don't know

what Morris intended for Hamilton to make of that perhaps pointed remark.

" 'We are all republicans, all federalists,' " I quoted.

"But," said Morris, "we are not all of us Virginians, are we?" Since no response from me was safe, I excused myself, realizing that Hamilton must now redouble his efforts to remove me from the scene.

Fortunately for Hamilton he had the aid of DeWitt Clinton, as well as of the journalist James Cheetham who was inspired by Jefferson to attack me at regular intervals in the New York *Citizen*, and from a Republican standpoint. As Jefferson used Callender to bring down Hamilton, he now used Cheetham to destroy me. According to Cheetham I had tried to take the presidency away from Jefferson.

My friends rallied round. John Swartwout fought a duel with DeWitt Clinton, and was wounded. As "Aristides," William Van Ness wrote a splendid polemic in my favour. I even allowed friends to bring a suit for libel against Cheetham. New York state was in a turmoil. Yet I did not think my cause hopeless. I was reasonably certain that I could be elected governor at the next election, despite Jefferson and the Clintons on the one hand, despite Hamilton on the other.

Meanwhile, I presided over the Senate. I also dined quite frequently with the President who continued to delight and fascinate me with his conversation, not to mention his wonderful malice which was positively Shakespearean in its variety.

Twenty-six

LEGGETT CAME TO SEE ME and Helen in our rooms just opposite the market. In the evening light the torn wall-paper looked almost new and the dusty furniture (Helen refuses to clean anything except herself) made a good impression.

"Such opulence, Charlie!" Leggett bowed over Helen's hand. "Such romance!" She rewarded him with her deepest scowl. I do not think he has been with her. She says not. It is curious that the more I see of her, the more she interests me. Yet the reverse ought to be the case.

We sat in the small parlour and looked out over the river: a view of ship masts in the foreground and Paulus Hook in the distance. Despite the summer heat, we ate a good deal of roast beef (Helen cannot—will not—cook and so buys her roasts already prepared). For half the dinner she talked most agreeably; then fell silent as a strawberry pie was passed about.

Leggett got down to business. He has now read all my notes on the Burr–Van Buren connection. "We have more than enough." He was delighted.

In the shadowy room I could not make out his face (for reasons of economy we never light more than a single lamp). Flies finished our dinner for us despite Helen's languorous banishing waves of the hand.

Leggett made a few notes in the dark: the play reviewer's knack.

"You are certain I have enough to go on?"

"What you don't have, you must invent. You have studied the manner?"

"Yes. By the way, did your Senator Johnson really kill Tecumseh?"

"We always say he did. I advise you to see the new five-act drama *Tecumseh* in which Senator Johnson is impersonated by an actor who wears the very same uniform Johnson wore when he struck down the turbulent Indian chief. Who is that?" Leggett gave a sudden start as he noticed a tall bosomy figure in the dark corner.

"Mrs. Cotswold," said Helen. "It's her dummy. I'm making her a dress."

"Very slowly." I was incautious. Helen is touchy

about her slowness with the needle. She cannot sustain effort for any length of time. But when she does at last finish the work, the result is admirable according to her few but patient customers.

I gave Leggett a draught of the pamphlet which I have been at work on for several days. "I'll take it with me. I'll give it the Leggett touch."

"Should we give Van Buren a black mistress to match your friend Johnson's two black girls?"

"That would be obvious." Leggett was amused. "Give him an Indian paramour."

"A sister of Tecumseh?"

"No. Mrs. Tecumseh. The raddled squaw herself."

"I knew an Indian girl once." Helen was dreamy. "She had two scalps she kept under her pillow. One was blond and one sort of brown-colored. She said her father took them off two soldiers. She thought the world of those two scalps. It certainly gave some of her visitors a turn." Helen chuckled in the darkness.

I do not allow myself to think of what will happen when the Colonel reads what I have written. Perhaps I should vanish first. Leave Helen. Sail for Europe. Leave Helen? No. Sail for Europe together? Why not?

Twenty-seven

THE COLONEL COMPLAINS of the heat. Most unusual for him. "It is Monmouth Court House all over again." He mops his brow. "And it's only July. What will August bring?"

The office is at a stand-still. Madame's action for divorce moves on its stately way through the courts. Mr. Craft has vanished into the depths of Pennsylvania. We are alone. The city is empty.

The Colonel is restless. Opens and shuts windows. Arranges papers on his desk. Suddenly goes to a cupboard and takes down a pistol. Is it the one?

"No. The pistols for our interview were supplied by Hamilton. But this is a close duplicate."

I find the pistol heavy but beautifully balanced as it rests on the palm of my hand.

"I have never liked fire-arms." The Colonel is unexpected. "In the Revolution I used a sabre." He takes his seat at the baize-covered table. Moves papers about. Shows me a newspaper cartoon of Jefferson and himself. Jefferson is holding a knife that he is about to thrust into the Colonel's back. From the Colonel's mouth appears a balloon containing the words "I have complete trust in Mr. Jefferson's policies."

Burr laughs as he reads aloud the words. "Actually I was not exactly a lamb brought to slaughter. More a snared eagle. And what a trap they laid for me." He lights a seegar. Puffs smoke furiously. Then he puts down the seegar with an odd expression: "A poor grade of tobacco. It is close in here."

I am grateful to be spared the smoke that usually leaves me with aching head and watery eyes.

Memoirs of Aaron Burr—Fourteen

BY THE END of 1803, I realized that between the Clintons in New York and Jefferson at Washington, my political career was drawing to a close.

Madison avoided me, sorrowfully I rather thought. Dolley, however, continued to be friends with Theodosia, and occasionally warned her of what Jefferson was about. Dolley was torn between friendship for me (not to mention gratitude: she was the only woman I have ever known with that cranial bump) and the necessity of pleasing the leader of our party and the fount of honour, for already it was assumed that once Jefferson's second term was completed, the secretary of state Mr. Madison would succeed to the presidential chair.

My presence in Washington, though constitutionally necessary, was a source of embarrassment to the Administration. Only Secretary of the Treasury Gallatin had the courage to defend me in Jefferson's presence. "You are doing yourself great harm, I said to zee President." Gallatin's French accent was much imitated by his detractors, among them Hamilton who at one point actually attacked the Republican party for being led by a "foreigner"—this from the West Indian who had for so long led the Federalists! But Hamilton was quite irrational the last year or two of his life, devoting much of his time to the creation of a Christian Constitutional party dedicated to Jesus and to Federalism, two elements not normally mixed.

"But zee President is adamant. He wants you gone from political life."

"Does he ever say why?"

"You know him. He never ceases to *say* why and yet never says anything." Gallatin's response to Jefferson was always somewhat ambivalent. He was one of the first to recognise that Jefferson was the master politician of our age. He also realized that Jefferson's limitations must be minimized in an administration that wanted no army, no navy, no trade, and no taxes. Wisely Jefferson left to Gallatin anything which had to do with finances. The resulting success of Jefferson's first term was entirely the work of Gallatin who indeed eliminated taxes, insuring Jefferson's re-election and the continuance of the Virginia junto. In fact, as the first term ended, the only spectre on the bright horizon of Virginia's dominance of the nation was Vice-President Burr.

In January of 1804, I requested a private meeting with Jefferson.

Through a thin rain, I rode across the ragged yard in front of the President's House. Gave the reins of my horse to an indolent black boy. Made my way through the red mud which affected to be a carriage drive. Climbed the "temporary" wooden steps to the front door. Pulled the bell; it did not work. Tried the handle. The door was warped. I gave it a satisfying kick and found myself in the freezing entrance hall.

A black slave in ill-fitting livery greeted me, and led me to the President's office. The interior of the "palace" was bare and full of echoes, and icy cold. The celebrated East Room was still unfinished, although Jefferson had recently used it to give shelter to the largest cheese ever made in the United States. This odoriferous miracle of American inventiveness most appropriately furnished that noble chamber until the electorate finally ate it.

The President had made himself a library-cabinet opposite the public dining-room, and here I found him seated at a long table covered with correspondence, books, maps, gardening tools, and a mocking-bird which, despite all of the President's requests both verbal and whistled, refused that day to emit so much as a single note.

Jefferson wore a heavy dressing-gown, a red stained waistcoat and much-worn slippers; his shirt front betrayed the breakfast eggs. "It is my fate," he said, "to live in unfinished houses."

"Better to build than to inherit."

"I think so. But the inconvenience . . ." He sighed. Then he motioned for me to sit opposite him at the table. Between us lay an unfurled map of the Floridas.

Aware that I had seen it, Jefferson declared, "It is our view that the Floridas are an integral part of the recent purchase of Louisiana. Certainly West Florida to the Perdido River is ours." Jefferson talked for some time of his famous acquisition. He had every reason to be pleased with his remarkable good luck. I say good luck because if the slaves of Santo Domingo Island had not overthrown their masters, Bonaparte would not have been forced to commit a vast amount of money and troops to the pacification of that island at a time when he was on fire to begin the conquest of Europe. Jefferson bought Louisiana for fifteen million dollars from Bonaparte, who was desperate for cash, thus doubling the size of the United States (and blithely violating the Constitution in the process).

Jefferson unrolled the map of the Louisiana Territory. He was jubilant. "And to think it is only a beginning."

"But what a beginning!" I noticed how deep the lines were about his mouth; how the dull red hair was going white beneath the powder.

"But we must obtain the Floridas. Together with Canada and Cuba our empire will then be safe, and freedom extended."

I asked him when Louisiana would be granted statehood.

Jefferson shrugged. "The people there are not like us, you know. Why, only one in fifty speaks English. And of course they are like children when it comes to self-government." He tapped a thick despatch. "An agent reports that the lawyers of New Orleans are not only opposed to the principle of trial by jury but to *habeas corpus,* too." He shook his head.

"Are they opposed to union with us?"

"How could they be opposed? How could anyone not want freedom?" At length Jefferson discussed the constitution he was writing for the lucky "children" whose territory he had just divided in two: the populous southern part to be called Orleans; the empty part Louisiana. We spoke of possible governors for these two territories. At that time a Virginian named Claiborne was governor of Orleans but his appointment was thought to be temporary. Claiborne was one of those representatives who supported Jefferson when the presidential election went into the House; some thought he might have supported me had I offered him high office. The name of the Marquis de Lafayette had recently been put forward as a Louisiana governor but Jefferson thought this "an impractical notion."

I proposed Andrew Jackson who had the support of the westerners in Congress. "Jackson? Good God, no! He is much too . . . contentious a man. Too violent. He would have us at war with Spain in a month."

"Is that a bad thing?" After all, Jefferson had once been ready to go to war with Spain in the matter of the Creek Indians.

"If war comes it must be by design not by blunder." Jefferson was cautious. "I do not trust Jackson. Any more than I trust the Creoles of New Orleans." Jefferson made it plain that he was in no hurry to extend to the 50,000 souls he had just bought any of those freedoms which he had once insisted must be enjoyed by all mankind, or at least by the white inhabitants of the eastern American seaboard at the time of the Revolution.

That seaboard was also on his mind. "I hear most disquieting news from Massachusetts and New Hampshire." He looked out the window at the gun-metal gray sky, as though the very elements were collusive. "Did you know that there are actually Federalists in those states who would *break up* the union?"

"They will make no move without New York."

"That is wise of them, isn't it?" He gave me a sidelong glance. When I made no response, he began to fiddle with his copying machine. This was an infamous contraption involving two pens. As you wrote with one pen, the other made an exact copy of what you were writing. In theory, this made a secretary unnecessary. In practice, Jefferson had work not only for a secretary but for a mechanic since the machine was almost always broken.

Jefferson placed a sheet of paper beneath each pen and, rather gloomily, started scribbling. "You know of New York matters," he said, knowing rather more than I did through the Clintons. "Does Hamilton support the dismembering of our union?" Eagerness— no other word could describe the expression that passed across his face.

"No. He is opposed."

"Curious." Jefferson was absently signing his name. To his surprise the machine was now, perversely, making fair copies of that celebrated autograph. He brightened noticeably.

"Since your acquisition of Louisiana, many New Englanders would prefer two nations. One centred on the Atlantic. The other on the Mississippi."

"In principle I quite agree with them." Jefferson was serene. "After all, both nations would still be American."

"Except that one would be slave-holding, and the other free."

Jefferson changed the subject. "I am told, Colonel, that you are now a grandfather." We discussed Theodosia's son, Aaron Burr Alston, and we discussed the President's daughters and grandchildren. We discussed old age. Jefferson was then about sixty and did not think it likely that he would survive a second term (assuming that the people would again honour him, et cetera). I said, most sincerely, that he would bury us all. I did not of course let on that I realized it was his intention to bury *me* as soon as possible.

I came to the point. "It is plain to me that you have made other arrangements for the vice-presidency next year . . ."

"I assure you, Colonel, that *I* have made no arrangements." One of the few good things Monroe ever said was "Jefferson's insincerity is always spontaneous; it is never contrived."

"I am passive in these matters as you know." Jefferson was studying the map before him. "No, that is not absolutely true. I confess that I was active on your behalf during the last election. You had impressed upon me the necessity of Virginia's support for your candidacy. And so I broke my usual rule and exerted myself on your behalf. But I did nothing elsewhere for you or for myself."

I let this nonsense go unremarked. "It is said that you have already decided on a vice-president."

Jefferson looked at me with true surprise. "I have *arranged* nothing, Colonel. In due course a Republican caucus will meet, and they alone will decide . . ."

". . . and since public opinion will not allow you to make a fellow Virginian vice-president, it is said that you will replace me with another New Yorker, with Governor Clinton."

"I have not discussed this matter with Governor Clinton . . ."

"Mr. Jefferson, I am willing to withdraw as gracefully as possible. But we must be candid with one another. Three years ago, I came to this place wanting to support you personally and politically. Yet from the beginning I have been sensible of your . . . disaffection for me. I do not know its cause. I have been told that you believe I tried to deny you the presidency. Yet I am certain that you cannot believe such a thing to be true for the excellent reason that you know that had I wanted the presidency I could have been elected on the first ballot with the aid of my friend Mr. Bayard of Delaware. Instead I forced him to give me up, and then I forced him to take *you* up, and here you are, Sir. And here I am."

I suddenly realized that it was an old man's face that looked at me across the maps of empire. Wrinkled and pale with a petulant look about the slit of a mouth—the only relic of youth the amber brilliance of eyes that now glared at me with perfect hatred.

"Colonel." The weak voice cracked with emotion. "I do not accuse you of ever being party to any plot to deny me what the people wanted me to have. But at times I have entertained certain doubts as to your republican principles. Your votes in the Senate have made me uneasy while your toast at the Federalist dinner . . ." Jefferson made his case; and it was nothing, as he knew.

"My votes in the Senate were based on the merits of certain legislation. My toast 'to the union of all honest men' was simply a feeble echo of your own inaugural address."

"No doubt there have been misunderstandings on both sides ..."

"No doubt. I still have a letter you wrote me when my election was in doubt, proposing that I take a post in your administration. I was honoured by your trust." I moved straight to the point. "In the course of my career I have never asked anyone a personal favour. Now I must set aside *my* usual rule. In order that our ranks not be divided, that bitterness not overwhelm our supporters, I should like to step down as vice-president, and take some other post, removing myself entirely from electoral politics."

"I see." The mocking-bird had suddenly flown to the mantelpiece. There was a moment of silence which I vowed I would not be the first to break; nor was I. "Naturally, Colonel, at the time I wrote that letter I recognised your claim to our party's gratitude. You had given us New York and New York had given us the country. But ... well, positions have been filled."

"The governorship of Orleans?"

"Mr. Claiborne has only just taken office."

"The governorship of Louisiana?"

"It is pledged."

"The embassy to France?"

"I must think hard, Colonel." The shadow of a smile began. "You have taken me by surprise."

"I hope you are not surprised by my desire to avoid the appearance of division between us."

"No. No. I am most grateful."

"Good. Otherwise, if I am not allowed to serve you in some appointive office, I shall return to New York next month and present myself for governor ..."

"As a *Republican?*" I did not know it then but DeWitt Clinton was already fearful that I might be a candidate, and so was doing everything possible to force his uncle to run again. But old Clinton had no desire to contest an election with me. For one thing, Jefferson had already promised him the vice-presidency. For another, I would beat him. Jefferson's dilemma was exquisite. He had removed from the contest the one person he believed could defeat me in New York. I later learned that even as we spoke DeWitt Clinton was pleading with Jefferson to bring pressure to bear upon his uncle to make the race against me.

"Yes, as a Republican. What else? Naturally, if the Clinton faction refuses to support me I shall propose myself as an independent Republican, and look for Federalist support."

The mocking-bird made a shrill sound. Jefferson and I both started in our chairs. Then he laughed. "This is not music, I tell the bird."

"Perhaps he is deaf."

"Ah, he hears. He hears."

Jefferson turned the subject to other matters and, as always, other matters invariably included the licentiousness of the press. We had both been suffering considerably that season. Cheetham in New York had been accusing me of extraordinary crimes while in Virginia James Callender had turned on his old employer and revealed to a fascinated world how Jefferson had paid him to slander Washington, Adams and Hamilton.

Callender had also been quite explicit about Jefferson's attempted seduction of Mrs. Walker as well as his long affair with the slave Sally Hemings. As it turned out, the nation was more amused than not by this unexpectedly human side to the apostle of democracy who directed our affairs with such solemn self-regard. But our philosopher-king was less than amused by Callender's libels, "particularly after my goodness to him."

"Cheetham is no different . . ."

But Jefferson was not in the least interested in my complaints. After all, Cheetham was Jefferson's creation. "Last summer I was fool enough to give Callender fifty dollars, out of pity, and then he writes me that the fifty dollars was 'hush-money'! That I paid him hush-money because he knew *things!* What things he knew I know not nor does anyone. Fortunately, he went and drowned himself. Otherwise I cannot think what I should have done."

"You can always invoke the Sedition Act." As usual, my pleasantry was taken literally.

"No. No. But," and the faded mouth became a harsh line in the old pale face, "I am convinced that what we need now are a few prosecutions of the most prominent and offensive editors. Such prosecutions would have a most wholesome effect upon the rest."

"But surely the First Amendment protects their freedom . . ."

"Is licentiousness freedom?"

"What is licentious to you may be truth to another."

Jefferson's response was grim, prompt and thought-out. "In 1789 Madison sent me a copy of the proposed amendments to the Constitution, and I wrote him that I thought he should make it clear that although our citizens are allowed to speak or publish whatever they choose, they ought not to be permitted to present false facts which might affect injuriously the life, liberty, property or reputation of others or affect the national peace with regard to foreign nations. Just the other day I reminded Madison of that sad omission in our Constitution, and he agreed that today's *monstrous* press is a direct result of the careless way the First Amendment was written."

I found this assult on the free press amazing, particularly from one who revelled in the name of republican. As usual, Jefferson had a way around the difficulty and, as usual, that way involved the inherent rights of the states. "Since the federal government has no constitutional power over the press, the states can then devise their own laws and . . ." The usual argument.

On a pleasant note, we parted. I went back to my house in F Street and wrote to my various supporters at Albany informing them that I was a candidate for governor.

Twenty-eight

THIS MORNING AS I WAS about to go into the office, Sam Swartwout came out. He looked most preoccupied. "Ah, Charlie!" I was flattered he remembered my name. "You must come see me at the Port."

"Yes, Sir." I was the eager junior.

"I can be helpful." He lumbered off through the shimmering August heat. Helpful in what way?

The Colonel was standing at the window, holding his hat behind his back in characteristic attitude. He was watching Swartwout. "Poor Sam is a conniver." The Colonel feigned sadness. "Loyal to me, and no one else. A sign of capital bad judgement, I should say."

"At least he is collector of the port."

"Yes, I got him that." The Colonel skimmed his hat across the room and it came to rest neatly on a lamp. "Jackson did me that favour when he became president. Did me a number of favours—by the Eternal!" Burr enjoys growling General Jackson's favourite epithet. "Unfortunately I cannot get the President to do anything directly for me. Not that I want anything save what is owing to me."

I have seen some of the correspondence between the Colonel and the War Department. As a former officer, the Colonel now receives a pension of $600 a year. He claims, however, that he is owed $100,000 not only in pay never collected during the Revolution but in money out of pocket: he spent his entire family inheritance on his soldiers. The government has shown no willingness to pay these arrears.

On the baize-covered table the duelling pistol still rested. As the Colonel prepared himself for the day's dictation, he hefted the pistol in a most military way and spun it about his finger, intoning suddenly an ancient bit of doggerel:

"O, Burr, O Burr, what hast thou done?
Thou hast shooted dead great Hamilton!
You hid behind a bunch of thistle,
And shooted him dead with a great hoss pistol."

He burst out laughing. I was slightly chilled by the
macabre air of the demonstration. "Well, here's the
'hoss pistol'—or a facsimile. The beautiful verse I found
attached to a set of waxworks on display up-state at
Rhinebeck, a serpents' nest of Federalism. There was
a tall, beautiful, noble Hamilton, all in wax, and a sly,
mean Burr, dark as the son of morning. Only the
thistle was absent. A sprout in the poet's head, I fear,
awaiting its moment to rhyme, so divinely, with
'pistol.'"

I copied out the poem. Then the Colonel began to
walk up and down the room, enjoying the equatorial
heat.

Memoirs of Aaron Burr–Fifteen

AMONG MY NUMEROUS CRIMES the chief is supposed to
be that I conspired to break up the union. Jefferson
wanted the world to believe that when I went west I
was bent on separating the new states of Kentucky,
Tennessee and Ohio from their natural ruler Virginia.
This was nonsense, and Jefferson knew it was nonsense.

Ironically, of the two of us, it was Jefferson who
believed that any state had the right to dissolve its
ties with the others. To him the federal government
was always "foreign," and should the federal government want a state to do something that a majority of
the state's landowners disapproved of (like abolishing
slavery), then it was Jefferson's belief that the state
had the right to nullify the federal government's laws,
and if nullification was not effective the state's proper
recourse would then be secession.

Although I never regarded the union as sacred, my
ambitions at the west did not involve secession. I was,
however, privy to the plot of 1804 to divide the United
States into two parts with the Hudson River as the
boundary.

Senator Pickering of Massachusetts led this most
respectable cabal in Congress. They wanted to detach
New England and New York from the rest of the
Virginia-dominated union. For these thoughtful men
the purchase of Louisiana had been the last straw.
They assumed, correctly, that Jefferson and the Virginia junto would carve up that vast region into a
number of slave-holding Republican states and that
New England would simply wither away, as the
Federalist party was doing. They affected also shock
at Jefferson's disregard for the Constitution at the
time of the purchase.

As Senator Plumer said to me, "If the President has
the right to buy a new state then he also has the right
to sell an old state."

"Perhaps," I suggested, "the Canadians would be so
good as to buy your own state of New Hampshire."
Senator Plumer was not charmed by this pleasantry.

My relations with the cabal were cordial but non-
committal. Yet Pickering was most insistent. "Everything depends on New York, Colonel. If New York
secedes with us we shall have a fine nation. Without
New York, we shall be a backwater like Ireland."

"Certainly New England has suffered at the hands
of Virginia and, as certainly, if you in New England
are to survive you must dominate Virginia." This was
the extent of my collusion.

"We intend to support you for governor of New
York."

"I shall need all the support I can get."

"If elected, you would be in a position to lead your
state into secession with us."

"Senator, I can assure you that my administration of
New York will do justice to all Federalists." Beyond

that I did not commit myself. Pickering was disappointed but he promised to use what influence he had to make me governor.

In March I was fairly certain of election. But by the beginning of April I knew that I was being damaged not so much by my Republican opponent but by that retired politician, that would-be Diocletian, the ineffable Alexander Hamilton who like the phoenix now rose from the ashes of the Reynolds affair to save the union.

Whether or not Hamilton was sincere in his desire to preserve the union, I do not know. I do know that he was horrified to find me, in effect, the standard-bearer of his own party in New York state.

Once again the slanders began to wheel about my head like so many bats at sundown. Apparently the brothels of New York were filled to bursting with women I had ruined. I was Caesar, Catiline. . . . It was a campaign of singular viciousness.

Yet at one point Hamilton came to Richmond Hill for dinner with Charles Biddle of Philadelphia and I have never found him so amiable. When I mentioned the libels of Cheetham in the press, Hamilton said, "Let the pistol decide. Call him out."

"I cannot. He is not a gentleman."

"Of course. Of course." Hamilton quickly changed the subject. I knew of course that he was doing everything possible to prevent my election but I did not think him capable of resorting to *personal* slander.

At this dinner I had Alexis produce a portrait of Theodosia (a great favourite of Biddle) so that we could toast her *in absentia*. Hamilton's toast was the most eloquent and enchanting.

I shall say no more of the election than that I lost it. I did carry New York City by a hundred votes but up-state the vote was heavily against me.

I had a number of projects at hand. I could return to the practice of law, and perhaps regain my place in politics (and my fortune!). Or I could go to the west where I was most popular. It would not have been difficult for me to be returned as a senator from either Kentucky or Tennessee, or as congressional delegate from the Indiana Territory. Best of all was the perennially interesting project to undertake the liberation of Mexico from Spain. To a man the people of the United States wanted the Spanish Dons driven from our hemisphere. Not even Hamilton could have found anything sinister in such a design for he too had secretly been dealing with various Latin worthies, hoping to be their leader. Hamilton dreamed of a Mexican empire for himself in alliance with England. I dreamed of one for myself, in alliance with the United States. Once again we were in competition; this time fatally.

I still possess a number of issues of a Federalist newspaper called *The Wasp* that was printed at Hudson, New York, under the editorship of a young man named Harry Croswell. During 1802 and 1803, young Master Croswell launched a series of attacks upon Jefferson.

Here is one: "Mr. Jefferson has for years past while his wife was living and does now since she is dead, keep a woolly headed concubine" (for the record, the hair of the concubine was not at all woolly but uncommonly fine and fair), "by the name of Sally— that by her he had several children, and that one by the name of Tom has since his father's election taken upon himself many airs of importance, and boasted his extraction from a president." The would-be seduction of Mrs. Walker was again retold. Most damaging, however, was the accusation that Jefferson had subsidized Callender when he was writing "The Prospect Before Us" (in which Washington was called "a perjurer, a robber and a traitor"). This was dangerous stuff because it was true: Jefferson had indeed given Callender money as well as private information.

After quoting from Jefferson's first inaugural, extolling Washington, Master Croswell wrote, "There he makes him a demigod—having already paid Callender

for making him a devil . . . will the word hypocrite
describe this man? There is not strength enough in the
term." This brought blood from Jefferson's thin skin.

The state Attorney-General was instructed to see to
it that Croswell was indicted for libel, which he did.
When Croswell asked for copies of the indictment
before he made reply, access was denied him. When he
asked for James Callender to be called as a witness,
the Attorney-General stated the principle that what
mattered in a libel case was not the truth or falsehood
of the statement but whether or not Croswell had
published a libel against the President. "The truth,"
said Jefferson's attorney-general, "cannot be given in
evidence."

Suddenly the "wholesome prosecution" had become
a most unwholesome attempt on the part of an
American president to abridge freedom of speech. It
was Hamilton who, unexpectedly, became the defender
of liberty against Jefferson the would-be censor.

It was a beautifully comic yet highly significant contest. The first round was won by Jefferson with the aid
of New York's Chief Justice who upheld the doctrine
that in such a case truth is not the issue. But the
Chief Justice then made the mistake of adding, "I very
much regret that the law is not otherwise." He then
directed the jury to determine only whether or not
Croswell had published the alleged libels. The jury
had no choice but to say that Croswell had indeed
published what he had published. Croswell's counsel
asked for a new trial, declaring that the jury had been
misdirected, and that truth must be given in evidence.

The second trial took place in February 1804. Although Hamilton had favoured the Sedition Act, he
was now, most eloquently, on the other side of the
fence. From all accounts, it was Hamilton's finest moment. In explaining his attitude toward the Sedition
Act he declared, disingenuously, that it had only been
aimed at what Jefferson liked to refer to as "false
facts" (the counter-term, no doubt, for "true lies").

Now the issue was to be truth-in-libel, and Hamilton elevated the discourse to Miltonic heights. "We ought to resist, resist, resist until we hurl the Demagogues and Tyrants from their imaginary Thrones." And, "it ought to be distinctly known whether Mr. Jefferson be guilty or not of so foul an act as the one charged."

I found it singularly delicious that Hamilton the Monocrat should be in a position to accuse Jefferson the Great Leveller of being not only Tyrant, but occupant of a throne!

Since Callender was by then dead, the actual guilt of Jefferson never did become an issue.

The judges divided two to two, and the legislature at Albany then prepared a truth-in-libel bill that is now the law of the land. Hamilton was again the idol of Federalism.

Unfortunately for Hamilton (and for me) I was, in effect, the Federalist candidate for governor and Hamilton could not bear this anomaly. At a dinner party in Albany to celebrate his victory in court, Hamilton indulged himself in a series of libels on my character in which truth, I fear, was hardly an issue.

About the middle of June I was sitting in the upstairs study at Richmond Hill with William Van Ness and his former law clerk Martin Van Buren. With some difficulty, I had just made peace between the two. Van Ness thought Van Buren disloyal for supporting the regular Republican for governor rather than me. I explained, as best I could, that Matty had to do as he did because "he is young and wants a career in politics." The two men were finally reconciled. But when Van Buren told me that he had supported the regular Republican ticket out of loyalty to his law partner, I told him that personal loyalty was the worst possible reason for doing anything in politics. "The important thing is to begin your career on the winning side. It makes a good impression—if only on the gods."

We were going through a number of newspapers just arrived from up-state, and enjoying some of the more fantastical portraits of me (including a learned dissertation on the precise number of women I had ruined), when Van Ness showed me a copy of the Albany *Register* dated April 24, 1804. It contained what looked to be a letter from Dr. Charles Cooper, reporting on a dinner party at Albany: "Gen. Hamilton and Judge Kent have declared in substance, that they looked upon Mr. Burr to be a dangerous man, and one who ought not to be trusted with the reins of government."

"That is hardly exceptional," I said. "Besides, I think Judge Kent voted for me."

Then I saw what had attracted Van Ness's eye: "I could," wrote Dr. Cooper, "detail to you a still more despicable opinion which General Hamilton has expressed of Mr. Burr." We looked in vain for that "more despicable opinion" but it was not given.

"It is the usual Hamilton diatribe." Matty did not take the matter seriously. Nor did I at first.

But in the night I began to meditate on just what was meant by "more despicable." Hamilton had already called me Caesar, Catiline, Bonaparte (while himself dreaming of a crown in Mexico should he fail to subvert Jefferson's feudal Utopia). What did he now mean by "more despicable"? I fear that my usual equanimity in these matters had been much shaken by the recent election. I did not sleep that night. The next morning I wrote a letter to Hamilton. Then I sent for Van Ness.

"I think this . . . *thing* demands an explanation."

"I agree." Van Ness was even grimmer than I. He would deliver my letter in person. The letter was short. I asked for "a prompt and unqualified acknowledgement or denial of the use of any expression which could warrant the assertions of Dr. Cooper." I enclosed the newspaper cutting. This was on June 19.

Van Ness delivered the letter to Hamilton who saw immediately the seriousness of the matter. "I shall answer Colonel Burr later today." But later that day

Hamilton called on Van Ness and asked if he might have another day in which to prepare his reply.

On June 21, I received a letter from Hamilton. It was long. There was a good deal of quibbling as to the precise meaning of "despicable." He then declared that he could not be held responsible for the inferences that others might draw from anything he had said "of a political opponent in the course of fifteen years' competition."

I answered him the same day, remarking that "political opposition can never absolve gentlemen from the necessity of a rigid adherence to the laws of honour." I pointed out that the accepted meaning of the word "despicable" conveys the idea of dishonour. I asked for a definite reply.

The next day Hamilton called on a friend and gave him a second letter to give Van Ness when he called. In this letter Hamilton complained of my peremptory style. He could not, he decided, give me a reply any more definite than the one he had put forward in his first letter. That of course was no reply at all. Meanwhile Hamilton's friend told Van Ness that he was authorized to say that Hamilton's recollection of the dinner party at Albany was somewhat hazy but to the extent that Colonel Burr was at all discussed the context was entirely political and bore upon the current election for governor. Apparently no reflections upon Colonel Burr's *private* character were made by General Hamilton.

It was at about this time that I learned exactly what it was that Hamilton had said of me, and knew that this world was far too narrow a place to contain the two of us.

Hamilton's friend made one further attempt to get him off the hook but only further impaled the slanderer by remarking that should Colonel Burr wish to enquire of any *other* conversation of Hamilton concerning Burr, a prompt and frank avowal or denial would be given. This was too much. I told Van Ness to set a time and place for an interview.

The friend made one last attempt to save his principal on the peculiar ground that General Hamilton
did not believe himself to be the *original* author of
any of the unpleasant rumours currently circulating
about Colonel Burr, excepting one which had been
cleared up years before: this had to do with my supposedly thrusting, as it were, Eliza Bowen into Hamilton's bed in order to learn his secrets. Actually she
thrust herself there, with his aid. And though she did
give me a copy of the pamphlet he had written attacking John Adams, he was forced to agree that I had in
no way solicited it.

Hamilton then complained of my "predetermined
hostility" to him. Van Ness replied for me, pointing
out that the phrase "predetermined hostility" was insult added to injury and that the evasive length of
Hamilton's correspondence seemed very like guilt.

It was determined that we would meet across the
river in New Jersey, on the heights known as Weehawk. Nathaniel Pendleton would be second to Hamilton. Van Ness would be second to me. Pistols would be
our weapons. Hamilton then asked that we delay the
interview until after the close of the Circuit Court.
It was agreed that we meet in two weeks' time on
July 11, 1804.

For two weeks we kept our secret from all but a
handful of intimates. I put my affairs in order; wrote
letters to Theodosia; prepared a will. I worried a good
deal about the debts I would leave behind if I were
killed. No doubt, Hamilton was in the same frame of
mind. If anything, he was in a far worse position than
I: he was deeply in debt largely due to The Grange,
a pretentious country seat he was preparing for himself several miles above Richmond Hill. He also had
seven children. Fortunately for them, his wife was a
Schuyler so the poorhouse would never claim these
relics.

I soon discovered that I had made a mistake granting Hamilton a two weeks' delay. He immediately
arranged for one Samuel Bradhurst to challenge me

to a duel with swords. I had no choice but to answer this gentleman. We fought near Hoboken. I was at a considerable disadvantage since Mr. Bradhurst's arms were about three inches longer than mine. It was Hamilton's design that I be, at the least, so cut up by Mr. Bradhurst that I would not be in any condition to succeed in our interview on July 11. Fortunately, I drew blood immediately. Mr. Bradhurst withdrew from the field of honour, leaving me unscratched.

On the evening of July 4, I attended the celebration of the Society of the Cincinnati at Fraunces' Tavern.

Hamilton was most poised. In fact, I have seldom seen him so charming. "I must congratulate you on a successful interview," he murmured as we bowed to one another in the tap-room.

"I hope your friend Mr. Bradhurst will make a swift recovery." I turned away.

Despite Hamilton's notorious arrogance and shortness with those whose minds worked less swiftly than his own, he had the gift of enchanting others when he chose. Suspecting that this might well be his last public appearance, he meant for all the world to remember him as he was that night, still handsome despite the fleshiness of too much good living, still able to delight with subtle flattery those older than himself, to dazzle with his brilliance those younger.

As we sat at table in the long room—a group of middle-aged men who shared nothing but the fact that we had all been young at the same time and had fought as officers in the Revolution—I too had the sense that this might be my last appearance upon the republic's brightest stage. There was a good chance that I would be killed. There was an even better chance that Hamilton would be killed. But whatever happened, nothing would ever be the same again in a week's time.

I felt curiously detached as I sat in the place of honour (despite my recent electoral defeat I was still vice-president of the United States); saw myself as from a great distance, already a carnival waxworks and no longer real.

Others have written that I was moody and distant that night. Obviously I was not in full command of myself. But then the ultimate encounter was at hand. The man who had set himself the task of ruining me during "fifteen years' competition" was now about to complete his work, and I must have known in some instinctive way that he would again succeed no matter what happened on the Weehawk Heights.

I was genuinely moved when at the company's request General Hamilton got up and in his fine tenor voice sang "The Drum," a song that no veteran of the Revolution can listen to without sorrow for his lost youth and the dead he loved.

Needless to say, I did not realize with what cunning Hamilton had prepared his departure from this world, and my ruin.

Twenty-nine

TODAY THE COLONEL was in a most curious and excited mood. "If it amuses you, Charlie, we shall go to the Heights of Weehawk and I shall act out for you the duel of the century, when the infamous Burr slew the noble Hamilton, from behind a thistle—obviously a disparaging allusion to my small stature. Yet Hamilton was less than an inch taller than I though now he looms a giant of legend, with a statue to his divinity in the Merchants' Exchange, his temple. While for me no statue, no laurel, only thistle!"

I was delighted and somewhat embarrassed. Burr almost never speaks of the duel; and most people, unlike Leggett, are much too nervous of the subject

ever to bring it up in his presence even though it is
the one thing everyone in the world knows about
Aaron Burr, and the one thing it is impossible *not* to
think of upon first meeting him.

"*He* killed General Hamilton," my mother whispered
to me when the elegant little old man first came into
our Greenwich Village tavern, after his return from
Europe. "Take a good look at him. He was a famous
man once."

As I grew older, I realized that my family admired
Burr more than not and that my mother was pleased
when he took a fancy to me, gave me books to read,
encouraged me to attend Columbia College and take
up the law. But my first glimpse of him at a table
close to the pump-room fire was of the devil himself,
and I half-expected him to leave not by way of the
door but up the chimney with the flames.

We walked to Middle Pier at the end of Duane
Street. "I've ordered my young boatman to stand by."

The Colonel's eyes were bright at the prospect of
such an unusual adventure—into past time rather than
into that airy potential future time where he is most
at home.

"It was a hot day like this—thirty years and one
month ago. Yet I remember being most unseasonably
cold. In fact, I ordered a fire the night of the tenth,
and slept in my clothes on a sofa in the study. Slept
very well, I might add. A detail to be added to your
heroic portrait of me." An amused glance in my direction. "Around dawn, John Swartwout came to wake
me up. I was then joined by Van Ness and Matt
Davis. We embarked from Richmond Hill."

The tall young boatman was waiting for us at the
deserted slip. The sun was fierce. We were the only
people on the wharf: the whole town has gone away
for August.

We got into the boat, and the young man began
to row with slow regular strokes up-river to the high
green Jersey shore opposite.

"On just such a morning . . ." He hummed to himself softly. Then: "My affairs were in order. I had set out six blue boxes, containing enough material for my biography, if anyone was minded to write such a thing. Those boxes now rest at the bottom of the sea." He was blithe even at this allusion to the beloved daughter: trailed his finger in the river; squinted at the sun. "What, I wonder, do the fishes make of my history?"

I tried to imagine him thirty years ago, with glossy dark hair, an unlined face, a steady hand—the Vice-President on an errand of honour. But I could not associate this tiny old man with that figure of legend.

"Love-letters to me were all discreetly filed, with instructions to be burned, to be returned to owners, to be read at my grave—whatever was fitting. My principal emotion that morning was relief. Everything was arranged. Everything was well-finished."

"Did you think you might be killed?"

The Colonel shook his head. "When I wroke up on the sofa, saw dawn, I knew that I would live to see the sun set, that Hamilton would not." A sudden frown as he turned out of the bright sun; the face went into shadow. "You see, Hamilton *deserved* to die and at my hands."

I then asked the question I have wanted to ask since yesterday but Burr only shook his head. "I have no intention of repeating, ever, what it was that Hamilton said of me."

In silence, we watched the steamboat from Albany make its way down the centre channel of the river. On the decks women in bright summer finery twirl parasols; over the water their voices echo the gulls that follow in the ship's wake, waiting for food.

Apparently the Weehawk Heights "look just the same now as they did then." The Colonel skipped easily onto the rocky shore. While I helped our sailor drag his boat onto the beach, the Colonel walked briskly up a narrow footpath to a wooded ledge.

"Ideal for its purpose," Burr said when I joined him.

The ledge is about six feet wide and perhaps thirty or forty feet long with a steep cliff above and below it. At either end a green tangle of brush partly screens the view of the river.

The Colonel indicates the spires of New York City visible through the green foliage. "That is the last sight many a gentleman saw."

I notice that he is whispering; he notices, too, and laughs. "From habit. When duellists came here they were always very quiet for fear they'd wake an old man who lived in a hut near by. He was called the Captain and he hated duelling. If he heard you, he would rush onto the scene and thrust himself between the duellists and refuse to budge. Often to everyone's great relief."

Burr crosses to the marble obelisk at the centre of the ledge. "I have not seen this before." The monument is dedicated to the memory of Alexander Hamilton. Parts have been chipped away while the rest is scribbled over with lovers' names. The Colonel makes no comment.

Then he crosses slowly to a large cedar tree, pushing aside weeds, kicking pebbles from his path. At the base of the tree he stops and takes off his black jacket. He stares down at the river. I grow uneasy; cannot think why. I tell myself that there are no ghosts.

When Burr finally speaks his voice is matter-of-fact. "Just before seven o'clock Hamilton and his second Pendleton and the good Dr. Hosack—Hamilton was always fearful for his health—arrive. Just down there." Burr points. I look, half-expecting to see the dead disembark. But there is only river below us.

"Pendleton carries an umbrella. So does Van Ness. Which looks most peculiar on a summer morning but the umbrellas are to disguise our features. We are now about to break the law."

Burr leaves his post at the cedar tree, walks to the end of the ledge. "Now General Hamilton arrives, with his second."

For an instant I almost see the rust-coloured hair of
Hamilton, shining in summer sun. I have the sense of
being trapped in someone else's dream, caught in a
constant circular unceasing present. It is a horrible
sensation.

Burr bows. "Good morning, General. Mr. Pendleton,
good morning." Burr turns and walks toward me.
"Billy." I swear he now thinks me Van Ness. "You
and Pendleton draw lots to see who has choice of
position, and who will give the word to fire."

With blind eyes, the Colonel indicates for me to
cross to the upper end of the ledge.

"Your principal has won both choices, Mr. Pendleton." A pause. "He wants to stand *there?*" A slight
note of surprise in Burr's voice.

I realize suddenly that I am now standing where
Hamilton stood. The sun is in my eyes; through green
leaves water reflects brightness.

Burr has now taken up his position ten full paces
opposite me. I think I am going to faint. Burr has the
best position, facing the heights. I know that I am
going to die. I want to scream, but dare not.

"I am ready." The Colonel seems to hold in his
hand a heavy pistol. "What?" He looks at me, lowers
the pistol. "You require your glasses? Of course, General. I shall wait."

"Is General Hamilton satisfied?" Burr then asks.
"Good, I am ready, too."

I stand transfixed with terror as Burr takes aim, and
shouts "Present!"

And I am killed.

Burr starts toward me, arms out-stretched. I feel my
legs give way; feel the sting, the burning of the bullet
in my belly; feel myself begin to die. Just in time Burr
stops. He becomes his usual self, and so do I.

"Hamilton fired first. I fired an instant later. Hamilton's bullet broke a branch from this tree." Burr
indicated the tall cedar. "My bullet pierced his liver
and spine. He drew himself up on his toes. Like this."
Burr rose like a dancer. "Then fell to a half-sitting

position. Pendleton propped him up. 'I am a dead man,' Hamilton said. I started toward him but Van Ness stopped me. Dr. Hosack was coming. So we left.

"But . . . but I would've stayed and gone to you had it not been for what I saw in your face." Again the blind look in Burr's eyes. Again he sees me as Hamilton. And again I start to die, the bullet burns.

"I saw terror in your face, terror at the evil you had done me. And that is why I could not come to you or give you any comfort. Why I could do nothing but what I did. Aim to kill, and kill."

He sat down at the edge of the monument. Rubbed his eyes. The vision—or whatever this lunacy was— passed. In a quiet voice, he continued, "As usual with me, the world saw fit to believe a different story. The night before our meeting Hamilton wrote a letter to posterity; it was on the order of a penitent monk's last confession. He would reserve his first fire, he declared, and perhaps his second because, *morally*, he disapproved of duelling. Then of course he fired first. As for his disapproval of duelling, he had issued at least three challenges that I know of. But Hamilton realized better than anyone that the world—our American world at least—loves a canting hypocrite."

Burr got to his feet. Started toward the path. I followed dumbly.

"Hamilton lived for a day and a half. He was in character to the very last. He told Bishop Moore that he felt no ill-will toward me. That he had met me with a fixed resolution to do me no harm. What a contemptible thing to say!"

Burr started down the path. I staggered after him. At the river's edge he paused and looked across the slow water toward the flowery rise of Staten Island. "I had forgot how lovely this place was, if I had ever noticed."

We got into the boat. "You know, I made Hamilton a giant by killing him. If he had lived, he would have continued his decline. He would have been quite forgotten by now. Like me." This was said without emotion. "While that might have been *my* monument up there, all scribbled over."

Thirty

I TOOK SAM SWARTWOUT at his word and went to him for help. He received me at the Tontine Coffee House where he holds court every afternoon. With him was Mordecai Noah, recently his aide at the Port of New York.

Noah recalled me pleasantly. Spoke at length of the Indians who are, he maintains, a lost tribe of Israel.

"Why else would I—of all people—have joined Tammany?" On this fantastical note, he departed.

"Well, how do you like poking about in our old cupboards?" Swartwout drinks Spanish wine by the hour; and is not always coherent. Worse luck for me.

"He's a great man, the Colonel is. And his life has been the greatest waste. You ought to hear General Jackson on the subject. 'By the Eternal, the ablest man in all our political life!' "

"Then why doesn't the President pay the Colonel the money owed him from the Revolution?"

"He don't dare. Don't dare do anything for the Colonel. Told him so quite frankly when he came through town last year."

"*They met?*" The Colonel has never so much as hinted at a meeting with the President.

"I was in the room." Swartwout winked. Called for more wine. "You see, Old Hickory—like me—is by way of being a protégé of the Colonel."

"Out west?"

"Out west. And before. Ever since Tennessee came

into the union, thanks to the Colonel who was in the Senate then. Old Hickory was the first congressman from the state and the first call he made when he got to Philadelphia was on Senator Burr."

Is this true? I don't know. I am simply taking it all down.

I asked what the Colonel's intentions were in Mexico but all that Swartwout would say was, "They arrested me. Did you know that? I was dragged around in chains for months. Massa Tom wanted to prove us all traitors. But if there was any traitor it was him not us." Swartwout's reminiscences then became somewhat disconnected. Finally, I asked him if we might meet some *morning*, and he said that he would be delighted. "Anything to be useful—to the Colonel, that is."

Before I left, I asked, "What was it that General Hamilton said of Colonel Burr that was so 'despicable'? That made him fight the duel?"

Swartwout gave me a long look from bloodshot eyes. "Don't you know?"

"No. And the Colonel won't tell me."

"I suppose he would not. An ugly story, and it was typical of Hamilton to spread it about."

"What did Hamilton say of the Colonel?"

"Why, he said that Aaron Burr was the lover of his own daughter, Theodosia."

Not until I was half-way home did I begin to wonder whether or not what Hamilton had said might, after all, be true.

"He loved no one else!" Madame's voice was shrill in my memory.

Thirty-one

Yesterday afternoon Mr. Craft and I were sent for by Mrs. McManus, "as I am most worried," she wrote. "The Colonel has had the stroke, and cannot move."

We took the ferry across to Jersey City. The day was cloudy, windy, prematurely equinoctial.

"He has a strong frame," observed Mr. Craft.

"But he is seventy-eight," I said.

I stared at the gulls. Mr. Craft stared at a group of Irish workmen. Though it was not eight o'clock in the morning, they were passing round bottles of whiskey. I wish I could regard them with the same long view the Colonel does. One day we were standing outside the court-house with a group of lawyers who were arguing a constitutional point. Finally, a lawyer appealed to Colonel Burr who was watching with his usual delight a near-by building site swarming with Irish workmen. The Colonel gave his opinion.

The lawyer disagreed. "Your view, Sir, is not that of the current expounders of our constitution . . ."

"My dear Sir," and the Colonel pointed at the Irish, "*they* are the current expounders of our constitution."

One of *them*, Jane McManus, opened the door of a small frame-house not far from the Jersey City landing. She was plump with a good-humoured face soiled by recent weeping.

"Oh, gentlemen, I thought he was good as dead, I did, when I came in with some tea for him and he was lying on the floor with his eyes wide open and not breathing. Well, then I called for our doctor, and he wasn't to be found. Are they ever? Then at sundown the Colonel opens his eyes—he's on the sofa now where the new maid and I put him—and he opens his eyes suddenly and he says, 'Am I dead?' and I says,

'No, Colonel, you are alive and with me here in Jersey,' and he says, 'my native shore' or something like that, always that little smile of his and then he tells me he can't move ... can't *move!*"

She wept for a time and Mr. Craft looked at her sternly until she stopped. I looked at an engraving of —yes, George Washington and his mother! Could the Colonel have bought it to remind himself of the conversation with Hamilton? Or does he perhaps spin his web of memory from the sights about him?

Done with her sobbing, Jane McManus showed us into the parlour where the Colonel reclined on a horsehair sofa, a blanket drawn up to his chin. He seemed cold despite the heat of a Franklin stove. On the table beside him was a stuffed bird beneath a dirty glass bell (a mocking-bird?). I grow suspicious.

"Gentlemen." The voice was weak. "It seems that I am paralyzed below the waist."

"But in good health, Colonel!" boomed Mr. Craft.

Burr winced—with pain? or simply at the idiocy of Mr. Craft. "Yes, Mr. Craft, I am in tip-top shape, saving the fact that I cannot walk."

"But, Colonel, you will, you will! Remember last time?"

"It's different this time," said Miss McManus. "The doctor said he's had a proper stroke. And he's not our usual doctor but one from across town who I found at the chemist's by chance."

"Most lucky," murmured the Colonel. "A natural healer who told me that at my age and with my medical history I should have been translated to a higher sphere at the first sign of headache."

"What was it like?" I fear that this was my first response. At least it amused him.

"Ever the alert biographer! Well, Charlie, it was like nothing at all. I was reading. I had a mild headache. Nothing unusual. Then I suddenly felt dizzy. Got to my feet—apparently for the last time ..."

"Colonel, don't say that!" cried Jane McManus.

"Then I found myself falling comfortably through

the air. Such a pleasant sensation, I thought to myself, as slowly the carpet rose to gather me to its cheerful Persian bosom. I go out just like a light, I thought. And so went out. Now I've been turned on again, at half-flame."

"What shall we do?" Miss McManus appealed to us as if the Colonel was not there.

"I shall tell Mrs. Burr . . ." Mr. Craft began.

"You will do no such thing!" The old voice was firm. "What you *will* do is find me lodging in New York. Near the office. I intend to go on as before."

"Yes, Colonel. And we have a lot of work to do." That was my tonic for him; it had a good effect.

"Indeed we have. That is why I want to be moved to the other side no later than Sunday."

"Oh, no!" wailed Miss McManus.

But the Colonel's "Oh, yes" settled the matter. We were commissioned to find him rooms in a boarding-house. Meanwhile, his cases pending would go forward as if nothing had happened.

"In fact, I would appreciate it if you were not to mention that I have had a stroke. Simply say that an old war-wound confines me to a chair."

So that is what we have been saying for several days now. But Leggett knows the truth and to-night told me I had best hurry up and extract what I can on the subject of Van Buren. Leggett is uncommonly cold-blooded. But then he is dying, too.

Thirty-two

TODAY WAS THE COLONEL's first day in New York. Since we have not yet found him a proper lodging, he stops for the present at Reade Street. Mr. Craft has found a German woman to act as nurse, and a cot has been made up for her in the room next to that of the Colonel, who regards her sombrely: he would prefer a man to look after him for the stroke has made him incontinent, but Mr. Craft's enthusiasm for Frau Witsch has so far carried the day.

Until noon the Colonel received clients, and for a time we thought that our fiction about the old war-wound was a success. But just as Frau Witsch was helping the Colonel to eat a heavy vegetable soup, a large thin figure appeared in the doorway. Dressed in sooty black and clutching an equally sooty book, our visitor pointed a bony finger at Burr and screamed, "Repent! Repent! Greatest of sinners! Murderer and traitor! Repent for thy moment of judgement is now at hand!"

The demented dominie was treated to the Colonel's most benign and courtly manner. "So good of you to be concerned, my dear reverend . . ."

"On your knees, sinner! Pray! Pray with me that God save your infamous soul!"

"It is my daily prayer."

"On your knees, sinner!"

"That is not alas, practical." The Colonel turned to me. "I do believe, Charlie, that the reverend father has forgot where the door is."

Frau Witsch and I then seized the maniac and hustled him out of the office. He resisted us like one inspired by God but by a so-so Mormonite kind of God: one got the sense that he had been ejected rather easily from more than a few sinful places.

Colonel Burr sighed. "It is the same as the last time I was ill. Every preacher in the city wants the honour . . . no, the glory, the heavenly glory of helping me out of this vale of tears and into Heaven—or worse. Apparently their fee is paid no matter *how* my case is disposed of."

Done with eating soup, the Colonel sends Frau Witsch away with a speech of appreciation in Dutch. She responds in German, and leaves us alone.

The Colonel is philosophic. "I can face death with some ease. I believe that I shall be able to face God with equanimity. But deliver me from his earthly agents!" Burr shudders; then motions for me to re-arrange his legs on the soft where he half-reclines, pillows at his back. From the waist up the Colonel is fully, even formally dressed; below he wears only his long shirt, and the blankets that swathe his dis-abled limbs.

Memoirs of Aaron Burr—Sixteen

AFTER HAMILTON'S DEATH, I remained at Richmond Hill for ten days. I confess that I was not prepared for the response to our interview. Apparently no one had ever fought a duel in the whole history of the United States until Aaron Burr invented this diabolic game in order to murder the greatest American that ever lived (after George Washington, of course). Over night the arrogant, mob-detesting Hamilton was metamor-phosed into a Christ-like figure with me as the Judas—no, the Caiaphas who so villainously despatched the godhead to its heavenly father (George Washington again) at Weehawk, our new Jerusalem's most unlikely Golgotha.

I confess that I was deeply and permanently dis-gusted by the extent and the variety of my country-men's hypocrisy. Ninety per cent of our newspapers were Republican and so had devoted the better part of two decades to the vilification of Alexander Hamil-ton. Therefore, it was with some wonder that I read in their pages of the saintly Hamilton's martyrdom at my wicked hands. I confess that during those days im-mediately following Hamilton's death, I ceased to want to live amongst such a people.

I did receive encouraging messages from a number of gentlemen who could not be regarded as friends. Among them was George Clinton who despatched a verbal message to me by way of Matt Davis. "You are perfectly innocent of any crime since the bastard Hamilton was under no obligation to meet you."

This was the private view of every gentleman in the country. How could it be otherwise? From DeWitt Clinton to Andrew Jackson, from Henry Clay to John Randolph, a large number of our leaders have been involved, like it or not, in similar affairs of honour. But no gentleman came to my defence in public. Hamilton had seen to that, for he had most shrewdly written a number of letters for posterity (where, apparently, one is never under oath: *ab mortuis nihil veritas*). So incensed was public opinion that a New York coroner's jury indicted me for murder—in *New Jersey*!

On July 21, I ordered a barge to take me from Richmond Hill. As my trunks were put on board, I said good-bye to The Little Band. We did our best to keep up our spirits, despite rumours of a mob with a rope in near-by Greenwich Village.

Suddenly we were startled by a loud cry. Then a black woman appeared from behind the slave cabin nearest the water's edge (where Martha Washington kept ice). It was Old Mary, a fixture at Richmond Hill.

"You won't ever come back, Colonel! Ever!" Old Mary wept and kissed my hand as she had kissed the hands of the two previous tenants Washington and Adams. But she was wrong. I came back to Richmond Hill last year and for fifty cents sat in the gallery and watched an indifferent tragedy. But, in a way, Old Mary was right. I never did come back to *her* Richmond Hill—or to mine. Today nothing but the shell of the house is left. The Minetta Brook, the farm, the park, the leafy river-side—all are now built-up and thoroughly John Jacob Astorized.

But I had no such presentiments when the barge finally departed for Staten Island at about ten o'clock in the evening. I recall only a marvellous summer night. Huge stars in a black sky. The soft slow sound

of the Hudson River all about me. Despite the danger
I was in, I was at peace—like a ghost released from an
unwanted body, or like an image freed from a shattered
mirror: Hamilton was dead, and I was not.

I stopped the next day with a friend at Perth Amboy,
and then moved on to Philadelphia where I was remarkably well-received, despite the ferocity of the
newspapers.

I stayed at the house of my friend Charles Biddle,
and a pleasant time we had, living the life of two
bachelors (his family had left the city for the summer).

Presently we were joined by the husband of Charles
Biddle's cousin Ann: the illustrious commanding general of the army of the United States, Brigadier-General
James Wilkinson. Yes, it was my old friend from Cambridge and Valley Forge and, most recently, New York
City where Jamie had come to see me in May in order
to convince me that now that my career in eastern
politics had been so thoroughly disposed of, glory
awaited me at the west. Combined with him, I might
again be what I was before the fatal contest with Jefferson and the Virginian junto.

Wilkinson and I sat up late one night in the comfortable library of the Biddle house (our host had tactfully withdrawn), and as Philadelphia's famous flies
buzzed in the summer night, occasionally immolating
themselves in the bright lamps, Jamie described to me
the situation at the west. "Our people hate the
Spanish. They want to drive them out of Mobile,
out of the Floridas, out of Mexico. They're sick of
Massa Tom, too. Sick of the easterners. Sick of having
to truckle to the Dons. All they lack is a leader, Burr.
All they lack is you.

Jamie guzzled port. He bore not the slightest resemblance to the boy general I had known at Valley
Forge. For one thing he had designed himself a uniform calculated to make a Napoleonic marshal look
drab as a Jesuit. For another the stocky youth of the
Revolution was now being impersonated by a fat, soft

man with loose jowls and a concentrated fierce gaze, rather like that of a sow about to cannibalise her piglets. The once clear voice had grown harsh from drink. Yet the boy general's exuberant charm continued. Jamie was as adroit at flattering others as he was at praising himself. For a politician—and that is what Jamie was—this is a gift of the gods. He used it well. But then he had no choice. After the Revolution, his army career ended somewhat confusedly and upon the dying fall (his accounts as clothier-general to the army never quite added up). It was as a civilian that he went west in order to make money at the rich Spanish port of New Orleans.

Some time in 1787, Wilkinson took a secret oath of allegiance to Spain in the presence of his friend Miró—the Spanish governor of Louisiana. This was usual for those Americans who wanted to trade in Louisiana without paying heavy duties. But Jamie could never be usual. Excited as always by intrigue (and making money), he proposed that Spain support him in a scheme to detach the western states from the rest of the United States and join them to Louisiana, either under the Spanish crown or as a neutral state. This ill-starred scheme (known later as the Spanish Conspiracy) had a good deal of western support, and Jamie took to calling himself, rather prematurely, the "Washington of the West."

I cannot think why Jamie was always so plausible to others, including me. If ever any man looked and acted the part of a scoundrel it was he. He was forever whispering "secrets" in his hoarse voice. He was forever trying to undo someone—from George Washington at Valley Forge to Governor Claiborne at New Orleans to, alas, one Aaron Burr. Yet for a time he managed to trick us all.

"I have been devoted to the independence of the western states for nearly twenty years." This was true. But that evening in Philadelphia I did not know why or in whose interest he was so dedicated. "I know every inch of Kentucky, Tennessee, Indiana, Mississippi, Louisiana. I know the leaders." Although it was unlikely that Charles Biddle was hiding behind the black lacquer Oriental screen, Jamie lowered his voice. "I went back to the army in 1791 so that I would be in a position to continue my work. *Our* work, Burr. Because a word from you and tomorrow morning every man in the west will rally to our standard!"

I was surprised. It had been my impression that the "Spanish Conspiracy" was a dead issue ever since the Louisiana Purchase gave the westerners New Orleans. Although the frontiersmen disliked the easterners, it was war with Spain they wanted, not separation from the Atlantic seaboard.

"Now I have also maintained good relations with the Dons." Indeed Jamie had! It was to take me three years to sort out his various intrigues. Fascinated, I watched as more and more wine went down his gullet. "With the Dons . . ." he repeated; blinked his eyes; was for an instant disoriented.

Jamie belched. Sighed. Complained. "Did you know that the Wilkinson family owned most of the land where the city of Washington now stands? and that my father sold that land for nothing, for nothing! My God, Burr, the money I would have had!" He struck his huge stomach a blow, as though that part of him had somehow collaborated with the feckless dead parent.

I had heard this story many times; and got him back to what interested me. "It is my impression"—I was cautious—"that the western states are now quite pleased with the Administration. After all, they have New Orleans. Except for Baton Rouge the Mississippi is American."

"But the Dons are still at Mobile. We still lack the Floridas! And they are ours by every right of treaty— yes, ours God-given!" Wilkinson suddenly sounded like Jefferson.

"What is the mood of the people at New Orleans?"

"Bloody, Burr, bloody! They hate Jefferson. Hate the Yankees. You—and I—could free that city with a thousand—no, with five hundred men."

I was amused. "Why do we need so many men since the defender of New Orleans is the commanding general of the American army—you!"

Wilkinson laughed—a sudden thick bubbling sound like German soup cooking on a Franklin stove (a quotidian simile, Charlie, if ever there was one). "Now you begin to see why I came back to the army five years ago. Why I got myself made commanding general." This promotion was not as lofty as it sounds. Since Jefferson preferred not to have any army, it was hard to find a self-respecting military man eager to take over the ridiculously under-manned "forces" of the United States.

"I had wondered." Until that night in Philadelphia, Jamie had only revealed to me bits and pieces of his intentions. We had been corresponding with one another since 1794 (in cipher, at his urging). But our correspondence was never of much interest. I apprised him of the political situation at Washington while he gave me news of sentiment at the west where my popularity continued to grow year after year. The westerners appreciated my role in the admission of Tennessee to the union, as well as my opposition to Hamilton. Distance, too, lends enchantment. By the summer of 1804, I was—next to Jefferson—the most popular American west of the Alleghenies.

"I saw my chance in 1799. When it looked as if there might be war with France, I told General Hamilton . . ." Jamie stopped; chin suddenly sagged over his collar; eyes popped like a light-snared toad's. Had he been tactless?

"The name does not distress me." I was soothing.

"Must say—never knew you was such a fine shot!" And Jamie giggled. He was good company, in his way, and for all his pomposity saw the humour in everything but himself. I am rather the reverse.

Jamie gave me his version of how he had got Hamilton to appoint him commanding general of the Mississippi Territory. "I was as frank with him as I am with you." This sentiment, no matter by whom proposed, invariably proclaims if not a liar a lie. "I said, 'General Hamilton, it is only a matter of time before we go to war with France. And now that France has got her hands on Spain that means all the Spanish territories like Louisiana and the Floridas and Mexico and the next continent down, the whole lot can be ours for the taking.' Well, he gave me that condescending look he was so good at and says, 'My dear Wilkinson, never tell a superior officer what he already knows.' Well, there were a lot of things I could have told him he didn't know but I was ever so polite and humble, the way he liked you to be, and that warmed him up enough to tell me how it was his idea—and General Washington agreed—that we make an alliance with England and with their fleet and our army we attack New Orleans, Havannah, Vera Cruz, and then go on to the next continent down."

I listened to Jamie's narrative with a certain bemusement. I recognized Hamilton's dreams. On the other hand, I could not believe that Hamilton dared use Washington's name in their support.

"Anyway, as soon as Hamilton knew I was as on fire as he was to go after the Dons, I got the Mississippi Territory."

I was in the Senate at the time of Jamie's return to the army as a brigadier-general, and I recall discussing him with the new major-general Hamilton who simply said, "Wilkinson's supposed to be a good officer. But you know him better than I. He's your friend, isn't he?"

Hamilton was awkward with me on this occasion, as well he might be: he had stopped my own appointment as brigadier-general. Although I think it unlikely that Hamilton knew Wilkinson was a Spanish subject, he did know of his connection with the Spanish Conspiracy because McHenry, the secretary of war, had told him bluntly that Wilkinson was so deeply involved with the Dons that he ought not to be allowed to command any troops near the border. "But Hamilton insisted"—McHenry made a face as he told me the story—"and whatever Hamilton wanted General Washington wanted so I could do nothing."

Why did Hamilton insist on promoting Wilkinson? The only answer is that he wanted to have under him someone as eager as himself to conquer Mexico and so he assumed that Wilkinson's new interest would cancel his old commitment to Spain. It was a stupid if not corrupt thing to assume. But then I was equally stupid, if not corrupt.

"You and I together—with a thousand men—can take Mexico in three weeks." The round, innocent, not entirely focussed eyes were fixed upon me, as though a steady point of reference in a dissolving world.

"Not without support from the sea." Although I had by no means decided what my future would be, I had like Hamilton thought much of Mexico, and studied in some detail that *vice-royaume*'s defences and knew, right off, that without at least one naval squadron to seize the port of Vera Cruz any invasion by land would fail.

"Details! Details!" Jamie was interested only in exciting me with thoughts of conquest. He was also interested in knowing the President's view of the subject. I told him that Jefferson would be delighted if Mexico were detached from Spain. "But I don't think he would look with a kindly eye upon *me* as the detacher."

I ought to have been more suspicious of Jamie than I was. But I could not, simply, take him seriously. No one could. That is how he came to deceive Washington, Hamilton and me, not to mention any number of other Spanish and American potentates, military and civilian.

The next morning, suffering seriously from headache, the Commanding General departed, after proposing that I meet with a certain Mr. Williamson—who turned out to be Colonel Charles Williamson, an old acquaintance from the Revolution. "You will find him trustworthy. And well-connected in England. He has the ear of Prime Minister Pitt. The Prime Minister will do whatever he says."

"But *what* does he say?"

Jamie looked at me over a third cup of steaming black French coffee provided by the Biddle butler. "He has a plan for the conquest of Mexico . . ."

"Who does *not?*"

"But he—*we* need a leader. We need Aaron Burr. Once you agree . . ." A low deep slow belch, memorial to Charles Biddle's port of the previous evening. "You spoke last night of needing naval support at Vera Cruz." No matter how much Jamie drank he not only missed nothing that others said but like a true conspirator never forgot a word that he himself had said. "Well, England has a fleet."

I was skeptical. Jamie overrode me. "You are the answer, Burr. See Williamson! He waits upon you at Oeller's Hotel. And now farewell, my commander, my superior!" I half-expected him to kiss if not my hand both cheeks in the Spanish manner. But Jamie merely saluted me—his salute every bit as sloppy now that he was commanding general as it had been when he was a thick crude boy at Cambridge.

That afternoon I walked to Oeller's Hotel. It was not easy for me to appear anywhere in public for, invariably, I would attract a silent crowd that would stare at me with the most intense interest. Fortunately, there was little outright hostility. But then I was protected not only by my office as second magistrate of the republic but by my ridiculous (and continuing) celebrity as a great marksman. No one wanted to offend me.

I felt clothed with invisible armour as I moved out of the sunny street into the cool dim interior of Oeller's where I was greeted somewhat shyly by friends, among them Colonel Williamson who saluted me. "We need you, Sir. We need you." Then he took me to a dark corner of the first-floor parlour and for an hour showed me maps; whispered knowingly of troops, of ships, of victuals. Finally, "I go to England presently. The Prime Minister wants a plan. I have the plan. He also wants a general. Shall I tell him that I have found the man we want?"

I was cautious. "You know my interest in the liberation of Mexico. Everyone's interest. I think I can even speak for the President when I say that he, too, would like Mexico liberated . . ."

"So we've heard!" Williamson was as impressed as I intended him to be.

"But one cannot make a move unless there is war between Spain and the United States."

"There is always trouble . . ."

"Not trouble—war."

"War might be arranged. General Wilkinson . . ." He did not need to finish. We both knew that Wilkinson could create a border incident with the Spanish whenever he chose.

I asked, "What can we expect from England?"

"Whatever we need. Pitt is with us!"

Several well-wishers approached at this point. I rose and shook hands. When they departed, Williamson said, "I am delighted, Colonel, with your attitude."

"I am interested, but no more."

"Of course. You want other assurances. And I have them. Right here in this hotel. Upstairs someone of the greatest importance is waiting for you." Williamson then bade me go to the second floor, to a corner bedroom, and there rap twice on the door. Reluctantly, I did as he asked.

"Come in." The voice was curt. I opened the door and there at the centre of the bedroom, looking most ill-at-ease, was His Britannic Majesty's minister to the United States, Anthony Merry.

"Vice-President, how good of you to come!" Merry gave me a small bow which I returned. We were as courtly as it is possible to be in a hotel bedroom with the bed unmade from the previous night's occupant, and a spittoon filled to overflowing with tobacco juice. Since there was nowhere to sit except upon the bed, we stood.

We spoke of our last meeting in Washington at the President's House. "I am glad, if I may say so, to be in Philadelphia. My wife and I have been spending a most agreeable summer here. A true city. Not like your capital which resembles, if I may say so, similar hamlets in Poland."

The Merrys had been accredited to Washington City for less than a year—a most unhappy year since Jefferson had managed to insult them at their first presidential dinner party. In the interest of demos, Jefferson had decided that season to forgo protocol. One did not go into table according to rank but, as he unfelicitously put it, "pell-mell." Shoved aside by guests intent on sitting close to the sun of democracy, the Merrys decided that England had been mortally offended, and Mrs. Merry never went back to the palace which pleased Jefferson who, invariably, referred to her as "that bitch-virago." Personally I found her delightful; large and fleshy in the English manner with a sharp humorous way of saying things. In other words, the sort of woman Jefferson hated on sight. I enquired after Mrs. Merry's health.

"My poor lady is most unwell. She has taken to her bed. And when Congress meets, I shall have to go back without her."

"We shall miss her at the capital."

Merry took his cue. "Then you intend to go back?"

"Of course. I must preside over the Senate in the fall."

"I see." Merry was the least diplomatic of diplomats. He looked at me so blankly that I felt obliged to explain.

"I am not under indictment for murder in Washington City, only in New York state."

"I see." He was plainly uncomfortable.

"The indictment against me in New York is of course illegal since the fatal business was transacted in New Jersey."

"I see."

"I could of course be indicted for murder in New Jersey, but so far no action has been taken." Actually, at that very moment, an indictment against me for murder was being prepared in Bergen County while New York state, having tardily consulted the law, changed its indictment of me from murder to that of the misdemeanour of having issued a challenge to a duel.

As subtly as Merry could, he spoke of Senator Pickering. Had I heard from him? As subtly, I indicated that I did not see much hope for the Federalist plan to separate New England from the rest of the union. "To succeed one must be certain of the majority's support in New England and our friends do not have that support. Also, to succeed, they need New York."

Merry nodded. "Your defeat, Vice-President, was a grave blow. Without New York . . ." He stopped. He did not need to say more. It was common knowledge that it was the British minister's policy to encourage the Federalists, or anyone else, who wanted to break up the union. Because of this policy or passion (there is some evidence that the British government did not share Merry's loathing of Jefferson), His Excellency and I now faced one another across an unmade bed at Oeller's Hotel. I noted with some distaste that the *vase de nuit* had not been emptied.

"You have heard Colonel Williamson's plan?" Merry placed a lace handkerchief soaked in eau-de-cologne over his nose, and inhaled as voluptuously as any snuff-taker.

"I think the plan reflects the dream of most Americans, to extend our empire west and south."

"Vice-President, would you be willing to undertake such a conquest?"

"*Liberation*, Minister! The liberation of a suffering colonial people from Spanish despotism."

"Of course. Liberation. Of course."

I moved obliquely. "Next March I step down as vice-president. I have a number of plans, and all involve the west. Naturally, I am tempted by any practical plan for liberating Mexico. I have reason to believe that my friends in Tennessee and Kentucky would rally to me. They hate the Dons. They claim to be attached to me. I believe I could raise a considerable army which I am also in a position to finance." This was a bold thing to say since I was known to be deeply in debt, but I did believe that I would have access to money for such an expedition since Mexico is every American's El Dorado and its conquest has an abiding appeal to our gamblers.

"I have been told that you could be in such a position if you chose."

"Unfortunately, any expedition would need naval support and that is beyond my means and capability."

"I see."

"In short, if England were to help me at sea, I can promise you a Mexico free of Spain *and* free of the United States." The handkerchief was withdrawn revealing a face foolish with calculation. "A Mexico in permanent alliance with England." Thus I made my bid.

"I shall report this to His Majesty's government. I know that the Prime Minister is interested in such a scheme."

"No doubt you are, too."

"I?" He looked befuddled. "Yes, of course. That is, I *reflect* His Majesty's government."

"No, Minister. I mean that it might be of interest for you to help—at a distance, naturally—in the liberation of Mexico. The rewards—if such things amuse you—would be considerable." It is not wise to underestimate the cupidity of any man.

"My assistance must be very much from afar." Merry mumbled about his duty to his sovereign but the seed, as they say, was well-planted.

From a near-by room came the whooping of westerners. Merry grimaced; he was never democratically inclined. "It is your president's *clothes* I cannot bear," he used to say with a shudder. "And those down-at-heel slippers!"

"You are most popular, Colonel Burr, at the west." Merry cleared his throat.

"I have been, I hope, of some use to the people there."

Merry then made *his* bid in what sounded to be a rehearsed speech. "Colonel Williamson has led me to believe that you might be interested in placing yourself at the head of the western states in the event that they might wish to dissolve their union with the United States."

I was startled at Merry's boldness; not to mention Williamson's presumption. I was forced to thread my way most delicately through the labyrinth. "Sir, I have never given Colonel Williamson, or anyone else, leave to speak for me in this matter."

"I am sorry, Sir. I had thought . . ."

"But it is no secret that I believe the western states will one day form their own nation centered upon the Mississippi."

"Do you think this a desirable thing?"

"I express no opinion, except to note that under the Constitution they have every *right* to secede. My view is identical with that of Mr. Jefferson."

Merry sneezed into his handkerchief. Blew his nose. Betrayed excitement. He now had a marvellous subject for his next report to the Foreign Ministry. "Surely the President does not want a secession."

"He claims to be indifferent. In his eyes we are all Americans, easterners or westerners, united or not."

"I see. I see."

I returned to my offer. I spoke plainly. "If your government will support me at sea in the liberation of Mexico, I shall most willingly mount an expedition by land."

The response was swift. "I shall certainly recommended that His Majesty's government support you. As for the western states . . ."

"With me at Mexico City, who knows *where* their eventual allegiance will be?"

I was careful to commit myself in no way to a breaking up of the union. My interests were, first Mexico; second, Texas; third, the Floridas. I never saw myself as King of Kentucky. Yet at this very moment I was, according to Jefferson, plotting treason.

"You must join Mrs. Merry and me for dinner before you leave Philadelphia."

"I thought she was ill."

"Only at Washington City where she suffers from acute Jeffersonitis. Philadelphia does her affliction a world of good."

"I shall dine with pleasure." This was sincere. I particularly enjoyed Mrs. Merry's disdain for our empire. A *propos* Jefferson's proud remark that with the addition of the Louisiana Territory the United States was now the second largest nation on earth, she said to me, "Your president is mad! Africa is ever so much larger, and its people ever so much blacker even than the Virginians, while London has rather more *white* people in it than there are in all of Mr. Jefferson's 'empire'! Mark my words, there'll come a day when you poor wretches will be crying for us to take you back and we won't, ever!"

Soon after our meeting at Oeller's Hotel, Colonel Williamson left for England to report to Prime Minister Pitt that I was willing to lead an expedition against Mexico. Meanwhile, I kept what company there was in Philadelphia, and Charles Biddle gave me a dinner party. By design, one of the guests was my old friend the Spanish minister Don Carlos Yrujo. He was well-liked—particularly on his wife's account for she was the daughter of Pennsylvania's Governor McKean. Until the purchase of Louisiana, Don Carlos had been close to Jefferson. Now relations were strained. Don

Carlos maintained that France had no right to sell Louisiana since it was a territory of Spain. He protested to Secretary of State Madison who was peremptory: "Since France has been ceded Louisiana by its ally Spain," said Madison, "France can certainly do what she pleases with what is entirely her property." A blunt way of saying that Bonaparte was Spain's master. Then Jefferson signed into law a congressional bill maintaining that West Florida was part of the Louisiana Purchase when, of course, it was not. Don Carlos was understandably furious. A mercurial man, he spoke English without accent and most kindly shared with friends superb seegars.

"Has Your Excellency been enjoying Philadelphia?" Don Carlos lit the seegar he had given me.

I puffed happily. Said that I always enjoyed seeing my Philadelphia friends, old and new. In fact, "I have been talking to your colleague Mr. Merry." I knew that sooner or later Don Carlos would hear of our meeting. "We discussed the war of protocol at the President's palace."

"It was terrible!" Don Carlos was genuinely upset; or affected to be. "The President was standing between my wife and Mrs. Merry before dinner. Then when dinner was announced, he left both of them and took in *Mrs. Gallatin,* leaving the diplomatic ladies stranded. Such an insult to England, to Spain, to us!"

I was surprised that Don Carlos seemed to take the matter quite as seriously as Mr. Merry who would have surprised me had he not. "I fear that our president really does believe that all white men are created equal."

"*Merde,*" said the Spanish minister to the United States. We then had a pleasant conversation in the course of which I told him that I considered Mr. Jefferson's claim to West Florida was specious. I also suggested that it might be worth-while for me to visit there during the course of the summer.

"Whenever you like, I will give you a passport." Don Carlos was most friendly. If he was curious about my future he made no reference beyond wondering whether or not he would have the honour of my company when the next session of the Congress sat in the wilderness. I said that he would see me at Washington City and that I would be happy to give him my view of how I had found things in the Floridas.

"General Wilkinson tells me that you are a good friend to Spain." Was Don Carlos suspicious at this point? I think not.

"Who cannot be sympathetic to Spain now that she suffers so much at the hands of Bonaparte." I thought that sentiment agreeable. So did he; so much so, apparently, that he did me a good turn. "The governor of New Jersey has just asked my father-in-law the governor of Pennsylvania to extradite you for murder."

"When was this?"

"The message came this morning. So I had better give you a passport first thing tomorrow."

"You are most kind."

"My father-in-law is your admirer, Colonel. We all are." A courtly bow, and I knew that I had been warned to flee Philadelphia as quickly as possible.

Thirty-three

It took me several days to obtain this last installment of the memoir. The Colonel has taken to repeating himself, to losing his train of thought. But then this morning he was once again his usual self and insisted on going over the text to change, add, refine. "After all, this is crucial evidence. One wrong word and I shall be indicted for treason all over again."

"How," I asked, "does Mr. Jefferson's version of what happened vary from yours?"

"According to him, I proposed myself to Merry as

a would-be British agent, ready to break up the union."
The Colonel shook his head. "You know, people extract from what one says only what they would like
to hear. Poor Merry *wanted* so much for me to agree to
his plan to divide the union that he finally thought
that I had. But all I ever wanted from him was a single
British flotilla at Vera Cruz—and a hundred thousand
pounds."

This evening we had a caller. "A Mrs. Keese." Mr.
Craft announced the lady with the air of one who did
not wish to assist at a seduction.

"I don't believe I know a Mrs. Keese." The Colonel
was smoking a seegar. "I also doubt the propriety of
receiving a lady this late at night and *en déshabille*.
Nevertheless, prepare her for the worst, Mr. Craft.
Charlie, stand by! She may be a creature of Madame—
intent on compromising me, on black-mail of the direst
sort." He was enjoying himself. He enjoyed himself
even more when the lady in question appeared, carrying a large hamper.

"Mrs. Overton!" The Colonel was delighted. "*Overton*, Mr. Craft, not Keese."

"It is Keese, Colonel." She was a good-looking old
woman of fifty, with naturally red cheeks and a Scots
accent. "I am re-married."

"Mr. Overton . . .?"

"Dead!" She sounded happy; but that is her manner.
"I have brought you a proper supper because, Colonel,
I know the stroke. Oh, I know the stroke as well as
I know how to roast a turkey . . ."

"She does that best of all." The Colonel explained
the lady to us. "I met Mrs. Keese's father during the
Revolution . . ."

"Oh, what a dramatic meeting!" Mrs. Keese began
to slice a turkey still warm from the oven. "Like a
ballad!" She roared a verse or two of Sir Walter Scott
in Scots. We did not understand a word.

"Near the Heights of Quebec," continued the
Colonel, "I had gone down to drink from a stream, my

pistol at the ready, when there at the water's edge was this British officer ..."

"*Scots*, Colonel."

"This Scots officer who was your father. Well, neither of us knew quite what to do. There is no protocol for enemy officers meeting like that. So her father offered me some water from his hunting-cup, and I put down my pistol and drank. Then he gave me a bit of horse's tongue, and I shared with him my last onion, and we chatted of this and that for half an hour and vowed that when the war was over we would meet and continue our acquaintance."

"And meet they did, thirty-six years later at my father's place in Scotland ..."

"Now here we are some sixty years later . . . Oh God!" The Colonel indeed looked pained. "*Sixty years later*! What am I doing alive? This is absurd. Everyone is dead but me."

"President Madison is still alive," I said.

"Chief Justice John Marshall is still alive." Mr. Craft intoned that great name reverently.

"Well, I must outlive them, mustn't I?"

"So you shall, if properly fed!" Followed by another booming unintelligible quotation, this time from Burns.

We had a splendid supper during which we learned that Mrs. Keese had been ruined financially by her first husband. Now, with her second husband, she ran a boarding-house in Broadway on the Bowling Green. "And there are two fine rooms for you, Colonel, in the basement but full of light because they're at the back, and look onto the dearest, greenest yard."

"Dear girl, I fear the prices in that neighbour-hood ..."

"Whatever you want to pay!"

Mr. Craft and I exchanged a glance. Once again the Colonel had fallen on his feet; if one could use an expression that does not quite fit.

"Tell me," the Colonel asked, "whose house it was?

I used to know every house from the Bowling Green to Wall Street."

"Why, it was the home of the old Governor John Jay."

"My joy is complete." The Colonel looked very happy. "Mr. Jay's cadaver will turn at least once in its grave at the thought of me in his cellar."

Thirty-four

So FAR IT HAS BEEN a cold depressing autumn. An election is in progress. On every wall one reads "Down with the Aristocracy." This Democratic slogan is said to be the invention of the elegant Mr. Van Buren whose candidate for governor is expected to defeat the Whig candidate. Mr. Davis and Leggett are deeply involved in the campaign, and so I avoid them.

Helen gives me trouble. She will not leave the house. I think of her all day long. I hate the world.

Fortunately Colonel Burr maintains his high spirits, even in the two small rooms Mrs. Keese has given him. Although not as full of light as she promised, they are as warm as the oven she roasts her turkeys in and our old salamander is happy.

The Colonel has so crowded his furniture, books, pictures into the two rooms that a visitor must hollow out a place for himself if he wants to sit next to the sofa where the Colonel reclines, the portrait of Theodosia on a table beside him. He has, incidentally, acquired a black man-servant who went to fetch me tea on my first visit.

"Most congenial fellow," the Colonel said. "Used to work for DeWitt Clinton of all people! Poor old fellow. I fear he is a bit addled. There are times when he thinks that *I* am DeWitt Clinton, and brings me a bottle of whiskey which I pretend to drink, simply to keep his respect."

The Colonel asked me about the office. Although he still works at briefs, it is tacitly accepted that he will never again visit Reade Street or set foot in a courtroom. Aaron Burr is, at last, incredibly, invalid.

"I have been preparing myself for you." Piles of documents and newspaper cuttings littered the floor beside the sofa. "I've also consulted Sam Swartwout. Not that he's much help. His memory is rather worse than mine. But Sam did find the letters that he wrote his brother John from the west, and they are helpful."

Mrs. Keese burst in, wanting to feed her lodger who declined feeding. "You don't know, Mr. Schuyler, what an honour it is, having him here!" Then she was gone, with a Scots war-cry.

Burr's response to her is—well, quizzical. "Women have played a considerable role in my life, and I wish I could discuss them freely but my code does not allow it. I could never be like Hamilton who kissed and published."

The Colonel then showed me a miniature of himself at the age of about thirty. "The property of a lady recently dead. Her son sent it to me."

The Colonel was remarkably handsome if the miniature is accurate: full mouth, straight nose, huge dreaming black eyes. Of what was he dreaming?

I asked him. He was taken aback. "Dreaming? Am I? Was I?" He put on his glasses; studied the miniature closely. "No. It is merely the artist's interpretation. Or yours." He took off his glasses. "No, I don't dream. It is not my nature. I . . . act. Take risks. Could never stay for long in one place. Wanted always to be moving, to be doing." He stopped. Touched the painting of Theodosia. "I used to think when I was away from her mother, who was sick, why, she'll soon be dead. Go home, I'd tell myself, be with her while you can. But I could not stop what I was doing, and when she died I was not there. Yet I might have had a half-dozen more years of her company if I'd not been—in motion."

The Colonel put the miniature of himself on the table face down before his daughter's portrait. "Now for that great American comedy: 'The Treason of Aaron Burr.'"

Memoirs of Aaron Burr—Seventeen

WITH SAM SWARTWOUT and a servant, I left Philadelphia in August 1804, and disguised as one R. King (tribute to the good Tory Rufus King who owned the Heights at Weehawk), I went to Georgia.

I pretended to be a London merchant (to explain my accent which the natives could not understand). Then I penetrated East Florida almost as far as St. Augustine. I talked to the inhabitants. Got the feel of the country. Made fascinating discoveries. For instance, did you know that even the finest Spanish ladies openly smoked seegars? Kept a journal for my daughter, which was lost with her. Made maps. All in all, the time was agreeably spent despite near-death during a hurricane that devastated the plantation where I was stopping, killing nineteen blacks and blowing out to sea the piazza where my host and I had been sitting. It was all like a bad dream, or the continuation of the terrible dream that I had had only the night before, a result of eating broiled alligator.

On the way back to Washington, I dropped my incognito and, to my amazement, was everywhere hailed. But then the southerners have no squeamishness about duelling, and Hamilton was not their hero.

At Savannah I dined with the governor of Georgia. Suddenly a band played music beneath the window.

"It is for you, Governor," I said.

"No, Colonel, it is for the Vice-President." And so it was.

At Raleigh, North Carolina, I was received with delight by the *Negro* population of the town. I can only attribute their enthusiasm for me to the fact that after travelling some 400 miles in a canoe, my ordinarily dark complexion had been turned by the sun to a truly luminous quadroon yellow.

By the end of October, I was at Richmond, capital of enemy territory, the mother to the Hydra-headed— no, that is an exaggeration—the many-limbed Virginian junto, the octopus with but a single Jeffersonian head and a thousand tentacles, all named James!

During a theatre performance in Richmond, I was recognised and applauded at the *entr'acte* by the (white) gentry. I daresay this ovation was reported to the chief octopus.

At the beginning of November, I appeared at Washington City, ready to preside over the Senate. Some people thought it indelicate of me to assume my constitutional duties as I was under indictment for murder in New Jersey. But I was a conscientious public servant. I was also a responsible citizen determined to go back to New Jersey and stand trial; until I was told that the judge for Bergen County had declared publicly that if I was not immediately hanged, there would be famine in Bergen and pestilence in Hoboken. New Jersey lost its magic for me. Meanwhile, I was gratified to learn that, at Jefferson's prompting, a group of senators were petitioning the governor of New Jersey to drop proceedings against me. Why was Jefferson so sympathetic? Love for me? A sense of justice? of honour? None of these things. He was in trouble and needed my help.

I got my first summons to the President's House two weeks after the Senate convened on November 5. The President's messenger tracked me down at the British minister's house—or rather houses. Merry had taken two brick buildings on K Street and transformed them as best he could into a fashionable embassy.

Mrs. Merry presided over tea before the fire. She

was in good form and we were all much amused by the latest symptom of her Jeffersonitis (as usual, I pretended not to hear anything unpleasant that was said of my sovereign).

But Mrs. Merry had other subjects. That afternoon she told us the fabulous story of old Mr. Collins and young Mr. Roper. Collins was an eccentric old Federalist who had a large estate near Alexandria. He was known to be mad, though I never saw any sign of it other than a tendency to quarrel with his *rib* in public; but if quarrelling with one's wife is to be mad then there are not asylums enough for us all. Roper was a young lawyer in Alexandria who was courting a favourite niece of Collins. Roper had any eye on the girl's money but to get at it he must first contrive to have old Mr. Collins confined to the madhouse.

"Well, young Mr. Roper has been foiled!" Mrs. Merry's harsh amused voice was like a parrot's. "He called yesterday on old Mr. Collins who said to him, 'They tell me you are mad!' Poor young Mr. Roper who had come to say the very same thing to his host was astonished! 'But I am not in the least mad, Sir.' 'But, Sir,' said old Mr. Collins, 'it is plain to everyone that you are quite mad. Fortunately there is a capital cure which did the King of England himself a world of good, and that is whipping.' Whereupon two large slaves appeared, pulled down young Mr. Roper's breeches and beat him unmercifully!" As Mrs. Merry wept with laughter, the President's messenger appeared, accompanied by the butler who intoned, "From His Excellency, the President, to Colonel Burr."

The messenger gave me a note and withdrew.

"It would appear, Colonel Burr, that you are soon to be pell to Mr. Jefferson's mell." Mrs. Merry was right. But this particular pell-mell was not social but political.

I dined alone with Jefferson the next day (he always took his main meal at three o'clock). I had not seen him for almost a year and thought him somewhat

haggard-looking—hair white, eyes tired and dull, the
tip of his vulpine nose oddly translucent, like alabaster.
The "palace" was still unfinished—cold, draughty,
empty. But the private dining-room was comfortable,
and original: Jefferson had installed a series of dumb-
waiters from which one served oneself.

"Life without servants," observed my host, "is the
last luxury . . . as well as the first privation," he quickly
added.

"They listen," I agreed.

"They also talk. Not that there is ever anything
said here which I would not be happy to see published." Jefferson tended to strike the self-righteous note
in much the same way as a clock strikes the hour and
like a familiar clock one does not hear the sound
unless one is anxious, as I confess I was, to tell, as it
were, the time.

I recall nothing of our excellent dinner except that
the French wine was not only good to drink but
promptly produced a lecture on the making of wine.
I herewith note for history that this lecture had in
no way changed its form from the last time I had been
honoured with it. Jefferson played his mind rather the
same way he played his fiddle, being especially fond
of the old tunes.

There was also a miraculous dessert that I had not
encountered before; it consisted of ice-cream served in
a shell of *hot* pastry.

No mention was made of the election I had lost in
New York. No mention was made of Hamilton except
for a rather tentative "I am told that your problems
in New Jersey will soon be resolved." He affected to
find the Merrys entertaining. "I understand from one
of my agents at London that Mr. Merry is known to
the Foreign Office clerks as *Toujours Gai*." Jefferson
knew from experience that this sort of thing was amusing and so, dutifully, repeated it to me, knowing I
would respond. If I had been Jonathan Edwards, he
would have quoted from "Samuel."

Jefferson asked politely about my adventures at the south. I told him that during my short visit to East Florida it seemed plain to me that the people in that part of the world were ripe for liberation.

Jefferson agreed. "Actually, we *have* liberated them by act of Congress and by executive order, but I fear nothing short of a war with Spain—or another purchase—can give us what is rightfully ours."

"The chances of a war seem excellent."

But Jefferson did not take the bait. Spoke instead of his difficulties with Bonaparte, of his difficulties with England. Then, as the fabulous confection was brought a second time by the French butler himself, Jefferson came to the point.

"I have never known, Colonel, to what extent the *nature* of our Constitution interests you."

"Hamilton made much the same remark. He found me equivocal."

"I trust I resemble Hamilton *only* in this matter." The smile was a swift baring of yellow teeth; the lips were gray tending to blue where most men are pink or red. I suppose it was the winter season that made him look like the last ashes of a once-fierce fire—soft, fine, white; no trace remaining of the foxy, red-haired man he had been save for the tarnished bronze of freckles.

"I suppose, at heart, I have never regarded the Constitution as a finished work."

"We agree . . . we agree!" He was too agreeable.

"It will evolve or be discarded."

"My own view . . ."

"There are two weaknesses that I see in it. The first is the so-called inherent rights of any state to dissolve its bonds with the union." I stopped.

Jefferson looked startled . . . no, embarrassed. God alone knew what he had heard of my dealings with the New England Federalists, or with Merry. "Am I to understand, Colonel, that you do not accept as inherent the right of any state to secede?"

"No, Sir, I do not."

"But of their own free will thirteen sovereign states came together and—"

"I know the argument." I was also damned if I would listen to Jefferson deliver this ancient lesson yet another time for my benefit. He was not rational on the subject. "I merely point out that no constitution can be effective if each state thinks that it has the right to nullify any federal law it pleases. I also think that as long as each state believes it has the right to secede, eventually one or more states *will* secede and there will be no United States."

"Yet we would all be American . . . cousins if not brothers." The usual sentiment.

"No doubt. But you have asked me my view of the Constitution and I must tell you what I think is one of its fatal weaknesses."

"I find it a peculiar strength."

"Then you no doubt agree with those New England Federalists who want to separate their states from the rest?"

In the wrong—or on shaky ground—Jefferson was always imperturbable; at his best, in fact. He smiled. "I do get occasional reports about those gentlemen." He was mild. "Madison tells me that I should be more concerned than I am. But I take the position that if Senator Pickering and the others can convince the people of their states to secede, then I will be the first to offer the hand of friendship to the new confederation."

"But of course you know that Pickering's people cannot command a majority . . ."

"I know so little of New England but admire so much what I do know." Jefferson was like silk. I could see what a figure he must have cut in his ambassadorial days. "What is at issue is a principle. And I uphold the principle—each state can do as it likes in reference to the others."

"Then what about Louisiana? Suppose the people of

New Orleans were to vote against union with us and to vote *for* a union with France or Spain, or for independence?"

He was not prepared for this variation on an altogether familiar air. He was hesitant. "I should say that in the light of the purchase, and of the very different nature of the inhabitants—"

The butler again entered (did Jefferson have a bell he could secretly push when he wanted a plate—or the subject—changed?) and poured the two of us champagne, a wine that had recently become popular at Washington City. The subject was changed. "You find a *second* fatal weakness in the Constitution?"

"Not necessarily fatal." But I was not about to blot further my copy-book and tell him that to me the second weakness is the imperial power assigned to the president. Instead I did the polite and necessary thing. I said what he wanted to hear. "The power of the judiciary."

The old face lit up. We were in agreement. We were friends. He could trust me. Out it poured, his fear of the courts, particularly of the Supreme Court in the hands of a monocrat like John Marshall. "The issue is so simple! Marshall believes that the courts have the right to set aside acts of Congress. This is intolerable! This strikes at the heart of our system of government! And, by Heaven, the fact that these judges can hold office for life—why, that sort of tenure invites tyranny!"

I was told the plot in straightforward (for Jefferson) terms. Samuel Chase was a justice of the Supreme Court. He was a brilliant, savage old Tory given to frequent harangues from the bench against the Republicans and what he called their "mobocracy." He had also taken pleasure in tormenting the journalist James Callender when he was still Jefferson's creature. As a result, earlier that year, Judge Chase had been indicted (with Jefferson's connivance) by the House of Representatives; he was charged with partisanship, unfairness, bad manners . . . for everything except what the Constitution said he could be indicted for, "high crimes and misdemeanours." Now the Justice must be tried by the Senate and I, as that body's presiding officer, would be in the position of judge. "Upon you, Colonel, falls the conduct of a trial which will determine the future course of our democracy."

"I shall be impartial, of course . . ."

"Of course. But I hope you will be partial to the principle which is not so much Judge Chase as it is the necessary subservience of the judiciary to the legislative branch. We must establish the precedent that judges may be removed at the people's pleasure."

"But the Constitution—"

"May yet have to be amended. But for now we must establish the primacy of the legislature."

"So that you will be able, if necessary, to rid yourself of the Chief Justice." This was the issue, bluntly put.

"That will of course depend upon Mr. Marshall's future behaviour." The voice was soft and lulling. "I suspect that if we remove Justice Chase, Mr. Marshall will understand that we are serious and so order his future conduct. I have found that in this world a warning is often quite enough."

I allowed Jefferson to think that I favoured his so-called principle. Actually I have always preferred a judiciary independent of the other two branches of government; and though life tenure tends to promote and protect incompetence, it has the perfect virtue of placing beyond the vindictiveness of the sovereign and the passions of the mob the one high thoughtful court of the land.

During the next three months, as the trial was made ready, I saw more of Jefferson than I had seen of him in the previous four years. We dined together at least twice a week. We often met privately. He was filled with suggestions for my conduct of the trial. He was somewhat fearful of John Randolph of Roanoke who was to handle the prosecution. "Poor Randolph is not

himself these days . . ." Jefferson looked discomfited.
Randolph had been shaken by certain land speculations
which had gone wrong, and so was not at his best.

"May I suggest that the self he normally is would
not be of much use during a trial." I was always
amused by Randolph, a strange long-limbed man of
indeterminate gender. Some thought him actually a
woman who had chosen to be a man. Whatever he
was, he had no sign of a beard; his curiously wrinkled
skin was tallowy; his long beautiful fingers were always
in motion when he spoke, while the voice was high
but clear like that of a boy chorister. Leaning against
a column in the House, wearing hunting clothes, drinking brandy given him by a slave, he would speak by
the hour, fascinating all with his mockery and his wit,
with a rhetoric that was unique in the republic's history.
In a way his public speaking was not unlike the private
conversation of his cousin Jefferson, but where Jefferson in company glimmered with shrewd novelties and
speculations John Randolph blazed in public like a display of Chinese fireworks. Incidentally, for some reason
he was most proud of his reputed descent from Poca-
hontas.

January 2, 1805, Judge Chase was summoned to the
Senate chamber which I had transformed into a replica
of Westminster at the time of the trial of Warren
Hastings. I thought the setting should be impressive
since, presently, we would decide what sort of republic
we were to have. The walls were hung with crimson
damask while to my left and right the senators sat
in a row like judges. I built an extra gallery for distinguished visitors. I even ordered cleaned the flues of
the two fireplaces and for the first time ever the
chamber was warm without smoke.

Just before Judge Chase appeared, I ordered the arm-
chair that had been set out for him in the well of the
chamber to be removed. "Let him find his own chair,"
I said very plainly to an usher. Several Federalist senators hissed me.

Judge Chase arrived, a tall commanding figure full of wrath. He had signed the Declaration of Independence. He had been appointed to the Supreme Court by George Washington. After Marshall, he was the most brilliant if the most cantankerous of the nation's judges. He had, also, in a famous decision, enunciated the very principle that Jefferson wished to deny: "There are unwritten, inherent limitations on legislative powers." He took himself and the issue most seriously.

Judge Chase looked about him. Then he said, "Am I to stand, Sir?"

"Bring the accused a chair since he does not wish to stand." Later I told one of the Federalist senators that in the House of Lords the accused always presented himself on his knees. My comment was much resented, as I knew it would be: the Federalists now assumed that I was entirely Jefferson's creature. He thought so, too.

Judge Chase asked for more time to prepare his case. I told him that he must return on February 4.

Jefferson was delighted. "They are already on the defensive. You have been masterful."

"Thank you, Sir." I then told him that I wanted my stepson, J. B. Prevost, made judge of the superior court at New Orleans, that I wanted my brother-in-law Joseph Brown made secretary of the Louisiana Territory, that I wanted General James Wilkinson made governor of the Louisiana Territory.

"Is that *all* you would like?" Jefferson attempted irony in order to mask his shock. He was not used to such open bargaining.

"If you could replace Governor Claiborne of the Orleans with me, my happiness would be complete. But I think that impossible."

Jefferson gave me one of his rare direct looks. Between us was yet another version of the famed copying machine.

"I do not like to combine the military with the civilian authority . . ."

"General Wilkinson is the most *civilian* general I have ever known, and I have known him a long time. He will be a credit to us at St. Louis."

"You want nothing for yourself?"

"No, Sir."

"Where will you go after . . . your term of office expires?"

"To the west. Kentucky perhaps. I own land out there."

"You will not go back to New York?"

"Hardly. Besides, I have nothing left to go back to. For the present," I added carefully. I assumed that he knew what everybody knew: Richmond Hill and its contents had recently been sold at auction to pay off debts. I was allowed to keep only the contents of the wine-cellars and the library.

Jefferson later claimed that I had asked, at this time, for a government appointment and that he had refused me. This was more than usually disingenuous of him. I had asked nothing for myself because I needed nothing (or so I thought). Jefferson understood perfectly politics and the business of buying what you want; he also understood how to give the appearance of being above all chicanery. Without demur, he gave me the three appointments I asked for in order that I help him destroy Judge Chase and the Supreme Court. I took his bribe and then, according to an unfriendly newspaper, I conducted the trial "with the dignity and impartiality of an angel, but with the rigour of a devil."

As I had suspected, John Randolph was a disaster for the prosecution. He knew no law nor was there much place on such an occasion for his usual vituperativeness—at least, with me in the chair. He finally went to pieces and spent his final oration stammering and sighing and moaning. At the end, he congratulated us all on "the last day of my sufferings and yours." This was gentlemanly of him.

On a largely partisan vote, Judge Chase was acquitted for the excellent reason that there was no true case against him.

The day after the trial, March 2, 1805, at about one o'clock in the afternoon, I was presiding over the Senate. The chamber was still a resplendent crimson place. But I had a sore throat; a low fever; and an overwhelming desire to go.

At the first break in the debate, I motioned for silence, and got to my feet. I suspect that everyone knew what would come next. I made a few improvised remarks. I am not what is regarded as a "warm" speaker but on this occasion I managed tolerably well to move my audience in the direction I wanted them to go.

I took my theme from the chamber itself, still dressed for the trial. We were all aware that we had together made history in that room. I reminded the senators of this and of their duty to preserve and to defend the Constitution. "This house is a sanctuary," I said (I paraphrase for there is no copy of the speech anywhere), "a citadel of law, of order, and of liberty; and it is here—" I indicated the temporary but to me significant placement of the senators' chairs: For a month they had sat not as mere legislators but in a row as judges. "It is here in this exalted refuge; here, if anywhere, will resistance be made to the storm of political frenzy and the silent arts of corruption; and if the Constitution be destined ever to perish by the sacrilegious hands of the demagogue or the usurper, which God avert, its expiring agonies will be witnessed on this floor."

I was aware as never before—or since—that I was holding entirely the attention of an audience. There was not a sound in that usually cold and bustling chamber.

"So I now say farewell, perhaps forever. I have, I hope, proved just in my dealings with you. But if on any occasion I have given offence, remember that my failure was simply human and not for want of the spirit to do good. May God bless those who sit in this chamber now, and forever after."

On that note, I left the Capitol, never to return. It has been reported that many senators wept at the end of my speech. Certainly they were so moved that they passed unanimously a resolution expressing, among many compliments, their "entire approbation of the Vice-President's conduct." This was satisfying. Later the Senate, not unanimously (the effect of my oratory had begun to fade), voted to give me the frank for the remainder of my life. The House of Representatives, however, mislaid this motion. So I have been paying for postage charges ever since.

Not long ago someone asked me just what "usurper" I was warning the Senate against. "Jefferson," I said, to his surprise. "After all, we had just witnessed his attempt to subvert the Constitution and shatter the Supreme Court. He would have succeeded if the Senate had not stopped him." But since none of this accords with legend, I am thought by many to have warned the Senate against *myself* as usurper!

I remained in Washington for two weeks, saying good-bye, tending to odds and ends, preparing for my western journey. I did not see the President again but he sent me word that my friends had received their appointments.

Attempts to fête me were discouraged. I wished quietly and silently to withdraw from the politics of the republic. On the surface my prospects were not glorious. I could not go back to New York or to New Jersey. I had lost Richmond Hill. I was bankrupt. I was a widower. I was forty-nine years old. Yet I believed that I was at the beginning of a great adventure. It was like being given a second life. I was happy, and envied no man on earth as I took the four A.M. coach for Philadelphia.

Wide awake, excited, expectant, I even found in-

vigorating the damp cold breeze from the mephitic
Potomac as the coach clattered past the pillory, the
stocks, the gallows.

Thirty-five

THIS AFTERNOON MR. DAVIS CAME to discuss a legal
matter with Mr. Craft. When he was done, he
came into the Colonel's office where I now work.

"Busy at your labours?"

"And you at yours?" It was inevitable, I suppose, that
I not like him for he is not only my tempter but also,
in a way, my rival. I have become as serious about the
Burr memoirs as I am about the pamphlet and the
money it will bring.

"It comes slowly." Mr. Davis sat in the chair where
I used to sit and take dictation. I put my feet up on
the stove, just like the Colonel.

Last week, as predicted, the Whig candidate for
governor was defeated. "But we are certain to win
nationally next year." Mr. Davis is always an optimist.
"With *your* help of course." The mockery was not
out-size.

"I'll be ready in a few weeks." Actually I have done
all the real work. I am now trying to capture the
slanderous manner.

"How is the Colonel?"

"His spirits are good."

Mr. Davis shook his head—either in denial or with
wonder. He is never not ambiguous. "He is a marvel."

"Who shot first," I asked, "Hamilton or Burr?"

Mr. Davis shook his head. "No one knows. And I
was there, watching through the bushes. I *think* Hamilton fired a second before the Colonel. I *know* that at

the first report the Colonel swayed—my eyes were on him—and I was afraid that he'd been hit. But he told me later there was a stone under his boot, and he was off-balance. We do know that Hamilton's shot was wide of the mark. Personally, I don't think he could see well, and so ought to have declined the encounter. Well . . ." Mr. Davis is not one for grieving over the past. The Colonel's example is infectious. Think always of the future.

"What will you do when . . ." This time Mr. Davis's inflection was not at all ambiguous.

"When the Colonel dies?"

"Unthinkable for those of us who are survivors of The Little Band."

"I don't know." I have told no one my plan to go to Europe with Helen and try to support myself entirely by writing.

"You are a lawyer, aren't you?"

"I haven't been admitted to the bar yet."

"But you could be? You have done the reading?" Mr. Davis's eyes were keen behind the steel-rimmed spectacles; he gave the appearance of sympathy.

"Yes, I could be. I suppose I will be."

"It is a good thing, you know. They say England is a nation of shopkeepers. Well, this is a nation of lawyers. For the lawyer, anything is possible. For the rest of us impossible." He gave a stagey sigh.

Actually I have not made up my mind whether or not to take the examination for the bar. Mr. Craft assures me that I will do well. But for me the law means politics which I hate. Like a fool I dream of the Alhambra—of Granada at night. Of roses growing wild in broken Moorish courtyards. Of Helen and me alone together on the moonlit terrace of some decaying villa above the Sorrentine—how marvellous to write the word!—peninsula, quarrelling bitterly.

Thirty-six

I SPENT THE EVENING with the Colonel. His spirits were low at first. He seemed distracted, asked me the same questions several times. Wanted to know trivial news. What had I seen at the Park? Three times I told him that I had gone with Leggett to see *Born to Good Luck* with Tyrone Power, who is nowhere near as good as Edwin Forrest in anything. I have written a review of his performance at the request of the editor of the *Mirror*. Their usual reviewer (who signs himself "Gallery Mouse") is ill. I think . . . *pray* that I will be asked to take his place and become their permanent Mouse.

I gave the Colonel our last chapter which he has already revised once. Usually he checks my fair copy but this time he waved it away. "I cannot gather my wits. Mrs. Keese feeds me too well. Pour me some claret. That often has a good effect."

I did; and it did. He cheered up almost immediately. "The servant found a number of bottles in the cellar, hidden beneath a bale of Federalist newspapers." Burr smiled and toasted the air. "To John Jay, with my appreciation."

Still thinking of the conversation with Mr. Davis, I asked him if he thought that I should take my bar examination.

"Certainly." The answer was brisk. "For one thing you'll qualify easily. I have seen to that—assuming you've read no more than half the books I suggested you read."

"But I don't want to be a lawyer."

"Well, who does? I mean what man of spirit? The law kills the lively mind. It stifles originality. But it is a stepping-stone . . ."

"So Mr. Davis tells me."

"You've seen him?" The Colonel frowned. "Poor Matt. He looks peaked, don't you think? Of course he has always had a sort of gray colour but lately the *shade* of gray has become somewhat sickly. Well, he's getting old." The Colonel chuckled. Then: "Move my legs off the grate. I think they may have caught fire."

I did as he asked. Then he hummed what I took to be some sort of Revolutionary ballad. Shut his eyes. Took us back thirty years to another time.

Memoirs of Aaron Burr—Eighteen

MY PLANS AT THE WEST were bottomed on two suppositions. First, that there would be war with Spain, making it possible for me to raise an army and descend upon Mexico. Second, that since Spain was now a dependency of France and France was at war with England, I would have English naval support.

When I left Washington in the spring of 1805, everyone from Jefferson to the Creoles at New Orleans not only expected but wanted a war with Spain that would give the United States the Floridas, fix the western border of the United States, and open for me Texas and Mexico. As for England, I saw Merry in Philadelphia (he had now decided that since his government did not specifically order him to live at Washington, he could as easily carry on his embassy at Philadelphia, far from the crudities of Jefferson's court).

We met in Charles Biddle's home, late at night. Merry was all business. "I have recommended to my government that you be supported."

"I must tell you, Minister, that we are ready to move no later than March of next year." This was an exaggeration. My actual plan was to begin the descent of the Mississippi the following autumn.

"I must wait for instructions." Merry was vague. We then discussed the situation in Europe which meant that we discussed, as everyone did in those days, the character of that remarkable adventurer Napoleon Bonaparte who had undone, the previous year, the French revolution by making himself emperor of France, and very nearly master of all Europe.

"It is plain that he means to conquer the entire world." Merry shook his head. "It is hard to believe that one man can be so powerful, so darkly evil."

"Worlds are there to be conquered." I was light but I meant what I said. We were living at a·time when for the adventurous and imaginative man anything was possible. Bonaparte had inspired, no doubt in a bad way, an entire generation. Certainly, thanks in large part to his example, I saw myself as the liberator of all Spanish America.

"Where do you go now, Colonel?"

"To the west, to meet General Wilkinson, our new governor of Louisiana."

"I see. I see." I think Merry enjoyed intrigue for its own sake. It is fortunate that he did since he had no gift for it; nor did I, as events were to prove.

From Philadelphia I proceeded toward Pittsburgh on the Ohio River. For nineteen days I rode through the wilderness, only to find that Wilkinson had not yet arrived. I think he moved more slowly than any general in history, with the possible exception of General Knox who was of course fatter.

I shall try not to mention too often the warm reception that I was accorded wherever I went. It is a curious sensation to be thought a hero in a part of the world every bit as strange to one as Cathay . . . well, not Cathay; as Monticello, Virginia!

Pittsburgh was then a glum frontier village, rich only in its rivers. On one of these rivers was a sort of Noah's ark that I had ordered built the previous year. My house-boat was about sixty feet long and fifteen feet wide with two bedrooms and a well-furnished kitchen with fireplace. There were no sails, no oars; the ark simply glided down the Mississippi—and this glid-

ing was so restful, so soothing, that I was forced sometimes to murmur my own name to myself, as a
reminder that I still existed, did not sleep.

Along the way, in mid-stream, I encountered Matthew Lyon, now a Republican congressman from
Kentucky and formerly a congressman from Vermont;
he had preferred me to Jefferson when the presidential
election went into the House but for reasons of his
own voted for Jefferson, and was duly rewarded. We
lashed our boats together and travelled in each other's
company as far as Marietta. Lyon did his best to convince me to settle in Tennessee, at Nashville, where
he assured me that I would be elected to the next
Congress—and the Speakership. I affected a degree
of interest for I still wanted to keep open every possible avenue.

At Marietta, Lyon left me. I continued south. The
next day I stopped at Blennerhassett's Island. Here a
romantic Irishman named Harman Blennerhassett had
built himself a mansion in the wilderness, and there
devoted himself to dreaming dreams in the company
of a delightful young wife so full of wit and fire that
one quickly overlooked her unusually large ears, turned-
up nose, small slant eyes; she had the face of an otter
or some such small bright river creature. Yet she was
a fine horsewoman; wrote poetry; recited Shakespeare.

"My husband adores you, Colonel! Becomes most
lyric when he speaks of you!" Having been told that
I was upon the island, Mrs. Blennerhassett had
hastened to the wharf to greet me. When I tried to
depart she insisted I dine *en famille*.

"Mr. Blennerhassett's away but even so, if I let you
leave like this, he'll never forgive me, never speak
to me again—and that is a terrible trial for a man who
talks all the time. Stay for dinner."

Stay I did, and the food was good; the company
tolerable; Mrs. Blennerhassett amusing, if rather desperate for conversation. It had not, obviously, been her
life's dream to end her days on an island in the Ohio

River. It was almost midnight when I was finally released from this Circe and allowed to set sail. I
promised to return.

May 11, I arrived at Cincinnati, a lively town of some
fifteen hundred people where, again, I was made much
of. Here I called upon the new United States senator
from Ohio, John Smith. This genial character owned a
large grocery shop where, in the back room, waiting
for me, was Jonathan Dayton whose term as United
States senator from New Jersey had expired in March.
The three of us were jointly involved in a scheme to
build a canal in Indiana (it was later built but not
by us). We were also involved in the movement to
liberate Mexico.

Amongst huge cheeses, beneath smoked hams, we
pored over maps.

"You'll have the support of every man and boy who
has a gun, and wants to get away from home." Senator
Smith was a most un-senatorial figure—large and blond
and wearing a sort of smock to keep his suit clean.

As always, Dayton was shrewd and imaginative. Of
all the group he was closest to me, and often acted
as go-between when I had dealings with the Spanish or
English authorities. Among my other confederates
were the former Kentucky senator John Brown and
the soon-to-be senator John Adair. Brown had been
eager for military adventure ever since the dinner party
on Jefferson's lawn at Gray's Ferry when we were
first told of Jefferson's scheme to provoke a war with
Spain.

John Adair had been a hero of the Revolution, a
celebrated Indian fighter, and one not able to bear a
peaceful—and certainly not a senatorial—life. Like so
many western adventurers he had dreamed of con-
quering New Orleans. Now that New Orleans had
been bought by Jefferson, his dreams had shifted south-
ward, to Mexico City.

Our plan was this: a force of 5,000 men from all
over the United States would assemble in small groups

at various points along the Mississippi. Should there
be war with Spain these men would immediately become a frontier American army. Under my leadership,
we would cross the Sabine River and, with American
naval support at Vera Cruz, liberate Texas and Mexico.

In the event that there was no war with Spain, then
a British fleet would replace the American, and we
would assemble our army at New Orleans. With the
support of the leading Creoles of that city, we would
set out by both land and sea.

Dayton wondered what would happen if the Administration openly opposed us. Senator Smith spat
a fine torrent of tobacco juice half across the room
and into an empty milk-jug. "They wouldn't dare!
After all, this is *our* war, our country, not theirs."

"But suppose Jefferson does betray us?" Dayton's
dislike of Jefferson was far more intense than mine
because he hardly knew the President and so could
despise him in the abstract. I have always found that
this sort of passion is the most fierce, the least rational
and the very stuff of which saints and conquerors are
made. "Shall we tell him to go to Hell?"

"Why bother?" Senator Smith bit into a piece of
tobacco dark as Mississippi mud. "He's two months
away in Washington—that's if you want to travel comfortably like I do, though why I go there I don't know.
I must confess, Colonel Burr, I don't like that Senate
you've got there in the woods and if it wasn't for Mrs.
Smith I'd stay right here, counting my apples."

"We'll need apples." I quickly changed the subject
to victualling the army. At this stage I was always
careful to suggest that the Jefferson administration
looked with a favourable eye on the liberation of
Mexico, which was true enough up to a point. I did
not mention that between Napoleon and me at Mexico
City, Jefferson would have taken Napoleon.

The next day I returned to my ark and drifted on
to Louisville; from there I rode to Lexington, Kentucky,
where I met Senator Adair. He had already received

a letter from Wilkinson to say that I "reckoned on" his support.

Adair assured me of Kentucky's good-will because "Our folks are as greedy as the old Romans when it comes to conquest. We want Mexico."

"We shall have it."

"But there must be war with Spain before we can move . . ."

"Senator, our friend Wilkinson can give us that war on an hour's notice." So I believed, trusting Jamie still.

From Lexington I rode to the state capital Frankfort, where I stayed with Senator Brown who assured me that "our old friend, Mr. Jefferson, just needs us to nudge him a leetle towards a war. Once he knows that's what we want."

"That's what *I* want." Mrs. Brown was emphatic. "If only to spite Sally Yrujo—and that Spanish husband of hers! I tell you the airs that woman puts on make me sick! Our own Sally McKean who's taken to speaking with an accent she thinks is Spanish." Mrs. Brown was one of the few political wives to work at her husband's side. Many thought that of the two she should have been the senator. She was a favourite of my daughter.

I found Kentucky hospitality lavish and bibulous—on the order of that bit of doggerel John Marshall produced when a lady asked him for a poem on the word "paradox."

> *"In the Blue Grass region*
> *A paradox was born.*
> *The corn was full of kernels*
> *and the Colonels full of corn."*

From Frankfort I rode through green jungle to Nashville in Tennessee, arriving May 29. I sent a message to Major-General Andrew Jackson of the Tennessee militia, asking if I might call on him. I then went to sleep in the best room of the new Nashville Inn. An hour later I was awakened by a crowd which had gathered outside my boarding-house. I showed myself, and was duly cheered. They rather liked the idea that I had killed Alexander Hamilton. They also knew that I had worked hard to admit their state to the union. Finally, they hated Spain and, like the Kentuckians, the Tennesseans were as greedy for loot as any Roman.

The next morning I was awakened at dawn by a great shouting below my window. I looked out and there was himself, General Jackson on a tall horse, swearing at a slave who had provoked his terrible temper.

When Jackson saw me at the window, he took off his hat, waved it around his head and bellowed, "By the Eternal, this is the greatest moment in the history of Tennessee! Now damnit, Colonel, get dressed and come on down and we'll have breakfast at my house." I did as I was instructed.

Jackson was then not yet forty but he had had a full career as a lawyer (though to this day he can neither read nor write with much ease) and as first congressional representative from his state. He served in the House of Representatives about three months; resigned to become senator and then, after less than a year, resigned from the Senate ("Damned boring place in those days, wasn't it, Burr?" he said to me when we met last year), and went home to be a judge of the state Supreme Court. When we met that summer day, he was busy transforming the Hermitage from a block-house to a mansion totally unsuitable for the wilderness. Hating the Virginian junto, Jackson wanted a house just like one of theirs. I only hope that if my old friend lives long enough to return home he will not end up as the Virginians did, dying in rooms emptied of furniture in order to pay off debts.

As we galloped toward the Hermitage, the wind combed back Jackson's thick reddish hair like a horse's mane (why did so many of our most famous leaders have red hair? Celtic blood? Or is there some magic in red? Need I add that our current President is over six feet tall).

Jackson shouted at me his view of the duel. "Never read such a damned lot of nonsense as the press has been writing! All that hypocritical caterwauling for that Creole bastard who fought you of his own free will, just like a gentleman which he wasn't, if you'll forgive me, Colonel! I know you couldn't have met him unless you *thought* he was one, but he was not, Sir. He was the worst man in this union, as you, Sir, are the best. The best and that goes for that pusillanimous spotted caitiff of a president we got. I only fear—aside from the damage it's done you, Sir, and that we'll undo quick enough—I fear that duelling will be stamped out and where would we all be then, I ask you? Why, there's a number of men right here in Nashville that one day I know I'll take a gun to, even if I am a poor shot, and that's the truth. It must be a flaw in my vision . . ." This rambling speech was delivered in fits and starts as we approached through a dense pine-wood the Hermitage.

Jackson is far keener on duelling than I but then the frontier spirit that he exemplifies depends a great deal on settling matters face to face rather than in the press or at law. Inspired by me, so Jackson claimed, he fought a duel the very next year with one Charles Dickinson who had spoken ill of Mrs. Jackson.

"You would have been thrilled by it, Colonel." I was at the Hermitage on a later visit, and alarmed to find my host still weak from wounds: a bullet was lodged near his heart—is still lodged there, and cannot be removed. Yet all he would ever say is that "he pinked me, no more."

"Well, Sir, I waited deliberately for that leper to fire first. Now mind you I am a poor shot, and he was a fine shot, curse him, and younger than I. So I just stood there, wearing this loose coat which made me look larger than I am. Well, he fired and I was hit. Luckily, it didn't knock the wind out, as I feared it might. So I was clear-headed, and knew that I wasn't mortally wounded, though I tell you, Colonel, even if I had been shot through the brain I would have lived long enough to do what I intended to do all along."

Jackson laughed grimly, the cold pale blue eyes fixed on mine. "You should have seen his face when I did not fall. Seen his face when I slowly raised my pistol and pulled the trigger. Seen his face when the god-damned hammer struck at half-cock. So we had a pow-wow. And the seconds allowed me another try. Well, Charles Dickinson was white as a sheet, and sweating. Did Hamilton sweat, too?"

"No more than I."

"But then you didn't have all the time I had to enjoy yourself and watch the devil squirm. Well, then I slowly raised my pistol a second time, the blood by now is streaming down my side and making a puddle at my feet, and so knowing I'd be unconscious presently, this time I fired fast, fired straight at him, and he was dead, Sir, *dead*, with a screech like a pig's on butchering day! You should have seen him fall!"

A duelling man, our president, but well suited for his place and this time. Also, a hanging man, as deserters were to discover at the time of the battle of New Orleans.

But I am ahead of my story. It is now the summer of 1805, and I dined for the first time with Jackson and his wife Rachel, a fat pleasant woman with a gentle manner. As everyone now knows, Rachel was married first to a man called Robards. They separated. She then fell in love with Jackson. Believing that Robards had obtained a divorce, Rachel married Jackson, only to discover that she was still married to her first husband. It took two years for a proper divorce to be granted and for Jackson to re-marry her. All this was reasonably innocent, if not exactly intelligent, and hardly im-moral. Unfortunately, when General Jackson became a presidential candidate in 1828, our eastern moralists made such a scandal that shortly after the election Rachel simply turned her face to the wall and died of shame. Needless to say, it did not improve the new president's disposition to lose a beloved wife as a result of our jackal press.

But all was sunny and fine those days I spent at the Hermitage (which was still a-building and put me in mind of my first and only visit to Monticello). I shall now record for history that with my own eyes I saw Rachel, with a shy by-your-leave, prepare, light and smoke a corn-cob pipe.

"Far better than snuff-taking like Dolley Madison!" Jackson deeply disliked the Virginia junto. After all, as a frontier aristocrat, if that phrase has any meaning, he has cause to resent the airs of those Virginia nobles who still regard our westerners as so much refuse swept from their own well-ordered society.

Jackson insisted that a public dinner be given me at Nashville, complete with parade, music, speeches. For an instant I almost regretted not having accepted Lyon's arrangement and become a congressman from Tennessee. But it is very hard to be a mere congressman when you are amongst a people who regard you as a leader, as one who will give them an empire. I was trapped by my own glory, and by the events of that summer when the west was more than usually aroused by Spain's various crude iniquities committed on their common, imprecise and so bloody border.

I stayed five days at the Hermitage and Jackson did his best to make me feel at home. "Though damn it, Rachel, we can't serve him food like this, fit for field-hands!" And he would shove an offending dish into the butler's hand. "Colonel Burr kept the best table I ever et at in Philadelphia, and with *wine*, Rachel, not this sour grape-juice!"

"Now, General," Rachel would murmur, soothing him the way one would a barking dog.

In private, Jackson and I discussed in detail my

scheme to liberate Mexico. As commanding general of the Tennessee militia, he was in almost as good a position as Wilkinson to begin the inevitable war with Spain. "And I will, Sir, if you give me the command. I hate the Dons worse than the devil himself—the devil is at least good company they say, and don't live within spittin' distance of the Sabine River, and capture our boys like they just did the Kemper brothers, and on *American* soil, too, God damn them!"

"Would you come with me, General, if there should be war?"

"You'd have to chain me to the door-post to keep me from killing Dons! And I'll bring the whole militia with me, too. That's a vow!"

"But suppose there is no war with Spain."

"We'll make one!" With an airy gesture, Jackson waved his pipe, making cottony puffs of white smoke between us, like artillery fire.

"But suppose the Spanish won't take our bait."

He frowned. "What you're asking is what do we do about the Dons if Jefferson loses his nerve."

"Yes."

"Well, that takes some thought."

"Yes, it does."

"Jefferson's never been keen for fighting. Remember how he hightailed it all over Virginia with the British chasing him like a fox—no, like a scared rabbit. Most comical! Most cowardly!"

"Do you think it would still be possible for us to cross the Sabine without a war *and* without Jefferson's permission?" I knew the word "permission" would distress him; it did.

Jackson damned Jefferson thoroughly. Then: "Personally, I would take the chance. Either you win Mexico and Jefferson writes you a real nice letter as one president to another or you get yourself hanged by the Dons and have no more interest in letters from Washington City."

Jackson had said what I wanted to hear; and I made my plans.

On June 3, in a boat supplied me by my host, I began the ascent of the Cumberland River to Fort Massac where Wilkinson was waiting. We were together four days. He showed me his list of recruits. I showed him mine. We decided that the following spring was the best time to launch our invasion.

"But we must have a war with Spain first." I mentioned the *sine qua non*.

Wilkinson thrust out his huge be-sashed belly. "You have but to say the word, and I will cross the Sabine River. I will force Spain to fight. I will even force Jefferson to fight. Count on me, as you would on the rising of tomorrow's sun!" Then Jamie gave me letters to various potentates at New Orleans and saw me off aboard a barge he had himself, most imperially, designed, all glittering with bright colours and manned by ten sailors and a sergeant.

I felt as if I was already emperor of Mexico as I glided into New Orleans—to the consternation of the idlers on the water frontage who had never seen anything quite so peculiar as my too exotic bark.

I was not prepared for the delights of the Crescent City. In fact, had I not been driven to do memorable things, forced always to move in a whirlwind, I would have been perfectly happy to settle down then and there, and live the rest of my life in some comfortable galleried house in the Vieux Carré, surrounded by the most attractive women in America as well as by a Creole society which I took to immediately—and I think they were attracted to me. After all, I was one of the few Americans who could speak intelligible French.

I stayed in the house of Edward Livingston who had fled New York City where, as mayor, he had been held responsible for the misappropriation of certain funds by an underling. Like so many easterners who have had a run of bad luck he went west, and did well for himself. In fact, two weeks before I arrived he had married a beautiful and wealthy Creole lady, aged nineteen. Presently he was to be a senator from

Louisiana. Currently he is our much admired ambassador to France.

"I was going to ask you if you missed New York," I said. "Now I don't need to." We sat in a tropical garden where the smell of summer flowers mingled deliciously with that all-pervasive odour of roasting coffee that is a characteristic of New Orleans. In his linen suit, Beau Ned looked more like an indolent planter than the beleaguered mayor of New York I had known in earlier days. He was bitter only on the subject of Jefferson and the arbitrary way in which the territory was being governed by Claiborne, a well-meaning but inadequate minion of the Virginia junto.

"Do you think now that you made a mistake in voting for Jefferson?" I teased Beau Ned who had once pledged his vote to me, without my asking. He had been a Republican member of the House of Representatives when Jefferson and I were in contest for the presidency.

Livingston blushed. "I was weak, Colonel. And now we have a weak president who is going to lose us Louisiana. Half the population here wants the Spanish back. The other half wants the French."

"No one," I asked, "wants independence?"

"There is always talk of separation out here: some of the westerners—particularly in Kentucky—are almost as bad as our New England Federalists. But the Creoles, quite sensibly, hate all Americans and who can blame them? They never wanted to become a colony of the United States."

Livingston had already heard rumours of what I was about and he was willing to be helpful. "You'll find the key to Mexico is the Catholic Church. Lately the Spanish have taken to taxing church property. As a result, every priest in Mexico wants independence. And what those priests want, they get!" He then arranged for me to meet the Roman Catholic Bishop of New Orleans. The Bishop so favoured my scheme that he assigned to me three Jesuit priests to act as agents. I was even received one afternoon by the Mother Superior of the Ursulines, and in her convent garden, over wine and cake, I met the sisters (two were quite presentable) and I was assured of the whole-hearted support of their order.

Although I never had any plan to separate the western states from the rest of the union, I did ally myself with a number of political figures like the senators Brown and Adair and General Jamie Wilkinson—who had in earlier times been involved in the Spanish Conspiracy. But that was all past. In the summer of 1805 there was no movement for disunion anywhere in the United States, outside of New England. I did believe—and still believe—that in time the various sections of the country will go their separate ways but not with any help from me. I should prefer the future disintegration of the United States to be laid to the man who most believed in the individual sovereignty of the states and their right to join and disjoin at will, Thomas Jefferson.

That summer I travelled from New Orleans to Natchez to Nashville (and a second visit with Jackson); from Nashville to Lexington to Frankfort; from Frankfort to Louisville to St. Louis, the capital of the territory of Louisiana where my confederate Wilkinson reigned supreme as governor.

I arrived at Jamie's capital September 12, my mind a confusion of parades and speeches, of feasts and thunderous vows to drive the Dons into the sea! Oh, Aaron Burr was a mighty conqueror that triumphant summer—if only in the floury back rooms of grocery shops or upon the shady verandas of those spacious houses that face so proudly upon the thick-watered Mississippi. The west was mine. So why not Mexico?

"We are recruiting every day!" Wilkinson was his usual exuberant self. He gave me the names of various army officers who would join us; and of others who might join us. I cautioned him not to reveal too much to anyone but his nature was to reveal every-

thing, or so I thought at the time. He also tended
to attack Jefferson in company—something I tried
never to do. Unfortunately, Wilkinson was (rather surprisingly for a compulsive scoundrel) a true Federalist.
"Jefferson is going to divide all property. You see if
he don't." This speech was regularly made after the
second bottle of claret. "He'll take away our money.
He'll level us all, *if*"—and here the red eyes would pop
and the voice lower with melodrama—"we do not stay
the tyrant's hand!"

Wilkinson also talked altogether too freely of the
desirability of separating west from east. I warned him
not to give a wrong impression of what we were about
but his reasoning was perfectly sound. "My friend,
leader, *Roi* . . ."

"In Spanish, *Rey*."

"No matter!" For one who had been so long involved with Spain, Wilkinson never deigned to learn
a word of the language of his other nationality. "Our
project depends on keeping the Dons in a good mood.
Now they're not fools. They know we're up to something. Well, I want them to think we're reviving the
old Spanish Conspiracy. And I've succeeded, let me
tell you."

Indeed he had! To the end Don Carlos believed
that we had no designs on Mexico. Unfortunately, in
tricking the Spanish minister we fell—or rather I fell,
as a result of Jamie's pushing—into Jefferson's trap.
The rumour was now being spread that I was involved
in a scheme to dismember the union, and anyone
listening to Wilkinson's hints and winks and talk of the
tyrant Jefferson would have thought the rumour true.

In August, the *U.S. Gazette* of Philadelphia
wondered aloud (the *query* is a nice journalistic way
of slander without legal risk) if Colonel Burr was con-
templating summoning a convention of those states
along the Mississippi and Ohio rivers in order to declare
them independent? The editor also "wondered" how
long it would be before I seized New Orleans as a
base for the reduction of Mexico. The first "query" was

what the Administration wanted the world to believe was my plan. The second was nearly true.

From St. Louis I moved east to Vincennes where I stayed with the governor of the Indiana Territory. William Henry Harrison was then a slight, horse-faced young Virginian in his early thirties. I delivered a letter to him from Wilkinson which he read, rather slowly, and said, as slowly, "Well, Colonel, he says the fate of the union depends upon your being returned to Congress as Indiana's delegate."

"General Wilkinson never exaggerates. I am sure he is right. But happily for your territory my fate takes me in another direction." That was the end of that "promotion."

Harrison is a most amiable man but his early rise in the world is as mysterious to me as his subsequent fall must appear to him. I am told that he is now clerk of the court of common pleas at Cincinnati after a career which took him from the governorship of Indiana to the United States Senate. Along the way he engaged in a small skirmish with the Indians which was exaggerated by the press into a great victory, rather on the order of Monmouth Court House. But that seems to be the American pattern. Despite our numerous heroic generals and colonels and coon-skin Indian fighters, Americans are almost always defeated in battle whether it be by the British or by the Indians or even by the Spanish. Since 1775 we have had only three proper victories: Gates at Saratoga, Lee at Charleston, and Jackson at New Orleans (a battle fought *after* we had already lost that particular war to the British). Yet so formidable is the national conceit that any man who has ever heard so much as a bullet's hiss is acclaimed a hero, no matter how fast he might have run from the enemy.

At Vicennes all that Harrison could discuss was Indians. "I write Mr. Jefferson almost daily, warning him against the tribes, but all I get from him is imprecise theories."

"My husband is *most* attached to Mr. Jefferson. As

was his father before him." Mrs. Harrison was protective.

"Yes, yes." General Harrison poured us more cider (he neither drinks nor smokes nor takes snuff while the dozen or so children he has had by his wife testify to his moral straitness in the Paphian sphere).

"Presently Mr. Jefferson is advising me to *lend* the Indians money against their lands. When they default in their payments, as he says they always do, I am to occupy their territories. But there is a flaw in this policy. We have no money to lend them. Oh, I tell you, Colonel, even while we sit here, comfortable beside the fire" (I was freezing in that draughty cabin), "the tribes are plotting our ruin. There will be a war out here such as the world has never seen. And why?" This was the only moment he displayed the slightest enthusiasm or passion during my stay. "Because concienceless men sell them spirits! Sir, I would hang any white man who sold an Indian so much as a teaspoonful of whiskey!"

"But we're not allowed to hang anyone." Mrs. Harrison was sad.

I got no support in that quarter. Harrison hardly knew where Mexico was. Worse, he disliked Andrew Jackson and it has been a rule with me to measure people by what they think of Jackson. Anyone who does not appreciate that frank and ardent spirit is an enemy to what is best in our American breed—by the Eternal!

I returned to Washington in November, and called upon Merry who said, "You have been betrayed, Colonel," and showed me a copy of the Philadelphia *Gazette*.

I put as good a face as I could on it. "It is not possible to set something like this in train without a thousand tales being told and of the thousand one is apt, by the law of averages, to be true."

Merry then made his confession. "I have received no instructions from London. I cannot think why."

"What of Colonel Williamson?"

"He is still in London."

"So we are where we were last summer."

"I fear that is the case."

I was disappointed to say the least. I needed British military aid. I also needed British money (the New York gamblers were not as generous as I had hoped). Since British gold could only be got by appearing to serve British interests, I was obliged to re-kindle Merry's enthusiasm. I told him what he wanted to hear: that the westerners were anxious to separate from the east. As for the people of Louisiana, "they detest the Administration," which was the exact truth, "and will fight, if they must, to break away," which might have been true. "They want me to lead them." Again the truth. "To set up a republic under the protection of England." This could be made true. At that time the people of New Orleans were desperate to rid themselves of the back-country American barbarians. If England would do this for them, then English they would become. "Otherwise they will apply to Paris." This had the desired effect.

"His Majesty's government would take a most grave view if that were to happen." I could do no more at this point. I had inspired him to write again to London. Now all depended upon Prime Minister Pitt's response.

The day after my arrival at Washington, Mrs. Merry insisted that I accompany her to the race track where each November from Tuesday to Saturday there were—are?—all sorts of horse-races culminating in the annual Jockey Club Ball, held at a near-by tavern. This was the event of the "season."

We stood beneath a canopy on a brilliant ice-clear day, and enjoyed ourselves tremendously. All around us the exuberant blades of Washington were having a fine time, swigging rum against the chill, and betting on the races. As always Mrs. Merry managed to surround herself with pretty women and intelligent men. I had quite forgotten my imperial dreams until, just before the last race of the day, a large lumbering bear-like figure came toward me from the far end of the track. It was the new vice-president George Clinton, looking old and uncomfortable.

"Burr!" he exclaimed, as though he loved me. "Good to see you here."

"My successor! My . . . *son*. I do feel like your father. No, like your father's ghost! Avenge me!"

"Mmm?" Clinton's mind was never a swift instrument. "We been hearin' about you in the west."

"Don't believe a word of what you hear."

"You was there all summer, they say. Well, that there part of the world better stay with us if they know what's good for 'em."

"Are you enjoying the vice-presidency?"

"Stupidest job there ever was, ain't it? And for me, George Clinton, the governor that was, and at my age!"

The following day, I dined with the President and a dozen members of Congress. I found Jefferson in good form and could not think why. I was so intrigued by his high spirits that I asked if I might see him privately; most readily he gave me an appointment.

I was received in the basement office, filled now with gardening implements as well as *two* copying machines. Apparently he had discovered a contraption that really worked. "Such a convenience, Colonel. You must get one."

"When I settle down, I most certainly shall."

"Yes." Not once did he look me in the face during an interview that lasted two hours.

I was almost entirely candid with him and for once he was as candid with me as his nature would allow.

"You have read of my supposed plans for the west." I began *in medias res*. I had vowed that there were to be no disquisitions on architecture or on the nature of music.

"I have read the newspapers." Jefferson fiddled with a globe of the world. He was seated in a chair of his own design which could turn this way and that, most disconcertingly, on a swivel.

"Let me tell you then that there is not the slightest chance in this world of the western states leaving the union."

"I am relieved." The attempt at lightness was plucky.

"I might add that you yourself are personally most popular in the west." This was true, as he of course knew.

"That is gratifying. I would like some day to go to that part of the world, when I'm free of this hateful place."

I promptly forstalled what I have come to regard as "The Presidential Lament." It is a constant song of self-pity first sung by Washington and taken up by all his successors, rather like part-singing. Last year even Andrew Jackson sang to me of that malign destiny which had made him our chief magistrate. I cut Jackson short; told him I was not in the least moved by his sad song. I will say that of the lot only Jackson has the humour to laugh at himself—not much but a little and that little is refreshing.

"Let me tell you how things stand at the west." And tell him I did, as accurately as I was able.

Jefferson listened attentively; asked precise questions; confessed, finally, that "I have never before been told so many things I ought to have known but did not."

"I enjoy sharing with you since what I have learned is of far more use to you than it is to me."

Jefferson spun the globe slowly on its axis. "I must tell you, Colonel, that I have not believed any of the more . . . sensational reports that I have read of your travels. I am certain that you would never attempt a separation of the western states."

Later Jefferson was to deny having heard at this time so much as a rumour of my "treasonous" activities. Actually there was little he did not know. After all, I was as open with him as I could be.

"General Wilkinson and I would like very much to raise an army—much like the one you had in mind at the time of the Michaux expedition—and liberate Mexico. As you know, this has been the sole object

of my western travels during which I discovered that
every American in that part of the world wants to
drive the Dons from our continent."

Jefferson did not answer for some time. He played
with the globe; turned it, finally, to Mexico. "You put
me in a difficult position, Colonel."

"It is my impression that this position is one that
you have for a long time wanted to be in. You have
always said that our empire would not be complete
without the Floridas, Canada, Cuba—and Mexico."

"Yes, of course. And we shall have the whole hemisphere one day. I am certain of that. But I can do
nothing unless there is war with Spain."

"It has been my impression that you have been . . .
and that you are . . . preparing for such a war."

"There are things, Colonel, that you don't know."
Jefferson pushed the globe away from him and sat so
far back in his peculiar chair that I thought he would
tumble over. "I have just received an offer from the
Emperor Napoleon. As usual, he needs money for his
wars. He has offered to 'persuade'—that was his ambassador's tactful verb—the Spanish government to let us
have West Florida. For this kindly act of persuasion
he would like two million dollars. I am tempted to
give the Corsican bandit his *pour-boire*."

I was astonished by the offer. I was even more
astonished by Jefferson's acceptance of it. "But you
are now buying what you have already paid for.
Wasn't West Florida part of the Louisiana Purchase?"

"That has always been my . . . uh, *construction* of
a somewhat unfinished document. But neither my construction nor Congress's acts will ever gain us a square
foot of Spanish territory."

"War will gain you the western hemisphere."

"No doubt. But the cost of sending an army—and
a fleet—to Mobile would come to rather more than
two million dollars. The Cabinet think that we should
hire the Emperor, on the ground that it will be
cheaper in the long run."

"This Congress will not appropriate the money."

"Properly approached, I am certain they will."

"Then there will be no war with Spain."

"I fear not." My obvious chagrin no doubt added to Jefferson's quite evident sense of well-being. He was complacent. "I do think that we are the first empire in history to *buy* its territory rather than to conquer it."

"There has never been any doubt, anywhere, of our uniqueness." I was thoroughly cast down by the news.

"What will you do now?" Jefferson pretended sympathy.

"I don't know." And I did not know. "I may settle on some property I've acquired on the Washita River . . . and wait for a war with Spain."

"I am sure that one day it will come."

"If not . . . what would your view be of a liberated Mexico?"

"I would applaud the result." Jefferson was again the diplomat at Paris. Each swift response rich with ambiguities.

"But the preparation . . .?"

"I give you the same advice that I gave Genêt and Michaux. Be quick, be successful, and do not implicate this government."

I rose to go.

Jefferson noted with surprise that we had been together for two hours. "I have never known time to go so rapidly, or so profitably." He walked me upstairs to the draughty entrance hall, filled with smoke from a faulty fireplace in the dining-room.

"We are having our problems with one of the flues."

"If you like, I'll rebuild it for you." When close to starving in Paris, I remodelled several chimneys for money. A useful talent.

"Colonel, you have touched my single . . . at least my most *noticeable* vanity! I alone tinker in this house."

"So be it."

An usher opened the front door. In the muddy front yard a groom stood with my horse. Jefferson looked at me curiously. "I must say that I had rather thought you would be coming back to live here."

"To this house?" I asked most pleasantly.

"Why not? But I meant to Washington City, to the Congress, representing one of the western states."

"It is still a possibility."

"You ought not to waste yourself, Colonel."

"I do not think that it is I who have done the wasting."

Jefferson blushed; and bade me farewell.

At this point I was willing to abandon the Mexican project. Without a Spanish war, most of my western confederates would refuse to risk the Administration's disfavour by taking up arms. Worse, despite Merry's efforts, I could get nothing from England.

Much discouraged, I moved on to Philadelphia where Jonathan Dayton tried to re-awaken my enthusiasm. I had also received a letter from Harman Blennerhassett who wanted to sell his island and throw in his lot with me.

"He's a fool but he has a good deal of money." Dayton and I sat by the meagre fire at Richard Dell's rather humble tavern, and I confess that I was as depressed as the winter day. Dayton did his best to rally me. "Let's approach Don Carlos."

I told him that I did not think Spain was apt to finance an expedition whose aim was to take Mexico away from her.

"That's not exactly the way I would put it to Don Carlos." Dayton grinned: he was a born peddler of snake-root. "Quite the opposite. I'd begin by saying that although we had once contemplated such an undertaking at the suggestion of the British minister..."

"The wise man never lies." I quoted the Jesuit aphorism, but to no avail.

"Everything I tell him will be true but inside out. Of course the Spanish know what we're about, and he's more apt to believe me if I admit to everything."

"So what do we have to offer Spain?"

"The revival of the Spanish Conspiracy."

Dayton had several meetings with Don Carlos who ended by giving Dayton $1,500, and wishing us luck. At the time I did not know just what it was that my colleague had said to the Spanish minister. I was not pleased when Dayton finally confessed to me that he had told Don Carlos that our real aim was to seize Washington, capture the President and the Congress, steal the money from the Bank of the United States, board the ships in the Navy Yard and sail to New Orleans where we would set up a western republic.

"You have now convinced Don Carlos that I am an out-and-out lunatic."

"What do you care?" Dayton was purest brass. "He takes the plan seriously enough to pay us money."

Sick of the whole business, I returned to Washington and applied to Jefferson for a government appointment. I was willing to take any post, no matter how humble.

Our interview took place on February 22, 1806. I humbled myself. Jefferson was ravished. I have never seen him so—*exalted*. There is no other word. With the serene justice of God Himself he told me, ever so softly, that since the public had lost its confidence in me, there was nothing he could give me in the way of an appointment.

"The lack of confidence shown by a few newspapers is hardly significant," I said. "We have all been tarred by them."

"True. But unfortunately *political* confidence in you has also been withdrawn."

"In the recent election for governor of New York, I not only carried the city but—"

"No, Colonel. I mean at the time of the last presidential election when, although you were the incumbent vice-president, you did not receive a single vote."

Jefferson rose and busied himself with the mockingbird's cage.

I had vowed to maintain a humble pose, but this was too much. "I did not get a single vote because the electors knew that I was *not* a candidate. The reason I was not a candidate for re-election as vice-president was *your* decision, not mine or theirs, and reflects not at all on either my competence or their confidence."

Jefferson released the mocking-bird from its cage and it flew to his shoulder. He sat down; again remarked that he was sorry. He could do nothing for me. Public confidence once withdrawn . . .

I stopped him short; reminded him that as recently as the year before when he had needed me in the Senate neither he nor the public had shown any lack of confidence in me.

"But since then, Colonel, we have heard so many things." His voice was dreamy. "The newspapers have alarmed the people . . ."

"That is their function."

Jefferson held out his finger and the mocking-bird lit upon it; and whistled.

"I confess, Mr. Jefferson, that I find it most remarkable, most strange, that you are not able to confide *any* task to the man who raised you to this place."

The fierce old mouth set. The hands fell to the table. The bird fled and perched on the mantel opposite. "It was the people, Colonel Burr, who did me this honour . . ."

"No, Sir. It was Aaron Burr who gave you your victory in New York state, and it was Aaron Burr who could have taken the presidency from you had he but said the word."

"But you did not say that word, Mr. Burr. And here I am." Like an axe his malice fell upon me; and we were done with one another.

I rose to go. "I wonder what the world would think if they were to know all the arrangements you made in order to become president."

"It is too late to change what is now the accepted version of our revolution." Jefferson put the mocking-bird back inside its cage.

But a good many of Jefferson's supporters were shaken when, two months later, my friends' suit against the journalist Cheetham came to trial in New York. Cheetham had charged me with trying to get the presidency for myself during the election of 1800. Duly sworn, Senator Bayard of Delaware stated categorically not only had Aaron Burr made no move to take the presidency from Thomas Jefferson but that Jefferson had been indecently quick to come to an understanding with the Federalists in order to get their support in the House.

Recently, when Jefferson's journal was published, one was able to read at inordinate length his dishonest response to this charge and his mad notion that I was entirely responsible for Senator Bayard's deposition which had, he wrote, been taken for no "other object than to calumniate me." Actually, I had little to do with the suit. It was Bayard who insisted that the truth be known. Currently the battle still rages amongst the heirs of the two men—who lied? Jefferson or Bayard? The Jeffersonians still maintain that it was simply coincidence that after the election of 1801, Bayard's Federalist friend was kept on by Jefferson as collector of the port of Wilmington, Delaware.

Despite the finality of our February interview, I dined with Jefferson once again in company. Then April 12, 1806, I went to say good-bye, and that was the end of that.

1835

One

LATELY I HAVE TAKEN to introducing Helen as my wife to strangers or slight acquaintances; not that we go to many public places—usually she refuses to leave the house. I assume it is because she is afraid she will meet men that she has known at Mrs. Townsend's (the thought alarms me, too). But she denies any such fear; says she does not care what anyone thinks. Yet when I urge her to go with me to this place or that, she says she prefers her "work" at home. When she does go with me, she is sulky while I . . . I feel a most extraordinary sense of triumph even though I know that I would be ruined if anyone suspected who and what she was. Certainly saying that she is my wife increases the danger. On the other hand, there is no reason why we cannot be married one day. All I have to do is make money; apply myself to the law; forget about going abroad, about leading the life of a Washington Irving—or even a Fitz-Greene Halleck, whom I saw to-night.

Sam Swartwout invited me to have supper with him

at the Shakespeare Tavern in Nassau Street. I accepted with pleasure. Once, on an errand, I took some papers to a client in the tap-room, and was amazed to see everyone from Edwin Forrest to James K. Paulding all drinking and smoking together in a most convivial mood. The Shakespeare Tavern is the unofficial club of the literary and theatrical people of the town; and to be accepted as an equal in that place is the dream of every would-be author or actor. Even politicians of the cheerier sort can be seen in the tap-room, not to mention members of the Kraut Club whose annual party starts at breakfast and continues until the last member has collapsed beneath the proud emblem of our Dutch heritage, the cabbage.

"You go alone. I want to work." For two weeks Helen has every day *not* worked on a dress already paid for by an impatient lady. A short quarrel, ending when she burst into tears—which is rare with her. "I hate everything!" she sobbed.

"Me, too?"

But Helen only blew her nose; splashed cold water into her face; sat at her dress-dummy, and started to work. She looked, as always, more like a lady than any of those who decorate the parlours of the City Hotel. I think this is why I like to show her off. I love the masquerade, and the danger.

Muffled against the arctic air, I walked through the darkening gray streets, trying not to slip on frozen cobbles, to avoid snow-bitches, to stay out of the path of the sleighs with their ominous thin tinkle and clatter of bells, and their terrifying propensity to slide wildly out of control, smashing the legs of horses—and of the poor who like myself walk.

I opened the green door of the Shakespeare Tavern, and was deafened by a roar of voices from the rooms to left and right; was overwhelmed by the powerful smell of spirits mingled with the odour of smoked goose and sauerkraut (despite my dislike of Dutchness I have Dutch tastes in food).

Ears tingling as heat replaced cold, I stepped into the tap-room and collided with a short stocky man who fell against the door-frame. We apologized simultaneously; then recognised one another. "Ah, the young protégé of Colonel Burr!"

I could not restrain myself, as usual. Like a fool I told Fitz-Greene Halleck that I had just finished reading the *Croaker Papers*; and admired them.

"Oh, dear!" Halleck talks as he writes—is highly whimsical. "Those old things." He gestured toward the back rooms. "We wrote them here, Mr. Drake and I." He gave me a penetrating if somewhat watery look. He smelled of rum. "I have just read your Old Patroon piece in the *Evening Post:* on eating your first love-apple—or I suppose one must now call it a *tomato*. I was filled with admiration for your courage. Like everyone in the world—except Indians and certain English eccentrics like Mrs. Trollope—I had thought the tomato deadly poison. Laughed at my grocer when he told me it could be safely eaten after all. But now, thanks to your intrepid spirit and literary skill, I shall, come summer, myself taste of that hectic scarlet sinister globe."

My face must have been cretinous with pleasure and confusion. Praise from Halleck! As I write this, I still cannot believe my luck for, "You must do more pieces so that we can make a book for you."

Halleck has a silly grin, the result of an under-slung jaw; but glittering, watchful, intelligent eyes. "Tell me exactly what it was like to taste a love-app . . . a *tomato*. How does it really taste?"

"An acid flavour," I said. "You must stew it first. Then put a good deal of sugar on it. Or syrup."

Halleck shuddered. "Not I! On second thought I shall forgo the experiment. After all, I have a young man of genius who will eat my love-apples for me in the pages of the *Evening Post*." Again the foolish but amiable grin. "I wish I could propose you for membership in our club. It is called the Ugly Club, and celebrates ugliness in all things—including *tomatoes*—but I'm afraid you lack the first qualification for membership. But come see me anyway. Any time."

Then he proceeded to the dining-room at the back while I went into the tap-room where I found Sam Swartwout standing at the circular bar which is supposed to be typical of English taverns. He was surrounded by a number of men, all playing the toady to him because not only is he the President's friend, but as collector of the port of New York he is the most important federal officer in the state.

"Come and sit down, Charlie!" Swartwout threw a heavy arm about my shoulder. "No girl to bring me?"

"No, Sir. She—the one who was to come—didn't ... couldn't come."

"Good! We'll have time for company later even if I'm not what I was, though I'm still better than the rest!" He steered me to a table and sat me down in a chair like a doll.

"Terrapin!" he shouted to a waiter who brought it to us in the time it would take most New York waiters to tell me that it was not possible to get terrapin in New York on any day except Midsummer's Eve. I hate terrapin but ate as he commanded, drank as he commanded; felt duller and duller. He, on the other hand, is enlivened by drink.

I tried to get him to talk of the past, but like the Colonel (and Mr. Davis) he thinks only of the future. Obviously the business of history is for the young alone. "Texas! That's the place. That's where you ought to go. Get out of New York. Away from soft, weak city-folk!" With a forkful of terrapin he indicated his cronies at the bar. (I must write a piece about the degenerative effect of city life on our vigorous American stock.)

"It was the Colonel, bless him, who got me onto Texas."

"His own Texas schemes were hardly a success ..."

"Ahead of the times! That should be on his tomb-

stone. Aaron Burr always saw the future first. Yet
never profitted by it. But he improves. That German
settler scheme was only a couple of years premature.
Now, in a matter of months"—the hoarse voice
dropped beneath that of the men at the bar—"Texas
is going to break away from Mexico *and the President
is involved."*

As he talked, I was suddenly transported back to a
time when men like Burr plotted for empires. But then
Swartwout is as much a relic of that era as Burr or
Jackson. Swartwout is now involved in something called
the Galveston Bay and Texas Land Company. The
attorney for the company is a former governor of Tennessee—a protégé of Jackson named Houston who broke
with his wife, resigned the governorship, went to live
among Indians (and took to drink). Now he is in Texas
where he is plotting, so Swartwout says, to liberate that
province from Mexico with the secret connivance of
Jackson. "And that's what they talked about, Colonel
Burr and the President, when they met here for the
first time since the treason trial thirty years ago."

Inadvertently, I started doing shorthand with my
fork on the scarred table; hope I am getting it all
straight now, three hours later—with a headache, and
much else on my mind.

Jackson's last visit to New York was June 12, 1833.
A fortnight later Colonel Burr married Madame Jumel.
I now understand why he needed Madame's money
to forward his Texas schemes: President Jackson had
told him things that others did not know.

"Ah, it was a sweet business, getting the Colonel
into the President's suite at the American Hotel. I had
to get the manager—old Boardman—to take us in the
back way and up the servants' stairs."

Without being told, a waiter set in front of us a
huge platter of pork ringlets and sauerkraut. Both
Swartwout and I ate as though starving—or Dutch,
which we are.

"Well, it was touch-and-go in the corridor where

the people wanting jobs was crowded but, finally, I
got the Colonel into a bedroom on the same floor, and
a secretary was told that someone special was there for
the President, and a minute later Old Hickory himself
came limping in. 'By the Eternal, Colonel Burr, I
never thought to see you again on this earth—or in
Heaven.'

"The Colonel was tickled by that. 'Well, Mr. President, if *you* get to Heaven it will only be in answer
to my daily prayers.'

"The President laughed so hard he had to sit down
. . . very shaky . . . he was—is—not long for this world,
poor old man. 'Now,' he says, 'I want to talk to you
about Texas.'

" 'The way we used to talk,' says Colonel Burr, 'in
the old days?'

"Well, General Jackson curled that short mean
upper lip of his back like a horse. 'Damnit, Colonel,
you almost lost me the election, you and your rascali-
ties!'

"But the Colonel was cool as could be. 'Lucky
thing,' he says, 'that your opponent Mr. Clay was also
a friend of mine.'

" 'Yes, Sir, that shut 'em up. By the Eternal, I
won't rest easy until I have shot Henry Clay and
hanged John C. Calhoun!' Then the President turns
to me. 'Sam, you go in the other room and have a
glass of Madeira. But only one while I talk to the man
I still admire the most in all the union.' So I wait in
the next room for maybe a half-hour. Then I'm called
back in and the President has tears in his eyes. He
says good-bye to the Colonel who says 'Farewell' to
him. When we were out on the street, I asked the
Colonel what they'd talked about but all he'd say was
'Texas.' "

As Swartwout ordered us an entire goose, Gulian
C. Verplanck walked by our table. Bowed briefly to
Swartwout, and moved on. I don't suppose he re-
members meeting me. Swartwout told me that Ver-

planck was married to the daughter of Fenno who edited the *Gazetteer of the United States* for Hamilton. They do stick together, our rulers.

Swartwout can think of nothing but Texas and the money that is to be made there. He told me how not long ago Jackson sent Houston into the territory to reconnoitre. "Because Sam Houston's got the same itch to be an emperor Colonel Burr had but I doubt if Old Hickory will let him get that far. The President wants Texas for the United States. And a lot more. Oh, he's sly, old Jackson. Here everybody's trying to get him to annex Texas, and he won't lift a finger. Keeps saying how he's got to abide by his treaty with Mexico. And he will. But do you know why? It's a precious plot, let me tell you. 'Sam,' he says to me one day, 'Texas is going to be independent in a year or two.' 'With our help?' Well, he lets that one pass. 'But I don't want 'em in the union right away.' 'Why not?' 'Well, suppose they was independent from Mexico. Suppose they was just another harmless little republic. And suppose they had trouble figuring out where their western boundary was because in that part of the world it *could* be anywheres. Now suppose this harmless little republic says their land goes all the way to the Pacific. Why not? And suppose they lay claim to the Californias and maybe to the fishing rights of the northwest and maybe to a harbour or two in the Pacific. Why, the Mexicans would just laugh, wouldn't they? And they'd tell that harmless little Texas republic to go to Hell because there's nothing a handful of Texans can do about kicking the Mexicans out of California.'"

A waiter offered Swartwout a section of venison pie. "With the compliments of the cook, Sir."

"Thank him. Thank him." Swartwout divided the section and with greasy fingers we ate the pie which tasted of cinnamon. Mouth full, Swartwout revealed Jackson's plot. A harmless little republic of Texas would lay claim to the Pacific Coast of our continent. After a decent interval, that republic would join the United States which would then claim all of Spanish California, "Giving us more territory than Jefferson ever did, that treacherous bastard! Oh, if I was your age, your age!" Apparently everyone wants to be my age except me.

Finally, unable to eat or drink more, Swartwout sat back in his chair and wanted to know exactly what I was doing "with this thing you're writing about the Colonel."

"Just that. His life."

"I hear it's really going to be a life of Matty Van Buren."

I said nothing; waited.

Slowly one large red hand dried the full red lips of goose-fat; then the hand was in its turn dried on the top of the table which began to shine. "You know, Matty Van tried to stop me from being collector of the port. He's a damned bad little fellow, and don't you forget it. But the real thing is," he looked thoughtful; belched softly, "we don't want the Colonel hurt, now do we?"

I shook my head, somewhat surprised at Swartwout's delicacy: he seems all push and bluster and false friendliness. "Well, now I think there's a way round a problem which must be bothering you, too." I tried to look impassive the way the Colonel does. But from the sudden heat in the tips of my ears I knew that they were now all afire and pink as a rabbit's.

Swartwout belched again, and tucked his heavy chin swag inside the tall starched collar. "I got a fair idea of what Reginald Gower is paying you. And I know somebody who will give you twice as much."

"But I've . . . I've made an agreement."

"Break it."

"I've taken money."

"Pay it back."

"But what's the point? The Colonel's involvement will be the same."

"Not if what you've written is taken and put inside of a book which someone else is writing."

"But we're still exactly where we were. The Colonel will think that I wrote someone else's book."

"He might if this was just another pamphlet written by Mr. Anonymous. But this is going to be a great big book by a very famous man whose very famous name will be all over the front, and nobody will ever connect you with him."

"Who?"

"I'll arrange for you to meet him." Although a man without secrets (as opposed to a man of many conspiracies), Swartwout enjoyed mystifying me. "He's coming to town soon, with his publisher. He's from Philadelphia—the publisher, that is."

At this point cronies joined the table and I knew it was time to go. Before I did, at my host's request, I wrote out for him Mrs. Townsend's address.

"Haven't seen that charming creature since . . . well, since she set up house."

I thanked Swartwout, and departed. Passing Verplanck's table, I recognised a number of writers and bookish lawyers. I wished that I had been of their company.

When I got home I found Helen vomitting. When she stopped, she told me that she was going to have a baby.

It is now four in the morning, and I cannot sleep. I sit and write and rewrite these notes, and stare at the dress dummy (progress has been made on one puffed sleeve), and wonder what is to become of Helen —me—the child.

Two

EARLY THIS MORNING it snowed, and Broadway is now covered with a thick white powder. Sleighs crowd the streets. Everyone is red-faced. My ears burn all the time when I am inside; freeze when I'm out.

Shortly after noon, I arrived at the Colonel's boarding-house where I found Jane McManus sitting beside the Colonel and holding his hand. Unembarrassed, she rose. "I must go, Colonel."

"As you like, dear girl." Odd to think that anyone could find this plump woman a girl, dear or otherwise. She promised to visit him soon again, and left.

"Poor child is still much shaken by Madame's raid on our happy nest."

The Colonel looks to be in good form, though he complains of the cold in a room so hot that my ears felt scorched. When I told him that I had dined with Swartwout, he indicated a thick folder of papers on the table beside his sofa. "Sam enters our story now. He was an attractive young man—like all the Swartwouts. Good-hearted to a fault . . ."

I was surprised at my own alertness, considering that I did not sleep at all last night. Unlike Helen who slept like a child and awakened this morning so sunny and pleased with everything that I did not have the heart to say a word to her about the trouble we are in. Yet she has not once mentioned marriage. I don't begin to understand her. I suppose that is why I gave her, impulsively, the only thing I have of value, Vanderlyn's miniature of my mother on a gold chain. She was thrilled; and put it around her neck.

Memoirs of Aaron Burr—Nineteen

IN THE FIRST WEEK of August 1806, I set out for the west expecting never to return. I had made arrange-

ments with several hundred ardent young men from
the best of American families to rendezvous with me
the first of November at Marietta on the Ohio River.

Wilkinson had promised me a war with Spain as
soon as I gave him the word. Before leaving Philadelphia, I sent Wilkinson that word in a ciphered letter
to be delivered by Sam Swartwout and Peter Ogden,
Dayton's nephew and the son of my old friend and
comrade at Quebec.

Since this letter was the principal evidence brought
against me at my trial for treason, I ought now to produce it. But the original is long-since lost or destroyed
by Wilkinson who then proceeded to fashion quite a
different document in order to incriminate me and
exonerate himself. He took my letter and added a number of his own windy phrases. Fortunately for me, he
bungled the job. He tried but failed to erase my first
sentence, "Your letter, postmarked 13th May, is received." This was a serious error because at first he
pretended that he knew nothing of the "plot" until
my letter. Despite his alterations, the letter established
two things damaging to him: we shared a cipher, and
he had written to me three months earlier.

What did I actually write Wilkinson? I told him
that our recruits would rendezvous November 1 on the
Mississippi. On November 15 we would descend the
river in light boats. At the Spanish outpost of Baton
Rouge we would decide whether to seize it or to pass
on. If possible, I would have liked to take Baton
Rouge simply to hearten Jackson and my other supporters who could not bear the thought of the Dons
so insolently lodged on *their* river.

I also reported that my agents (those three Jesuits
at New Orleans) had assured me that the people of
the country to which we were going would rally to me
if I swore to defend their religion (an oath I had
already taken in the presence of the Bishop of New
Orleans). I said that Wilkinson would be second-in-
command only to me, that he could draw on me for
money, that the business would be accomplished in

three weeks. I assured him that we had British naval protection—which was not true. I ended by saying that further instructions would be given him by Sam Swartwout whom I presented (somewhat insincerely) as a dazzled admirer of the Washington of the West.

Those further instructions were very simple: create an incident on the Sabine River. This should have been an easy thing to do because the previous year the Spanish had crossed the Sabine and occupied Bayou Pierre and Nona, two outposts on American soil. This insolence drove even Jefferson to action. In February of 1806, he directed the War Department to remove the Spanish troops. But Wilkinson ignored the Secretary of War, and the Spanish remained where they were. I assumed Wilkinson was waiting to coordinate his movements with mine.

In June, the President directly ordered Wilkinson to leave St. Louis and take personal command of our forces on the Sabine and drive out the Spanish. Yet at the time of my letter (late July), Wilkinson had not stirred from St. Louis, and everyone at Washington was of the opinion that Jefferson would soon remove his dilatory commander.

I told Dayton to write Wilkinson to warn him that he would soon be replaced. I thought that this would stir our commander to' action; he would now have no choice but to seek a new world. Instead, I fear, Dayton's warning convinced Wilkinson that he must do something to restore himself to Jefferson's favour. That something was to betray me.

This, then, was the background to my letter. Needless to say, I did not mention Mexico by name nor did I propose that Wilkinson provoke a war with Spain. I assumed that this would happen as soon as he obeyed the orders of his other commander-in-chief.

In my letter I said what I believed to be true: that in three weeks the place to which we were going would be ours. At my trial the prosecution sought to interpret this to mean New Orleans not Mexico. Considering the support I had in that city (and with the aid, as I then thought, of the commanding general of the American army), New Orleans would have been ours not in three weeks but in three hours. My letter referred only to Mexico.

By the middle of August, I was at Pittsburgh. It was here that I made the error of dining with Colonel George Morgan, a vain foolish man whose intelligence had not improved with age. I had come to his house not to see him but to recruit his three lively sons. In the course of dinner, I made a number of cheerful remarks about Jefferson, indicating a lack of admiration for that chieftain—but no animus. When the Colonel complained of the deterioration of the American army and the encroachment of the Dons, I said, "But that is Mr. Jefferson's policy. Why, he has so weakened our military establishment that you and I with two hundred men could toss President and Congress into the Potomac." Never joke with an old and addled man; particularly one who has for many years been trying to get the government to assign to him a disputed tract of Indiana land. Inspired by righteous greed, Colonel Morgan decided to warn a number of local worthies of my dark plan for drowning Mr. Jefferson. He also wrote my intended victim in the most emphatic, if incoherent terms.

Shortly after my arrival at Pittsburgh, I received a letter from Wilkinson (who had not yet got mine). After a good deal of the usual bombast, he declared "I am ready." All things conspired, it seemed, for our success.

I took it as a good omen that Theodosia's health (injured by the Carolina weather) had so improved that she was able to join us on the Ohio River.

At Blennerhassett's Island I finally met the legendary islander himself. Near-sighted to the point of blindness, a formidable talker, an inadequate listener, a constant dreamer, this splendid eccentric was positively deranged at the thought of obtaining at least the marquisate of Vera Cruz, not to mention my embassy to London where he intended to pay off ancient scores. I soothed him; fed the flame.

Mrs. Blennerhassett was as clever and as febrile as before and on very short notice gave us a magnificent dinner party. I must say I always found it marvellously strange in the west to dine grandly off silver-plate, to drink champagne from Irish crystal, to be served like a lord in a mansion that had been dropped as if by magic in the midst of a primaeval wilderness.

Theodosia delighted everyone, myself most of all. I had missed her, as I do miss her every moment of my life. We could say anything to one another; said everything.

After dinner, the ladies withdrew to the long drawing-room while I sat with Blennerhassett and those lieutenants who had come with me. We spoke of provisions, of money, of the future.

Blennerhassett was all afire, and despite a tendency to want to discuss Voltaire when I wanted to talk of barrels of pork, he was good company and not entirely useless; he contributed what money he could.

It was during our first stay on the island that Mrs. Blennerhassett took me riding through gardens hacked rather unconvincingly from the forest. In a beech grove, beside a gazebo, she intimated that we were in some rich strange way special souls. I was kindly (as befitted her sovereign) and confirmed to her what I had already secretly granted her husband, my embassy to London.

"But we cannot go back! He knows that!" She reined in her horse. Yellow leaves set off her red riding-habit; she looked heraldic.

"Why not?"

"Because we—we have—we are—not like others."

Not married, I thought immediately, as I gazed at her solemnly, imitating Solomon as reported in my grandfather's favourite book. She started to weep; then shouted to me her terrible sin: "*I am Harman Blennerhassett's niece!*" My horse shied; hers whinnied.

"But what is wrong with that?"

"Wrong? I have married my own uncle! They would burn us in Ireland!"

"But in England, surely, they will fête you!"

"Do you think so?" The moment of high drama was swiftly replaced by her natural high spirits. "I'm not at all certain. It is a complicated matter." She dismounted. I did the same. In the course of a pleasant hour she told me the amazing, the unique, the extraordinary story of her life, and the periodic need in it for change. It is my rule always to listen to this story with the sympathy that it deserves.

In less than a week the island was transfromed into a workshop. Corn was dried and ground into meal. Barrels of supplies from Marietta arrived and were stacked on the island's wharf. Against my counsel, the Blennerhassetts packed all their belongings: they would go with us to the Washita Lands and there await the conquest of Mexico.

At this point I had heard nothing beyond the "I am ready" letter from Wilkinson. For once both Jefferson and I were kept in precisely the same suspense by the Washington of the West.

When would Wilkinson obey Jefferson's orders (not to mention mine!) and confront the Spaniards on the Sabine? As it turned out, he did not leave St. Louis until the first week in September. Then slowly, slowly, he proceeded to Natchez where he wrote senators Adair and Smith that he was now ready with fire and sword to rid American soil of the Dons. He also wrote Adair that "the time long looked for by many and wished for by more has now arrived, for subverting the Spanish government in Mexico."

Adair sent me a copy of this letter, and I was delighted though puzzled. Why had Wilkinson not written to me? I confess that it occurred to me that he was toying with the idea of himself striking at Mexico—betraying both Jefferson and me.

Toward the end of September, Wilkinson sent word

to the Spanish commander that if he did not withdraw from the west bank of the Sabine River, there would be war. To everyone's surprise (and to my consternation), the Spanish did exactly what he ordered. On September 27 they were gone from American territory.

During these weeks, I had continued to make preparations for either the settling of the Washita River lands or the invasion of Mexico. In either case, the assembly of men and supplies was the same.

On September 27, I was in Nashville where Andrew Jackson gave me a public dinner at Talbot's Hotel, proposing the antique toast "millions for defence; not one cent for tribute!" As a commander of the Tennessee militia, Jackson was in a position to make possible the war which now seemed imminent. On October 4, at my request, he gave the order for a general alert. He vowed that he would ride at my side into Mexico.

A few days after the alert in Tennessee, Sam Swartwout and Peter Ogden delivered my cipher-letter to Wilkinson who was now at Natchitoches on the Mexican border. It had taken them two months to find the commanding general of the American army who had, finally, obeyed the President and arrived four months late at his post.

Swartwout gave Wilkinson my letter. After Wilkinson read it, he asked Swartwout to help him prepare a coded answer whose burden was, as usual, "I am ready." Wilkinson despatched the letter to me. Then, suddenly, mysteriously, he had second thoughts. He sent a messenger to intercept his own letter and had it destroyed. I only know the gist of the contents from Swartwout.

On October 20, Wilkinson wrote Jefferson that there was currently afoot a western plot to seize New Orleans. He mentioned no names. He did not have to. One nice touch: the conspirators were bent, he declared, on causing an insurrection of the blacks in Louisiana. Jamie knew how to distress Massa Tom.

According to Jefferson's recently published journal, he was convinced as of October 22, 1806, that I was guilty of treason for it was on this fateful day that my proposed expedition was discussed by the Cabinet. Despite my "guilt," it was agreed in Cabinet that as I had committed no indictable act, the government could do nothing beyond warning the western governers to be on their guard against a traitor who had, as yet, not committed treason. This was Jeffersonian logic at its most glorious.

Unaware of the attention I was getting in Washington, I continued to assemble men and supplies.

October 6, I left Nashville (with my newest recruit, a nephew of Mrs. Andrew Jackson) and went on to Lexington where I met Theodosia and her newly arrived husband.

In November, I planned to begin the descent of the Mississippi. Wilkinson was now on the border and despite his curious behaviour with the Spanish I expected, as did everyone, a war with Spain.

Earlier in the year, two sodomites had started a scandalous newspaper at Frankfort called *Western World*. They now accused Wilkinson and me of trying to revive the old Spanish Conspiracy. As a result, an ambitious Kentucky politician named Joseph Daveiss decided to intervene directly in my affairs. For some time Davciss—a dedicated Federalist—had been trying to establish that certain distinguished westerners were secretly in the pay of the Spanish government. By an odd coincidence, each of these distinguished figures was a power in the Republican party. Among those he named were the senators Adair, Brown, Smith and Breckinridge, as well as the senator-to-be Henry Clay, Governor William Henry Harrison and General Andrew Jackson—apparently all were involved with Spain in a plot to separate west from east. At the head of this list of worthies he now placed Wilkinson's name and mine.

Daveiss wrote Jefferson his suspicions. The President

was no doubt as delighted to find me in command of
such a conspiracy as he was appalled to learn that most
of his western political supporters had also been
branded traitors by young Mr. Daveiss, brother-in-law
of the arch-Federalist himself John Marshall. Warily,
Jefferson asked for more information.

The relentless young Federalist went to St. Louis
in the spring to talk to Wilkinson who talked altogether too much, revealing to Daveiss that he had sent
out a regular army officer named Zebulon Pike to
blaze a possible trail into Mexico, preparatory to an
invasion. Daveiss then began bombarding Jefferson,
Madison and Gallatin with letters, passing on every
rumour afloat, and there was at least one tall tale for
every gossip in Kentucky. In his zeal to damage the
Republican party, he made so many reckless charges
that Jefferson ended by ignoring him. But unfortunately
it was not possible to ignore Daveiss on his home
ground for he was the district attorney of Kentucky
and in a position to make a scandal, which he now
proceeded to do.

After a cursory inspection of my vast fleet and provisions at Louisville (five flat-boats and some barrels
of flour), Daveiss went back to Frankfort and on
November 5 presented to the local judge an affidavit
to the effect that I was planning an invasion of Mexico
to be followed by a separation of the western states
from the east. He was thoughtful enough to admit to
the judge that although there exists no law forbidding
anyone from inciting a state to secession (if there
was, Jefferson would have long since been in prison),
I ought anyway to be bonded over in order to stop such
a dangerous conspiracy. The judge denied Daveiss's
motion. Daveiss then asked for a grand jury to be
empanelled, which was done November 12.

I was at Lexington when Daveiss first presented his
affidavit to the court. I rode as swiftly as possible to
Frankfort in order to put a stop to the proceedings.
But I was too late. I found a most confused situation.

Charges and counter-charges filled the press. A dozen
careers were destroyed; among them that of my friend
John Adair who, failing to be re-elected to the Senate,
resigned in favour of the twenty-nine-year-old Henry
Clay, reputedly the state's best lawyer. When I saw
how far things had gone, I engaged the senator-elect
to defend me.

Not until the first week in December did I appear
before the grand jury. These gentlemen were of the
opinion that an expedition against Mexico was not
such a bad thing. In fact, after listening to me and
to my eloquent counsel, the grand jury returned "no
true bill" with a further address to the effect that both
Adair and I were pretty fine fellows. Needless to say,
Henry Clay's ringing oratory had much to do with
this happy result.

In passing, I continually marvel at how different
today's lawyers and politicians are from us of the first
generation. We did not possess a single orator to compare with the present crop. Jefferson and Madison
were inaudible. Monroe was dull. Hamilton rambled
and I was far too dry (and brief) for the popular taste.
Fisher Ames was the nearest thing we had to an orator
(I never heard Patrick Henry). Today, however, practically every public man is now a marvellous orator—
no, actor! capable of shouting down a tempest, causing
tears to flow, laughter to rise. I cannot fathom the
reason for this change unless it be the influence of a
generation of evangelical ministers (Clay always makes
me think of a preacher a-wash in the Blood of the
Lamb who, even as he calls his flock to repent, is
planning to seduce the lady in the back pew); and of
course today's politician must deal with a much larger
electorate than ours. We had only to enchant a
caucus in a conversational tone while they must thrill
the multitude with brass and cymbal.

On November 25, Wilkinson arrived in New Orleans.
That same day his first letter of warning reached Jefferson. Two days later the President issued a proclama-

tion, "warning and enjoining all faithful citizens" to abandon any illegal conspiracy against Spain. This proclamation did not reach the west for some weeks.

On December 11, Blennerhassett's Island was invaded by the county militia in order to forestall what the local judge had determined on his own was a major insurrection. Since there was no one on the island except poor Mrs. Blennerhassett, the troops drank up all the wine and then wrecked the house in order to show their contempt for civilisation. At the time none of this was known to me. In fact, it has taken me thirty years to work out the chronology of events that I now record.

I left Frankfort after a glittering ball in my honour where the senator-elect Henry Clay imitated barn-yard creatures most authentically.

At Nashville I was visited by General Jackson and his friend John Coffee at the Clover Bottom Tavern.

Jackson was terrified. "Colonel, you have got yourself and me in a most terrible pickle."

I have never known that fierce man ever to lower his voice for fear of being overheard but now his brazen voice was a hoarse whisper as we huddled in a corner of the tavern's main room, a rack of newspapers partially shielding us from the gaze of the curious. John Coffee waited just out of earshot.

I told Jackson what I was soon to grow weary of repeating. I had no separatist designs. "Why would I? It is Mexico, Mexico, Mexico."

"Not so loud!" Jackson looked alarmed. "I have had the worst reports—about you and Wilkinson."

"What of Wilkinson?"

"You trust him?"

"No. But I trust his self-interest. Jefferson is planning to remove him. He has nothing to lose and everything to gain by continuing with us."

The thought of Jefferson deflected for a moment the familiar catechism. "You've always said . . . well, you've sort of let on that Jefferson knows what you are doing."

"He has known all along, and he is just as anxious as you and I to reduce Mexico."

"Without war?"

"Preferably."

Jackson looked nervously about him; then he whispered, "Do you know what Wilkinson's relations with Spain are?"

"Years ago he swore an oath to the Spanish crown so that he could trade at New Orleans and Mobile but . . ."

"That's nothing! Better men than him took that same oath. Don't mean a thing. But did you know that he was . . . do you know that he still is a Spanish agent?"

"You have been reading the newspapers."

"I have been reading reports from Mexico. From friends of mine. And I have proof that James Wilkinson has been Spanish agent number thirteen for at least fifteen years and that he is still Spanish agent thirteen, pensioned by the King of Spain."

"I don't believe you. It's not possible." For once I was not capable of disguising either my amazement or my alarm.

I think Jackson realized that I was not dissembling. With grim pleasure, he went on, "Well, Colonel, you have been properly dished. Now Wilkinson's in trouble with the Spanish and he's in trouble with Jefferson. This year his pension from the Spanish is going to stop while it looks like Jefferson is going to remove him as commander of our army. *Our army!* By the Eternal!" Jackson's voice suddenly filled the room and startled everyone; himself, too. He dropped his voice. "You must admit we got ourselves a precious horse's ass for president, and that is the plain truth. Who else, I ask you, but Jefferson would turn the American army over to a Spanish agent?"

I was in no mood for Jacksonian mordancy. "If this is true . . ."

"It's true. I got all the proof you'll ever need, short of seeing the bastard's actual commission."

It was all depressingly clear. I understand now why Jamie had disobeyed Jefferson, why he had refused to go straight to the Sabine River and why, when he did, the Spanish melted away.

"Colonel, you got your head in a noose, and you got my head half-way in as well. Well, I'm taking my head out. I've already written the President, written that fool of a governor in New Orleans, written everybody I can think of, saying that though I hate the Dons with a passion I have nothing to do with you and Wilkinson and that I will take my stand for the union forever . . ."

"We are not for separation . . ." I was mechanical, thinking hard.

"I'm sure you're not. After all, you ain't stupid. But by the time Jefferson gets through with you every one will think you're the greatest traitor since Benedict Arnold. As for Wilkinson . . ."

"He will denounce me." I stated the obvious.

"Yes, and Jefferson will be pleased as can be. After all, he's got to prove to everybody that his general is loyal while his enemy is a traitor."

"Does Jefferson know that Wilkinson is a Spanish agent?"

"The man who told me—a Don, no less—says that Jefferson was informed as early as last spring."

"My head *is* in the noose" was all that I could say, or think.

"Well, I'll stick by you, Colonel, as best I can. Now let's play-act for my old friend John Coffee. You still have that blank commission you showed me, signed by Jefferson?"

In the interest of verisimilitude, I usually carried with me a blank military commission, given me by my frend and ally the Secretary of War. I said that it was in my jacket.

"Good. Now we'll have us a row in front of old John and I'll accuse you of not coming clean with me, and then you'll say what you always say about

Mexico, and I'll say does the President approve? And you'll pull that sheet from your pocket and say, 'Here's a blank commission, signed with his name,' and I'll scratch my head, like the dumbest darky you ever saw, and agree that that *looks* like the real thing."

"It is."

"Why, then so much the better." Jackson's good humour was restored and we acted out our charade for John Coffee. I hope he was impressed. My own thoughts were elsewhere. There is nothing more humiliating than to be outwitted by a man one knows to be a fool.

Wilkinson next appeared in New Orleans as its defender against Aaron Burr "whose accomplices," he declared, "stretch from New York to this city and whose army of invasion numbers twenty thousand desperate men."

Despite the feeble objection of Louisiana's governor —and the loud objection of everyone else—Wilkinson declared martial law, jailing Dr. Bollman (a German recruit to our adventure), Peter Ogden and Sam Swartwout. To forestall any attempt at *habeas corpus*, Dr. Bollman and Swartwout were put in chains and taken aboard a ship in the harbour, bound for Washington.

While Wilkinson played Caesar at New Orleans, I was floating down the Cumberland River with two flat-boats. On December 27 I was joined by Blennerhassett's "flotilla." In all we now had ten small boats, and about fifty men. I told our discouraged company that I could not for fear of spies tell them our exact destination but that it ought to be plain to anyone that a group as small as ours was not about to do any fighting. We were now, in fact, what I had always wanted us to be in appearance—genuine settlers, headed for the Washita River lands.

It was on January 10—an oddly balmy day—that I stopped at Bayou Pierre just north of Natchez and went ashore to stay with an old friend who greeted me with a copy of the *Natchez Messenger*; and what a messenger! Not even Mercury himself ever delivered such a series of surprises. First, I read the President's proclamation. Second, I read Wilkinson's version of my ciphered letter. Third, I read that the acting governor of the Mississippi Territory had ordered my arrest.

"Well," I said to my friend, "here I was looking forward to some of your venison."

"You shall have it." We dined most heartily. What else is one to do in the gallows' shade?

Three

"IT IS MOST ENJOYABLE." Mr. Bryant stared at me across his book-stacked desk.

"I hope it is not too *macabre*."

"Not for our readers."

"But an *unsolved* murder . . ."

"Bad morality, perhaps, but then we are used to bad morals now-a-days."

"Like those of the anti-Abolitionists?" Oh, there is nothing I will not say or do to ingratiate myself with Mr. Bryant, or with any editor. I must have money.

Mr. Bryant laughed as he was intended to do. "We shall be delighted to publish—at our usual rate."

I will not record the next exchange. But I managed to get five dollars more than the usual rate. As a potential father, I have become a kind of jungle animal, stalking New York editors. Last night I worked until dawn, describing the murder of Elma Sands and the defence of her supposed assassin by Burr and Hamilton. I am now using the Colonel's memoirs as a quarry.

We discussed other possibilities. "I wish you would take a look at the city for us, through the eyes of Old Patroon." Old Patroon was conceived by Leggett a year ago. Since then he has become unexpectedly popular. I find it easy to write in his character, once I find a subject. Old Patroon is a thundering Tory who will try anything, after a show of reluctance.

"But I do look at the city."

"I mean *see* it. See the ugliness we are making here. Contrast the old Dutch houses of honest stone with what is being built now, with those miles and miles of painted brick houses. Just think, Mr. Schuyler: *painted* brick!" He shook his head.

I had always taken it for granted that brick houses are supposed to be painted red with each brick carefully outlined in white. Apparently not.

"Painted brick is something modern, and peculiar to New York. Like the clothes our women wear. Those monstrous hats, the piled-up hair . . . Well, no, we had best not offend the ladies. But do *look* at our city and tell us exactly what you see. Or rather what your noble Old Patroon sees."

I blinked my eyes, as one who boxes might flex his arm; eager to show Mr. Bryant that I was ready to look as hard as I could, to earn my—our bread. As I rose to go, he motioned for me to stay, was sombre.

"I have the notion that you are turning pamphleteer."

Who in New York does not know about my pamphlet? But then politics is the consuming passion of half the town.

"I must tell you, Mr. Schuyler, that I am convinced that Mr. Van Buren will prove to be one of our greatest presidents." Mr. Bryant sounded as if he were delivering a commencement day address or reciting "Thanatopsis." "And he will certainly continue the noble work General Jackson has begun."

I said nothing. There was nothing to say. How explain the fact that I am living with a prostitute from Mrs. Townsend's establishment, that the girl is pregnant, that I must now marry her while dreaming, simultaneously, of freedom in another world, on the

Mediterranean, far from brick houses painted red, from talk of elections, from money-making? I am in a cage: *but will get out.*

"Have you seen what I have written?" Some days ago I gave a copy of the pamphlet to Leggett. I have shown it to no one else.

Mr. Bryant nodded. "Yes, I have read it."

"I am surprised Leggett gave it to you since you favour Van Buren and he does not."

"The situation is changed. As he will tell you."

I have not been able to discuss the pamphlet with Leggett; he is home sick.

"You see, Senator Johnson is no longer a candidate. The gallant slayer of Tecumseh has privately agreed to be Mr. Van Buren's vice-president."

"Then Leggett is for Van Buren?"

"*Faute de mieux.* But I predict that he, that every-one will be pleasantly surprised by the Van Buren administration."

"If there is one."

"If there is one." Mr. Bryant wiped his quill pen clean with a piece of paper. Then wiped it clean again.

"There are other contenders," I said, not about to concede an election I have for some time deluded myself that I alone would decide. "There's a candidate from Tennessee, isn't there?"

"Hugh White. Yes, he has some western support."

"And there is always the Whig candidate Henry Clay."

"Yes, there is always Henry Clay." For a third time, Mr. Bryant started to clean his pen; then stopped, aware of the redundancy. "Mr. Schuyler, your pamphlet can do the most extraordinary harm."

"That was Leggett's intention when he asked me to write it." Firmly, I assigned the responsibility.

Mr. Bryant grimaced. "Yes, I suppose it was. Our friend is always too fierce, too swift in his judgements."

"You would prefer that I not publish it?"

"Yes." Mr. Bryant's response was both swift and fierce.

Lately desperation has made me cunning. "Mr. Bryant, I am soon to be married."

"My felicitations . . ."

"Thank you. I have no money. I have not yet taken my examination to be admitted to the bar. Actually, I had hoped, as you know, for a career as a journalist."

Mr. Bryant tried to contain his alarm. "At the moment, I fear there are too many journalists and too few positions . . ."

"No, Sir. I do not want a job."

Relief was evident. "Of course whatever you write, if it is of this quality," he tapped *The Mystery of Elma Sands*, "will be published here—and proudly. After all, you have a following." A dim smile. "Fitz-Greene Halleck has praised you to me. Because of Old Patroon he plans to eat a tomato, or so he says."

Ordinarily I would have been blushing and speechless with delight. This morning I hardly noticed the compliment. "To support myself, I will write all I can. But it seems to me that there ought to be something more, particularly if I . . ."

"If you *don't* publish?"

"Yes. After all, I will be giving up five thousand dollars." Cold-bloodedly I multiplied by five my fee. It was an outrageous stroke but Mr. Bryant seemed to believe me.

"That is a very large sum." He tugged at his side whiskers. "But then many people are desperate to destroy Mr. Van Buren."

"Yes, they are. But I am not. As you know, I came in here one day with a piece about Colonel Burr's marriage and before I knew what was happening, Leggett had persuaded me to write about the Van Buren connection."

"I'm afraid our friend Leggett has got you—and us—into trouble. I realize it is not your fault, nor anyone's. Simply the partisan passions of our age." Mr. Bryant was philosophic but then how could he not be when he looks like a bust of Aristotle, with side whiskers?

"I could abandon it, I suppose." I paused. Looked

away. Noticed on his desk Irving's latest book, A *Tour of the Prairies*. A bronze paper-knife was stuck in the first chapter—like a murderer's weapon, I thought, and wondered suddenly who did kill Elma Sands? I must ask the Colonel whom he suspected.

"We have no influence with the Administration." Mr. Bryant also found comforting the sight of A *Tour of the Prairies*.

"If I don't publish, and if Van Buren is elected . . ."

I stared at him, genuinely at a loss. What to ask for?

"I will talk to someone who might be helpful."

"Will it be soon? I am to see the publisher on Monday."

"I will do what I can for you. For Mr. Van Buren, that is."

"I should warn you that I detest politics."

Mr. Bryant turned Irving's book on its face. "When I was young I wanted only to be a poet of the purest kind, like Milton. No, no, like Thomas Gray. After all, Milton was political. Then I came here." He gestured at the bound files of old newspapers that lined his cubby-hole like so many yellowed tombstones memorializing dead news. "I had to live somehow. But then, gradually, I began to care about these things."

"I never shall."

"But you are much interested in Colonel Burr."

"As a character . . ."

"I was once a Burrite." Mr. Bryant suddenly smiled. "At thirteen I wrote an attack on Jefferson. In verse. It was called 'The Embargo.'" The voice suddenly dropped a register.

> "Go, scan, philosophist, thy Sally's charms
> And sink supinely in her sable arms;
> But quit to abler hands the help of state."

He laughed; broke off. "One ought never to publish at thirteen. Nor at thirty. Nor perhaps ever!"

"Obviously you were political from the beginning."

"So it would seem. But now . . ." Mr. Bryant turned to me. "Young man, I must confess to you that I fear Colonel Burr to this day. I fear his mind. I fear his example."

"I think him a great man, Mr. Bryant. Others would, too, had he not lost the game he was playing, the game Jefferson won."

"There! You've made my point. What was a *game* to Burr was a contest between good and evil to Jefferson." The sententious and moralizing William Cullen Bryant suddenly replaced the practical editor. "I grant you Burr has an acute and active mind, but he did not—could not rise to intellectual greatness. As for his morality . . ."

"Hardly worse than that of anyone else at the time, or now." I rose to go.

Mr. Bryant was taken aback. Usually it is he who terminates our interviews. He was placating. "Well, what are we anyway but so many critics in the stalls, criticising the grand performers?"

Mr. Bryant walked me to the door. "There is," he said, "an honest shoemaker living in Naples, on the Murgaleena" (I am guessing at these Italian spellings), "on the right hand as you go toward Poteswollee. Every morning, just the sun comes up, his little dog runs out of the house and barks at Vesuvius."

Four

I WENT UP to Fourth Street. At first Leggett's wife did not want me to see him but when he heard my voice in the hall, he shouted down. "Come up! I die of ennui! Not to mention yellow fever, malaria . . ."

I entered the bedroom, as he was finishing the list of

his complaints. ". . . catarrh, and the consumption."
Leggett did look as if he might die at any moment;
his face was sallow and beaded with sweat, and the
room stank of quinine and the flesh's corruption.

I sat at some distance from him and described my
interview with Mr. Bryant. Leggett laughed, coughed,
wheezed, spluttered, was amused. "You seem to have
got him on the defensive. Good for you. He only
mentions that little dog in Naples when he's nervous.
It's like a tic with him, that story is." He pushed the
blankets away from his chest. "Well, I got you into
this and now I must get you out."

"I'm to meet the publisher next week."

"What do you want?"

"What do you think? Money. Helen's pregnant."

"Well done." Leggett was as sympathetic as a man
dying of several diseases can be. "Will you marry her?"

"I want to."

"*She* does not?" Brows arched with surprise.

"No. Or so she says. But whatever we do, I must
start practising law, publishing more articles . . ."

"You will stay in New York?"

"What choice do I have?"

"A government appointment might be possible."

"Before next week?"

"That's not much time."

"No, it is not." Whatever I can extract from Leggett
and Mr. Bryant I will, and with a clear conscience;
just as I will take whatever I can obtain through
Swartwout's publisher. I mean to be as ruthless with all
of them as they have been with me.

Curious. Sitting here, watching Helen at work in
front of the dress-dummy (she is now industrious), I
am certain that the child will be a girl, and I am
actually pleased at the thought of being so completely
stopped in my tracks, of being forced to struggle like
everyone else in this city while lacking the motive of
everyone else which is to make money. All I ever
wanted was a life to myself, inside my own head. Now

I must work for two other people to the end of my days and the thought of such long servitude does not depress me; quite the contrary. I am a fool. I think my mother would have liked Helen.

"Bryant said he would make inquiries?" Leggett dried his face with a towel.

"Yes."

"That means he will do something. So will I. Between the two of us, there's no reason why you could not get a consulate."

I stared at Leggett with wonder. None of my dreams had ever been so ambitious.

"Usually a consulship is a reward for services rendered to the party, but in your case," Leggett grinned his broken-toothed smile, "it will be for services triumphantly *not* rendered."

"You can actually get this for me?"

"In time, yes. It is possible."

"Time . . ." I frowned.

"For God's sake, Charlie, don't publish that damned thing! If you don't, I swear to you—on the head of Bryant's little Neapolitan dog—that we'll get you something good. That's a solemn oath, Charlie!" He slapped his muscular, death-riddled shield of a chest, and so I swore to him that I would not publish the pamphlet. But can I take seriously the "chaunting cherubs" of the *Evening Post*? Have they such power? I refuse to dream of the consulship for if I do it will pass me by.

Five

COLONEL BURR WAS AMUSED when I told him that Mr. Bryant had once been a Burrite. "I shall now read him with a warmth which hitherto has been lacking." The Colonel gave a place of honour to the *Evening Post* on the table beside his sofa. Then: "Pour me out some claret. I've a chill today."

I poured us each a glass. The Colonel seems to be growing frailer in body but the mind is clear. At least today it was. Other days he is forgetful, puts words in the wrong order—to his own annoyance. "Old age is not to be encouraged, Charlie."

"Should one die young?"

"No. Simply avoid ageing. There must be some way. I thought I had found it."

"And what was that?"

"The love of women. But at a certain point not even their flesh can keep us from shrivelling up like old apples. Well!" He finished off the claret.

"What sort of government did you have in mind for Mexico?"

"Government?" He looked at me blankly. Shook his head. Appeared to think back. "That would have depended on what we found there."

"Everyone thinks you meant to be emperor."

"Oh, no! I was far too modest to want to appropriate the title of the great Napoleon. King would have been sufficient for my purposes. *Yo el Rey* as the Spanish king begins his correspondence. Bleak but to the point. 'I the King . . .' "

"But to what end a king?"

"To make a civilisation on this God-forsaken continent!" Suddenly in the Colonel's face I saw a glimpse of something I had not seen before, a kind of fury and contempt that was usually masked by the exquisite irony, the serene good humour. "Between the dishonest canting of Jefferson and the poisonous egotism of Hamilton, this state has been no good from the beginning. Now it starts to change with old Jackson. For the better, I hope. But I can assure you that that early republic of ours was no place for a man who wanted to live in a good world, who wanted to make a true civilisation and to share it with a host of choice spirits, such as I meant to establish in Mexico. Unfortunately,

I was not able to be a king—though I very nearly was
a president—but in my way I have been lucky for I
have always been able to indulge my true passion
which is to teach others, to take pleasure in bringing
out the best in men and women, to make them *alive*,
and though I did not achieve any sort of kingdom in
this world, I have established small human dominions
along my way, proved to the doubting that women had
souls, and trained a hundred boys to make the best of
their life, without complaint, or dishonour."

For a long time after this uncharacteristic outburst
(the result of swallowing too rapidly a large tumbler
of claret) the Colonel was silent, staring at the coals
in the stove's grate. Then, without any preamble, he
began the day's work.

Memoirs of Aaron Burr—Twenty

I GLADLY SURRENDERED myself to the governor of the
Mississippi Territory on January 17, 1807. I say gladly
because I knew that if I were to come under Wilkinson's jurisdiction, I would not live long enough to
have my day in court, or anywhere else. The governor
of Mississippi was deeply embarrassed once he discovered that the army with which I was to seize New
Orleans consisted of fewer than fifty men, and no
weapons beyond what settlers of a new country would
use for hunting.

"I apologize, Colonel Burr, but I fear we have been
misled by the dictator of New Orleans."

The Governor was polite to me and contemptuous
of Wilkinson whom he referred to not only as the
'dictator' but as the 'pensioner.' Apparently everyone
in the west knew that Jamie was in the pay of Spain—
except me.

I rode to the town of Washington, the capital of
the Mississippi Territory, and was bound over in
$5,000 bail by one Judge Rodney whose claim to fame
was that he had fathered Jefferson's attorney-general

and so knew his political loyalties rather better than he did his law.

Since the grand jury did not convene until February, I rejoined my poor army and navy. For the next few weeks my principal task was to avoid being kidnapped by Wilkinson's agents. He knew that if I got to the east alive, his part in our "conspiracy" would come to light.

In due course the grand jury found me "not guilty of any crime or misdeameanour against the laws of the United States." They also went out of their way to condemn both Wilkinson and Jefferson for recklessness with the law, and for putting in jeopardy the Constitution.

Judge Rodney was so deeply distressed by the jury's findings that he refused to release me from bail. I daresay this case is unique in American legal history. A man found innocent by a grand jury is still guilty in the eyes of the judge. Meanwhile, Wilkinson had sent a certain Dr. Carmichael and two army lieutenants into the territory with instructions to kill me. I am happy to record that the governor of Mississippi was appalled when he learned of their mission, and successfully dissuaded Dr. Carmichael from his sanguinary task. The two military men, however, were faithful to their commander; they were also every bit as incompetent as their commander and I was able to evade them easily.

I sent word to the court that whenever I was needed I would present myself, preferably under guard; but that for the present I preferred to go into hiding since my life was in danger. My bail was promptly (and illegally) forfeited, and the Governor was persuaded to offer $2,000 to anyone who might capture the dangerous Aaron Burr.

This was the end of all my hopes. I met with my Little Band. I told them to go on, if they chose, to the Washita Lands. I then gave them my boats and everything else that I possessed. So it was that we parted.

A few days later my friends were all arrested; illegally, as usual. Fortunately all were soon freed, except

for Blennerhassett and two others. I should note that
to this day I receive letters from my one-time praetor-
ian guard. Most of them settled in and around Natchez.
Most still dream of what might have been.

With a guide, I vanished into the vast piny Mississippi forest. My disguise was shapeless pantaloons
and a coat made from a blanket; on my head was a
wide-brimmed soft hat to disguise as much as possible
my perhaps familiar features. I also wore a leather
strap across one shoulder from which hung a tin cup
on the left and a scalping knife on the right. I must
confess that at this point there were a good many scalps
I would have liked to detach from their owners' pates,
beginning with Jamie Wilkinson's.

I have never in my life seen so much rain as fell
that February in the endless Mississippi forest. Our
clothes were never dry. Even when the rain for a moment stopped, we managed to get wet again as we
forded swollen, muddy streams in which we soon grew
accustomed to the snakes that swam alongside us like
so many sticks of wood come slimily alive.

On the night of February 18, reasonably lost but
travelling in the right direction (toward Pensacola in
Spanish Florida where I hoped to set sail for England),
we came to a clearing in the woods that turned out to
be the fateful village of Wakefield (I have never since
been able to read Goldsmith!).

I knocked on the door of the nearest cabin and
asked for the house of an old friend of mine. The
young man to whom I spoke later declared that despite
my shabby clothes and muffled face, the extraordinary
lustre and beauty of my eyes convinced him that there
on his own door-step was the diabolic Aaron Burr
while practically in his pocket was $2,000 worth of
reward money. I suspect it was not the glory of my
obsidian orbs but the incongruity of a pair of New
York boots that gave me away. After all, westerners
looked first at a man's rifle, then at his boots. Eyes are
the last feature to be noticed.

We went to the house of my friend who was away

from home. But his wife kindly made us welcome, and bade us sleep in the kitchen. Within the hour, the sheriff arrived, having been warned by the young man that the traitor Burr was in town. After a brief discussion, the sheriff decided that to arrest the potential conqueror of Mexico was hardly in the public interest. He, too, hated the Dons. So the three of us spent the night comfortably in the kitchen.

The next morning the sheriff most amiably offered to show us the way out of his county. Unfortunately, the young man had meanwhile alerted the local army garrison. Two miles outside Wakefield, I was arrested and taken to Fort Stoddert.

The garrison was well-disposed toward me, and though I dreaded Wilkinson's long arm, I knew that I had nothing to fear from those good-natured young men. In fact, their commander confessed to me that "one more week here, Colonel, and they'd have followed you to Mexico."

I was sent on to Washington City, in the company of eight soldiers.

We travelled at the rate of forty miles a day, our tired horses slipping and stumbling in the slick red mud as huge black crows mocked us. My companions soon discovered that whatever the President thought of me, I was hardly a traitor in the eyes of the western people. After several rustic ovations, my escort thought it wise to avoid towns altogether, and so we slept each night in the cold wet woods.

En route we were advised that our destination had been changed from Washington City to Richmond, Virginia, where I was to be tried for treason. It had been decided that my alleged treacheries had taken place on Blennerhassett's Island which was a part of Virginia. With this change of venue, Jefferson must have thought my fate already decided. What chance would Aaron Burr have on trial in the capital of the President's own state?

On March 26, 1807, we arrived at the Golden Eagle

Tavern in Richmond where I was locked up in a second-floor bedroom, filled with newspapers assembled by the thoughtful manager. I was most grateful to him as I studied what had been happening during the weeks that I was out of the world. I read with particular interest how, on January 16, John Randolph (who was no longer a friend to Jefferson) demanded that the President clarify for Congress his proclamation. Just *who* were the mysterious conspirators, he asked, and to what end did they conspire?

On January 22, Jefferson sent his answer to the Congress. He named Aaron Burr as "the principal actor, whose guilt is placed beyond question." Categorically, Jefferson declared that I had wanted to sever the union at the Alleghenies but that when I had found the west impervious to my schemes, I had then decided to seize New Orleans, rob the local banks, and go on to Mexico. Jefferson was never a fanatic when it came to evidence. Although he mentioned various letters he had received testifying to my guilt, he did not say who had written them. He did praise by name General James Wilkinson ("with the honour of a soldier and the fidelity of a good citizen") for having arrested a number of the conspirators.

I have since discovered that two days after Randolph's question in the House (and four days before Jefferson's response to Congress), Wilkinson's version of my ciphered letter arrived on the President's desk. This explains, I think, the recklessness of the message to Congress with its extraordinary assertion that I was guilty "beyond question." Of all people, John Adams asserted the moral—not to mention legal—principle. "If Burr's guilt is as clear as the noonday sun, the first Magistrate ought not to have pronounced it so before a Jury had tried him."

But Jefferson was now in a state of delirium. The day after his message to Congress, he instructed his Senate whip, Giles of Virginia, to call a secret session of the Senate in order to suspend the constitutional

right of *habeas corpus*. This was aimed at keeping
Swartwout and Dr. Bollman in government custody.
Despite my friend Bayard's eloquent speech against
this monstrous perversion of the Constitution, the
Senate obediently suspended *habeas corpus*.

The House of Representatives was not so craven.
Right off, they refused to meet in closed session. Then
Jefferson's own son-in-law (who knew his wife's father
altogether too well) declared that "never under this
government has personal liberty been held at the will
of a single individual." The House refused to suspend
habeas corpus. Nevertheless, Dr. Bollman and Swartwout were still in a military prison at Washington
City and for the moment beyond the reach of the
Constitution.

Now, most comically, noble democrat Jefferson and
Spanish agent Wilkinson were confederates. Forgotten
was Wilkinson's disobedience. Ignored was Wilkinson's
military dictatorship at New Orleans. When the Governor of Louisiana protested Wilkinson's actions to the
President, the author of the Declaration of Independence responded with a remarkable letter of which
I possess a copy (given me by Edward Livingston).
"On great occasions," announced the scourge of the
Sedition Law, "every good officer must be ready to
risk himself in going beyond the strict line of law,
when the public preservation requires it." Jefferson
then acknowledged that the Administration's political
"opposition will try to make something of the infringe-
ment of liberty by the military arrest and deportation
of citizens, but if it does not go beyond such offenders
as Swartwout, Bollman, Burr, Blennerhassett, etc.,
they will be supported by the public approbation." In
other words, if public opinion is not unduly aroused
one may safely set aside the Constitution and illegally
arrest one's enemies. Had this letter been published at
the time, an excellent case might have been made for
the impeachment and removal of a president who had
broken that oath he had taken to defend and to pro-

tect the Constitution by conspiring to obstruct and pervert the course of justice.

On January 23, Dr. Bollman was taken from prison and escorted under heavy guard to the office of the Secretary of State. There he found Madison and, to his surprise, the President.

"I had never seen Mr. Jefferson before," Dr. Bollman told me later, "and I was not prepared for this unusual man. He was extraordinarily nervous. He complained of headache, and kept pressing his eyes all through our interview. He never once looked at me. Mr. Madison did most of the questioning. Finally I said that I would tell them everything that I knew about your plans on condition that nothing of what I said would ever be used for any purpose other than their enlightenment.

" 'That is fair enough,' said Mr. Jefferson. 'I give you my word I will abide by that.' Then the two of them, like a pair of court recorders, I swear, sat and took notes while I told them how you had intended to revolutionize Mexico.

" 'But surely,' said Mr. Madison, 'Colonel Burr had designs on New Orleans.' I said what you used to say: that since the artillery at New Orleans was the property of the French, you felt no compunction about seizing it, as well as what *foreign* shipping you might be able to commandeer on the way to Vera Cruz. My two scribes were disappointed.

"Mr. Jefferson asked, 'What about Colonel Burr's plan to separate the west?' I noticed that his hands trembled as he turned a page of the copy-book. I said there was no such plan.

" 'But we know,' said Mr. Madison, 'that Colonel Burr proposed such a plan to the Spanish minister.' I told them the truth, that it was Senator Dayton's trick to raise money, and that it had failed.

" 'What about Colonel Burr's conversations with the British minister?' asked the President. I told him a lot of nonsense in order to protect Mr. Merry—told them how England only wanted to aid your Mexican adventure. I ended by advising the President that he would do the United States a great service by promptly declaring war on Spain and allowing you to continue your work. He broke his pen on that. Then Mr. Madison gave me a twenty-page version of what I had said which I read carefully and signed.

" 'This paper, Dr. Bollman, will never leave my hand,' said the President, and he sent me back to prison."

A writ of *habeas corpus* was issued on Dr. Bollman's behalf by that poetical lawyer Francis Scott Key. But before it could be properly served, Jefferson hurled a charge of high treason at my associates, and they were kept in jail.

At this point the redoubtable Tory, the drunken, the brilliant, the incomparable Luther Martin (easily the best trial lawyer of our time) came forward to their defence, and applied to the Supreme Court for their deliverance.

February 21, 1807, Chief Justice John Marshall delivered his opinion. After reading Wilkinson's version of my cipher-letter, as well as the rest of the "hearsay evidence" collected by the government, Marshall was obliged to observe that under the Constitution no act of treason had been committed by anyone. Unfortunately, in his garrulous way he gave a loose and dangerous definition of what constitutes a treasonable act. This *obiter dictum* I will come to in due course. By the Supreme Court's order Dr. Bollman and Swartwout were freed.

This was the background to my charming season at Richmond where I was able from various places of detention to observe the marvellous flowering spring in that part of the world, to delight in daffodils and dogwood, to indulge myself in the pleasures (never denied me by my gallant gaolers) of knowing Richmond's elegant ladies.

Jefferson's ill luck continued (as opposed to his ill

luck I must put upon the scales my own far heavier and singularly maleficent destiny!). In his haste to try me in his own state, Jefferson had overlooked the fact that the presiding judge of the circuit court at Richmond was none other than his old enemy the Chief Justice. I *assume* that Jefferson had overlooked this fact. John Marshall, on the other hand, thought that the selection of Richmond was deliberate.

"He wanted to catch me out, just as he tried to catch out Justice Chase," said Marshall to Luther Martin some years after the trial. "It was a deliberate attempt to destroy the Supreme Court. All I need do was show the slightest favour to Burr, mis-step once in the law and Jefferson would have *me* on trial in the Senate, and with me the Constitution." Fortunately, Marshall was not about to mis-step. Nor for that matter was I.

The Chief Justice and I met March 30, 1807, in the tap-room of the Golden Eagle Tavern. This comfortable hostelry was famed for having over its front door the biggest sign in the union: an eight-by-five-foot golden eagle with wide-spread wings, the work of the then unknown Thomas Sully.

The tap-room was crowded with what I suppose was every lawyer in the state. Some of the finest legal talent in the nation was already assembling for my defence. Needless to say, most of them were Federalists. Like it or not, I had become, over night, the symbol of opposition to Jefferson and to his high-handed administration.

As I stepped into the room, I recognised the tall figure of the Chief Justice. He wore dusty riding-clothes (he was even more untidy than his presidential cousin) and his dark hair needed combing. I, on the other hand, wore new small-clothes of black silk and my hair was freshly powdered and queued (I had even got rid of the fleas that had so loyally accompanied me from the west). As I moved through that assemblage, I had for the first time in months the sense of being once more in control of my destiny. Where there is law, I fear no man.

I bowed to the Chief Justice; he bowed to me. "I think, Colonel, we had best remove ourselves to a more private place." And so, to the distress of the onlookers, we withdrew to a small side-room where I explained why I had left the Mississippi Territory.

Marshall heard me gravely, without comment. I asked to be set free. The United States attorney George Hay then asked that I be committed over to a grand jury on a charge of misdemeanour for having plotted a war against Spain, and of treason for having plotted a war against the United States.

I was then released on $2,500 bail and the court was adjourned until the next day when we would meet in the state capitol (a pompous pseudo-Greek monstrosity designed, I believe, by Jefferson himself).

The next morning, surrounded by well-wishers, I climbed the steep slope to the classical portico where I was allowed to observe the view of Richmond, lovely in the first yellow-green of the season.

Then pushing past several goats who were feeding on the turf at the foot of the capitol's steps, I followed the sergeant-at-arms to the Chamber of Delegates which resembled the interior of a country church with its rows of uncomfortable pews, each thoughtfully equipped with a box of white sand in which to spit tobacco.

Our first day was spent listening to George Hay press his charges. He wanted me imprisoned and held without bail.

On April 1, Marshall delivered his opinion in this matter. He said that a prisoner could only be let go when it appeared that the charges against him were "wholly groundless." He did not believe that I fell into that category. On the other hand, he stated firmly that the law may not allow "the hand of malignity" to "grasp any individual against whom its hate may be directed or whom it may capriciously seize, charge him with some secret crime and put him on the proof of his innocence." Although this was deliberately directed at Jefferson (and was so interpreted by everyone), Marshall later remarked, most demurely, that he had not Jefferson but Wilkinson in mind.

Marshall saw no convincing evidence at this point that I had assembled troops for a treasonable purpose, and so bailed me in the sum of $10,000, and bade me answer the charge of misdemeanour (plotting a war against Spain). The grand jury was convened for May 22.

Jefferson now took over the prosecution. Day after day he sent messengers to the west to collect (or create) evidence and witnesses. It ought to be noted here that in a number of Jefferson's private conversations during this period, he admitted quite freely that my designs were obviously on Mexico. Yet, publicly, he persisted in his efforts to mark me as a separatist and so a traitor. Mark me? No, hang me!

During the three weeks before the grand jury met, I was fêted by the good people of Richmond. Jefferson was not popular amongst the gentry. The common people, however, admired him and I heard a rhetorical tailor drink a toast at the Golden Eagle bar to "the hemp which will be Aaron Burr's escort to the republic of dust and ashes."

Almost a week after my release from detention, I was invited to dinner by my chief counsel, John Wickham, a charming and gregarious man whose dinner parties for the legal profession of Richmond were celebrated.

"You are to be guest of honour," said the invitation I received at the Golden Eagle. So on the afternoon named I repaired to the Shockoe Hill district.

As I entered the drawing-room, I was astonished to see that John Marshall was a member of the company. If he was startled to see me, he made no sign. Later Wickham told me that Marshall quite properly questioned the wisdom of a judge dining with a man who

must soon appear before him on a grave charge;
nevertheless, he had decided to attend the dinner.

We bowed to one another across the room, and I
promptly sought the company of my various lawyers
(I would have preferred the company of ladies but
none ever attended Mr. Wickham's legal dinners).
That season, by the way, was a splendid one for the
ladies; or perhaps I should say for their admirers. The
so-called Empire fashion had swept America and even
the most respectable of maidens (and, alas, the most
mature of matrons) wore high bodices two-thirds bare.
It is a moot point which issue most concerned the
republic in the summer of 1807: my alleged treason or
the brazen and ubiquitous baring of breasts that called
forth from every pulpit warnings of the wrath of
Jehovah. The lascivious press was in an ecstasy: teats
and treason—could any other combination be more
popular?

After dinner I suddenly realized that John Randolph
had sat down next to me. Those huge hollow eyes
glared at me and I noticed, as always (and with an
involuntary shudder), the curious silky down on his
cheeks like that of a young boy, or of a girl who has
been too much in the open. "I saw you pass my house,
Colonel, some weeks ago."

"My triumphal procession!"

"Perhaps it was a triumph. We'll soon know." The
voice in my ear was reedy and disagreeable. Yet on the
floor of Congress it could be most beautiful and seduc-
tive. The long delicate fingers were dirty; the nails
broken and black. "I shall be most curious to learn
how you intended to break up the union with only a
hundred men . . ."

"Forty-seven . . ."

"Half again as formidable if we are to apply my
Cousin Tom's peculiar method of reckoning."

What a family to have produced Randolph, Marshall and Jefferson! The first mad, the second eccentric,
the third a passionate hypocrite. To add to the com-

plication of shared blood and madness, the three
detested one another.

"Let me say, Colonel, that to my mind you have
every Constitutional right to *try* to dissolve the union."
Randolph was even more devoted to the integrity of
the states than Jefferson. "Cousin Tom ordinarily would
agree with you. Are we not all brothers, all Americans?"
He mimicked the President cruelly.

I was polite, and non-committal.

As we left the dining-room, Marshall and I spoke to
one another for the only time that evening. "I have
been reading," I said, "your life of Washington." I had
indeed been doing my best to navigate the first four
volumes of that remarkably tedious work (so deeply
reflective of its subject).

"Oh, it is very bad, Colonel."

Although of all this world's creatures, the author is
the vainest, Marshall was a notable exception. But then
perhaps his vanity was the greatest of all: to undertake
such a huge work without the slightest qualification.

Despite my flattery, Marshall was adamant in con-
demning himself. "I was forced to publish too soon.
And so there are errors. Worse, parts of it make no
sense at all. I have not had time enough what with
. . ." he gestured diplomatically, ". . . all this."

"But you have finished the last volume?"

"Oh, yes. It has gone off to the printer. I deal with
Washington's presidency. It is better than the rest. At
least I pray that it is."

"I found your first volume most original." The Chief
Justice had required a whole book just to get his hero
born, like Tristram Shandy.

"No one else does. My publisher tells me that many
subscribers are asking for their money back."

"You had ten thousand subscribers, I am told."

"Nowhere near so many. Of course there might
have been more except . . ." Marshall stopped, conscious of indiscretion.

I finished for him. "Except that the Administration

regards your work as a political attack on the Republican party."

Marshall nodded, pleased to have said nothing. Then he added, "You know, books are sold to subscribers through the postmasters. Mysteriously, the Republican postmasters to a man have refused to sell *The Life of Washington.*"

"Most mysterious," I agreed. Then we joined the others. That is the only "private" conversation I had with John Marshall during the seven months we were together at Richmond. Needless to say, the Republican press made much of our encounter, and demanded that Marshall be—what else?—impeached.

On May 22, 1807, at 12:30 P.M., the United States circuit court for the district of Virginia opened its doors for business in the House of Delegates.

It is like a play, I thought, as I looked about me. Men so crowded the court-room that some were obliged to stand in the open windows (it was to be such a hot summer that even I was sufficiently warm).

There in front of me were the elegants of Richmond society, looking like courtiers to the late French king. Crowded in next to them were frontiersmen and Piedmontese with coon-skin caps and leather jackets, promiscuously spitting jets of tobacco; in such close quarters, they often missed their target, dirtying many an expensive London jacket.

I saw a number of friendly faces. Some known to me, most not. I particularly noticed day after day an enormous, heroically built young man who stood on the huge lock of the main door. Like an avenging angel, he towered over the room. Twenty years later I saw him again at Albany, in the house of Martin Van Buren. It was General Winfield Scott, then a tyro-lawyer. He was most sympathetic. "May I say, Colonel, that I have never seen a man so composed as you were at Richmond? You were as impenetrable, as immoveable as one of Canova's marbles."

John Randolph was also there, leaning in his priv-

ileged way against the judge's tribunal, flicking his
riding-whip against one long leg, a planter's hat
jammed down on his head.

Most reassuring of all was the presence of Andrew
Jackson. He stood at the back of the room, staring
balefully at anyone who testified against me.

A few days later Jackson was nearly mobbed when
he addressed an anti-Burr crowd in front of a grocery
shop on the edge of the capitol green. But he held his
ground and, with many an oath, declared that I was
the victim of political persecution and that anyone
who believed a word James Wilkinson said was a god-
damned fool for Wilkinson was a liar, a bastard from
Hell, and in the pay of the Spanish government. My
poor friend had a difficult time in Richmond and I
fear—hard as it is to believe now—that the plebs
actually *laughed* at their future idol Andrew Jackson.
I at least blessed him for the friend he was.

The grand jury was empanelled. I was able to keep
Jefferson's creature, Senator Giles, off it. But not John
Randolph who was made jury foreman, even though
he told the court that he was absolutely certain of my
guilt.

Despite the lack of evidence, the Administration
wanted me indicted for treason. The lesser misdemeanour did not satisfy them. Also, treason was not
bailable and the Administration affected to believe that
I would flee their justice rather than face in court
their witness Wilkinson. Finally, Marshall was obliged
to require of me a total bail of $20,000.

I began my defence by pointing out that three times
in the west I had been tried for the same offences and
three times found innocent. I spoke of the illegality of
my arrest by the military. I spoke of Jefferson's political
interest in the matter. I spoke of Wilkinson's chicanery.
I think I made an impression not so much on Marshall
as on the populace packed in the hall before me, an
audience whose physical presence I came to dread,
smelling as it did of cheap tobacco and harsh sweat.

For a time Jefferson counted on Dr. Bollman's "confession" to convict me of the misdemeanour of planning a war against Spain. Although Jefferson had given his word that Dr. Bollman's deposition would never leave his hand, he sent a copy of it to Hay, with a signed pardon. If Dr. Bollman allowed the deposition to be admitted in evidence, he could go free. Dr. Bollman refused the President's pardon on the excellent ground that since he had committed no crime he could not be pardoned. He also denounced the President as a dishonourable blackguard who had broken his word. Jefferson's response was swift. "Convict Bollman," he wrote Hay, "for treason or misdemeanour."

It is my private (and entirely unverifiable) view that during this period Jefferson was mad. I say this having spent seven months in and out of court observing his two cousins and so was able to note not only their numerous eccentricities but their curious resemblances to one another and to him. Jefferson's headaches and irascible outbursts combined with his extraordinary expenditure of money to produce or create evidence against me (Jefferson *never* spent public money) was proof to me of his irrationality that season. Certainly it was not the act of a sane man to rest the government's case against me on the evidence of someone he knew to be a Spanish agent, a man who ought not to have been allowed to command even a platoon much less the entire wretched army of the United States.

Jefferson's behaviour was like that of a woman who has decided to destroy the man—or rather the men (Marshall was as much his target as I)—who spurned her. As the case against me slowly collapsed, the furious President shifted his guns to the Constitution itself. Blamed everything on "a judiciary independent of the nation." Threatened to amend the Constitution. Judges ought to be removable, he trumpetted, at the pleasure of president and Congress.

Fortunately the canny John Marshall avoided one

by one Jefferson's traps as the long summer days
lengthened and three generations of lawyers advanced
(or set back) their careers by appearing either for the
government or for me.

On my side I had, amongst a galaxy of legal talent,
the celebrated Virginian Edmund Randolph who had
been Washington's attorney-general. The government's
only distinguished lawyer was the unwholesomely
elegant and actorish William Wirt. The government's
principal prosecutor, George Hay, was not much of a
lawyer. But then he did not need to be since he would
soon be son-in-law to James Monroe. The junto, the
junto!

The first weeks of skirmishing established little.
Until Wilkinson's arrival the government could not
begin its prosecution. Meanwhile, I decided to amuse
the grand jury and perhaps make law.

I read to the jury Jefferson's message to Congress,
drawing their attention to the part in which he refers
to various letters he has received about my activities
as well as to certain orders he subsequently gave to the
army and navy.

"I have, may it please Your Honour, applied to the
Secretary of the Navy for copies of these orders. He
has refused to produce them. Attempts to obtain
copies of any of the letters written to the President
have also failed. Now I cannot prepare a defence
without full knowledge of what my accusers have said
of me. I must also know what orders the President or
his secretaries gave to the army and navy in regard to
my person. Therefore, may it please this honourable
court, I must request that there be issued a subpoena
duces tecum to the President of the United States . . ."

I paused and enjoyed the sound of several hundred
tobacco-y breaths exhaling simultaneously. ". . . and
that the Honourable Thomas Jefferson come to this
place and bring with him the documents which are
necessary to my defence, and to the promotion of
justice."

Hay sprang to his feet and spoke so rapidly that he stammered. "Naturally, Your Honour, I will do what I can to obtain these papers which the court—and only the court—deems material but . . ."

"But, Mr. Hay," murmured the Chief Justice in that low voice which at times so much resembled the whispery tone of his presidential cousin, "how is the court to decide *what* is material when the court has access to nothing?"

"Your Honour surely cannot respond to this . . . to this impudent . . . to this, uh, to this attempt to call the Chief Magistrate into court."

"The court considers the point moot, and will reflect upon the matter. We now stand adjourned until to-morrow morning."

The next day Hay made the specious point that since this was only a grand jury proceeding, I was not entitled to any of the usual privileges of the legal process.

Then Luther Martin took the stage. Sipping from a stone jug of whiskey, he advanced to the well of the chamber. He was a dishevelled figure, to say the least. For two nights running he had slept in his clothes on the floor of my bedroom at the Golden Eagle; nor had I tried to move him. I knew from experience that when Luther Martin decided to sleep on the floor (or in a cupboard—he was unnaturally partial to cupboards), it was pointless to protest. He would stay where he fell, snoring loudly and, presumably, content. But what a man of law, drunk or sober!

Luther Martin suspected, as did I, that somewhere in the War Department there might exist an order to Wilkinson intimating that my death would be convenient to all concerned. With this in mind, he explained to the jury the difficulties we had encountered in procuring government documents. Most puzzling, he said. Most puzzling. Then he took a long restorative swig from the stone jug, and the crowded stuffy room became absolutely still. I have never seen on any stage an actor who could hold an audience as he could.

"This is a peculiar case, Sir." The small red eyes rolled up toward Marshall, then back toward the grand jury. "We have here a most peculiar case in which a president, no less, has undertaken to prejudice my client by declaring in a message to Congress, no less, that, and I quote, *'of his guilt there can be no doubt.'*" Luther Martin shook his head mournfully at man's base nature, at all human perfidy.

Tension mounted in the chamber. The idol of the crowd, the god Jefferson himself, was being summoned to appear before them like any other mortal. Worse, the apostle of the rights of man was being condemned not only for vindictiveness but for prejudicing the judicial process.

"It would seem"—Luther Martin's voice was now in the tenor range: a special *piano* he affected before the *fortissimo* storm—"that the President has assumed to himself the knowledge of the Supreme Being." A gradual elision from tenor to baritone. "He has proclaimed his late vice-president a traitor in the face of that country which has rewarded him. He has let slip the dogs of war, the hell-hounds of persecution." The baritone became Jovian bass and the room began to resound with that powerful voice. No one moved. "And would this president of the United States, who has raised all this absurd clamour, attempt to keep back the papers which are wanted for this trial, when a life itself is at stake?" The question ricochetted like a fatal bullet from the rafters.

Luther Martin then levelled a stubby finger at Hay, *in loco presidentis*, and demanded: "Are we to assume that the President would be *sorry* if Colonel Burr's innocence were proved?" A roar of indignation from Jefferson's partisans. The Chief Justice threatened to clear the court of spectators.

For several days the issue was furiously debated. Could a president be summoned before any court? Hay said as president, no; as a private individual, yes. Not a helpful illumination of the Constitutional landscape. He also maintained that "confidential communications" of the executive were privileged, and so on.

On June 13, Jefferson's answer was read to the grand jury. He reserved to the president of the United States the right "to decide, independently of all other authority, what papers coming to him as president the public's interest permit to be communicated." What he deemed permissible he would of course supply. He agreed to give us a copy of Wilkinson's October 21 letter to him but he would withhold those parts of the letter he thought immaterial. As for the army and navy orders, well, if we would just tell him which orders we would like to see he would do his best to comply. This put us in a nice situation: we were to specify which military orders we would like to see, having seen none!

Marshall took up the challenge. The issue was simple. Could a president be summoned into court, and if he could, ought President Jefferson be summoned in this case? Marshall resolved the matter neatly. Yes, he declared *ex cathedra*, a president could indeed be summoned. Nothing in the Constitution forbade it, or in any statute save—and the "monocrat" Marshall was plainly enjoying himself—"in the case of the king." But, Marshall was happy to note, a president was not entirely like a king (there was a positive gnashing of Republican teeth in the hall as they heard the apostle of the democracy compared by a Federalist judge to that most hated of this earth's monsters, the crowned despot).

"I mention two essential differences," said Marshall, most mildly, but speaking more loudly than usual. "The king can do no wrong, that no blame can be imputed to him, that he cannot be named in debate. Since a president can do wrong and since he can be named in debate, he is not an anointed king and so like any man is answerable to the law." John Marshall then summoned President Jefferson to Richmond.

There was nearly a riot in the court-room. Not

until the next day did we begin to realize the extent of Marshall's subtlety. First, he asserted the power of the court to subpoena a president. Then, he avoided a Constitutional crisis by adding—almost as a postscript —that the court would be perfectly satisfied if the *original* letter of General Wilkinson and related documents be despatched. Once they were in the hands of the court, the President need not make the tedious journey from Washington to Richmond.

I am told that Jefferson was, literally, deranged by this decision and insisted by return post that George Hay arrest Luther Martin for treason on the ground that since he was an old friend of mine he must have been in my confidence from the beginning and so was party to treason. No president has ever behaved so; let us hope no president ever shall again. Luther Martin, needless to say, was not arrested.

A number of documents were duly sent to the court from Washington, and the constitutional crisis was at an end. Jefferson, however, had a number of bitter things to say about the court's power to summon a reigning president. He was particularly annoyed by Marshall's sly comment that "it is apparent . . . the President's duties as chief magistrate do not demand his whole time, and are not unremitting." This reference to Jefferson's long absences from the capital brought forth the cry, "I pass more hours in public business at Monticello than I do here every day!" The cousins knew how to wound one another.

As luck would have it, on the same day that Marshall summoned the President, James Wilkinson arrived at the Golden Eagle which was crowded to bursting. But then Richmond itself was crowded to bursting. From every part of the nation people had come to observe the great treason trial, and all agreed that it was better than any theatre; for as even the most ignorant backwoodsman knew, at issue was a struggle to the death between the President and the Supreme Court, between nationalists and separatists, between

Jefferson and Burr who at even this late date was still a hero to the New England Federalists and might have been able—had I so wished—to lead that part of the country in a revival of the now moribund Federalist party.

I was in the Golden Eagle parlour when Jamie made his entrance. He was ablaze with gold lace, epaulets, and whiskey. He moved like a turkey, wattles a-quiver, sway-backed, stomach thrust forward as though if he walked normally the centre of his gravity would so shift to the paunch that he would fall flat. He was accompanied by a host of aides and "witnesses" from the west.

When Jamie saw me surrounded by my Little Band, he made a curious, almost placating gesture with his right arm and hand, the palm upward; and I caught a glint of what looked to be pleading in his eyes. Then he was led to another room.

Sam Swartwout was all for challenging him to a duel. "Not the happiest solution to our problem," I said.

"But the bastard put me in chains for two months, and stole my gold watch!"

"Challenge him!" Andrew Jackson was now entirely my partisan, and recklessly outspoken. But then he could afford to be; his letters to Governor Claiborne and to Jefferson had so cleverly established his loyalty to the union that the prosecution had originally wanted him to testify against me but as Jackson stormed about Richmond, proclaiming my innocence, the government came to regard him as a perfect nuisance, and dangerous to their weak case.

Luther Martin was mellow. "My boy, you're not to touch the whoreson until I have had my fun with him in court."

But the next morning, a Sunday, as Wilkinson was taking the air in front of the tavern, Sam Swartwout marched up to him and with one strong shoulder, shoved the commanding general off the side-walk and into the gutter. Aides drew swords. Distraught admirers helped the Washington of the West to his feet.

"Your seconds will find me at the Golden Eagle," said Sam. "Be honoured that I treat you like the gentleman you are not."

Face scarlet, Wilkinson made no answer. Sam returned to the tavern from whose window, I am sorry to say, General Jackson and I had observed the scene with some delight on the ground that what we could not prevent, we ought at least to enjoy.

"My God, I feel better for that!" Young Sam was exhilarated.

So was Jackson. "I'll be your second, boy. But first we'll do some practising with the pistol. Always a good thing before a duel, don't you agree, Colonel? Even when you're up against a sack of guts which, I swear by the Eternal, must be the largest target this side of the Alleghenies."

"Jamie will never meet you," I said to Swartwout, drawing on my superior knowledge of the double—no, triple agent; and I was right. Even when Swartwout published a broadsheet denouncing Wilkinson as a coward, the brigadier made no response. Unlike most villains I have known, Jamie was a physical coward.

The commanding general arrived in court on Monday like a conqueror. After all, was he not the President's creature? Come to the heart of the President's own state?

Comically, Jamie bowed this way and that as he made his way to the witness-stand, spurs clattering, leather harness creaking like a superannuated farm horse.

I ignored Jamie until his name was called. Then I turned and glanced at him briefly. So much for our confrontation.

The principal evidence of the prosecution was my cipher-letter to Wilkinson. Luther Martin questioned him about it. Why had the General made alterations in the text? Why had he tried to erase the first sentence which made it clear that Colonel Burr's letter was in answer to one of his own? And why had he said that his ciphered correspondence with Colonel Burr had begun in 1804 when evidence showed that the correspondence in question had actually started as early as 1794? Wilkinson stammered, contradicted himself, committed a number of perjuries.

It was then that John Randolph decided that the General was "a villain from bark to core," a sentiment he expressed that same evening to the crowded taproom of the Golden Eagle, within hearing distance of the villain himself.

As jury foreman, Randolph began to harp on the ciphered letter. Why *had* Wilkinson made changes? Was it to avoid implication in Colonel Burr's plot? To mislead the President? To disguise the fact that the General had been a prime mover in the Spanish Conspiracy fifteen years earlier? Abruptly, John Randolph turned to the Chief Justice and demanded that General James Wilkinson be forthwith indicted for treason.

The prosecution was demoralized. Wilkinson was incoherent. The grand jury then retired to determine whether or not to indict the government's chief witness. One can only imagine Jefferson's response when he learned that seven members of the grand jury favoured indicting his general, with nine opposed. An ominously close vote.

On June 24, the grand jury indicted Blennerhassett (*in absentia*) and me for the misdemeanour of launching an expedition against a Spanish colony and for treason against the United States. I was not surprised. After all, the grand jury was made up almost entirely of Jefferson's partisans. Nevertheless, as I was taken under guard to the Richmond Municipal Jail, I could at least congratulate myself upon the fact that the only important witness Jefferson was able to produce against me had himself narrowly escaped being lodged with me at the public's expense.

Six

SAM SWARTWOUT ASKED ME to meet him this evening in the bar of the City Hotel. I must say I find
it hard to associate this portly red-faced man with the
fiery boy who once challenged the commanding general
of the American army to a duel, with Andrew Jackson
himself as second.

"That challenge was the beginning of my glory,
Charlie!" Swartwout was drinking hot rum and cloves.
"Because then and there General Jackson decided that
if he had had a son it would have been a crazy young
hot-head like me, and that's the way he still thinks of
me, thank God!"

"Did Colonel Burr ever seriously discuss the separation of the western states?"

"Of course he did. We all did. Why, in Richmond,
during the trial, I listened to John Marshall and John
Randolph talk about separation. We were in the bar-
room late one night—Colonel Burr was in jail at the
time—and a group of us, maybe a dozen, all clever
lawyers except old Sam here, started in on the subject
and John Randolph said, 'If I did not think Virginia
could leave the union whenever she chose, I would
leave these states and find myself a home in the
farthest antipodes.'

"And John Marshall laughed at him and said, 'Better
find yourself a boat, Cousin John, because no state will
ever have that right.'

" 'No matter what the Constitution says, Cousin
John?'

" 'No matter what it says and, more to the point,'
said the Chief Justice, 'what it *don't* say!'

" 'Why, Cousin John, you are a bloody monarchist!'

" 'And you, Cousin John, are a bloody Jacobin, and
a perfect democrat.'

" 'No, Cousin John,' says John Randolph, 'not perfect. I love liberty but, by Heaven, I do despise equality!' Oh, they were a precious pair, those cousins."

Swartwout put down his rum. "Now, Charlie, you are going to meet the man with his publisher who is going to buy this thing you've written."

"For how much?"

Swartwout blinked. "How much you getting from the other people?"

"Two thousand to start with, two thousand when I finish." I was pleased that I could bargain so well.

Swartwout grunted with surprise—respect? "So you got two thousand already?"

"Which I'll have to pay back."

"Then ask for five thousand, settle for four."

"I'll ask for seven and settle for five." My head spun at such extraordinary sums: in Europe, Helen and I and our child can live comfortably for more than five years on that amount.

At the end of a long dusty corridor on the second floor, we stopped in front of a door. Swartwout rapped loudly. The door opened. A small worried head looked out. "Come in. Come in," the head whispered. "You're late. He's almost gone. We'll have to be quick."

We stepped inside. A man in shirt-sleeves lay wrong way round in the bed, stocking feet up on the brass head-board. In his right arm he cradled a demijohn of whiskey. Opposite him, on a spindly wicker chair, a second small worried-looking man sat. He rose as we entered.

"This is the publisher." Swartwout indicated the first of the worried pair. "Mr. Robert Wright of Philadelphia." We shook hands.

"And this gentleman will be actually writing the book." Mr. Wright indicated the other worried-looking man. "In fact, he has already written most of it for our friend." Mr. Wright glanced nervously at the figure on the bed who was humming softly to himself. The eyes of "our friend" appeared to be shut beneath a mat of wild graying hair.

"I look forward," said the gentleman who would be writing the book, "to your assistance."

"Of course." I was at sea.

Suddenly a voice thundered from the bed: "Damn you all for a passel of Mexican cornholers!"

"Cornholer? Sam Swartwout's no cornholer!" And Swartwout leapt upon the recumbent figure. Drunkenly they embraced. Then the wild man brushed the hair out of his small red eyes; and glared at the rest of us.

"I spoke a mite too soon, Sam. But jest you look at them three. Now there is three Mexican cornholers and don't dispute my word because I got a keen nose for their likes." I do my best to reproduce the speech of the professional frontiersman.

"Come on." Swartwout was brisk. "Sit up. I want you to meet a friend of mine, Charlie Schuyler . . ."

"Cornholer—*Mexican* cornholer," muttered the wild-eyed man, taking a long swallow of whiskey and refusing my out-stretched hand.

"Charlie, this is Colonel Davy Crockett." So it was that I met the famous 'coon-skin' congressman from Tennessee. He is considered a delightful figure. I can't think why. Last year he published the so-called story of his life which I have no intention of reading. It is supposed to be very funny, in the western style, and sold a good many copies. Currently he is a star of the Whig party, and an enemy of Jackson and Van Buren.

"And now"—Mr. Wright glanced apprehensively at his sodden "author"—"we are writing a second book. A very secret sort of book, you might say. But not a secret to you, Mr. Schuyler, since, I gather, you know the subject . . ."

"Me, I know the title. That's something, ain't it, Sam?" Colonel Crockett pulled himself up on the pillow. "My book is going to be called *The Life of Martin Van Buren, Heir Apparent to the Government and the Appointed Successor of General Andrew Jackson . . .* a Mexican cornholer of the first water."

"That's not part of the title," said the actual author. I never did learn his name.

"And I won't hear a word against Old Hickory!" Swartwout took the jug from Crockett and drank deeply. They are a good deal alike, these two aged roaring boys. Crockett must be at least fifty years old.

"Old Hickory's cornholed every last Indian in the west. Cornholed my friends the Creeks, the Cherokees, best people in this damned country—so what does he do? goes and breaks our treaty with 'em and why? because he wants to steal their land for hisself . . . Oh, he's a crooked man, Old Hickory, but to compare him, bad as he is, to Matty Van, is like comparing a diamond to shit."

Mr. Wright tried to smile; and disagreeably failed. "Our book will concern Mr. Van Buren only—not the President . . ."

"The title!" shouted Colonel Crockett. "I didn't finish givin' my title. *The Appointed Successor of General Andrew Jackson. The Mexican* . . ."

"Cornholer. We heard you, Davy." Swartwout gave the Colonel back his bottle.

"*Containing Every Authentic Particular by which his Character has been Formed, with Concise History* . . ." Crockett's chin suddenly dropped onto his chest. He appeared to sleep.

"I understand you have some interesting material for us." The actual author was staring at the manuscript in my coat pocket.

"He certainly has!" Swartwout played the honest broker. "He has actually gone and proved that not only is Matty Van the son of Aaron Burr but that he is also the political creation, the amanuensis, you might say— no, worse, the homunculus of that very same traitor Aaron Burr!" Swartwout gave me a wink which the others did not see because their eyes were upon the manuscript that I now held in my hand.

"Proof?" asked Mr. Wright, reaching for the sheaf of papers.

"As conclusive as possible." I was cool. "You see, I'm also the Colonel's biographer."

"I thought," said Mr. Wright rather sharply, "that Matthew L. Davis was the biographer."

"We both are. But Mr. Davis must wait until the Colonel's death. I am not so bound."

"Do you mind if we . . . well, *look* at a few pages?" Mr. Wright's hand had a life of its own. Without waiting for me to give him the pages, he took them.

For nearly an hour actual author and publisher read to one another passages that I had written, occasionally checking with me or with Swartwout for further details, additional verification. "Not that we need be too meticulous," Mr. Wright assured me. "The Davy Crockett style is so much that of the tall story that we can say nearly anything we please."

"This is marvellous for us. Absolutely marvellous." The actual author's bright eyes revealed not only normal human greed but the unexpected zealotry of the true Whig.

"You think you can lick Matty Van with all of this?" Swartwout was curious.

Mr. Wright nodded gravely. "After all, whatever Davy Crockett writes . . ."

"Never wrote a damned thing! Hate books. Spellin', grammar's all contrary to nature." Davy Crockett's eyes were still shut.

"Your material, Mr. Schuyler, couched in the Crockett style, will destroy Van Buren both as a politician and as a man."

"*Not* a man," from the bed, "why if it wasn't for them perfumed whiskers you couldn't tell if he was a woman or not, dressed up the way he is, in *corsets*, that ineffable, spotted Mexican . . ." The voice trailed off; he snored.

For an hour we haggled. At the end I got $5,400, and Mr. Wright got everything that I had written as well as certain documentation I agreed to supply (court records from Albany, etc.). Apparently the Crockett book is already written but the actual author says that it will be an easy matter to incorporate my work into the existing text. We shook hands all around.

I ran home through fast-falling snow. I kicked open our door and shouted to Helen, "We're rich!" To which she answered, rather blandly, "We had better be rich, that's all I can say!"

"As soon as the baby's born we'll leave New York. Go to Spain. To Granada. To the Alhambra!"

Helen smiled happily; not understanding a word.

To-night has been the most wondrous of my life. I am rich (although I must pay back the $500 I received from Gower). I can now marry Helen. And leave New York. Best of all, I have done no injury to Colonel Burr. Not only will he never associate me with Davy Crockett but if the Crockett style is what I think it is no one will take seriously a word that's published in the name of that drunken fat-head. My troubles are at an end.

Seven

I WENT TO THE Reade Street office this morning for the first time in a month.

Mr. Craft has taken a new partner, and added a clerk (in my place); he received me with surprising warmth in what had been the Colonel's office, now newly furnished and bright with vases of spring flowers. "My daughter has done this." He apologized for the flowers. "She is to be married in June."

I congratulated him; promptly told him, "I shall be married, too." I can never *not* say what I mean; or rather what I'm thinking about.

"That is good news. Do we know the young lady?"

"No. She's only recently come to New York from

Connecticut to stay with her aunt—in Thomas Street."
Why must I always sail so close to the wind? if that
is the proper nautical expression.

"I assume you have abandoned the law?" I had
ceased to come to the office shortly after the New Year.

"For the present."

"You ought really to take your examination before
the bar."

"There is always time for that. I'm writing for the
newspapers now."

Mr. Craft nodded. "I know." I am always delighted
when people tell me that they have read what I have
written. "I've seen many of your pieces in the *Evening
Post*. You are Old Patroon, aren't you?"

I confessed that I was. I did not tell him that in
other newspapers and magazines I am Skeptic (who
praises the Whigs) and Gallery Mouse who reviews
plays and thinks Edwin Forrest the greatest actor of
our time and said as much when he recently sailed for
England (although Mouse was obliged to admit that
he was not entirely happy with Forrest's interpretation
of *The Broker of Bogota*).

"Many literary men are also lawyers. Look at Mr.
Verplanck. Look at . . ."

But I did not let him pursue the subject. I did the
business for which I had come (collecting Colonel
Burr's private files), and departed.

I found the Colonel seated beneath the rear basement window. A watery April sun shone on his up-
turned face: he seems to draw to himself light and
heat, like some ancient sun flower unexpectedly rooted
in a cellar.

I gave him the bundle of documents. He put them
on the floor beside his chair.

"How was the theatre last night?"

"James Sheridan Knowles held a benefit for himself."
I reviewed for the Colonel the various scenes Knowles
acted out from all the plays he has written, including
The Hunchback, a noisy work the audience loves.

"I confess to missing the theatre." This was the nearest the Colonel has yet come to a complaint. He turned from the light; no longer sun flower, more ancient mole returning to its burrow.

"On with the trial of the century!" Burr held up a large volume. "This is a *précis* of my trial. The actual record runs to some eleven hundred pages. If you are ever morbidly disposed, read it. But for the moment, I shall condense the issues, in a way entirely favourable to me!"

Memoirs of Aaron Burr—Twenty-one

IN THE MATTER of treason, the Constitution is explicit: two persons must witness the traitor in the act of levying war against the United States or of adhering to their enemies, giving them aid and comfort. Since the place where I was supposed to have raised my "army" of insurrection was Blennerhassett's Island, in the month of December 1806, it was necessary for Jefferson to establish that I had indeed committed the crime he had told Congress I had committed.

Yet the facts were unimpressive. All that the prosecution could prove was that some thirty men associated with me stopped at the island on their way down the Ohio. They were not armed. They committed no acts of violence (unlike the local militia). They threatened no one. They said they were en route to the Washita River lands. But because General Wilkinson maintained that these unarmed men meant to seize New Orleans and revolutionize Mexico, they were accused of levying war against the United States *by construction*, and since I was thought to be responsible for their movements (even though I was in Kentucky at the time this "war" was levied against the United States in Virginia), I too was guilty of treason *by construction*.

May I say that the entire concept of *constructive*

treason is unconstitutional and was known to be so by
every lawyer in the United States, save Jefferson. But
he was desperate. Although he had assembled nearly
fifty witnesses to denounce me (of whom more than
half perjured themselves), there was never any proof
that I had levied war against the United States, or
advised the thirty men on Blennerhassett's Island to
levy such a war.

During the trial, the Governor of Virginia very nicely
assigned me a three-room suite in the new penitentiary
outside Richmond. I have seldom been so well looked
after. The jailer received me most courteously, and
hoped that I would be comfortable.

"I am certain to be," I said, graciously.

"I trust, Sir, it would not be disagreeable to you if
I should bolt this door after dark?" He indicated the
front door to my apartment.

"By no means, Sir. I should prefer it—to keep out
intruders."

"It is also our custom, Sir, to extinguish all lights
at nine o'clock."

"I fear, Sir, that that is not possible. I never go to
bed before twelve, and always burn two candles." I
did not add that I never go to bed but with regret,
and by violence to myself.

"Just as you please, Sir. I should have been glad if
it had been otherwise . . ." A sigh. "But as you please,
Sir."

We became excellent friends, particularly when I
shared with him the gifts that were hourly brought me
by liveried servants—oranges, lemons, pineapples, rasp-
berries, apricots, cream butter and even ice, a luxury
in that equatorial zone.

On August 2, Theodosia and her husband arrived,
and moved into Luther Martin's house. Theodosia
swiftly became the queen of Richmond society, presiding at the Golden Eagle with such charm—despite
ill health and natural anxiety—that Luther Martin
said, "I must marry her, Colonel. I shall kill her un-

worthy husband, and then she will be mine, by right of conquest."

"You have my blessing." At that moment I confess that I should not in the least have minded anyone murdering my son-in-law who had all but denounced me in order to avoid being arrested by Jefferson. Alston was a man of weak character with but one interest—his wife and his son. For that shared passion, however, I forgave him everything.

Meanwhile, Blennerhassett had joined me. He, too, was under indictment, and somewhat out of sorts. Our first meeting was not harmonious, largely because he saw fit to pay a call upon me just as a lady of Richmond (a young widow, I hasten to add) was stealing from my presence, with the good jailer's assistance.

"I do not wish to criticise you, Colonel . . ."

"Then *indulge* your wish, my dear friend, and refrain from criticism."

"But immorality of any sort, *licence* of any sort . . ."

"Come now." I did my best to soothe the incestuous uncle.

". . . and in a *penitentiary!*"

"Ah, it is not *fitting.* I see what you mean."

"No, it is not." He then told me that he wanted back the money he had contributed to our venture. Since I was not able to oblige him, he most quixotically refused to hire a lawyer to defend himself. Fortunately my cohort of attorneys was willing to save him from the gallows.

The government had been led to believe that my son-in-law would testify in their behalf. But we undid them. On the day of the trial, August 3, Alston and I entered the court-room together, my arm through his.

It took us a week to assemble a jury from the usual panels. As it turned out, every prospective juror was of the opinion that I was guilty. We might still be at Richmond if Marshall had not ruled that an opinion of the defendant's guilt which was *lightly* held—as opposed to *deliberately* held—did not disqualify a juror. This exquisite decision pleased George Hay. But the wrangling continued.

Finally, I moved to pick any eight men from the existing panel, *if* the prosecution would accept them. Startled, Hay agreed. After all, the entire panel thought me guilty—and none appeared to hold their opinion with much lightness. Almost at random, I picked eight men, making the point that I was certain I could rely on the fairness of gentlemen. This proved to be an excellent move, and I won right off a convert or two, not that it much mattered. I knew that only the law could save me; the jury was irrelevant.

Next to Wilkinson, the government's most important witness was William Eaton, an adventurer who called himself "general" as a result of some interesting skirmishes in North Africa that had gained him a degree of celebrity, a fascinating costume inspired by the Berbers, and a long outstanding claim on the United States government for services supposedly rendered.

I had met Eaton in Washington, had mentioned something to him of my plans for Mexico. He had shown interest, and that was all. Now, suddenly, he had a marvellous tale to tell. Apparently I'd planned to seize the capital, murder the President, and so on. To forestall me, he told the court, he had gone to Jefferson and suggested that I be given a foreign embassy to remove me from the scene. Out of tact he forgot to mention to Jefferson that I intended to murder him.

In court I probed Eaton on the subject of his claim against the United States. Had it been paid? He tried not to answer. Finally, reluctantly, he admitted that shortly after my arrest the government suddenly saw virtue in his claim and he had received some ten thousand dollars.

The Morgan family also testified. Their reports of my conversation were sketchy, and self-contradictory. Nevertheless they, too, were rewarded by Jefferson, who saw to it that the government granted them the disputed Indiana land.

My chief of staff the good French Colonel de Pestre was secretly offered a commission in the American army if he would testify against me. He refused. Even Blennerhassett was approached by Jefferson's henchman, the editor Duane, and told that if he would fully incriminate me all charges would be dropped against him. Surprisingly, Blennerhassett refused. I suppose he thought that if I was hanged he would never see so much as a penny of the money he had lent me. The other witnesses for Jefferson made little impression.

Finally, Marshall asked Hay if he had any further "evidence" that Burr had been at Blennerhassett's Island on the famous December 10 when an act of "war" had been supposedly levied against the United States. Hay said that he had none.

John Wickham then moved that no further testimony be admitted. He also entranced the court for two days, making the point—and re-making it in a hundred subtle ways—that it was not possible to commit treason unless the traitor was himself present when war was levied against the United States. This argument was essential to my defence. Quite simply, I had not been at Blennerhassett's Island December 10. But the constitutional argument was even more important than my neck (which I would have, perhaps, denied at the time).

Wickham's target was the ancient notion of "constructive treason." In its purest sense this phrase means that anyone who might have wished well a potential traitor was as guilty as the traitor himself even though the well-wisher was miles away from the act of war. Wickham reminded the court that the Constitution is a unique document in which treason is exactly and narrowly defined. The traitor must actually be caught in the act of levying war against the United States. These absent figures who wish him well, who might even have inspired him, are nowhere mentioned in the Constitution, and so are not traitors.

This point had to be spelled out with great care because John Marshall had made a serious error in his earlier ruling on Bollman-Swartwout. Although Marshall had not found any evidence of any war of any kind being levied on Blennerhassett's Island, he did declare—no doubt wanting to impress Jefferson with the court's impartiality—that "it is not the intention of the court to say that no individual can be guilty of this crime who has not appeared in arms against his country. On the contrary, if war be actually levied, that is, if a body of men be actually assembled for the purpose of effecting, by force, a treasonable object, *all those who perform any part, however minute, or however remote from the scene of action, and who are actually leagued in the general conspiracy, are to be considered as traitors.*"

I am told that to the end of his days, Marshall regretted this extraordinary blunder, redolent of the medieval Star Chamber. As he himself was soon to recognise, if such a wide net is to be cast into the sea who cannot be caught in it if he has had the ill fortune to have said "God-speed" to a man who later levied war against the United States?

The prosecution was slow to use the weapon Marshall had forged for them. They were so intent on proving that I was on the island December 10 that when I was able, easily, to prove that I was elsewhere, their set-back made more of an impression on the jury than it ought. They would have been better advised to confine themselves to my *distant* leadership of the men on the island and to the treasonable words I was supposed so promiscuously to have said to the various perjurers Jefferson had paid to come to Richmond.

The task of the defence was now to modify Marshall's doctrine of "constructive treason." The Chief Justice, however, was moving in a different direction. He was going to evade as much as possible the trap he had set for himself by attending to the simpler issue of whether or not an act of war against the United States had indeed been levied December 10, and if it had could the government produce two witnesses to that act, as required by the Constitution?

Wickham's presentation proved so thorough and so masterly that the prosecution asked for a recess (which was granted); they also asked for more witnesses to be heard, and heard they were—to no avail.

Then the counter-attack began. William Wirt insinuated himself into the history of American prose if not of law by a splendid flowery description of Blennerhassett's Island as a perfect and innocent Eden to which Aaron Burr, the Devil himself, came as the sulphurous tempter of poor Blennerhassett (a monstrous composite of Adam and Eve), deliberately, cruelly changing to Hell a pristine island Paradise. I am told that this remarkable effusion is still taught in every school of the country as an example of—God knows what! I do suspect that my continuing dark fame in this republic is now almost entirely due to the fact that the only thing that three generations of American schoolchildren know of Aaron Burr they have learned while committing to memory William Wirt's oration. Not long ago I had the pleasure of listening to one of my wards proudly recite by rote Wirt's philippic against Aaron Burr, not realizing it was her kindly old Gamp she was denouncing in such rich, hyperbolic phrases.

Now on the defensive, George Hay not so delicately chose to threaten John Marshall, reminding him that for pre-judging a trial Justice Chase had been impeached. The defence made much of this threat. Wisely, Marshall made little. Luther Martin and Edmund Randolph then closed the case for the defence on Friday, August 29.

John Marshall spent Saturday and Sunday preparing his opinion. On August 31, he read it to us for three hours. From the legal and constitutional point of view,

the opinion is often weak and contradictory. Having
nearly undone himself (and the Constitution) with
the Bollman-Swartwout ruling, he ignored, as best he
could, his own previous statement that anyone who
had contributed to the levying of war against the
United States was as guilty as the actual leveller of
war, and addressed himself to quite a different issue.

In order to prove treason, the government was
obliged, first, to prove that an act of war had been
levied against the United States and, second, to prove
whether or not a given individual had been involved in
that act. The case, in other words, had been presented
backward. The government had arrested Aaron Burr
for complicity in an act of war which had yet to be
proved. Further, it was the government's contention
that Burr was present when the as yet unproved act
of war was levied. Marshall briskly dealt with that: the
court was satisfied that Burr was elsewhere.

Then Marshall affected to deal with the prosecution's crucial point: had Burr incited others to treason?
and if he had was he guilty of treason? Marshall now
edged with elephantine grace away from his own earlier
position. He pointed out that Burr had been indicted
for acts of war against the United States on a certain
day and at a certain place. Now on that day Burr was
not present in that place. Nevertheless, the question
remained: was he guilty of inciting to treason those
who were there? If he was, then the court must point
out that the government had *not* indicted him of this
crime for the excellent reason that incitement to treason was no crime under the Constitution. There was
a murmur from the lawyers in the court as they saw
which way our legal history was about to go.

"To advise or procure a treason," and Marshall's
voice became suddenly loud and clear, "is in the
nature of conspiracy or plotting treason . . ." He paused,
no doubt aware that the obvious always sounds novel
when stated with unexpected emphasis. Then he made
his point, and took his place in history, "which is

not treason in itself." With this formula, he undid his own decision of six months before.

As the murmuring increased in the court-room, Marshall patiently explained that no doubt there *ought* to be such a law, but since for the present it did not exist he would move on. Meanwhile, he was still not satisfied that "a secret furtive assemblage" on Blennerhassett's Island had ever been intended as an act of war but even if it had been so intended, the absence of Aaron Burr made him no party to it, and what advice he might have given the men there futively assembled could not be considered an act of war against the United States, as defined by the Constitution.

That was the end of the government's case. George Hay slammed down his papers on the prosecution's table for which diversion he was favoured with Marshall's full attention yet mildest tone.

"That this court dares not usurp power is most true." There was complete silence in the court. Everyone knew that Jefferson's wrath would now be focussed upon the Chief Justice. How would the Chief Justice respond? John Marshall was direct: "That this court dares not shrink from its duty is not less true." He spelled out as plain as any Martin Luther where he stood, and why he would not move, despite Jefferson's threats of impeachment and the breaking of the Supreme Court. On that note the jury was sent out to do its duty.

The next day, Tuesday, the jury found me "not proved to be guilty under this indictment by any evidence submitted to us." I was relieved; I was outraged. I was not to be hanged; I was also not to be exonerated. The jury had broken with all custom by refusing to answer simply "guilty" or "not guilty." Marshall chose to allow the jury's phrase to remain in the indictment while signifying that the court's record would be decorated with the usual, unadorned "not guilty."

The next day I was released from prison, on bail, and attended a dinner party given by John Wickham to celebrate our victory.

Theodosia was my consort for the evening, and we presided over the revels—and were happy except that I knew that my days in court were not yet finished while I was troubled by my daughter's health. I prayed it would not follow the same course as her mother's. Yet that evening she was witty, resplendent, triumphant.

Eight

THE COLONEL STOPPED suddenly. "I cannot go on."
I put down my pen. "Are you ill?"
He shook his head. "No. Tired."

"Shall I get Mrs. Keese?"

"No." He sat back in the sofa; took a deep breath . . . I half-expected it to be his last but he is not ill as far as I can tell.

For some minutes I sat watching him, wondering whether or not to go. Finally he opened his eyes, turned toward me. "I am only tired," he repeated, "unexpected as that may seem. It is not easy for me—re-living all this."

The Colonel indicated the volumes of legal reference he has been using. "You must go through them yourself. Decide what you would like me to comment upon. I don't seem to be able to . . ." He stopped.

"We've been doing too much." I apologized at length.

But the Colonel was not listening. He was staring at the portrait of Theodosia. Finally, "Actually there isn't much left to tell. We stayed on at Richmond for another two months and I was found innocent of the misdemeanour of wanting to invade Mexico. But Marshall was becoming frightened. Almost every evening he and I were burnt in effigy, an honour I was used

to but one which distressed the Chief Justice who was
—quite sensibly—fearful of Jefferson's ability to stir up
the people. So Marshall ruled that I be tried in Ohio
for the misdemeanour of trying to levy war against
Mexico. It was a shameful collapse before Jefferson
and popular opinion—reminiscent of King Henry's
before Jack Cade. Fortunately Ohio never pressed the
suit, and I was free—but shadowed.

"I went with Luther Martin to his home in Baltimore, but was forced by mobs to leave. Then I went
to Philadelphia, and tried to re-assemble my life. I
still had hopes in Mexico—with English or French aid
something might yet have been done. There was also
Texas. I had support there . . ."A long pause.

Then the voice changed from disjointed elegy to
dry narrative. "Disguised as Mr. H. E. Edwards I
sailed for Europe in June of 1808. By the middle of
July I was in London, just in time to learn that
Napoleon's brother Joseph—yes, our New Jersey neigh-
bor who ate pork and cabbage in Madame's kitchen—
would become king of Spain and, of course, of Mexico.
That was the end of my Mexican venture. King Joseph
was not about to help me dismember his newly-ac-
quired empire. Nor was England about to dismember
the empire of the previous king, in whose name
England presently invaded Spain in order to drive out
the Bonapartes . . ."

Another long pause. Then, "Four years I lived from
hand to mouth. The English would not let me stay
so I went to Sweden. The people were warm; the
weather not. I moved on to Germany, to various
princely courts. At first France would not let me in.
When at last I was admitted, they would not let me
out. I was watched day and night. I failed to be presented to the Emperor though I had plans which might
have interested him."

Suddenly the Colonel opened his eyes, very alert.
"You know, Charlie, Paris reminded me exactly of
Albany before the Revolution. The same filthy streets
with a gutter running down the middle. This meant

that every hack driver could splash the pedestrian to his black French heart's delight. But Albany reformed itself while Paris would not admit the evil."

At this point the man-servant entered with the news-papers. Seeing that the Colonel was exhausted, he gave me a reproachful look. "The Governor has missed his nap," he proclaimed (he invariably calls the Colonel "Governor," a habit contracted while working for Governor Clinton).

"Yes, the 'Governor' is not himself." The Colonel gave me a quick smile. "Unless this *is* himself. In which case may God mend the Governor for man cannot."

Loaded down with reports of the trial, I departed.

Nine

IT IS THE FIRST of June, 1835. If I don't write it all down, I shall never be able to.

START again.

A week ago Martin Van Buren and "Tecumseh" Johnson were nominated for president and vice-president by the Democratic convention at Baltimore. Mr. Van Buren said that he did not seek the honour. Most of the state delegations said they did not seek the *dis*honour of raising to the vice-presidency the paramour of two black women but they were forced to accept Johnson.

No. Start again.

At about four o'clock this afternoon George Orson Fuller, professor of phrenology, came to pay a call on Helen and me. Some months ago I wrote about him

in the *Evening Post*. He now thinks that I should do
more articles on the science of phrenology, and so
do I, and so does Leggett who is not only up and
around but in charge of the newspaper while Mr.
Bryant is in Europe.

Professor Fuller. He is small, with tiny hands like a
monkey's paws; he wears a black stock that nearly
covers his mouth. He is bald and every bump of his
distinguished cranium shines like the plaster demon-
strator's model he carries about with him in a woman's
hat-box.

"Mrs. Schuyler, an honour. A true honour." The
Professor bowed to Helen who helped clear a place on
her work table for the life-size plaster head with its
numbered divisions like a map of the German states.

"Everything's such a mess," Helen apologized, eyes
intent on the head. "Would you like tea or sugared
water?"

"Water. I never touch stimulants." The Professor
tapped the beginnings of his side whiskers, just in
front of the left ear. "That's the source of Alimentiveness." Helen looked blank. "When over-developed
it means gluttony, an addiction to food and strong
drink," he explained. "As you see, I lack *any* development then. You," he blinked his eyes at me, "like
your food."

"He does," agreed Helen. "He'll get fat, too, the
way he eats."

While Helen prepared to feed and starve respectively
our Alimentive bumps, the Professor told me how
much he had enjoyed Old Patroon's observations on
the new science of phrenology.

"Though we're not so new as people think. Our
founder, properly speaking, is Professor Prochaska of
Vienna whose work on the nervous system in 1784
linked what is *inside* the skull—the brain—with what
is *outside*—the contours of the head."

Helen gave the Professor his water, staring at him
as though he were an exhibit at the museum. Lately

she has asked me to bring people home. "If you're not ashamed of me. I get lonely sitting here, even with *this* to keep me company, kicking all day she is." She would stroke her stomach fondly.

"Now, Mr. Schuyler, I have something for you which I think Old Patroon—and the *Evening Post*—will agree is unique." He drew from his pocket a much folded sheet of drawing-paper. Carefully he opened it to reveal a head exactly like that of his model except for certain numbers, which had been underlined. "This is the first phrenological examination of the head of Martin Van Buren, obtained by a colleague of mine at Washington City."

My heart sank. Am I ever to be free of Mr. Van Buren? "I think the *Evening Post* will be delighted—if it is authentic."

"A very big head," observed Helen.

"A very *superior* head." The Professor loves his work; and I am impressed by the thorough-ness of this new science and tend more to believe in it than not. At some length the Professor revealed for us the Vice-President's head and character. Highly developed are Secretiveness (posterior part of the squamous suture) and Self-Esteem. Also, Cautiousness (high development on the parietal eminence) and Firmness (a lofty sagittal suture from behind the bregma to the front of the obelion).

Although I have not yet examined in detail the chart Professor Fuller left with me, I am fairly certain that Old Patroon will be impressed—after his usual fulmination against modern credulity.

I queried the Professor as shrewdly as I could. Noted objections to his science. "For instance, it has been recorded that the playwright Sheridan's bump of Wit was not well-developed. Yet he was the wittiest writer of his age."

"But he was *not* witty. Oh, what a superb critic of literature as well as of man our science is!" The Professor revels in the subtleties and paradoxes of his science. "You see, Sheridan's wit was not *true* wit and phrenology has at last confirmed what no critic could ever have known: that Sheridan's most notable bumps were Memory and Comparison. Now those two in powerful conjunction can give the appearance of wit (after all, Sheridan *remembers* other men's clever words and then *compares* them to the ideal in art) but the appearance of wit, as his writing absolutely proves, is not Wit itself."

"How is my Wit?" Helen leaned forward, with a smile at me.

"Small, I am thankful to say. Wit is unbecoming in the gentler sex. Do you mind? May I?" The monkey's paw lightly tapped Helen's head here and there; as he did, he buzzed to himself like a bee.

"Very good," the Professor said at last. "Your Philoprogenitiveness is *highly* developed." He tapped the back of the model head. "There. On the squama occipitis. See?" Helen was bewildered. "It means a love of children. It is highly pronounced in most women and apes since in both women and apes the love of children is greater than it is in men."

"Well!" Helen felt the back of her head. Then, to my astonishment, she said, "I think I need something strong, to fortify me," and in front of Professor Fuller she poured herself a small glass of Dutch gin.

The Professor laughed a bit nervously. "You *seem* to be lacking in Alimentiveness . . ."

"I am. It's just very close in here. If you'll excuse me." Helen went into the bedroom and shut the door.

"You, Mr. Schuyler, have an excellent bump of Constructiveness, as do I."

The Professor touched himself midway between eyebrow and side whiskers. "You know, the meaning of that bump was discovered by Professor Gall of Antwerp, in a most interesting way. He went one day with his wife to the leading milliner of Antwerp and noticed that the lady was highly developed in that region. Since her head was in no other way un-usual, he logically ascribed this development to her celebrated talent for hat-making. But of course in science one specimen is never enough. He needed con-firmation. It finally came years later when on a trip to Italy Professor Gall was allowed to examine what is reputed to be the skull of the painter Raphael and lo and behold! there was the *same* bump."

From the next room I could hear the sound of Helen being sick. Since this was not unusual, I paid no attention; listened instead to the Professor who was oblivious to everything save his own voice.

"I should now like to confide to you my plan." The Professor delicately mopped his bright cranium with a handkerchief, stimulating, caressing the bumps of his genius.

"Since the beginning of history, man has dreamed of being like the gods." I feared that I was in for a lecture, and I was, as Old Patroon will soon record for the readers of the *Evening Post*.

"Well, Mr. Schuyler, it is now possible for us to become gods. Do we want Shakespeare born again? Yes? We do? Good! Then simply provide me with a healthy male infant and I shall fit him out with *this!*"

Professor Fuller took from the hat-box a curious mesh of leather thongs and wooden disks. "I will fasten this patented machine upon the child's soft still-unformed skull and gently, gently, as the child grows, the bump of Ideality, the bump of Construc-tiveness will grow, responding obediently to these gentle but firm pressures. By the time the head is full grown, its owner will have the capacity of Shakespeare *without* the Bard of Avon's immorality . . ."

At that moment, Helen screamed.

When I got to her she was sprawled on the floor beside our bed, legs spread wide like a marionette when the strings are broken.

"I'm sorry," she said, staring at her white skirt which was slowly turning scarlet. First a few pretty drops, like a scattering of rose-buds; then, as I stared foolishly, the full awful tide.

It was I who screamed next. Sent Professor Fuller running for a doctor. Called in a woman neighbour who has had nine children and, thank God, knew what to do.

Helen sleeps, heavily drugged by the doctor who came too late to be of any other use.

"It should never have happened," he kept repeating. "Your wife is quite normal. I cannot think what went wrong." He was good enough to take away in an old pillow-case the body of our son.

Ten

July 9, 1835

I HAVE MADE Professor George Orson Fuller happy even though I was obliged to anticipate the expected outcry from those who disapprove of moulding heads. After all, as Old Patroon so wisely remarked: Suppose one of the straps got loose and instead of Constructiveness. Destructiveness was over-developed? And a future architect became Attila the Hun?

Leggett and I were together this morning in his office. "Drunkenness. That's your next theme." Leggett sat with his feet up on Mr. Bryant's desk. Washington Irving's book is still in its place, and still unread. Leggett looks like death but affects to be in the best of health. He is certainly cheerful, though I cannot think why. Every day he is threatened in the streets by the Anti-Abolitionists while every window of the *Evening Post* has been broken at least once.

"You think I have exhausted phrenology?"

"You have exhausted me. Here." Leggett gave me a number of pamphlets. "Apparently there are a half-million hopeless drunkards in the United States. The result of sin, according to a reformed wine merchant who should know. But according to me the result of the unhealthy life we lead in the cities." A fit of coughing . . . to demonstrate the unhealthiness of New York City's air.

"So examine the city man. Describe the classic Yankee type: the lean, leathery-skinned, long-jawed, small-headed conqueror of the wilderness. Show how he is being replaced by a sickly, pasty creature with sunken chest and a soft belly from too much spirits."

"I prefer the replacement."

"Is that the view of Old Patroon? Or of Dutch Charlie."

"Both." Like all the Dutch, I was born resenting the clever, ruthless Yankees who took our country from us. It is hard for me not to be proud of Van Buren, and hope that he will be the first Dutch president.

Mr. Sedwick appeared at the door to say that an advertiser was in the outer office.

Leggett swung his legs off the table. "They come to the office as advertisers. They depart as *former* advertisers." We both rose. "Helen?" he asked.

"In good health."

"Her spirits?"

"She has made a good recovery." This was true. But her character is much altered. Where before she wanted only to hide at home, now she wants to go out all the time, to meet new people, to be amused. I cannot say I find this change in her agreeable. I work most of the day and often into the night. When I don't work, I read, and until lately I thought she enjoyed our silent communion—each at work in his own way. But now silence of any kind makes her sullen. She fidgets. Complains. I cannot wait to get us both out of New York.

I asked Leggett about the consulship. Until today

I have not mentioned it to anyone. I am even reluctant to make any reference to it here. Superstition.

"The machinery turns. Van Buren knows what you have done, and he is grateful for your heroic restraint."

"He's certain to be elected, isn't he?"

"As certain as it is that that last window-pane over there will be broken." Leggett then asked me about the publisher Reginald Gower "and the unsavoury Matt Davis."

I told him that I had paid Gower what I owed him. "I think they were both rather surprised." Gower had also been angry while Mr. Davis had been deeply— and correctly—suspicious. Fearing a rival offer, he suggested to Gower that he pay me a bit more than the price agreed on but I said that I simply could not bring myself to betray the Colonel's confidence and Gower said that even if I was so minded he was damned if he would give me a penny more than we had agreed upon. Mr. Davis then said it was a tragic waste of "material" and did I not want to protect the United States from Van Buren? and I said—with perfect truth—that I did not care *who* was president, and so I lost their interest, earned their contempt.

I left Leggett, carrying with me a dozen indictments of whiskey.

In Broadway, I suddenly found myself face to face with William de la Touche Clancey.

"Well!" A long drawn-out syllable, in which fear and condescension were unpleasantly mingled. "What is the young Old Patroon about to turn his hand to next?"

"The Vauxhall Gardens, I should think." My dislike of Clancey is almost physical. Yet I stare at him with fascination; note that his protuberant eyes are yellowish; that he scratches himself compulsively; that his tongue darts in and out of his mouth like a lizard's catching flies.

"Of the delicious nymphs you disport with there?"

"Of the delicious fauns, too—and their goatish friends."

"Uh-huh . . ." A long drawn-out attempt at sounding amused failed of its object. "I hope you realize that your editor's unholy passion for the Negro grows more embarrassing each day. If I were he I should beware. He might simply *vanish* one dark night."

"Murdered? Or sold into slavery?" Clancey recently delighted his admirers by proposing that since the institution of slavery has been an integral part of every high civilisation (and peculiarly well-adapted to those nations that follow the word as well as the spirit of Old and New Testaments), poor whites should be bought and sold as well as blacks.

"I don't believe that poor sick Mr. Leggett would command a high price in the bazaar. Only his *diseased* mind would have a certain morbid interest to the special collector. You, on the other hand, ought to fetch a pretty price."

"More than the usual two dollars you pay?" Two dollars is the current rate for a male prostitute.

"Much more! Why, just for those pink Dutch cheeks alone!" It would be nice to record that I thought of something terminal to say but in my rage I could think of absolutely nothing and so left him with the last word.

Noted in a bookstore window: Colonel Crockett's new book will be on sale this summer. As yet, there is no title.

Eleven

COLD FOR JULY. Today I visited the Colonel for the first time in some weeks (guiltily reminded of him by this morning's newspapers with their long obituaries of John Marshall).

"Fortunately I am able to bear up under the calamitous news." The Colonel gave a sly and, I fear, almost toothless smile. Saving the splendid eyes, there is nothing left of Burr's legendary dark angelic beauty.

"Now only Jemmy Madison and I are left. And which do you think will go first to glory? That's a horse-race to bet on, by General Jackson!—who will probably precede the two of us, poor old man, despite," and the Colonel held up a bottle of patent medicine labelled Matchless Sanative, "this delicious restorative. When I saw the President in New York, he told me not once but three times that he owed his health to this particular medicine. Since I have never seen a man look worse, I was not impressed. But then I thought, here is Jackson with a bullet lodged next to his heart and suffering from a dozen diseases and the fact that he is not dead may well be due to Matchless Sanative. So I take it daily, always careful to follow the instructions on the bottle. The General warned me to follow the instructions to the letter. And I will say that I find it refreshing: a combination, I should guess, of opium and apple-jack." I record all this with a certain wonder. When two historic figures meet after thirty years their talk is of Matchless Sanative!

I told the Colonel that Leggett has read the memoirs and would like to discuss them with him. "Why not? What else can I do now but talk of the past." The sudden bitterness was interrupted by the man-servant who announced in a low voice, "Congressman Verplanck to see the Governor," and there was Verplanck himself, heavy and old and gouty.

"Mr. Verplanck is now the lawyer's lawyer," said Colonel Burr, introducing us.

"I met you, Sir, with Mr. Irving," I began.

"I recall. You are Old Patroon, aren't you?"

My ears went scarlet; I could feel the heat of my own blood rising. "Yes, Sir. I try to . . ."

"I like Old Patroon a good deal better than Mr. Irving's nonsense. At least you're a Dutchman and don't write about us as if we were a variety of elves with our quaint wood shoes and our quaint wood noggins."

Mr. Verplanck is trying to persuade Congress to grant Colonel Burr the money owing to him from the Revolution. He is optimistic. But then the Colonel has that effect on people.

Twelve

August 27, 1835

I WRITE this date . . .
START again. From the beginning.

Yesterday morning Leggett asked me to join him in the park where the Anti-Abolitionists were planning to hold a rally, with the Mayor himself presiding. In the last few days there have been riots all round the country, the work of those New England and New York lunatics who insist on immediate freedom for the slaves and so have unleashed the fury of that white majority which supports slavery and hates the blacks. The Abolitionists will not be happy until they have destroyed the United States. Yes, I am now an Anti-Abolitionist.

All in all, a terrible summer, cold and stormy and strange . . . and disastrous for everyone, particularly now for me.

Helen has been odd. Yes, cold, stormy, strange ever since the death of our child. But yesterday I thought she was again her old self, loving and at ease with me. On my side, I have been making an effort to work less when I am home, to talk to her more, to take her out almost every night.

"Will there be fighting?" Helen was not in the least alarmed when I told her about the meeting.

"I hope not. The Mayor will be there."

"Then I'll wear the new hat." A mountainous affair of dyed feathers, the work of some milliner's Constructive concavity.

Leggett met us at the agreed-upon spot: a block of masonry that had recently crashed onto the side-walk in front of Astor's unfinished hotel.

Helen gave Leggett her boldest look. "Well, what about the moon?" She pointed to the red disk just visible above the hotel's unfinished façade. "Have you been reading what the people who live there are like, in the *Sun*?"

Leggett laughed. "It sounds a perfect hoax."

"That's because you're jealous of the *Sun*," said Helen.

She was quite right. Leggett is jealous. All New York editors are jealous of the penny paper that makes a fortune by each day giving the public some atrocious novelty. Currently the *Sun* is doing a series of articles on the way people live on the moon, as observed through the telescope of a British astronomer; absolute nonsense, accepted as gospel by the simple.

The meeting in City Hall Park was predictably dull. One speaker after another denounced the Abolitionists on the ground that slaves are property and all property is sacred. Much praised was President Jackson's recent order to the postmasters to destroy any abolitionist literature they deem inflammatory. Leggett has been surprisingly tolerant of the President's abridgement of free speech. But then radicals like Leggett are as quick to surrender principle when it suits them as they are to decry the same absence of principle in others. Old Patroon seems to be taking me over. I am becoming very conservative, and intolerant of everyone.

To Helen's disappointment, the meeting ended without a battle. "My hat's safe, of course, but even so I'd hoped for some rioting. I'll go back now."

I was surprised. Hadn't she wanted to spend the evening in company? "No, no." Helen was decided. "You two go on."

We were at the edge of the park. The huge moon was now half-way up the sky and still red . . . war among the lunar people?

I insisted on walking Helen to our street. I was upset that she (careful, be accurate) . . . I was *glad* that she was going home (the truth, may I be damned for a fool); glad Leggett and I would be able to make the rounds together the way we used to in earlier days.

Just back of the Washington Market, Helen said good night. As she walked toward our building, the huge hat wobbling on her head looked absurd, and touching. At the door she stopped; waved to us. When she had gone inside, Leggett and I hailed a hack and set out for the Vauxhall Gardens.

At midnight I came home, having drunk too much beer. Careful to make no noise, I lit a candle; undressed in the parlour; crept into the bedroom, and got into our cold and empty bed.

Helen had left a note pinned like a medal to the bosom of the dress model. "I am going now. Don't look for me anywhere. There is a milk delivery tomorrow and I owe the boy for two weeks you pay I keep forgetting to pay him and to tell you I am sorry Helen Jewett."

All I can think as I sit staring at the note is what does "sorry" refer to? Leaving me? Or forgetting to pay for the milk?

Thirteen

MRS. TOWNSEND WAS straightforward. "Yes, Helen's here. And she does not want to see you."

Mrs. Townsend's room—no, chapel—was filled with vases of bright autumn leaves. Despite my anxiety, I

could not help but wonder if having abandoned the
Buddha (the gold idol was gone), she had now re-
verted to Pan or some other earth spirit.

"Could I just speak to her, to tell her that . . ."

"Mr. Schuyler, you are unethical." This came like
the clash of chisel on marble, my epitaph, my doom.
"You first came here in what I took to be good faith
and in good faith I received you into our family—and
that is the word for us in Thomas Street, a family.
I also received you into my confidence, admitted you
to this room where we have had so many inspiring
exchanges. *Then* . . ."

Grimly, Mrs. Townsend lowered the wick of the
lamp: no waste of oil on me. "You steal away a simple
girl, a happy girl despite the usual small disaffections
of family life. I have since fired that thieving nigger
woman Helen took exception to, and because of whom
and *only* because of whom—if you can bear the truth—
she left my roof for yours. I now have a respectable
Irish woman who takes a particular interest in Helen,
bringing her hot water a dozen times a day as if this
were the Grand Union at Saratoga Springs and Helen
taking the cure. Mr. Schuyler, forget her. You have
nothing to offer her."

"I want to marry her."

Mrs. Townsend reached for her Bible and held it to
her stomach, as though to ward off evil. "I repeat,
Sir, you are not ethical. Some things are fitting. Some
things are not. Helen understands this. You don't."

"*You* don't understand. We were happy together."

"I think not. Certainly when she used to come to
see me . . ."

"*Before* last night?"

"She would come at least once a week." The
triumph in Mrs. Townsend's face made me suddenly
understand the impulse to murder, to hold a neck
between one's fingers and crush out the life. "Oh,
she kept our visits a secret from you. She was terrified
you would find out."

"Helen came *here*?"

"I do not receive at the City Hall."

"She came here and saw men?"

Mrs. Townsend's snow-drift of a face turned to ice. "It is not polite of you to ask me that question nor for me to answer. But she did come here to weep, to tell me of her unhappiness with you, of the unnaturalness of her life."

"I don't believe you!" Yet at such moments one does believe the worst. "She wanted to be a mother, to be my wife . . ."

"But she is neither and that is the fact of her condition. I think you had best go, Mr. Schuyler."

"She certainly did not want to spend her life as a whore."

Mrs. Townsend rang the dinner-bell beside her chair. "You are impolite, Sir. Mrs. O'Malley will show you to the door."

I was ready to smash up the room. "I shall tell the police . . ."

"Tell them what? That the girl you lived with in sin, that you made pregnant, has returned to me and is happy? They will laugh at you, as would I if there was any laughter in me. If there was anything in me other than regret and a sense of all-contaminating sin."

Mrs. O'Malley came in from the front hall. "Which room's he to go to, Ma'am?"

"He's to go *out* the door, Mrs. O'Malley, and to a church if he's wise."

"Oh, it's that bad, is it?" Mrs. O'Malley looked at me as if I had just revealed to her the leonine face of the leper.

I left the house in Thomas Street and did not once look back for fear I would see Helen in a window—laughing. No, she does not laugh at such things, nor weep either. She would simply appear vexed.

Like Pygmalion I have spent over a year inventing my own Helen Jewett and now she has gone back to being her own Helen Jewett. Or is she entirely Mrs.

Townsend's invention, occasionally on loan to me, on loan to anyone who will pay the price?

Would Helen see me if I paid? The thought is so disgusting that I can think of nothing else. How did I make her unhappy?

Fourteen

November 20, 1835

TODAY I SUPPOSE William Leggett must be the most hated man in New York; certainly he is the most courageous. I have been with him a good deal this autumn and though my contempt for politics persists I have enjoyed watching him stir up Tammany Hall. The members are supposedly pro-Jackson; yet since a good many braves are secretly subsidized by the Bank they are Whigs like Mr. Davis and Mordecai Noah.

A few weeks ago I went with Leggett to a meeting at the Tammany Wigwam. As we entered the crowded assembly-room, Mordecai Noah was denouncing the immigrants. "They will destroy our democracy!" he shouted. Although Noah himself is not popular, the line he was pursuing was calculated to excite the audience; and did. "We must stiffen our voting requirements. Make it more difficult for this human refuse—this *Papist* human refuse . . ." The dread word had been said, and the room was still. ". . . to come to our shores, as they do now, by the thousands, bringing with them the fever, the plague of Popery for, mark my words, Popery and despotism are synonymous!" Shouts of approval; in fact, an ovation led by Mr. Davis.

Leggett slumped in the chair beside mine. "Unspeakable," he murmured.

Mr. Davis then spoke for something called the Native American Democratic Association. "Since July our organization has attracted much support in the city and we hope for your complete support here in the Society of St. Tammany. Our newspaper *The Spirit of '76* . . ."

Leggett was on his feet. "Mr. Davis, is your Democratic Association going to support the Democratic candidate Mr. Van Buren or is it a secret Whig contraption to takes votes away from the true Democratic party?" There were a number of loud boos from around the room.

Mr. Davis was smooth (he lies with a kind of integrity). "Our association exists simply to protect native American institutions. Certainly no one here wants our electorate to be dominated by depraved foreigners, blindly and passively obedient to an ambitious priesthood, intent on making us into a replica of a Catholic European state." A few boos for Mr. Davis; nevertheless, anti-Popery is a popular issue and the Whigs exploit it at every turn. I understand perfectly the appeal. I dislike the Irish and their priests but thanks, I daresay, to Leggett I know that the immigrants are a good deal less dangerous to us than their political enemies.

"It is my view, Mr. Davis, that your latest campaign —ostensibly against the Pope—is really against President Jackson, and is paid for—as you are paid for— by Mr. Biddle and the Bank!" A round of applause from the radicals; angry shouts from the majority.

"I was not aware, Mr. Leggett, that you were such a partisan of General Jackson." Mordecai Noah was again on his feet. "Our good President—may all the Christian saints preserve him, as they say in the Ninth Ward—has recently forbidden anti-slavery literature to go through the mails. Our good President has said that he does not want a civil war over slavery. What about you, Mr. Leggett? Is our good President right or wrong?"

Leggett was true to himself. "I am against having any two-penny postmaster decide what the people of this country can read." He was almost booed down by the Anti-Abolitionists in the room. "I also favour"— Leggett's voice is a powerful instrument when he chooses—"the protection of the Abolitionists no matter how fanatic they are!" The room reverberated with fierce cries; fists were shaken; riot was in the air. Practically to a man Tammany hates the Abolitionists.

Noah shouted above the crowd. "Would you protect a man with a torch who wants to burn down the White House?"

Leggett bellowed, "Force cannot defeat fanaticism!" But the force of several hundred angry voices now defeated him. Since he could not be heard, he rose to go. I followed him down the aisle. A half-dozen admirers did the same.

There was a sudden hush; all eyes turned to observe our departure.

Mr. Davis spoke quietly to the room. "Mr. Leggett does not support the President in his efforts to avert civil war. We of the Native American Democratic Association do support the President."

Leggett stopped at the door. "I support freedom of speech before I do any president."

This angered everyone in the room. For the average American freedom of speech is simply the freedom to repeat what everyone else is saying and no more.

Noah shouted after him. "You are for civil war, Mr. Leggett! And no friend to General Jackson!"

This was the end for William Leggett. The next day the post office cancelled its advertising in the *Evening Post*. Shortly after, Tammany ceased to publish its notices in the *Evening Post*. Worse, Leggett's usual following, the workies, turned against him. That hurt the most.

"I don't understand it. Workies are slaves, too. Yet they hate free black men in the north."

"They are afraid for their jobs." I gave the usual

reason, having no other to give. I cannot say I much like black people free or slave but I admire the way that out of principle Leggett puts himself squarely in the path of everyone—Jackson, the workies, Tammany, the Abolitionists *and* the Anti-Abolitionists. He is like Colonel Burr. No, he is nobler. Through no choice or fault of his own, Colonel Burr was in the way of the New York magnates and the Virginia junto and when they combined against him he showed his nobility only in the way he endured misfortune. But Leggett has chosen to take arms against our rulers. Now he has lost.

In a low bar near the Five Points, Leggett said, "I have this afternoon laid down the burden." He is uncommonly cheerful despite illness and defeat. "I have resigned from the *Evening Post*."

"What will you do now?"

"Start my own newspaper."

"What does Mr. Bryant say?"

"Well, he has *twice* mentioned the little dog who barked at Vesuvius. But he is kind." Leggett drank mug after mug of beer. "Now I would like to go to Mrs. Townsend's . . ." He stopped short. "Too many memories for you?"

"Too many," I said. Leggett thinks that Helen has gone home to Connecticut.

A new nightmare: Leggett goes to Mrs. Townsend and is sent up to Helen's room. Mrs. Townsend would happily do that to me. Would Helen?

We went to a place that has just opened next to the Swedenborg Chapel in Pearl Street. I think Leggett forgot his cares. I did. The girls are mostly German, and very clean. Best of all, there is no Mrs. Townsend. The owner is a pleasant old German gentleman who was once a clown with a circus in Hamburg (I am getting into the habit of writing for myself as if I were Old Patroon writing for the *Evening Post*—facts, facts!).

We did not leave until dawn.

I think I may have the clap. A burning sensation when I pass water, and the foreskin inflamed. What would Old Patroon say?

Fifteen

December 18, 1835

LIKE EVERYONE ELSE in the city, I was awake the whole night. Half the First Ward has burned down.

It was Dante's Hell: ice and fire together. A horrible racket of bells pealing, of fire-engines clattering, of houses collapsing. At midnight the sky was like a red dawn. Today every New Yorker who knows how to read mentions *The Last Days of Pompeii*.

I am thankful that I won't be required to describe what I saw. Memory too crowded with fiery images. Wall Street in flames. A freezing wind full of fire—an anomaly.

Suddenly the new Merchants' Exchange vanishes in a long wave of flame. A moment later I was able to see *through* the walls to the statue beneath the dome of Alexander Hamilton.

From nowhere, a half-dozen young sailors raced into the building and tried to save the statue. They pulled the figure off its pedestal but then the police forced them out of the building just in time for with a hissing sigh the dome fell in and Hamilton was seen no more (his would-be rescuer was a young officer from the Navy Yard—a banker's son, what else?).

Firemen turned their hoses on the flames but the water from the pumps did not flow. Or rather flowed for an instant, then turned to stalactites of ice.

Today everyone is red-eyed from the smoke; not to mention grief. Some nineteen city blocks have been destroyed (about seven hundred buildings). The total loss in property is close to fifteen million dollars, which means that as of this morning every insurance office in the city is bankrupt.

At noon Leggett and I walked along Wall Street. The ruins are still smouldering. In fact, the fire itself is still burning with diminished force near the North River.

"Like the end of the world" was the best that I could say.

"If only it were. For some of these business men." Leggett was hard-hearted.

A group of drunken Irish approached us, each clutching a looted bottle of champagne. Leggett was recognised and one said, "They'll be making no more of them five-per-cent dividends, will they now?" I confess it took us both some seconds to penetrate the man's brogue but when he made a thumbs-down gesture at the wreck of the Merchants' Exchange (it now looks like a ruined Roman temple) and said something about the "aristocracy," we got his range and Leggett grinned and gave him a thumbs-up.

In the side streets shopkeepers were gloomily digging among the ashes to see what the fire had spared. In Pearl Street there are miles of scorched cloth stacked on the side-walks. In Fulton Street furniture. Nearly every street is like an open bazaar of ruined goods. The poor steal whatever they can, particularly food . . . as do the pigs, who have declared themselves a national holiday and are now rampant. In armies they trot along the streets, rooting among the ruins, gorging themselves on a million burnt dinners, the only contented sound in the city is their squeaking and snorting as they turn up delicacies where once were taverns, grocery shops, homes.

At noon we were ushered into Colonel Burr's presence. The Colonel was genuinely pleased to see Leggett again. "Do sit down. Tell me something pleasant.

I am very old, you know." The Colonel turned upon Leggett a glance that was not old at all.

"The Merchants' Exchange is a ruin . . . is that pleasant?" Leggett played up to the Colonel.

"Such a new building, so expensive . . ."

"The statue of Hamilton was destroyed." My contribution.

"Ah, the flames, the cleansing flames! Not only for the flesh but for its leaden surrogate." The Colonel shivered though the room was stifling. "Now, Charlie, you begin to understand my craving for heat. I am preparing for the next world by indulging myself as a sort of prophylaxis."

The Colonel told Leggett that he was sorry to learn of his departure from the *Evening Post.* "Because you tried to—deal with politics in moral terms, a unique approach."

"Doomed, apparently." Leggett coughed as discreetly as possible into a huge handkerchief. The Colonel and I both looked away.

"Quite doomed," the Colonel agreed. "Although Americans justify their self-interest in moral terms, their *true* interest is never itself moral. Yet, paradoxically, only Americans—a few, that is—ever try to be moral in politics."

"It is the influence of your grandfather."

"Would that he had had *any* good effect."

To my surprise Leggett was not in a challenging mood. Never mentioned the Mexican adventure. Instead he asked the Colonel about his years in Europe. I took notes though I have no way of relating this conversation to the memoirs as they presently exist.

"You actually knew Jeremy Bentham?" Leggett's tone of awe did not exactly delight the Colonel.

"Yes, and Jeremy Bentham actually knew me, Mr. Leggett."

I confess Bentham until today was just a name to me, best known in legal circles for having written an attack on Blackstone, accusing that giant of the law of grossly favouring the powerful and so making impossible legitimate reform.

"I think him the best mind of our age." Leggett has said this of others but his enthusiasm is always genuine.

"Well, he was unique," the Colonel agreed. "When I met Bentham in 1808 he had been writing for forty years. Yet only two men in America had ever understood him, Gallatin and me. I believe him superior to Montesquieu. Certainly he understood law as no one has before or since. I used to stay with him at Barrow Green outside London. A quaint dwarf-like little man." As usual, the Colonel speaks of the smallness of others with no self-consciousness.

"I often quote him on democracy."

"Do you?" The Colonel was polite. "Bentham was certainly drawn to democracy, having experienced so little of it. He enjoyed repeating the old saw about 'the greatest happiness of the greatest number.' "

"In which you do *not* believe?"

The Colonel was delicate. "Who does not *want* such happiness for so many? I simply question if we can achieve it here."

"Well, I will grant you that we have not . . ." Leggett began. But the Colonel was not listening. The past is now more vivid for him than the present. He is, finally, old.

"In Bentham's house at Barrow Green, we would work at the same long table, with a huge fire at our back—neither of us was ever properly warm. We would work in silence for hours. Occasionally he would ask me questions about American law. He was codifying the law for England. *Codifying.* Did you know he invented that peculiar verb? He also invented 'minimize.' I rather like 'codify' but I shall never take to heart 'minimize.' "

"Or maximize?" My single effort to keep up.

"And of course Bentham was interested in the liberation of Mexico. For a time he wanted to go with me. Together we would set up an ideal society. At one point, he assembled all the material that he could on Mexico. The flora, the fauna, the economy. The climate particularly appealed to him until he noted the death-rate. 'Very ominous,' he said. 'I must live a long time, Burr. I have so much work to do and the odds are that I shall not survive a year if I become one of your subjects. They die in vast quantities, of unpleasant diseases, at a young age.' I tried to tell him that together we would lengthen—even maximize—their lives as well as our own but he was skeptical."

"Do you accept Bentham's principle of utility?"

"Who cannot? Except Charlie who has never heard of it."

I was the butt for the day. So I quietly made my notes, as though in school. Apparently Bentham thought that human beings had but two desires, gain and pleasure, and he accepted those desires as the facts of our condition (he hated St. Paul) and tried to make of them a philosophy whose keystone was an eloquent defence of usury. He would have been at home in New York.

They talked then of the Colonel's travels. Leggett was particularly fascinated to learn that Colonel Burr had visited Weimar at the beginning of 1810 and there met J. W. von Goethe.

"I must confess that Mr. Goethe was not my chief interest in Weimar." The Colonel lit a seegar. "Weimar was some seventy miles out of my way but I took the *détour* in order to pay a call on a lady of the ducal court. She was charming, and so was Weimar. A country in miniature, with this stout noble figure in charge of everything, including the theatre where I saw a play performed in French, the language Mr. Goethe and I used together. Not that we had anything memorable to say to one another. At the time I had read nothing that he had written while his interest in the United States was disappointingly slight. Curious. He has entirely faded from my memory but I recall vividly his mistress who was very fat and his wife, a former mistress, also very fat and, best of all, the elegant Baroness Von Stein who was the Madame Récamier of the duchy and if not his mistress his beloved friend. She, too, was stout. I also recollect that Mr. Goethe was interested in animal morphology. He had found a bit of monkey bone—from the jaw, I think—which he thought similar to the same bone in man. This excited him."

Leggett asked questions about various Napoleonic figures Burr had met in Paris. Among other things we learned that Talleyrand's table manners were particularly disgusting. The great minister would pile forkful after forkful of food into his mouth. Then when that orifice was completely filled, he would slowly, hideously, chew with mouth ajar. The Colonel was full of anecdotes, but no politics. He is wary with Leggett; with all journalists.

Leggett's single reference to the western adventure produced nothing more than, "Poor Jamie Wilkinson came to a sad end. I have just learned that he died in Mexico, addicted to the smoking of opium. His last years were devoted, most appropriately, to distributing Bibles for the American Bible Association."

The man-servant entered: it was time to go.

"I look forward to reading *your* newspaper, Mr. Leggett."

"So do I."

"Charlie, you must come again soon, and I will try to collect my scattered wits."

I said that I would come next week. The Colonel is pleased that I am writing so much for the newspapers. "But do recall that the two splendid men we have discussed today, Bentham and Goethe, were both lawyers."

"I won't let him forget," said Leggett.

The day has become unexpectedly mild. Pale smoke hangs like fog over the east side. Everywhere the shadowy figures of thieves searching for loot. The wind smells of wet ashes.

I have never been more wretched.

1836

One

April 11, 1836. Sunday

AFTER A LONG EVENING with Fitz-Greene Halleck at the Shakespeare Tavern, I intended to sleep the whole morning.

But at sunrise the landlady burst into my room and said, "Run, Mr. Schuyler! They've come for you!"

I stared at her stupidly, with a sore head. "Who's come for me?" But she had herself run upstairs, presumably to hide in the attic.

They were the police. Two fragile-looking men with fierce moustaches, clutching their sticks. "You Charles Schuyler?"

"Yes." I was now awake; and thought myself truly dreaming.

"Well, you come with us. Get dressed now. Don't do nothing stupid."

I jumped from bed; they leapt backward, more alarmed than I. "Don't do nothing stupid." This was their principal advice. So I did nothing at all, except to get into my clothes.

They would not tell me why I was being arrested—an omission they will soon be reading about in the *Evening Post*.

At the police headquarters the captain received me with, "Well, you didn't get far, did you?" He then congratulated my escorts for their keenness and courage.

By then my first fear (everyone is guilty of *some* crime in the theatre of his imagination) had been replaced by anger. Old Patroon was not about to be treated like a common Irish thief. "First, I want to know why you're holding me. Then I want you to send for my lawyer, Mr. W. D. Craft in Reade Street . . ."

"You're being held for murder, Charlie boy. So if you're thinking about bail . . ."

"Murder?" I wanted to sit down. Elma Sands. I killed Elma Sands. That was all I could think. I was out of my mind. Yet I heard my voice say very coolly, "And whom did I kill? and why? and where?"

From a cold distance, I heard a voice say, "Last night between eleven and twelve P.M. you were admitted to the room of one Helen Jewett who lived in a disorderly house kept by Rosanna Townsend. With a hatchet, you murdered said Helen Jewett on her bed. You then set fire to her bed, and escaped through the back window. You climbed over the fence in the back. Then you . . ." The cold increased all about me. The voice continued but I did not. I fainted dead away.

I was free before nightfall. Mrs. Townsend confessed to a mistake. From the new maid's description of Helen's last "caller," she had thought it was I. The actual slayer is one Richard Robinson who is now in Bridewell prison. He has been identified by the maid. Also, a piece of material found on the hatchet came from the cloak he was wearing while his trousers were stained with whitewash (the fence behind the Thomas Street house had been newly coated). Finally, at the time of his arrest, Robinson had in his possession the miniature that I had given Helen.

Two

I TOLD THE MAID that if Mrs. Townsend would not see me, I would bring suit against both of them for false arrest and slander.

Mrs. Townsend saw me. "The description our new maid gave of the young man misled me."

"You are a liar as well as a whore."

"I am paid by your sort to be both." Abruptly Mrs. Townsend turned away; her flaring skirt swept a pile of religious circulars to the floor.

"Who killed her? Why did he kill her?"

"I will only lie to you."

I moved so close to her when she was speaking that I could smell the faded scent she wears, the frightened acid of her breath. "Richard Robinson."

"Who is he?"

"A clerk to Mr. Hoxie. He's nineteen. He's been seeing Helen regularly. Unfortunately, the new maid had not seen him before last night and so . . ."

"Why did he do it?"

"I don't know."

"If he went up to her room at eleven o'clock, then . . ."

"No, at ten. At eleven the maid brought them champagne. Helen looked to be asleep. The boy was lying on the bed, reading a newspaper. Later the maid saw smoke coming from under the door which was locked. We broke the door down. Helen was on the burning bed, most horribly, most bloodily killed."

"Why did he do it?"

"Why did you take her away from here?"

"Because I was . . . because I wanted her to be with me."

"Then the same *force* that impelled you to take her from home impelled him to kill her. Lust is stupid, Mr. Schuyler, and so is harmful to its object."

Three

I GAVE MR. BRYANT my account of the false arrest.
He read it carefully and tore it up. "You are lucky
that no newspaper has yet mentioned you in any connection with this . . . this deeply sordid, this truly
dreadful affair."

Mr. Bryant was more shaken than I have ever seen
him. Yet I am calm; am filled with energy, with a
strong desire to kill someone, preferably Richard Robinson or Rosanna Townsend.

"I am, I confess, surprised that you could ever have
met such a young woman in any society."

"I knew her before this episode in her life." Literally, I spoke the truth.

"Please. I do not want to hear about it, Mr. Schuyler.
I am sure your relations with her were most innocent.
I know perfectly well that no gentleman could ever
have visited such a . . . such an establishment or have
known such a girl."

I cannot believe that Mr. Bryant means a word that
he says. Has he had *no* life at all? But I accept his
wisdom. He told me rather pointedly that if I want a
government appointment I am mad to advertise my
connection with Helen.

Helen is dead.

Four

June 6, 1836

THE JAY MANSION is to be torn down.
All week friends and relatives (on the Edwards
side of the family) have been moving the Colonel's
possessions to Winant's Hotel on Staten Island.

We crowd in and out of the basement apartment, carrying books and papers and pictures. Every day I see Mr. Davis, Sam Swartwout, Judge Ogden Edwards —the Colonel's cousin who lives on Staten Island and inspired the move (he is the very same Judge Edwards who recently declared that for the workies to form any sort of labour union is "criminal conspiracy"; he is not a favourite of Leggett).

Mrs. Keese weeps a good deal but vows she will visit the Colonel often, with food. The man-servant has already found himself another "governor."

The Colonel is low in spirits. I suppose now he sinks. Yet when he chooses to speak (which is not often) he is as sharp as ever.

Some days after Helen's murder I came to see him. He noticed that I was depressed though I did not tell him why. I made no mention of Helen even when he discussed the case, as everyone does; in fact, people talk of nothing else and it is all I can do to stay silent, to pretend indifference.

"You are disturbed, Charlie. You keep biting your knuckles. A bad sign."

"I am sorry. But it *is* a bad sign. I am disturbed, and wonder sometimes how I'll ever get through life."

"One *lives* through it, Charlie."

"Some things seem to kill one."

"Then die. We must all do that. But die, as they say, game."

SAM SWARTWOUT AND I accompanied the Colonel on the boat to Staten Island. The day was fine. A warm wind out of the west broke with silver the gray surface of the river.

The Colonel lay on a litter and watched New York City recede into the distance for the last time. This is easier to write than to believe. Secretly I think we both expect him to wake up one morning, leap out of bed, and shout "Heigh-ho for Texas!" and begin all over again his splendid life.

A large hat shades the Colonel's head from the sun; hides his eyes from us. Silence as he stares at the ships' masts that screen the water frontage at what was Richmond Hill.

"I dreamed of Quebec last night." Burr's voice was so low that only I could hear him. "At least I think it must have been Quebec. I was on a sled. On the side of a snowy hill. Moving down very fast. Most agreeable sensation."

Sam Swartwout deserted the bow of the ship where he had been posing, a portly figure-head. "You'll like Staten Island, Colonel. You know, it's still pretty much the way it used to be with all those big houses and gardens."

"Oh, Sam, Staten Island is an earthly paradise!" The Colonel's impish side still shows itself. "When I was there in the Revolution, a young boy, younger than Charlie here, slipping in and out of the coves on dark nights, stealing through the woods." He stopped as if he had lost his train of thought; but he had not. When he continued, the voice was unexpectedly sad. "Luckily it was almost always night when I was on the island. If it had been day-time, I might have looked in this direction and if I had I might've seen myself here on the river half a century later, half a corpse on a barge—imperial to the end!" He shook his head. "I don't know what young Aaron would've thought . . . what he thinks if he's still lurking up there in those green woods and looks our way."

Judge Edwards is waiting at the dock. With him are a doctor and (to the Colonel's horror) the Reverend P. J. Van Pelt.

I walk beside the Colonel's litter as we cross the landing to Winant's Hotel.

En route the Colonel whispered, "If you should hear that I have died in the bosom of the Dutch Reformed Church, you will know that either a noble mind was entirely overturned at the end or a man of the cloth has committed perjury."

"I shall include that in your memoirs. But why not shock everyone and get well."

"It is no longer my wish." The Colonel winced as the porters jolted the litter. "Not that I am absolutely done for. After all, I had an uncle who lived to be a hundred, which makes me practically a stripling with twenty years left in which to seek my elusive fortune."

Winant's Hotel is small but clean and pleasant. The Colonel's rooms are on the second floor with a balcony where he can take the air in good weather. The hotel-keeper is a slow man with a red face who seems most sensible of the honour the Colonel means to do him by dying in his hotel. Mr. Winant is even more impressed by his neighbour Judge Edwards, a brisk dapper man not in the least like the Colonel but obviously fond of him, awed by him.

Five

June 7, 1836

THE TRIAL IS OVER; it was very like the trial of Elma Sands except that where there was some doubt that Levi Weeks actually killed Elma Sands, there is no doubt at all that Richard Robinson killed Helen Jewett.

I have spent the last three days in court and most hard it was to find a seat. Fortunately Old Patroon is welcome everywhere.

The first day in court I knew that I had seen Robinson somewhere before. He is a handsome ruddy youth who dresses in the height of fashion. He is also very popular: half the court-room was filled with young clerks just like himself and they provided him with a sympathetic *claque*; for that matter so did judge and jury.

Mrs. Townsend charmed no one while her Biblical references inspired laughter. The girls did no better as, one by one, they testified to Robinson's presence in Thomas Street on the night of the murder. Whenever a girl spoke, the clerks would giggle until the witness was reduced to blushes and stammers.

By the second day of the trial it was apparent to everyone that Robinson had murdered Helen (for reasons never established); it was equally apparent that since he was an attractive, well-spoken youth who had fallen among sinful women, he deserved the court's compassion. And what, after all, was Helen Jewett to this court but so much debris to be swept out of sight? Certainly no one except me wanted that strong rosy neck stretched and broken on the gallows in the Tombs.

Oh, what I would give for just one hour in which to be Tamerlane loose in the streets of New York. Mrs. Townsend disembowelled. The judge's head on a pike. Robinson slowly quartered, slowly dismembered!

I was awakened from my day-dream of vengeance by a familiar figure squeezing past me to get to the aisle. It was William de la Touche Clancey who scowled when he saw me. With good reason. I remembered everything.

Clancey and the male prostitute skulking in the shadows of the Vauxhall Gardens; and Helen had mocked the boy, mocked Richard Robinson.

I wanted to shout, "Stop! I have proof!" But I said nothing; have no proof of any kind. Can only guess at what happened.

According to Mrs. Townsend, Helen had liked Robinson while he had "thought her very nice—for that sort of—well, person—in a place to which I was enticed by—well, I could not stay away from, Your Honour, and I wanted to stay away, wanted to save my money so I could—marry." Tears started in the large blue eyes.

Since motive was never established by the prosecution (and it ought to have been, either real or invented), the incriminating details were one by one explained away by the clever defence. Fresh whitewash is on many a fence and door and therefore on many an innocent trouser leg. The miniature (will I ever get it back? do I want it back?) was *given* Robinson some weeks before the murder. The shreds of tassle on the hatchet? Well, no one denies that his cloak had rested on the hatchet which had been left in her room by the maid O'Malley.

But if Robinson was innocent, then who was guilty?

The defence's answer to that obvious question was masterful. "Shortly after Robinson left the house, around midnight, someone else came to Helen Jewett's room. Now let us pause a moment and consider the various details we know in a new light. For instance, the passage *from* the house which the prosecution suggests that Robinson took—that is, across the yard and over the picket fence—might well have been the passage *to* the house that the real murderer took and, may I say, there are excellent possibilities of our finding *him*, gentlemen of the jury, yes, excellent possibilities."

I had stopped breathing at this point, aware that the entire court-room was listening to my heart beat.

"For there exists a man in this city with whom the unfortunate Helen Jewett lived. By whom she had a child that did not live, a jealous man, a vindictive man from whom she fled, fled in fear of her life. And because of this monster that satanic house in Thomas Street became not just a den of vice for Helen Jewett but, Heaven help the poor girl, a last safe—she prayed—refuge."

It was some time before I breathed again, before my heart ceased to flutter. As coldly as I could, I reviewed the law in my head. Considered evidence. Saw little likelihood of an indictment, and no likelihood of a prosecution. After all, I had been with Fitz-Greene Halleck until two in the morning.

After fifteen minutes of "deliberation," the jury set Robinson free. Because the case is still open, I now wake up in the night after exactly four hours of drugged sleep and lie awake until dawn, wondering if they will arrest me.

I just looked at myself in the mirror and said, "*You* killed Elma Sands!"

Six

June 30, 1836

THIS MORNING I RECEIVED a letter postmarked Washington City. It contained a thick white card engraved as follows: "The PRESIDENT, Requests the honour of (written in) *Mr. Schuyler's* Company at dinner, *Monday, the 9th July, at 5 o'clock.* The favour of an answer is desired." That favour was granted in the several minutes it took me to write an acceptance and the twenty minutes it took me to hurry to the temporary post office where I was delighted by the postal clerk's expression when I slipped the letter to him with its austere address plainly visible: "The President, The White House, Washington City."

"I guess everybody wants a job!" was the best the poor man could do. I smiled graciously, paid for my letter, and went to Pine Street.

Mr. Bryant was pleased but not surprised. "Mr. Van Buren is punctilious about these things. But then that is the secret of his success. He never forgets a debt or an injury."

"I never expected him to act so quickly."

"Perhaps General Jackson wishes to meet Old Patroon." I was suddenly nervous at the thought of finding myself face to face with that famous warrior.

"I think it shows Mr. Van Buren's confidence in you, asking you to the White House *before* he is elected."

"Not to mention his confidence in himself," I was impelled to remark. "But one way or the other, I shall leave New York with or without a government place."

"Old Patroon will be missed. But then you will write to us from Europe. And of course one ought to go abroad when young." Mr. Bryant is still distressed by my involvement with Helen Jewett. Although Leggett has tried to convince him that I was an innocent youth led astray, Mr. Bryant has given me up as one who will not be saved. He is right.

He then read with pleasure (or so he said) my description of Old Patroon's terrifying journey on the recently completed Brooklyn-Jamaica Rail Road. After paying me, he excused himself to write a memorial of James Madison who has just died.

Seven

THE COLONEL IS WEAK; does not leave his room. I found him sitting up in bed, newspapers all over the coverlet, an unlit stump of a seegar in one hand. He had already heard the news. "Well, I *am* the last, aren't I? And you're in time to help me write a letter to Dolley. I understand she has not a penny to her name. Her son ran through everything." The Colonel seemed moderately pleased. "I can't think how she will live, poor girl. She dearly likes to spend money."

The Colonel dictated an agreeable letter which he signed with some difficulty; his hands have developed a tremor. Then he sat back exhausted as I sealed and addressed the letter. "Jemmy was at least five years older than I," he murmured, looking out toward the Atlantic.

"Have you seen much of the Reverend Van Pelt?"

"At every opportunity, he pays me a call. But he is

tactful. So far he has not asked to hear my confession. But then he is not young and it would take a decade once I was truly launched. Actually he has been *un*-tactful only once. He asked me if I expected to be "saved." A most impertinent question, don't you think?"

"What did you tell him?"

" 'On that subject,' I said, 'I am coy!' "

I told the Colonel of the invitation from the White House. He was intrigued. "Now who arranged that, and to what end?"

"Leggett and Mr. Bryant. I . . . I am to write about General Jackson in the White House."

The Colonel looked at me thoughtfully. "You'll find Matty a most agreeable and good man. He will take to you. In fact, I have written him about you."

I looked at the Colonel as innocently as possible. "Do you think Mr. Van Buren will be at the dinner?"

"Every likelihood, Charlie!"

"Do I mention you?"

"If you don't, he will." The Colonel then asked me if I would read aloud to him. "I know it is dull for you but for me being read to is better than laudanum."

From off the table beside his bed, I picked up *Tristram Shandy* and read for an hour. We were both amused. The book is better read aloud than to one-self. "I am partial to Sterne," said the Colonel, "and regret that I came to him so late in life. In fact, when I was young, if I had read more of Sterne and less of Voltaire I might have realized that there was room enough on this earth for both Hamilton and me."

Before I left, the Colonel gave me advice on how to comport myself in the White House. "It can be most unnerving, particularly when there is no lady of the house." He smiled at a sudden memory. "Dolley used always to carry a book in one hand so that she and a stranger would immediately have something to talk about. 'What book is it?' my daughter once asked her. '*Don Quixote*,' said Dolley, 'always *Don Quixote*.'

When Theodosia asked her what she thought of Cervantes, Dolley said, 'If I *read* the book I should have nothing to say. But over the years I've learned quite a lot about the plot from nervous guests.' "

The Colonel chuckled. "Dolley will do well, with or without money. I am told that Daniel Webster is in love with her and since he takes every bribe offered him, he will have enough money to keep her in style."

Eight

July 8, 1836. Washington City

IF THIS IS NOT HELL, it will do. I have never been so hot. I can see why Colonel Burr wanted to be president—to revel in the stifling damp heat of this depressing tropical swamp.

Congress adjourned July 4 and everyone assures me that the town is empty. I don't see how they can tell since there is no town. In front of the Indian Queen Hotel where I am staying there is a stretch of paved road which soon becomes dirt and vanishes into woods. Washington has no centre, or rather there are several centres. One is the Capitol, an impressive if slightly ridiculous building on its wild overgrown hill. The White House is also impressive at the other end of Pennsylvania "Avenue"; however, the want of much of anything between these two majestic poles tends to diminish the grandeur of each.

I spent the morning at the Capitol. The interior of the Senate chamber is particularly handsome but the carpetting is black and gummy with tobacco juice despite the presence of a hundred large spittoons. Two slaves were scraping at the carpet in a lazy way. Even the black men are vanquished by the heat.

I called upon the Vice-President but he was out. I

left my card. There were a number of people Leggett thought I should try to see. I tried and soon gave up. With Congress's adjournment everyone has fled to the mountains or "gone home." Apparently no one stays in Washington during the heat of summer except the blacks who are everywhere. They make me uneasy for I have never been south before and so have never, consciously at least, seen a slave. Incidentally, the word "slave" is never used in this part of the world. If nothing else, the Abolitionists have made the southern whites self-conscious. They speak of their servants, their blacks, their people, but never of their slaves.

I spent the evening in the hotel bar, drinking with some westerners. They were filled with anecdotes about Old Hickory. To my astonishment I did *not* tell them where I was having dinner tomorrow. My character improves. I learned that President and Vice-President both leave the city on the tenth. So tomorrow afternoon will be the last White House dinner of the season.

Nine

July 9, 1836

TEN O'CLOCK. A stifling night. Mosquitoes are humming about the bed and I ought to turn out the light and sleep but cannot. Must describe my evening.

At four-thirty I started toward the White House, moving very slowly in the shimmering heat; afraid the starch in my new collar would melt. It is an odd feeling to be dressed for a palace reception and then be obliged to walk across empty dusty fields with only small black children to note one's splendid progress along "streets" yet to be built; their future sites marked, however, with rough stones carved optimistically with such legends as "Connecticut Avenue."

At the White House a single tobacco-chewing guard paid no attention to me as I walked up the path to the main portico where the other guests were arriving by carriage. Apparently I was the only one to come by foot.

I got to the portico just as Edward Livingston and his wife were descending from their new Hansom cab. For someone who is known as Beau Ned, Mr. Livingston is a rather plain-looking man. Mrs. Livingston might have been beautiful in early days but now she is heavy with deep dark circles under her eyes.

I followed the Livingstons into the cool main hall where a Negro porter or usher (must check on what presidential servants are called) wearing curious yellow slippers (in order to move quietly?) bowed deeply to each guest and indicated that we go into an oval room.

Right off, I was struck by the shabbiness of the furnishings. The faded curtains are full of dust, most of the chairs have been broken and are casually repaired; the carpet is splotched with tobacco juice despite a wealth of spittoons disgustingly full. But the room itself is impressively proportioned with a splendid view of the Potomac River and the smoky blue-green hills of Virginia beyond. On the brown lawn below the window I saw the first firefly of the evening.

"A good *situation* for a palace." I had been addressed by a young man who turned out to be on some sort of mission for the British government. I never got his name but was duly grateful to have someone to talk to. Washington politicians are no different from the ones who hang about the bar at the Tammany Wigwam. They stick close to one another; talk in low voices, laugh loudly at what has *not* been said while regarding with suspicion those of other tribes.

"Who are those famous people?" the young Englishman asked.

I confessed that "I'm a stranger, too." But at least I was able to point out the Livingstons whom I know by sight from New York. Otherwise we were both at sea, staring at the colourful democratic menagerie, at frock-coated statesmen sweating and (may I say what Old Patroon cannot) stinking in the hot room. Several westerners were got up like frontiersmen while their squaws, on the other hand, affected the latest Paris fashions. I note that the westerners are all yellow-faced. Malaria? While the southerners tend to be red-faced. Whiskey.

Quietly the Vice-President slipped into the room, and as if in response to some pre-arranged signal the guests spread out before him like a fan so that he might, starting from right to left, go from first one to another, speaking to each in a quiet voice. He was easily the most elegant figure in the room and even the loud westerners were forced to acknowledge true natural distinction by lowering their voices when they spoke to him. Some of their ladies actually curtsied, as though he were already sovereign.

Van Buren knew immediately who I was. "Mr. Schuyler. You were good to come."

"I was most honoured, Sir, most . . ." I was incoherent.

"The honour is ours, if I may speak for the President." I noticed again that we are exactly the same height.

"I want you to know, Sir, that I . . . well, was not partisan. I mean in all of this business."

"Of course. Of course." The gentle voice firmly prevented me from indiscretion. If the bumps of Diplomacy and Secrecy are inherited, one knows their origin in Van Buren's case. He is remarkably like the Colonel. "We enjoy your Old Patroon articles. Most pleasurable." Then he said something to me, rather sharply, in Dutch.

"I'm afraid, Sir . . ."

Again the charming smile. "You have not our dying language?"

"No, Sir. I speak no Dutch."

There was a commotion at the opposite end of the room. I heard several voices murmur "the President."

Mr. Van Buren continued, however, to devote his attention entirely to me. "What news of Colonel Burr?"

I confess that as I told him about the Colonel's removal to Staten Island, my attention (though not my gaze) was on the doorway through which General Jackson had just entered the room.

"You must tell him I shall go and visit him, if I am able to, before the election." I did not look as startled as I was. No man who wants to be president can openly visit Colonel Burr. "But," he continued blandly, "if I do not get to Staten Island, tell him my thoughts are with him."

Out of the corner of my eye I was aware of a tall thin figure dressed in black, standing at the room's exact centre.

"You missed a good deal, Mr. Schuyler, not having known Aaron Burr in his prime. He was a god to us."

"I think him splendid, Sir, and like no one else."

"He is most fond of you. He has written me recently to that effect." With a small bow and a whispered "by your leave," the Vice-President turned from me and approached the old General who stood very straight beneath a dusty broken chandelier.

The fan arrangement occasioned by Mr. Van Buren's entrance was now replaced by the more utilitarian wheel at whose centre axis was the President, holding in his left hand a black cane like a sceptre.

One by one the guests circled him like so many spokes. Although each was presented by a secretary, the President appeared to know most of the guests and usually made his greetings right through the secretary's presentation.

Not so with me. "Mr. Schuyler of New York," said the secretary, consulting a list.

I felt dizzy for a moment as I took the surprisingly soft hand of the victor of New Orleans. I bowed low. The President said, "Good evening, Sir. Mr. Van Buren speaks well of you. We are honoured at your

presence." The stately formula was perfunctory but
the eyes were not. They never leave one's face when he
speaks to you. Eyes of a predator, I thought, of a killer,
until I recalled that the eyes of Richard Robinson were
like spring forget-me-nots. No, Jackson's eyes are those
of some merciless punishing angel or devil presiding
over the agonies in Hell. It is the bold alert indifference
of his blue gaze that makes for such a disquieting and
cruel impression. I have seen such an expression in the
eyes of a caged wolf. I have no idea what we said to
one another. Fortunately, dinner was announced.

The President gave his arm to Mrs. Livingston and
led the company into the dining-room. I noticed that
he moves slowly, as if in pain. The dead-white face
combined with the white plume-like hair gives him the
look of an attenuated snow-man, diminishing in summer sun. It is a miracle he has lived this long into his
second term.

At table the President ate only rice, and touched no
wine. The rest of us gorged ourselves. How avoid it? I
have never dined so well or eaten so much.

The lady on my left was so engrossed with the
senator on her left that I talked to her not at all, but
the wife of a western congressman (who told me her
name twice and I have twice forgot it) was more than
kind. "I think the General does wonderfully well with
no wife to help him. Of course his girl was sweet when
she was here but it's not the same thing as a wife, is
it? But he does know about food. Why, I have never
had such good meals in this house as since he's been
here. The Adamses gave you boiled beef and a very
frosty time."

Everywhere in Washington it is whispered that the
President is ruined financially; and goes home tomorrow to try to save his estate. If he is bankrupt, I can
see why. He is much too generous with his guests.

We sat at a long table with tall lamps at regular
intervals. We were attended by some twenty waiters in
livery. At each place was a napkin, folded to resemble

a four-leaf clover. In the centre of the napkin was a slice of light bread, a relief from the corn-bread that is usually served in the south. To the right of each plate was a forest of crystal glasses of different sizes for the different wines. I counted nine glasses.

Parallel to the table where we sat was a second table of equal length covered with elaborate dishes hot and cold. From this table the waiters selected the courses and passed them from guest to guest, murmuring in one's ear, "Beef, Sir? Pheasant, Sir?"

The first course was a fish chowder served with a plate of boned fish. Sherry was poured.

My companion praised the chowder. "Maryland crab!" she exclaimed, dipping her spoon happily into the steaming contents. "Crab is one of the few pleasures of this place." I found that to a man (and woman) those whose lives have been spent trying to get to Washington City in order to live at the public's expense spend the days of their glory in lamenting their lot. To hear them tell it Detroit, Cincinnati, Memphis are far more brilliant than the capital.

After the fish course (the crab was the best I've ever tasted), canvas-back duck and pheasants were brought round. I watched with wonder as my companion seized upon a drumstick of duck and a quarter-pheasant. "You know, my husband—he's so full of fun! —he shoots these ducks from our hotel window. You see, we're at the other end of K Street where the marshes begin. So there's such excitement when he takes to picking off the birds, even if some of your mean old Yankees in the hotel do complain about the racket."

I don't care for duck; could learn to like pheasant if it is not tough. Mine was. Just as well. The next course was an entire ham and an entire turkey on the same vast platter; they rose like twin mountains from alternating foot-hills of mutton chops, sweetbreads and partridges.

My companion smacked her lips. Yes, she was very

fat. I'm afraid Old Patroon is not doing his duty. This description is coming out in bits and pieces, the way the President's dinner finally came up. I am ill. "Oh, that's one of the hams from the other side of the river, close by Alexandria. What a smoke-house this old Negro man has! We all go to him." She took ham and turkey (but not a drumstick); she took a chop (her fork hesitated over a second chop then fell upon the sweetbreads). I did my best to keep pace with her.

"You write about politics, Mr. Schuyler?" My connection with the radical, *disgraceful* (she giggled to show that she was serious) *Evening Post* had been established early.

"Not very often. I describe things. Like old New York and the theatre and . . ." What *does* Old Patroon do? Denounce all things modern in order to please those elderly readers who are—or were—displeased by Leggett.

The side-dishes were now being passed about. My companion tried each one. I tried every other one. There was macaroni and oyster pie (which I can still taste), spinach, sassafras, cauliflower, braised celery . . . and all the while our glasses were filled with nine different foreign wines.

We were two and a half hours at table; I saw the President's wisdom in eating only rice. Was he bored with us? It is hard to say. Mrs. Livingston on his left looked to be vivacious company while a foreign lady on his right was very handsome. Occasionally he would speak across the ladies to this man or that but I could not hear a word he said. His voice is high-pitched but not unpleasant; certainly it is not loud. The imitation everyone does of him shrieking "by the Eternal!" like some demented old rooster seems far from the fact. He is the soul of dignity and elaborately courteous, rather like Colonel Burr and the other relics of the Revolution. If Van Buren is elected in November, he will be the first of our presidents not born a subject of the English king.

I stare at Andrew Jackson, thinking Old Patroonish thoughts but despite he splendour of the setting I am mostly aware that the pale old man at the head of the table is in physical pain and that his false teeth do not fit; one can see them shifting about in his mouth as he purses his thin lips trying vainly to make himself comfortable.

"Gracious!" My companion spit—there is no other verb—a mouthful of bird-shot into her plate. "This poor partridge was in a war, not a hunt!"

Duly warned I ate turkey; drank Madeira. The lady from the west was full of praise for Mr. Van Buren who sat opposite us, smiling benignly and hardly speaking to anyone beyond a polite phrase or two. "We call him 'the little magician' here in Washington. And he is! He is! Why, the way he gets things done politically! Well, you know, my husband says Matty Van moves like a tiger in the night his object to achieve!" Liking the phrase, she repeated it so that I would be sure to ascribe it to the congressman from Ohio (I recall now that their home is Toledo).

"Naturally we are happy . . . *thrilled* he's going to be the president no matter what Mr. Clay thinks— who is the nicest man in the Senate in spite of all the spirits he drinks, all the gambling he does. I am temperance."

Old Patroon gave her some interesting statistics on the number of drunkards in the United States. She was not interested.

"But again we shall miss the lady's gentle touch. Mr. Van Buren is not only a widower but there aren't even any daughters or daughters-in-law. So we shall just have to make do with another bachelor in this lovely house. Of course a wife can sometimes be a trial. I am told that Mrs. Monroe was so stuck-up that she had a platform built in the East Room where she used to sit on a *throne* and receive the *hoi polloi* like she was a queen."

I told her about Dolley Madison and *Don Quixote.*

I must have got the story slightly wrong for she saw nothing droll in my version.

Ice-cream moulded into fantastic shapes made the rounds, accompanied by blancmange, cakes and custards. Next we were offered pyramids of fruit. I thought I would die. I was also drunk, as was most of the company. But then Washington City is a southern town governed by westerners. This means that although people drink a good deal more than they do in New York, they seldom appear drunk in public.

Toasts were proposed in champagne. We all drank the President's health. He drank ours. Mr. Van Buren proposed a toast to the President's safe—and successful —journey tomorrow. The President proposed a toast to the Van Buren administration. And so on.

Then the President rose and led the company into a reception room where waiters stood about with dishes of coffee.

Mr. Van Buren asked me if I had enjoyed myself.

"Yes, Sir, only I have never seen so much food. I could not do it justice."

"Come now, I am sure that Old Patroon can keep pace with these Yankees any day." Most comically, he said not "Yankees" but "Jankes," the Dutch word for a barking dog. Then he was taken from me by others with a greater claim on the future source of honour.

I talked for a time with Edward Livingston who was most amiable and wanted to be remembered to the Colonel. With drunken courage, I mentioned the election of 1800.

Livingston was not unwilling to discuss "a most trying time. Most dangerous, too. For a time it looked like we might never elect a president."

"But you supported Jefferson through every ballot."

"Oh, yes. Despite temptation."

"From the Colonel?"

Livingston was cryptic. "Colonel Burr wanted very much to be elected president."

I could not believe it; said as much: "After all, if he

had wanted the election, he had only to say the word to Mr. Bayard of Delaware."

Livingston smiled. "He could not say the word because he meant to come into the presidency as a Republican. Besides he had all the Federalists anyway. What he needed was for me and Lyon and Claiborne and one or two other Republicans to change our votes."

"Did he *ask* you to change your vote?"

Livingston affected not to hear the question. "Colonel Burr was a very poor adventurer, and I told him as much when he came to see me in New Orleans. But he would have made a better president than Mr. Jefferson because he was in every way the nobler man. We made a mistake, I fear. And everyone has suffered."

I cannot wait to ask the Colonel whether or not there is any truth to what Livingston says. The Colonel has always maintained the Livingstons were bribed by Jefferson. Did he mean that they were bribed *away* from him? A mystery.

I got as near as I could to where the President was standing. Only to find—to my discomfort—that he was discussing the death of Colonel Crockett in Texas.

"Over the years I had my differences with the Colonel. But I confess that he made a fine and manly end." The President looked solemn. A westerner then gave us the latest and most heroic version of how Colonel Crockett and a handful of Texans were slaughtered by the Mexican Santa Ana who was then himself taken captive by Sam Houston. Ironic that what was treason in Aaron Burr thirty years ago is now, according to the press, "The Hand of Providence Pointing the Union's Necessary Way Westward."

"What's *your* view of Colonel Crockett, Matty?" a heavy-drinking westerner teased the Vice-President.

"I agree entirely with the President. He made a fine and manly end." The little magician waved his hand over the scene. "Of course I, too, had my differences with him."

"Yes, Sir," said the President, suddenly grim, "and

Davy put those differences in a book which I would
not have in this house." There was the beginning of
colour in Jackson's face. There was, doubtless, none in
mine.

"I have not read the book but I am told Davy's treatment of me was most . . . most humorous." Discord
was swept away, to my relief. So far no one has connected me with Colonel Crockett's book. But then
hardly anyone has read the book, including me. The
author's marvellous death has quite obliterated his
foray into political libel. The world much prefers to
recall Davy Crockett as a legendary hero fighting hordes
of Mexicans with his bare hands until at last he falls in
the ruins of the Alamo, by Mexicans overwhelmed . . .
cornholed?

Ten

MR. BRYANT WAS PLEASED with my description of
"A Dinner at the White House" and helped me
add a political detail or two.

"You stand well with Mr. Van Buren," he assured
me.

"I have no way of knowing. He *said* nothing."

"When does he ever? But he will be elected in
November, and you are sure to get an appointment.
Now let me give you a small European intinerary."
And for an hour the busy editor of the *Evening Post*
wrote me out a list of places I must visit. Curious how
many of America's writers are drawn to the Mediterranean: Irving to Granada, Cooper to Sorrento, Bryant
to Rome; not to mention all those like me who would
live in that part of the world if they had the money.

I left the office in Pine Street and started toward

Broadway when I heard a woman's voice call—no, bellow—"Charlot!" I turned and there behind me was the golden pumpkin of a coach containing Madame.

"Get in, get in!" I did as directed. Who does not?

I had not seen Madame for two years but she is unchanged. "I have been to Saratoga Springs, *pour la santé*. To the Battery!" she shouted to the coachman, adding with a ghoulish smile, "Through the ruins!" She turned her bloodshot gaze upon me. "I confess to a certain *frisson* when I look at what the fire has done to so many wicked worshippers of the dollar." I had never thought to hear Madame criticise the source of her distinction, as well as her abiding passion. "Why is it I have not seen you, Charlot? Why have you deserted me?"

"I have been so busy."

"I know. *J'ai lu vos pièces!* What talent! You must write about my house. It is the *last* of New York. Now tell me. Tell me the truth. How is *he?*" Last things obviously come together in her mind.

"I've not seen the Colonel since July when he was very weak. He hardly spoke."

"Oh, poor man! Do I dare see him before the divorce is granted? That will be middle of September." Suddenly she frowned. "*Mon Dieu!* When I divorce him, will I have to change my coat of arms?"

I stared at her stupidly.

"And I thought Old Patroon notices everything." Apparently the doors of Madame's coach are decorated with both the seal of the vice-president of the United States and the Burr family crest.

"You will," I said firmly and with pleasure, "have to paint them over."

Madame sighed. The world was continuing to use her ill, but a glance at the charred buildings in William Street did her good. Beggars are still digging among the ruins despite numerous signs threatening scavengers with punishment. The entire lower part of Manhattan Island will now be occupied by commercial buildings.

The former residents are moving up-town to Fourth Street and even farther. I am moving out.

On the Battery the carriage stopped; we remained inside, watching the usual parade. Just opposite a man selling buckwheat cakes reminded me that I have eaten nothing all day. "I have never known—*sauf l'Empereur*—such a man." Madame sniffed suddenly. Tears? No, catarrh.

"You should visit him."

"Is he comfortable?"

"I think so. Judge Edwards looks after him and everyone goes to see him." Yet I have not seen him since I got back from Washington City. I did write him a note but got no answer. I shall see him in the next few days to report on President Jackson's insolvency: the thought of *any* president dying in penury revives the Colonel marvellously.

"Our love has always been a tempest, Charlot." Madame gazed with longing across the North River, as though half-expecting to see her ancient lover roll toward us like a storm from Staten Island. "From the beginning when I was a *jeune fille en fleur* and we met at the French confectioner's and the Colonel was the handsomest man I have ever seen and adored by every lady in New York—from that very first moment he vowed and I vowed one day we would be together. And we were! That summer night we married when he held me in his arms for the first time," I could not believe my ears, "I thought—*enfin* I am home. But, no, I was too trusting, too romantic. I did not realize—how could I?—that it was too late for me, for him, for us. Because *his* character was entirely formed and it was not possible for him to break all the selfish habits of bachelorhood. The day I learned of his Jersey City *garçonnière* and Mrs. McManus, that slut, I knew the love I had dreamed of all my life—the totalness of it—was *pas possible!* '*C'est ça,*' I said to myself and instructed Mr. Alexander Hamilton to file for divorce."

"So it was not the way he spent your money that disturbed you?"

"Who gave you that idea?" said the one who had. "Money exists to be spent, *n'est-ce pas?*" Madame's tune has entirely changed. "No, I am a woman, Charlot, of passionate nature, and of total—total . . ." She stopped, sought the word. So many words occurred to each of us that I was silent for fear that I might let slip a fatal one.

"I wanted a hero, a man. He was both. But he was never entirely mine. Even so . . ." In one eye a whiskey-tear tried to fall. "Tell him that I remember him daily in my prayers."

"I shall."

Madame blew her nose softly, wetly. "I shall go see him once the decree is final."

Madame ordered the coachman to take us up-town to Leggett's house. "Since you will see my beloved Aaron before I do, tell him that my heart is his forever. Also, tell him that if he has a receipt for the sale of the horses and carriage I would appreciate a copy, for my records. He will understand."

Eleven

September 14, 1836

A T 2:00 P.M. THIS AFTERNOON, Aaron Burr died; aged eighty years and seven months.

I was at Leggett's house working on the first issue of the new paper when word was delivered me by a messenger from Mr. Bryant.

"You will write the obituary for us?" Leggett was cool.

"No, no. I must go see him." I was in an odd state of confusion.

"But he is not *there*," said Leggett, "to be seen. Your old friend is gone."

"Even so, I have to go where he is." And I went

across to Staten Island; found the parlour of Winant's Hotel crowded with friends and relations.

"You will want to go up," said Mr. Davis when he saw me. "I'll take you." Together we climbed the narrow stairs. "It was an easy death. He was conscious almost to the end. His last word was 'Madame.'"

I was startled. "His wife?"

Mr. Davis shrugged. "We don't know. I suspect it was addressed to the lady who was sitting with him, a Mrs. Keese. She is still with him."

In the pale evening light Mrs. Keese wept into both hands, making a silhouette framed by the sea-view. Beside her, head bowed, the Reverend Van Pelt prayed.

On the narrow bed lay the Colonel, a sheet to his chin. A single lamp overhead lit his face. Old people in death are supposed to look wondrously young. The Colonel looked exactly the way he did on my last visit except for bits of what I took to be lather in his side whiskers but proved to be plaster; the death-mask had already been taken. Although the face was as usual (he looked to be napping, with a slight frown), I could not help but notice in death what one was seldom conscious of in life: how very small he was—like a half-grown boy.

On the table beside the bed the portrait of Theodosia had been turned to the wall. Next to the portrait was an open book. *Tristram Shandy*? The Colonel's octagonal glasses marked his place.

Mr. Davis regarded the Colonel solemnly. "He will be buried at Princeton College on the sixteenth. It was his wish, and theirs."

Suddenly a deep voice filled the room. "'The fashion of this world passeth away.'" It was the Reverend Van Pelt.

"Corinthians," sobbed Mrs. Keese. "Seven."

"All is vanity!" observed the holy man vainly.

"Did he die in the church?" I asked.

The Reverend Van Pelt shook his head. "No, he did not. I fear that I failed him. At the end he wanted ..."

We were interrupted by Aaron Columbus Burr who burst into tears at the sight of his dead father. Rosary in hand, he dropped to his knees beside the bed. This so affected Mrs. Keese that she began to weep even more loudly than before while for the first time the Reverend Van Pelt looked as if he, too, might weep—at the popish display.

I ran from the room, hot-eyed, wishing that I had the Colonel to talk to one more time.

In the parlour, whiskey was being poured. Among the drinkers was Jane McManus, surprisingly calm. "I was with him only yesterday," she said to me. "The Colonel knew that he was going. 'It's like floating,' he says, 'on the river, on a barge, getting farther and farther from shore.' That was all he said. He talked very little the last days. There was no pain. At the end he just floated out too far, that's all, and left us."

I thought of a sled descending a snowy hill, cold wind in the face, a sense of falling, flying. All done.

Predictably, Sam Swartwout was the heart and soul of our wake. "Drink up, Charlie! He'd want us in a good mood, you know."

"But I don't think I am in a good mood."

"Well, this will make you laugh!" Swartwout withdrew a legal document from his pocket. "I swear to God it arrived an hour after he died. *It's his divorce.* Colonel Burr is no longer married to Liza Bowen. He's a free man, Charlie!"

1840

December 8, 1840, at Amalfi;
in the Kingdom of the Two Sicilies

At sundown I was on the terrace, wondering how to capture in words the exact way the sea below looks in winter light; the way the gradations of milky blue and green abruptly father darkest sapphire (no, no mention of jewels—that is cheating); give birth to a deep black-blue like . . . like the deep black-blue of the Mediterranean at the end of a sunny winter day. I have never been able to describe what I see every evening from the villa's terrace. Must make do with plain statements like the mist that signifies good weather eliminates the line between sea and sky so that they look to be the same element and one has the sense of being at the centre of an opal's cool fire. Well, *one* jewel only. Washington Irving would have used a dozen.

I attempt this description for the hundredth time in order to give my pen something to do as I try to sort out what has happened to me since Pantaleone appeared on the terrace with the alarmed look he always has when an American comes to call and a barbarous name must be announced.

"Signor Consul, c'è un americano, un colonello."
"Svaduz" was the name I heard. Since it is my job to be at home to American travellers—particularly colonels —I told Pantaleone to show the visitor onto the terrace.

I straightened my frock-coat. I was formally dressed, for today was the Feast of the Immaculate Conception and I was expected to represent the United States during the festivities in the piazza.

From the white arch that opens onto the sea terrace, a large slow figure stumbled into view. "Well, Charlie, if you're not glad to see me—and why should you be?—I'll turn right around and go down all those stairs I just climbed. I swear to God I've never seen so many steps that they call streets. Let me get my breath! Well, you've done all right by yourself, I'll say that. Look at your view!"

By the time all this had been said, Sam Swartwout had crossed to where I was standing. I stared at him like an idiot. What was I supposed to do? Send him away? Call for the police? As I stood, frozen to the spot, I was aware that I was not representing the glorious republic with much brilliance. What, I wondered desperately, would Washington Irving have done?

Like a large dog expecting to be hit, Sam tentatively extended a paw. Numbly I took it, to his relief.

"Haven't seen you for a long time, Charlie."

"A long time," I echoed stupidly. At least I did not repeat my own name.

Fortunately a few loud fireworks went off below us in the port of Amalfi, ending the first phase of our conversation. "What's that?" Sam leapt as though someone had fired at him.

"Fireworks. It's the beginning of the *festa*. There'll be a procession and . . ."

"I figured there was some kind of Fouth of July going on down there."

"Sit down." That was the best I could do. He praised the view. Who does not? The villa I have rented is next to the ruined watch-tower of the old mad queen of Naples. Below us is Amalfi wedged in its rocky ravine: white walls, red roofs, a Saracenic cathedral with a cupola of glazed green and yellow tiles. Above the town narrow terraces are bright with oranges and dark with wild laurel. In this setting Sam Swartwout is like a Fourth Avenue street-car in Arcady.

"I wasn't certain it was you who was consul till this American skipper in the port described you to me and I figured there just couldn't be two of the same name and looks. That's my boat." He pointed to a handsome sloop that I had noticed this morning when I made my consular round which consists mostly of visiting American ships and discussing with their captains how best to free the sailors arrested the previous night. I am a combination of justice of the peace and chaplain, obliged to carry about with me a greasy Bible for Americans to take their oath on—by kissing. I call it the perjurer's book.

"I've been here a year and a half . . ."

"I know. And before that you were at Antwerp. And just the other day I saw a copy of the book you wrote while you were there. Something about taking these little trips in the Lowlands."

"Something like that, yes." No one has ever been able to remember the title the publisher with such acumen chose for my first book.

"Have you been home since you got the job as consul in Antwerp?"

"Vice-consul. No. I haven't been back."

"Me, I left over a year ago."

"Yes. I know you did."

A rocket from the harbour slowly crossed the pale sickle of the new moon, and burst into white flames.

"You know, Charlie, I was caught in the depression of thirty-seven. It was really bad, as I guess you know. You see, I had everything tied up in England in these coal-mines. Good as gold, everyone said, and like always everyone was wrong. Well, I was wiped out. So I had to . . . I left."

In August 1839, Samuel Swartwout, collector of the

port of New York, sailed for England. A few weeks later it was discovered that he had stolen from public funds one and a quarter million dollars: the most money ever stolen by an American official if not, very simply, the most money ever stolen by an American. Sam Swartwout will no doubt become a folk hero once the first wave of indignation ceases. Meanwhile, he has damaged the reputation of former President Jackson who was responsible for putting Sam in the way of being a thief on the largest scale. Worse, the scandal of his theft helped the Whig candidate William Henry Harrison defeat President Van Buren in the election last month. The poignant result of all this history is that there will be a new American consul at Amalfi next spring. As much as I am impressed by the extravagance of Sam's crime, I cannot say that I like losing my job because of it.

"There's been a lot of confusion back in New York." Sam stared at the smudge of smoke where the rocket had burst above the moon. "And a certain amount of misunderstanding over my . . . uh, affairs."

"I should think so."

"I travel a lot. Spain. France. We've been sailing down the coast of Italy for weeks now. After that North Africa. They tell me Algiers is a nice place."

My wife appeared on the terrace. Sam got to his feet. I made the introductions.

"An honour, Donna Carolina." Sam kissed Carolina's hand with some grace.

My wife apologized for not being able to speak English which is to say she will not speak it if she thinks she is apt to be bored. Actually, she is accomplished in English, German, French, and of course Italian; her father is the Swiss Baron Jost Josef de Traxler who was a chamberlain at the court of the last King of the Two Sicilies as was her mother's father (a Neapolitan of Spanish descent). I met the Traxler family when I was first presented to King Ferdinand at Caserta. After a year of bitter wrangling with her family over religion and property (they have a good deal of each while I have neither), we were married six months ago. Our first child will be born in June.

"Can we serve you coffee?" Carolina used her careful slow English voice.

"If you have no spirits."

After Carolina withdrew, Pantaleone brought Sam a bottle of brandy which he drank like tea. "I must tell you, Charlie, I'm home-sick. Never thought I'd be, what with all this." He waved toward the sea. As he did, a star fell. My consulship.

"I don't suppose you'll ever be able to go back." I wanted him to suffer a bit for what he had done to President Van Buren not to mention me.

"Well, now, I think once the *whole* story is known . . ." He mumbled into silence. I was grateful that he did not have an "explanation." Then he turned to me. "What about you, Charlie? When are you going to take your beautiful wife to live in God's country?"

"I think she prefers living in Pope's country."

"What about you?"

"I don't know." I was not about to tell Sam that Carolina has no desire ever to see America, that it is her dream one day to live near Stans in Unterwalden, Switzerland, where the Traxler castle is. Unfortunately, Switzerland is much too placid, too romantic for my present taste. I am no longer interested in roses and Moorish arches. Instead I am fascinated by the political situation at Naples (having found tedious the doings of Tammany!). I wait eagerly for the next round of revolution that is as certain to erupt as smoke-plumed Vesuvius. And when it does . . . what shall I do? Run out and bark. That is plainly my nature. I am turning into Leggett as he turns to earth.

Swartwout was talking of Leggett. "You have to say one thing for Matty Van, he never holds a grudge. When that paper of Leggett's went out of business, Matty Van made him minister to Guatemala without even being asked."

"But Leggett always supported the President."

"Not always he didn't." Sam winked. Then drank deep; struck the maudlin note. "Poor fellow. He never got to Guatemala."

A year ago May, when Leggett died, I wrote the widow who answered me at length; unfortunately, the pouch containing her letter was dropped by mistake into the bay of Salerno and all the ink ran. I still do not know the details of Leggett's death but can guess.

"You're welcome to stay here," I said, realizing from the lights below in the piazza that the procession was beginning to form and I would soon be obliged to represent our nation.

"No, no. Thank you. I stay aboard the ship. I've got a good English crew. A fine captain—English, too, and partial to brandy and whist, like me."

"I must report for duty in the piazza," I said.

Sam got to his feet. "They seem like a cheerful people." Sam's interest in foreigners is slight.

Since Carolina had already gone down, Sam and I together descended the thousand steps from my villa to the main square of the town. A green sky touched a green sea, sharing the same stars, the sickle moon.

"What's become of your book about Colonel Burr?"

"I'm waiting for Mr. Davis to publish his biography first."

Two years ago Mr. Davis published the Colonel's journals, and though he bowdlerized a number of passages the result was still shocking to the American public and the Colonel's reputation is now more Satanic than before.

Swartwout paused. Took a deep breath. He was drunk. "He was most fond of you, the Colonel, most fond."

"I was fond of him." Not wanting to discuss the Colonel with Swartwout, I moved on ahead, said good evening to a family of peasants as they hurried past us, late for the *festa*.

"Yes, Sir, he liked you best of the whole lot . . . or almost best."

"I'm glad." I put my head down and hurried on.

Swartwout managed to keep up with me. "In fact, the Colonel wrote Matty Van about you . . . from Staten Island."

"Yes, I know he did."

"Asked him to look after you. Fact, he asked him to give you this job." Swartwout laughed. "Oh, the whole business tickled the Colonel. You know how things that shock most people always made him grin. 'Why shouldn't Matty look after young Charlie?' the Colonel said to me. 'After all, he's his big brother.'"

I stopped with a crash at a turn in the stairs. "What did you say?"

Swartwout came to an unsteady halt: a huge swaying figure in the twilight. "I'm sorry, Charlie. I thought you knew."

"I did not know."

"I'm sorry," Swartwout repeated.

In the piazza, we parted.

Coloured lights were strung from artificial trees. The crowd was packed in so tight that only with the aid of a carabiniere was I able to get through to the bottom of the cathedral stairs.

Hardly conscious of where I was, I walked up the steps to the wooden platform that had been built for various dignitaries. Here I was greeted by the Mayor, by the agent of the King, by my wife. In the narthex of the cathedral a uniformed band played marches. Fireworks exploded in the port. I was deafened, dazzled.

Although I bowed to this one and that, affected interest in the ceremonies, I could think of nothing but Colonel Burr and what we had not said to one another: he through tact and I through ignorance.

"*Ecco la Vergine!*" Carolina clapped her hands. A moaning from the crowd as the tall richly-clothed image of the Virgin was borne into the piazza on a high litter. Incense from censers swirled about the idol. A splendid bishop led the way.

Rockets exploding. Showers of white stars over the dark sea. A dazzle of red, yellow, green lights. Loud music. Cloying incense. The edges of the world suddenly began to recede from me. My eyes went in and out of focus. "Must not faint. Must not die," I said to myself, holding onto Carolina's arm and so, through an exercise of will, did not die, did not faint.

Silver robes flowing in the sea-wind, the crowned figure of the Virgin was now directly opposite us.

"*Ah, chiedi una grazia! Chiedi una grazia!*" Carolina spoke into my ear. "Make a wish. Quickly! She will grant it!"

But there was no wish that I could make that I have not already been granted by my father Aaron Burr.

Afterword

WHY A HISTORICAL NOVEL and not a history? To me, the attraction of the historical novel is that one can be as meticulous (or as careless!) as the historian and yet reserve the right not only to rearrange events but, most important, to attribute motive—something the conscientious historian or biographer ought never do.

I have spent a good many years preparing and writing *Burr* and I have tried to keep to the known facts. In three instances, I have moved people about. James Wilkinson did not arrive at Cambridge until a year after Burr departed. There is a case that Jonathan Dayton was not on the Canadian expedition with Burr. The elegiac conversation between Charlie and Edward Livingston in July 1836 becomes entirely explicable if somewhat supernatural when one recalls that two months earlier Ambassador Livingston died a few miles from my old home in Dutchess County. I revived Edward Livingston because I needed him at that point. Otherwise, the characters are in the right places, on the right dates, doing what they actually did.

Obviously I have made up conversation, but whenever possible I have used actual phrases of the speaker. Certainly the opinions Jefferson expresses in the book are taken from life, and often represented in his own words. He wrote and talked a great deal about everything. All in all, I think rather more highly of Jefferson than Burr does; on the other hand, Burr's passion for Jackson is not shared by me. Although the novel's viewpoint must be Burr's, the story told is history and not invention. In fact, all of the characters in the novel actually existed (including Helen Jewett and Mrs. Townsend) except Charlie Schuyler, who is based roughly on the obscure novelist Charles Burdett, and William de la Touche Clancey, who could, obviously, be based on no one at all.

I had thought to give a bibliography but it would be endless, and political. As a subject American history is a battleground today and I would prefer to stay out of range. I will, however, admit to a bias (and hear already the charming sound of bullets, as Washington would say) for a small brilliant work by Leonard W. Levy called *Jefferson and Civil Liberties*.

Errors and anachronisms *ought* to be few. If they do occur, I take full responsibility like Richard Nixon, casting no blame on copy editor Lynn St. C. Strong or on historian-researcher Mary-Jo Kline, who have not allowed me to get away with even the smallest of shortcuts.

G.V.
June 7, 1973

ABOUT THE AUTHOR

GORE VIDAL was born in 1925 at West Point, but he grew up in Washington, D.C., where his grandfather, Thomas Gore, was the distinguished senator from Oklahoma. Growing up in the Washington of the turbulent thirties, Vidal breathed the heady air of New Deal and World War II politics. Enlisting in the army at eighteen, he promptly made the literary scene with a fine first novel, *Williwaw*. Since then he has remained one of the most active, versatile and successful American writers.

His eleven novels include the controversial *The City and the Pillar*, *Julian*, *Washington, D.C.*, *Two Sisters*, *Messiah* and *Myra Breckinridge*. Two of his plays, *Visit to a Small Planet* and *The Best Man*, had long runs on Broadway. His critical articles and essays have been collected in a volume called *Reflections on a Sinking Ship*.

In 1960, Vidal ran for Congress from New York State's 29th district. Although he lost, he ran better in the traditionally Republican stronghold than any Democrat since 1910.

Today Mr. Vidal divides his time between New York and Rome, writing novels and literary commentary for periodicals.

From the master
of the epic historical novel...
GORE VIDAL

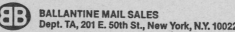
TA-26